X 75

D1421340

Empress of the Endless Dream

Empress of the Endless Dream

FIFTH BOOK OF THE OROKON

TOM ARDEN

VICTOR GOLLANCZ
LONDON

This edition published in Great Britain in 2001 by
Gollancz
An imprint of the Orion Publishing Group
Orion House, 5 Upper St Martin's Lane,
London WC2H 9EA

A CIP catalogue record for this book
is available from the British Library

ISBN 0 575 063742

Typeset by Datcon Infotech, Frome, Somerset

Printed in Great Britain by Clays Ltd, St Ives plc

TO

Fiona Mark

Empress Song

Come, meet the Empress of the Endless Dream!
Now nothing will seem the way it seemed to seem:
> *Gold will gleam,*
> *Time will stream*
When you meet the Empress of the Endless Dream!

Ah, see the Sister of the Sacred Night
Who looks upon your face with blinding sight:
> *Endless light,*
> *Timeless flight*
Is yours with the Sister of the Sacred Night...

Embrace the Daughter of the Damned and Saved
Who always waited on each road you braved:
> *You roared, you raved*
> *Like those enslaved*
Still, you loved the Daughter of the Damned and Saved!

Look to the Mistress of the Mystic Quest
Who longs to take you to her sacred breast:
> *East or west,*
> *Final rest*
Awaits you with the Mistress of the Mystic Quest!

Can this really be the Empress of the Endless Dream?
Can nothing still seem the way it seemed to seem?
> *Ah, yet light will beam,*
> *Love will teem*
Between you and the Empress of the Endless Dream –
You, and the Empress of the Endless Dream...

Players

JEM, *the hero, seeker after the Orokon*
CATA, *the heroine, beloved of Jem*
RAJAL, *loyal friend to Jem, beloved of Aron Throsh*
MYLA, *Rajal's younger sister, now much older*
LITTLER, *their small companion*
EJARD ORANGE, *a most remarkable cat*
POLTY (POLTISS VEELDROP), *Jem's implacable enemy*
BEAN (ARON THROSH), *accomplice of Polty, beloved of Rajal*
LADY UMBECCA VEELDROP, *evil great-aunt to Jem and Cata*
NIRRY, *formerly her maid, now landlady of the Cat & Crown*
WIGGLER, *loyal husband to Nirry*
EAY FEVAL, *a distinguished man of the cloth*
KING EJARD RED, *rightful ruler of Ejland: see* BOB SCARLET
HIS IMPERIAL AGONIST MAJESTY KING EJARD BLUEJACKET
HER ROYAL MAJESTY JELICA, *his wife, the former Jeli Vance*
TRANIMEL, *their First Minister: see also* TOTH-VEXRAH
FRANZ WAXWELL, *the apothecary*
WIDOW WAXWELL, *his aunt, and much else besides*
CONSTANSIA CHAM-CHARING, *former great society hostess*
TISHY CHAM-CHARING, *her unmarriageable daughter*
LADY MARGRAVE, *friend to Constansia*
FREDDIE CHAYN, *heir to a worthless principality*
PROFESSOR MERCOL *of the University of Agondon*
BAINES, *also known as the 'one-eyed beauty'*
MORVEN *and* CRUM, *hapless young recruits*
BLENKINSOP, *a brown rat, pet to Crum*
CHOKEY, *keeper of an exclusive gentlemen's club*
MR BURGROVE ('JAC'), *a ruined man of fashion*
MAJOR-GENERAL HEVA-HARION *of the War Lords*
PRINCE-ELECTOR JAREL *of the War Lords*
GENERAL-LORD GORGOL *of the War Lords*
BARON-ADMIRAL AYNELL, *formerly Rear-Admiral*
VARBY & HOLLUCH, *one man, not two*
WEBSTER, *of coffee-house fame*
JAPIER QUISTO, *Agondon's finest gentlemen's tailor*
JILDA QUISTO, *his ruined daughter*

HEKA QUISTO, *his other ruined daughter*
MASTER CARROUSEL, *the great hairdresser*
XAL, *'Great Mother' of the Vaga tribe*
The FLYING MENTINIS, *remarkable blind acrobats*
MISS TILSY FASH, *the 'Zaxon Nightingale'*
SERGEANT FLOSS ('CARNEY'), *a drunken Bluejacket*
ROTTSY *and* SUPP, *also Bluejackets*
MISS VYELLA REXTEL, *an unfortunate young lady*
The BACK-UP BABY
ALEX ALDERMYLE, *young society buck*
Other ALDERMYLES, VENTURONS *and* BOLBARRS
MAZY MICHAN, *wife of the Zenzan governor*
SIR PELLION PELLIGREW, *withdrawn from society*
MISTRESS QUICK, *making a cameo appearance*
GOODY GARVICE, *her trusted second*
ARCHMAXIMATE *of the Order of Agonis*
CANON FLONCE, *who is soon to change his state*
LECTOR ARDEN, *soon to change his*
RIPANDER, *last of the celebrated Castrati of Wrax*
The CLUMPTON CLOWNS
PUG, *a dog, but not in fact a pug*
The CONGREGATED *in the Great Temple*
QUALITY-FOLK *at the Wrax Opera, also at the Ball*
FOREIGN DIGNITARIES *invited to Agondon*
COURTIERS, SERVANTS, GUARDS,
SOLDIERS, RABBLE
&c.

REDJACKET REBELS:
BOB SCARLET, *rebel chief: see also* KING EJARD RED
HUL, *a scholar, loyal member of his rebel band*
BANDO, *not a scholar; even more loyal*
RAGGLE *and* TAGGLE, *his two young sons*
LANDA, *beautiful young Priestess of Viana*
The FRIAR, *another of their band*
FOLIO WEBSTER *of the rebel scholars*
ROLY REXTEL, *Cantor of Varby, whose sister has vanished*
ONTY MICHAN, *cousin of the Zenzan governor*
DANNY GARVICE, *a wizard with explosives*
MAGDA VYTONI, *great-daughter of the philosopher*
SHAMMY THE HOOD, *underworld leader*
'SCARS' MAJESTA, *another one, even worse*
OFFERO THE MOLE, *another one, even worse*
The SKIVVY *or the* SLUT, *his downtrodden daughter*

FIGARO FINGERS, *corrupt turnkey of Oldgate Prison*
PETER IMPALINI, *ex-sword swallower, good with knives*
MOLLY THE CUT, *notorious female felon*
HARLEQUIN *of the* SILVER MASKS
CLOWN, *his longtime companion*
PRISONERS *of Xorgos Island*
Bluejacket DEFECTORS
&c.

IN THE CRYSTAL SKY:
STARZOK, *a mysterious old man*
BLAYZIL, *his mysterious son*
SILAS WOLVERON, *father to Cata; not really dead*
BARNABAS, *a magical dwarf; certainly not dead*
LORD EMPSTER, *Jem's treacherous guardian: see also* AGONIS
ONDON, *Lord Secular of the Children of Agonis, long ago*
FATHER-PRIEST IR-ION, *an ancient Father-Priest*
AVATARS *and* FALSE AVATARS *of the gods*
BEARERS OF THE VEXING GEM
MALLARD DUCKS
ACOLYTES
&c.

OFF-STAGE – OR DEAD:
ZOHNNY RYLE *and family, back in Varl*
TOR (TORVESTER), *uncle to Jem, and a harlequin*
LECTOR GARVICE, *formerly of the Great Temple*
STEPHEL, *missing father to Nirry*
WYNDA THROSH, *mother to Bean, and Polty too*
LENY, VEL *and* TYL, *members of Polty's old gang*
Starzok's family, MISHJA, EKIK, LANZIK *and* JAMAJA
NATHANIAN WAXWELL, *Irion's physician*
BERTHEN SPRATT, *a servant*
The LADY LOLENDA
ZADY, *a Vaga-man*
GAROLUS VYTONI, *the great Zenzan philosopher*
'MISS R—' *the distinguished authoress*
'FANNY O', *not a distinguished authoress*
MR COPPERGATE, *a distinguished author*
MR BELFORD SLIPSLOP, *not a distinguished author*
DR TONSON *of Speculator fame*
MR CREDULON, *the noted stage designer*
THELL, *ancient author of the Theatricals of Thell*
The composers ELGNAR, STROSSINI *and* BACHOVEN

The artists RAPHIAN *and* BELLORETTO
Many other LIVING PEOPLE
Many other DEAD
&c.

GODS AND STRANGE BEINGS:
OROK, *Ur-God, father of the gods*
KOROS, *god of darkness, worshipped by the Vagas (purple)*
VIANA, *goddess of earth, worshipped in Zenzau (green)*
THERON, *god of fire, worshipped in Unang Lia (red)*
JAVANDER, *goddess of water, once worshipped in Wenaya (blue)*
AGONIS, *god of air, worshipped in Ejland (gold)*
EMPRESS OF THE ENDLESS DREAM
PENGE, *a most important part of Polty*
W'ENGE (WOODPENGE), *his woody avatar*
TOTH-VEXRAH, *the evil anti-god: see also* TRANIMEL
The LADY IMAGENTA, *his mysterious daughter*
HAWK OF DARKNESS, *his mysterious servant*
The MAUVERS, *mysterious purple birds*
CHORASSOS, *or the Unbeing Bird*
The serpent SASSOROCH
The HARLEQUIN
Other CREATURES OF EVIL
&c.

The Story So Far

It is written that the five gods once lived upon the earth, and the crystals that embodied their powers were united in a circle called THE OROKON. War divided the gods and the crystals were scattered. Now, as the world faces terrible evil, it is the task of Prince Jemany, son of the deposed King of Ejland, to reunite the crystals.

The anti-god, Toth-Vexrah, has burst free from the Realm of Unbeing. Projecting his powers through his Creatures of Evil, Toth is determined to revenge himself on Orok, the father-god who rejected him. If Toth grasps the crystals, he will destroy the world. Only Jem stands in his way.

An unlikely hero, Jem was born a cripple, but gained the power to walk after falling in love with the wild girl Catayane. Cata was later trained as a lady, and Jem's old enemy, Poltiss Veeldrop, sought her for his bride.

Escaping her tormentors, Cata was briefly reunited with Jem, but now is a member of Bob Scarlet's rebel band, fighting Ejland's Bluejacket régime; meanwhile, Polty and his long-suffering friend, Bean, have become servants of Toth.

So far, Jem has found four crystals. His companion Rajal bears the purple Crystal of Koros, Cata, the green Crystal of Viana, their small friend Littler, the red Crystal of Theron, and Jem, the blue Crystal of Javander.

Now, racing back to Ejland in a magical flying ship, Jem must still find the golden Crystal of Agonis, then bring together all five crystals. But all is not well. Myla, Rajal's magical sister, is ageing rapidly owing to an evil enchantment, and Toth, unknown to Jem, has only been biding his time, waiting for Jem to find the crystals before he seizes them.

Soon, the anti-god will reveal his secret weapon.

LAMASERY of the WINDS

AGONDON HILLS

Great Temple
of Agonis

Koros Palace

OLLON FIELDS

THE ISLAND

Cham-Charing
House

The Embankment

R I V E R   R I E L

AGONDON NEW TOWN

AGONDON
CAPITAL OF EJLAND

PART ONE

Darkness Visible

Chapter 1

KILLER'S KISS

The snow has possessed the city again, fluttering down over spires and spiky railings, battlements and gables, alleys, cobbled streets and broad, sweeping boulevards. In the day, like weary soldiers, ragged teams sally forth, struggling with shovels and coarse brooms to hold back even a fraction of the tide; with nightfall, the mocking whiteness has triumphed once more. On and on come the frozen waves, rolling out of the darkness like a strange enchantment.

Time-bells toll. Still it is early, but when darkness descends in mid-afternoon, evening might as well be the depths of night. Light comes only from a thin, seeping moon, and sometimes from the fugitive glimmer of a lamp, insisting its way through a shuttered window. It is the night before the Festival of Agonis. From the rank tenements of the Vaga Quarter to the elegant terraces of Agondon New Town, from the suburbs that sprawl across Ollon Fields to the ancient, imperious edifices of the Island, the city lies suspended under a shimmering pall.

And yet there are stirrings, here and there. On the Island, a fine coach-and-four rumbles down the steep incline of Aon Street; at the Wrax Opera, just across from the Koros Palace, quality-folk assemble for an evening's performance. In more than one alley, a drunkard slithers and slips; hopeful harlots wait for trade; along the Embankment, the rampart that circles the old city like a collar, stonily dividing it from the river below, a huddled figure makes its shivering, stumbling way.

It is a woman, with an infant in her arms.

Labouring through the snow, the woman turns her head this way and that. She peers behind her, towards Regent's Bridge and the darkness of the New Town; she gazes up into the different darkness before her, into the steep, forbidding maze of streets, as if she cannot quite remember her way. When a patrol goes by, ominous in trudging boots and bearskin coats, the woman fades like a wraith into a doorway, cringing from the rays of a swinging lantern. Then she looks down at her swaddled infant and hurries onwards.

In her haste, her headscarf slips; for a moment, moonlight reveals her face. Now an observer, if observer there were, would see that she is barely more than a girl; decidedly, no common girl. If there is not quite nobility in her face, still there is evidence of breeding, of distinction.

She hurries on as best she can, making her way round the curve of the Embankment. But all her striving has taken its toll; in an alcove that curves back in a high wall, the girl staggers, breathless.

She looks up imploringly. In the alcove is a fountain, one of many in Agondon, of the type known as a Foretelling. Here, surmounting a marble bowl, are the Lord Agonis and the Lady Imagenta, united as they have never been united in this world. Life-sized, they look across the frozen river. In seasons of heat, water arcs over their naked marble bodies, and in the bowl beneath they shimmer in shifting green; now, icicles cover them in a glittering crust and the waters beneath, like the bowl that holds them, might almost be made of marble too.

The girl slithers to her knees in the snow. Hugging the infant tighter at her breast, she offers up a prayer. Moonlight, through a gap in the clouds, shines with harsher radiance, illuminating the tableau of desperate piety.

But now the girl hears a clatter of hooves. Chains rumble over the paving-stones. It is a coach, and there are voices; the voices of men. She staggers upright; the infant whimpers and she rocks it nervously, whispering to it to hush, hush.

The infant squeals, but there is a howl of wind, bearing away the high-pitched cry. Fresh snow flurries into the girl's face. She flails forward, almost tripping over her skirts; she turns, then turns again. Which way? There is only darkness; darkness and snow. Now, perhaps, she will sink down; snow will cover her, and she will be still.

But there is something else, suddenly there. The girl gasps. Has her prayer been answered? Wind whips her headscarf away; she is oblivious. Wonderment fills her face; snow lashes her; the infant struggles and cries, but the girl can only flail towards the mysterious, glowing vision that has appeared before her.

It is a woman dressed in flowing robes, like a Sister of the Enclosed, but this woman's robes are of no austere black, and instead shine with all the varied brilliance of a rainbow. The woman – the lady – stretches forth her hands; the lady, it seems, is an embodiment of goodness, though strangely, disturbingly, she has no face, and there is only golden, streaming light where her face should be.

Mysterious music fills the air, insisting its way through the wind and snow. The girl stumbles forward, moaning, sobbing. Visionary ecstasy fills her; she has no thought for the coach she has heard, or the voices of the men. There is only the lady, the beautiful lady.

But now there is a man, too, stepping towards her.

'What's this, my beauty? Out in such cold?'

Sharply, the girl draws in her breath. At once, the lady is gone; now, before the girl, there is a very different figure, mountainous in a bearskin coat. If there is lamplight behind, it is an orange haze; refracted, juddering through the swirling snow, it makes the man only darker, more mysterious. The girl almost cries out as he steps closer, reaching for the child that she clutches so hard.

His voice comes urgently: 'Are you lost, my beauty? Abandoned? Have you been cast out? And what's this? An infant, in weather such as this? Come, I think I must assist you. Come, let me take this burden from your arms.'

Perhaps, at that moment, the girl would scream; perhaps she would turn, even try to run; but all at once the man is upon her.

Bewildered, she feels his hungry kiss.

It was over in an instant.

The girl, enveloped in the hot, sudden embrace, could not have seen the blade that plunged decisively through her bundled garments, ripping up through her abdomen. Perhaps, in her shock, she barely felt the pain, or the slithering, steaming lengths of intestine, discharging like an abortion beneath her skirts.

Her eyes grew wide. She stumbled, swayed.

Smoothly, as if with practised ease, the man plucked the infant from her arms.

Moments later, the coach moved away, rumbling slowly up the cobbled hill. In the cushioned interior, the killer sank back, satisfied. He had covered the infant's mouth to stop it crying out; still he kept his glove over the tiny face.

'Fool, you killed that girl, didn't you?' From the gloom inside the carriage came a peevish voice. It was the voice of an elderly man, a man accustomed to wielding authority, but one to whom authority, evidently, gave little satisfaction. 'Couldn't you just have knocked her unconscious? The cold would have done your work well enough. The Watch would think she was a drunken harlot, passed out in the snow.' A sigh. 'Another death on our hands, and for what?'

'Sir, I had to do it. That girl was strange. Trouble, I'm sure.'

'Trouble?' Disbelieving. 'How so?'

'Mad, sir – cracked. Why, when I approached her, she was staring wildly, alarmed—'

'At *you*? And that was mad?'

'No, as if – as if at some vision. Some dream.'

'Dream?' Disgusted. 'What are you talking about?'

'Her eyes, sir – trouble, sir, definitely.'

The sigh again, dismissive this time. 'Well, the snow shall cover her, soon enough – I dare say the Watch won't find her for a while. They'll think she was just a harlot, at least.' Then, alarmed: 'But the brat! You're not smothering *this* one, are you?'

The killer shifted his hand. 'N-no, sir, of course not.'

The infant made a gurgling, gasping cry.

'You *were*, weren't you? Fool, if this one dies before we need it, I don't rate your chances high of finding another, do you? Tonight? In this weather? Just remember, Veeldrop, my patience may be infinite, but Brother Tranimel's is decidedly *not*.'

'Y-yes, sir. Y-yes, Major-General.'

The infant let out a piercing shriek.

'Oh, make it shut up!' cried the old man. He rapped with his stick on the roof of the carriage. 'Hurry, Throsh, hurry! Don't you know I'm late? Don't you know I'm expected at the Wrax Opera? In the *royal box*?'

The driver cracked his whip.

But all is not quite over.

On the Embankment, the corpse is already half-covered; all, perhaps, might be as the Major-General has predicted. But the rainbow figure comes again, stretching forth mysterious hands; and now the golden beam, shining from where her face should be, flares with an intensity greater than before. Perhaps it is a summons. A call.

A wraith arises from the murdered girl, shimmering in the darkness like a tremulous flame.

Chapter 2

A NIGHT AT THE OPERA

'Look at the woman!'

Constansia Cham-Charing rolled her eyes. At another time she might have restrained herself; now, over the hubbub, she would speak her mind.

'Really, just look at her!'

'One would rather not,' said Lady Margrave.

'There are those of greater charms,' said Freddie Chayn.

'Some,' Professor Mercol murmured, 'amongst this present company.' With twinkling eyes he smiled at Miss Laetitia Cham-Charing, a scholarly young lady who had been persuaded only with difficulty to relinquish her book.

Laetitia looked abashed; her mother, for her part, was not to be beguiled. All around the Opera House, the audience had risen for the arrival of the Queen. As the stirring, familiar strains of the royal anthem boomed up from the orchestra, Lady Cham-Charing could not forbear from further remarks. Her family box was exactly opposite its magnificent royal counterpart. Maliciously, she gazed across the auditorium, past stiff-backed clusters of Bluejacket guards.

'Why, the creature is even wearing a tiara! Has she forgotten the respect she owes to the *crown*?'

The lady's tongue made a series of sharp little clicks. The object of her attention was not Queen Jelica, but the huge, toad-like, decidedly non-royal personage who swelled beside her, for all the world as if the anthem were her personal tribute. It was an outrage. Just a moonlife before, His Imperial Agonist Majesty had announced a contest to fit words, at last, to Mr Elgnar's time-honoured tune; the fat woman, by all accounts, was to chair the board of judges. Waggishly, Freddie had suggested that the sure way to win would be to submit an ode in praise of Lady Umbecca.

But what would one praise? Her ability to eat?

'Of course, she has *no* breeding at all,' Lady Cham-Charing went on. 'Would you not say so, Freddie? Would you not say, Professor Mercol? Why, just look at that gown! Imagine, Tishy, had it been *your* good fortune to be chosen as the bride of His Imperial Agonist Majesty! Should I have paraded about in the gaudy raiments of – of a *harlequin*, whilst my daughter confined herself to royal blue? Should I not have appeared only as a virtuous dowager?'

With infinite grace, the Queen – young, blonde, radiant, the very embodiment of the 'Ejland rose' – waved benevolently to the adoring public who had braved the elements to be here tonight. Thunder filled the theatre, and only the guards failed to join in the rapturous applause.

'And where,' murmured Freddie, 'is the Queen's husband?'

For a moment, Lady Cham-Charing considered suggesting that His Imperial Agonist Majesty was obscured, as well he might be, by the immense bulk of his wife's fat aunt.

Of course, it was a joke. With Her Majesty occupying the Opera Throne, and Lady Umbecca in the Chair of the Consort, the position was clear: no superior personage was here tonight, or would be. Once again, Ejland's not-quite-rightful monarch was – as so often happened – indisposed.

But now Lady Cham-Charing saw another figure, looming in the background of the royal box. She blinked. She coloured. Would she have one of her turns? In late moonlives, Constansia's once-brilliant eyes had assumed a watery appearance, which no powders or potions seemed able to allay; worse, her head had begun to wobble, just a little, as if in the grip of a perpetual mild shivering. How she would survive the Festival season, with its myriad engagements, was anyone's guess.

Lady Margrave leapt in. 'Dearest Constansia, you are right, as ever. Have we not known already the blessings of married love? Do we not appear gladly in black? (Ah, but still I sorrow for my dear, late lord!) For what reason does a woman don finery – unless, of course, she is abandoned to all virtue and shame – if not first to *win* her husband's love, and then to reflect glory upon him, for the choice he has made?'

It was an impressive speech; Tishy appeared to have some reaction to it, as did Professor Mercol; even Freddie was not unmoved.

Constansia, unfortunately, was not paying attention.

The anthem had ended now and a rousing overture had taken its place, a rag-bag of melodies from popular marches, ballads and novelty songs, such as always introduced the Last Night at the Opera. Anticipation rippled round the theatre, but Constansia could only gaze upon her enemies.

Umbecca Veeldrop was bad enough. Eay Feval was worse. Far worse. Could it be less than a cycle ago that Constansia's merest word, uttered almost casually in the Archmaximate's ear, had consigned that gossiping creature to the furthest provinces? (The Tarn! How much further could he go?) But now that fat, common old trollop – a merchant's daughter, of all things – had brought him back!

Constansia's only consolation was that Feval, for all his unctuous ways, could surely be given no distinguished position in the capital. Let him be canon of some vulgar suburban temple – Cantor Lector of Ollon-Quintal, at the most. But even Constansia, who saw decadence on all sides, could hardly credit the rumours that Feval was a candidate for Lectoracy of the

Great Temple, following the death of Great Lector Garvice. Never. Absurd. Not even the Archmaximate would sink so low.

In the box beside Constansia's, a party of young bucks – raucous young fellows, in the dress uniforms of a fashionable regiment – passed a bumper of ale back and forth. Already they appeared a little the worse for wear.

Lady Margrave shot them an angry glance. Why could not all military gentlemen – excepting, of course, those of the *highest* rank – assume the impassive, respectful demeanour of guards? The sentries, stationed all around the theatre, were fine models of manhood, common in origin though many of them must be. The bucks, by contrast, were sniggering loudly, and for a moment the terrible thought came to Lady Margrave that they were sniggering at Constansia.

Or at *herself*.

Surely not. Must there not be *some* deference, even in this degenerate age? Lady Margrave raised her voice, perhaps a little too much.

'Indeed, Constansia,' she sailed on, 'not only are we women of refinement, but we are Agonists – Agonists, whose piety is no mere sham! Would we, in widowhood, in this Javander-season of our lives, seek admiration for mere *outward* beauties, like parading, painted strumpets – or like giddy girls, fresh from Mistress Quick's, lined up in the Koros Palace to make our Entrance?'

She gestured to the balcony across the way, where Mistress Quick herself, stiff-backed and white-haired, and her redoubtable deputy, Goody Garvice, sat surrounded by the latest pupils from that great establishment where gens of Ejland's fairest flowers had been, as they would put it, *finished* in the womanly arts.

The great educationalist did not look towards them, but nonetheless Lady Margrave halted, alarmed not so much by her unintended comparison of Quick-girls with ladies of the night as by the recollection of certain misfortunes which had attended the Entrance of young – though no longer quite so young – Miss Laetitia.[1] Pleadingly, Lady Margrave turned to Freddie Chayn, who likewise complimented the 'Great Cham' (as the girl's mother was known) on her immaculate refinement.

Poor Constansia was by no means mollified.

'Really, I just don't know what the world is coming to,' she sighed. 'Did I tell you, Elsan, I had a letter just this morning from dear Mazy Michan?' (She had: several times. Their old friend – Mazy Tarfoot that was – was the wife of the Zenzan governor.) 'Shocking news! Remember that peevish cousin of hers, who went to visit her in Wrax? Waylaid on the way home, she was, by that vicious Bob Scarlet! Shot dead! Found in the woods!' Constansia shuddered. 'And her loyal old servant, Baines, has disappeared, lost without trace. Oh, what a world is this—'

---

[1] *The King and Queen of Swords*, Ch. 27

There was more in the same vein. In the box beside them, the sniggers had risen to guffaws.

'Oh, be careful, do!' came the whisper. 'Can't you come back here? Quick, on your mark, on your mark!'

The young woman twitched the plush curtain back into place and turned, smiling, to her fellow performer. 'I had to have a look, didn't I? Just a peep?'

'Chance enough for *that* when the curtain goes up!'

'Really? It's all I can do to remember those dance-steps.'

Her companion rolled her eyes, or attempted to do so. Having already assumed her opening pose – arms curved gracefully above her head, left leg jutting towards the wings – she was concentrating hard on not letting it slip. She staggered a little, trying to resume her fixed, dazzling smile.

'Are you on your mark *yet*?' she muttered through her teeth.

'Trying. I tell you, if I don't fall on my face, it's going to be a miracle. I don't think I've ever felt so ridiculous.'

'Not even when you were at Mistress Quick's?'

'Close. But not enough.' Poised in the midst of an elaborate set – the drawing-room, supposedly, of a country house – both young women wore frizzy yellow wigs and the black and white lacy uniforms of parlourmaids. Each carried a colourful feather duster. 'This is hardly what I thought I'd be doing when I joined Bob Scarlet's band, is it?'

'We had to be backstage tonight. What better way than this?'

'Backstage? We're *on* the stage.'

It was hard to believe they had come this far. When Bob Scarlet first devised this evening's scheme, the others thought it the merest fancy. Perhaps it was. Soon they would know whether a moonlife's careful planning had all been for nothing. The evening would end either in triumph or disaster. One or the other: one or the other.

Of course, there was Plan B. There was always Plan B. But that, thought Cata, was even worse than Plan A … No, they would never have to resort to *that*.

The overture ended with a last flourish. There was a signal from the wings. Applause thundered. As the curtain rose, the two young women pirouetted and pranced, flicking at the furniture with their dusters. Behind them, Lexion windows opened on what appeared to be a sunny, luxuriant garden. In moments, mercifully, the glamorous figure of Miss Tilsy Fash would emerge through those windows; the gentlemen soloists, then the chorus, would burst from the wings.

The young women brightened. Really, this was not so bad, was it? Mugging absurdly, they bobbed up and down, swinging their dusters from side to side.

This is what they sang:

> *An enchanter threw a hex upon*
> *The Widow of Midlexion*
> *To make her irresistible*
> *To every man she sees!*
>
> *This widow fair with magic arts*
> *Would gladly break a hundred hearts:*
> *She loves to see fine gentlemen*
> *A-scrabbling on their knees!*

It was the beginning – but only the beginning – of Strossini's best-loved comic opera. Soon, after the celebrated Miss Fash had flicked away a brace of lovers, sung several choruses of *Widow Am I, But Young* (though the diva in question was hardly young) and curtseyed expansively to the royal box, the oft-told tale would proceed no further. The drawing-room would vanish into the wings and flies, to be replaced by a wholly different spectacle.

Such was the way on the Last Night of the Opera. Each year at this time the three chartered theatres – the Wrax Opera, the Volleys and the Theatre Royal, Juvy Lane – were obliged to close in deference to the Festival of Agonis. But on the night before closing, the Wrax Opera, most opulent of all – named for its great counterpart in the Zenzan capital, where the operatic arts had achieved their finest flowering – would stage an extravagant royal gala. There was no pretence of a coherent programme; rather, it was a motley collection of popular turns, musical, dramatic, acrobatic, hippodromatic, said to be chosen personally by the monarch. Neither the Volleys nor Juvy Lane attempted to compete; apart from anything else, their finest performers would invariably be filched for the Last Night.

The two young women faced each other, wide-eyed, index fingers poking their cheeks:

> *For vengeance on the stronger sex*
> *The Widow sought this spell:*
> *But is it such a blessing after all?*
> *Can blessings pall?*
> *Watch, and we shall tell…*

And twirling their dusters, they retreated to the sides of the stage as Miss Tilsy Fash made her elaborate entrance. Over the applause, the young women managed the following exchange:

'You were right – I didn't dare look up. But you *did* see her, didn't you? She's in place?'

'A sitting target. Just think – at Mistress Quick's, she was my greatest friend. Landa, what if she recognises me?'

'Got up like that? Cata, don't be silly!'

But Cata was worried. From the beginning, this scheme had struck her as mad. Only now did she see just how mad. Bluejackets everywhere! How could a little band of Redjacket rebels manage – here, tonight – to kidnap the Queen of Ejland?

Stumbling, Cata made it to her next mark.

Chapter 3

WHEN A GIRL MARRIES

'Laetitia, will you put that book *down*?'

By now, Miss Tilsy Fash and the chorus had completed their excerpt from *The Widow of Midlexion*. A tedious clown act had taken the stage: Pierrot, Pantaloon, Columbine, and a dog in a ruffle that leapt through hoops. Queen Jelica, it appeared, found them most diverting; Miss Laetitia Cham-Charing evidently did not.

In those days – long before the politeness of the present era – the auditorium in a theatre would be lit throughout the performance. Nor would the audience necessarily attend, with any particular ardour, to the traffic of the stage; instead, the evening proceeded to the accompaniment of gossip, assignations, and the frequent comings and goings of those intent more upon promenading. Quality-folk, after all, were as keen to look upon each other as upon mere performers; for the merchant classes, gathered on benches in the pit, and the lower orders, jammed into the high galleries, the spectacle of their betters was no doubt quite as edifying as the official entertainment.

There were, however, less orthodox ways to take advantage of the light.

Lady Cham-Charing snapped, 'Laetitia!'

Tishy, who did not look up, muttered annoyingly beneath her breath. For the purposes of this evening the young lady had assented, if grudgingly, to her mother's demands that she dress with some decorum. Forgoing her customary green shift and stockings, she wore instead a beaded, puff-sleeved gown which at least revealed something of her admirably white shoulders. She had even permitted the application of curling tongs. But why, *why* would the girl not desist from those horn-rimmed eyeglasses? And *must* she pursue her studies, even here?

How Tishy would survive the Festival season was anyone's guess. What could a mother do but despair? Think of tomorrow. The day would begin in the Great Temple, with the service known as Agonis Inaugural. Early as it was, anyone who was anyone would be there, not least because the Archmaximate was to reveal, at last, the identity of the new Great Lector (certain to be Canon Flonce, Lady Cham-Charing thought with confidence).

In the evening, still more importantly, was the Masquerade in the Koros Palace. The 'Bird Ball', as it was called, was the last great official gathering before the year – 999*d*, penultimate of the present cycle, and, said some, of the Time of Atonement – ended with the five secluded days

13

known as the Meditations.[1] Of course, quality-folk held many additional functions during these 'god-days', in order to assist them in their pious thoughts. No time of year after the Varby Season, Constansia had always maintained, was more vital for securing a girl's prospects. How many unmarried daughters – here, at this very moment – were aflame with anticipation? Yet Tishy carried on implacably, straining her eyes over a useless dead language!

Lady Cham-Charing's liver-spotted hand hovered for a moment above the grammar-book. Would she dare seize it, flinging it contemptuously into the pit below?

'Mother, please, I'm declining.'

'You certainly are, you wretched girl.'

'I meant, Mother, that I am declining verbs.'

'Verbs? And what man wants a wife who knows *verbs*?' Lady Cham-Charing dropped her voice. 'Tishy, don't you realise that unmarried gentlemen are watching you – now, right now? Why, I can see several handsome fellows staring in your direction, entranced by your beauty! Yes, young Baron Aldermyle – see him over the way, leaning across Reny Bolbarr? He was glancing this way, I'm sure of it. Now take off those horn-rims, and put that book *down*. Professor Mercol, won't you tell her?'

The Professor smiled uncertainly. His position in the Cham-Charing circle was a delicate one, and he knew it. On the one hand, he had been engaged as Tishy's tutor; on the other, no one, apart from the girl herself, expected him to take his duties seriously. What point was there in teaching a girl the ancient languages? Could she attend the university? Could she enter the learned professions? What could learning do but ruin her lovely eyes?

In engaging Professor Mercol, Lady Cham-Charing had attempted to call her daughter's bluff. Poring idly over books was one thing, but a mere girl would surely soon tire of a rigorous programme of classical learning.

Or so everyone, Tishy excepted, had agreed.

In truth, the girl had taken to the ancient languages with an alacrity – indeed, an ability – that Mercol had seldom seen in his young gentlemen at the university. Constansia was furious. More than once, the distraught mother had determined that the lessons would cease, but the Professor had dissuaded her. What good would it do, he argued, to make the girl even more contrary?

Of course, he had his own motives. Once or twice in the course of her lessons, Tishy had removed her eyeglasses, and the Professor – who had begun to think that there might, after all, be something to be said for the education of women – had seen that this particular young woman was

---

[1] Cf. Appendix, 'Time in The Orokon', in the first volume in the sequence, *The Harlequin's Dance*.

nowhere near as plain as she might at first appear. Was she not the very image of Constansia, as Constansia had been in her youth?

If Constansia recalled little of the young Phineas Mercol, Phineas Mercol recalled the young Constansia only too well. How he had sighed for her, when he was a lad!

The old scholar cleared his throat, his hand fluttering to the handsome periwig with which he was always careful, in Miss Laetitia's presence, to conceal his hairless and somewhat bumpy head. Now here was a dilemma: should he take Tishy's side, or Lady Cham-Charing's?

'It is – hm – the beginning of wisdom,' he observed sagely, 'to recognise that there is a time and place for all things. Yet – hm – does not the life of the mind know its own rules?'

Mother and daughter alike shot the Professor a grateful look; then both scowled, thinking they had misunderstood. Flustered, the learned gentleman would have attempted a second sally, but just then Lady Cham-Charing's attention turned again to Baron Aldermyle, who had joined the party of young bucks in the box next door. There was much renewed sniggering and the passing of the bumper; oblivious, Lady Cham-Charing inclined her head.

'Of course, Baron' – she gestured expansively, as if inviting him to leap into their box – 'you *know* my daughter Laetitia.'

The Baron beamed. Oh, but was he not a handsome fellow? To be sure, these friends of his were a *little* wildish – there were rumours, indeed, about the Baron – but would not the love of a virtuous woman tame him soon enough? And might he not dance with Tishy at the Ball?

The lady's smile widened; the gentleman's too. Tishy raised the grammar-book, covering her face.

'Hah! These girls and their romances!' cried her mother. 'You understand, Laetitia is desperately excited. Like every young virgin, of what does she think but Balls, Balls, Balls? Why, Baron, when I was the merest slip of a girl, was not I, too, filling my empty little head with dreams?' Her manner became grave, even reverent. 'But as I tell my Tishy, how soon such dreams must come to an end – I mean, of course, when a girl marries.'

'How soon indeed,' muttered Freddie Chayn, who was saved from Lady Cham-Charing's matchmaking only by the worthlessness – it was widely agreed – of the principality to which he was the heir. Bitterly he reflected that the Aldermyles were lords of several of the fattest counties of The Inner.

'How does Mr Coppergate put it?' Lady Cham-Charing plunged on – then broke off, forgetting the quotation. She might have asked the Professor, but could not risk losing the Baron's attention. 'Oh, it was wise, at any rate. Something about a girl's dreams. Something about what happens to them when she marries. Indeed, what need has she *then* of dreams?'

15

'More than ever before,' contributed the Prince of Chayn, who recalled the quotation. He might have proceeded to further ironies, had Lady Margrave not dug him in the ribs.

The Baron's smile had become a smirk. He leaned forward; if his words were for the lady alone, nonetheless they carried clearly enough to her companions – and to his own.

'Romances?' he enquired. 'And tell me, Lady Cham-Charing, were you a great reader of Mr Belford Slipslop?' (The lady blanched. Mr Slipslop, an author of no breeding at all, was the favoured reading of kitchenmaids; often, indeed, he was cited as a strong argument against literacy for the lower orders.) 'Or "Fanny O"?' (Now the lady reddened: Madame 'O', a Zenzan courtesan, had been the authoress of a memoir particularly unsuitable for polite reading, and consigned long ago to the Chamber of Forbidden Texts.) 'Or perhaps you favoured the estimable "Miss R—"?'

And with a glance towards the royal box, the gentleman turned back to his companions. The bucks guffawed; one of them passed the bumper and all applauded loudly as he glugged it down. Heads turned. Further applause rippled round the theatre. (But of course: of all Agondon's young quality-folk, who was more celebrated than Alex Aldermyle?)

Professor Mercol looked bewildered; Tishy did not emerge from behind her book; Freddie only looked down at his programme, hoping that honour did not compel him to challenge Baron Aldermyle. (Surely not: Constansia was only his cousin-by-cousin. And had not the Baron *shot* young Lord Lensky, just last Theron-season?)

Elsan Margrave shuddered with contempt. Were her companions all cowards? But she would not dignify Alex Aldermyle with a response, she would not! Expansively she gestured to the stage, where the tedious clown act must surely soon end.

Did Constansia, she urged loudly, recall last year? Had not Mr Credulon made a tremendous impression, with his staging of the battle scene from *Wars of the Vast*? This year he was treating them to the Storm Aria from *The Flying Zenzan*, was he not? And had Ripander, last of the celebrated Castrati of Wrax, really been lured out of retirement again? And what of the Flying Mentinis? Could any pleasure be greater than to watch them fly? 'Why, Laetitia, you shall cast aside your book when you see the Flying Mentinis!' Lady Margrave boomed. 'Shall she not cast aside her book, Constansia?'

All this was to no avail. Lady Cham-Charing would not be distracted. She was mortified. Which was worse – the implication that *The Story of Fanny O* was a book she might have actually have *read*? Or the Baron's heartless allusion to 'Miss R—'? Many a time Constansia had heard rumours that Queen Jelica's aunt had been the mysterious authoress she had so loved in her youth. Impossible, it had to be – that fat, gaudy old strumpet? – but Constansia knew well enough why the Baron had pointed to the royal box, and the particoloured, immense figure that sat beside the Queen.

Poor Constansia! How far she had fallen!

The water from her eyes spilled down her cheeks and her head wobbled more precariously than before. Had she really once been Agondon's most celebrated society hostess? In her glory days, she would never have been insulted by the likes of Alex Aldermyle. The drunken cad would have *begged* to marry Tishy! In those days, a mere invitation to Cham-Charing House had been prized above gold, and its mistress had reigned in Agondon – so all agreed – as a rival Queen. How had she lost her place? How could it have happened?

Of course, there was really no need to ask. Lady Cham-Charing had long been in eclipse. Had not Lady Venturon's salon, cycles ago, cast the first shadow? Had not Baroness Bolbarr and her circle, with all the cruel exultation of youth, hastened Constansia into the darkness? It was inevitable. Cham-Charing House, that rambling old palazzo on the edge of the Island, could hardly look other than shabby compared with the new mansions of the Venturons, Bolbarrs and Aldermyles, rising imperiously across the river.

But if Constansia's fall had many a cause, the great lady thought only of one – the final one, the decisive one. Resentfully her gaze burned through her tears, lingering obsessively on the royal box.

Oh, worse and worse! Now the Queen's party had been joined – and late, too! – by that pompous fool, Major-General Heva-Harion. Really, what trash was not allowed in the royal box now? Since the disappearance of Constansia's old friend, Mathanias Empster, Mander Heva-Harion had risen to unwarranted prominence in The Ascendancy. Who was he, after all, but a *younger son*? Besides, he had lost no opportunity to spread the foulest calumnies about poor Lord Empster. And about Constansia.

She blinked away her tears. She struggled, and failed, to still her wobbling head. Very well, she was old: she was a widow: her glory days were gone. But did she not bear the noble name of Cham-Charing? If the Umbecca Veeldrops, if the Eay Fevals, if the Mander Heva-Harions were to triumph, what then? Why, it was the end of Ejland society! Somehow, Constansia must fight them. Somehow – she did not know how – she must have her revenge.

The tedious clown act finished at last; Ripander, the great castrato, took the stage. The frail, elderly eunuch's strange high voice silenced even the rowdiest amongst the audience. Even Alex Aldermyle was entranced, but Lady Cham-Charing barely listened, thinking only of revenge, revenge.

Chapter 4

TAVERN SCENE

A little away from the Wrax Opera, further down the sloping sides of the Island, lies the celebrated square known as Redondo Gardens. Named after the noble Tiralon family who once kept the mansion bordering one of its sides, in olden times this square did indeed contain gardens, a lush oasis in the very heart of the city, surrounded by a high wall. The wall is gone now and so are the gardens; now, all that is ever green here is spinach, lettuce, celery and cardoon, and the only blooms are from flowers cut and tied in bunches. Redondo Gardens is Agondon's main greengrocers' market.

The fine houses decayed long ago, slipping into usages less noble by far. By night, 'the Gardens' is a byword for iniquity. But this is not quite fair. If there are harlots to be had here, if dealers in illicit potions and powders beckon from dark doorways, still there is a pretty chapel, a hospice for decayed gentlefolk, and a tavern by no means disreputable. In a half-timbered Elabethan house, jammed between Flowerdew Lane and the ramshackle premises of a moneylender, the tavern bears the sign of a marmalade cat with a crown on its head. Where the sign has its origins, who can say? But for all who live round the Gardens, the Cat & Crown is famed as an excellent establishment.

And how was business, on the Last Night of the Opera?

One might imagine it could hardly have been booming. But the Opera is not for everyone, and that night in the Cat & Crown, I am certain – beneath the snowy eaves, behind the shutters and the drawn curtains – sufficient barrels were rolled up from the cellars, sufficient cuts sliced from the spit, and quite sufficient quantities of smoke swirled round the thick, dark rafters. Fires roared in big old fireplaces; there were toasts, jokes, merry songs, and in the second-best parlour, opposite a table of young rowdies, a Bluejacket in a shabby sergeant's uniform had drawn a certain barmaid on to his knee.

'Ah, Baines, there's been many a lass in my life,' the sergeant slurred. 'Well, it's natural, isn't it, me being a man and all? And shifted from place to place I have, ever since I was a lad, *tramp-tramp* here, *tramp-tramp* there. All over this kingdom I've been – farmer up in Harion, whaler off the Varl coast. Gamekeeper in Vantage, poacher in Chayn. Why, I've been a footman in the grandest house in Agondon – that's Lady Cham's to you, my dear. Been detained at His Majesty's pleasure too, but you'd say I'd fell on my feet, wouldn't you? After all, I fetched up with the Blue Irions.'

Not without pride, he stroked his regimental badge.

'You're saying, then, that you've met a lot of ladies?' Baines, ever so gently, urged the sergeant back to his theme. The tale of his wanderings was familiar enough; seldom had he mentioned matters of the heart.

Now *that* was promising, very promising.

'Ladies?' He flashed a set of brown dentures. 'Well, it's not a word *some* would use.'

Baines simpered. Whether she understood the implication, who could say? She was a woman of virtue, but when Sergeant Floss had accosted her, she had hardly resisted. Now his head pressed against her bosom; smoke from his clay-pipe filled her nostrils, and when the rowdies at the next table toasted the beauty of this or that young lady, Baines could almost believe the toast was for her. Why not? Lamps glowed hazily in the tavern air, imparting a hint of beauty even to a servant-woman, no longer youthful, with a grey face and only one eye.

The sergeant was saying, 'With these two eyes of mine, Baines, I've seen the lasses in Zenzau and Tiralos; I've seen them in the Tarn and in the Lexion Lands. There was a widow in Midlexion – I don't mind telling you, *she* was something.'

He gulped from his ale and a moustache of foam appeared on his upper lip, wobbling absurdly; Baines wondered if she should wipe it away. Or lick it.

'But I wouldn't have you thinking I was one of your *fast* fellows, me love. Not old Carney Floss. Oh, there's been a few things I've regretted – me being a man, and all. I mean, when I was younger. Can I help it if these two eyes of mine like to wink at a lass?'

He winked; the foam jiggled up and down.

'Like I say, I've seen many a lass. But do you think I've seen another like the one here in this tavern?'

Baines felt her heart flutter. *Dare* she lick the foam?

As if in answer, the sergeant shook his head; the foam dripped down and he wiped it away.

'Yes, love, there's been many a lass I'd liked to have married. This is not the first time and won't be the last. Story of my life, Baines – too late, always too late. Dear Nirry! Dear, dear Nirry!'

'Nirry? *Nirry?*' Now Baines was confused, but before she could say more, a voice cut through the haze. And the voice called her name.

'Ah, the celestial tones!' sighed the sergeant.

Flushing, Baines slipped off his knee, grabbing up her ale-jug and slate. Dutifully, she bobbed at her mistress.

'And what do you think you're doing?' Her mistress, arms akimbo, would not be placated. 'There's customers in the front parlour, customers in the snug, *and* upstairs, too. Not to mention this lot' – she gestured towards the rowdies – 'who'll be wanting refills any moment, I'll wager.'

There were cries of assent from the rowdies, whose toasts to this or that young lady had assumed, in the last moments, a coarser cast.

'And enough of that.' Sternly, Nirry Olch stabbed a finger into the air. 'This is a respectable hostelry, this is, not one of your bawdy-houses. No swearing, no spitting, no smut. And no brawling either – ooh, I know what you menfolk are like. Them's the house rules at the Cat & Crown, and if you don't like 'em you can sling your hook. Got it? And keep down your noise – there's *quality* up in the best room ... Now fill them tankards, Baines, and don't forget to mark it on the slate.'

The rowdies grinned, abashed; Nirry turned, gimlet-eyed, on Carney Floss. Could the sergeant be mistaken, or was there a hint of laughter in the landlady's eyes?

Her voice dropped and she struck him on the shoulder with the back of her hand. 'As for you, shame on you! Saucy fellow, didn't I see the way you were making up to Baines? I'm telling you, I won't have you leading her on. Don't you know she's only got one eye?'

'I know one lass who's got two. Lovely ones, they are.'

Nirry sighed. How many times had she been through this routine? Grinning, the sergeant tried to catch her hands. She slapped him again, harder this time. 'Carney Floss! Have you forgotten, I'm a respectable married woman?'

'Nirry, dear Nirry—'

'That's Goody Olch to you, and you can put that in your pipe and smoke it. Try your tricks with me and you'll have my Wiggler to answer to.'

The sergeant did not look much alarmed at this prospect. He sat back, eyes twinkling. 'And where's my wiggly-eared friend tonight? Thought he might have run off and left you, I did. Didn't I warn you about them fellows from the Fifth?'

'Ooh, you! Now don't you go running down his regiment. My Wiggler's ever so proud of it, though for the life of me I can't see why. Wouldn't he be dead by now if I hadn't bought him out? Made a fair hole in my savings, it did. But if I'd had to pay ten times over it'd be worth it, to get my Wiggler out.' Nirry's eyes misted. 'As I always say, Carney, would I have a purse full of gold, or see my Wiggler lying in his grave?'

'I'm still in *my* regiment,' said the sergeant, 'and I'm not dead.'

'The Blue Irions!' Scoffing, Nirry blinked away her tears. 'And when do you ever do a stroke of *anything*, that's what I'd like to know? Lounging round, sucking on your clay-pipe, cluttering up my respectable establishment night after night. Life of leisure, if you ask me. That's right, toss back your tankard! The Blue Irions, indeed!'

She turned on her heel, but the sergeant called after her, 'So where *is* Goodman Olch, eh?'

'Up serving the *quality*, that's where.'

'Quality *here*? On the Last Night of the Opera?'

'Don't sound so surprised. Not all them can fit in that there Opera House, can they? And them that can't, they know where they can come. We've had some *fine* folk in here, Carney Floss. You'll be surprised, one day you'll come sniffing round and we won't be taking riff-raff like you any more.'

'Sure you wouldn't take *me*, love? Just once?'

But Nirry – fortunately, perhaps, for Sergeant Floss – had already made her escape.

'Oh Carney, Carney!'

Nirry breathed heavily, leaning against the panelling in the back hall. For a moment – but just for a moment – she held her face in her hands. If only Carney would go, just go! There were times when she wished his regiment would be posted far away – back to Zenzau, at the least!

But no, she didn't want that, not really; besides, even Wiggler's lot were back in Agondon now, and didn't she know it? What a trial she had, to keep him away from his old army cronies! And she could hardly keep his cronies away from the Cat & Crown. More than once, the place had filled to the rafters with Bluejackets, Bluejackets, Bluejackets. What if one of them – just one of them – were to guess something? What if *Carney* were to guess something?

Poor Nirry! How she cursed the day she'd met that wretched Bob Scarlet! Wasn't it hard enough running a respectable tavern without some murdering rebel turning it into a base?

And if tonight's plan came off, they'd be in greater danger than ever. Nervously Nirry looked upstairs, towards where the so-called quality had gathered.

Quality, indeed!

But she could hardly go getting herself into a state. Could Baines look after the downstairs by herself? With one eye? It wasn't *nearly* enough! And Wiggler would be having trouble upstairs if past experience was anything to go on, which his wife had found it usually was.

If there weren't drawn swords by the end of the night, Nirry would be surprised. Very surprised.

Chapter 5

TURKEY DRUMSTICKS

'Please, Aunt?'

'Child, *no*.'

'But ... I want her.'

'Want? What ever for?'

'I like her. Isn't that enough?'

Umbecca Veeldrop rolled her eyes. 'My dear child, one does not *like* theatrical performers. Have you ever seen *me* liking such a person? But you are being perverse. Surely you are sensible of the chasm which must exist between those of *our* breeding and mere entertainers?'

Queen Jelica pouted. 'You smiled at the Clumpton Clowns, Aunt. I saw you.'

'Smiled, yes. At the proper time, one finds such persons diverting: that is their function. But should one, because they performed it adequately, thereby invite these *Clumpton Clowns* to share one's supper?'

This, the Queen might have retorted, was a privilege which her aunt would, ideally, extend to no one else at all, lest they reduce the available quantities of food. Instead she explained, somewhat laboriously, that she wasn't talking about the Clumpton Clowns. 'And I didn't say anything about supper, either. It's only interval.'

'Indeed it is, child: hence *not* the time to meet this Zenzan Nightingale. Remember, the evening ends with the Backstage Walk.'

'A cold formality!' The Queen had lost her patience. Really, one would think she was still at Mistress Quick's, not Queen of Ejland! It was not that she cared that much about Miss Tilsy Fash – but she was bored, bored! 'My mind is made up.' She gestured to her maid. 'Jilda, take my message. Miss Fash. Here. Now.'

Umbecca's eyes blazed. 'Child, this is most unorthodox.'

'Well, so am I.' And the Queen sniffed, tossed back her head and flounced away from her aunt.

This, no doubt, would have been a diverting spectacle for the audience, rather more diverting than the Clumpton Clowns; unfortunately, the little party had already retired to the withdrawing-chamber, the private apartment behind the royal box.

It was not a place the Queen much liked. Oh, it was adequate enough – there were chairs, books, a roaring fire; there were cold meats, cakes and pastries; footmen stood with trays at the ready, laden with glasses of

22

glittering Varl-wine. But how dreary it all was! The chamber was not only shabby, but entirely masculine, suited to the tastes of a coarser age. That fox's head above the fireplace! That looking-glass, framed in antlers!

But then, beside the fire, almost blending into the dark panelling, was Widow Waxwell. Poised demurely on one of the slithery dark chairs, Aunt Umbecca's old friend from the provinces pecked, bird-like, at a slice of ham.

In her wisdom, the Queen's aunt had decided that it would be improper to permit the Widow into the royal box. Instead, she had graciously allowed her friend to listen from the withdrawing-chamber, keeping the door just a little ajar. Ruefully, the Queen found herself thinking how different a personage was this Widow from the glamorous figure portrayed by Miss Tilsy Fash. Berthen Waxwell was stick-thin, withered, and had only a stump where one of her hands should be.

The Queen shuddered. Turning, she snatched a glass from a tray, flung back her head and would have drunk down the Varl-wine like medicine, but the bubbles went up her nose.

Impatiently, she thought of the morrow. Not the tedium of the Inaugural – that was merely duty. But the Masquerade! This year, the theme was Birds of the World. The Queen had been supervising the production of her costume for at least a moonlife.

With pretended fascination she gazed upon the sporting prints – gentlemen on horses, jumping over stiles – that hung, speckled and faded, against the reddish flock wallpaper. How many times had she been in this chamber before? Had she not implored her husband to have it renovated?

Indeed, and he had agreed; but nothing had been done yet, nothing at all. Dimly she was aware of her shimmering image, swimming away from her in the looking-glass.

A hand grazed her arm. The Queen jumped.

'Your Majesty, may I tender again my *sincere* apologies?'

It was Mander Heva-Harion. The Queen had never much liked him. Eay Feval was one thing, and *he* was a man of the cloth. Heva-Harion, recently promoted by her husband – or rather, by the First Minister – to the rank of Major-General, had no such excuse. Try as she might, the Queen could not help but find him repulsive. Was it his purplish lips, parting over a porcelain smile? His wrinkled, hard face, hanging like a mask beneath his steel-grey wig? The smoke from his tobarillo? Besides, he was *nobody*, wasn't he? Only Javey Heva-Harion's uncle. No titles, no lands of his own. Yet how swiftly he had risen in The Ascendancy! Often, as tonight, he would appear as proxy for the First Minister.

Fulsomely the creature expatiated upon the snow that had *so* delayed his passage to the Opera House, and hinted at his duties that were *so* greatly pressing; the Queen only nodded, in a dazed sort of way, and was even grateful when Aunt Umbecca appeared again.

The fat woman had been preoccupied with the cold meats. Having rapidly stripped several turkey drumsticks – grease rimmed her little mouth
– she had heaped a plate high with as many more as was practicable. She
only hoped there was time to allay her hunger. Often she had complained
of the inadequacy of these intervals; after all, there were only three of
them in the entire performance, and supper was still far away.

Anxiously she eyed a platter of cream horns, an enormous round pud-
ding and a gooseberry tart, wondering if she need point out to her niece
that it would *not* be the done thing to offer any refreshments to Miss Tilsy
Fash.

The Major-General repeated his apologies to Umbecca. Softening,
the fat woman informed him with a smile that of course she understood,
and asked if he would be attending her little supper party after the
performance. This, she hinted, would be an elaborate affair.

The Major-General could hardly doubt it. Since coming to the Koros
Palace, Lady Veeldrop had taken a particular interest in the kitchen
orders. Through her influence, the catering budget had been substantial-
ly increased. Arrangements for the Bird Ball, tomorrow night, were
rumoured to be of an extravagance unprecedented even in the most
decadent foreign Court.

So it was with all the more regret that the Major-General had to shake
his head, declaring that he must return to his duties as soon as the
performance was over.

Umbecca permitted herself to look a little crestfallen. She had rather
taken to the Major-General, who was, she had decided, a fine figure of a
man – a *man's* man, as they say. Everyone said he should have inherited
his brother's title. Only that feckless nephew stood in his way – what was
his name? Javey, yes: Fifteenth Marquis of Heva-Harion.

Still, thought Umbecca, the problem was hardly *insoluble*.

'But poor Major-General, to work so late! Do the wheels of government
never cease to turn?'

'The Major-General perhaps refers to his *military* responsibilities?'
Eay Feval turned from the table where he, too, had availed himself of
the buffet. Umbecca shot a glance at the contents of his plate. (Ham.
Pickles. Thank the Lord Agonis!) He smiled, with his best air of clerical
benevolence. 'Is there not talk of the Redjackets rising again?'

'Redjackets?' said the Queen. 'But I thought—'

Turkey spluttered from Umbecca's little mouth. 'Redjackets! How can
they rise, when they have fallen so utterly? You forget, Eay, that I lived
through the Siege of Irion. Did I not witness their utter defeat? Did not my
dear, late husband dispatch their pretensions – and their Pretender – once
and for all?'

'Indeed, dear lady,' Feval said soothingly; secretly he cursed himself for
his carelessness. Were not the Redjackets a sensitive matter for Umbecca?

24

Had not her beloved nephew, Torvester, been hanged as a traitor? Had not Jemany, her great-nephew – equally beloved, *more* beloved – followed a similar path?

Smoothly he turned to the Queen, asking how she was enjoying the evening's performance. Again, Umbecca wished he had not spoken, rolling her eyes as the girl – oblivious alike to the merits of Mr Credulon, Ripander and the Clumpton Clowns – lavished naïve praise upon Miss Tilsy Fash, whose animated efforts at *opera buffa* had both opened and closed the first part of the programme.

If Umbecca had entertained suspicions before, by now she was sure that the Palace should not have approved this particular performer, who had returned from a season in Zenzau especially for this evening. By all accounts, Miss Fash was a woman of questionable character. Besides, she was well past the first flush of youth. Couldn't even Umbecca tell when a voice had gone to pack?

Perhaps she should mention the Flying Mentinis. Yes, that would be an idea. What thought could Jelica have for that raddled old screecher when she had seen those extraordinary young acrobats – two brothers, both blind – whizzing on the high trapeze above the very heads of the startled audience?

But then, thought Umbecca, it was best not to refer to the high trapeze, not yet. One did not want to upset the Widow, who would only be able to hear the accompaniment. Let Berthen think it was a musical item, and she would be content.

Umbecca would have introduced the subject of the anthem, and the great quest to provide it with words – a safe subject, surely a safe subject – when Eay Feval interjected, 'It's those *blind* fellows next, isn't it?'

The fat woman glanced at him murderously. 'But you *are* enjoying yourself, child?' she grimaced, taking a fond step towards the Queen.

'There's just one thing.' The lovely brow furrowed. 'It's my seat. Can't I change with you, Aunt?'

Umbecca laughed lightly. 'Perverse child, that is the Opera Throne, is it not? When your husband is not in attendance, it is your place to occupy it, as it is mine to take the Seat of the Consort. That is how things are *done*. Is there more to be said?'

The Queen might have remarked that if *she* were so important, surely she should have the most comfortable seat; instead she said, 'It's too *big* for me. Aunt, can't we switch? You take my seat and I'll take yours.'

A smile flickered over Umbecca's lips. Eagerly she bit off a mouthful of turkey. That she was tempted, she could not deny; if proper form was an obsession of hers, still more was she preoccupied with her own grandeur. For a moment she saw herself in the royal throne; she even heard the anthem rising around her, imagining it fondly as a song in her praise. In the provinces long ago, Feval had promised her that she should be a great lady; by the grace of the Lord Agonis, this had come to pass, but was it not absurd that her stupid young niece – and all for the sake of a fleeting, girlish beauty – should occupy a position greater than her own?

Besides, Umbecca's seat *was* a little small.

But what was she thinking? 'Child, really! What would the world be coming to, answer me that, were we to question the most commonplace items of protocol?'

'Oh, *protocol!*' Turning away, the Queen grabbed another glass of Varl-wine, tossing it back.

How restless she was! And where was that wretched maid? Where was Miss Fash? The interval must be half gone already. Let Jilda bring Miss Fash to her, and bring her *now!*

Heva-Harion had drawn Feval aside. 'His Majesty, I take it, is indisposed again?'

'The usual. One can only hope he will attend the Masquerade. Not to mention the Inaugural.'

'To witness your triumph? You *would* think of that.'

'I think, Major-General, of the good of this realm.'

'Of course.' Politely, Heva-Harion inclined his head. 'But alas, I was late. What of the pit? What of the galleries? Were the common folk disconcerted when they knew their ruler was not to appear before them?'

Feval gestured to the Queen. 'Shall we say, the absence of *another* might have distressed them more?'

The Major-General drew deeply on his tobarillo. 'Indeed, the girl is a valuable asset to our cause.'

Feval, evidently, was expected to agree; instead, a stiffness came into his face and he wondered who this Heva-Harion thought he was, talking like this. *Our*, indeed! Just how highly did the fellow rate himself? Was he any more than a transitory politician, a functionary of the First Minister? If Feval were conscious of one thing, it was the dignity attendant upon his own station.

Or rather, the dignity he was soon to acquire.

As if with sudden interest he turned to the Widow Waxwell, enquiring if she was looking forward to these flying foreigners.

'F-Flying?' she said, puzzled.

The Queen, just then, cried, 'Jilda!'

'Miss Tilsy Fash, Your Majesty.' And the maid stood aside, revealing the many-feathered, extravagantly gowned and coiffured figure of the woman once dubbed the 'Zaxon Nightingale'.

Umbecca's little mouth set hard. Nightingale, indeed! More like a big, ugly vulture! But of course, she thought with sudden charity, Miss Fash had been a mere girl when she acquired her amusing designation – and that, undoubtedly, had been *long* ago.

Uneasily, Umbecca eyed the cream horns.

'The *what*, Bean?'

'The Clumptons. The clowns.'

'What about them?'

'They say they're good.'

'They, who's they?' Polty stamped on the carpet, shaking the snow from his boots and hat and coat.

'I don't know,' said Bean. 'People. Lots.'

Polty sighed. 'People are stupid, Bean. Don't you know that? And when they all agree on something, it's a fair bet they're wrong. Let's face it, it's not even a bet.'

Bean flushed, shame-faced. His friend's words were alarmingly loud; indeed, they might have been directed to the interval crowd that milled around them, spilling out from the stalls. But these were respectable folk, weren't they? Merchants and the like? Bean could hardly believe they were all stupid.

Not *all* of them.

'I just thought they might cheer us up. The clowns, I mean. We've got tickets.'

Polty's hand, black-gloved, gripped Bean's shoulder. 'Only one thing can cheer *me* up,' he said. 'Fool, haven't you learnt even that?'

Bean gulped. The hand was hurting him. 'Can't you be just a *bit* cheered up, Polty? In the meantime? I mean, while we're waiting?'

'Why, can you? Can you *really*?'

With a flash of contempt, Polty turned away, droplets spraying from his glistening coat. There were murmurs amongst the merchants. Bean's flush deepened; his friend lurched towards the stairs and he followed, struggling to keep up, suddenly hot in his heavy furs.

Rudely, Polty pushed past a servant.

'We've probably missed them anyway,' said Bean, rubbing his shoulder through his coat. 'But we might be in time for the Flying Mentinis.'

Polty rolled his eyes. 'Don't be so wet, Bean.'

'What's that, Polty?'

They had reached the first landing. Gold threads glimmered in blue wallpaper. Quality-folk glided here and there; there was urbane laughter, and the clinking of glasses.

'I said, don't be so wet.' Polty's voice dropped to a murmur. 'Those tickets are for the stalls, or haven't you noticed? Do you think I'm sitting down there, squashed in with a lot of dirty peasants, while Mandy Harion lords it in the royal box? Not to mention Aunt Umbecca,' he added savagely. 'Come on, we're having a drink.'

The Gentlemen's Lounge loomed before them, a warm cavern of mahogany with its big marble fireplaces, blazing with orange light. Polty glimpsed the long bar with its array of gleaming bottles. He smiled, pulling the hat from his head, tugging at a glove. But a footman on the door, elegant in epaulettes, looked suddenly alarmed, and raised a restraining hand.

'Excuse me, sir, I don't think—'

Polty's eyes flashed; threateningly, he stepped closer to the footman. 'What do you think we are, common guards?' he muttered. He fumbled in his jacket, searching for the badge of the Special Agents. But the footman merely twitched his mouth, eyes hardening.

Quickly, Bean stepped forward. Quality-folk had turned to look. And wasn't that Baron Aldermyle coming this way? Oh, if only Polty would not make a scene! Gently, Bean urged him to come away. 'There's the Merchants' Lounge,' he whispered. 'There's always the Merchants' Lounge.'

Polty's red hair blazed; for a moment, Bean imagined it bursting into flames.

But the moment passed. 'Damn this place. Come on, Bean. Let's go to Chokey's.'

'Not Chokey's.' Appealingly, Bean looked at the footman. 'We *can* go in the Merchants' Lounge, can't we? We're waiting for our master – I mean, our commanding officer ... waiting, that's all, while he's at the Opera...'

But already the footman had turned away, smiling sycophantically at an elderly gentleman in an opera cloak, hobbling on a cane towards the bar. Did the gentleman need help? Could the footman assist? Ah, but let him take the gentleman's arm!

Disgusted, Polty thundered downstairs.

'Waiting for your *master*, indeed!' he said furiously. 'And what are you, Bean, Mandy's coachman?'

'These days,' Bean said glumly, 'I pretty much am.'

'Oh?' Polty bridled. 'So what am I?'

Bean thought it best not to answer. Imperiously, they swept into the Merchants' Lounge.

Chapter 6

RED MOON MYSTERY

'There. It's red, see?'

  'What's that, Littler?'

  'Red. Jem, didn't you see?'

Jem yawned. He had not turned. 'Littler, put it away. I've got one too. So's Raj.'

  'What?' Clambering on to the plushly cushioned bench next to Jem, Littler patted the bag that hung over his heart. Since it had fallen to the young Unang boy to bear the crystal of his race, he had taken every opportunity to display it proudly, turning it in the light, polishing it, looking wonderingly into its depths. But Littler said he hadn't been talking about the Crystal of Theron. Not this time.

He meant the moon.

'Red? Like your crystal?' said Jem.

'Like blood. Peered out from behind the clouds, it did. Then it was gone again.'

Jem hunched wearily over the levers, wheels and dials. 'The moon's not red, Littler. Anyway, I'd have seen.'

'You were asleep.' There was a certain cockiness in the little boy's voice. 'You were nodding off, Jem. Wasn't he, Ejjy?'

Ejard Orange, who had guzzled up the last of his milk some time ago, and most of the other provisions too, had been padding irritably about the narrow cabin. If anyone were eager for this journey to end, it was the big, hungry cat.

With a resigned *miaow* he leapt up between Littler and Jem, curling into a warm, furry ball.

'Now *that's* nodding off. Well, let's hope so.' Jem looked through the wide window, where the cabin's dim, unflickering lights palely reflected the scene within. Ghostly images of his own face and Littler's hovered against a billowing blackness; in the background, slumped and sleeping, were Rajal and Myla. On and on their warm cocoon fizzed and thrummed through the chill, occluded darkness.

It was their third night on the skyship. Dusk had already declined into darkness when the little party first set off, hearts heavy with sadness, after Captain Porlo's burial at sea. That first night, they had gazed with grave wonderment at the tropical skies, spangled with thousands upon thousands of stars; when day came, the sun seared through the windows and

29

the sea glittered below like a second starry field. The next day had been one of deserts, then waters again, then greener, cooler lands; Ejland, Jem was certain, could not be far off now.

On the first night, even the second, he had taken his turn to sleep.

Now he did not dare.

Littler urged, 'But you *must* Jem. What about on the magic carpet? That was much more dangerous, and you slept all the time.'

'Didn't.' Jem grinned. 'Well, it was comfortable.'

If only they still had their wonderful carpet! In his haze of tiredness, it was extraordinary to Jem that Littler even remembered their strange journey to Wenaya. How long ago it seemed! Were it not for the sea-blue Crystal of Javander, nestling warmly beneath his tunic, Jem might have thought their adventures in those island realms no more than a troubling dream.

He winced at a fizz of lightning crackling from the skyship's blue, metallic hull. He rubbed his eyes, saying that things had been different on the carpet.

Littler looked round dubiously, almost fearfully, at the dark wood and leather and curves of riveted brass. 'The skyship's flying of its own accord, isn't it?'

Jem blinked. 'What are you getting at, Littler?'

'I mean, how do you know where we're *going*, Jem?'

'The skyship seems to know. I suppose Oclar must have told it the way. Well, not *told* it – oh, I don't know.'

'Face it, Jem, you're just looking out of the window.'

This was not entirely fair. Before Jem and his friends had left Wenaya, the Prince of Tides had given Jem a number of instructions on how to work the skyship. He knew how to veer from high mountains, thunderstorms and flocks of birds. He knew how to make the ship fly higher or lower, and how to make it land.

What he could not do was set its course.

'Littler, why aren't *you* sleeping tonight?'

'I've tried. I'm too stirred up.'

'Well, so am I.' But Jem had to yawn again. He shook his head. Anxiously he looked towards the back of the cabin, where Rajal slumped, breathing heavily, beside the couch where his unconscious sister had been strapped in place. 'Poor Raj, at least *he*'s getting some sleep. At last.'

'Funny, isn't it?' Littler said sadly. 'We can't sleep at all. And poor Myla can't do anything else.'

'Not,' said Jem, 'if she's going to stay young.'

'But she's so much older already!' There was a crack in Littler's voice. He clutched his crystal and his brow screwed up tight. 'And yet she's *really* still the same age as me, isn't she?'

'Used to be, Littler. And will be again, we hope.'

Littler blinked back the tears in his eyes. Poor Myla! How he cursed the evil that possessed her! 'I … I know I only met her once, Jem. Properly, I mean. But oh, how I wish she'd come back! Sometimes I want to shake her, just to see her awake again.'

'I know, Littler, I know. If only you'd seen her as she used to be, before she fell into the Spidermother's grip! Back in Ejland, I don't think I knew anyone more alive than Myla.' He looked down. 'Well, only one.'

Cata's image loomed painfully in Jem's mind.

'Don't worry,' he added quickly. 'We'll make Myla good as new. Promise.'

Littler gulped. 'Really, Jem? Young again?'

'We've got no choice. After all, if we fail with Myla, we've failed with the quest too.' Jem turned gravely to his young companion. 'We've found four crystals. Only one more. But Littler, it's still 999*d*. There's a whole year till the End of Atonement, have you thought of that?'

The little boy looked blank.

'Never mind, it's the Ejland calendar. But we're not going to fail.' Jem's voice was not quite convincing, even to himself. 'We *can't* fail now, can we?'

Littler only looked solemn, and gulped again.

'These bird-men—'

'Men, really—'

'They're Vagas, aren't they?'

'Vagas? Of course not.'

'Not *our* sort, no. But Vagas from *somewhere*?'

'Come, my love, if they were any sort of Vagas, they'd hardly be performing before His I.A.M., would they?'

'They're not. Ejjy Blue's not here, is he?'

'Well, he was meant to be.' A sigh. 'And we came out in this weather, too!'

'Oh, Japier, you're not complaining? We've seen Queen Jel, haven't we? That's the main thing. Do you know, she's even lovelier than her engravings? When she first came out – why, I nearly died!'

The conversation was between a merchant and his lady in the pit just below the Cham-Charing box. Freddie Chayn listened sardonically. Everything this couple said revealed them as *new money*. They had tried hard, but everywhere there was that fatal vestige of vulgarity. Indeed, more than a vestige – in the lady's hair, for example, a mess of cheap dyes, frizzed, burnt with tongs, and piled up extravagantly in imitation of her betters.

Oh, the middle classes!

But they were always rising.

31

'Those Clumptons looked like Vagas to me,' the merchant's wife was saying. 'Not that I mind, mind. I mean, we used to enjoy them Vaga-fairs, didn't we? And what about them Silver Masks? They've performed for the highest.'

'Not any more. Outlawed, they are.'

'What for, love? I've never known why.'

'We've got the Vagas' measure, that's what!' snapped the merchant. 'Dirty beggars took us in before. Not now, though, with Ejjy Blue on the throne. Brought us back to greatness, the blue king has.'

The fellow swelled with pride. But pride in what? With a start, Freddie realised that this merchant was more of a patriot than he had ever been. But then, had not Freddie's worthless principality once, long ago, been an independent state? So was he an Ejlander, or was he not?

Freddie could never quite make up his mind.

Interval was almost over. The one-gong had rung, and now the two-gong; slowly the auditorium was filling again. All around there was chatter, laughter and the clinking of glasses; in the orchestra-pit, the viols were tuning up, emitting a succession of catlike squeals.

Freddie shifted uncomfortably in his seat. When interval began, the others had refused to leave the box. Lady Cham was in some kind of distress, her head wobbling a little more than usual; Lady Margrave endeavoured to console her. As for Tishy, the girl had put a question to the Professor, some nonsense about verbs; the old man was still answering it even now, muttering interminably away.

All this, and not a servant to be had. It had been left to Freddie to fight his way out to the foyer and bring back a tray of drinks, which he had virtually had to wrestle from a footman's hand. Alas, he had spilled one of them on the way back. Politeness compelled him to assume it was his own.

He sighed impatiently, wondering when the curtain would rise again. Baron Aldermyle and the young bucks had returned noisily to the next-door box. In the course of the interval they had acquired several ladies – or female creatures in the garb of ladies – and would appear to have imbibed large quantities of rum-and-orandy; further supplies were on hand. Freddie, with pretended casualness, averted his eyes. He looked towards the stage. He looked up to the ceiling. He looked across to the royal box, where the Queen and her party had yet to return.

His fingers drummed on the balustrade.

A boy – a son, presumably, awkward in wig and velvet suit – was sitting in between the merchant and his wife. For a time the boy had been silent, swinging his foot distractedly back and forth; now, in a piping, unbroken voice, he began a series of questions about the Flying Mentinis. Didn't they sound much more exciting than the Clumptons? Or that old gentleman with the funny high voice? Or that *screeching* lady? But they couldn't really be blind, could they? And could they fly? They couldn't, could they?

'Wait, my boy, just you wait,' the merchant said, his tone becoming kindly.

'It must be some sort of wires. Is it wires?'

'They leap. They jump. But it's as *if* they fly. They'll soar above our heads, our very heads.'

'When they're blind? Really blind?'

'Just you wait, my lad.'

The three-gong rang in the foyer outside.

'But what if they fall?' said the merchant's wife.

'The Flying Mentinis?' The merchant laughed.

'Well, I never!' The wife shuddered, adjusting her shawl. 'Dear me, I'm sure I shall be frightened.'

'Come, my dear, they never fall. Not the Mentinis.'

'I'll protect you, Mama,' piped the boy.

Freddie became aware that he was biting his knuckles. He ceased abruptly, snapping his eyes open. Ladies fluttered their fans. Gentlemen adjusted their waistcoats. In Mistress Quick's party, Goody Garvice was scolding some of their charges; Baron Aldermyle made lewd gestures, illustrating a bawdy story.

But Freddie's gaze was fixed upon the royal box. Could his eyes be mistaken? Through a gap between the Opera Throne and a curve of velvet curtain, he could just make out a door with a quilted back. It was the door to the withdrawing-chamber, and now it opened.

Figures emerged. Feval. Mandy. The fat woman.

And there amongst them was Miss Tilsy Fash.

The Queen embraced her and the great songstress withdrew, disappearing down a corridor, while the royal party lingered on the threshold of the box. A servant gave a signal; in the pit, the conductor raised his baton. There was a fanfare and the audience rose to its feet, applauding the reappearance of the Queen and her companions.

Freddie's mind reeled. As he dutifully clapped his white-gloved hands, he could think only of Tilsy. But he had seen her at the beginning of interval, when he went to get the drinks! He had clutched her hand. She had smiled at him, whispering that all was going to plan.

And then she had gone to the Queen?

A horrible thought flashed into his mind. His hands stopped working and he sank back into his seat.

Elsan Margrave hissed, 'Freddie! The Queen!'

Her Royal Majesty was still on her feet. Like a rocket, Freddie leapt up again, flushing darkly. Had others seen his blunder? But he barely cared. At another time, this might have been a disaster; now, other thoughts were far too pressing. Could Tilsy … could Tilsy have been *warning* the Queen?

No, it was impossible!

But now, to Freddie's astonishment, there was an altercation in the royal box. It lasted just for an instant. Many – most, perhaps – might not even have seen it. A matter of gestures, flashings of eyes. But what happened next was clear to all. Smirking, the Queen slipped into the Seat of the Consort – and her Aunt Umbecca, first awkwardly, then imperiously, took her place in the Opera Throne.

The applause subsided raggedly; quickly, the orchestra burst back into life and Freddie Chayn sat with a hand across his mouth, his secret burning like acid in his eyes. Bewildered, he gazed at the still-unrisen curtains.

He pushed back his chair. 'Excuse me, I—'

'Freddie, what's wrong?'

But Freddie was gone.

Chapter 7

ANOTHER VANTAGE

'Hm? What?'

'The Mentinis. The acrobats.'

'I've told you, Bean, no, you can't.'

Bean looked miserably into his flattening ale. He had barely touched it. 'I was only saying they'd be *on* by now. I can hear the orchestra, can't you? Just faintly?'

Polty was not listening. He banged on the bar for another Vantage. Bean grimaced, not daring even to look at the barman as the fellow splashed out a fresh dram. What was this, the fifth? Sighing, the side-officer gazed with pretended interest around the Merchants' Lounge, at the overstuffed chairs and the Tiralon carpets and the portrait of His Imperial Agonist Majesty, swelling in his blue garb above the stone fireplace.

The merchants, if merchants they were, had all returned to the auditorium; only Polty and Bean were left behind.

'Those hearth-chairs are free now,' Bean said gently. 'You'd like to dry out your boots, wouldn't you?'

'I still think we should go to Chokey's,' Polty muttered.

Bean gulped, 'In this weather? Besides, we're on duty. What will the Major-General say if we're not here when he needs us? You know we can't take chances. Not any more.'

A cloud passed over Polty's face. He leaned forward, his breath gusting hotly. 'Come on, Bean, this rubbish goes on for aeons yet. Wouldn't you like another visit to Chokey's? We'll be back before the old bastard wants us. Get the coats. Come on, you enjoyed it last time. You're shy, but you're getting a taste for it, I know you are.'

This was not true; Bean did not even want to think about the notorious establishment where his friend squandered so much of his time. He stood up, gesturing to the hearth-seats. 'Polty, it's freezing outside. Let me get you another dram. Let me – let me get you a bottle.'

There was a moment of tension; then Polty lurched upright, staggering towards the fire. Thank the Lord Agonis! Now, thought Bean, his only problem – hardly a new one – would be to get Polty back on his feet later. After all, there would be things to do. Duties.

Best not to think of that.

And yet, for an instant, the tasks of this night flashed vividly across Bean's mind. He saw himself, stiff-faced and shivering, driving uphill as

35

the dead mother lay behind them in the snow. He saw them pulling up at the Great Temple; he saw the robed figure stealing out to meet them, taking the infant from Polty's arms. Yes, everything was ready, wasn't it? And nothing here was new. But when Bean thought of what would happen later, he found himself shuddering violently, as if he were still out in the freezing night.

He slumped into the hearth-seat beside his friend.

'Now this is nice, isn't it, Polty?' He poured Polty a fresh glass; Polty tossed it down. They put their feet on the fender; steam rose from their boots. Bean leaned back. Could he, even for a moment, be happy? It was possible, wasn't it, if one could just *forget*?

Perhaps that was happiness: the ability to forget.

His head rolled against the warm leather; he gazed at Polty through half-closed eyes, lingering upon the creamy, pale face and the carroty hair, bright as the fire. Perhaps Bean might have drifted into sleep, dreaming about Polty at the height of his glory; instead, as if prompted by some evil imp, Bean found his eyes opening wider. The mists cleared and he saw the frog-like ballooning at Polty's jowls; he saw the buttons straining on the blue tunic.

Poor Polty! At the very end of his boyhood, just when he had appeared condemned to a life of ignominy, a curious magic – if magic it had been – had transformed him from a rolling ball of lard into a young man of devilish, sharp-jawed beauty; now, it seemed, the magic was slipping into reverse.

Polty lolled across the little table between them, grabbing, almost cuffing at the Vantage bottle; after another dram – the seventh? eighth? – he reached into his tight jacket, producing a tobarillo from a little silver case. Smoke clouded the air; Polty inhaled deeply and his face twisted, as if beset by troubling thoughts.

Bean tensed himself. This was not good.

'You know it's all *her* fault, don't you?' Polty said.

Bean might have asked his friend to explain; he might have changed the subject. Either course would be dangerous. He had heard this speech again and again, whenever Polty was in his cups. It was best not to encourage him, but to lurch into an another topic could also be unwise: Polty might grow angry.

Best to say nothing. Polty must be drowsy in the heat of the fire; perhaps he would forget about Catayane.

No such luck.

'I tell you, Bean, it's *her* fault. Isn't she my wife, my rightful wife?' (She was not. But Bean was silent.) 'If the bitch hadn't run away, it would never have happened, would it?' (Here, Bean did not know *what* to say.) 'I had to use a *bit* of force, didn't I? A gentle bit of force, just to teach her a lesson?' (Bean wished Polty would lower his voice.) 'I just wanted to break

her in, didn't I? For her own good? I tell you, if it hadn't been for her ...'
(Tears burst from Polty's eyes. His shoulders shook.) 'And then that
Sultan ... he wouldn't have done what he did, would he? He couldn't
have ... could he?'

Bean was scarlet. Nervously he looked across to the bar. 'P-Polty, I
couldn't have a drop of that Vantage, could I? Just a—'

Polty stood sharply, knocking over the bottle. 'Chokey's. Come on.'

'Polty, no!' Bean was up, too. Dark liquid soaked into the carpet round
their feet.

'My coat,' Polty snapped. 'And what are *you* looking at?'

The barman swivelled nervously away.

'My coat, Bean! My coat!'

Despairingly, Bean began to flutter about his friend. Really, Polty
couldn't want to go to out again, could he? Wouldn't it be nicer to sit by
the fire? Yes, let them sit down again, and Bean would get *another* bottle –
wouldn't that be best?

Polty lurched forward, clutching his soft belly, and would have fallen if
Bean had not caught him.

'Poor Polty, but you're not well! Here, lean on me. Yes, that's right.
Come on, let's get you to the garderobes.'

'Just a peep?'

'Cata, no.'

'Just to make sure?'

Only moments now. The stage loomed, dark and waiting, behind the
purple glimmer of the curtains. This time there was no crack of light in the
middle, but in the left curtain Cata saw a hole, a circle of sharp gold like
a little star.

Just at eye level. Just right.

'No, Cata.' Landa gripped her friend's arm. 'You heard the fanfare.
She's back in her seat. Quick, on your mark.'

'You're right.' The two young women hugged quickly, each aware of
the other's nerves strung taut like tensile wires. Applause, like thunder,
boomed through the curtains. Cata skittered across the stage, taking her
place in the chorus line.

The painted flats behind them, glimmering in the gloom, depicted a
high, remote mountain range. Before it, the many girls were curved in an
arc, Landa at one end, Cata at the other.

Cata peered at her co-conspirator. All the girls, as the Mentinis had
demanded, were dressed in black shifts. They wore no wigs and had tied
back their hair; their only striking features were their faces, which were
painted a blank, dazzling white. As a disguise, thought Cata, this was
dangerously thin.

Would Jeli recognise her? Or Aunt Umbecca?

Cata calmed herself. So far, all had gone to plan. To be sure, certain of the other girls had resented them – nobodies, shoehorned into the chorus line on the whim of Miss Fash. More than once Cata had felt an envious glance, or sudden, seemingly accidental pushings and shovings. Sometimes she longed to lash out. Yesterday, a girl had jabbed an elbow into Landa's eye; today, in dress rehearsal, another had tripped Cata, and only Landa's restraining arm had held her back.

Were the girls merely envious? Might not some of them have suspected something – tittle-tattled about them to rich, powerful lovers?

Still, that danger was over now. There was only Jeli to worry about.

And Aunt Umbecca.

Cata shuddered. For an instant, she had a flash of an old nightmare. With the Mentinis in mid-flight, the Queen would leap up, crying out her old schoolfriend's name; then Aunt Umbecca's voice would boom down, demanding that the guards seize her runaway niece. It would all be over; it would all have been for nothing, all Bob Scarlet's careful planning, all the secret coaching from Miss Fash.

All Hul's hopes. Bando's. Nirry's.

No, it was absurd. It was too late already. In moments, the Mentinis would have done their work.

And Cata – Landa, too – would be far away.

Now the curtains rose. From the orchestra pit, surging up majestically, came a certain rousing melody of Mr Bachoven's, adopted as a theme by the Flying Mentinis.

Cata's heart thundered. For a moment, the stage remained still, with only the mysterious white faces staring out from the gloom. Then, dancing and dazzling, came a beam of limelight, picking out just one figure, a gentleman on a gleaming trapeze that descended above the auditorium.

The applause gathered strength. The gentleman had a shaven, slightly pointed head, surmounting a body of formidable strength. He might have been an image of physical perfection, but for the one detail that disturbed: the smooth, unbroken skin where his eyes should have been.

The gentleman was oblivious to his disability. Dressed in a tight costume of blue and white stripes, he flung out one arm confidently, generously, like a host inviting the audience to step with him into a different world.

A second trapeze descended, with a second Mentini, identical to his brother but for his suit – not blue and white, but red and white. Elegantly the brothers swung towards each other, gripped hands, flipped through the air and swapped trapezes.

The audience gasped; the blind men did it again, then again, this time turning twice, always in time to their surging theme.

For Cata, it was like watching some remarkable mechanism, repeating ever more complicated actions with precise, clockwork certainty. What would happen next? She knew exactly. She saw the brothers whirling like impossible dancers, blurring together into a purple streak. She saw them swinging on the same trapeze, the blue brother balanced on the bar, the red balanced on the blue's shoulders, first on his feet, then on his hands, then on one hand, then on just a finger. She saw them on the high wire, scuttling on tip-toe from side to side, then swaying, leaping, landing on the wire again.

And all the time the girls in the chorus would raise their voices in incongruous comic songs, nonsense about daring young fellows and tumbling and turning, merrily, merrily, meet in the middle and *bump!*-sa-daisy.

All this Cata had seen before, again and again in rehearsal. But then would come the things she had not seen, the things that could happen only tonight. First the sudden, startling battle in mid-air, blue against red, red against blue; then red's swinging fist, then blue crashing down, and the audience freezing into bewildered shock.

Then, while every eye sought the fallen figure, wondering if this could be part of the act, the red brother would swoop out one last time, strike like lightning at the royal box, grab the Queen and sweep her away.

That is, if all went according to plan.

Chapter 8

A GENTLEMEN'S LAVATORY

Which was the way?

Freddie Chayn blundered along a corridor. He plunged down a flight of stairs. This was a floor for the merchant classes. Here and there were sets of doors, all shut now, leading into the stalls. He heard the swell of the orchestra, muffled and distorted. But was this the way? He should have known. Had he not slipped backstage in the interval? Had he not waylaid Miss Tilsy Fash just outside her dressing room?

He rounded a corner and saw a pair of Bluejackets standing at the doors that led backstage. Damn it. The same ones as before? He thought of them hovering in the interval, sniggering and smirking at the feckless young gentleman making a fool of himself over a singer. But the guards had been the fools. Or so Freddie had thought then.

They eyed him curiously. It was interval no longer. He had no reason to be here.

But perhaps his pallor was reason enough.

'I ... I'm n-not well,' he mumbled, covering his mouth.

Yes, they were the same ones! The sniggering came again, from one of them at least; the other, with admirable restraint, merely smirked and pointed upstairs, indicating the way to the Gentlemen's Lounge.

Gurgling, Freddie acknowledged his mistake. Too far down. Of course. Yes.

'But I don't – don't think I can quite...'

'Not the quality? Will the *commons* do?'

The pointing finger lowered; Freddie lurched off, ignoring the fresh guffaws behind him. Was he not a prince? But what did that mean? The Ejlanders had made Chayn into nothing more than a province, installing a military governor, closing the Court. What was Freddie's title but a mockery? Why, he wasn't even rich any more! Just one of Constansia's hangers-on.

These days, even the guards knew it.

He propelled himself down a second flight of stairs. Not the quality, the commons: yes. He had studied the layout of this mouldering old labyrinth. The garderobes for the merchants had once been for the players; there was a connecting panel, leading backstage. That would be the way – but when he got there, what would he *do*?

40

He slumped in despair. *Oh, Tilsy!* Could she really have betrayed them? Had he not been by her side through long moonlives in Zenzau? Had he not been with her when Bob Scarlet held up their coach, and Tilsy, instead of fainting away, had embraced the highwayman? Boldly she had declared that they would be partners, dedicated to the downfall of the Bluejacket régime; and Freddie, in a rush, had seen that there was more, much more to Miss Tilsy Fash than he had ever dreamed. In that moment he had known that he loved her.

What was he to think now? Had it all been a bluff?

Freddie almost wished he had abandoned all caution, yelling out his warnings in the auditorium. *No, stop it. No, don't.* Everyone would have thought he was mad, or waking from a nightmare. Everyone, that is, except the Flying Mentinis. But how could he warn them now?

He struggled back to his feet. Like a man who was really about to be sick, Freddie plummeted into the Merchants' Lounge.

The garderobes! Which was the way?

'There … that's better, isn't it?'

Polty, for some moments, did not reply. Bean sighed. There had been a time when his friend, like any good Tarn lad, drank only ale; now it was nothing but Vantage, notorious through all Ejland as the fiercest of spirits. Bean would be staggering after a single dram! But look at Polty: so early in the evening, and here he was slumped on his knees, his head hanging over a circular, stinking hole. From time to time he moaned; strings of vomit swung from his lips.

'Here, let me wipe your mouth.' Bean looked round anxiously. No cubicles separated the latrines, not for commoners; if anyone were to walk in, his friend would present a pitiful, even comic sight.

And Polty would not like that.

The drunkard sniffed loudly, drawing in a long, gurgling stream of snot. 'I tell you, Bean, if I see her again …' His voice echoed down the stinking hole. 'But I *will* see her again, Bean, and this time I'll break her … *I'll break her, I tell you!*'

'*Shh*, I know … Polty, can you stand?' Bean curled an arm round his friend's shoulders.

'Where … where is she, Bean?' Leaning heavily on his lanky companion, Polty clawed his way upright. His face was green. His breath was foul. Bleary-eyed, he looked around him, as if his lost beloved might be lurking here, mocking him from the corners of this dingy, cold chamber. 'Do you think … do you think she's back in Ejland? Or still in Unang Lia? Do you think she's still with that crippler-boy? Or … or…'

'*Shh*, Polty, *shh*. She might be far away, she might be close – for all we know, closer than we think.'

Polty stumbled, almost slipping to the floor. 'I'll find her, Bean ... *I'll find her, I tell you!*'

'*Shh*. I know, I know ... Polty, can you walk?' And Bean dared to add, 'You know we're still on duty, don't you? No more Vantage tonight, hm? No more. Not tonight.'

These, Bean knew, were daring words; at another time, Polty might have turned on him, but now he was barely listening. To Bean's horror, he broke into guttural sobs, sinking again to the stone-flagged floor.

'Bean, Bean,' he cried, 'why won't she love me? Cruel Cata! Doesn't she know she was made to be mine? Doesn't she know I was made to be hers? That bitch, that evil bitch! Doesn't she know I love her more than life itself?'

'*Shh!* Polty, please ... not here...'

In Bean's life there was much to endure, and often he was filled with horror. That night, there had been bad things already; there would be worse before it was over. But of all his fears, none was worse than that poor Polty would break down for good, his mind snapping like a thread.

Bean slid to the cold floor, urgent in his ardour to comfort his friend.

The door burst open. Polty reeled.

'Wh-what's *he* doing here?' he burst out.

'P-Polty,' Bean hissed, 'we're in a *garderobe—*'

Freddie Chayn's eyes grew wide. He skidded to a halt, staggered back at the sight of Polty and Bean.

'I said, what's *he* doing?' Polty's voice cracked into a screech. Desperately, Bean tried to silence him. To be refused entry to the Gentlemen's Lounge had been humiliation enough; to be ejected from the Merchants' Lounge would be *far* too much. Polty had his pride. Was he to be seen in so abject a state by this perfumed, periwigged society fop? Bean gulped; Polty swayed back to his feet.

Shadows played on the tiles and flagstones.

Freddie faltered, 'If you'll pardon me, officers, I have, as you will appreciate, an *urgent* need...'

'Here? This is for merchants!' Polty's face, green before, had now turned red; he dashed away his tears and snuffled furiously. 'I've seen you. I know you. Society gadfly. Dirty little parasite. Think you're the finest quality, don't you? You're not even on the map. When I come into *my* title, I'll wipe you out. Oh yes, I know who you are. I know.'

Bean covered his face in his hands. This was exactly the scene he had feared.

And here, in a garderobe!

Freddie could think only of the panel at the back. Yes, he could see it. There was no time to lose. *Warn them, warn them.* Who cared about these drunken fools? Let them think what they like!

He took a step forward.

42

So did Polty. Freddie stepped back.

'Polty, leave him alone. He's just a fop.'

'You think so, Bean? I think he's *spying* on us!'

'Don't be silly,' Bean snapped. 'Let's just get out of here. We're on duty, remember!'

Bean might as well have been silent. Freddie gulped, screwing up his courage. Again he stepped forward; this time, Polty pushed him in the chest. 'Come on, fop, who sent you? What did you hear?'

'Polty, enough,' said Bean. 'Come away.'

In a moment, they would; but first, Freddie took another step.

This time, Polty lashed out. How he laughed as the Prince of Chayn fell, cracking his head on the flagstones! The periwig slipped off, revealing the sparse auburn hair beneath; Freddie twitched, then was still.

Bean groaned, 'Polty, what have you *done*?'

But Polty was smiling. He clapped an arm around his friend's shoulder. 'What, Bean, loitering in a garderobe? Come on, I need another dram.'

> *Blind they may be but they fly so fast*
> *They'd never see what was going past:*
> *Twirling and whirling round till at last*
> *They meet in the middle and* bump!-*sa-daisy*,
> *Bump! bump! bump!*

Triumph or despair: had to be.

Triumph: or Plan B.

Plan B: despair.

Bump, bump! Of all the silly songs Cata had learnt for tonight, this was the silliest. Back and forth she swayed in time with the other girls, raising her voice in a joyous lilt as the blind acrobats swung above the audience, turning and tumbling in their stripy costumes, bumping hips, bouncing back like balls. Such power! Such precision! In the stalls, every face was turned upwards in wonder. From all over the theatre came gasps and cries, even from the quality-folk.

How brightly the trapezes flashed!

> *Men? Yes they are, but they might just be*
> *Birds from the way that they fly so free:*
> *Up, down, around and then look, d'you see?*
> *They meet in the middle and* bump!-*sa-daisy*,
> *Bump! bump! bump!*

It was the climax of the act. Cata struggled to keep the smile on her face. In the corner of her eye she could just make out Landa, like her own mirror-image across the stage. Her friend – Landa, after all, was a

Priestess of Viana – had counselled her in a dreamy voice to banish all fears, concentrating only on the lilt of the orchestra, on the to-and-fro of the dance steps, on the silly words of the *Bump! bump!* song. Just let it happen, Landa had said. Empty your mind. Then, when the real action starts, it will just *happen*, too. Over before we know it.

If only! Cata screwed up her forehead. Nervously she shuffled round in a circle, arms linked with the girl beside her. *Bump!* she sang, *bump! bump!*, but all the time she was aware of another rhythm, of her heart pounding ominously out of time with the merry *one-two-three, one-two-three...*

Too often lately, Cata had felt a sudden, alarming lurch of sickness. At first, she had denied its cause, even to herself. Only in the last moonlife had she come to accept the truth. It all added up – that night with Jem in Unang Lia, in the Sanctum of the Flame ... how could Cata have been such a fool? And yet, how she longed for this child!

So far, only Nirry knew of Cata's condition. But Cata wondered for how much longer she could keep her secret – and for how long she could keep up her rebel life. Nirry would look after her, Cata knew that much ... But still she was frightened, not least of all of the weakness, the helplessness that soon must overcome her.

For now, she prayed only that she wouldn't throw up. Or trip. Nothing must spoil what was about to happen.

Soon, the girl whom Cata had known as Jeli Vance would whizz down to the stage, shrieking in the arms of Mentini Red. Cata and Landa would leap forward, Cata grabbing one hand, Landa the other, lashing them together with cunning cords. Helpless, the Queen would soar into the air, while Cata and Landa grabbed ropes of their own, rushing up into the flies to grab Jeli, bundling her out through a trapdoor in the ceiling, across the roof of the house next door, then down into an alley where Hul and Bando, disguised in stolen uniforms, awaited in what appeared to be a Bluejacket coach.

Meanwhile, Mentini Blue would have bounded back to the stage, swung up to the flies with his brother, and both would have vanished across the rooftops, too; the stagehands who had operated the machinery would have made their escape in the confusion, while Miss Fash and Freddie Chayn would look entirely innocent.

Any moment now, thought Cata, *any moment now*. Round and round she swung on her partner's arm, desperately fixing her smile again.

Please, let this work: please, please.

Key change. Final chorus.

Bump! bump! The white faces of the other girls had become a blur. Turning, Cata took in the scene in the auditorium. She saw the blue stripy costume and the red, meeting and parting precariously in the air. The trapezes, flashing silver. She saw the royal box, just glimpsed it for an instant, unobscured by the limelight's dazzle.

Cata's heart stopped. How could this happen? What about Freddie? What could this mean? A spasm shook her; she stumbled, losing her place in the chorus line. The girl beside her bumped her. Cata was oblivious. *Bump!* Could something really be wrong?

All had been planned with the utmost precision, every move engraved upon the senses of the brothers. And now the moment had come. The waltzing rhythm rose to its climax. Back they came, one blind brother, another blind brother, ready to *bump!* one last time.

No: this time, Mentini Red lashed out, striking his brother. The blue figure crashed into the stalls; there were cries. The conductor turned, startled. The orchestra lost its place. Viols squealed; the harpsichord faltered. In the royal box, Queen Jeli cowered; the Lector and the Major-General exchanged shocked glances. But there was no time for their gallantry. Shrieking, rising imperiously from the Opera Throne, an indignant Aunt Umbecca repelled the attacker who grappled and clawed at her mountainous form.

'*Unhand me, sir, unhand me!*' the fat woman cried, swinging back a sausage-fingered hand. The Major-General lashed out with his stick, but it was Umbecca's blow that connected first.

Her fist was like a rock. Mentini Red crashed down.

Umbecca sank back, clutching a hand over her enormous breasts. Gentlemen fluttered around her; footmen sprang forth. Rapidly, rapidly, she flapped with her fan.

Below, guards swarmed through the stalls. Mentini Blue bounded up as if to save his brother. No good. Shots rang out. The theatre was a chaos of screaming.

Cata, despairing, covered her face. 'Plan B! Oh *no*—'

'Quick!' Landa cried. 'Let's get out of here—'

'But the Mentinis! We can't just—'

'There's nothing we can do! Cata, *quick*—'

The ropes, at least, had fallen from the flies.

Chapter 9

CEREMONY IN THE CRYPT

Not once! Not once, she would wager!

Goody Olch, formidable landlady of the Cat & Crown, bustled importantly into her back hall. She must check on the kitchen. It needed checking, no doubt about that. Oh, there was a local girl to help out, but she was useless – worse, if worse she could be, than some of the trollops Nirry had had to put up with as a regimental cook. Had the spit been turned in the last couple of fives? Had the ragoût been stirred, even once?

Nirry grabbed a candle from a side-shelf, lighting it impatiently with a tinder-stick. Steely-eyed, she was about to storm down to the basement when all at once there was a commotion on the landing. At first, she was alarmed. But this, she realised, was a familiar thunder.

'Boys!' she called. 'Boys, stop that at once! What do you think you're doing, racing round at this time of night?'

In a trice, Nirry was on the landing too, sternly separating two identical, swarthy urchins who rolled and tumbled, pummelling each other.

'Am I going mad,' she said, 'or didn't I put you two to bed? I'm sure I did, didn't I, and blew out your candle, too? Now what's this all about? Raggle? Taggle?'

Raggle snuffled loudly. He squirmed in Nirry's grip, his little nightshirt billowing, his fists still tightly clenched. Taggle hung his head. In the candlelight, Nirry saw tears in Raggle's eyes. Above, from behind the door of the private chamber, came muffled guffawings, clinkings of tankards. To Nirry, the sounds were ominous.

She must get the boys back to bed.

'Boys, this isn't like you, is it? Racing round my tavern like wild things I expect – but *belting* each other? In the middle of the night? What's this about? You'll tell Aunt Nirry, won't you? Come on, Raggle, put down that fist.'

Slowly, Raggle obeyed.

'Taggle,' he sniffed, 'Taggle said—'

'Did not!' Taggle burst out. 'Said *might*, that's all—'

'Stop, stop!' Nirry knelt down. Exasperated, she looked between the brothers. 'Now who said what? Hm?'

'Taggle,' Raggle blurted, 'said Papa's been *killed*.'

Nirry felt her heart turn cold. The fate of her own father, Stephel, had been much on her mind. The last she had heard, the old steward and coachman had been dismissed from Lady Umbecca's service. Whether he was still in Agondon, Nirry did not know. Fondly she dreamed of finding him and looking after him. But if Nirry feared losing her father, still worse was her fear that these little boys might lose theirs.

'Now why ... why would you say a thing like that, Taggle?' she asked. 'Papa was here only today, wasn't he? Didn't he come and see you? Doesn't he always come and see you?'

'*Might* be killed,' said Taggle, '*might*.'

How should Nirry reply? That Bando *might* be killed was possible, even likely. Wiggler was one thing; she could keep him safe in the tavern. A certain scarlet fellow had promised Nirry that Wiggler would not fight in any war, so long as the rebels used her tavern as a base. It was one of Nirry's few comforts, and the only thing, by now, that reconciled her to the rebels. But Bando? The old rebel was reckless. If he got himself killed, what would happen to these boys?

Nirry faltered, 'Raggle ... Taggle ... you know it's safer for you here. You don't want to be stuck out in that nasty farmhouse, do you? Don't you like it here at the Cat & Crown? Tried ever so hard to make it nice, I have, and here's my two bestest guests telling me they hate it! How do you think that makes me feel?'

'You're saying ... Papa *won't* die?' said Taggle, after a moment.

'Papa's brave,' said Raggle. 'He's a *hero*.'

'What about Mama?' Taggle's voice cracked. 'She was a hero, wasn't she? She was a warrior-woman, but she's dead.'

And Taggle, at the thought, burst into tears.

'Cry-baby,' Raggle taunted, but half-heartedly. He was trying to stop himself from crying, too.

'Shh!' Anxiously, Nirry glanced towards the private room. 'Boys, I'm not going to hear another word of this. There's your Papa, out being a hero, fighting for' – she steeled herself – 'for *freedom*, and here's his own two boys fighting each other. It's not right, is it? Is it?'

Raggle shook his head; Taggle sobbed again.

'Come on, Taggle, up here with you.' Nirry took him in her arms. 'Ooh, what a big lump you are! You know, you get heavier every day. Raggle, pick up the candle, hm? And take my hand, that's right. Now come on, I'm putting the pair of you back to bed, and if there's any more trouble, then ... then there'll *really* be trouble. Make no mistake, I'm talking trouble of the *no breakfast in the morning* sort!'

This silenced the boys, for a little at least. Raggle gulped, then Taggle sniffed, rallying, 'Aunt Nirry, will you tell us about your old mistress again, and the big breakfasts she used to eat? And the big lunches and dinners?'

Raggle tugged her hand. 'Aunt Nirry, yes! You'll tell us about the fat lady, won't you?'

Nirry sighed. Would she ever get back to the bar? Curses sounded from the private room. The boys were used to the sounds that echoed every evening round the Cat & Crown. But to Nirry, these were no usual sounds.

The quality – the quality! – were getting restless.

Labouring up to the turn of the stairs, Nirry wished she had not been so eager to take Taggle in her arms. She was about to tell him that a big boy should walk on his own two legs, if he was lucky enough to have them, when an alarming *thump!* came from outside the window.

Nirry gasped, letting Taggle slip down.

Raggle's eyes were wide. 'Aunt Nirry! What is it?'

There was a scuffling, then a squeak, from behind the curtains; a gust of cold air, and the candle blew out. Someone had come through the window.

Nirry shrieked. Raggle and Taggle squealed with glee.

'*Shh!*' The dark figure, breathing heavily, put a hand to Nirry's lips. Through a crack in the curtain came a glimmer of moonlight. 'It's only me, can't you see?'

Excitedly, Raggle and Taggle capered round the newcomer.

'Stop that!' Nirry cried. She rolled her eyes. 'Really, Miss Cata, can't you come in the door like an ordinary person? As if I didn't have enough to cope with. I'll never get these two little beggars down for the night now. And look at you, dressed in only a shift – and you in a delicate condition, too! And what's that white stuff all over your face? Silly girl, it's a wonder you know you're born! Now come on, let's get you down to the fire, and get you a nice snifter of—'

'*Shh, shh!*' Catching her breath, Cata had to laugh. But there was nothing to laugh about. 'Nirry, I'm escaping. I've come over the rooftops.'

'Escaping? Miss Cata, you don't mean—?'

Cata's voice was low. 'It's failed. Everything's failed.'

Nirry squealed again. This time she put her own hand to her mouth, but forced a whisper through her fingers. 'No one's dead?'

'Nirry, it's all right.' Tenderly, Cata clutched Nirry's shoulders. 'Bando's not dead. No one's dead.'

'Papa's alive! He's alive!' cried Raggle.

Anxiously, Taggle piped up, 'But he's still a hero?'

'Oh, Taggle!' Cata ruffled the boy's unruly hair. 'Of course he's still a hero. *And* he got away – we all did.' *Except the Mentinis.* But Cata would say nothing about the Mentinis, not in front of the boys. 'There's still tomorrow night,' she continued brightly. 'Plan A didn't work, so we just go to Plan B, that's all. Didn't I say Plan B was better? Didn't I … didn't I always say that?'

'Ooh, but your highwayman friend didn't, did he?' Nirry pointed to the private room. By producing his prisoner – a prisoner he had been certain he would have tonight – Bob Scarlet was to have cemented his authority over the disorderly, often wayward, Rebel League. But now? 'You're telling me I've got a room full of cut-throats, all ready to see … to see a *certain person*, all gagged and trussed up – and she's not going to be there? So how's our Master Scarlet going to tell them *that*, Miss Cata, hm?'

Cata looked down. Shivering in the thin black shift, she rubbed her arms.

'Actually, he's not,' she said, abashed.

'What!' Nirry's eyes blazed.

'Bob's gone to Corvey Cottage with Hul and Bando. Landa's with them, too, she thought she ought … well, Bob thought they ought to get out of the city before the Bluejackets start crawling everywhere.'

'They did, did they? That's nice, isn't it?'

'Nirry, Nirry!' Cata shook her head. 'I'll tell the Rebel League, don't worry – that's why I'm here, isn't it? Do you think I'd leave you and Wiggler alone with that lot? Now why don't you take these two scamps to bed? In a moment I'll come up and change, then help you and Baines downstairs.'

Sighing, Nirry shook her head too. 'I don't know how I put up with it, Miss Cata, all this rebel nonsense,' she hissed. 'If it weren't for keeping my Wiggler safe, do you think I'd put up with any of it? If them down there aren't just as bad as the Bluejackets, I … ooh, I just hope you know what you're doing!'

'Nirry, I *do*.' Cata knelt down, kissing the boys. 'Now off to bed with the pair of you.'

With that, Cata flitted downstairs while Nirry took the boys firmly by the hand, tugging them after her into the darkness.

But she turned again, lingering, as lamplight from the private room spilt across the landing. For a moment the sounds of carousing were louder, and Nirry glimpsed poor Wiggler – ale-jug in one hand, Vantage-bottle in the other – waiting upon the shifty, piratical-looking fellows who called themselves the Rebel League.

Eagerly the cut-throats turned to the door, intent upon the sudden appearance of a lovely, dishevelled young girl. Then the door closed.

And her in a delicate condition, too!

Midnight.

Now, as snow sleeps whitely on the dark city, something is happening in a labyrinth below. Moonlight, seeping through clouds, strikes a mirrored glass, then another, channelling down from a spire to a subterranean chamber. Here, amongst columns and vaulted arches, black-cowled figures gather in silence. Stranger beings – bird-like, purple and glowing – hover near the ceiling.

All are expectant.

And now he comes, their white-garbed leader. Tolling bells die as he raises his hands. Ecstatically, he gazes into reflected moonlight, his face a dazzle of shadows and gold. In rapture he addresses his Brotherhood – and the bird-creatures, new accomplices in evil, that he refers to as *Mauvers*.

He speaks of a being they await, a being that is soon – soon now – to lead them to what they think of perhaps as the salvation, perhaps as a damnation they all desire. He speaks of the morrow, of the Canonical of Inauguration with which it will begin, of the masquerade – the Bird Ball – with which it will end. What are these events, in truth, but preparations for things greater, grander, vastly more evil than any this city has known before? He speaks of the five god-days that will follow, and all that he is certain will come to pass.

His voice rises. He speaks of a villain he calls Jemany Vexing, who now – even now, he cries – is coming into his clutches. He speaks of the power of the Orokon, of the Crystals Five that soon – soon and certainly – will be his, and his alone. Flinging back his head, he laughs at the fools in the city above, benighted in their ignorance, who do not know, who do not guess the new world that is about to come.

'Rejoice, my Brothers – Mauvers, Rejoice!'

Behind the altar, a black curtain billows. But is this not a curtain that has ripped away before, bringing Toth-Vexrah into the Realm of Being? What new horror can lie behind it now? What can it be, this salvation, this damnation?

The Brothers chant. This is their mantra.

> *Unbeing Bird, mighty bird of fire,*
> *Come to us, come to us, fill our desire:*
> *Come to us, come to us, fuel our desire!*
> *Unbeing Bird, mighty bird of flood*
> *Come to us, come to us, bathe us in blood!*
> > TOTH *who is Sassoroch waits now for you,*
> > TOTH *who is Chorassos will fly with you!*
>
> *Unbeing Bird, mighty bird of ice,*
> *Come, let us offer up our sacrifice!*
> *Unbeing Bird, mighty bird of snow,*
> *Come to us, take us where the saved must go:*
> *Take us to the mountains of the ice and snow!*
> > TOTH *who is Chorassos waits now for you,*
> > TOTH *who is Sassoroch will fly with you!*

Feet stamp. Spit flies. Mauvers flap and cry. On and on, round and round it goes.

Then all at once there is silence, and standing beside the altar – but have they not been there all this time? – are two figures we know, dressed in the uniforms of Bluejacket soldiers. One is lanky and tremulous; one is flame-haired, defiant. It is the flame-haired one who holds in his arms the gagged, struggling infant.

In moments, the infant will struggle no more.

And blood will stain the whiteness of the leader's robes.

'See, Jem? What did I tell you?'

'A red moon, you said.'

'I was right, wasn't I?'

'Seems you were. Strange.'

Jem stared as the blood-like disc vanished again into the deep, cloudy blackness. Last night, and the night before, the moon had been a brilliant gold, so clear and close they might have plucked it from the sky. What were they to make of this sinister redness, burning as if with secret shame? Uneasily, Jem wondered how far they were from Ejland.

If only it were light, and the clouds would clear!

'Shall I try the Orb again?' Littler said now, as if in response to Jem's thoughts. Eagerly he picked his way across the shuddering cabin, returning with his gift from Princess Bela Dona. When the little boy was not displaying his red crystal, often he was hovering over this mysterious glass sphere, searching for visions in its glittering depths. 'Perhaps it will show us where we are.'

'You think so?' Jem did not much like the Orb. When it had been lost, he had been glad, or would have been, had it not fallen into the grip of Toth-Vexrah. Really, had the wretched thing been of *any* use except for channelling Toth's evil powers? 'You can't see anything, can you, Littler?'

'Don't sound so cocky.' Littler hunched cross-legged over the gleaming sphere. 'Takes time, that's all.'

'So does this ship.' Idly, Jem flicked at one of Ejard Orange's ears; the ear flicked back, but otherwise the big, curled cat did not stir. He purred rhythmically; Jem yawned. Flurries of snow spattered against the glass, gleaming eerily in the skyship's blue lightning.

'Jem,' Littler said after a moment, 'tell me about Ejland.'

'What, bored with that thing already?' Jem smiled. 'I knew it didn't work. Except for Toth.'

Littler sniffed. 'A good reason to keep it, then.'

'So Toth can't have it? More like a good reason to smash it, I'd have thought.'

'I don't think you can. Not the Orb of Seeing.' The Unang boy moved his small hand over the glass. 'But Jem, about Ejland. It's a cold place, isn't it? With snow and ice?'

'Sometimes. Well, a lot of the time. What do you know about snow and ice?'

'I've seen pictures, haven't I? But what are we going to do when we get there, Jem? We've no big thick coats, have we? Or furry hats?' Littler looked down at the Orb again, circling it with his finger. 'I hope we find somewhere warm, that's all I can say. Somewhere with a big roaring fire, where Ejjy can curl up all nice and cosy…'

Jem rubbed his eyes. Was there something strange, something distant in Littler's voice? It was as if he were slipping into a trance, and taking Jem with him. Jem reminded his young friend that they could hardly expect a comfortable time, not where they were going. Gravely he indicated the crystals at their chests, then gestured towards the unconscious Myla, as if there could be no more to say.

Littler's voice grew softer as he said he was sure they would shiver all the time, and wished he were back in Unang Lia. 'What a dark city Agondon is! So grey, so lifeless! Where are the colours of Kal-Theron? Where are the bright splendours of Qatani? Oh, those high houses with their pitching roofs! Those chimneys, belching smoke! Those heavy, hanging gables, almost touching over the narrow lanes!'

Jem murmured, 'Littler … you can *see* this, can't you?'

Littler rushed on, 'And the frozen River Riel! That Island in the middle! That high, forbidding Embankment! Those heavy, stone columns of the Great Temple!'

This was not Littler. *This was not Littler.*

The voice was just a whisper now, but still more intense, still more strange. 'And the snow in the streets … and the snow stained with blood … and Toth, Toth everywhere, thudding under it all like the pulse in your wrist, like the heartbeat in your chest—'

'*Littler!*' Jem shouted.

His hand swooped, grabbing the Orb. Littler cried out as if he had been scalded; in the same moment, the Orb blazed with dazzling light. There was a mighty BOOM! and the skyship lurched, flinging Littler and Jem to the floor. The crystals at their chests burned with mystic fire.

'Evil … something evil—' This time it was Myla who screamed, jerking at the straps that held her in place.

She slumped back, insensible, as her brother leapt up.

'Myla … Jem … Littler!' Rajal's crystal was burning too. 'Wh-what's happening?'

'It's Toth,' cried Jem, 'it has to be Toth!'

Lightning zigzagged over the windows. Jem shouted. Littler grabbed Ejard Orange. They ducked, Rajal flinging himself across Myla as the window in front and the portholes in the sides burst inwards, showering the cabin with glass.

Still the crystals seared; still the Orb blazed, rolling across the buffeting floor and walls, whizzing through the air like a bouncing ball.

Icy winds roared all around them.

'Look ... l-look!' Jem clambered up. He was bleeding from somewhere. Fire seared his chest. Desperately he pointed through the ruined window.

Rajal twisted round, convulsing with pain; Littler gasped, almost strangling a protesting Ejard Orange. The dark clouds had parted and the bloody red light that spilled across the sky now came not from the moon, but the rising sun. Wheeling below the skyship was the vista of a harbour, of islands, of a jagged delta, of a darkly magnificent city clutched in hands of ice. Here was what Littler had seen in the Orb, suddenly beneath them, suddenly real.

'Agondon,' Jem burst out, 'it's Agondon—'

'Never mind that!' cried Rajal. Frantically he reached for his sister. *Oh Myla, Myla!* Had she been through so much, only for it all to end this way? 'Jem, we're going to crash! Toth's going to kill us—'

Jem wrenched at levers. He punched dials. Still the Orb rolled round and round, alive with light, as if indeed they had plucked down the moon. Ejard Orange, scratching and scrambling, leapt from Littler's arms, pouncing upon the gleaming sphere as if it were his prey.

Cat and Orb rolled together, Ejard Orange hissing and spitting; Littler fell back, clutching at his crystal.

He writhed towards Rajal. 'The Amulet of Tukhat! Raj, *wish*—'

'What do you mean, *wish*?' Rajal gripped the talisman that circled his wrist.

'Don't you know anything?' Littler shouted. 'Just *wish*—'

'We're not going to make it—' Jem cried, despairing.

Down and down the skyship plummeted, careening over houses and streets. The thrumming of the vessel had become a tortured shrieking; smoke trailed behind them. Orb-light, crystal-light pulsed and whirled. Once, twice, three times, Jem managed to jerk the ship upwards, gaining a little height, but the magic that had made them fly was guttering, almost gone.

Rajal's eyes blazed. He gripped the amulet.

'*Wish!*' Littler cried again. 'Raj, *wish* ... Jem, hang on—'

It was no good. They were going to crash.

Jem managed, at least, to get them over the city.

The crash came in the snowy hills beyond.

Chapter 10

SAUSAGES AND BACON

'Nirry … Nirry!'

Blearily, Umbecca reached for her bell.

A hand stayed her. 'Your Ladyship, I'm sorry, I—'

'Ignore her, Master Waxwell,' came a bored voice. 'Every morning, she forgets that Nirry's gone.'

The apothecary bowed, murmuring politely; the Queen cast herself into a window seat. Though dressed only in a diaphanous nightgown, she was unconcerned at the presence of a gentleman. Behind her, drawn curtains disclosed the bleakness of the morning; she turned her back to the white glare, looking about her with a superior expression.

Dominating the apartment with its ornate carpets, its monogrammed wallpaper, its priceless porcelains and rococo furnishings, was the vast canopied bed where the fat woman lay. How grotesque she looked, bloated and insensible amongst her ruffles, her tassels, her golden-threaded embroidery!

Umbecca stirred again, moaning this time. Might she be recalling her ordeal? All night the apothecary had not left her side, fearing, he would say, for the balance of her humours. More than one leeching had been necessary, and potent doses of Jarvel-orandy. Now, with his best professional tenderness, the smooth fellow crooned to the lady to *hush, hush*, and again held a potion to her little mouth. Umbecca moaned once more; dribble ran into the furrows between her several chins.

The Queen – but let us call her Jeli – turned away, humming a snatch of melody. 'Did you ever meet *Nirry*, Master Waxwell? One of my aunt's old servants. In the provinces.' She shuddered, presumably at the thought of the provinces. 'Do you remember *Nirry*, Widow?'

Widow Waxwell sat by the fire, darning stockings stretched across a specially adapted frame. For a woman with only one hand, she displayed an admirable dexterity. Breaking off, removing pins from her lips, she would have embarked upon a polite and full answer, but Jeli was not really interested.

'*Nirry*, indeed!' she swept on, oblivious. 'And why should quality-folk even *recall* the names of former servants? A servant is a type of machine, no more. Take Jilda. Necessary as she is to me at present, I'm sure the memory of her would fly my mind like chaff were she no longer present to my eyes.'

With this, she flashed a stern look at Jilda, who had entered just at that moment. The maid – a plumpish, pretty girl, no older than Jeli – bore a breakfast tray which she had laid out in the Queen's apartments, then been obliged to take up again when her mistress flitted into this adjoining chamber.

The maid coloured and the breakfast things rattled a little too loudly as she set them down anew on a handsome marquetry table. Unloading teacups, kippers and the like, she kept her eyes low, as if dreading the Queen's gaze; emotion burned like a flame between the two young women.

Impatiently, Jeli flicked her away.

'My aunt must miss provincial life,' she declared, crunching at a finger of toast. She reached for the marmalade. 'Can a woman eke out her life in rustic obscurity, then with ease become a fine lady in Agondon? Must she not long for her old simplicity? What cares she for the delicacy of the finest sauces, against the rough, brute bulk of peasant fare? Would you not say so, Widow? Would you not say so, Master Waxwell?'

The Widow might have pointed out that neither her friend nor herself had lived in Irion as grovelling peasants; indeed, they had been the local quality-folk. But the old woman had no time to remove the pins from her mouth, even if she had dared to speak.

Her great-nephew had more presence of mind. At once he left off his fussings at the bedside. Bowing low to the royal personage, eagerly he professed his humble assent.

Jeli speared a rasher of bacon. 'And when a provincial woman attempts finery, what then? Last night, did my heart not flutter in anguish at my aunt's gaudy garb? Many were the courtiers who laughed behind their hands! She might have been one of the Clumpton Clowns! Yet it could hardly be otherwise: has she not spent almost all her life in the garb of Agonist piety, such as the Widow wears? And could the Widow dress as a lady?'

The Widow's face sagged a little more and she looked sadly at the stump where her right hand should have been. Her great-nephew's smile hardened, ever so slightly. His patient was coming round. Whatever happened, he must not offend Lady Umbecca.

A politic fellow, Franz Waxwell had considered Umbecca Veeldrop deeply, even intimately. Without doubt, he owed his present prominence to this lady. To be a Waxwell had set him on a firm foundation; the lady had once been tended by Great-Aunt Berthen's husband. But it was the excellence of the younger Waxwell's art, he was certain, that had won him this most desirable of patients.

When he had first encountered her, in the spa-town of Varby, she had been a mere commoner. Devoid even of a title, Umbecca Veeldrop had been little more than a Duenna, hopelessly attempting to marry off an ungrateful minx called Catayane. What had become of the little slut, the apothecary did not know; but when the fat woman had come to Court – ennobled, summoned to the new Queen's side – it was soon clear that she would not forget the elegant, skilled fellow who had treated her with such solicitude … Dear Lady Umbecca! He would not betray her, not even for the Queen.

Besides, she had *much* more power.

The Queen, with controlled violence, cracked a spoon over a hard-boiled egg.

'Hardly surprising that her experience of last night should have thrown my aunt into confusion,' she mused. 'What has she known, in provincial life, of the splendours of the Opera? How her head was turned by the Mentinis! How her eyes shone with wonderment! Then, how much worse the reversal that came! I fear we should have sat her in a safer place, side by side with the Widow in the retiring-room…'

She burbled on. But if the apothecary had no thought for her words, he began to pay more attention to her person. Was her radical moisture, he wondered, quite as it should be? Had her radical heat risen too high? There were drippings of egg-yolk at the corner of her mouth and her thighs, beneath her nightgown, were decidedly parted.

Hm. The girl leaned back in the window seat and it occurred to the medical man that she might soon require a certain intimate examination. Until now, he had never dared recommend it, not for Her Royal Majesty. But he could hardly risk her health for such foolish scruples. Affliction was no respecter of station, and a lady, after all, could never be too careful.

There was a rapping at the door.

It opened at once, and slipping into the apartment came Lady Umbecca's spiritual advisor, Eay Feval. Jeli, a little flustered, rearranged her nightgown; turning, the apothecary found his smile slipping – if only a little – as he as he looked into the Lector's blandly handsome face.

Gliding towards the bed, Feval leaned over his swooning lady. He kissed her forehead; Umbecca moaned.

'You've been here *all night*, apothecary?' he enquired.

What hints are carried in the commonest words! Something in the Lector's address – so thought Franz Waxwell – implied that he considered the apothecary the merest tradesman. Icily, he replied that he had barely finished attending upon His Imperial Agonist Majesty when he had been called to the lady's side – seven, eight fifteenths ago.

In the depths of night, at any rate.

'And *still* the lady lies languishing?' said Feval.

Bright spots appeared in Waxwell's cheeks and he remarked that a woman of Lady Umbecca's refinement could not but suffer from such an ordeal. To be sure, her humours were sadly out of kilter; why, they might never be in balance again.

'Then I dare say you must attend upon her more frequently,' remarked Feval. 'But the Inaugural? You hardly propose to deny her the Inaugural?'

Jeli's eyes flashed. 'What about the *Ball*?'

'Both events, I had heard, might not go ahead.' Forgetting himself, the apothecary smiled, as if he were glad to be the bearer of these tidings.

His pleasure was short-lived.

'The Ball!' Jeli wailed. She flounced up, fork in hand. 'Has Tranimel ordered this? Where is he? Bring him to me! Why … why wasn't I told? I … I won't have it! Are rebels to deny us all our pleasures? Double the guards, triple them, quadruple them! But the Ball – oh, the Ball!'

A sausage hung forlornly from the end of the fork.

'Your Highness, I fear Master Waxwell distresses you needlessly.' Now Eay Feval smiled; the apothecary blanched. 'The Court, it is true, has been awash with rumour. Is it not unfortunate that those fools of guards should have shot the Mentinis? Without doubt, the fellows were not working alone; without doubt, they were pawns in a greater game. But who would concoct so elaborate a scheme? Who would dare to abduct a Queen?'

Grease dripped from the sausage. 'Me? Abduct *me*?'

The Lector, it appeared, had distressed the royal personage far more effectively than the apothecary.

But still he smiled. 'Indeed, Your Royal Majesty. Must not those blind fellows have planned their moves in advance? And had you not changed places with your aunt, moments before their act began?'

'Me,' said the Queen under her breath. 'Me, *me*?'

And turning away, perhaps not so distressed, she did a little twirl, her nightgown billowing.

She swung back. 'But the Ball?'

'Your Royal Majesty, fear not. There will, of course, be many more guards; invitations, and guests, will be scrutinised intently. But are we to throw away our noble traditions, bowing meekly to terror's yoke? Meekness is not the Ejlander way; nor, if I may say, is it the Agonist way.'

The Lector was proud of this last touch; as a man of the cloth there were privileges he could invoke, and he would be a fool if he failed to invoke them. The Widow, he noted, clutched her Circle of Agonis, her wizened lips moving in a virtuous litany; Waxwell and the Queen looked humbled.

Feval struggled to conceal his triumph.

'So you see, apothecary,' he could not forbear from adding, 'your rumours are not quite correct. I take *my* intelligence from the First Minister. Tonight, the Queen shall shine at the Ball, as she was always fated to do. And so, I trust, shall this great lady.'

Fondly he looked towards the bed. 'But first there is the matter of the Inaugural. The morning ticks away. As all know, Lady Umbecca is a woman of the utmost piety. She must soon rise, must she not, if she is to attend the Great Temple? And rise, I think, she will.'

Umbecca emitted a pig-like snort; as for the apothecary, his look was grave. 'That the lady may rise in course of time is my fervent hope. Whether she may attend the Ball must be in doubt. But the Inaugural? What manner of physician would I be were I to release her from my care so soon?'

'It is spiritual counsel,' the Lector suggested, 'to which this lady most responds.'

'We must both tend to our separate spheres.'

Politely, Feval acknowledged the apothecary's wisdom. Inwardly, he burned with fury. Was his noble profession – his sacred calling – to be seen as equivalent to this quack's trade? Oh, but he had seen off one Waxwell, breaking the villain's grip on his lady's heart!

He would see off another, or his name was not Feval.

He squatted by the bed, anger cracking through his bland mask. 'Apothecary, she reeks of your potions. What have you given her?'

'Dear Lector, do you suggest I would keep this lady in a stupor? Last night, it is true, a sleeping draught was necessary. Now I seek to raise her radical moisture, escalating the infusion of radical heat, returning the humours to a proper balance – in short, I would have her wake.'

'You *would*, would you?'

Feval rose suddenly. Jeli, bored again, was lolling on a sofa, flicking her tongue across the greasy sausage. With surprising curtness, Feval demanded it.

He strode back to the bed.

Dear Umbecca! How he prayed this noble heart would be restored! A tear glittered in the Lector's eye as he wafted the sausage under her nose.

The moaning returned, this time as a deep, cow-like lowing. Umbecca's eyes fluttered urgently open. The eyes grew wide. She reached out, grabbing the fork.

Dear, dear Umbecca! Waxwell's mouth twisted; the Lector exulted. In an instant, the sausage filled the little mouth; in another, the lady sat up, propped on pillows, bellowing for her breakfast.

But still she was a little confused. 'Nirry … Nirry!'

Chapter 11

THE LADY'S DRESSING ROOM

'Wh-where am I?'

Something soft buffed at Jem's face. Blearily he looked into golden-slitted eyes and heard the rumble of a purr. Ejard Orange? Jem was aware of cold, gloom and a strange, pungent smell. He rubbed his eyes. A snowflake fluttered against his cheek; he felt something prickly beneath his back and arms and legs and pressing into the skin of his neck.

He looked up. Then he understood.

He was lying in a hayloft in a tumbledown barn.

Overhead, there was a jagged hole in the roof; a little away from him, half-buried in the hay, was the unconscious Myla. To his relief, she was still breathing; beside her sprawled Rajal, moaning faintly, amulet glittering on his outflung wrist.

Jem supposed they had been thrown free from the skyship. But where *was* the skyship? And what about Littler? Jem peered about anxiously. Though the hole in the roof disclosed a white haze of sky, the barn's interior was deep in shadow.

'Glad to see you've woken up. At last.'

Jem turned sharply. Littler, huddled in a blanket, sat on a throne-like bale of hay. Between his crossed legs was the Orb of Seeing, not glowing now, but dull, almost metallic.

'I tried to wake you, but you were out cold, the lot of you.'

'Cold? You can say that again.' Jem rubbed his arms. 'Myla's got Raj to keep her warm. How about sharing that blanket of yours, Littler? But ... how did we get here?'

Littler moved over, letting Jem share the blanket. 'You don't remember? You got the hatch open as we were coming down. Said we should all bale out. Take our chances.'

'I did?' The blanket – it must have been lying in the barn – was not, thought Jem, such a good idea. It was scratchy, stank abominably, and was no doubt filled with fleas. He would have told Littler, but just then Jem felt a throbbing in his thigh. There was dried blood on his breeches, a clinging sliver of glass.

'Raj got Myla unstrapped just in time,' Littler went on. 'We hurtled through the air, towards this snowy slope. And it was the barn roof! We were lucky, Jem. You never know what might have happened. I might have lost the orb!'

59

'Oh yes?' Picking up the glass sphere, Jem weighed it suspiciously. He furrowed his brow. Why had the orb glowed so brightly? And what, precisely, was its connection with Toth? He would have hurled the thing away, but Oclar had been certain they should take it.

Gently he handed it back to Littler.

'We might have broken our legs and arms, or cracked our heads, or anything,' Littler burbled on.

'Might have frozen,' said Jem. 'Still might.'

'If it weren't for the amulet, we'd be been done for.'

'The *amulet* now?' Jem remembered their fall well enough. But he looked dubiously at Rajal's golden band. He gestured to the hay. 'And what about this convenient barn? Not to mention the hole in the roof?'

'They helped too. Anyway, we're all right. Except for Myla.'

'She's not worse?' Wincing at the gash in his thigh, Jem scrambled across the hay. Earnestly he peered into the altered face. He turned Myla's head. Fixed upon her brow was the Lichano band, her own magical talisman, glinting in a pale shaft of light.

He pulled back a strand of dark hair. Could it be that Myla had aged again? But she had woken only for a moment! She had performed no magic, had she? But perhaps another magic, Toth's magic, had touched her. Picked out harshly in the cold light, Jem saw lines around Myla's eyes and mouth.

Rajal stirred at last. 'Jem ... what's happening?'

'Let's just say your amulet may have come in useful.'

Rajal turned to his sister. 'Myla? You're all right?'

Shivering, Jem looked round the dilapidated barn again. Spoked wheels and horse-collars hung against the walls. A ladder led down to a dirt-floored region cluttered with crates, barrels, a cart. There were rusty hoes and scythes. Big doors rattled in the wind.

'We've got to get help. That's the first thing.'

'Help?' Rajal looked up. 'What do you mean, *help*?'

Jem made for the ladder. 'We're cold, and getting colder. We've got no proper clothes. And we're going to get hungry soon.'

Ejard Orange miaowed, as if on cue.

'Poor Ejjy!' said Littler. 'There must be rats here.'

'Frozen ones?' said Jem. 'He'll break his teeth.' And, grimacing at his gashed leg, he climbed down the ladder.

'Jem,' said Rajal, 'where are you going?'

'This is a barn, isn't it? There must be a farmhouse somewhere near.'

'Haven't you noticed, this place looks abandoned?'

'Then perhaps the farmhouse is too. We can hole up there while we sort ourselves out.' Wryly Jem looked up at Rajal's lugubrious face, peering down at him from the hayloft. 'Buck up, Raj! At least we're back in Ejland.

Home territory.' The wind sang bitterly through the barn doors. 'Littler, you couldn't throw me down that blanket, could you?'

'All right, Jem. But I'm coming too.'

'You're not, you know. You stay here with Raj and Myla. Take care of Ejjy. I'll scout around, and be back as soon as I can.'

'Never. Never, never.'

'Your Royal Majesty, please.' There was anxiety in Jilda Quisto's voice, there was something like entreaty. The time of the Inaugural was drawing near, and still the Queen wore only her nightgown. What was she to do? Send word that she was unwell? But this was no ordinary public occasion. Today, of all days, the First Minister would be furious if the royals did not appear. How would this look to the common folk, if not that they were running scared from the rebels?

The maid ventured again, 'Your Royal Majesty?'

Miss Jelica Vance – as the Queen, in secret, still thought of herself – did not turn from the window. Sighing, she gazed down upon the city, with its snow-heaped roofs, its spires and gables and chimney pots, staggering down towards the frozen River Riel.

Already the morning was far advanced. On the river, circling like black, mysterious insects, was a party of skaters. Oh, to glide across the glistening ice! In imagination, Jeli was there too, sweeping round the Island, soaring past the Embankment, scything under Agondon Bridge and Regent's Bridge, too.

Her heart exulted; then sadness filled her and again she whispered *Never*. Never would Her Royal Majesty Jelica, Bluejacket Queen Empress of Ejland, Zenzau, Zaxos and the New Colonies, Princess Sacred of Varl, and Grand High Consort of Tiralos, feel the slashing skates beneath her feet. It would never be allowed – but vividly she recalled a time when Miss Jeli Vance swooped and circled with a certain boy, a handsome boy with haystack hair, who had vanished shortly afterwards, as if he had never been.

He had said his name was Nova. *Nova.*

Cautiously, the maid touched the royal arm.

Jeli started. 'Quisto, you useless baggage! What are you thinking of? Have you forgotten I must be at the Inaugural? Am I to be disgraced before my husband, before my courtiers, before the empire's noblest families? Look at me – hair unpinned, face unpainted! Have you laid out my petticoats, my gown, my brooches, my rings?'

The maid had done some of these things, or attempted to do so, between myriad other tasks – clearing crockery, making the bed, emptying the royal close-stool, and such. By rights, these lowly tasks were the province of inferior servants, but then, for a Queen's personal maid, Jilda

Quisto was accorded scant respect. She hardly expected it: not from Poison Jelly, as the girls used to call her at the Quick Academy.

Poor Jilda! As she bustled in and out of the royal dressing room, she thought how much she had envied Jeli back in their schooldays. What had their last Speech Day been, with its valedictory addresses, but a series of odes and arias to beautiful little Miss Vance? To Jeli had gone the Regency Memorial Award, the Cham-Charing Cup, the Ejard Certificate – even that year's presentation copy of Mr Coppergate's *Poetical Works*, inscribed in the poet's own shaky hand. One would hardly have been surprised if the old fool had scribbled a new sonnet in it, just for her; in any case, Jeli's glory was assured. And with what rapidity it had claimed her! Everyone said she would marry soon, and well; so she had. And yet – Jilda smirked – look at her now. Yes, look at her now.

Poor Jeli! The Queen, Empress, Princess Sacred, &c., &c. slumped disconsolately at her dressing table. She picked up a powder puff, toying with it idly; she studied her reflection, pulling back her nightgown from her pale shoulders, turning her neck this way and that. There was a fine dusting of powder on the glass (really, that Quisto!); the fire flickered in the haze behind her, a bright orange-red. She leaned forward, wiping a hand across the glass. *No. Oh no.* The light was poor, but was there not a hint, just a hint, of sallowness in her features? She pulled back her blonde, dishevelled ringlets. Oh, and there were dark shadows under her eyes! Her destiny had hardly been glorious. And yet – Jeli permitted herself just a little, malicious smile – at least she was better off than Miss Jilda Quisto.

'Quisto ... what was it like when you were ruined?' The maid looked alarmed. The Queen had asked this question before. Many times. 'Was he a handsome man? Did you love him?'

'He ... *was* handsome, Your Royal Majesty. And ... I thought I loved him. But that was before—'

'I suppose you can hardly remember. Since then, there must have been *so* many. How many?'

'Please—' Jilda might have said more, but already the Queen appeared bored with her questions. Again she gazed into her glass. Might she be dreaming fondly of love? Jilda was aware that the mistress had been, in a manner of speaking, as much a whore as the maid. Both had been sold, though Jeli's price had been far higher. Jeli ... Jilda. Jeli, Jilda. What was the difference, in the scheme of things?

Jeli snapped out of her distracted state. 'Quisto! Come here! The Inaugural, the Inaugural!'

Flustered, Jilda left the royal garb – it would just have to wait – rushing to attend to the royal hair, the royal teeth, the royal face and hands.

Quite a task. The royal hair, for a start, was filthy, slick with grease; Jilda was liberal with perfumes and pomade, but alas, one could not say she performed her work well. She had hardly been born to a life of service. Jeli knew it. Jilda knew it. Quisto was clumsy. Quisto was useless.

'Quisto,' said Jeli (as the maid applied paint, somewhat precariously, to the royal eyelids), 'do you still see that sister of yours?'

Was there a harshness – just a hint – in the royal tone? A sly malevolence? Again waves of resentment washed through Jilda Quisto. Tears pricked her eyes; the hand that held the brush wavered as she explained – not for the first time – that she was no longer permitted to see her sister.

'Then you've not … heard the *news*?'

'News?' Icy light spilled across the carpet; Jilda Quisto's heart beat hard. The Queen, humming lightly, swung towards the glass again, studying her maid's merely adequate handiwork. Those circles, those dark circles! Could it be true what she had once heard, that the beauty of an 'Ejland rose' might dazzle, but soon would fade? She was tired, that was all. Too little sleep. Too much fretting.

A rankness rose from the royal armpits; Jeli reached for a pungent cologne.

'Your Royal Majesty?' Jilda had to prompt.

'What's that, Quisto? Oh … oh yes.' And with seeming casualness, the Queen contrived to mention – she had heard it, she said, from her husband this morning – that last night there had been another of those nasty knife-murders down by the Embankment.

And who had been the latest victim of the rebels? Some shiftless indigent? Some drunken harlot? Alas, but no! Who but a certain Miss Heka Quisto?

Jeli's smile returned as her maid crumpled.

Chapter 12

THE LADY VANISHES

Really, it was filthy!

Jem drew the blanket tighter around him. And how could it stink so much, in all this cold? He supposed it was a horse blanket; he wished he had the horse. Gritting his teeth, screwing up his eyes, he lifted his feet comically high, trudging out into the flurrying haze.

Snowflakes stung his face. Hilly fields lay heaped in bright whiteness, their contours obscured, their colours hidden. Up ahead was a line of bare trees, their branches heavily burdened. Jem looked miserably from side to side. No sign of Agondon. No sign of a farmhouse. Icy wetness squeezed through his shoes.

But what was this – something bright, something blue, glinting from a snowdrift just up ahead? The wreckage of the skyship, covered in snow? He might have gone to investigate, but there was no time. Already the cold was biting through the blanket; besides, the ship had to be wrecked beyond repair.

Jem felt for the Crystal of Javander, pressing it roughly against his heart. But there was something else, wasn't there? Something he valued more? Anxiously he dug into his breeches pocket, bringing forth a heavy, swirling-patterned coin. It flashed gold in his hand; he gripped it tightly.

Oh, Cata.

Now the snow was falling faster; soon, Jem thought, he would barely be able to see. And the cold! He floundered forward. Where *was* the farmhouse? Beyond the trees? In the warm season, the trees would form a rich, green avenue. There must be a road under the snow, mustn't there? A lane?

And a lane must lead somewhere.

A small bird, some way off, was the only sign of life. From one barren branch to another it hopped; at its breast, Jem saw a familiar burst of red.

'Say, you're a Bob Scarlet!' He smiled, hoping that this might be a good omen.

Thoughts of the highwayman filled Jem's mind. What were Bob's rebel band up to now? Was Cata still amongst them? He struggled towards the little bird, as if the Bob Scarlet could give him answers, but as he drew near, it flitted away, vanishing in the falling snow.

Jem peered down the lane, a hand like a visor held above his eyes. There were ruts in the snow; a glimpse of green. Had a cart come this way? By now he was shivering violently, and his feet and hands were numb. Looking back, he could no longer see the barn.

Just a little further. See where the lane went.

Moments later, Jem saw something curious, looming through the whiteness. What was this sudden fluttering of robes, this vision of rainbow colours in the snow? Could this be a woman, stretching forth her hands – hands, like Jem's, that wore no gloves? She might have been a sister from an Order of the Enclosed, incongruously clothed in the five colours of the Orokon.

'Who are you?' Jem whispered, stepping forward. Her features were concealed, for she hung her head. Then, as he approached, the lady looked up.

Jem gasped. Billowing back, her headdress revealed no human visage, but only a glowing, golden ball of light.

'Who are you?' Jem urged again, but already knew the answer. This was a vision. This was a sign. He sank to his knees in the freezing snow, oblivious as the blanket slipped from his shoulders.

Mysterious music hovered on the air; Jem felt his heart pounding like a drum. Still the lady stretched out her hands; Jem reached back, thinking of Cata; for a moment, it was as if the lady *were* Cata.

Exulting, he would have touched her, but the lady began to retreat from him, not turning away, but only moving back, back along the barren avenue, too fast to follow.

Still he tried. He called, pleaded. There was so much she could tell him! He floundered forward, but the lady was vanishing. Still the hands stretched; still the light streamed; but ever further she retreated, the snow closing around her like a chill, diaphanous veil.

'Come back!' Jem gasped, but it was no good.

He slipped. He fell. Dazed, he lay unmoving.

And the snow was falling harder.

'Never! Never, never—'

'Really, Quisto, don't take on so! I've told you it was a joke, haven't I? Silly girl, I thought you'd be amused! Why, I thought you hated that stuck-up sister of yours ... Oh, what's the use? One tries to be pleasant to one's servants, and where does it get one? Back to my dressing table, girl, and quick about it! The Inaugural, the Inaugural!'

To the Queen's relief, her maid complied at last. Why she had said that Jilda's sister was dead, Jeli could not be sure. Some mirthful imp had prompted her: a harmless joke, that was all. Quisto – there was no getting away from it – was becoming a bit of a bore.

Still, Jeli was nothing if not benevolent. (Her virtues in this regard were praised regularly – indeed, worshipped – in every Temple of Agonis in the empire.) So it was that as Jilda, yet again, applied herself to the royal hair, Jeli returned to her original theme. She had meant to say that a certain Miss Quisto – so noted the Court Circular, some days earlier – had been contracted in marriage to the Prince-Elect of Urgan-Orandy.

'A splendid match, is it not, for the daughter of a mere threadneedle?' Sincerity filled the royal voice. 'Think of it – not one, but *two* royal connections for the household of Quisto! No doubt your father must be very proud.'

For some moments Jeli enthused in this manner, for all the world as if Japier Quisto, Agondon's finest gentlemen's tailor, had not disowned his ruined daughter Jilda; as if, too, 'Binkie' Urgan-Orandy were anything other than a fat, provincial boor.

As it happened, Jeli had heard rumours about Miss Heka Quisto. Some said the minx had lost her virtue already, perhaps to Alex Aldermyle, even to Reny Bolbarr – who was known, after all, to keep more than one mistress. There was even talk of a confinement.

Spite, no doubt; Jeli knew all about the machinations of rumour. Did Jilda recall the talk about Miss Jelica Vance and 'Binkie'? Of course there had been nothing to it. Who would marry a slobbery-lipped drunkard with reeking breath, gambling debts as long as the River Riel and the inability to dance with a girl without crushing her feet?

Heka Quisto, that's who! What could her father have been thinking of? The fool, no doubt, had let 'Binkie' dazzle him – with his title, with the rings on his hands, with the quantities of fabric that went into his suits. If his first daughter had gone to the bad – so the threadneedle must have reasoned – the second, at least, could be a princess. Didn't he understand that he was ruining Heka as surely as some seducer had ruined Jilda? Already the pride of the Quistos had been battered; now it was about to be crushed underfoot.

But the Queen, of course, said nothing of this. 'Ah, how Heka shall become her new station! Was ever any girl from the ranks of *trade* better suited to rise into the quality?' (Many, many: without a doubt.) 'But how shall she accustom herself to provincial life? She always was a *vivacious* girl, was she not?' (She was not: Heka was – what was the word? – *insipid*. What could Alex have seen in her? Or Reny? No, these rumours were hardly to be believed!) 'But Heka, without doubt, will acquit herself admirably. Shall the Prince-Elect e'er rue the day when he took a threadneedle's daughter for his bride?' (What did 'Binkie' see in her? A father's fortune, that's what: the hard-won fruit of cycle after cycle of fawning over the quality. If Alex and his like had their scruples, 'Binkie' would hardly be too proud to squander the fortune of a jumped-up little threadneedle.) 'Hm? What's that, Quisto? Quisto, but you're crying!'

There had been no shriek of anguish this time, no sudden crumpling. The maid, as her mistress spoke, had first turned away, a hand covering her face; trembling, she had perched upon the day-bed by the fire, clawing distractedly at a velvet cushion. Now she slumped down, tears flowing thickly.

Jeli went to her. 'Quisto, Quisto … Jilda, hush!'

The royal hand reached out, stroking the maid's back; stretching beside her, whispering soothing words, Jeli curled against her old schoolmate. A log flared and crashed in the fire. For a moment Jeli was sorry for her cruelty, and wished that Jilda could just be her friend again.

Or just be her friend.

The royal voice was a hollow whisper. 'Jilda, don't you know how unhappy I've been? I knew this was wrong, even before the wedding. Didn't I know it, from the time the King took my hand, and said he could not love me, but that we must marry? They sold me, Jilda – Aunt Vlad and Uncle Jorvel, they sold me, don't you see? Oh, but I tried to resist, I did! I ran away, did you know that? It was in Uncle Jorvel's house, that's where they brought him to me. And I ran, I burst away and ran downstairs, down corridors I'd never seen before.

'Jilda, that's where I saw you – down in that place the gentlemen call Chokey's, underneath my uncle's house. Of course, there was nothing I could do, not then; but in my heart – my *heart*, Jilda – I vowed that I would save you. And I have, haven't I? Oh, we play our little game of mistress and maid. But we're friends, aren't we, Jilda? Aren't we really friends?'

Jilda would not leave off her ugly bawling. Would she wet all the cushions with her tears and snot? Rapidly the royal patience frayed and Jeli disengaged herself from the shaking figure. Gazing back towards the dressing table, she caught her reflection in the powdery glass. At first, her face looked formless, strangely askew.

Then it hardened. Jeli spoke to the air.

'This has to stop, Quisto. You were brought here on trial. You knew it was only a trial, didn't you? You committed the cardinal sin of your sex. You were ruined, fitted only for a harlot's life. There was one – I speak, as it happens, of Aunt Umbecca – who went so far as to call me a fool, even to think of saving you. Yet save you I did. I knew you not to be a vicious girl. What did I say? That only the arts of the basest seducer could have made my Jilda yield! If Jilda's virtue had been lost, said I, what virgin was there who could count herself safe?'

Still the sobbing persisted, if a little more softly; Jeli, still gazing into the powdery glass, found herself reaching blankly behind her, running a hand beneath the maid's skirts. The eyes glowed like coals in the royal face.

'Jilda' – the voice was harder now – 'I fear you have given me but poor recompense. Am I not your Queen, as well as your friend? And yet I am met with ingratitude! Have you studied to be my maid? Have you honoured me as your mistress? Have your prosecuted your duties with all dispatch? Your ineptitude shames me – now these vulgar, violent emotions! Yes, your lot has been hard: but can your sufferings compare to mine? I was raised for greatness, achieved it, and found that it brought me only sorrow. Jilda, though your ruin is regrettable, remember you are still just a threadneedle's daughter. It is mine that is the tragedy, Jilda ... Quisto. Do you hear me, Quisto? Quisto, I forbid you to weep, unless for me!'

The maid struggled to govern herself, raising herself up, wiping at her eyes. Had she felt Jeli's hand, playing beneath her skirts? Impossible to say. She grunted, groaned. Snorted, sniffed. Repulsed, her mistress leapt up, looking down sternly upon the ruined girl.

Her forefinger stabbed the air.

'Quisto, I have but one thing to say. Become what you are meant to be, or pay the price. Play your role, or it's back to Chokey's. I mean it. Aunt Umbecca would send you back at once. Uncle Jorvel longs for your return. My compassion, only mine, keeps you from a harlot's shame.'

'No ... please!' Gulping air, Jilda staggered forward, collapsing into the royal arms. 'Your Royal Majesty ... Jeli, Jeli, please!'

Jeli? The Queen would have pushed her away; instead, she found herself sinking, swooning. Loneliness rose in her like an immense darkness, and she held her old friend roughly in her arms. Brutally, royal hands dug into the maid's hair, pulling it back behind the girl's ears. Savagely, Jeli kissed Jilda's lips.

The door clicked open. 'Your Royal Majesty?'

Jeli gasped. She sent the maid sprawling.

'Ah, but I see you are indisposed.' It was the First Minister. The Queen was outraged. How dare the man intrude like this? But he registered no surprise at what he saw. His close-cropped head was like a mask, stiff and cold, suspended above his white monastic robes. 'You will pardon me if I interrupt you, but may I confirm your attendance at the Inaugural?'

'The ... Inaugural?' Confused, Jeli put a hand to her head. 'Oh, but it's so early! Why is it so early?'

The Inaugural, as it happened, had once been held at dawn, and over the years had been progressively put forward, in deference to the delicacies of quality-folk. The First Minister might have pointed this out; instead, he said there would be a luncheon meeting with the War Lords – his military advisors – as soon as the religious service was over.

'And this, I trust, my Queen will *also* attend? Perhaps even my King – but my Queen in particular. My advisors, I have found, are far more likely to agree to sensible measures when they are in the presence of beauty. And are we not *particularly* in need of such measures now? You shall inspire them, my dear. Make them less violent ... The War Lords, my dear. I'm speaking of the War Lords.'

'Oh … oh.' Flushed, Jeli gazed into the strangely glowing eyes. Her voice came softly, murmurously. 'Of course. My maid is about to … dress me. My maid…'

Jeli wrenched her eyes from the intruder. Sweeping round, she turned on Jilda, demanding that the little slut get up from the floor.

'This instant, Quisto! Quisto, do you hear?'

Chapter 13

DISCOMFORT FOR NIRRY

'Myla? Myla, did you speak?'

Worriedly, Rajal leaned over his sister. Her eyes were closed. Her face remained impassive. But still he was certain her lips had moved. *Please, let her sleep!* He clasped the Crystal of Koros, muttering out a prayer to the god of his race.

Instead, she stirred.

Rajal said, 'Littler, what can I do?'

'Something's happening.' Littler looked up from the orb. 'I can see ... something bright. Like a rainbow.'

'Forget that thing! I'm talking about Myla!'

Rajal huddled against her, heaping extra straw over her tattered gown. Shudders passed through her, but she did not wake. He held her shoulders, looking earnestly into the lined, mature face. He shivered. *Let her sleep. Just let her sleep.* The barn was growing colder.

'Like ... like a rainbow,' Littler said again.

Distantly, Rajal registered the words. 'I'm sorry, Littler. You still miss him, don't you?'

Fondly he recalled the rainbow-patterned dog, once Littler's shabby mongrel, who had laid down his life for their little party. He caressed the Lichano band that circled Myla's forehead. Once Rainbow's collar, it was said to magnify the powers of the mind. Oclar had said it would protect Myla. But how?

Snow fell, more heavily now, through the hole in the barn roof. 'We'll have to move her soon, Littler ... Littler?'

There was a hiss, like escaping steam, and Rajal turned sharply. Littler was on his feet, his mouth gaping wide, his small hands no longer touching the orb.

Glowing, it hovered before him in the air.

The hiss came again. It was Ejard Orange, backing away from the magical sphere. His back arched. His fur stood on end.

'There was ... a rainbow,' said Littler. 'Something like a rainbow. It's Jem. Something's happened. I don't know what, but something's happened.'

The orb began to spin.

'Toth?' Rajal breathed. 'Can it be Toth?'

Before Littler could answer, there was a cracking, then a crash. A beam fell from the roof, slamming into the straw. Littler cried out. Rajal flung himself over Myla. The barn, it appeared, was about to collapse. Straw flew up, whirling round the hayloft. Wheels and horse-collars fell from the walls; the doors banged violently back and forth.

Then, as suddenly as it had begun, it was over. All was still, but for the falling snow.

Rajal uncovered his head, looking about him. He saw Littler, blinking amidst the debris, clutching a miaowing Ejard Orange; the glowing orb had vanished. Rajal raised his eyes. The hole in the roof had widened and there was a jagged gap in the barn wall too. 'Well, that's just what we need. Now we'll really freeze ... Littler, what's wrong?'

The little boy stumbled forward, pointing. Rajal staggered up, lurching in the straw. Through the gap in the wall, hovering in the air, was the orb. Like a beacon, it illuminated the gloomy haze. At the back of the barn, the ground fell away rapidly, and in a hollow below, almost concealed amongst thick pines, was a rambling old cottage, its gables and tall chimneys burdened heavily with snow.

'So that's the farmhouse?' said Rajal.

'Must be. And Jem went the other way.'

'We've got to find him!' Rajal burst out. He looked round anxiously. 'But ... I can't leave Myla.'

'I told you,' said Littler,' something's *happened* to Jem—'

'What do you mean, *happened*? You don't mean he's—'

Littler cast his eyes towards the doors. One had fallen open and an icy wind whirled through, carrying gusts of snow. 'I'm not sure,' he muttered. 'I can't understand everything in the orb, but I know we won't find Jem if we go that way. He won't be back for us. And how long will we last here?'

Setting down Ejard Orange, Littler clambered out through the gap.

'Wait,' said Rajal, 'what do you think you're doing?'

'Scouting round, of course.' Littler pointed to the farmhouse. 'You stay with Myla. I'll check the lie of the land, then we can carry her down – well, you can. I might even get help, if anyone actually lives there. I just hope they've got some furs, is all I can say. Or blankets.' He rubbed his arms; Ejard Orange miaowed again. 'That's right, Ejjy. And food, too. Lots of food.'

'Hold on,' said Rajal. 'What if it's not *safe*? What if—'

'We're in trouble anyway, aren't we? Coming, Ejjy?'

With a sigh, Rajal watched as Littler trudged precariously downhill, slipping a little, then righting himself. Ejard Orange was much more nimble.

'Say, Littler?' he called, with sudden generosity. 'We're going to need another name for you soon. I always thought you were just a little pest. And you're not so little any more. Not really.'

But Littler did not hear.

For a moment the orb hovered far above him, golden and glowing; then, to Rajal's surprise, the sphere burst, vanishing like a soap bubble.

Littler, it seemed, had not noticed it go. His small form vanished into a clutch of pines. Rajal peered through the greyness. The falling snow had relented, just a little. He saw a plume of smoke, curling up from the farmhouse chimney, and wondered if Littler had seen it too.

'Taggle! Stop that!'

Taggle, who was not sure what he should stop, looked up, startled. Nirry flashed him a stern look; he remained startled, but at least he had stopped. Nirry ruffled his hair and told him to be good. Taggle squirmed. So did his brother.

From behind her veil, Nirry gazed about her with satisfaction, as she always did when she brought her little party into the Great Temple. As members of the commercial classes, Goody Olch and Co. could take their places – if somewhat lowly ones – in Merchants' Row, a long, handsome-ly cushioned tier of pews which ran along the western side of the nave.

Candles shimmered in the holy gloom. Incense hovered thickly on the air. All around were the pious citizenry of Agondon – quality-folk to the front, commoners to the rear – ready to commemorate Agonis Inaugural. It was a solemn affair, more solemn than usual. All were shocked by the events of last night. Bluejacket guards were out in force, stationed in large numbers throughout the Temple.

'Brr, it's not half freezing, love!' said Wiggler, a little too loudly. He rubbed his hands. 'Just as well we've got these here cushions, or I reckon my—'

'Wiggler Olch, don't you dare!' hissed Nirry, though she could not help but smile. 'We'll have none of your *vulgar-itties*, thank you very much. Remember the boys – not to mention Baines and me. *Some* of us are women of piety, even if you're not.'

'Eh, love? Of course I'm not a *woman*, am I?' Grinning, Wiggler dug Baines in the ribs. 'Eh, Pirate?'

Baines simpered, fluttering the lashes of her single eye; Nirry fumed. Sometimes she was not sure about Baines. Did the woman realise the privilege that was accorded her, being counted amongst the Olch party? By rights she should be up the back with the servants. Still, Nirry had to make allowances; poor Baines was a decayed gentlewoman, after all, and not without talents.

For some time, determined to be equal to her new station, Nirry had struggled to teach herself to read. She had not got very far, but Baines could read as naturally as speaking; she could even cast accounts. More than once, Nirry had wished that her servant would instruct her in these arts. But a mistress, she had decided, could hardly request such a thing;

besides, Baines must be straining that eye of hers quite enough. It wasn't as if she had one to spare, like most people.

'Raggle?'

'Aunt Nirry?'

'Don't do that, hm?'

To Nirry's relief, Raggle desisted. The surge of the pipe organ filled the nave; at any moment, the service would begin. Nirry smiled, raising her veil. Once again she took in the screens and monuments, the soaring columns, the massive stained-glass windows.

Back in Irion, she would never have dreamed that one day she would worship in a place so splendid. Would she have dreamed that she might worship at all with anything other than a sense of duty? Since coming to Agondon, Nirry had felt the love of the Lord Agonis rising within her. Perhaps it was this magnificent temple, filling her with sacred awe; perhaps it was her new life, and all the blessings that had come her way. Now if only she could find her old father ... if only she could keep Wiggler out of the wars ... *if only* a few other things, besides. But already the Lord Agonis had been more than generous.

She reached for Wiggler's hand and squeezed it tight.

'Quite the little family, aren't we?' she whispered, gesturing to the boys. 'And if we pray hard, Wiggler, we might have some of our own. Just because it hasn't happened yet—'

'Course it'll happen, love. Just a matter of time.' Wiggler leaned closer, grinning. 'But I don't think *praying*'s got much to do with it, eh?'

'Wiggler Olch!'

But Nirry had to grin too. Fondly she looked into her husband's face. 'Ooh, but your shiner's come up something huge! Now why have I kept you out of the wars, if you go and get one of them? What will people think?'

'They'll think you've been keeping me in line, love. Wish I'd brought the steak with me, I do.'

In Temple? Nirry tut-tutted; Wiggler was unrepentant. More than once, as the little party had trudged, crocodile-fashion, through the chill morning, he had scooped up handfuls of snow, squashing them against his smarting eye. No wonder he complained of the cold. The silly man had got his mittens wet through – the new ones Nirry had just knitted, too!

Things could have been worse. That Wiggler's eye had been the only casualty last night in the Cat & Crown had been something of a miracle. The news that Bob Scarlet's plan had failed had driven the rebels to fury. Swiftly they had fallen to fighting amongst themselves. Some decried Bob as a villain, declaring that they would trust him no more; others turned viciously on those who attacked him. There were oaths, execrations, flying fists – and Wiggler was in the way. Nirry could barely believe they had got all the rebels out by the back stairs without stabbings, let alone gunshots. The drunken fools had made a terrible commotion. She told Carney that the quality-folk had quarrelled over an inheritance.

'I just hope Miss Cata's all right,' she mused aloud.

'That one?' Wiggler said admiringly. 'She's all right, never you mind. Should have seen her with them rebels, love! Could have done with that one in the Fifth, we could.'

'Don't you go telling Miss Cata that. Used to be a lovely lady, she did, and now look at her...'

Nirry might have added that Miss Cata, to cap it all, was in a delicate condition; might have said the girl would lose that baby, the way she carried on. But that was women's business, and not for the likes of Wiggler ... And could Nirry believe Miss Cata was an honest woman? Could she really have married Master Jem in some wretched foreign temple? It wasn't right, it just wasn't right!

But Nirry only murmured, 'It's a rum do, a lady like her, running round with riff-raff like Bob Scarlet.'

'What about Miss Landa?'

'She's foreign. But Miss Cata? Ooh, and I wish she'd come to Temple, I really do!'

'She's one of them Vagas, isn't she?' said Baines. 'Well, something like that. Don't have to come.'

Wiggler muttered, 'Wish I was a Vaga, then.'

Nirry pinched her husband's arm. 'Vaga, indeed! If you think you're off to the Realm of Unbeing while I go to the Vast all by myself, you've got another think coming, I'll tell you that much! Temple for you, regular as clockwork, or my name's not Nirrian Jubb!'

'But it's *not*,' laughed Wiggler. 'Not any more.'

Nirry had to laugh, too. But her laughter was short-lived. As the mighty heft of the organ swirled through the nave, the choir assembled in the choir stalls, the Cantor Lector and Temple Canons took their places, and persons of particular quality emerged through special doors into their ornate private pews. Nirry had always said she had no vulgar desire to gawp upon her betters; still, it was with a thrill of pleasure that she glimpsed, as usual, the gorgeous Lady Bolbarr, the dashing Baron Aldermyle, the noble Lady Cham-Charing, with that *rather* unfortunate daughter.

And this morning, someone else.

Nirry breathed, 'But I thought...'

'What is it, love?' Wiggler was alarmed. His wife had turned pale and clutched a hand to her mouth. She turned to him, wide-eyed.

'I ... I thought they worshipped in the royal chapel! And here she is!'

'Your old mistress?' said Baines. 'Well, I never!'

'The *fat lady*?' said Raggle and Taggle, both at once.

Nirry cursed herself for a fool. Of course she should have known that the royal party came to Temple *sometimes*. When else if not on the Inaugural?

'Come on, love, the old bag's leagues away,' Wiggler said kindly. 'She'll hardly see you from there, and what if she does? You were a servant, not a slave! You're your own mistress now. Besides, quality don't gawp at the likes of us, not the way we gawp at them.'

'I … I never wanted to see her again,' was all Nirry said.

In a fluster, she lowered her veil.

Chapter 14

MORE DISCOMFORT FOR NIRRY

'So this is Ejland? What a place!'

By the time he reached the bottom of the hollow, Littler was so cold he had barely any feeling in his hands or feet. He wished he were back in Unang Lia. Miserably he scanned the shabby farmhouse with its shuttered windows and locked doors. For an Ejlander house, it was commonplace enough. But Littler had never seen one like it before. Ivy wreathed the walls and the gables loomed darkly under the grey burden of the sky. How sinister it looked!

Littler gulped; when Ejard Orange buffed his leg, he jumped. 'Ejjy, stop it!' His voice was harsh but he softened at once, scooping the heavy cat into his arms. 'Poor thing, your paws are frozen! We can keep each other warm, at least. What's that, Ejjy?'

Miaowing, the big cat looked over Littler's shoulder. It was only then that Littler remembered the orb. He turned, expecting the golden sphere to be hovering over their heads; seeing that it was gone, his fears welled anew. He gazed into the sky, but did not see the smoke from the farmhouse chimney.

He shook his head. 'Never mind, Ejjy. What do we need with that silly orb? Jem's right. More trouble than it's worth. Now let's find a way into here. Abandoned barn, abandoned house. Nothing to be frightened of. Besides, it must be warmer inside than out, mustn't it? Just a bit?'

By now, Littler had tried the forbidding door, set back in a gabled, evil-smelling porch. He would never get in that way. Numbly he trudged from window to window, rattling at shutters.

'What about this one?' At the back of the house was a window smaller than the others, with shutters in the last stages of rottenness. 'Sit on the sill, Ejjy, that's right. Just let me get a leg-up here, then I think we can pull this thing away. *Ouch.* One more time. *Ouch.* Well, another time. There, that's done it.'

Littler flung down the rotten wood. Luckily, there was no glass. Nimbly, following Ejard Orange, he thudded down into a darkened chamber.

'Ejjy? Now stick by me. What's that? You *can* see in the dark, can't you?'

After the crisp glare of the snow, Littler could barely see anything. Only slowly did he make out the dispiriting scene. The floors were bare; the walls were daubed with obscenities. Fallen plaster lay here and there; dirty-looking bedding was heaped in corners. Ah, but here was a blanket! Gratefully Littler grabbed it, wrapping it round his shoulders like a cloak.

And what was that smell? His blanket caught against a chamber-pot. With a clang, the pot upended on the floor. He whisked the blanket away from a spreading, dark pool.

Only after a moment did Littler think what this must mean. A chamber-pot with liquid, stinking contents? The place, then, could hardly be abandoned.

But by then he had moved beyond the mean back chamber into a long hallway, very dark. He shuddered, wondering if he should escape. But it was warmer here; besides, Ejard Orange had flitted on ahead.

'Ejjy,' Littler whispered, 'where are you?'

Should he call out? Littler did not dare; then he began to smell something else, something more pleasant than the chamber-pot. A waft of cooking drifted down the hall. Breakfast! Ejjy must have smelled it first, and followed his nose. Littler's stomach rumbled and he almost swooned. Light flickered from a doorway up ahead. His heart pounded hard. Doubts assailed him. A floorboard creaked; then a hand, like a vice, gripped his shoulder.

'Got you, you little villain!'

And Littler could only cry absurdly, 'Help, help! Jem, Raj – *help*!'

'Is it really her?' Raggle urged.

'Of course!' said Taggle. 'Look how—'

'Boys, boys!' Nirry snapped.

They could barely contain themselves. If the boys, at another time, might have been enthralled to see His Imperial Agonist Majesty, their father's great enemy, in the flesh – or rather, the ermine, velvet and gold – for now, they had eyes only for the *fat lady*, presiding like a vast, bejewelled slug between the shabby-looking King and his still unabducted Queen.

At the altar, the Cantor Lector raised his arms. With much shuffling and coughing, the congregated rose for the first of the Songs of Inauguration. Nirry held her Cantorate high, nudging Wiggler to do the same. Never mind that the Olches could not read, they hardly wished their neighbours to know – though any who glanced at Wiggler might have seen that he held his Cantorate upside down.

In any case, Wiggler only opened and shut his mouth; Nirry, for her part, followed the lead of Baines, while the caterwauling of Raggle and Taggle bore little relation to the sacred words. It was as well that several thousand other voices rang all around them, filling the nave to the top of its high, vaulted ceiling.

And so we gather here to praise
Our god who stayed on earth:
The sacred seeker who forsook
His element of sky
    To walk our ways,
    To walk our ways.

Wiggler's Cantorate soon slipped. Not for the first time, a terrible thought possessed him. After running away from her mistress, Nirry had not only bought him out of the army, but bought the lease of the Cat & Crown. She said she had been saving. But had she stolen from her mistress? Wiggler prayed that his suspicion was false. Would Nirry have come to Agondon, had it been true?

But then, when they had taken the Cat & Crown, Nirry had not *known* that her mistress was in Agondon.

A mirrored girl from him did fly
And in her flight so shook
All goodness, virtue, trust and worth,
That since, through all these days,
    We can but cry,
    We can but cry.

It was one of the harder hymns and Nirry rapidly gave up too. Trembling, she thought of that fateful night when she had left her mistress. Often, in these last moonlives, she found her time in service almost hard to imagine, though for so long it had been all she had known. How Nirry had changed! Her old life filled her with horror. Of course there had been good times, when Lady Ela was alive; there had been Lord Tor, little Barnabas, Master Jem.

But looming over it all, dominating it all, there had always been the mistress.

But now a new age comes to birth:
With every passing phase
This long Atonement's end draws nigh,
And no more must we brook
    This time of dearth,
    This time of dearth.

Nirry had not always seen the mistress clearly. For a long time she had thought of her only as an exasperating old harridan, easy enough to placate so long as food was forthcoming. Her hypocritical piety had bothered Nirry no more than her father's maudlin drunkenness; when the fat woman had taken up with Chaplain Feval, Nirry had seen the funny side.

Then came the terrible night when the chaplain, goaded on by the mistress, had murdered Lord Margrave. Concealed in the dense greenery of the Glass Room, Nirry had seen it all. Together, the chaplain and the mistress had ensured that nothing would stand in the way of Governor Veeldrop's peerage; so it was that the mistress had acquired her position in society.

The next day, Nirry ran away with Miss Cata.

> *For now that shepherd with his crook*
> *Shall with his might defy*
> *The welling evil of these days:*
> *Once more shall joy and mirth*
> > *Shine in each look,*
> > *Shine in each look.*

Sometimes Nirry tried to convince herself that it was the chaplain who had corrupted her pious, well-meaning mistress. She was not sure she believed that – and now, peering from behind her Cantorate, gazing upon Lady Umbecca, Nirry knew she did not believe it at all. She shrank behind her veil, wishing they had sat at the back with the lower orders. How her pride was punished!

Fearfully, she tried to imagine her father's fate. Could the old bitch simply have thrown him out on the streets, after so many years of service?

Oh, she was evil, evil!

> *So with his goddess in his gaze*
> *The lordly one soars high,*
> *And all that evil's forces took*
> *Shall come back to the earth*
> > *For all its days!*
> > *For all its days!*

The hymn came to its stentorian end.

Further Songs of Inauguration followed, some by the choir alone, some by the congregated, some by the massed forces of congregated and choir. There were readings from the El-Orokon and from the Lives of the Sainted; there was an incantation and a blessing, led by the Maximate of the Inner in his pointed hat and gleaming white surplice. Softly gleamed the gold, the ebony and the marble; all the time the sacred candles fluttered, incense wafted and the glare of morning through the stained glass cast a five-coloured rainbow high in the gloom, arcing between the great carved columns.

Yet for all the splendours a chill wind skirled along the aisles, and even the quality-folk, swathed in furs, soon became uncomfortable. There were furtive sippings from Vantage flasks, and many were the longings for chamber pot, coffee cup or tobarillo by the time the Archmaximate, Leader Most Holy of the Order of Agonis, ascended to the high, ornate lectern of stone to introduce the new Great Lector.

At last! Nirry's interest quickened, and she forgot her thoughts of the mistress. Like all who attended the Great Temple, Nirry had been saddened by the death of old Lector Garvice, and intrigued by the rumours surrounding his replacement. Some had put their money on Chaplain Etravers from the Royal Ejard Guards; some on Lector Arden of Varby; there was talk of Canon Flonce, most trusted of the old Lector's aides.

Since Canon Flonce was the only one Nirry had seen, she was biased in his favour, especially since he was a handsome man, in a plump, benevolent sort of way. If there were those who said he was common, numbering servants and tradesmen amongst his relations, Nirry still hoped he would receive his reward for all his devotion to Great Lector Garvice.

A buzz of murmuring filled the nave. Twisting Raggle's head towards the lectern, Nirry gazed nervously at the Archmaximate, spiritual father of All Ejland. In the Order of Agonis, the Great Lectoracy was the next most important role, for the Great Lector would almost certainly be Archmaximate in his turn.

For now, the present incumbent raised his arms in blessing. The murmurings died. In a quavering voice, the old man began a long oration, reiterating the virtues of the late Lector Garvice and reflecting on the moral, intellectual and spiritual excellence which must be found in his successor if this great metropolis, citadel of civilisation, fulcrum of the world – &c., &c. – were to be guided safely through the testing times ahead.

The Archmaximate, it seemed, would go on interminably, so it was a surprise when he broke off abruptly, stepped back and gestured towards the arched door of the vestry. The organ burst back into life, the choir too, and the door opened to reveal a magnificent robed figure, crossing the altar with stately steps and ascending to the lectern.

There were gasps, even cries; the guards, stationed about the temple, became for a moment more obtrusive. Raggle and Taggle craned their necks, wondering what this meant. Nirry was open-mouthed and the colour drained from her face.

'Eh, steady on, love!' Wiggler whispered.

'Goody Olch, what's wrong?' hissed Baines.

Nirry could only gaze round wildly, just in time to see a certain old lady fainting in the Cham-Charing pew, and the proud, triumphant smile on the face of the mistress.

Fearing she might throw up, Nirry struggled to listen as Eay Feval announced the text of his sermon.

80

Chapter 15

HAND IN GLOVE

'Myla? Myla, did you speak?'

Again Rajal leaned over his sister; again, she stirred. Still her eyes were closed, but Rajal was certain that she no longer slept. He looked around him, as if there were something, anything he could do. How lonely he felt, with Jem and Littler gone. Right now, he would even be glad to see that fat, annoying cat. Despairingly, he looked into his sister's face, so strange, so waxen in its unaccustomed pallor. He felt her skin. Oh, but she was frozen. Cold winds rattled through the holes in the barn; snow scurried from the grey, hazy sky.

That was when the light came overhead.

Gulping, Rajal looked up. It was Littler's orb, spinning and spinning.

Then came the voice.

Brother Raj, it's a summons. The summons we need—

'M-Myla?' Rajal whispered. His sister had still not opened her eyes. Or her mouth. 'You ... you can see the orb?'

I see everything. Brother, take me in your arms—

'Wh-what? I ... I don't understand—'

Take me in your arms—

Rajal wanted to protest, but was not sure why. Awkwardly, he scooped up his strangely aged sister, feeling sharp bones beneath her blue, crumpled robes. *How light she is*, he thought, looking like a lover on her deathly face. Peering up through the shattered roof, he saw the golden sphere spinning away, vanishing in the haze, as if it were the sun abandoning a world it did not wish to illuminate any longer.

Your shoulder, carry me over your shoulder—

Now the wind came, wilder than before, bursting open the barn doors. Staggering, Rajal saw the orb again, hovering over the snow. Could it be calling him?

Take me, just take me, where the orb wants to go—

With his sister swaying precariously over his shoulder, Rajal made his way down the ladder from the hayloft. By the time he trudged out into snow, he was sweating more than shivering, as if on the verge of a dangerous fever. He looked behind him, back into the cheerless barn that felt suddenly almost comforting.

This was the direction Jem had gone.

And where, Rajal wondered, could Jem be now?

The orb juddered forward, a little sun again, this time a shifting, beckoning sun. Rajal made out something up ahead, something bright and blue. The skyship, half-concealed beneath a snowy mound.

The orb bobbed above it.

'Sister, tell me, what does this mean? It's wrecked, it's ruined, it has to be—'

The skyship. Take me to the skyship—

This, Rajal discovered, was harder than it looked. Approaching their crashed vessel, he found his sister growing strangely heavier; his steps grew leaden too, and the distance – really, no distance at all – was too much.

His fever, if fever it were, was worse.

'Sister Myla ... oh, but I must rest—'

Strange images filled Rajal's mind, images of white mountains, of ice, of a vast, fantastical palace. But why? The amulet on his wrist began to turn and turn, chafing him, and he felt the crystal burning at his chest.

And the band at Myla's forehead flashed with silver light.

Rajal fell. 'Sister, no I can't ... no, no I—'

But that was when Myla rose up in the sky, floating towards the spinning, sun-like sphere.

Rajal, like Jem, might have passed out in the snow. Instead, aware of her insistent summons, he looked up in astonishment to see his sister in the air, blue robes billowing, above the skyship where the orb had been. She raised her hands to her temples, pressed her fingers to the Lichano band.

Now the snow was slipping from the skyship.

And the ship was rising, rising in the air.

'Hardly the most sensible behaviour now, is it? To lie in the lane where the carts come by, that would be bad enough – in Theron-season, bad enough by far. But on a morning like this? In the snow? You *are* listening, aren't you? Jem, you are listening?'

Jem, in truth, was not *quite* listening. His eyes were closed and he was pleasantly warm. Dimly he was aware that he was swaying, just a little, from side to side, and jogging lightly up and down. He smiled; the voice was a pleasant droning. And there was something in his hand. Something warm.

'Oh yes, Jem. A few moments more, you'd have been covered completely. Invisible in the white. And then where would you have been? Lucky, weren't you, that I came along? You might even call me your saviour. – But you're listening, aren't you? Jem?'

It was then that Jem opened his eyes. He saw that he was on the box of a cart, his head slumped on the driver's shoulder. The white lane stretched ahead and trails of steam rose from the nostrils of a big, plodding cart horse.

He straightened up quickly. 'I … who are you?'

Snow fell no longer: the sky was iron-grey. To the side, a hare bounded through a field; the driver watched it, averting his face. Jem saw only that his companion was tall, and dressed in thick, dark furs. He looked down, opening his hand. Gleaming in his palm was the harlequin's coin.

'Who are you?' he asked again.

Perhaps Jem's companion could not hear. 'Oh yes, it could have been bad for you,' he said, hunching forward, urging on the horse. A high collar, like a rampart, still concealed his face, but the voice, Jem thought, was strangely familiar. 'Death by freezing is a nasty business. And few enchanters can reverse it, did you know that? Try as they might to bring the dead back to life, it's a difficult business at the best of times. But if a fellow's been frozen? – You're listening now, aren't you? Hm? Jem?'

'You know my name?' Jem said at last.

By now he was not so much alarmed as puzzled. He was by no means a prisoner. No bonds held him; he imagined leaping from the cart, but something made him stay. Was it that he still wore his thin, inadequate garb? No hat on his head, no gloves on his hands, no stout boots of leather: yet Jem seemed not to feel the cold at all.

Was it – but it must have been – the gash in his thigh? Jem had forgotten the gash in his thigh. But when he looked down, he saw that it was gone.

Gingerly, he prodded his flesh. *Cured. Cured.*

The driver said, 'Jem, of course I know your name.'

'And yours?' Jem breathed, astonished. 'What's yours?'

He thought he knew; Jem might have pulled at the high collar, exposing the visage he was certain would be there. But was there any need? The cart rounded a corner. Below them, mighty and magnificent, was the capital of Ejland, sprawled across the delta of the River Riel.

Ah, Agondon, City of Aeons! Agondon, royal throne of kings! Frozen under the cold sky, the city was a vision of mysterious splendour. And most splendid of all, gold against the grey, was the noble spire of the Great Temple, heart of the city, heart of the empire, heart of all the world.

In fearful rapture Jem gazed ahead, even as his companion turned his face towards him. Now the fellow made the horse stay; from their point of vantage in the Agondon Hills, they might have been poised to take flight, swooping over the city below.

'Jem, I don't have much time. But you know that, don't you? Down there, amongst the narrow, winding streets of the Island, there is a tavern. Oh, it's not a place you'd have been before, not in your days as Lord Empster's ward. A simple establishment, its customers are common, but you will be more welcome there than in the gilded halls of quality-folk. Its sign is the Cat & Crown, and it is there that you must go.'

Jem was alarmed. 'But Raj ... Littler?'

'Fear not for your friends. Already they have found their own parts to play.'

'And Myla? What about Myla?'

'Jem, think only of the Cat & Crown. The time, I say, is short, and I must go.'

Only now did Jem turn to his companion. 'Go? But where?'

The silver mask flashed. 'It is not my destiny to live in this world. Like the one whose semblance I bear – remember, once, how you called me by his name? – I should have departed from it long ago.'

Jem gulped. He knew, of course, that this visionary harlequin was not one and the same with Uncle Tor, who had run with Vagas, worn motley and performed his harlequin's dance on the village green. No, Tor was dead; Jem had seen him hanging from the gallows, grey-faced and broken-necked, betrayed by Aunt Umbecca.

But must not this harlequin be Tor's Essence, guiding Jem from beyond the grave?

'Enchanters bring people back to life,' he murmured. 'Harlequin, you said so. What is destiny, measured against enchantment?'

The harlequin told him that his words were idle. 'You are *destined*, are you not, to reunite the Orokon? You are *destined*, are you not, to wear this kingdom's crown? Yet Toth's enchantments work against you all the time! Ask, perhaps, what enchantment might be, pitched in a battle against what is ordained; never allow that Toth might triumph, lest in thinking, you make it so.' The harlequin looked down. 'I say, I must depart; yet soon, my child, we shall meet again, when your quest at last is at an end.'

Alarm surged in Jem. Snow was falling once more, and he gestured helplessly over the city below. 'Harlequin, wait! There's so much you must tell me! Who was that lady, that rainbow lady? And where's Cata? Won't you tell me how to find the golden crystal, here in this epicentre of Toth's power? Won't you give me a clue? A sign?'

The mouth beneath the mask twisted into a smile. Now, through a gap in the swathing furs, Jem caught a glimpse of the particoloured costume.

'Jem, Jem, have you not had signs enough? Perhaps you cannot believe your work is nearly done.' A gloved hand reached out, touching his chest. 'The Crystal of Javander. And the Vaga has the Crystal of Koros, does he not – the little Unang, the Crystal of Theron? The wild girl possesses the Crystal of Viana ... Yes, the avatars are almost in place. It is simple, Jem. Join again with Wolveron's daughter; bring together your little band, and the four crystals, their powers conjoined, shall bring you the fifth. There is no mystery here. When the avatars present themselves at the Lamasery of the Winds, then all is over. Then the time has come.'

Jem's mind reeled. '*No mystery?* Ava-what? Lama-what? Harlequin, but—'

'I can delay no further.' The mouth beneath the mask smiled again and the harlequin gripped Jem's hand; it was the hand that held the coin. 'My child, after today, only one more time can I come to you; one more time, then I vanish for ever. Call on me when you need me. But *only* when you need me. Then I shall come.'

'But today ... today, I didn't call you—'

'If you hadn't called, I should never have come.'

Jem could only gaze into the harlequin's mask, staring into the eyes behind the curved, polished silver. Love filled his heart, for how could he believe this harlequin was not his Uncle Tor?

The mask began to vibrate, almost to dance. 'Harlequin! What's happening?'

'Remember, Jem, the Cat & ... Cat &...'

This time, the voice was far away; then, quite suddenly, the harlequin was gone, leaving behind only his empty coat ... his hat ... his gloves ... his boots.

Bewildered, Jem gazed around him, clutching the coin so tightly that it hurt. He shivered violently. *So cold, so cold!*

Still the Temple's spire shone through the snow as Jem blinked away the tears in his eyes. Swiftly he donned the discarded clothes, then took up the reins of the steaming, stamping horse.

'Gee-up, boy – the Cat & Canary!'

Slowly they made their way downhill.

'Or ... do I mean the Cat & Crown?'

Chapter 16

EARTHLY POWERS

For the time that was to come, he said, would be a Time of Atonement,
when all would live in sorrow for the errors of the past.

Ork. Juv. V.54/7–9

With the confidence of an experienced performer, Eay Feval leaned forward, the sleeves of his robes draping luxuriously over a huge, ancient El-Orokon, fixed to the lectern by a golden chain.

A smile played over his sharp, handsome features. There were shufflings, bowings of heads; Wiggler tried to keep his ears still, and Baines rapidly blinked her single eye. In the Cham-Charing pew, a harried Miss Laetitia alternately wafted smelling salts beneath her mother's nose and flapped her Cantorate back and forth like a fan – much to the annoyance of Lady Margrave, who sat on the other side of the Great Cham. Freddie Chayn (a little concussed from the night before) and Professor Mercol were there too, looking abashed.

The Lector breathed deeply. The smile slipped from his face and suddenly, startlingly, he thumped the holy book.

'Women and men of Agondon,' he declaimed, 'know ye what is written here? Pray that ye do, for it is by thy allegiance to this book, by this and this alone, that ye shall be judged when the time comes. Obey these teachings, engrave them on your hearts, and eternal bliss shall be your reward, as ye are spirited up to the glories of the Vast; forget them, and like flotsam in a storm, the Keeper of the Portal in his righteous wrath shall cast ye down to the Realm of Unbeing, there to know such unending torments that all the agonies of your earthly flesh shall seem in comparison like the shudderings of pleasure!'

It was a stunning opening. Umbecca looked on proudly; First Minister Tranimel, who had slipped into the nave just moments before, permitted himself a wry smile. Even the Cham-Charings, mother and daughter, were startled into attention.

But Eay Feval was a cunning orator. Fire and brimstone was only one weapon in his arsenal. Soon his tone would change, then change again.

'I ask, know ye what is written in this book?' He hunched over, speaking rapidly and low, as if he might be imparting a confidence to each and every woman and man assembled there. 'It is written that once we lived in the Vale of Orok, in that first age of this world which we call the

86

Juvescence. It is written that this Vale was racked by wars, when the forces of Theron and his sister Javander fought against the forces of Koros and Viana. Only Agonis, greatest of gods, desisted from the vicious folly of these wars. Still it was that when these wars passed, the Ur-God rose from the darkness of his death, deep within the Rock of Being and Unbeing, and decreed that the five races must go forth in exile from the Vale of Orok. Thus did the Juvescence end and the present age begin, this era we have called the Time of Atonement.'

Feval's eyes flickered over expectant, fearful faces. Anguish thudded in Nirry's brain. How could this man – this vicious, scheming murderer – be Great Lector of Agondon? What did her faith mean if such a thing could happen?

Of course, she might have wondered how such a man could belong to the Order of Agonis at all. She knew he had been in some sort of disgrace. Wasn't that why he had been banished to Irion? How, then, could he rise to such glory?

In many ways, Nirry Olch remained a simple woman. The thought came to her that the Lord Agonis must surely appear – right here, now – and strike Feval down.

The Lector's manner became expansive. From time to time he would shake his head, like a man moved by sad reflections.

'So it came to pass that we left that place of our innocence, thence to endure great hardship and peril in quest of this realm where now we dwell. So, legend will say, the Lord Agonis – his heart bleeding for our sufferings – disobeyed the command of his father that he must return to his home in the Vast. Instead, the god of our race began his long roamings in quest of his beloved, the Lady Imagenta, whose dazzling visage had sparked the wars that destroyed our first and most splendid earthly home.

'This, I say, is but legend, which the holy book neither confirms nor denies; but through the ages the belief has been strong that when Our Lord finds His Lady at last, this present ordering of things must end.'

Baines gulped, blinking at the tear that filled her single eye. Wiggler shifted uncomfortably, then became still more uncomfortable as he saw the expression beneath his wife's veil.

Bewildered, angry, Nirry gazed between the smooth, self-satisfied Lector and the proud, beaming Umbecca. How they had triumphed! Wildly, she imagined lurching up from the pew, screaming out the truth.

She would not dare. In her foggy way, Nirry had always thought the world was well-ordered, with a place for everything, and everything in its place. Only for the sake of Miss Cata and Miss Landa had she taken up with the rebels. Now, all at once, she understood their cause. Ejland languished in the grip of evil. Somehow, whatever it took, that grip must be broken.

She trembled violently. She clutched Wiggler's arm.

'But when shall it be, this End of Atonement?' Eay Feval stabbed a finger at the congregated. 'Women and men of Agondon, is it apprehension I see in your faces? It is, for do we not gather here this morning to commemorate the start of the Festival of Agonis, the Meditations that end this present year? In a matter of days, we must number the year no longer as 999*d* but 999*e*, the last before the Thousandth Cycle begins. And what then? What fears must we face, in the brief space of a year?

'Ah, I know what some will say! Some rant on street corners, some whisper it behind their hands – but many are those who think the impending Thousandth Cycle, even in the very moment of its dawning, must mark the end of all we know. But whether this ending shall be joyous or dire, that is a matter of fervent debate.'

The Lector stroked his chin. 'And what of you, my children, foregathered here this morning? What do you imagine? Do I delude myself that *the end, the end*, tolling like a bell, finds no echo in any hearts here? Women and men of Agondon, I do not. Let me look amongst you.'

With exaggerated gestures, a hand above his eyes, the Lector peered into the holy gloom. There were stirrings of anxiety amongst the common folk. 'Ah yes, I see a fellow at the back, red-faced and fleshy – a shoemaker, I surmise, or a tallow-chandler. Or, perhaps, a dealer in intoxicating liquors.'

Guffaws came, and many were the necks that craned in several directions to see just where this fellow was to be found.

'And what is it that you envisage, my friend? Demons, perhaps, from the Realm of Unbeing – demons, bursting through the walls of this dimension, massing to destroy this ancient city?' The Lector's eyes blazed like hot coals. His whisper hissed through the vaulted stonework. 'Ah yes, I think you do. *I think you do.*'

Frightened gasps replaced the guffaws as his gaze roved again, this time alarmingly close to the Olch party. For a terrifying moment Nirry thought she might be singled out. *And you, my veiled one? Come, show us your visage.* She trembled; Baines, by contrast, permitted herself some discreet primping.

As it happened, Feval appeared to have lighted upon a lady a few pews away, though which lady neither the relieved Nirry, nor the disappointed Baines, could be quite sure.

'And you, my good woman? From the place where you sit, might I not guess you to be a merchant's wife, as prosperous as you are plump? 'Might I not compliment you upon – for yes, I am sure they are – the latest Varby fashions?'

Titters filled the air, and more than one wife amongst the merchant classes flushed, conscious that her garb was not *quite* of the latest.

'Ah, my fair one, I mean no offence. In your husband's establishment I am certain you are the finest of ornaments, and a woman of deep and profound piety. Perhaps that is why your fond heart dwells – for yes, I am sure it does – upon thoughts that the Lord Agonis shall soon be amongst us, His Lady at his side at last. Then, with but the spreading of his arms, shall there not begin a new, eternal era of peace?'

Titters were transformed into gasps of joy. Feval smiled, conscious of a mastery honed by long practice in the Temple of Irion. How he had despised his provincial exile! Now his sufferings were paying off. And now – but obliquely, playfully – would begin his vengeance upon the authoress of those sufferings.

His eyes turned towards the private pews. There were confused murmurings. Surely not even the Great Lector would single out a person of quality, not here amongst this promiscuous fray? But this time there could be no doubt as to his victim. He pointed with a long, rapier-like finger. Laughter rippled and heads turned to Miss Laetitia Cham-Charing, flushing, mortified.

'And you? What of you, my Greenstocking beauty? Your reputation for learning has spread far and wide; already, some say, the wisdom of the ages is contained between those immaculate ears! Let us hope your husband shall not be tempted to *box* them, exasperated as he must be at your superior learning ... But of course, I forget you have yet to *find* a husband.'

The laughter was louder now, almost ribald.

'Poor child, what a trial to your mother you must be. And what a pity you display so little concern for her as the poor woman slides into the twilight of senescence, sustained only by memories of her lost glories!'

As if in sorrow, the Lector shook his head; by now, the laughter that had begun amongst quality-ladies had spread to encompass the entirety of the congregated. Lady Cham-Charing slumped back, her face fixed in a rictus of horror, while Tishy, scarlet and sweating, could only gaze and gaze at her tormentor, fighting the impulse to block her ears, to scream, to rush down the aisle in tears. Like lashes, the hootings of the mob rained upon her, booming from the heights of the vast vaulted ceiling.

The Lector assumed a conversational air. 'But what thoughts, I wonder, revolve beneath that sternly pulled-back hair on this pressing topic of Atonement's End? Ah, Miss Tishy, I feel I can almost see behind those pretty little horn-rims, into the whirling cogs of your brain! And what thoughts come to you but *Nonsense ... nonsense*? No, my Greenstocking, deny it not, for is it not your pride and presumption to look with contempt upon the simple faith of your sisters and brothers, gathered here in the love of the Lord Agonis?'

Cries of *Shame!* and *For shame!* rang out until the hapless girl was reduced to tears, clutching her face in convulsing hands. Professor Mercol struggled to comfort her; Lady Margrave held the shaking Constansia;

Freddie Chayn could only sink into himself, despising himself, while the Lector stood back, secure in his triumph.

He had destroyed Lady Cham-Charing. In a single morning, the woman's lingering pretensions had been entirely undone. What woman was there now, even amongst the commonest, who would not look upon the old bitch with contempt? What man was there who would marry her pathetic, ugly daughter? Ah, vengeance was sweet!

But all this was incidental.

Feval had barely warmed to his theme. He breathed deeply, surveying the sea of faces. In a moment, he would crash down his fist on the El-Orokon, sweeping aside his three victims – liquor dealer, merchant's wife, even Miss Laetitia – with a booming cry that all were *wrong*, WRONG, WRONG in their paltry imaginings.

The Thousandth Cycle, he would declare, was of shattering significance. But was humankind to be released from earthly bondage into easy oblivion – either annihilation, *or* sensual bliss? (How the merchant's wife would blush!) Never! What was this, in truth, but a time for that renovation of the heart, that fervent renewal of faith which alone could ensure that the Lord Agonis never ceased his vigil over this great and ancient kingdom? What was it but craven to expect anything other?[1]

For yes, the Thousandth Cycle would begin an age of glory, but glory here on earth as the mighty forces of Ejland, supreme amongst nations, first crushed the rebels who dared challenge the rightful reign of His Imperial Agonist Majesty, then swept on in triumphant Holy War against all this world's benighted and inferior races. So their dominance would

---

[1] What Feval outlines here is the Doctrine of Perpetual Atonement, or 'Effective Perpetuity'. Increasingly in favour amongst the divines of Temple College as the Thousandth Cycle drew near, this was ratified in the Encyclicals of the Archmaximate, Moonlife of Sendal, AC 998*e*.

Though there was much dissent, especially amongst the vulgar, the official view of the Order of Agonis held not that Atonement would *literally* never end, but rather that it was endless from our present worldly perspective. The faithful, therefore, were adjured to regard the 'Foretelling' of the reunion of Our Lord and His Lady (as depicted in innumerable Agonist statues, murals and stained-glass windows) rather as a depiction or symbol of spiritual aspiration than of an event which could be expected to come to pass within the lifetime of any of those presently living.

Many and furious had been the arguments against this view. Some divines believed Effective Perpetuity could only diminish the faith of the masses; its proponents, by contrast, argued that it was folly to promise happenings which could not be certain to eventuate. The Agonist ministry, they declared, must stress the necessity to endure our worldly sufferings in hopes of an eternal reward in The Vast, where all the sorrows and injustices of the present order would be rectified.

endure for another thousand cycles, then another, then another, in the sacred name of King Ejard Bluejacket, representative in human form of the great and all-merciful LORD AGONIS!

Ah, it was a brilliant oratorical performance, the greatest Eay Feval had ever devised. Standing there at the lectern, he saw the remainder of the sermon laid before him, like a hill he must climb to his magnificent peroration. He held his audience in his hands, and held them utterly. His fame was secure. He was Great Lector, and soon – soon, when that old fool was out of the way – he would be Archmaximate, spiritual leader of the world's mightiest empire!

Feval could have thrown back his head and laughed. Already he imagined reports of his triumph, blazoned across column after column of the *Gazette*, surmounted by a noble engraving of his visage. He saw the commemorative busts, the icons. He saw himself elevated to the ranks of the Sainted. He swelled out his chest, ready to continue.

He never had the chance.

After the events of last night, the Temple that morning was thronged with Bluejackets, eyes peeled for the smallest signs of trouble. The mob, as they entered, had been scrutinised carefully. All had been searched for weapons; some had been turned away, some detained.

What no one reckoned on was the extent of rebel fanaticism. Or rebel cunning. So it was that when a certain lady – the merchant's wife, many would maintain, the one singled out in the Lector's sermon – burst from her pew, rushing towards the royal party, at first no one understood what was happening.

Lady Umbecca was the first to scream.

Shots rang out. A guard sprang forward, stabbing with his bayonet. Blood spurted. The rebel reeled and the heavy, high wig fell away, revealing the hairless male pate beneath. He crashed against the lectern. There was another shot, then another, but this was a suicide mission.

The bomb was primed and ready.

It all happened so quickly that Eay Feval had no time to move. An instant more, and bits of the pretended lady – limbs, organs, hanks of hair and last year's Varby fashions – exploded in a deafening, bloody cascade.

Feval caught the full force of the blast.

Chaos filled the Great Temple.

In those terrible moments, no one knew who was alive and who was dead, or if another bomb might be about to explode. Screaming, crying crowds battered towards the doors. Quality-folk and commoners, choristers and canons bundled wildly together. Some started in one direction, only to be carried off in another by the surging, swarming tide. The guards were helpless. Shots rang again. Fists flew. There were torn dresses, blackened eyes, arms wrenched from sockets. Candles overturned. There were sudden, leaping flames.

And somewhere in the fray, a certain respectable married lady, desperately clutching two small boys, found herself borne back towards the ruined lectern. There, just after someone had ripped the veil from her face, she bashed against a huge, gaudy form that struggled, gasping and sobbing, towards the Lector's mutilated form.

There was an instant of recognition – the little mouth opening wide, the gasp of *Nirry!* – before a fresh surge came from behind and Nirry and her young charges were propelled away, hurtling rapidly down the aisle.

Raggle and Taggle shrieked in glee.

END OF PART ONE

PART TWO

Waiting for the Miracle

Chapter 17

RAT-A-TAT-TAT!

And then? What did you do?

'I've told you. I took the child in my arms. I took him to the river. The sun was bright, and I took him to the river.'

And? Then what did you do?

'I said I took him to the river. In the sun.'

Was it bright? The sun?

'It sparkled on the waters. And on the waters there were mallard ducks. The child was so excited! We splashed in the reeds, so green, so high, so … spiky—'

Sharp? Like swords?

'N-not like swords—'

Knives, perhaps?

'Not knives … no, not knives.'

But the reeds? Was there something in the reeds?

'You mean … a body?'

What?

'I … I don't know why I said that.'

Perhaps you should tell me what happened then.

'I've told you. I took the child by the hand, and—'

Oh, this river! But there weren't really ducks?

'The river was frozen. The night was dark.'

Dark? And you didn't take him to the river, did you? No, you took him away. Took him from his mother, when the night was dark.

'N-no, that wasn't me. That wasn't *me*!'

You blame your boon companion – only him? Come, my friend, the child was taken. Taken – and then?

'We took him to the Temple. We prayed.'

The Temple?

'I took him. Yes.'

And prayed?

'I … no, we didn't pray.'

So tell me what you did.

'I … but you know! You know!'

You've got to say it. Tell me.

'No … no, I—'

95

Until now, Bean had murmured his replies, staring at the figure that hung before him in the shrouded light. Only with these last words did his voice break into a cry, but it was a cry he stifled at once. Anxiously he looked over to Polty's bed, relieved that his friend had still not stirred.

Bean rubbed his eyes. The phantom had gone, but it would be back. Whether it were real, or only a creature of his troubled mind, he did not know. In any case, it would come to him again and again. Before he slept, he would shudder and sweat in twisted sheets, his heart hammering, his mouth dry. Then, when he lapsed into uneasy sleep, slowly he would become aware that something was there, that *something* ... With a start, he would wake, and before him would billow the phantom, coloured only black, white and grey, with its striped robes and headdress and the gleaming light where its face should have been.

Why had it come to him? Ah, but Bean knew the answer well enough! Huddled, stiff with fear, on the edge of his bed, he could only be glad that – this time at least – the phantom had vanished before its questions went further. He shivered, clutching his face in his hands. No sun. No reeds. No mallard ducks. He thought of the child in the filthy cell, somewhere in the labyrinth beneath the Great Temple. There the walls dripped with slime, the stench was like a sewer, and there would be no light but the light of Bean's taper when he came with Polty to take the child away. How Polty would grin as he slid back the bolts, his red hair lurid in the taper-light!

Bean doubled over, sick with shame. Did he see himself caressing the filthy, frightened child, speaking to it softly, bidding it to hush as Polty strapped it down on the sacrificial slab? Oh, it was he who deserved to die! Appalled, he saw the Brotherhood of Toth; he saw the knife in Tranimel's hand. Night after night, in the fastness of his heart, Bean had cried out against these monstrous things. Had he not tried to explain this to the phantom? Had he not begged the phantom to listen?

Night after night: and the phantom would not.

Bean forced himself up from the bed, his long limbs cracking. Quickly he pulled on his breeches, stockings and shoes. Polty had fallen asleep in his clothes again. Bean should have undressed him, but he had been too tired. He was still tired, but it was no good trying to sleep again now.

Morning must be far advanced. A purplish, greyish light filled the chamber, pressing behind the long curtains. Bean parted them, screwing up his eyes against the brightness of the snow. Yes, *far* advanced. Why, they must have missed the Inaugural! Not that Polty would care ... Bean's teeth chattered and he rubbed his arms. He must make up the fire, get Polty's breakfast, clean Polty's boots.

Wearily he shuffled about the disorderly chamber, with its dusty carpets and crumpled playbills, its strewn garments, its greasy plates and empty, glinting bottles. In their status as Special Agents, Polty and Bean were not required to reside in Ollon Barracks, nor in any of the common billets dotted about the Island. Instead, they occupied an apartment in Clumpton Castle. Formerly the royal residence, now it was merely a wing of the rambling, ramshackle edifice that was the Koros Palace.

There must have been a time – in Good Queen Elabeth's day, perhaps – when this chamber was luxurious. For military men it was still impressive, with its dark mahogany panelling and moulded ceiling, its ornately carved fireplace and diamond-paned casement. There were those who would have been sensible of so great a privilege; Polty and Bean had abused it, as usual.

Bean lit the fire, piling on playbills as the flames took. Holding out his hands, he knelt before the crackling warmth; he might almost have drowsed again, stretching out on the hearthrug like a long cat. But no; Polty would be stirring soon.

Rolling over, Bean gazed towards his friend. Face down on the bed covers, Polty snored with little irregular, swinish grunts. After they returned from the ceremony in the crypt, he had downed a whole bottle of Vantage; the bottle still lay beside him on the covers, clasped lightly in his curled hand.

He shifted a little, burying his face deeper into his pillow. It was hardly guilt that prompted his indulgence. No, Polty had other concerns, represented – one might have said they took physical form – in a certain glass jar he kept beside his bed, covered in a chequered cloth. To Polty, there was nothing but this glass jar: the centre of his being.

Don't think of these things. Bean beat his forehead with the heel of his hand. But if he didn't think of the jar, he would think of the crypt; then he would think of the shrieking child. How high the blood had spurted! Last night it had been a crimson fountain, drenching the First Minister's white robes. So much blood, from so small a child!

Don't think of these things, he told himself again. He wished they were at the Inaugural. When Polty was not looking, Bean might have prayed. Instead, he would empty the chamber-pot. Yes, that was it. The cold air from the window would clear his head. Besides, didn't it stink in here? Polty must have thrown up in the night again.

Blearily sniffing the air, Bean crawled on all fours over discarded coats, shoes, rumpled carpets. The pot, where was the pot? He groped blindly under Polty's bed, retrieving a fashionable cravat, a missing foot-stocking and several snotty handkerchiefs. What was that he could hear, scurrying out of range? A rat, perhaps, or an enormous cockroach?

Gingerly, Bean shifted his hand; as his fingers slithered back across the dusty floorboards, they caught in a twisted leather strap. He pulled the strap; attached to it was a truncheon-like, cylindrical object. Indeed, Polty must have woken in the night; in his stupor, he must have tried to lace the object on before lapsing into unconsciousness again.

Gently Bean held the long, thick cylinder, untangling the straps at the flattened base, picking flecks of dust from the mushroom-capped tip. He stroked the long shaft, his fingertips bumping over the artfully carved veins.

The handiwork of an expert craftsman, the object in question was known – to Polty and Bean – as Woodpenge, or W'enge for short. If a little larger than the part which had served as his model, nonetheless W'enge was an admirable approximation. Amongst Bean's most important duties was to oil and polish him. W'enge looked like he needed polishing now. If everything else in these chambers was filthy, W'enge, at least, would be gleaming. Glistening.

Rising to his feet, Bean permitted himself just a moment's indulgence. Once, when W'enge was new, he had attached the thing to his own person. *I was only checking the straps*, he had protested when Polty found him and blazed into fury. Of course, Bean had been doing more.

Anxiously he glanced at the sleeping Polty. This time, Bean merely held the thing in place. It was enough; he shook his head in wonderment. Why, W'enge was monstrous – elephantine!

Bean scurried to the looking-glass. He turned on his side. If he half-closed his eyes, could he not imagine that W'enge was attached to his own person? He thrust the thing forward; he waggled it back and forth; he passed the straps round his hips and thighs, knotting the laces with a greedy recklessness.

It was just for a moment. Only for a moment.

In truth, it was for somewhat longer that Bean pursued this dangerous path, going so far as to develop a little routine. He would call it – hm – *The Wedding Dance of W'enge*. The dance involved various more elaborate wagglings, not to mention swoopings, plungings and proddings.

He had just succeeded in standing on his hands when a sharp *rat-a-tat-tat!* came at the door.

Bean collapsed in a heap.

The *rat-a-tat-tat!* came again. Urgently he tugged at the knotted laces while Polty called, his voice muffled in his pillow, 'Bean ... Bean, damn you, see to that door!'

'I'll ... I'll get rid of them, Polty!' Bean cried.

Oh, but these knots! Suddenly W'enge weighed heavily upon his person; at once he was aware of the base, pressing painfully against his own less prodigious parts. What a fool he was! What had he gone and done?

He pulled. He picked. Where was a knife? Must he cut the laces? But Polty would be furious! Polty would beat him!

The knocking came again, this time a persistent *rat ... rat*; again, Polty called out. This time, Bean did not dare delay. Hoping only that his friend would not turn, he scurried to the door and opened it, just a crack, peering into the hallway.

The rat-a-tatters were not quite what he expected. In the gloomy light stood two very young and lowly Bluejackets. One – evidently rat-a-tatter-in-chief – was a fellow almost as scrawny as Bean, if by no means as tall; big eyes blinked from behind round eyeglasses. His companion, standing behind him, was a thickset little fellow, clearly of peasant stock, whose face was fixed into a foolish grin.

The thickset fellow was about to speak, but the scrawny one hushed him quickly, gulped – the apple in his throat bobbing up and down – and enquired, 'M-Major P-Poltiss Veeldrop?'

Bean said he was not, adding quickly that he was side-officer – it was a dignified calling – to the gentleman in question; whatever message they had for Major Veeldrop, it could be entrusted to him.

'Well, tell him—' the thickset one began, then broke off with a yelp, 'Ouch! Morvy, them's my toes you're treading on!'

The scrawny fellow sniffed, gulping again. 'I am Recruit Plaise Morven, of the Fifth Royal Fusiliers of the Tarn, Royal Watch, Island Secondment,' he said importantly, 'and am to tell you that I am empowered to deliver my message only to Major Veeldrop in person. He is within?'

'He's *what*, Morvy?' said the thickset one. 'You said he was a war hero. This Veeldrop' – the fellow, all innocence, looked enquiringly at Bean – 'wasn't he the one that saved Zenzau, back in the Orvik campaign? We was in that campaign, you know, me and Morvy.'

'Crum, be quiet!' his companion hissed; Bean, for his part, thought it best simply to ask 'Morvy' by whom he was (as he put it) *empowered*.

Bean had no wish to be contrary; he just didn't want to open the door.

'By Sergeant Bunch,' said Morven, 'of the Fifth Royal, Royal Watch, Island Secondment. But he, I understand, is empowered by Major-General Heva-Harion, who is empowered by Tranimel – I m-mean, His Loyal Excellency, Protector Most High of the Crown and Realm, First Minister to...'

'Yes, yes.' Bean sighed. This Morvy, it seemed, was something of a pedant; in fact, *everything* of one.

Excusing himself, Bean drew back from the doorway. Polty was stirring; now this was going to be tricky. Doubling over, Bean reached down, thrusting W'enge painfully between his thighs. Clamping his knees together, he raised himself slowly to a standing position, thrust his hips outward, and crossed one foot over the other.

Yes, that was about it. Ah, but … he pulled out his shirt from the waist of his breeches, letting it hang over the tell-tale straps. Yes, *that* was it. So long as he kept his legs tightly closed – struggling to ignore the shooting pains, stabbing up through his tender parts – no one would guess he was concealing W'enge.

There were throat-clearings from the hallway; Bean feared renewed *rat-a-tats*. Creeping back on crossed-over legs, he opened the door, smiled – though the pains, the shooting ones, made his face jump – and in the manner of a society hostess, welcoming her noble guests, instructed the young Bluejackets that Major Veeldrop was to be found upon the bed.

He gestured graciously, face twisting.

'Wait here, Crum,' Morven hissed, to his companion's disappointment. Hoping to meet the war hero, Crum might have protested, but Morven was firm. Blinking behind his spectacles, he looked with astonishment about the foetid, filthy chamber. Could these chaps really be officers?

Morven saluted. 'M-Major Veeldrop?'

Bean sighed. With an agile swing, he had positioned himself against the wall just inside the door. Unfortunately, the door was still ajar and the soldier called Crum hovered outside. If Crum could not see Polty, he could see Bean, and grimaced at him. The fellow, it appeared, was trying to be friendly. Didn't he know that Bean was a lieutenant? In any case, Bean responded only with a sharp facial tic; Crum did likewise. He must have thought they were playing a game.

A rapid succession of face-pullings followed, involuntary on Bean's part, voluntary on Crum's.

'M-Major Veeldrop?' Morven saluted again.

Bean rolled his eyes, turning away before Crum mimicked him again. 'Of course he's Major Veeldrop! Didn't I say so?'

Gingerly Morven reached out, touching Polty's shoulder. Now this was not a good idea; Bean never touched Polty unawares. With a startled cry, the flame-headed figure leapt up from the bed, clutching Morven's jacket.

'Crum! Help, help!' Morven staggered back, then fell, musket clattering; Crum blundered in, musket at the ready – just as Polty turned green, doubled over, and threw up – all over the unfortunate Morven's jacket.

Polty slumped back on the bed, wiping his mouth. Crum turned savagely, this way and that, as if about to give covering fire, before tripping over one of his bootlaces, stepping into the chamber-pot, and crashing to the floor.

But Crum, *in extremis*, had no thought for himself.

'Morvy!' he cried. 'Morvy, are you all right?'

Flushed, Morven clambered back to his feet, hissing to his companion, 'You fool, Crum! Can't you see these are officers? They'll have us on a charge!'

'You called for help, Morvy,' said Crum, not unreasonably.

'Crum, they're on our side,' said Morven, *un*reasonably.

'But where's the hero?' whispered Crum. Reasonably.

'Are you all right, Polty?' Bean called from the wall.

'Of course I'm all right,' Polty glowered, pushing back a strand of his shaggy curls. He sniffed sharply. What a stench from that chamber-pot! Well, no time for that now. 'Bean? What have you been doing? Where's my hair of the dog? Haven't you got my hair of the bloody dog?'

Crum wondered where the dog might be and looked around, concerned for its safety; Morven fished for a handkerchief. Gulping, Bean calculated the distance to the wardrobe, where – as it happened – he had stashed a fresh Vantage bottle, just for this occasion. Could he ask one of their visitors to get it for him? He supposed not; the trick was to walk very quickly before anyone noticed that his legs were crossed.

'Bean,' said Polty, 'I know this may be a foolish question, but can you explain why you're walking that way?'

'Cramp, Polty. Got a cramp in the night, you know.'

Polty's eyes narrowed. 'And what about your face?'

'My face?' Bean's face leapt. 'I … twisted a nerve.'

For a merciful moment he vanished behind the wardrobe door, availing himself of the opportunity to readjust W'enge. If only he had a knife! There was nothing for it: he would have to cut the laces, replacing them before Polty found out.

Bean lurched forward, almost flinging the Vantage at Polty; Polty grabbed the bottle, glugged down much of its contents, then turned back to his visitors with an expectant smile.

Now what could these fellows want? For now, the one called 'Morvy' was concerned only with his handkerchief, which was already sodden, and the vomit on his jacket only half wiped up. Looking round helpfully, Crum spied a certain cloth, covering a certain jar, on the little table beside Polty's bed. The thickset fellow reached out: Polty grabbed his wrist. Tears sprang to Crum's eyes. What a grip! Polty smiled, holding it for several painful moments.

Abashed, Crum stepped back, mutely signalling his resignation. Really, it was only an old cloth, wasn't it? But the ways of officers, Crum knew, were strange.

And where *was* the hero? Not this chap, surely!

Furtively Crum scraped his boot on the carpet, then bent over, devoting his attention to his bootlace. Meanwhile, wanting a barrier between Polty and himself, Bean began to edge behind the bending figure.

101

Crum took an inordinate time over a lace; truth to tell, he had spied a little whiskery muzzle underneath the bed. A mouse? A rat? To the tender-hearted Crum, any little animal was a source of wonderment. How he wished he had some cheese, to tempt it forth!

Polty stood up, Vantage now coursing pleasantly through his veins. He paced before Morven. 'Now, what *could* you fellows want?' he asked in a tone by no means unkindly. He was prepared to be indulgent; that these fellows had any important mission was unthinkable. Some trivia, no doubt. Some meaningless protocol.

Morven's throat-apple bobbed and he saluted again, bringing his heels together in a sharp click. Looking behind him, he would have urged Crum to a similar show of respect. But he had tried Major Veeldrop's patience quite enough.

The rank stench rose from the chamber-pot.

'S-Sir,' Morven began, 'you've been s-summoned—'

Polty started. Oh, but his temper was as fiery as his hair! He leapt forward, clutching Morven's throat. 'Summoned! What, is there a warrant? What cur's put a warrant out against me?'

Morven, with his throat-apple trapped, could hardly reply; nor did Crum, who still pretended to tie his lace, certain that the rat would come out at any moment. As for Bean, his face gave an involuntary jerk. *A warrant? Against Polty?* Terrible thoughts filled his mind and he had to remind himself to keep his knees clenched. He gazed at Crum's broad posterior, straining against the fabric of his blue breeches.

At last, Polty thought to release the trapped apple, and after it had bobbed freely for some moments Morven managed to gasp out that he was *empowered* (as he put it) to summon Major Poltiss Veeldrop, Special Agent, most urgently to attend upon the presence of His Loyal Excellency, Protector Most High of the Crown and Realm, First Minister to His Imperial Agonist Majesty King Ejard Bluejacket and Chief of the Ascendancy, Ethan Archan Tranimel.

Crum, who saw the little furry muzzle again, made beckoning noises. As for Polty, his demeanour altered at once.

'Tranimel?' he cried. 'He wants to see *me*?'

Relief shook through Bean; more urgently, he clenched his knees and his face went into a spasm. Excitedly, Polty pushed Morven out of the way. He pirouetted round Crum, who was straightening up at last, furtively secreting the rat into his jacket. Polty gestured to the jar beside his bed. 'Bean, Bean, do you know what this means? His promise! He's going to fulfil his promise!'

Bean nodded; Polty slapped his friend on the back.

It was badly timed. Just then, a fresh spasm passed through Bean's frame; just then Crum, who had been more interested in the rat than his boots, realised that he had failed to tie his lace properly. The peasant lad bent over: Bean staggered: W'enge shot up, striking the broad posterior like a battering ram.

'*Yeow!*' Crum leapt forward. His hands flailed out and he struck the cloth-covered jar, sending it spinning, glittering, through the air.

'*Yeow!*' Polty grabbed the jar, saving it just in time. At once, he turned furiously upon Bean.

Bean cowered. 'Polty, wait! You won't need him any more! Don't you see? *You won't need him!*'

What these words might mean, neither Morven nor Crum could have known. But their effect was clear enough. Slowly the fury drained from Polty's face; and yet, as in a tableau, his fist remained raised, suspended in the air above his friend.

At last Bean said timidly, 'Do you think you could ... cut my laces, Polty?'

For the moment, Crum lay spreadeagled across Polty's bed, so it was left to Morven to look on – goggling, open-mouthed – at the extraordinary spectacle of these two officers, one with this monstrous, artificial appendage, the other clutching a glass jar which appeared to contain, preserved in greenish fluid, a bodily organ of the same type, and of almost equal dimensions.

No, surely not! It was an eel, it had to be!

Morven's cheeks burned. To grab Crum, salute, and make a swift retreat was almost as much as he could do. In the corridor, he shook his head in astonishment. 'Dear me, dear me ... I know there's some funny things in the ancient plays. But officers? In Agondon?'

Crum, who was not listening, reached inside his jacket. Sudden relief overspread his face. 'Oh, thanks be for that. He's all right, Morvy! I was worried, I'll tell you.'

'What?' said Morven. 'Well, so was I. There was something queer about those fellows, Crum.'

'I'll say. And I've got the sore arse to prove it.'

Chapter 18

ARTS OF LOVE

Tishy Cham-Charing screamed.

It was not for the first time that day.

'My dear, shh! Calm yourself, it's all right—'

'Professor Mercol? But where are we? It's *dark*—'

'Never mind, there'll be a lamp-bracket below. Just a few steps first …
Take my hand, I can feel the way.'

'To where?' Tishy's voice trembled.

'Somewhere out of the fracas.'

'But Mama! What about Mama, and—'

'Lady Margrave won't let any harm come to her, will she? Besides, we
can hardly find them in all that crush. I think we'd do best to wait until
the chaos dies down, hm? In the meantime, I've something to show you
… Your hand, your hand.'

Tishy hesitated, but the Professor took the girl's hand nonetheless.
Bewildered, stumbling, she followed him down a dark spiral staircase.

It had all happened so suddenly. In the chaos that filled the Great Temple,
Tishy had found herself borne away by the pressure of the crowd. Swept
into a chapel somewhere off to the side, she was crushed against a wall,
gasping and crying, when all at once a hand had grabbed her shoulder;
Professor Mercol's. Then a door had opened, clanging shut behind them.

Tishy adjusted her spectacles, as if they could be of any help in the dark.
If she was more than a little frightened, she was powerless to resist. What
a gamut of emotions she had run, all in so short a time! 'But Professor,
where are we going? Is … is there a way out?'

'*Five*, my dear, through the cross-tunnels. But we'll hardly need them.'

'We won't?' Tishy would have asked what *cross-tunnels* were, but the
Professor had paused, patting at the wall with mutterings and cursings
before he managed to light a battered-looking lamp. A golden glow suffused the dank, ancient stones. Tishy shivered, gazing at her companion.
How different he looked! He had lost his periwig and underneath he was
wholly bald, but for the few white tufts that sprouted above his ears. His
eyes glittered strangely as he took her hand again, leading her almost too
rapidly along a sinister, arching passageway.

A door loomed ahead. It was dark and forbidding, fashioned from
blackened iron. 'Come, my dear, we'll be safe in here. Of course, it's a
place I take only my *favourite* pupils.'

Tishy blinked, puzzled, as the Professor, thrusting the lamp into her hands, produced a bunch of large, jangling keys, several of which he inserted successively into the lock. At first, Tishy thought he was trying to find the right one; then she realised that he was turning each key in a particular, well-remembered pattern of clunks and clicks. When the door opened at last, he ushered Tishy in before him, pushed the door back into its heavy frame, and began to repeat the locking code from the other side.

Click. Clunkety-clunk. Click.

'Raise the light a little, my dear, hm?'

Tishy obeyed distractedly. She had wondered whether she should enter. Now, as she gazed about her, her doubts were replaced by astonishment. She had expected a dungeon; instead, glimmering in the lamplight, was a cavernous chamber with a thick, ornate carpet, leather chairs, fine mahogany tables and walls lined entirely with books – thousands upon thousands of them, lushly bound with gold-stamped spines. It might have been the library of a gentleman's house, transferred bizarrely to this subterranean place. The smell, a musk of leather, paper, parchment and dust, was intoxicating to a young woman of Tishy's tastes.

Hastily she placed the lamp on a table, rushing to inspect the laden shelves.

'I've made it more cosy over the years,' mused the Professor, moving round the walls, lighting several additional lamps. 'There was a time when it was quite devoid of civilised comforts, would you believe? A mere place of storage. But comforts are *so* essential, are they not? Especially for a man in his declining years. *Brr!* But let me light the stove, and then we'll *really* be cosy.'

Tishy nodded obliviously. The shelves puzzled her. In so respectable-looking a library, a scholar might have expected to recognise many books, if only by name. Where were the classics? Volume after volume was entirely unknown to her – yet these, it seemed, were works of learning. Well, some of them.

> *The Reign of the Regent Queen.*
> *A Commentary on the El-Orokon.*
> *On Oppression: A Political Philosophy.*
> *Dialogues Concerning the Order of Agonis.*
> *Boudoirs of the Beauties of Agondon.*

The Professor shut the blazing stove. He rubbed his hands. 'Come, my dear, let me help you with your coat – that's right, that's right ... Why, what a pretty dress! Now, how about a tipple of Tiralos? But sit, my dear, make yourself at home.'

'This library,' said Tishy, 'why is it here?'

'Should not a Great Temple have a great library?' The Professor handed her a glittering little glass. '*Chin-chin*, my dear, *chin-chin*.'

105

Tishy did not touch the ruby-red liquid; the Professor downed his with a greedy gulp and poured another.

'But why,' urged the girl, 'should a library be *hidden* in these vaults? Behind these doors?'

If the Professor laughed, it was an affectionate laugh. 'Sweet child, this is the Chamber of Forbidden Texts.'

Uncertainly, Tishy perched upon a sofa. 'Forbidden? Why?'

The Professor sat beside her. 'My dear, these are *evil* books – heretical, subversive, immoral. Such books, not unnaturally, must be sought out and burned, but always one copy is preserved in this chamber.'

Tishy knew that books could be enthralling; she had never considered they could be evil. Gazing at the imprisoned volumes, she felt a mysterious fear, but a stirring excitement, too.

'Why here?' she said. 'Why keep them here?'

'I know, my dear. Many times I have urged that they be transferred to the Royal Ejard Library, but the committee can never agree. Besides, tradition is strong. Some say the holy power of the Temple neutralises the evil – the Archmaximate, I gather, inclines to that view. And of course, we're at the intersection of the cross-tunnels here—'

Tishy interrupted, 'But *why* keep these books? Why keep them at all, if they're evil?'

'My dear, must we not be familiar with all evil's wiles? This collection is a record of all we must fight against if we are to preserve this noble empire. Why was it, after all, that the Queen was almost abducted? Why has the Temple just been bombed? Such, my dear, are the consequences of subversive ideas.'

It occurred to Tishy that banning books had not, in that case, done very much good. She also thought that anyone who had bombed Eay Feval might not, from all points of view, be an enemy. A sympathy with her mother stirred within her; she could not bring herself to feel any for Feval.

Tishy shook herself. 'But who decides? I mean … *how* do you decide that a book is to be banned?'

'Not just books, my dear.' The Professor twirled his Tiralos glass. 'Pamphlets, newspapers, banners, etchings – some *very* diverting etchings, not to mention paintings, though of course not displayed openly on the wall. Oh, many are the treasures of this chamber; much is the work the committee must do. I've chaired some lively meetings, I can assure you! But come, drink your little tipple.'

At last – she was not sure why – Tishy took a sip.

She made a face; fondly, the Professor took her hand again. 'Poor child, you've had some nasty shocks this morning. You're hardly well, are you? Curse that brute, Feval! I knew he was to be Lector, that much was clear. But if I'd had any *idea* he was planning to – well, I…'

'You *knew* he'd be Lector?'

'My dear, half of Agondon knew. But your mother, alas—'

Tishy stared. 'Then you're on his side, aren't you?'

'*Side*, my dear? What can you mean?'

Tishy, as it happened, was not really sure. Confused, she said that the Professor was an important man, a powerful man, a man who served on committees.

He was also a man who was stroking her fingers.

The Professor spoke softly. 'Oh, I'm not so important, my dear, not important at all. Of course, like any gentleman, I have my perks.' He pulled a rolled parchment from his pocket. His voice became wry. 'It is I, for example, who nominate the Aon Fellow. Fill in a name on this document and the lucky chap receives Ejland's most prestigious scholarship. A career will be made, and all down to me. Call that power if you will – but *real* power? There was a time when Phineas Mercol would be consulted on the highest matters, when his expert opinion was eagerly sought. Not any more, not since Tranimel ... well, let's just say the First Minister has made a few changes. Still, I have my keys to this chamber, have I not? He can't take *everything* away from me, can he? No, not everything...'

He rambled on, but Tishy was no longer listening. With some alarm she looked down at the leathery, veiny hand moving over her own hand in a strangely sinister rhythm. The Professor edged closer, squeaking across the sofa. Tishy looked into the loose elderly flesh, sagging beneath the speckled, bald dome.

Until now, he had always kept a respectful distance. And his young pupil had never looked at him so closely. What bushy eyebrows! What juggy ears! What a receding, rabbity chin! Purple veins crawled across the Professor's cheeks and webbed his bulbous, porous-looking nose; yellow teeth loomed behind colourless, wrinkled lips, and the look in his eyes, Tishy realised, was unlike any he had ever given her in the course of their lessons.

She broke away, pacing the carpet. 'Professor,' she said brightly, 'you said you'd brought pupils here before ... favourites, you said. Have there ... have there been a lot of them?'

The old man smiled. 'Of course not, my dear! Don't you know, you're the first member of *the sex* I've taught? I'd never even taken on private pupils before, but for Lady Cham ... why, I remember when a man would climb to the moon for Lady Cham!' The smile became a sad one. 'No, I always held to the conventional line, declaring that ladies were unsuited to scholarly work. Since meeting you, I've changed my mind.'

'You have?' Tishy brightened. 'But Professor, that's marvellous! You mean you think ... you think ladies should be admitted to the university? Then ... you can order it! You can make it happen! Of course, I enjoy our private lessons – but to be at the university...'

The roll of parchment had fallen to the floor. Laughing, Tishy seized it. She clutched it to her heart. 'The Aon Fellowship! Imagine, if you could nominate *me*! Oh, Professor, I should die of happiness!'

Indulgently, the old man shook his head. 'There are other forms of happiness, my dear. Do you forget, you must marry soon?'

'Marry? For what?' Tishy whirled, her arms wide, taking in the vista of books, books, books. 'Professor, I want to be a scholar, like you! You're not married, are you?'

'No,' he said, 'but that is not something I declare with satisfaction.' He came closer. Tishy stepped back. Lamplight caught in the lenses of her spectacles, flashing like a warning. A strand of hair escaped its bonds, rolling down her neck in a wanton wave. Ah, but what would she look like with *all* her hair untied? 'Child, did I not witness your sorrow when the Lector said that you would never be married?'

'Professor, you don't understand—'

'On the contrary, I understand everything. And may I say I think Feval was wrong? Very wrong! Dear, sweet Tishy—'

She flushed. 'Who – who *were* they, then? These favourites?' she said quickly.

Of course, she was wondering how she might escape. Then she thought of the books, and longed only to stay. Oh, but it was confusing!

'No favourites, none—'

'You said there were *some*—'

'None ... but one.' The old man turned away, his demeanour altering. Tishy eyed him as he reached for the shelves, grabbing what was evidently a familiar book. 'Never again, never. See this little tome, my dear?'

Tishy took the book. Carefully she opened the fraying cover. '*Liberty or Licence?*' she read aloud. '*Being a Discourse or Investigation by Mr Vytoni into the Nature, Desirability and Attainment of the State of Freedom, Political, Social and* ... it all looks very hard.'

'I should never have trusted him,' the Professor sighed.

'You mean this ... Vytoni?'

'My dear, no! I mean a young fellow called Eldric Hulverside. Who was he but my Aon Fellow? Oh, it was long ago now, but still it saddens me to think of it. Such brilliance! Such promise! And such ... such treachery! They say he's running with the rebels now. Rebels, I ask you!'

Tishy gazed on the book with awe, almost as if the book and this Mr Hulverside were one and the same. *Rebels, I ask you.* 'Professor, these rebels – I've heard so much about their evil, their wickedness, but ... who *are* they, really? And *why* are they rebels? This Mr Hul—'

'Is that eagerness I hear in your voice? Such hunger for knowledge! Yet many would envy your girlish innocence – many, indeed, are those in the highest circles who wish they knew so little of the Redjackets, and all their works and ways!' And taking back the book, the Professor tossed it contemptuously to the floor.

Tishy was more than a little shocked.

'Such a *little* book,' the Professor sighed, 'to cause so much trouble! But enough. What could it profit an innocent girl to fill her head with *rebels*?'

A sudden daring surged in Tishy. 'I ... I almost feel they are on my side.'

'My dear, really! Don't go saying things you'll regret.'

'Why do people say that? Sometimes ... sometimes you don't *know* what you feel until you say it out loud.'

'Does not Ovanal say as much, in Canto the Third of *Arts of Love*? But I forget, your studies are at an early stage.' The Professor poured himself a fresh glass of Tiralos. He turned back thoughtfully. 'Often we are afraid to say what we feel. We hold it inside; deny it to ourselves. Later, we may regret that we have done so – indeed, regret it bitterly. Did I not say that once I would have climbed to the very moon, just to please Lady Cham? Of course, she was not Lady Cham then. Consy Grace, she was – little Consy Grace! Ah, my dear, you are so much like her. Without those glasses, with your hair a little different – I declare, you should be the image of my Consy! Darling girl—'

Tishy looked round. Randomly, she seized a book from the shelves. 'Professor, look – this one's in Juvescial! Shall I translate? You know you like to hear me translate. Now, let's see, what's it called? *Something* – oh, what *is* that word? – *Something of the Winds: A Prediction*. No, *A Prophecy*. Professor, look, this word here—'

'Tishy, Tishy, put down that book—'

'You've brought me into a library!' She attempted a laugh. 'Professor, you know I can't resist—'

'And nor can I!' The old man clutched her. The book fell to the floor. 'Fear not, sweet child, your virtue is sacred to me! Can't you tell that my intentions are honourable? Can't you tell I seek nothing but marriage? One kiss, just one kiss is all I ask now—'

'Professor, no – please—'

'Call me *Phineas*—'

To Tishy, this was obscene. 'I won't, I won't—'

He backed her against the bookcases. Urgently a leathery hand reached up, tugging the band from her hair. Auburn locks tumbled round Tishy's shoulders; Professor Mercol gave a wolfish smile. 'Oh, I should have lady pupils a-plenty, could they all be as pretty as you! Come, let me remove those little horn-rims—'

'Professor, I said *no!*' Tishy pushed the old man violently; she stumbled away, but at once he had slithered to the floor, wrapping his arms around her knees. His face pressed into her thighs; revolted, she saw the bald speckled skull, like something diseased and loathsome, a huge, hard fungal growth, rolling, almost butting into the front of her dress. 'Tishy, Tishy, I've waited so long! Dearest child – dearest *Consy*—'

'No!' Again, Tishy wrenched herself free. Desperate, she grabbed *Something of the Winds: A Prophecy* from the floor. She brandished it like a weapon.

The Professor laughed. It was not a big book.

He lunged.

She brought down the book.

He fell, cracking his head against the stove; he groaned, and then was still.

Tishy gasped. 'Professor! Professor Mercol, are you all right?'

Chapter 19

PICKLE IN A JAR

'Bean, what's wrong with you? Hurry, hurry!'

Gasping under the several burdens he carried, Bean floundered after his friend. No doubt about it, Polty was excited. In rapid succession, Bean had helped him rinse his mouth, untangle his hair (Polty, whose own hair was magnificent, would wear a wig only for disguise), shave, wash his face and neck, change his linen and squeeze into his dress uniform.

If, since his accident, Polty had gained a little weight – indeed, more than a little – nonetheless he could still be an imposing sight, with his flaming curls, his epaulettes and the long, ornate scabbard of his dress sword clickety-clacking behind him.

How splendid to see him this way! More than once – even as his loyal friend buffed his boots, shone his buttons, or thrust the stuffing-stocking down his tight breeches – Polty had muttered curses at Bean. Any side-officer worth his salt, he said, would never have let him have so much Vantage. It was true; worried, Bean imagined Polty lurching into the First Minister's presence, slack-jawed and bleary-eyed, as if into the tenth tavern on a tavern-crawl.

But Polty had rallied. Nobly, like the hero he had once been, he strode through the labyrinth of the Koros Palace. Chest outflung, he swept across cobbled courtyards, through long corridors, up and down stairs, past nodding courtiers, bobbing servants, saluting guards.

'Bean!' he flung back. 'Stop dallying!'

While Bean did his best, he was hardly fool enough to risk his burdens. Admittedly, some did not matter. There was his jacket, slung across his left arm, which Polty had not given him time to don; his left boot, which he could hardly, at present, put on his foot; the hat that still hung from his left hand. Then, wedged beneath his left arm, was a large box. It contained certain papers; one of them was vital.

Still more vital was W'enge, in his leather case, which Bean carried under his right arm, and – clutched securely in Bean's right hand – the fleshly original, sloshing in its cloth-covered jar.

What spectacle he presented to the courtiers, servants and guards was of no concern to Bean. Breathless, dripping sweat, he was careful only to clutch his burdens tighter as a great oak door opened at last and he followed Polty into a handsome chamber with book-lined walls, plush carpets and chairs of purple leather, arranged around a bright, leaping fire.

His Loyal Excellency, a guard explained, was presently at luncheon with the War Lords. If they would wait, the First Minister would attend upon them forthwith.

'Luncheon?' The guard withdrew, the door clicked shut and Polty, a little crestfallen, slumped into a chair. How rapidly the day had advanced! 'Didn't I tell you to hurry, Bean?'

Bean, who had placed his burdens down, fell to pulling on his left boot. The blue jacket he could do without, but he must wear it out of respect. Alarm passed through him. This *was* the clean one, wasn't it? Not the one with those stains?

Polty brightened. 'But he'll be back soon. It's not every day you have an occasion like *this*, is it? War Lords, indeed! Who are the War Lords?'

'Important generals,' said Bean, misunderstanding. 'Heroes of—'

He broke off, mopping his brow. Nearly a nasty mistake there. After all, what was Polty if not a hero of Ejland? If anyone should have been a War Lord, it was him. And he would be, if any justice prevailed. But perhaps, before this afternoon was over, it *would*. Perhaps the War Lords, even now, were discussing the role he might play.

With a smile, Bean hinted as much; Polty, excitedly, sprang up from his chair.

He paced before the fire, watching the flames. An Olton-clock ticked, too loudly, on the mantelpiece; above the mantelpiece was a curious painting, depicting all manner of mythical beasts and birds. Loping, crawling, slithering and flapping, they clustered round a collection of ivied ruins. Had this painting, Polty wondered, been here before? Hadn't there been a portrait of the King?

Troubled, though he was not sure why, he turned towards the books. Bound in red, and latterly blue, they were dull, worthy tomes – official histories, peerages, almanacs, statute books, volume after volume of *Proceedings of the Ascendancy*. He toyed with the scabbard of his dress sword; he whistled; he spun a globe of the world and watched it whirl. Round and round went the Lands of El-Orok. 'I suppose we're meant to make ourselves at home?'

On a table near the fire was a decanter.

'Polty, I'm not sure—'

'Oh, don't be such a wet blanket!' With the faintest of tremors, Polty sloshed a little, then a little bit more, of the rich liquid into a tumbler. 'War Lords?' he mused urbanely, swirling the liquid in the glass, then in his mouth. 'A peerage? I've been thinking along those lines, Bean, of course. I've served my time, haven't I? Suffered enough?'

'More than enough, Polty. Much more.'

Grinning – how long since he had last grinned? – Polty strode across to Bean, slapping him on the shoulder. 'It's happening, friend – I tell you, it's happening at last. And when it happens, do you think I'll forget who helped me through this difficult time? I owe you a special debt of gratitude, Bean.'

A lump came to Bean's throat. 'You do?'

'Of course. I don't forget, do I? Did I forget Vel, back in the Tarn?'

'You killed him, Polty,' Bean said admiringly.

It had been Polty's first great feat. Ah, innocent days!

Polty winced, just a little. 'Not *killed*, Bean. Vel met with an accident. Let's just say I introduced him to it.'

He paced again, scabbard clinking, back and forth across the yielding carpet. The chamber was immaculately clean. Curtains were drawn against the cold, pale day; lamplight sparkled in the rich, dark Vantage.

'No, I never forget anyone, do I?' Polty continued. 'That's why – mark my words, Bean – there'll come a time when everyone gets what's coming to them. Everyone. You, Bean; yes, and your ma, too – you know I always liked old Wynda, didn't I? Who else? There's Umbecca, of course, not to mention Eay Feval. They've *definitely* got something coming.' He paused, as if relishing the thought. 'Then, of course, there's a certain young lady.'

Bean stiffened. For Polty to mention his heart-mother was bad enough. Since her elevation to greatness, the fat woman – urged on, Polty was certain, by Feval – had refused even to receive her son-by-marriage, apparently regarding him as beneath her. It was an outrage; but galling as this was, it was nothing against the infamy of Miss Catayane Veeldrop.

Inevitably, Polty expanded on this theme; Bean pursed his mouth. Ah, but it *had* all been Cata's fault, all the things that had happened to them in Unang Lia and since. Under the terms of his father's will, Polty might have possessed a peerage long ago – why, he need never have sailed to Unang at all – had Cata only agreed to marry him. Instead she had fled him, and all for the sake of a crippler-boy from Irion.

'Think, Bean! If she hadn't been with the crippler, I'd never have had my accident, would I? If she hadn't resisted, would I have pulled out Penge?' There was a catch in Polty's voice; he doubled over, clutching his groin. 'Oh, has ever a man suffered so? That girl deserves no mercy, Bean. I'll find her, I tell you, as soon as I'm back to my old self.'

While Polty rambled on, Bean struggled to think only of his friend's terrible accident, pushing away the memories of all else that had happened in Unang Lia. Had he been under an enchantment? How else could he account for the fact that he had travelled in a van with Cata, Rajal and Amed across the burning sands to the Sacred City? How else to believe that he had been Cata's friend, and seen Polty – for a time – as Cata saw him?

And what of Rajal? On that last night, could Bean really have held Rajal's hand, looked in his eyes and known that Rajal loved him?

And that he loved Rajal, too?

It had all been madness. Bean belonged to Polty.

He said with difficulty, 'I've been thinking, Polty, these purple chairs … last time they were blue. Have you noticed that? Last time, they were blue.'

Polty, by now, had slithered to the floor. Tenderly he took up Penge's jar; impatiently he pulled away the concealing cloth, gazing upon the prodigious pickle. Poor Penge, but he had shrunk a little, had he not? How tragic to see him so greenish, so mottled! Pray, pray that Penge could be himself again, standing strong and proud like his wooden brother!

Fingers caressing the cold glass, Polty whispered to Penge as if to a lover. But Polty, Bean was certain, had never spoken to a lover like this.

'Sweet beloved, can you forgive me? It was an *accident*, Penge! Would I have tugged you from your concealing fastness had I known the Sultan would strike you down? I was maddened, my darling, enraged! There was a woman – Penge, was there not always a woman? – to whom I would have had you teach a lesson. It would have been the glory of your reign! Poor Penge, cheated of so sweet a triumph! But don't you know you shall teach that lesson yet? Don't you know your reign will resume? This is the merest interregnum, Penge. Cata will be your first triumph, I swear it, when again we are united! Darling Penge, that time will be soon!'

And not only Polty's fingers, but his lips, too, slithered up and down the glass.

❄   ❄

'Bean, you brought the contract?' Polty looked up sharply.

'I … of course!' Bean fumbled in the box. There had been no time to sort through the mess of army papers, tradesmen's bills, dunning letters and the like. Where *was* that parchment? Polty drummed his fingers; at last Bean drew forth the roll of vellum, signed in blood, on which his friend had agreed to serve their master.

'Read me what it says,' Polty sighed. 'Just the best part, you know the part.'

Bean knew it only too well. His eyes zigzagging downwards over the elaborate Gothic script, he read, in a suitably declamatory tone:

> *…And when I deem his service at an end,*
> *Again to me I'll call my flame-haired friend:*
> *And suffer once again his grief to see,*
> *For all that he has lost in serving me.*
> *This accident, if accident it were,*
> *For long he must decry! But let it spur*
> *His efforts in my service, for the day*

When his most grievous loss I do repay.
Yes, let him serve me faithfully and long,
And with my magic I will right this wrong.

'Why do you think he wrote it in verse?' said Bean.

'What?' Still Polty hugged Penge's jar, stroking it and sighing. 'He's an evil anti-god, of course he's going to write it in verse. It's more ... I don't know, more *magical*.'

'It's not very good,' said Bean.

'Since when are you a critic?'

Bean screwed up his mouth. An old doubt nagged him and he said incautiously, 'What does it mean, this bit about *if accident it were*? That sounds almost threatening. And this bit, *serve me faithfully and long*? How long? And why should our service be at an end? Why now?'

'What are you talking about?'

'Well ... it's only *been* a few moonlives.'

Polty bristled, breathing out slowly. Carefully he placed Penge's jar on the hearth – poor Penge, how cold he must be! – and rose, adjusting his stuffing-stocking.

'A *few* moonlives? Yes, a *few* moonlives I've been shoving this stocking down my breeches. A *few* moonlives I've been squatting over the pisspot like a girl. A *few* moonlives I've been strapping on W'enge to remind myself what it was even *like* to have the proper equipment of my sex – and you think it's not *enough*? Friend, fellows like you may be troubled only seldom by manly desires. A bit of furtive jerking in a garderobe, once or twice a moonlife, that's enough for you! Yet *you*, in your bloodless way, are nonetheless a man, possessed – if in paltry form – of a man's parts. Goad them into life, and those parts will give you ease.'

Polty paced again, drawing forth the sword from his scabbard. With a cryptic expression, he turned the glittering blade. Was he thinking of the scimitar that had severed Penge? Perhaps of Penge, this blade, and the qualities they shared?

He slashed the sword through the air.

'P-Polty?' Bean was nervous. Still he perched upon the purple chair, half-turned away from the glowing fire. 'P-Polty, put the sword away.'

Instead, Polty darted forward. Bean jumped. The sword zipped past his eyes and he looked down to see the blade, shaking violently, hovering above his groin.

Polty's lips drew close to Bean's ear. 'Friend, have you forgotten the Lands of Unang? In those realms, there are those who are *wholly* unmanned. Such a fate seems cruel, does it not, the cruellest a man can suffer? Yet have you considered my crueller fate? Crueller I say – for what is it to possess those parts that *fuel* desire, yet lose the part which, alone, can quench it? Have you even *considered* this, Bean?'

115

Bean had, many times. His friend's face, flushed before, had grown strangely white; his red hair seemed redder than ever and his voice was a crazed whisper. 'What can you know of my torments, my shame? Do you *know* how I've suffered? How could you know? How could anyone know?'

Poor Polty! He must not upset himself. Gently, Bean touched the hand that held the blade. 'I know … I know.'

'You can't!' The blade swung back.

'No! Polty, no—'

'Damn you, Bean—'

But whether Polty, in his frenzy, would have attacked Bean, neither Polty nor his friend would ever know. Polty gasped. The blade, as if by magic, was arrested in the air, immovable, behind his flaming head.

Swivelling, he looked into the eyes of Tranimel. The door had not opened. There had been no sound. But here was the great man, white-robed, bold as life, thin lips twisting into a cold smile.

And what was that sound? Polty and Bean heard a steady *drip-drip*, as of something liquid, thudding to the carpet in big, heavy drops.

Then they saw. Tranimel held his hand aloft, clutched tightly round the blade of the sword. Blood flowed, turning his sleeve a rich, wine-like purple.

Chapter 20

TOTH'S INNER SANCTUM

Tranimel cast aside Polty's sword.

Without sound it fell to the carpet; a little later, Bean would glimpse the First Minister's palm and see upon it no trace of the blade's deep cut.

Stepping across to a book-lined wall, Tranimel drew forth a shabby volume bound in red. The robed figure assumed a deliberate air, leafing through the pages in the manner of a scholar, seeking a quotation.

A hand stroked his chin. 'Extraordinary. Did you know that under the Act of Deliverance (Zaxos), AC 859c, there were quotas – quotas, I ask you! – on the monarch's powers to raise an army from the province in question? Now why should that be, do you think? Is one to annexe a province, then grant it privileges – *rights*? Nonsense, nonsense!'

He ripped the Act from the statute book, feeding it to the fire.

Bean had risen respectfully; Polty stood trembling, toying with the empty scabbard at his side. The lamps hissed and there was a thud at the curtained window, as if a bird had flown against the glass. Tranimel kept tearing; Polty, clearing his throat, indicated the jar, glittering on the hearth, in case the great man had failed to see it.

'I – we ... we brought Penge, Your Loyal Excellency. I mean, my – my ... and W'enge, we brought W'enge, too.' A note of anxiety had entered Polty's voice. Almost angrily, he gestured to Bean, who at once fumbled in the leather case.

'It's so ... so you can see what Penge looked like,' Bean explained, jabbing the wooden organ into the air. 'B-Before, I mean ... Of course he's made of wood, and not attached to Polty, and ... I mean, not unless he straps him on, but – he's a *very* fine copy, really quite remarkable. A *bit* bigger, I'll admit, but quite ... remarkable...'

Flushing, Bean trailed off, but Polty jerked his head and grimaced until the puzzled side-officer added his own refrain of *Your Loyal Excellency*.

But what could be happening? In the presence of this man – this being, this *creature* – it seemed to Bean, and Polty too, that reality was slipping, fracturing. Both tried to recall their last interview with Tranimel, after he had whisked them back from Unang; somehow that, too, was a blur, with only the contract signed in blood as proof that it had ever taken place.

Both thought of the vaults beneath the Temple, where they had seen this white-garbed figure wielding a bloodied knife. This was the man. The being. The creature. And the chamber, slowly, was beginning to tilt.

Tranimel – tired, it appeared, of tearing – at last flung the entire statute book to the flames. For a time he looked on, smiling coldly, as the laws of Ejland vanished into smoke. The great man paid no attention to Polty, to Bean, to Penge or W'enge.

But then he pointed above the mantelpiece, speaking again. 'My friends, you have noted this painting? Striking, is it not? Found, I believe, in the palace vaults, along with a thousand sacked treasures from here, there and everywhere in the empire, though why it should have been hidden I cannot imagine. A most interesting find, most interesting.'

Striding before the fire, the great man gestured with an expressive hand at the canvas in its golden frame. 'The manner, I'm sure you've noted' – they had not – 'is a pastiche, and a creditable one, of the great sacred paintings of Raphian or Belloretto, such as may be seen in the temples of Ana-Zenzau, Wrax and Tiralos; some have gone so far as to attribute it to Belloretto, though I am inclined to see it as the work of a pupil – *school of*, definitely. And would Belloretto leave his work unsigned? No other instance is known to us; yet curiously, on the back the canvas is *titled* in what appear to be characters of blood.'

'B-Blood?' says Bean.

The chamber had been tilting; now it tilted more. 'The title, I admit, is both inelegant and confusing. *Atonement's End Ended: An Allegory*,' said Tranimel. 'But what is the allegory, answer me that?'

Oh, but this tilting! Polty clutched Penge; Bean, W'enge. Neither spoke, but both nodded eagerly as Tranimel pointed instructively to the painting.

'See these creatures, flapping and loping, crawling and slithering in the purple twilight? See the serpent, massy and vast, heaving his coils over the ruined steps? The great lizard with hooded eyes, peeping from behind the fallen stones? And lo! the bat on leathern wings, circling like a vulture round the crumbling bell-tower! One beat of those mighty wings would send what remained of that tower crashing down. And look at these creatures that are stranger still – this one, with the shell of a tortoise and a spider's legs! This giraffe-necked giant beetle! This slinking, slavering, many-headed wolf! This immense frog with horns and a slimy tail!'

The tilting got worse. Bean stumbled; Polty, too.

Tranimel rushed on, 'What can they be, these hideous things, but beings such as existed in the ancient days, before the Ur-God descended into this world to give it order? What can they be but Creatures of Evil, whose banishment was vital if this world were to be other than a dark, terrible chaos?'

The First Minister turned at last to Polty and Bean; by now, they were cowering and stumbling in a swirling, darkening chamber. The lamps guttered, the fire too; for a moment, light came only from a crack at the window, where another bird, then another, thudded against the glass. The purple painting vanished in the gloom.

But then, suddenly, the canvas flared up, lit from within by its own eerie light. Vividly, the painted monsters writhed with impossible life.

'Creatures of Evil?' Tranimel cried. 'Or the true, original owners of this world, falsely called evil by those who bow in servitude to Orok and his five snivelling children? Creatures of Evil? Or Rejects of Orok, cruelly banished, who yet shall return in glorious vengeance? Creatures, in truth, whose time has come, now that The Atonement speeds towards its end? And when Atonement's End is ended? What is the allegory? No allegory, but prophecy, of an *eternity* of evil – evil, so called, by canting fools!'

Between staggerings, Polty and Bean could only look on in astonishment, transfixed by the writhings of the purple picture.

With a snapping jerk, Tranimel spun round. At once, the writhings were over. The floor lurched no longer; the lamps, then the fire, burst back to life. 'But my friends, forgive my impoliteness! Am I to entertain such *trusted* familiars in this cold, formal chamber? Come, come.'

And, striding to a book-lined wall, he pressed a switch, bidding Polty and Bean to follow. Hesitating a little – still clutching tightly to Penge and W'enge – the friends stepped through a sliding panel.

A pallor played around them, tinged with purple, red and blue; rising from below came voices, clinkings, chinkings.

Surprise filled their faces. They were standing on a gallery, bathed in the light from stained-glass windows. The gallery stretched round the walls of a large chamber; beneath them, a lavish banquet was in progress. They heard a peal of laughter, a brief guffaw; then voices, more subdued.

The First Minister put a finger to his lips. Motioning to his companions to do the same, he ducked beneath the level of the gallery, beginning a rapid, absurd *scuttle-scuttle-scuttle* towards a door on the other side. Polty hunched, Penge against his chest, sloshing in the pickle jar; Bean jammed W'enge under an armpit and bent his lanky form, as if he had more joints than an ordinary man.

Scuttle-scuttle-scuttle round the gallery they went, concealed from the diners. But as they scuttled, they listened to the voices; and more than once, here and there, Polty and Bean dared to peek over the gallery. At first, they marvelled only at the words they heard, realising that they appeared to have missed something important. Whatever had been going on while they slept?

'The rebels have thrown down the gauntlet,' said an old gentleman with enormous white moustaches. 'This outrage at the Inaugural is the last straw.'

'Last?' said another. 'Hah! Lone bombers are just the beginning. It's rum enough when fellows are prepared to dress as ladies. But when, as a ship is fitted into a bottle, a time-bomb is secreted – begging your pardons – in an *intimate* orifice, what limit can there be on Redjacket depravity?'

'But Agondon?' burst out another. 'Could they *dare* to march on Agondon?'

'This "Bob Scarlet" is more than we imagined him to be, the very lynch-pin of a vast rebel network,' said 'Mandy' Heva-Harion – for yes, it was he. 'Many a rebel may we have imprisoned on Xorgos Island, but too many are free. And their numbers are growing. Soon, I am certain, secret armies will rise up and attack. There is no alternative but civil war.'

Frightening words; but Polty and Bean, by now, were rather more interested in the persons at the table. Could that be the Queen down there, radiant and silent – bored, perhaps desperately bored – sitting opposite the slobbering King? Even the talk of intimate orifices did not seem to have roused her.

Then they saw something *very* strange.

'Bah! Let the wretches attack, we will be ready,' said a bluff, red-faced fellow. 'But no more demands on Zaxos – no more, that's all I ask.'

The reply came coolly. But who was this, presiding at the head of the table between the King and Queen? 'The Act of Deliverance (Zaxos), AC 859*c* has been *repealed*, I think you'll find. But is there any measure at which we can demur?'

It was the First Minister, as real down there as he seemed here on the gallery.

'The final conflict is coming,' he went on, 'the conflict which shall determine the fate of our empire. And yes, we shall be stalwart. Yes, we shall not fear. Is there any war it is possible for us to lose? – But another toast, Your Imperial Agonist Majesties. Another toast, my lords.'

He raised his glass. '*Ejland ever glorious!*'

And astonished, Polty and Bean could only scuttle after Tranimel – *their* Tranimel – into the door on the far side of the gallery.

'*Ejland ever glorious!*' rang the toast as the door shut behind them, silently but firmly.

They found themselves in a chamber very different from the one in which the interview began.

Oh, some things were alike: drawn curtains, books, a leaping fire – indeed, more than one, for though the chamber was immense, heat blazed in the gloom. Then there was the stench, a sour, assailing rottenness; the rubble strewn across the floor; the fallen plaster, upended shelves, ruined chairs and tables. A rat, then another, scurried through the debris. There was a vast looking-glass, shimmering strangely.

Tranimel – but now, to be sure, he must be Toth – leapt into the air, impossibly high. Gasping, Polty and Bean looked up to see him, eyes glowing evilly, hanging from the ceiling like a mighty bat. Was he, in truth, the vulture-bat from *Atonement's End Ended*?

Other creatures from the painting came forth from the looking-glass, surging into being in phantom form. Round and round the ruined, foetid chamber they writhed.

Bean cried out. Polty stumbled. They sank to their knees amongst the plaster, the ruined books, the rats. Whizzing towards them, dancing around them, came the tortoise-spider, the beetle-giraffe, the rhinoceros-toad.

Toth laughed merrily. 'Do you see my pretties, do see them all?' Joyously he leapt about the ceiling and walls, sending more plaster crashing down. Jumping into a fireplace, like a grinning gargoyle he squatted amongst the flames. 'Yes, see my pretties! Relish them, for they are my brothers, and when Atonement's End is ended, this world shall belong to them – along with my devoted *human* servants,' he added slyly – then quickly, contemptuously, jerked a hand towards the banqueting hall. 'The fools, speaking of the final conflict! Wars? Armies? What is all that but a prelude to the glorious day that soon will come?'

And, trailing flame, Toth leapt from the fire, spinning round in the air, cutting like a scythe through the phantom monsters. Suddenly he dropped between Polty and Bean, scattering phantoms, scattering rats. Leering, he draped his arms around his servants, one around Polty, one around Bean.

Compelled, they walked with him. By now, Toth's face was a decomposing mass; his limbs misshapen, scaly. But his voice was low, almost tender. 'And why, you wonder, do I say this day *soon* will come?'

Polty faltered, 'Because … you're the anti-god?'

'Because your powers tell you?' shrilled Bean.

'Indeed,' smiled Toth, 'my powers tell me much. For example, they tell me, right now, that the Key to the Orokon is back amongst us.'

'The crippler?' Polty's throat tightened.

'Veeldrop, of course. And does the fool, I wonder, think he is safe from me? Does he think he can defeat me? I have bided my time, that is all. But now I shall bide my time no more.' A hand clawed into Polty's shoulder. 'You hate him, don't you, Veeldrop? You hate him? You would destroy him?'

Polty winced. 'Great Lord, of course.'

The voice dropped lower. 'Then you shall have your chance. His doom begins tonight. I need you, Veeldrop – you, and your useful friend. Do you think I don't appreciate just how *much* I need you?'

Polty nodded. He was flushed, trembling; now he grew bold. He held out the pickle jar; helpfully, Bean jabbed W'enge beneath the hole where Toth's nose should have been.

Had the moment come? But the monster broke from his servants, leapt about the walls again, crashed his head against the ceiling several times and dropped back to the floor, grinning hideously with his lipless mouth.

'Oh Veeldrop!' he laughed. 'Did I not say I *needed* you?'

Polty gulped, 'Great Lord, I know, but ... will not your servant need all his strength, all his power for the task that lies ahead? I have served you as best I can, but – but ... would I not serve you better, *even* better, if I were restored to my rightful self?'

Toth had to laugh. '*You*, served me well? I called you here to impress upon you the gravity of your task, not to release you from the contract you have signed!'

Polty's face fell.

'Your duty,' said Toth, 'has barely begun. Listen to me, and listen well. Tonight, you are to seize another child – but this time, no ordinary child. Go to a place known as Flowerdew Lane, just off the square called Redondo Gardens. There, precisely at dusk, you will find a boy-child playing – just one, in himself a child of no importance, but one upon whom this world's fate now turns. Take that child – that child, and no other! – for through him, I foresee, the Key to the Orokon shall come to me at last.'

Toth whistled grotesquely through his lipless mouth. 'Yes, the fool shall walk right into my trap. And the crystals shall be mine! Do you understand me, Veeldrop?'

Crushed with disappointment, Polty could only nod wordlessly. A heavy, ancient curtain crumbled from the window, filling the chamber with harsh, pale daylight.

And the anti-god was gone.

Chapter 21

POOR LITTLE RICH GIRL

'Guards! Guards!'

Umbecca's voice was deafening. Jeli rolled her eyes; from across the bed, His Imperial Agonist Majesty waved at his wife as if in sympathy, waggling three fingers and a thumb. Disgusted, she shuddered. How could she not be disgusted by this hand, from which the middle finger had been severed at birth? And all for nothing: what need was there for this to distinguish Ejard Blue from his brother Ejard Red? How Jeli wished she could have married the brother!

The luncheon with the War Lords was over at last, and the First Minister, monarchs in tow, had come to look in upon Lector Feval. Franz Waxwell, with a pious expression, hovered like a presiding spirit round the bed. From time to time the apothecary changed the leeches, wiped the hot forehead and dripped spoonfuls of expensive, syrupy potions between the patient's lips. Widow Waxwell, perched at a distance, had descended into annoying, guttural sobs.

'Guards! Guards!' Umbecca called again, flinging her huge bulk across the carpet. Silver trays lay upon a low mahogany table. Distraught, she dived for them. Grabbing a drumstick, she stuffed it into her mouth, ripping greedily at the pale flesh. Juices squirted down her magnificent gown until, suddenly, she tore the little limb from her mouth and flung it into the fire.

A guard appeared in the doorway at last.

'Thank the Lord Agonis!' Umbecca cried. 'Is there *word* yet? Have you found her?'

'No word, ma'am, I—'

'Find her, I say! Oh, out of my sight!' Slamming the door in the guard's face, Umbecca rolled back towards the big bed where her friend, her beloved, the mastermind of all her triumphs, lay stricken, close to death. She slumped down on the bed's edge, moaning. 'Eay, I swear the murderess will be brought to justice!'

'Really, Aunt,' snapped Jeli, 'you don't know if this woman had anything to do with it. Besides, we *saw* the killer being blown to bits, didn't we?'

Umbecca's eyes blazed and she seized the royal arm. 'It was a woman who attacked my dear Eay, was it not? A woman of the merchant classes?'

'Aunt, no, it was a man in disguise, and—'

'It was Nirry! I saw Nirry!' Umbecca shrieked.

'For Orok's sake! First Minister, tell her, please—'

But Tranimel only smiled thinly. 'Your Royal Majesty, you were *at* our luncheon, were you not? I put it to you that a perpetrator for this outrage *must* be found. Should that perpetrator be a weak woman, is it not all to the good – in demonstrating the guises rebels may wear, and the vigil we must keep, constant and unflagging, against their infiltration into our midst?'

Jeli screwed up her forehead. 'What?'

'I am *saying*, Your Royal Majesty, that whether Lector Feval lives or dies, someone is guilty of an offence for which public punishment must follow swiftly and mercilessly. I am *saying* that this Nirrian Jubb, as Lady Veeldrop implies, was undoubtedly behind the attack – even if the bomb was not secreted upon her person. And I am *saying* that she must – *will* – be found.'

'It's ridiculous!' Jeli protested. Turning away, she tossed back her pretty blonde ringlets. Her Royal Majesty, alas, was more concerned to be contrary than to see that justice was done; still, she might have said more.

But when she turned back to Tranimel, he was gone.

Really! And he had not even bowed!

Sourly, Jeli looked about the Lector's private chamber. Holy icons glinted against the wallpaper and a big golden Circle of Agonis hung above the bed. It was all horrible. But the whole day had been horrible. The War Lords luncheon had been far too rich, for a start – Jeli was determined to keep her figure – and she had had to make sure she threw up immediately afterwards. Now she was starving. She craned her neck towards the low mahogany table. Typical! Her aunt had eaten the entire cold collation, or tossed it on the fire. When would Jilda bring afternoon tea? Damn the little baggage!

The chamber smelt abominably of burned meat.

Jeli paced. Oh, what did she care for Eay Feval? She was tempted simply to flounce out of here, returning to her own apartments. Didn't she have the Ball to prepare for? But something held her back. An ache pressed behind her eyes. And she should have been so happy!

After the outrage in the Great Temple, Jeli had been terrified that the Ball would be cancelled; worse still, that too many of the guests would be scared of another bombing and stay away. Fortunately, the First Minister had decreed that the great gathering was compulsory. The rebels must not think they had the upper hand. Everyone who was invited had to come, or be barred for ever from future royal gatherings. It was a brilliant threat – a social death sentence! Anyone else might have been grateful to Tranimel, but Jeli could hardly feel any such thing for someone who was, in her eyes, nothing more than a functionary.

She paced, paced. Jeli felt an urge to be angry with someone, an urge to do something vicious and cruel. She looked round sourly at her companions. Still Widow Waxwell snuffled piteously; Umbecca let out a cow-like lowing. Now she seized the apothecary's hand. 'Good Master Waxwell, is there *nothing* you can do? Is there *no* way you can restore him?'

A pained look came into the apothecary's face. If one thing was certain, it was that his bill was swelling, bloating like the leeches with every moment that passed. To a man of his professional pride, the implication that he was doing less than everything was hardly welcome. A certain coldness crept into his voice as he expatiated upon the damage done to the patient's humours.

And to other parts besides.

Suavely he indicated a sofa by the fire where three cylindrical objects lay wrapped in bloodied cloth; another was propped in the bath chair which waited near the patient's bed, as if in anticipation of his speedy recovery. The objects in question were the Lector's limbs. Three had been blown off in the blast, while the one in the bath chair had been injured so grievously that amputation had been the only possibility. They had all agreed it was just as well: Feval, if he survived, would at least be *even*.

Master Waxwell picked up one of the legs, carefully peeling back the stiffened wrappings. The stench sharpened; sadly he looked upon the burned, bloodied flesh, nauseating in its hues of purple and black.

Umbecca swooned. For a moment it looked as if she might fling her bulk across the limbless, leech-covered torso on the bed. Fortunately, restraint held sway and she clutched her face in her hands as Waxwell – with that hint of malice employees sometimes assume with powerful but hated employers – pronounced his professional judgement on the thing in his hands. Appropriately, his manner took on a clerical air.

'Alas, Lady Veeldrop, to fix back this limb would be a task only gods, not men, could accomplish. Whether Lector Feval will survive this night I cannot say, but I am afraid that never again shall he walk upon this noble part that once carried him so ably. Thank the Lord Agonis that – if nothing else – he was spared the indignity of losing certain *other* parts, which I have seen happen to one of my gentleman patients.'

'Gentleman?' said Jeli, sensing gossip. 'And which gentleman might *that* be?'

Waxwell could not forbear from smiling. Saucy little minx! Yes, he must *insist* on that internal examination ... Pondering his reply – the right effect was crucial – he was on the brink of remarking, with an urbane laugh, that the gentleman in question might be expected to attend the Bird Ball in the guise of ... *Woodcock*. But perhaps this would be going a little too far? The Queen, on the other hand, might demand he go further and reveal the gentleman's name.

Fortunately, before the apothecary was compelled to break his professional confidence, the door opened and Jilda entered, bearing a heavy tray.

'Thank the Lord Agonis!' cried Jeli, darting for the tray before her aunt could get to it.

His Imperial Agonist Majesty, meanwhile, had been busying himself with medicinal rum-and-orandy, intended for the patient. Upon Jeli's entrance he brightened – less, one might suspect, from the prospect of tea than from the sight of his wife's fetching little maid. The King had taken quite a shine to Jilda, and was eager to let her know it. He waved at her, careful to use the hand that was whole, and grinned imbecilically.

Jeli had been stuffing herself with cake; now she bristled. If she had ignored her husband almost entirely since their wedding, permitting him certain distasteful intimacies only for the purpose – *still* fruitless – of securing an heir, nonetheless she was by no means happy that his attentions should ever wander.

So, he liked little Jilda, did he? Very well, let him know all about her! Stalking to the other side of the bed, Her Royal Majesty sat beside her husband. (Umbecca, relieved, descended upon the tea-tray.) Jeli snapped her fingers, motioning her maid to join them.

The King grinned. (Umbecca gorged.)

'Come, Jilda,' the Queen muttered, just loud enough for maid and monarch to hear. 'My husband and I have grown dull, waiting for old No-Limbs to wake up or die. Perhaps you would like to entertain us with reminiscences of your distinguished career at Chokey's?'

Jilda blanched. But if the Queen's cruel words had the desired effect on the maid, they appeared to have made little impression upon His Imperial Agonist Majesty. The King had turned on his side and, with the two girls in his sights, was shutting first one eye, then the other, so that he saw first Jeli, then Jilda … Jeli, then Jilda.

A delightful game!

'M-Morvy?'

A tremulous eagerness filled Crum's voice. Morven grimaced. As they trudged through the snow, he had been contemplating a most interesting intellectual issue and was in no mood to be interrupted. Hadn't he told Crum to shut up? Twice? 'What is it now? If it's something else about that silly rat you're hiding in your tunic, I don't want to know. Or is it another of your famous rat *stories*? Perhaps about the time Zohnny Ryle cut off the tail of your best racing one? Because if it's anything like that, Crum, there'll be trouble, I'm warning you.'

'What sort of trouble, Morvy?' Crum asked innocently.

'I mean … well, I'll be very annoyed,' Morven snapped, and with a defensive air he adjusted the strap of his musket, which *would* keep slipping off the shoulder of his bearskin.

Evening was falling rapidly over the streets and the air was a haze of flurrying snow. They must be close to the Cloth Quarter, mustn't they? Along with other sentries, who had gone in different directions, Morven and his companion were in search of a certain rebel suspect; the Cloth Quarter was the area they had been assigned. It was the sort of job they often had to do, tedious and no doubt pointless, involving endless checks of identity papers. Poor Morven! Couldn't Crum let him have a little peace before they had to begin? One might have thought the fellow had enough to keep him occupied, with a mangy old rat squirming round in his tunic. The very thought!

'You don't appreciate the concentration necessary to the life of the mind, Crum. I know you're only a simple peasant, but could you not at least *attempt* to imagine that some might not share your fascination with the works and ways of rats – not to mention the Crum family and the Ryle family, on their neighbouring farms in Varl?'

'I suppose so,' said Crum, his lower lip protruding. Then he brightened. 'But it's not about Blenkinsop.'

'Blenkinsop?' said Morven, puzzled.

'My rat. That's his name.' Affectionately, Crum patted his chest. 'It's not even about Zohnny Ryle. Besides, he only did it once – cut off Bomber's tail, I mean … Well, he only had one, didn't he? – Bomber, not Zohnny.'

Morven rolled his eyes.

'No, this is something else, Morvy.'

Perhaps, thought Morven, he could simply *not listen*. Yes, that was the way. Let Crum rattle on, reeling out his tales of rats and peasants; let Morven cultivate a shield of deafness, behind which he could carry on his elevated cogitations. Crum would hardly notice, would he?

The Varlan began an anxious address; with a determined air Morven struggled to think only of the subject that obsessed him now. During the composition of his prize-winning essay, *Issues of Prosody in The Jelandros, With Special Reference to the Provenance and Propriety of the Great Caesura*, Morven had puzzled over a passage in the play which appeared to allude to certain artificial appendages favoured amongst the sportsmen of ancient times. In 'Mercol', as it was known,[1] a phrase (IV.ii.189) which translated roughly as *battering at the back door* had been said, by Mercol, to pertain to the custom in which a suitor would hold one of these appendages in his hand when he came to knock upon the door of his beloved; now, illuminated by events in Major Veeldrop's quarters, Morven was certain that Mercol was wrong.

[1] Officially, the Definitive Annotated Edition, Agondon University Press, 12 vols, AC 992e–994d (Gen. Ed. Phineas Mercol, B.Juv. (Hons.), M.Juv., D.Litt, Phil.D., O.M., F.R.S.E., Ac.Ej).

Excitement and frustration possessed him in equal measures. Of course it was all dreadfully immoral – the ancient plays often were – but the eye of the scholar could not flinch from the truth. If only he could repair at once to the Royal Ejard Library! There were learned works he must consult, but Morven was sure his theory was correct. Rapturously he imagined the paper he would compose, complete with innumerable footnoted references to the depraved customs of ancient times. He would deliver it to the Juvescial Society at college – no, better yet, by special invitation, to the Academy Ejlandica, the members of which would rise to their feet, applauding thunderously, some declaring that this brilliant young man was the only fit successor to Mercol's chair, some even murmuring – no, shouting over the commotion – that a new edition of *The Jelandros* was called for at once, under the editorship of Plaise Morven.

Imagine Mercol's chagrin!

But Morven's was worse. Again his excitement subsided, leaving only frustration. More than once over the last moonlife, he had written to Professor Mercol and even, unsuccessfully, attempted to see him. Morven was desperate. Through an old student crony in Webster's Coffee House, he had heard that the Aon Fellowship was unexpectedly vacant. Eustace Bolbarr – a society fop, all agreed, who should never have been appointed in the first place – had proved himself a failure, withdrawing with his dissertation incomplete. The new candidacy was in Mercol's gift. And who better to receive it than Plaise Morven? With the Fellowship in his grasp, Morven would not even have to buy his way out of the army – why, they would have to give him an exemption! No more parades. No more patrols. No more Crum.

If only Mercol would come round!

'He knows I'll supersede him if I'm on the scene, that's it,' Morven muttered. 'And haven't I just thought of a *brilliant* dissertation topic? And one that will show him up for the old fraud he is? I'll bet he even *hopes* I've been killed. The Aon Fellowship, there in his hand, and what has he done for me? Left me like this! A scholar of my ability, trudging about the Cloth Quarter on a rebel round-up!'

Crum burst out, 'But that's just it! Morvy, weren't you listening?'

Morven turned, annoyed. How ridiculous Crum looked in his bearskins! The hat kept slipping over his eyes, there was a squirming lump in his chest and he wasn't even trying to shoulder his musket, just plunking it in the snowy cobblestones, bayonet downwards, *plunk, ker-plunk* like a walking cane.

'You idiot, what are you talking about?'

'I was trying to tell you, this isn't the Cloth Quarter. We're lost, Morvy.'

'What? You can't get *lost* on the Island.'

'But *we* are,' Crum insisted.

Morven sighed. He supposed it was up to him to take a rational approach. 'Well ... where's the *lamp*, Crum? It's got dark rather quickly, hasn't it?'

'I ... I think I left it at our billet, Morvy. Or I might have put it down at that corner back there – when I had to tie my bootlace, remember? Say, did I tell you about the time Zohnny Ryle's bootlace came undone when we were out bird's-nesting? – Well, *he* was bird's-nesting, I always said you should leave the poor birdies' eggs where they—'

'Crum, shut up!' Slivers of light shone through many a shutter and the hanging moon gleamed palely on the snow. Morven wiped his spectacles. 'Now, listen to me, I've spent years as a student in this city – *years*, Crum, enough to deserve the Aon Fellowship...

'Let's see, there's a square up here. Now if I'm not mistaken, that's Corvey's Corner, where that water fountain is ... that's the chapel ... that's the hospice ... that's Bulgani's, the moneylender's – the college rowdies always went to him when the duns were on their trail. And see that tavern? That's called the Cat & King, or something. Rowdies went there, too, shocking place it was ... Crum, this is Redondo Gardens.' Triumphantly, Morven strode ahead. 'Lost, indeed!'

'But ... we're not where we're supposed to be, are we?' Crum said, reasonably enough.

'I suppose we must have come the wrong way,' Morven admitted. 'The Cloth Quarter's over the other side.'

Crum wailed, 'Morvy, what are we going to do?'

'Turn round and go to the Cloth Quarter, of course!'

'Couldn't we just go back to the billet?' Crum stamped his boots. 'I know, let's just say we couldn't *find* this rebel lady. Sergeant Bunch isn't going to know, is he?'

Morven looked dubious.

'Couldn't we just knock up some houses round here? That'll *do*, won't it? Morvy? Blenkinsop's tired, and so am I.'

Scraps of cabbage blew across the empty marketplace. Here and there, even in the icy darkness, harlots plied their trade, leering out of lighted doorways.

Morven gulped. 'I don't think it *will* do, Crum. Besides, Corporal Supp and Soldier Rotts are doing this bit, aren't they? What if we ran into them? We'd be in trouble, Crum.'

'We're in trouble *now*, Morvy.'

A harlot sashayed towards them, crooking a beckoning finger. Morven and Crum scurried across the square as fast as they could in their bulky coats.

Outside the Cat & Crown, Crum looked up at the painted sign. Longingly, he rubbed his mittened hands. 'Morvy? You don't think we could have a hot toddy, do you? In this tavern, I mean?'

'Hot toddy!' Morven cried, disgusted.

He was not quite sure *why* he was disgusted.

'Didn't I tell you about the time Zohnny Ryle was out looking for Woolly, but he didn't know Woolly – that was his favourite lamb – had already come back the other way? Silly Zohnny, you should have seen the look on his face!' Crum grinned. 'Anyway, after the search party found him, they took him home for a hot toddy. Granny Ryle always used to say you should have a hot toddy if you'd been freezing to death.' The grin became a grimace. 'Well, I'm freezing to death right now, Morvy. So's Blenkinsop. And if we're frozen, we're not going to be much good at finding rebel ladies, are we?'

For once, Morven had to agree with Crum. Apprehensively, the hapless recruits pushed through the doors beneath the squeaking sign. They found themselves in a narrow lobby, opening on either side into two different bars. Peering to their left, into the snug, they spied a Bluejacket soldier, hunched over, almost concealed in a corner by the fire.

Quickly they stepped back, but Crum resisted when Morven tried to bundle them outside again. The fellow, after all, was not from their regiment. It wasn't Rottsy; it wasn't Supp. Besides, the parlour on the right looked safe, empty in the dark afternoon but for a few traders, here and there, and one or two wizened-looking almsmen. The new arrivals shed their wet bearskins, positioning themselves as close as they could to the fire.

Eagerly Crum ordered the hot toddies, explaining to the one-eyed lady at the bar all about the time when Zohnny Ryle went looking for Woolly.

Chapter 22

THE SHINING

The fire roared up the chimney.

'Cold? I say, you must have been! I can tell just by looking at your swarthy little face that you come from somewhere hot, my boy. (Eh, Ginger, out from under my feet.) How you can stand it here even for a moment, I don't know. Me, I'm from Holluch-on-the-Hill, and I'll tell you, if I didn't have these furs over my cassock, even here indoors, I just don't know how I'd cope. (Those furs of yours all right, my boy? Old discards from Bando's brats, I'm afraid, but we have to make do, don't we? – Ginger, down I say!) What, so there's a fire? Yes, and guess whose job it is to keep it stoked ... But what's a fire, against weather like this? *Ooh*, what I'd give for a nice warm monastery down in Tiralos, or Down Lexion! (If only you didn't have to get up too early.) Rebels! Don't get mixed up with rebels, my boy, if you ever want a moment's peace or comfort again!'

The scene was a shabby, low-beamed sitting-room in a certain country cottage in the Agondon Hills. On and on burbled the podgy Friar, his tonsured head glinting in the lamplight. To Littler, the words blurred into a haze; lying on a sofa in his borrowed furs, he gazed up at a pattern on the shadowy ceiling, like a map made of brown, seeping damp. His eyes flickered shut and the visions came again. Somewhere, as if from far away, he saw the hovering Myla, with her blue, billowing robes; then he saw the blue robes turning rainbow-coloured and Myla's face disappearing into the golden, dazzling light.

But no, it was not Myla any more.

Then Littler saw the skyship, rising again.

'Hungry? I say, you must be *very* hungry. I was always hungry when I was a boy. All the time. To tell the truth, I'm hungry now. *And* all the time.' Sausages sizzled and a kettle sang. 'So's Puss-cat, by the looks of him. Come here, you big lump, let me pet you. Listen to him miaow! (Just don't think you're getting too much, Ginger. One sausage, and that's it. Gave you a dish of milk, didn't I? Last of the milk, too!) But really, the provisions we get here! Count yourself lucky I've got these sausages, my lad, that's all I can say. This is a better high tea than any we've had here in Corvey Cottage for I don't know how long! Now why I can't be based in that nice tavern, right in the middle of town, I really don't know ... Rebels! But really, what can you expect?'

131

Now Littler saw the skyship swooping, looping, plunging. It could have been a vision of the vessel before it crashed; but no, this was the vessel as it would be again, ready for one last, desperate flight. Marvelling, Littler saw mysterious powers flattening the dents in the metallic sides; as if time went in reverse, he saw shattered glass cracking back into place and the cracks smoothing away. He saw the skyship screaming through the darkness; he saw the mountains of ice and snow. He saw Jem. And Rajal. And Myla.

Littler jerked awake. A hand went to his mouth.

'Frightened? My dear, don't even *talk* to me about frightened.' Clattering by the fire with his plates and cups, the Friar was serving out Littler's tea. And his own. He heaped his plate high. 'Now if I'd had any sense, do you think I'd have taken up with that man in a mask? (Eh, Puss-cat, your tea's on the way. No need to get quite so ... what's *with* you, hm?) Not to mention the others. Rum lot. That Miss Landa's a heathen for a start, a positive heathen. (Eh, Ginger, you're running round like a mad thing. Calm down, eh?) I'll tell you, I'm only glad Bando's brats aren't here in Corvey Cottage. Vulgar little tearaways! Would you believe, they used to call me *Capon*? And me a man of the cloth! It's the father who encourages them, that much is certain. Now you, I'm sure, are a *much* nicer lad – but what's wrong? Little boy, what *are* you doing?'

Suddenly Littler flung himself across the room, following the bounding, capering Ejard Orange. Thick curtains obscured the window. He ripped them back, looking out over the black, snowy fields. And into the sky.

Littler clapped his hands. The skyship!

❄ ❄

'Sorry, Piebald, but I think I'd be faster on my own now.'

Jem patted the carthorse on the nose and left it standing at the corner. He strode ahead, then looked back guiltily. Already the day had darkened and snow fell more thickly.

Piebald looked decidedly glum. All the way from the Hills, Jem and the carthorse had braved the cold, the slush and the Bluejacket patrols that had stopped them numerous times, demanding to know where they were going and why. Affecting an Inner accent, Jem had pretended to be a draper from a Hills village, heading into town for a consignment of cloth. It was as well his pale skin left no doubt of his race or he could have been searched, or forced to pay bribes.

The draper line wouldn't work any more; Jem was nowhere near the Cloth Quarter. He thought he ought to be stealthy; with so few people in the streets, he could easily attract attention. Shaking his head, he looked between Piebald and the cobbled streets that angled up towards the top of the Island. Scurrying back, he rapped on the shutters of a chandler's shop, hoping the chandler would be grateful for a faithful new carthorse. But Jem was off again before the chandler appeared.

Straining hard in the harlequin's coat, he made his way up through the twisting streets. Now where was this tavern called the Crown & Cat? Jem knew little of Redondo Gardens, only that it was in one of those parts of the Island known, in quality circles, as a Decayed District, deserted long ago by gentlefolk who had migrated across the river to Agondon New Town. Quite what the place might hold for him now, he could barely imagine. But he had to trust the harlequin.

Jem knelt down to a beggar in a doorway. 'Crown & Cat? Or Cat & Crown?'

With a broken smile, the beggar waved an instructive hand. Thanking him, Jem dug in his pocket for a coin, then realised with a start that the coin, the only one in his possession, was the harlequin's. Quickly he snatched it back just as the beggar reached for it.

The fellow cursed and would have given chase, but fell down drunkenly in the snow instead.

Upset by the incident, Jem blundered into Redondo Gardens before he realised quite where he was. Snow swirled through the darkness. He looked round uneasily at the hunched shapes of the almshouse and the old chapel. Behind him lay a half-timbered Elabethan house; across the square he saw leering doorways, with female forms hovering.

A linkboy trudged past, lighting the way for a sedan chair. The gentleman in the chair – if gentleman he were – was evidently making for one of the harlots. He bellowed impatiently and Jem stepped out of the way, looking behind him just as the light from the linkboy's torch flared luridly over the tavern's creaking sign.

Jem gasped. 'Ejard Orange!'

He had hoped for some hint that he was on the right trail. Now he had one. Resplendent in a shining, cat-sized crown, the cat on the sign – no doubt about it – was the spitting image of Ejard Orange.

Still, it was not without caution that Jem entered the lobby. Peering into the parlour to his right, he felt a stab of alarm.

Bluejackets!

He saw them only briefly, and from behind, but Jem could tell that one of them was speaking to the barmaid – earnestly, and at length. That day he had heard more than one guard muttering the word *rebels*. Were these fellows looking for strangers, combing the city for suspicious types?

Jem thought he would turn and go. But that was absurd; of course the city was filled with Bluejackets, crawling with them. What could he expect? He looked into the snug. Thinking it was empty, he made his way in.

Only when it was too late did Jem see another Bluejacket, a decidedly drunken sergeant, propped up in a corner by the fire.

'Ah, a friend!' The fellow waved him over. 'Don't know you from the Lord Agonis, lad, but you'll do, you'll do! Come and have a jar with old Carney Floss!'

Reluctantly, Jem complied.

❊   ❊

'Guards! Guards! What, still nothing?'

Umbecca cursed as the news came – or rather, did not. Nirry couldn't just have vanished, could she? Since this morning? No, the vile murderess was hiding somewhere, up some filthy alley, down some stinking sewer, planning more outrages against good, pious, Agonis-fearing folk. She would not get away with it. If they had to ransack all of Agondon, even all of Ejland, the guards would find Miss Nirrian Jubb, find her and bring her to her outraged mistress.

With a part of her mind, Umbecca knew that she was hardly being rational. But how could she be rational after all that had happened? From the walls, from the carpet, from the curtains in the window she would see Nirry's face, then the word MURDER, blazing before her eyes as if written in fire.

Nirry. MURDER. Nirry. MURDER.

In the looking-glass: REDRUM.

The fat woman flung herself about the chamber. She picked up one of the severed legs, cradling it in her arms. She whimpered. She moaned.

'Good lady, calm yourself,' the apothecary crooned. 'Alas, the distresses of the day have caused your radical heat to rise dangerously high. Let me fix you a sedative,' he added kindly. 'I have just the thing in my bag, a new mixture in what many of my ladies find a *most* attractive flavour – not wholly unreminiscent, I might add, of strawberry cheesecake.'

Normally this would have tempted Umbecca, but now she ignored the apothecary. All this time the Widow Waxwell had been snuffling and sobbing, as if the Lector's tragic fate could possibly distress *her* as much as it distressed Umbecca. Still, Umbecca had tolerated the performance – willing for Berthen to act, as it were, the part of a chorus.

But now the wizened crone – who, after all, had been *no one*, absolutely *no one*, until Umbecca deigned to notice her – hobbled forward, as if to claim the place of a principal! Taking up another of the Lector's swaddled legs, the Widow cradled it like an infant against her breast.

Umbecca's reaction was instant and overwhelming. With a roar of rage, she banished the Widow from the sickroom. Whimpering, letting her bloodied burden fall, the old woman scurried out as fast as her decrepit legs could carry her. Had she hesitated even a moment, Umbecca would certainly have clouted her with the Lector's other leg.

'The crone is mad, mad!' she shrieked.

A second drama of banishment was happening on the other side of the sickbed. As the apothecary once again busied himself with his leech-dish, His Imperial Agonist Majesty resumed his foolish game with the Queen and her maid, winking at one, then at the other.

If he winked fast enough, they blurred together.

'Jeli ... Jilda! Jeli ... Jilda!' the King exclaimed delightedly.

'Really, this is absurd!' Jeli burned with shame. She would have broken away, but her husband trapped her wrist, then the maid's too.

Jeli struggled; Jilda gasped, helpless as the King, with a triumphant yelp, flung her across the sickbed. Waxwell yelped too as his leech-dish went flying. He would have protested – but dare he, to the King?

Besides, the King was now attempting to mount the pretty maid, all the time giggling, 'Jeli ... Jilda! Jeli ... Jilda!'

Jilda shrieked; Jeli shrieked; so did Umbecca.

But Umbecca went further. Wielding the Lector's leg, the fat woman burst forward. 'Monster,' she cried, 'you'll squash Eay! You'll squash Eay, you monster!'

Fortunately, this tragedy was averted. The torso, after all, took up little space in the bed, and the leg, with all the weight behind it of Umbecca's bulk, succeeded in cracking His Imperial Agonist Majesty a savage blow to the skull, just as he was about to rip down his breeches.

The King crashed to the floor.

Spent, Umbecca staggered back.

Waxwell wondered quite what to do.

It was left to Queen Jelica to command the scene. Guards burst in, bewildered, anxious to discover the cause of the commotion; their bewilderment grew as they looked between the King, collapsed in a heap, and the sobbing maid, lying over the sickbed with her uniform ripped. Assuming an admirably regal demeanour, seldom seen in her since the day of her wedding, Jeli delivered a speech she had rehearsed many a time. If her words were too florid for the ears of guards, she did not care. Eyes flaring, ringlets shining, she pointed in righteous anger to the bed.

'Guards, this servant has betrayed my trust. Thinking the creature had been ill-used, I raised her from the lowliest degradation known to woman, hoping in this display of compassion to gladden the heart of the Lord Agonis. I see now that I was mistaken, for sometimes wrath is the only path of righteousness. None could reclaim so wanton a harlot; and yet, I would not forgo compassion altogether. Death should be her portion, but I stay my hand. Take her back to Chokey's!'

And here the scene would have ended, but for a happy coda. A moan broke from the Lector's lips.

Umbecca rallied, rushing back to him.

'My potions!' Waxwell clapped his hands. 'Didn't I tell you they'd do the trick?'

Chapter 23

ROUND EVERY CORNER

'Biddy-biddy-bobble!'

'Diddy-on-the-double!'

'Boys, please!' Nirry cried. Struggling to keep the annoyance from her voice, she was not quite successful. She forced a smile. Raggle and Taggle rolled on the kitchen floor, several times almost tumbling down the open hatch of the cellar. 'Be careful, do! You'll break something, you will, and if it's not my best crocks it'll be one of your heads! – Eh, haven't you finished them tankards yet?' she added to the skivvy at the washboard. 'And don't grimace like that, girl – just be glad you're not over the other side of the Gardens, where you belong!'

Huddled into herself, Nirry sat by her kitchen fire. From time to time she would rise halfheartedly, stirring a cauldron or turning the spit. There was no disguising that she was not herself. How she envied the boys! To Raggle and Taggle, the dramas of the morning were long gone.

Wiggler climbed up from the cellar, his back burdened under the weight of a barrel. Wiping his brow, he set it down on its side. He glanced at his wife.

'Eh love, buck up! It's all over now.'

'Is it? I'm telling you, Wiggler, the mistress knew me, sure as hamhocks.'

'And I'm telling you, that old cow's not your mistress any more. Come on, love, this isn't like you! Not like my Nirry!' Wiggler went to her, taking her hand. 'If it was anyone else, you'd be saying they was a fool to carry on so. And my Nirry can't be a fool, can she? Don't I depend on her to be the brains?'

Nirry managed a little smile. Wiggler wiggled his ears and the smile grew.

But only for a moment. 'Raggle! Leave that barrel alone! What do you want to do, crush Taggle? As for you, Wiggler Olch, what do you mean, leaving that cellar door open? I declare, sometimes you hasn't got the sense you was born with!'

Wiggler grinned. Now *this* was more like it!

A thudding came in the back hall. Turning, Nirry peered through the open doorway. There was a glint of guns, of knives, of unshaven faces and shaggy brows. *Tramp, tramp*, went one pair of heavy boots, then another, up the stairs to the Royal Ejard Room.

'Wiggler, I don't like it.' Nirry drew back, troubled. 'I didn't like it last night, and now I like it less. What's Bob doing, calling them all together again so quickly? I don't see the point.'

'The point, love, is that they bombed the—'

'Shh!' Nirry put a finger to her lips. '*Someone* did,' she hissed, 'but that was mad, that was—'

'*They're* mad, the lot of them.'

'Yes, and they're in my tavern! Ooh, if only all this were over! There'll be shootings, riots – and Carney's in the snug again right now! The whole place could be crawling with Bluejackets! Why can't we have some peace and quiet?'

This last line, delivered stridently, was directed towards Raggle and Taggle, who had left off rolling on the barrel and were now chasing each other round and round the kitchen, Raggle holding a cauldron lid above his head, Taggle beating on the lid with a ladle.

A new voice rode above the clamour. 'What's this, what's this? Warriors bold, fighting in Nirry's kitchen? How could they dare?'

It was Cata, coming in from the back lane. Snow speckled her hair and her clothes.

'Miss Cata, really!' Nirry protested. 'Haven't I told you you'll catch your death, going out without your coat?'

'Just checking the lie of the land, Nirry.'

'Oh? Rebels in all directions?'

'Don't look so glum. You like *some* rebels, don't you, Nirry?' Cata smiled mischievously. 'Because look who I've found!'

Standing aside, she revealed two figures in riding costume, emerging into the lamplight. Nirry and Wiggler broke into smiles, but it was Raggle and Taggle who squealed with delight.

Bando's rifle clattered to the floor. He held out his arms. With a merry grimace, Hul stepped out of the way as the boys cannoned into their beaming father. They scrambled up his paunch. They pulled his hair and moustaches and tugged the red bandanna he wore around his neck. Merrily their father swung them through the air, one after the other.

'Ho, so fat! Madam Nirry has been good to you, I see!'

'They're just growing,' smiled Nirry. '*And* growing. *And* growing. Wiggler, go and fetch some ale for our guests, eh? Ooh, and you'd better get upstairs after that. All them rebels'll be here soon.'

Bando pinched Raggle's cheeks, then Taggle's. 'Ah, you scamps, you won't eat so well when you're back with your old father. Just wait, after the big battle, when we're back in Zenzau, then you'll have to earn your keep!'

'But you're fat, Papa!' Raggle cried.

Taggle shrilled, 'Papa, you're fatter than—'

Bando cuffed him playfully.

But Nirry's smile fell. 'Battle ... Zenzau?'

Cata drew Hul to one side. 'Things must be coming to a head, mustn't they?'

The scholar nodded solemnly. 'Those fools in the Rebel League have forced our hands. But we've one trick up our sleeves. The Bluejackets have no idea how big our forces are. I know they beat us in Wrax, but we had a chance, didn't we? Well, we've got another one now ... But today's meeting is vital. If we're going to take on the Bluejackets, this time we've got to have a disciplined, fighting army. Bob's *got* to win over these rebel leaders.'

'I don't know what's happened to Wiggler,' said Nirry. She yelled at the skivvy to go and find out. 'And bring us back some ale, do you hear?'

'So where *is* Bob?' Cata continued.

'Don't worry, he'll be here.'

Cata's look was wry. 'I couldn't believe what he did last night. What was he doing just skulking round in Corvey Cottage? Reading the *Gazette*?'

'He has his ways, Cata.'

'Hul, you're too good to him! If only we could trust him!'

The scholar looked pained. 'You mustn't speak like that.'

'I wish I didn't have to. But I'm not the only one who feels this way, am I?' Ominously, Cata looked up to the ceiling, which echoed with the thumpings and scrapings from the Royal Ejard Room. More footsteps came, tramping up the stairs.

The skivvy, returning with a tray full of tankards, bent and whispered in Nirry's ear. Nirry rolled her eyes, jerking her thumb towards the front parlour. 'Typical Wiggler. Holed up in there with a couple of regimental cronies, on today of all days! And who's going to wait in the Royal Ejard Room, that's what I want to know? Regimental cronies, indeed!'

'They're still *in* the regiment?' said Cata.

'Bluejackets, Miss Cata, through and through! As if Carney Floss weren't bad enough – ooh, and I dare say he'll be coming out here to pester me soon, once he's got his dander up. Perhaps Master Hul and Master Bando'd better get upstairs, hm?'

Both of them were now piggy-backing the boys.

'Ho, such heavy lumps!' Bando laughed. 'Not like that little boy at the cottage, eh, Hul?'

'Certainly ... not,' Hul gasped, relinquishing, with some relief, the squirming burden of Taggle. 'No, that little chap's light as a feather!'

Cata's brow furrowed. 'What little chap?'

'Oh, something very strange.' Hul sipped appreciatively from his tankard. 'This morning a little boy – dark, foreign fellow – just wandered in from the snow. No shoes, no coat, dressed in the skimpiest of rags, would you believe? Must have got in one of the back windows, we think ... Well, the Friar found him, and the little boy collapsed. We've put him to bed, but I can't believe he doesn't have any friends or companions.

Landa was getting together a search party, just as we left.' He looked towards Bando. 'Come on, old friend, let's get upstairs, see if we can calm the rabble—'

'Hul, wait.' Cata clutched his arm. 'You said this little boy's *foreign*. Where from, do you think?'

'Wenaya? Unang Lia? Oh, and there was one other thing. I don't know if it's a caste-badge of his tribe or something, but under his tunic the little boy was wearing, would you believe, a leather bag—'

'A bag? Over his chest?'

'That's right. And inside the bag was a stone, a sort of … *crystal*, I suppose – I say, steady on!'

Cata bolted towards the door.

Nirry cried, 'Miss Cata, where are you going?'

'To Corvey Cottage! I've got to get down there!'

'Tonight? In your condition? Ooh, what's the girl talking about?' Helplessly, Nirry looked between Hul and Bando, then flung up her hands and called out, resigned, 'Miss Cata – don't forget your coat.'

A door banged shut. From the yard came a whinny, then a thunder of hooves.

❉   ❉

'Aye, she's a grand girl,' Carney Floss slurred. He guzzled his ale. 'Don't suppose you've ever had a grand girl like that, eh, lad? Bet you've never!'

'I … I *know* a grand girl,' Jem said defensively.

'Wouldn't send her my way? Eh? – No, lad, that's a joke, a joke.' The fellow rested a hand on Jem's forearm, almost as if he were clamping it to the table. 'Look at it this way … look at it that way … any way it's the same. There's only one girl for Carney Floss!'

'Hm, so you've said.' Jem permitted himself to sigh. He had thought it best to be polite to this Bluejacket. Now he found himself wanting to be rude. Surreptitiously, he peered at the regimental badge, almost concealed beneath a fold of cloth. The Blue Irions? A pang filled him and he wondered if this fellow really came from his own home town. Probably not: people said the regiments were all mixed up nowadays.

The barmaid bustled in, refilling their tankards with an automatic air. This 'Carney Floss' was evidently a regular. A regular bore, no doubt. A regular burden. Jem wished he had gone into the other room instead. This Cat & Crown, most likely, was a false trail, but maybe something would happen. Or someone would come. He thought again of the picture of Ejard Orange, swinging from a bracket in the snow outside.

He had to get away from Carney Floss.

Jem was about to ask where the latrine might be when the sergeant's grip tightened on his arm and he burst out tearfully, 'Aye, she's a grand girl! Oh, my dear Nirry!'

Baines narrowed her single eye. 'Now you stop that, Carney Floss, or I'll—'

'Nirry?' said Jem. 'Her name's *Nirry*?'

'Aye, Nirrian Jubb,' said the sergeant, 'and never a—'

'Goody Olch to you,' said Baines, 'and don't you—'

She broke off, shrieking, as Jem clutched her. Wrenching free from the sergeant's grip, blundering to his feet, the young stranger almost overturned the table; as it was, he knocked over a tankard of ale. It soaked into the breeches of the bewildered sergeant.

'Where *is* she?' he demanded. 'Where's Nirry?'

Baines gulped. And they said Bluejackets were dangerous! 'In ... in the kitchen out the back. But sir—'

There was no time to say more. Jem bolted out of the snug.

'Useless girl! Don't you know there're openings on the other side of the Gardens for those who can't make good with respectable work? – Worse luck, too. Why, I've a mind to go over there with my best broom and clear off those dirty trollops myself ... It's not right, letting that sort of thing go on, and only a few streets away from the Great Temple!'

Nirry stabbed the air with her peeling knife. There was no reply, but she expected none since she was talking to herself. Roused from her torpor, she was busy preparing potatoes. Such work was beneath her, of course, but she had sent the skivvy to help out upstairs.

Hul and Bando had also gone up; Raggle and Taggle, forbidden to follow, kicked their heels in the back hall. Morosely they looked round for some new delight, though there was nothing to replace their father.

'Ah, the quality will come back to the Gardens, I'm sure of it. Just you wait and see what the Cat & Crown becomes! Think it's a common sort of place, don't you? Fit for the likes of you, and no better? I've seen your superior looks, my girl, and never you mind. Rebel's daughter, but don't you think you're just a common trollop to me? I'm telling you, one of these days we'll have a footman on the door, and if you're not quality, do you think you'll get house room in the Cat & Crown? None of your rebel's daughters! And none of your rebels!'

Pausing in her reverie, Nirry peered anxiously at the ceiling. What was going on up there right now? And where was Bob Scarlet? If he didn't show, there'd be pandemonium. But if he *did* show, might there not be pandemonium, too? Nirry was only grateful that Master Hul was there. And Master Bando. She could trust *them*, at least.

Amongst those she could not trust were Raggle and Taggle. At that moment, donning their little snowcapes, the boys were stealing out the back door. They ran into the stableyard, then into the lanes beyond, delightedly scooping up handfuls of snow.

'Ooh, I know what you're thinking,' Nirry continued. 'Dream on, Goody Olch, but this part of town is far too common. Well, if you want a tavern, you have to take what you can get, don't you? Yes, I'd have liked the Champion; yes, I'd have liked the Lion & Eagle – but I could *afford* the lease here. And if there's one lesson in life you need to learn, my girl, it's this – don't try and live beyond your means.' Nirry prodded again with the peeling knife. 'You hear me, girl?'

'I don't think *she* does. But I do, Nirry.'

Nirry turned, startled. Only one lamp burned in the kitchen and the gloom pressed from all sides. She clutched her throat, her heart beating hard, as a slender, blond young man stepped forward from the doorway.

'I … I don't believe it! *Master Jem!*'

Rapturously the Prince of Ejland and the former servant ran into each other's arms. Jem whirled Nirry around, far off the floor. She hugged his neck, clinging tightly.

'Master Jem,' she gasped, 'but how, but why – you've been away so long, I thought … Ooh, Miss Cata told me some funny stories, but I didn't know what to believe, I … I don't know whether to laugh or cry!'

Jem hugged her again. 'I think you're doing both!'

A voice burst out: 'Nirry, how could you!'

Nirry jumped. 'Cripes, it's Carney! C-Carney, this is an old friend from Irion, I mean, my old—'

Enraged, the sergeant advanced on Jem. Baines hovered behind, helpless, wringing her hands.

'M-Mistress, I tried to stop him, but—'

'I saw you kissing my Nirry, you, you—'

The sergeant swung his fist at Jem, missed and fell into a tangled heap. He scrambled up at once, this time determined to fling his bulk forward, bringing Jem down. He was a burly fellow and might have pummelled Jem hard; but after all, he was also very drunk.

Jem grabbed a saucepan and banged him on the head.

'Ooh, that's torn it, Master Jem!' said Nirry. For a moment, her look was grave, then she burst into helpless giggles. 'I'm sorry,' she gasped. 'It's just that Miss Cata once did exactly the same thing – knocked him out with my best saucepan! Poor Carney! Looks like he's gone and disgraced himself, too.'

'It's ale – sorry, I spilled it,' Jem explained. 'But Nirry, what's this about Cata? You mean you've seen her? You know where she is?'

'Of course, Master Jem—' Nirry clapped a hand across her mouth. 'Ooh, but she's gone! I understand now, she must have thought—'

'Gone?' cried Jem. 'Where?'

'To Corvey Cottage. In the Agondon Hills, leagues away! In the dark, I ask you, and in her con—'

'But I've just *come* from there! When did she leave?'

141

'Just now, she's—'

'I've got to catch her! Nirry, have you got horses?'

Nirry nodded, waving towards the yard, and Master Jem was gone as suddenly as he had appeared. Bewildered, Nirry slumped over the kitchen bench, wiping tears from her eyes. What a day it had been!

But it was not over yet.

Chapter 24

REDJACKET! BLUEJACKET!

'I don't like it, Hul. Where's Bob?'

'Bando, you don't believe he'll let us down?'

'I believe *you* don't believe it, old friend. Perhaps that should be enough for me. Ah, but I wish I could trust him as you do! We were rebels before we fell in with him, weren't we? Aren't there many factions? Aren't there many leaders? Just look around us.'

'I am, Bando. And I'm not sure I like what I see.'

Uneasily, standing by the fire, Hul surveyed the hot, crowded chamber, a fug of sweat, drying clothes and tobarillo smoke. The rebel leaders sat impatiently around two dark, wormy tables.

Some of them, the ones at the front, were brave and true-hearted, fellows – and a lady – Hul would be proud to fight alongside. There was Folio Webster, son of the Webster of coffee-house fame, who controlled a secret network of student radicals. There was Roly Rextel, Cantor of Varby, aggrieved brother of the society beauty, Miss Vyella Rextel, who was missing, believed murdered (Roly blamed the Bluejackets). There was big, shambling Onty Michan, renegade cousin of the Zenzan governor; there was wiry Danny Garvice, a wizard with explosives, and beautiful, dark-eyed Magda Vytoni, great-daughter of the famous philosopher.

But then, at the back, there were Shammy the Hood and 'Scars' Majesta, Offero the Mole and Figaro Fingers, corrupt turnkey of Oldgate Prison – sordid, shifty-eyed fellows all. Though rebels should have been fired by political commitment, Hul had to admit that many were simply the dregs – or perhaps the cream – of Agondon's criminal classes, who saw in the chaos of revolution a chance for pillage and plunder on a scale hitherto unprecedented. What else was one to think of Peter Impalini, one-time sword-swallower with a carnival troupe, who was given to random acts of violence, generally involving knives? Or Molly the Cut, notorious female felon, with her big hoopy earrings, foul mouth and gap-toothed smile?

As for the silver-masked harlequin, known as 'Mask', and the clown who was his constant accomplice, Hul did not know what to believe. Separate from all the others, they sat in two stiff chairs against the wall, solemn and inscrutable.

Clutching a sturdy walking cane, Mask bent his lips close to Clown's ear. 'I fear for the issue of this, old 'panion,' he was muttering, 'I fear it much indeed.'

'Issue? You should be lucky to have any,' said Clown.

'Droll. You are a fool, but not such a fool as that. I speak not of the infirmities of our age, but of what might fall out should this highwayman fail us. Look around you. Who else is to bind together our disparate ranks?'

'Disparate? You mean desperate?'

'I mean both. And I mean we must be bound.'

'But why? Think of the power we wield amongst the Vaga-kind.'

'I do, and know it is not enough. Are Vagas to achieve, here in Agondon, what even the forces of the Green Pretender failed to achieve in Wrax?'

'I know, I know. If only Tor were here!'

'Indeed, old 'panion. But Tor was defeated too.'

'More ale, slut!' cried Shammy the Hood, seizing the skivvy as she roamed towards the back table, bearing a heavy jug.

'Careful, you'll spill it!' the girl squealed.

'Hah! That's what her mother said,' grinned Offero the Mole, whose daughter she was. 'And don't I wish I hadn't?' He blew out a cloud of smoke. 'Get over there, girl, and sit on Figaro's knee. He'll need a bit of cheering up, he will, when it's me that takes over this motley crew!'

'What do you mean, *you*?' snarled Fingers, exposing golden artificial teeth, bought with the many bribes with which he had enriched himself in his capacity as turnkey.

'We're loyal, aren't we?' said Peter Impalini. 'Aren't we still loyal to the highwayman?'

'Oh, shove your sword up your arse, Impalini!' said Molly the Cut, lighting a fresh roll of Jarvel-rough. 'The highwayman, always the highwayman! And where is he? Off pissing himself with fright, that's where! He won't show, bet you he won't!'

'How about *you* show us something, Molly?' leered Shammy the Hood. 'Like your tits, for a start.'

'Good idea! Let Molly sit on my knee,' said Fingers, sending the skivvy sprawling to the floor. 'Offero's spawn is all skin and bones!'

'They could be right,' said Roly Rextel at the front table. Puffing on his briar, he exchanged a worried glance with Danny Garvice.

'About Offero's girl?' smiled Onty Michan.

'About the highwayman,' said Danny. 'I couldn't believe it when the abduction failed. But I won't believe Bob's lost his touch, I won't!'

'And if he has?' Magda Vytoni arched an eyebrow. She smoked a long, thin cheroot and her voice was cool, calmly rational. 'Think of all his promises that have never come true. Didn't he say we would storm Xorgos Island, releasing all the rebel prisoners? Think what that would have done for our cause! I've said it before and I'll say it again: we should *elect* a new leader, on fair, honest and open principles. What is this highwayman but the biggest bully? Did my greatfather die as a martyr in order that we should fall into idolatry over a criminal, for all the world as if he were a king?'

'Yes, Magda, and *you* wouldn't want a king either,' sighed Folio Webster. 'But open your eyes. Are the common folk ready for anything else? How far do you think your *fair and honest principles* will take you? If we're going to get anywhere, we *need* the biggest bully.'

Magda spat, 'But the principle of the thing—'

'Look at it this way,' said Onty Michan. 'Before we can do anything else, we've got to defeat the Bluejackets. Agreed, friends? So let's be practical.'

Folio, Roly, and Danny nodded; Magda only glowered, then grimaced in disgust as Peter Impalini smiled at her invitingly.

At the front of the room, Hul and Bando were increasingly uneasy. Where could Bob be?

'I feel like a schoolmaster,' said Hul, 'in an unruly class.'

'Hah! If you were a master, these would be boys and you could beat them all.'

'I'm not sure I could,' said Hul, 'not these.'

He wiped the mist from his spectacles. How vilely this chamber stank! And how hot it was, here by the fire! Flames roared up the chimney like dragon's breath and their flickering shadows, mingling with the lamp-light, reached even as far as the curtains at the window. Red rep flickered as if it, too, were on fire. Hul thought he might rip the curtains open, flinging the casement wide. But he hardly wanted to pass the back table, not just now. With sinister intensity the light played over earrings, sword-hilts, pistols, golden teeth.

He was just returning his spectacles to his nose when a knife whizzed past his ear. Hul gasped. Bando roared, clattering his musket into place.

Laughter came from the back table. Peter Impalini smiled thinly.

'Picture,' was all he said. 'Picture.'

'Oh. Yes,' said Hul, flustered. 'It's all right, Bando.'

On the wall above the mantelpiece was a portrait – or, it might be said, an iconic representation – of His Imperial Agonist Majesty, clear-eyed, youthful, resplendent in blue robes. In Ejland, such paintings were commonplace, turned out in vast numbers by the royal studios to decorate public places and patriotic homes. But this was a special one, and highly illicit, of a type known as a *slider picture*.

Feeling for a hidden catch in the frame, Hul released an ingenious mechanism. In an instant, the blue portions of the painting rolled away, replaced by red; thus was Ejard Blue converted into his deposed brother. So cunningly did the sliding sections mesh with the fixed parts that only the most minute examination of the picture could have revealed its secret.

Impalini applauded as his hero was revealed; the others at the back table jeered – as they would, no doubt, at anything sacred.

'Can it be true,' said Clown, 'that there are many such pictures? Even in the homes of the highest?'

'We must hope so, old 'panion,' was Mask's reply. 'Often, when we performed in the homes of quality-folk, I used to have my suspicions. Getting close enough to check, that's the thing. One drops a few hints, but the quality are nothing if not cautious. Ladies especially.'

'Indeed,' sighed Clown. 'How I miss our performances! Will we Vagas be free again when the Redjackets triumph?'

'We must hope so, old 'panion,' came the reply again.

At the front table, Magda raised a scoffing hand to the picture. 'A king? A dead king?'

'A *red* king! Can't you see he's a symbol?' said Folio Webster.

'Yes, of tyranny. Bluejacket, Redjacket, bobbing up and down like those puppets in the booths! Why not Yellowjacket? Why not Greenjacket, what does it matter?'

'Right now, quite a lot,' said Danny Garvice.

Bando had turned to study the picture. 'He was noble, was he not, your Redjacket king? Ah, if only he were still amongst us!'

'Er – indeed,' Hul said awkwardly, then yelped as another knife shot through the air, juddering into the panelling of the wall behind his head.

'We're bored!' demanded Peter Impalini. 'Where *is* he?'

'There's not enough ale!' cried Shammy the Hood. 'And only this slut to serve it, what's the good of that?'

'Eh, that's my daughter you're talking about,' said Offero the Mole, who sometimes, unexpectedly, would find himself filled with fatherly tenderness towards the child whom, at other times, he would see abused with impunity. He reached for his dagger.

'Dear me, this is what I was afraid of,' muttered Hul. In an instant, the hot chamber was a scene of chaos, with feet stamping, fists flying. Hands dived for pistols. Mask and Clown cowered. Bando brandished his musket, ready to fire.

'Please, no shots!' Hul wailed.

But a shot rang out, zinging through the air.

There was a scream. It was Magda. For a moment Hul thought she had been shot, but she raised a trembling finger, pointing towards the window where the red rep curtains had been pulled back – from the *other* side.

Standing in the window was Bob Scarlet.

Silence fell. The scarlet-garbed figure in his black mask and three-cornered hat presented an image at once terrifying and romantic. Twirling his pistol on his finger, he blew the smoke from the end, then cut a rapid swathe across the room, leaping with extraordinary grace from tabletop to tabletop, his cape billowing behind him.

Scattering not even a single tankard of ale, he landed before the fire and spun round on his heels. Looking over the assembled rebels, the eyes behind the dark mask flickered and flashed; the mouth beneath curled cruelly.

'Greetings, friends. I'd wondered what you'd say about me if you thought I wasn't here. Interesting – *most* interesting.'

'Eh, Wiggler, remember that time Bunchy bawled us out about being the slackest lot in the army? Said we might as well be rebels? Said we was on their side, the way we carried on? – Well, I know he said it a lot, but I mean when he went to climb up on Bluebell right after. You know, he was going to ride off real quick – make an impression, and all that – but he didn't even turn round to look at her, he just *thought* she was there, but—'

Wiggler finished the story. 'But she wasn't, and he fell in the dirt!' He drummed his hands on the table. 'Good old Bunchy! Always funny when he was on his high horse, wasn't he?'

They laughed merrily, then Crum shook his head. Stroking Blenkinsop, he was feeding the little brown rat a sliver of cheese. Now a frown crossed his face. 'Eh? No, you don't get it. He *wasn't* on his horse, not that time.' Crum looked at his hand, calculating. 'And Bluebell, she wasn't what you'd call a *high* horse, she'd be – oh, let me see…'

Wiggler guffawed, wiggled his ears for good measure and punched his old crony on the arm. 'Crum, Crum, same as ever! How do you put up with him, Professor, eh?'

Morven had fallen silent. Much as he would like to have stayed in this parlour, with the steam rising from their hot toddies, with the fire leaping merrily in the grate, he was worried. What if they were found out? He was about to suggest they should be on their way, but he brightened at the word *Professor*.

A nickname? No, a prophecy! Excitedly, Morven began to tell his friends about his major scholarly discovery, and the Aon Fellowship, and the golden future before him – or rather, he would have done, had Crum not run away with his monologue and turned it into a description, considerably embellished, of the worm that used to live in one of Morvy's books.

'Remember how he used to pop up his little head, Morvy? And wave it all about? You'd have loved it, Wiggler, it was all wiggly like you. I think he must have been an old worm, though, because it was ever such an old book. Your favourite, wasn't it, Morvy? Didn't you have a name for it, just like I had a name for the worm? *Vy*-something, that's right, *Vy Tony*—'

'Crum, *shh!*' Anxiously Morven looked about them. Fortunately, the syllables which would have provoked a shocked silence in his old college dining hall, or in Webster's Coffee House, appeared to hold no meaning for the simple patrons of the Cat & Crown.

But Morven added, to be on the safe side, 'You must be thinking of some other book – someone else's. Dear me, but I think we'd better be off soon. Duties, duties—'

It was to no avail. Drunk already on a single hot toddy, Crum was hardly listening. 'Your rebel book Morvy,' he sailed on, 'you know the one. Would you believe, Wiggler, me and Morvy was almost rebels once. Well, almost. Remember that time we went missing, just before the Battle of Wrax? You were gone by the time we got back, married and all that, so we never *did* tell you the story—'

'Yes, fancy you being *married*, Wiggler,' Morven cut across, in a booming voice, adding, with a tilt of his tankard, 'Our compliments to your lady wife!' And he dropped his voice, muttering into Crum's ear, 'We *really* ought to go—'

Crum blinked. '*Go?* But we've just met Wiggler. And poor Blenkinsop's all nice and warm! We can't *go*, Morvy, don't be such a silly!' The peasant lad drained his tankard, wiped his mouth and burped happily. 'So tell us, Wiggler, about your lady wife. It must be amazing, having a fine place like this, running it together, and all.'

Wiggler smiled shyly. 'Well, it's the wife that runs it, really. And it's no bed of roses, don't get that idea. She can be a hard taskmaster, she can, just like Sergeant Bunch, but I wouldn't go back to the old days, no sirree, no matter how many barrels of squincy I have to lug up from the cellar. Aye, she's a good sort is my—'

Crum leaned forward, screwing up his forehead. 'But Wiggler, how did she lose her *eye*? I was wondering, see, because Zohnny Ryle's puss-cat—'

Astonished, Wiggler blinked, then burst into laughter. Just as well Baines was out the back, for she would hardly have been flattered by his hilarity at the very idea that he might have married *her*. 'Oh Crum, Crum, that's not my—'

Morven gasped. A gust of cold air had skirled through the parlour. New arrivals, that was all, in the front hall. But through the parlour door he glimpsed a face.

He grabbed Crum, dragging him under the table.

Wiggler dived down with them, astonished. 'Morvy! Crummy! What's up?'

'*Down*, don't you mean?' Crum giggled. His hand darted upwards, seizing Blenkinsop. 'Morvy, what are you playing at?'

'It's Rottsy and Supp! We're supposed to be in the Cloth Quarter. Wiggler, we've got to get out of here, or we're *for* it—'

Wiggler thought quickly. 'Out the back—'

Swiftly the two recruits made their escape, although it was only an escape of sorts. Of course they should have run through the hall, out into the yard and the lanes beyond. But Crum, drunk, thought it was all a game. Stuffing Blenkinsop back inside his tunic, he whooped, laughed, and thudded up the stairs.

Morven followed, struggling to catch him.

Meanwhile, Corporal Supp and Soldier Rotts looked appraisingly about the front parlour, eyes flickering over the common patrons. Yes, this was the place. Hadn't they heard a few things already from the spiteful harlots across the Gardens? The Nirry woman had been bad-mouthing them, it seemed. Well, now she was going to get her come-uppance. And *what* a come-uppance.

Supp looked beadily at the gulping Wiggler. Impassively, the corporal held up a parchment in his gloved hand, intoning, for perhaps the fiftieth time that afternoon, 'In the name of His Imperial Agonist Majesty, we are empowered to search these premises, and inspect the identity papers of all persons within. We have a warrant for the arrest of Miss Nirrian Jubb.'

Wiggler's face betrayed him at once.

So did his voice. 'Nirry? Not my Nirry!'

Chapter 25

THE WAY OF THE WORLD

What was she to do?

Tishy Cham-Charing had deliberated long and hard on the problem of Professor Mercol. The old man did not appear to be dead; he was breathing, if slowly, and a weak pulse still flickered, somewhere amongst the folds of his neck. He just would not wake. Nothing would wake him.

Time and again, Tishy had tried the keys in the lock. Impossible. If only she had noted the order; all she would have needed to do was turn each one the right way, the right number of times. Instead, until someone else came, or the Professor came round – and both prospects, right now, seemed decidedly remote – she was trapped in the Chamber of Forbidden Texts.

She did not despair. In fact, Tishy was more than a little excited. For some time, lamp in hand, she wandered about her comfortable prison, finding it to be of an extent greater by far than she had first imagined. Shadowy corridors between certain of the shelves led away into annexe after annexe. How Tishy wished she could absorb all these books, just by breathing in their delicious odours! It was a feeling that always overcame her in libraries, a sort of rapture. She did not believe for a moment that these books were evil, even if some of them were a little immoral.

Only the fear of being lost – the *chamber*, in truth, was a labyrinth – propelled Tishy back to where the Professor lay. In a cupboard near the stove she found, amongst extensive supplies of paper, ink, quills and the like, a coffee-pot, some coffee-grounds, a generously proportioned Varby cheese and a box of digestive biscuits. The Professor, to give him credit, had set up this little sanctum rather well.

Laying out the provisions on the table – and provisions, for her, included paper, quills and ink – Tishy carefully settled a cushion beneath the Professor's head, picked up the parchment that lay beside him and the little book he had tossed so contemptuously to the floor (she could not bear such disrespect), and prudently extinguished all but one of the little flickering oil lamps. Then she sat down in a circle of light, applying herself to her studies.

But what was she to study? At first, thinking she must practise her Juvescials, Tishy returned to *Something of the Winds: A Prophecy*.

Now what was this about?

I.

*Know that when the time came called the Time of Atonement, many and
many were those daughters and sons of man who from the Vale of Orok
ventured forth: to wrest new lives from perilous places, where hitherto
had dwelt only Creatures of Evil, these daughters and sons did go.*

II.

*And know that of these daughters and sons, none were at once so blessed
and cursed as those whom Agonis had held to his heart: by decree of Orok,
the dying god, blessed beyond others were the Children of Agonis, yet
cursed beyond others too were the Children of Agonis.*

III.

*For it was decreed that the Children of Agonis had proved themselves
unworthy of this fairest of the gods, and that the fate before them should
be harsh: no place of laving sun, warm sands or seas should thus be home
to them, nay, nor no green and wooded lands.*

IV.

*Instead, it was to northern lands of ice and snow that Orok, the dying
god, would send this tribe, that they should eke out their lives amongst
the Crystal Sky: for only there, the dying god decreed, in mountain
ranges mighty and remote, these Children of Agonis should Atonement
find.*

V.

*Yet many and winding are the paths of destiny, and many and winding
are the ways of man: for it happened that, under the command of a lord
called Ondon, the Children of Agonis came upon a green and wooded
land, when yet the icy mountains still were far away.*

Tishy sighed. How long had it taken her to get this far? The problems
of translation were huge; the book, alas, was written not in Juvescial
Standard but in that convoluted, ancient variant known as the Tongue of
Agonis; it was more than a little advanced for her, and she almost wished
Professor Mercol would wake up just so that he could help her – if, that
is, he *would* help her.

With a stab of alarm, Tishy wondered whether today's incident meant
the end of her lessons. She hoped not; she was quite prepared to forget
what had happened, if only the Professor would do the same. They had
both been overwrought, that was all. What man of learning could regard
such an incident as anything but trivial, set against the life of the mind?

So Tishy reasoned; nonetheless she was not quite convinced, and was too distracted to concentrate on Juvescials. She pulled other books from the shelves; soon the table was cluttered. Idly, she unrolled the Professor's parchment. Her heart thrilled. At the top, in elaborate script, was the name *University of Agondon*; at the bottom, squashed out in red, was the university seal. In between lay densely printed paragraphs, setting out the terms – such generous terms! – of the Aon Fellowship.

There was also space for the candidate's name. To Tishy's surprise, this was filled in already; there, in Professor Mercol's blotty scrawl, was the name *Plaise* – was that *Alexander*, or *Aloysius*? – *Morven*. Tishy frowned, revolving in her mind various young men from Agondon society. Plaise Morven? No, she had never heard of a Plaise Morven – lucky fellow, whoever he was.

If only the name could be her own!

On a mischievous impulse, she reached for pen and ink, scratched through the name of this Morven fellow, and – carefully imitating the Professor's scrawl – substituted *Laetitia Elsan Constansia Cham-Charing*.

If only, indeed!

Just a joke, of course.

Tishy sighed. It was no good fretting; the way of the world was the way of the world. Sitting back, she sipped her coffee, thinking over the day's extraordinary events. She thought of Mama – was Mama all right? She thought of Eay Feval; she thought of the rebels, and remembered the book the Professor had flung down, the book his former favourite had taken so much to heart.

Discourse on Freedom. By Mr Vytoni.

Oh well, at least it was in Ejlander.

For the first few pages Tishy continued sipping her coffee, nibbling on a digestive, shifting restlessly. After that, her eyes began to flick ever more rapidly over the pages. She let the coffee go cold and did not stir again until she had read the little book all the way through.

In the Royal Ejard Room, Bob Scarlet paced before the fire, pistol spinning in his hand. Smoky lamplight churned through the air and the slider picture, switched to red, loomed behind him mysteriously.

How tall he was, how handsome! His mask could not disguise that he was a fine figure of a man; he wore his three-cornered hat like a crown. The rebels found their doubts receding. Some, like Offero the Mole, were cowed and trembling; some were filled with sudden, wild happiness. Beautiful Magda Vytoni gazed upon him intently, her cheroot burning unregarded in her hand; Molly the Cut forgot the violence in her heart, while Figaro Fingers, despite himself, flashed his golden smile. The highwayman always had something of this effect. This was why, for all the stirrings against him, none had ever threatened him directly.

Flanked by Hul and Bando, the highwayman addressed the rebels in the cultured voice which revealed that, whoever he might be, he was no common member of the criminal classes. Wryly he spoke of his sorrow for the events of that morning, excoriating the folly of whichever rebel leader had ordered the bombing.

'That some of our followers will *do* such things is no reason why such things *should* be done. Gladly I would lay down my life for our cause, but would I conceal explosives upon my person and fling myself into a gathering of quality-folk? Some might call this a hero's death; I call it a coward's, and an act of grossest folly. What can it achieve but greater vigilance on the part of the Bluejackets? Are not our operations dangerous enough? Day after day we run the risk of discovery.

'Oh, I know what lay behind it. One of you ordered it, did you not? Perhaps it was the work of Figaro Fingers, perhaps Offero the Mole; perhaps Peter Impalini, even Folio Webster harbour secret resentments, behind their seeming loyalty to me. No, my friends, no protests, for many wear masks, for all that their faces appear to be bare. Harlequin, have you not found it to be so? I'm sure you have; sure, too, that *you* could be behind this outrage, quite as easily as any of these others. Might you not, in the very crudity of this display, have disguised the hand that once devised such exquisite entertainments in the days when your troupe was welcomed in the houses of the highest? Come, Clown, close your mouth, you might at least show the dignity of your inscrutable friend.'

The highwayman turned with a theatrical sigh. 'But not my Magda, beautiful Magda? Not big, shambling Onty Michan? Alas, I could not put it past even *you*; then, too, it has occurred to me that young Danny Garvice is more than a little adept in the arts of explosives. Hush, Danny, for have I not said that no great skill was needed for this operation? On the contrary, one might find in it more than a touch of Shammy the Hood, or 'Scars' Majesta. Ah, and if we speak of crudity, do we not think of Molly the Cut? No, Molly, you know it is so … But I have said, too, that in its very crudity this outrage may be meant to throw me off the trail. Roly Rextel, I have not spoken of you. A man of the cloth, from quality-stock – who more unlikely to bomb the Great Temple? Yet, from another view, who *more* likely?

'Enough, I weary of this. One of you ordered this action, and your intent, I am certain, was as much against *me* as against the Bluejackets. Oh, I could seek you out, and no doubt I could find you. But my friends, we have not the time to waste. If we are divided, we can but fall. Would I not rather secure your loyalty, *all* your loyalty, than indulge in recrimination? Let me admit it: last night's campaign was a failure. But must there not be failures on the path to success? The Wrax Opera was only the first of our plans. The odds against it were massive, but have we not learned from the mistakes we have made? Have we not, Hul? Have we not, Bando?'

The highwayman leaned against the mantelpiece, looking up at the slider picture. His voice dropped and the rebels strained to hear. 'Tonight, the Koros Palace is the scene of a masquerade, known as the Bird Ball. Already intelligence has reached me that the Ball will go ahead, despite today's events. It is not to be wondered at: are quality-folk to forgo their amusements, which are all that distract them from the guilt and secret fears that gnaw at their hearts? Besides, to cancel so important an occasion could have the gravest of consequences. The First Minister, I gather, is forcing his quality subjects to attend, or face vicious reprisals. It is a fitting irony. Let the Ball go ahead. And before it is over, the so-called Queen, the usurper's wife, shall be in my clutches!'

He turned decisively. 'My friends, doubt me not, for all is in place. Such a coup shall rock this régime to its foundations. Yet it is but the beginning of a greater, nobler plan. With the vast ransom the Queen must command, our forces will at last have the supplies we need. Then there can be no more delay. As I am your supreme commander, you must be my generals, forging our various bands into a united army.

'I had thought we must wait until Viana's season melted the harsh snows. Now I see we can wait no more, for the evil of the Bluejackets grows apace. Speed must be our weapon, and surprise too. For yes, my friends, the crisis is upon us. The final conflict is coming, when we take Agondon or die. For the man who holds Agondon holds this empire; such has always been the way, here in these chill northern lands. And who shall hold this empire but Robin Scarlet?'

It was a rousing speech, and might have ended there, with applause thundering round the hot chamber. For a moment, Hul thought it *had* ended. He marvelled: only a short time before, his leader's power had seemed at its lowest ebb, liable at any moment to slip from him entirely. Hul had feared a coup, that very day … Yet now, at first slowly, then all in a rush, new fears filled Hul's chest as the scarlet figure raised his hands for quiet, then resumed in a very different manner, filled as much with sadness as with rebel fervour.

'My friends, is there *still* doubt in your hearts? Can any amongst you think I speak empty words? I say to you, our victory is certain – I say to you we must triumph, for what true son of Ejland would not rally to our standard when at last it flies red and brazen over the fields? Ah, my friends, but for long I have carried a great and secret burden. I had thought to keep it until victory came at last, revealing myself only to the Bluejacket king, in the moment before I took his hated life. Now I see the folly of my pride, for what is my secret but the last and greatest spur our rebel forces need to secure our victory?'

Hul hissed, 'S-Sire, are you s-sure—'

His leader stayed him. 'My friends, look upon me in this mask for the last time. You have known me as Robin Scarlet, gentleman highwayman, scourge of the Wrax Road. But there was a time when I went by another name. Only Hul has been privy to my secret, but now it is a secret I share with you all.'

So it was that the rebel leader bowed his head, removing his three-cornered hat. Blondish locks cascaded down; then, slowly, he detached his mask.

Quiet had descended but for the crackling of the fire and soft patter of snow at the window. Then came the gasps as one set of eyes, then another and another, shifted from the figure that stood before them to the looming image in the slider picture – then back again. A smile came to the face of the rightful king as all who gazed upon him, even the coarsest, slipped from their chairs, sinking to their knees in awkward reverence. Had some of them prayed, it would not have been surprising. It was a tableau more holy than any that had been witnessed for long cycles in the Great Temple of Agonis.

But a tavern chamber, perhaps, is not the place for such a tableau – especially when someone has failed to lock the door.

Voices rang out – *Can't catch me!* and *Crum, come back!* – as all at once the door burst open and in floundered two hapless blue-garbed figures, tumbling together and crashing into one of the tables.

The King's eyes blazed. 'Bluejackets! Seize them!'

Chapter 26

RAY OF LIGHT

'*Whoa!* Whoa there, girl!'

After cantering away from Nirry's tavern, Cata had rapidly slowed down, aware of the dangers in the darkness and snow, and the ominous signals from her black mare. Through the twisting, narrow streets of the Island, they had proceeded for some time at a slinking pace. Rounding a corner, Cata glimpsed the lanterns lining Regent's Bridge. A patrol passed: Bluejacket guards. Oh, this was absurd! How long would it take to get to Corvey Cottage now? What dangers would she face on the way? Cata half-thought she would turn and go back; yes, she could go to the cottage in the morning.

But no. If Littler were back, she had to see him. She had to know what had happened to Jem. Another corner. Across the bridge. Then the flatlands: it would be easier there.

That was when the mare shied, slithering dangerously on the cobble-stones. Only with difficulty did Cata gain control again.

'*Shh. Shh.*' She leaned down, patting the mare's black neck. 'What is it? Tell me, girl, what is it?'

Calling on her Wildwood powers, Cata attuned her mind to the mare's. Something was wrong here, but nothing of the sort that Cata had expect-ed – no commonplace warning of Bluejacket evil, or villains lurking in dark doorways. To Cata, this city was a forest more dangerous than the forest she had known in her strange girlhood. She had not been fright-ened in the Wildwood and was not frightened now, not of any villains, whether blue-garbed or in rags.

But this was different.

The mare had turned towards a dark alley. And now, at the end of the alley, was the vision.

'Wh-what is it? Who is it?' Cata's breath came slowly. Her heart thumped hard. She put a hand to her forehead.

Then came the ray of light.

> *Come, meet the Empress of the Endless Dream!*
> *Now nothing will seem the way it seemed to seem:*
> > *Gold will gleam,*
> > *Time will stream*
> *When you meet the Empress of the Endless Dream!*

'Are you real?' said Cata. 'Or illusion?'

The rainbow lady came forward, gliding over the snow, light streaming from what should have been her face. And the music came from nowhere – sounding, Cata was certain, in her mind and nowhere else.

A second verse came:

> *Ah, see the Sister of the Sacred Night*
> *Who looks upon your face with blinding sight:*
> > *Endless light,*
> > *Timeless flight*
> *Is yours with the Sister of the Sacred Night…*

'Are you evil? Are you good?'

No answer came from the faceless one; only the music, only the song. From her earliest days, Cata had seen magic aplenty, but in this rainbow lady she sensed a magic more profound than any she had ever known before.

More profound, and more ominous too.

> *Embrace the Daughter of the Damned and Saved*
> *Who always waited on each road you braved:*
> > *You roared, you raved*
> > *Like those enslaved*
> *Still, you knew the Daughter of the Damned and Saved!*

'For me? Have you come for me?'

Quite why she asked this, Cata did not know. Gazing, entranced, into the golden light, she felt a shudder deep within her being, and knew it had nothing to do with the cold, with the night, or even with the unaccustomed fear that filled her now.

It was a sense of loss. Deep, impossible loss.

> *Look to the Mistress of the Mystic Quest*
> *Who longs to take you to her sacred breast:*
> > *East or west,*
> > *Final rest*
> *Awaits you with the Mistress of the Mystic Quest!*

Cata murmured, 'No. No, I won't come.'

She wrenched her eyes from the vision. All at once she knew her course was wrong. She must not go back to the cottage, not tonight. Jerking at the reins, digging her heels into the mare's flanks, she turned back to the tavern.

The song echoed behind her as she cantered away.

> *Can this really be the Empress of the Endless Dream?*
> *Can nothing still seem the way it seemed to seem?*

Ah, yet light will beam,
Love will teem
Between you and the Empress of the...

A Bluejacket patrol, checking her papers, was to delay Cata's return to the Cat & Crown. When she got back, she would find a certain small child – alone, shivering and sobbing – in Flowerdew Lane. Jem, she would gather – Jem! – had urged the child to flee to the warm tavern, before making a sudden, shocking departure.

This was to come. But what happened first?

'Come on, rebel! It's Oldgate for you!'

While Morven and Crum fell into rebel clutches, Wiggler and Baines, in another part of the tavern, wailed and wrung their hands. Desperate, they could only look on as Bluejackets hustled Nirry away, charged with conspiracy and crimes of terror. Bewildered, none of them could believe what was happening, least of all Nirry; but all knew that the sight of Sergeant Floss, lying senseless on the kitchen floor, could hardly bode well.

Meanwhile Jem, oblivious to all this, stood shivering in the lanes behind Redondo Gardens. Rushing out, crazy with longing for Cata, he had never even bothered to commandeer a horse. Now he knew it would be useless anyway. Already Cata would be far away. And how was he to find Corvey Cottage tonight? He would just get lost in the darkness and snow.

Miserably, he made his way back. He had left his coat inside and his teeth were chattering. He didn't care. He scuffed his boots in the slush; distantly, he heard the tolling of a bell. How strange to think it was only afternoon: the cold was deeper than any he remembered, even in the Valleys of the Tarn. He hugged himself, wishing Cata's arms were around him.

'But what a fool I am,' Jem said aloud. 'Why, I'm closer to Cata now than at any time for – oh, I don't know how many moonlives! We're *almost* together again, aren't we? Here we are, both in Ejland where we belong, and the quest's almost over. Didn't the harlequin say so? Oh, I *am* a fool! What's one night, when soon we'll be together – for eternity?'

With that, Jem forgot his chattering teeth. He could look forward to an evening with Nirry, couldn't he, in her nice warm tavern? What tales they could tell each other; what memories they could share!

It was as he was passing through deep shadows, under a heavy overhang of eaves, that Jem was startled by a powdery projectile, striking the wall behind his head. He heard a laugh and a small figure in a snowcape crashed into him, almost knocking him down.

Jem grabbed the child. 'Say, you're a little bruiser!'

'Let me go!' The child kicked and flailed.

'Hey, steady on!' With a struggle, Jem turned the little boy upside down, holding him by his ankles. The snowcape fell about the woolly-hatted head. 'What a brat! Didn't your mother tell you it's not polite to kick?'

'My mama,' came the muffled reply, 'was a warrior woman. She kicked who she liked. And my papa's a dangerous brigand, so you'd better watch out!'

'Wait, I know you!' Gracelessly Jem turned the child again, pulling down the concealing cape. A shaft of moonlight stuck a swarthy, indignant face. 'Now if ever anyone were the spitting image of his papa, it's you. Raggle, isn't it? Raggle, don't you remember me?'

'If you put me down I might.'

Jem put him down. 'In Zenzau, remember? But Raggle, what are you doing *here*? Are you living at Nirry's? Is your papa there? Is he there now? And where's Taggle? Come on, Raggle, tell me.'

The child pouted. '*I'm* Taggle.'

'Oh,' said Jem. 'So where's Raggle, then? I thought you two were inseparable.'

Raggle, as it happened, had been there only moments before, throwing the snowball that had failed to strike his brother. Now – so Taggle intimated – he would have skittered ahead, ready to burst from concealment, ammunition at the ready, when his brother came in search of him.

'He's hiding?' said Jem. 'I think we'd better find him, don't you? You boys shouldn't be out here in the dark. *Brr*, I wish I had a snowcape like yours.'

'It wouldn't fit you,' Taggle scoffed. '*And* it's mine,' he added indignantly, pulling back when Jem, with a laugh, tried to take his hand.

The little boy trudged ahead, calling for his twin. 'Brother, come out now! Brother, we're caught!'

In truth, it was only Raggle who was caught.

They turned a corner into Flowerdew Lane, the alley behind the Cat & Crown. Here snow fell more thickly, and in the pallid moonlight neither Jem nor Taggle could at first make out the hunched, sinister bulk of a Bluejacket coach, stationary at the end of the lane.

But they heard the sudden, high-pitched cry.

And saw the assailant, soon enough. Hefty, muffled in coat, scarf and hat, the figure dragged a small, kicking form along the lane, clapping a hand over the child's mouth.

Jem started forward. 'Hey! Leave him—'

A cloud obscured the moon. In the blackness, Jem felt a fist smashing the side of his head; he rallied, but then came a kick, and another, and heavy footsteps thudded to the end of the lane. Raggle screamed; there were shouted words. Jem scrambled up, but collapsed again.

When the moon came back, he was lying on his side, his head bleeding. Whimpering, Taggle hovered above him. Struggling back to his feet, Jem

159

heard a whipcrack and the rumble of the coach, driving away; then, shuddering, he recalled certain shouted words he had heard, moments before, in voices he recognised only too well:

'Shut your noise, brat! Save it for the sacrifice!'

'Have you got him, Polty? – Polty, quick!'

END OF PART TWO

PART THREE

In the Labyrinth

Chapter 27

BLENKINSOP IS INNOCENT!

Traditionally, Ejlanders had thought of the Festival of Agonis as a time for miracles.

In this darkest part of the year's round, when light failed early in the afternoons, when icicles hung from the gargoyles on the walls, there were those who would say that magic must be close at hand. Think of skaters whirling on frozen rivers, of children flinging snowballs in fields of white. Think of little bobbing, red-breasted birds, skittering in the branches of barren trees. Must this not be a time when the Love of the Lord Agonis, so often cloaked and secret, would long to make itself known in the world? How could their god not respond to the songs that rang out in his praise, all across the empire? How could he not manifest himself, witnessing the rapture in the faces of children, opening their god-day gifts?

Such were the superstitions of common believers in what must seem to us a more innocent age. Now, far into the reign of the Bluejacket king, few were the Ejlanders who expected miracles. In the provinces, no doubt, there would be sightings of the Lady Imagenta, as before; reports would come of miraculous cures, here and there. But all this was dismissed as the ignorance of peasants. Agondon had embarked upon a rational age, a hard, unforgiving age. So it was with all the more astonishment that many would hear what had happened on the evening of the Bird Ball.

Before that evening ended, the strangeness would be manifold; reports, next day, would be convoluted and wild, to be dismissed by many as madness, illusion. It all began with sightings of a certain extraordinary craft, a sort of ship of the sky, swooping and plunging through the cloudy air.

And what did observers make of the skyship? What thoughts filled them, apart from fear? This rather depended on who the observers were, and exactly where they had made their observations. Some, who had been on Regent's Bridge, spoke of the ship plunging terrifyingly down, scattering a Bluejacket patrol; in Ollon-Quintal, there was talk of a bolt of fire, shooting from the ship towards Ollon Barracks. Often those who purveyed these reports revealed in their faces a secret joy, hinting that a new and powerful enemy – a secret, magical enemy – had risen against the Bluejacket tyranny.

Others saw the skyship differently. Fleeing from the swooping vessel, they thought only of the colour of the riveted, metallic hull, and the crackling, fizzing aurora that played all around it. What could this be but a

Bluejacket secret weapon? What could this be but a warning to the rebels? And some would smile, some collapse in sobs, at the thought that the Bluejackets were invincible.

If only they could have looked inside the skyship!

Here, hovering against the padded ceiling, was a mysterious female form. A strange glow suffused her skin; a wild, unearthly music issued from her mouth. And below, two frightened boys and a big orange cat looked up at her, wide-eyed, between the sickening lurchings of the ship.

'B-But where are we going? What can this *mean*?'

'It's magic, Raj! Oh, if only I still had my orb!'

'Forget it, it vanished when Myla rose up—'

'Vanished? But how can it just have—'

'I don't know, I don't understand—'

'At least she's Myla again, not—'

'At least she's no older, but—'

'She's using her power—'

'And how much can—'

'Using it all up—'

'But why—?'

'*Aargh!*'

'*No!*'

❄ ❄ ❄

'We're ready, Hul?'

'Just waiting for Cata.'

'Drat the girl, where is she?'

'Wh-what about us?'

The speakers, in order, were Bob Scarlet, Hul, Bando and Morven. Crum was present too, but unable to speak; he had made so much noise upon being captured that the highwayman had insisted upon gagging him as well as binding his hands. Gulping, the Varlan looked apprehensively around the Royal Ejard Room, where the rebel convocation had now broken up. Tankards glittered on the emptied tables; some rolled on the floor. He shivered; the fire was dying, but no one added fuel.

Bob Scarlet spun his pistol on his finger, pacing before the slider portrait. The highwayman looked set to ignore Morven's last question, which disappointed Crum; after all, it was a very good question.

But he turned, as it happened, to the captive Bluejackets. 'Do? With you? I think we know what to do with double-crossers, don't we, Bando? Don't we, Hul?'

Crum gulped; Hul cleared his throat. 'Bob, I've said I'm not sure about this. Morven and Crum *were* on our side, weren't they? In Wrax?'

'Yes, and didn't they scuttle back to the Blues just as soon as they had the chance?' said Bando. 'If there's one thing I hate more than a coward,

164

Hul, it's a traitor. If you want their measure, look at the colour of their jackets.'

The highwayman, as if in agreement, brought his pistol against Crum's temple with a sharp *click!* 'Are they really idiots, or just pretending to be? They're slippery customers, that much is certain – but no more. This is one trap they won't worm their way out of!'

Crum's eyes goggled and, despite himself, he found himself thinking of the long worm, long as a snake, that Zohnny Ryle had found in the north field one Koros-season and taken home for a pet. Poor old Widdershins! If Crum had not been gagged, he would have told the story at once—

'P-Please sir,' said Morven, 'but we *are* idiots! – No, I mean, Crum's an idiot. – I mean, I'm Plaise Morven, author of the Jagenam Plaque-winning essay, *Issues of Prosody in the Jelandros, With Special Reference to the Provenance and Propriety of the Great Caesura*, aren't' I? – So I couldn't be an idiot, could I?'

Hul smiled. Bando snorted.

'It's just an accident that I'm in the army at all,' Morven went on, 'I should be at the university, but that doesn't mean … I mean, Juvescials, that's my field, b-but I didn't just study the Theatricals of Thell, I'm not a narrow specialist, I … you see, I've read Vytoni, the *Discourse on Freedom*, and—'

The highwayman gave a loud sigh.

'What I mean to say,' Morven added quickly, wishing he could adjust his spectacles, 'is that we had an accident, we ended up in the infirmary, we had no choice but to go back to … and then the rebels were defeated, and we were back with the … I mean, I mean, we never betrayed you, Master Scarlet, and we never would, never!'

Hul's smile returned and Morven puffed out his chest as far as he could – which, admittedly, was not far.

'I mean, Master Scarlet – s-sir,' he resumed uncertainly, 'if our jackets were the same colour as our hearts, they'd be red, red through and through! – And don't mind Crum.' Morven attempted a smile. 'He's never going to win the Jagenam Plaque, but he's as much on your side as I am – aren't you, Crum?'

It was perhaps as well that Crum could not reply. The Varlan had never had much time for Morven's rebel sympathies; so far as he could see, it all came from reading too many books and not knowing which side his taters were buttered, as old Farmer Ryle used to put it. But then, at this particular moment, all their taters were very much on the highwayman's side.

Crum gulped again, feeling the prodding of the silver pistol.

Bando was impatient. 'Can't we finish them off, Bob? We're wasting time.'

'Don't be ridiculous, old friend,' said Hul. 'They're on our side, I tell you! But yes, we're wasting time – let's untie them. They're with us now.'

The highwayman, ignoring both his old cohorts, eyed Morven with frank disdain. 'A pretty speech, but am I to be impressed that your *hearts* are red? The same is true of every man, as you will know, young fellow, when you have taken as many lives as I. Oh, we could change the colours of your uniforms quite easily, here and now—'

Crum wanted to point out that red and blue would make purple, and was annoyed that he could not; he was also annoyed that Blenkinsop was squirming uncomfortably inside his uniform.

Bob Scarlet could not help but notice. 'There's *something* odd about your hearts, I see – or one of them.'

'That's just B-Blenkinsop, s-sir,' said Morven, flushing.

'Oh? And who – or what – is *Blenkinsop*?'

'A brown rat. Crum found him somewhere, and—'

With a deft movement, Bob Scarlet ripped off several buttons from Crum's uniform, extracting the squirming, quivering little animal. He held up Blenkinsop by the tail – which Blenkinsop, unsurprisingly, did not appear to enjoy much.

Crum, for the first time, struggled in his bonds.

'We're wasting time,' Bando said again. 'By Viana's dugs, where's Cata?'

'Wait!' said Hul. 'That's it!'

'What's *it*?' Bando said irritably.

'Bando, Bob – it's the missing piece in our plan, don't you see? Let me explain...'

Hul's enthusiasm was so great that even Bob Scarlet deigned to listen. Plan B revolved around the 'cross-tunnels', the largely forgotten network of subterranean passages that radiated from the focus of the Great Temple. Hul had learnt of the tunnels from an old map he had found long ago in the university library, rolled up in a dusty corner with some mouldering illuminated manuscripts. Designed as 'routes of sanctuary' in ancient times, the five branches of the Agonist cross led to Temple College, the White Friars monastery, the Koros Palace, the Wrax Opera and the university. It was through the latter route that Hul, in his days as a rogue scholar, had made his illicit visits to the Chamber of Forbidden Texts: a crumbling wall in the basement of Webster's Coffee House led into the bowels of the university library, where a trapdoor opened the way into the tunnels.

In Plan A, the Wrax Opera scheme, Hul had wanted to bundle the Queen out through the tunnels, but the others had voted for the rooftops instead. The tunnels, it was true, were difficult and dangerous; tonight, nonetheless, they were the only way. Reconnaissance had established that the tunnel into the Koros Palace emerged in one of the nine retiring rooms that flanked the Imperial Ballroom. Each of these chambers, Hul had explained, was named after one of Ejland's Nine Provinces, and had a large painting of that province on the wall; the cross-tunnel door lay, evidently abandoned, behind a panorama of the Valleys of the Tarn, surmounted by the high mountains called the Kolkos Aros, or Crystal Sky.

The plan was this: Hul, Cata and Bando would make their way to the Tarn Room, from which Hul and Cata, in appropriate bird-garb, could easily slip into the Ball; Bando, meanwhile, would wait in the tunnel to assist with the kidnapping when Cata, calling upon her old friendship with the Queen, lured the startled girl into the retiring chamber.

'You're going to abduct … *the Queen*?' Morven gasped.

Crum's eyes grew wider. His knees trembled.

'Really, this plan is full of holes,' said Bando. 'How does Cata even recognise the girl if everyone's in a mask?'

Bob Scarlet smiled. 'I see you know little of protocol, my friend. The identities of the royals are never concealed – *that* would be quite improper. Besides, the guests unmask at midnight. No, I should imagine that silly girl can be taken easily enough. Hm, Hul?'

Hul was less sanguine. 'I'm afraid Bando's right. The plan *is* full of holes. But now we've just filled up a large one! Morven and Crum are Bluejackets, right? I'll bet they're on guard duty in the palace tonight—'

'We are, actually,' said Morven, 'and nearly late—'

'But you won't be,' said Hul. 'Because that's where you're going, right now—'

'Old friend, are you mad?' Bando burst out.

'No, Bando, listen. We *need* Morven and Crum. They'll keep guard on the Tarn Room. That way we'll make sure nobody's there when we're coming and going. They can say the room's been closed or something, keep people out until the coast is clear—'

'You *are* mad!' said Bando. 'How can we trust them?'

Hul clapped a hand on Morven's shoulder; for a moment, as they stood side by side, the two bespectacled scholars looked remarkably similar. 'I got to know this young man pretty well last time,' Hul said, 'and I'd swear he's a goodhearted fellow. I'd trust Plaise Morven with my life, and I don't mind saying it. After all, he's a follower of Vytoni.'

Bando groaned. 'And the *other* one?'

Sweat rolled down Crum's forehead. Anxiously he looked at Blenkinsop, who still swung back and forth in the highwayman's hand.

Poor Blenkinsop, he must be dizzy!

'The idiot?' said Bob Scarlet. 'We might keep *him* hostage.'

'That's it,' said Bando. 'His friend seems fond of him.'

'Yes,' said Hul, 'and what's he going to say when Crum's missing, hm? Or won't anyone notice?'

'S-Sir, I swear that—' Morven began.

'Yes, he's fond of him,' said Bob, jabbing his pistol in Morven's direction. 'But not, perhaps, so fond as the idiot is of *this* fellow.'

The pistol jabbed at Blenkinsop's stomach. *Not Blenkinsop! Blenkinsop is innocent!* Crum screeched behind his gag. His face was purple. His eyes popped.

'He'll do anything, I swear it,' Morven cried, 'if only—'

'So I thought,' said the highwayman, stuffing Blenkinsop into a pocket of his coat. 'Untie them, Bando.'

'You m-mean it, s-sir?' Morven gasped.

The hapless recruits had almost collapsed in gratitude when a wild cry split the air. The door burst open.

The highwayman spun round, ready to shoot.

It was only Wiggler – but this was Wiggler as no one had seen him before. His periwig was lost and his natural hair stuck up at angles, as if he had been pulling at it by the roots. His face was flushed and glazed with tears. Slumping to the floor, he beat at the carpet, making inarticulate cries. In his delirium of grief, he did not even notice the peculiar fate that had befallen his old army cohorts.

'Come, Goodman Olch, don't take on so,' cried Baines, blundering after him, 'it's not over yet—'

'But what's happened?' cried Morven. 'Wiggler, what—'

Baines sank beside the sobbing young man, whose stiff red ears looked incapable of wiggling ever again. She stroked him, rocked him, begging him in a maternal voice to *hush, hush*.

Only as his sobs subsided could Wiggler reveal the terrible truth that Morven and Crum, with a rush of horror, had already suspected.

'Nirry … *Jubb*?' cried Morven. 'But that's who we were—'

'Morven, what do you mean?' said Hul.

'That's why we were here … looking for a rebel, the one behind the bombing, or the one they say … we were lost, and Rottsy and Supp, and … oh, this is a terrible mistake, it has to be! Crum, quick, we've got to see Sergeant Bunch *at once*, we've got to—'

Morven plunged forward, but a brutal hand flung him back. He smashed into the wall, his spectacles falling askew.

He cowered. Crum sank to his knees, shrieking through the gag that still bound his mouth.

'Mistake?' cried the disgusted highwayman. 'Do you think the Bluejackets will admit a *mistake*? What do you take me for, as big a fool as you? So, you fellows were in on this, were you? You *knew* this would happen—'

Hul gasped, 'No, Bob, I told you, not Morven, not Crum—'

'W-We thought … we didn't … we didn't *know*—'

Bando cocked his rifle. 'I'll finish them, boss!'

'Bando, no!' Hul swung the barrel angrily aside. 'Don't you see, this makes our plan more urgent than ever? Don't you see how much we *need* Morven and Crum? Listen, Morven: there'll be no going to sergeants. You'll carry out the plan, just as we agreed – hm?'

Morven nodded earnestly. Crum gurgled through his gag.

'But what about my Nirry?' wailed Wiggler, who still huddled piteously on the floor. 'Those brutes, they'll kill her—'

'Not right away, they won't,' Hul offered helpfully, 'and when they—'

'A traitor's execution?' mused the highwayman. 'Hm, they'll advertise that *widely* before—'

'She's not a traitor!' Wiggler cried.

'Well actually,' said Baines, 'when you *think* about it—'

'I was going to say,' Hul said quickly, 'that they won't kill her at all. Not if we've got something to bargain with. And that's *exactly* why we need the Queen—'

Wiggler was oblivious. 'They'll take her to … to Oldgate, won't they?' He struggled upright, shaking off the clinging Baines. 'I've got to go to her. I'm her husband, they've got to let me see her—'

'Oldgate?' said Bando. 'But Figaro Fingers, surely we can—'

'Don't even think about it,' Hul snapped. 'Fingers might do something for petty thieves, harlots, backstreet murderers. But the Temple bomber? I mean … I mean that'll be top security, the Bluejackets won't risk—'

'Old friend, a man is losing his wife!' Bando seized Wiggler, pinching and pummelling the poor fellow's cheeks. 'Ah, the tears that fill his eyes! Hul, you cannot know such suffering! *Cold* Hul, *cruel* Hul—'

'On the contrary,' Hul cried, 'that's precisely why—'

'I'm going to Oldgate!' Wiggler wrenched away, blundering to the door.

'Not so fast, my friend.' Bob Scarlet barred his way. 'Your pretty little wife might squeal out quite a few secrets before the Blues have done with her—'

'Goody Olch? Never!' Baines cried, shocked.

The highwayman ignored her. He looked levelly at the distraught Wiggler. 'And what about you, my friend, hm? What would *you* reveal, in vain hopes that your wife might go free?'

Wiggler faltered, 'I … I – no, I swear—'

'The Queen,' Hul said firmly. 'It's the only way.'

Snuffling, Wiggler nodded. He slumped against the wall.

'Now quickly,' said the highwayman, 'we must leave this place and not return. The Blues could be back at any moment.' He reached up to the frame of the portrait over the fire, clicking it back to the image of Ejard Blue. 'Morven, Crum, off you go.' (Crum, who was still gagged, made an inarticulate protest.) 'The rest of you, come with me. Everything's ready for tonight, Hul?'

'Everything,' said Hul. 'Only … where's Cata?'

As if in answer, the door flew open. It was Cata, with a sobbing Taggle in her arms.

'Cata, where *have* you—' Hul began.

But Cata's expression made him stop. A terrible hollowness filled her eyes.

'I – I found him in the alley,' she breathed. 'Something's happened. Something terrible—'

The cry that broke from Bando's throat was longest and loudest.

※　※　※

In the Koros Palace, another drama was preparing itself.

The sparse chamber which Umbecca had provided for the Widow Waxwell was little better than a servant's quarters. One might have called it a cell: the walls were whitewashed and there was only a narrow bed, one chair and a brass Circle of Agonis hanging on the wall.

The Widow was on her knees, praying, her single hand clasping her mutilated stump. Terrible thoughts filled her mind. For how long, how cruelly long, had she held back her feelings about Lector Feval! Oh, there were things she was not meant to know; but things she had realised long ago. She thought of the severed leg she had taken in her arms; she might have sunk down, sobbing, but her eyes remained dry, gazing on the Circle of Agonis.

Strength. She must pray for strength.

She thought of Umbecca's sudden, wild anger. Meekly the Widow had scurried away; now, she could almost wish she had stayed, wish she had shouted the terrible truth into that bloated, stupid face.

Lost in these thoughts, she did not at first see that a servant had entered; only slowly did she realise that the girl, as she stoked the fire, was snivelling back tears.

The Widow turned. 'What is it, my dear?'

'I … I'm sorry, ma'am,' gulped the maid, wiping her eyes.

Painfully, the old woman rose to her feet. 'But child, what *is* it? Tell me, what's happened?'

And all at once, the girl collapsed into her arms. 'Ma'am, I know it's not my place, but it's not right – it's just not right! It – it's Jilda, ma'am. They've – they've sent her back to Chokey's!'

A shudder passed down the Widow's spine. 'No. No, this cannot be!'

She rocked the servant-girl, stroking her hair. And gazing again upon the Circle of Agonis, the old woman could only hope that her prayers would be answered.

Strength. She needed all her strength.

Chapter 28

SCREAMING SKIN

Polty! But how could it be?

With icy hands, curled like claws, Jem clung to the back box of the swaying coach. The whip cracked again. Precariously they swivelled through twisting lanes, rumbling under eaves burdened heavily with snow. Bluejackets passed, lanterns swaying. *Squish, squash* went their boots through the slush. How Jem envied them their bearskin coats! And how he prayed the patrols did not see him, clinging to this government coach!

Ah, but for how much longer could he hang on? Fresh snow flurried; Jem's teeth chattered and he clenched them tight. Soon he would be frozen, falling rigidly to the cobblestones.

He must think of Raggle. *Yes, Raggle.* Jem shut his eyes, but it was the little boy's captor that rose up in his mind, grinning and leering like a depraved vision of evil. *Oh Polty, Polty!* Jem saw his enemy as the bloated bully in Irion, tormenting him, then as the handsome Bluejacket he had become after Commander Veeldrop owned him for his son. Rage burned in Jem's heart. He thought of what Polty had done to him, and worse, far worse, what Polty had done to Cata. If Jem could revenge himself on Polty, he would. But, as if he were a child again, he saw Polty straddling him, pinning him down; he saw a hard fist, swinging savagely back.

And yet, what of Polty as Jem had seen him last, convulsing on a cracked, shimmering floor, deep within the Sacred City of the Unangs? Screaming, Polty had clutched a bloodied, eel-like organ, severed moments earlier by the Sultan's scimitar.

For Jem, there had been no time to see what happened next; he supposed that Polty had bled to death, vanishing into the Realm of Unbeing where he belonged. But then, thought Jem, he had known for a long time that Polty had become an agent of Toth. Hadn't he seen Polty in his demon guise, skin turned blue, flames rippling upwards from his blazing hair?

Jem snapped his eyes open, dispelling the vision. The coach strained uphill; from inside he heard a gasp, then a scream, then the scream was swiftly muffled. He heard Polty's laughter. Jem cursed. Wildly, he imagined hauling himself over the top of the coach, flinging open the door, pummelling Polty, wrenching Raggle from the monster's arms ... Impossible. Jem could never equal Polty's strength. Besides, the cold had almost paralysed him. For now, to cling to the back of the coach was as much as he could do.

Linkboys squeezed past. Torches flaring brightly, the boys led two huddled, muffled gentlemen down the dangerous incline of the street. Jem heard elderly, quavering voices:

'An outrage! In a holy place, I ask you!'

'The holiest! They've gone too far this time!'

'We must strike back, and fast!'

'Strike without mercy!'

The words chimed with others Jem had heard as he made his way into the city that day, through the check-points and heavily patrolled streets. Something had happened, that much was clear. But what had this to do with Polty and Bean and whatever foul game they were playing now? There had to be a connection, Jem was certain. He had to find out where they were taking Raggle.

Already Jem had a terrible suspicion.

Soon enough, he knew he was right. A mournful carillon sounded on the air, as if immense bells were directly overhead. Then came the tollings, once, twice … Yes, Jem knew where they were going now. Moonlight shone through the ragged clouds and he made out the familiar Temple Precinct, sinister in the snow.

The bells tolled a third time, then a fourth as the tombyard gates swung open. Flattening himself against the back of the coach, Jem prayed the sentries would not look behind them. Now the bells had tolled five times, six. Jem guessed there would be more sentries ahead, guarding the entrances to the Great Temple. Bracing himself, he leapt from the box, rolling into a heavy drift of snow, heaped on the verge of the crunching drive. Quickly he scrambled into the shadows of a tombstone, huddling, shivering, in the impassive darkness. Still the bells tolled, seven, eight.

Jem peered from behind the massy stone. Through swirls of snow he saw a lantern, juddering in Bean's arm, then Raggle, struggling in Polty's grip. There were words, too, perhaps curses, threats; from this distance, Jem could not make them out, but once he thought he heard *dungeon*, and once, *sacrifice*. It was what he had feared. Bleakly, the bells resounded for a ninth time, then a tenth, and Jem recalled what he had witnessed in the crypt on the night Myla almost met her death. Then it had been Tranimel who led the child-killings, before Toth broke from the Realm of Unbeing. What worse excesses had the anti-god contrived, what hideous depravities to feed his evil energies, now that he inhabited the First Minister's body? Anger surged through Jem like a flame, almost driving out the cold that besieged him.

Eleven tollings, twelve. For a moment Bean remonstrated with his master, until Polty gestured contemptuously; he swung Raggle over his shoulder and Bean could only scurry after him, lantern swinging violently, as he made his way towards a side entrance of the Temple. Between two vast buttresses of ancient stone was a low door, almost obscured in the gloom. Sentries parted to let them through. They were gone, and the bells tolled thirteen.[1]

Jem dashed his fist against his head. He cursed his helplessness. What could he have done? Rushed forward? He'd have been captured, killed. He hugged himself tight. The cold had seeped into his very bones. He supposed he could get help, but where? Could he even find his way back to Nirry's tavern? Would there be time? Despairingly he gazed around the dark tombyard, a deathly garden with its hunched slabs and headstones and tangled, barren trees. Forbiddingly, like a vast, impregnable fortress, the Temple rose above him. Guards would be everywhere. It did not matter. Somehow Jem must find his way inside.

'Harlequin,' he murmured, 'can you help me now?'

But Jem's teeth chattered and his words were lost.

❀ ❀ ❀

'Shut up, brat! Want me to dash your brains out, eh?'

The stairs were spiral, turning and turning; the crypts that lay below were a dark labyrinth. With each downward step, Bean's heart sank, and sank more as Polty swung his burden through the air. Raggle's skull scraped the slimy walls, almost smashing into the hard stone. Louder and louder his squeals came, bursting through his makeshift gag. Polty chuckled, crushing the child against his breast again in a parody of tenderness.

Bean, with the lantern, stumbled behind. 'P-Polty, careful!'

'The brat's going to die anyway, isn't he?' Still came the squealings, muffled in bearskin. 'Can't you see I'm being merciful, Bean? Let him lose a bit of his useless brain, and he might just keep still. Perhaps I could break a limb or two, eh, or poke out his eyes?' The chuckle came again. 'Remember last moonlife? Remember the fun we had with the tobarillo?'

'Yes, Polty,' Bean said miserably. He had tried to forget the incident in question, when his drunken friend, grinning all the while, had prodded a baby's eye with a lighted tobarillo. First the tender lashes and lids had burned away, then the eye-flesh sizzled like poaching eggs until, like the contents of a lanced boil, the vile jelly burst from inside. Polty had cursed, furious at the waste of a good tobarillo; still, he lit another one which (while Bean vomited in a corner) he applied eagerly to the baby's other eye.

'I d-don't think you should try that again, Polty,' said Bean. 'R-Remember what the First Minister said.'

---

[1] The bells, that is, have rung in the 'Thirteenth Fifteenth'; in our world, the time would therefore be just a little after seven o'clock at night. *Vide* the Appendix, 'Time in the Orokon', in the first book in the sequence, *The Harlequin's Dance*.

Polty sighed grudgingly; eye-burning had been only one of his excesses. He had broken a child's fingers, one by one; he had pulled out a baby's tongue by the roots; he had slit noses, sliced off ears, gelded an annoying, snivelling little boy and carved his initials into the bellies and thighs of several infant girls.

There was more he would have done, but after a limb-lopping session Toth had demurred, demanding (not unreasonably) that his victims come fresh to the altar. With ill grace, Polty had restricted himself since then to a little playful slapping, some arm-twisting and some gentle violation of the prettier girl-children, sometimes with the aid of W'enge.

If Bean was relieved, still he feared that Polty might get carried away again.

'R-Remember, Polty, this one's special.'

'Hah! Just a brat like the others, if you ask me.'

'But T-Toth said so! You've got to trust him, haven't you?'

Bean should have known this was dangerous territory. A foul corridor stretched before them, glistening dankly in the light of the lantern. They had reached the lowest and most ancient level of the crypts, hard by the echoing chamber where the First Minister, watched by his black-garbed Brotherhood, would carry out his depraved rituals.

Bearing tonight's victim towards the cells, Polty turned back angrily. 'Trust Toth? What do you mean, trust him? Wasn't he going to put Penge back today? And here I am, still in the same miserable, mortified state! Bean, if there were any other way, I'd break with him now.'

'Really, Polty? You're thinking about it?'

Polty's eyes narrowed. 'What are you *saying*, Bean? You think it's a good idea?' Fishing in a pocket, he produced a bunch of keys, jabbing one, then another, into the lock of the cell. 'Here, let me have some of that light. We'll put him in with the back-up baby, eh? A bit of company for the brat. Who says I'm not filled with the milk of human kindness?'

Bean shuffled closer. He had hoped he could get through tonight without seeing what Polty called the *back-up baby*. The sight was always distressing; lately, it had begun to upset him more and more.

He said quickly, 'Polty, but *could* we break with Toth, do you think? Go off somewhere, just you and me, perhaps to another country, and—'

'Bean, don't be so wet!' The child had resumed his struggles; visibly, Polty resisted the temptation to bash its head against the wall. 'Idiot, how can I leave before Penge is restored?'

'B-But you just said you can't trust him! He's mad, Polty! He talks about destroying the world, and—'

'What good's the world to me, with Penge in a pickle jar?'

This was not going as Bean had planned. How he wished they could escape! For all that he had seen of Toth's power, still Bean could not quite believe it encompassed the world. If only Polty could forget Penge, contenting himself with W'enge! What happy days they could still share, master and servant, far away, luxuriating in some warm exotic clime!

Often Bean had attempted to expand upon this theme, but always Polty had silenced him viciously; now he simply opened the door of the cell. 'Ugh, that stench! The back-up baby's getting worse, eh, Bean?'

Revealed in the lantern light was a squalid, mean chamber with damp mossy walls and a straw-lined floor. Polty cast down his burden with relief, expertly grabbing Raggle as the child tried, inevitably, to break away. Pressing a knee on the little chest, Polty swiftly bound ropes around the wrists that were too thin for manacles.

A groan sounded from the darkened end of the cell.

'Did you bring Vy a crust, Bean? Don't forget, we've got to feed the back-up baby.'

'I thought *you* liked to do that, Polty.'

'I don't feel like it, all right?' Polty snapped. '*And* I'm busy.' He turned back to his task, applying a tighter gag to the little boy's mouth. 'Never mind, brat, it won't be for long. Just keep Vy here company, eh? What have you got to worry about? Soon you'll be on the slab and it'll all be over. Easy.'

Polty might have been taunting the child, but Bean detected a pathos in the words. Poor Polty! Bean would do anything to relieve his friend's suffering. But did Polty believe him? Polty, Bean thought sadly, had never trusted him quite so much since a certain event in Unang Lia, one in which Penge had been notably involved. But what other side-officer would serve him so well? One day, perhaps, Polty would see that Bean was the best friend he had ever had, the only friend who would never forsake him.

Such are the ways of deluded love.

Sighing, setting down the lantern, Bean searched his coat for the stale, somewhat mouldy chunk of bread which was all that Polty thought appropriate for the nourishment of the back-up baby. For a time, Bean had secreted other little treats in his pockets, apples and carrots and biscuits and once a slice of chocolate cake, which had made rather a mess. When Polty found out, he became enraged, speaking of treachery, of betrayal. Only through copious tears and pleas had Bean averted disaster.

Shifting the lantern, he exposed the stinking, spreadeagled figure that was chained against the far wall. It was a grown woman, naked and heavily pregnant. Her hair was matted; worms and cockroaches crawled across her flesh; rats had gnawed away several of her toes. Between her legs were piled quantities of straw – in anticipation, no doubt, of the happy event; the straw, at present, was caked with excrement.

Gulping, Bean ripped off a corner of the crust. Soaking it in a pannikin of stale water, he held it to the woman's mouth. She turned her head away, moaning again. Gingerly, Bean tried to push it between her lips.

How he loathed these duties! How he loathed himself! But Bean was a prisoner, just as much as this pitiful victim.

'You've got to eat, Vy. Come on, for the *baby*.'

A stertorous breath was the only reply. The woman could no longer speak, and Bean was sorry; there had been a time when they had conversations of a sort, before Polty had smashed in her teeth. Like a fool, she had protested a little too loudly at one of the baby-tortures it amused Polty to carry out in front of her. If only she had heeded Bean's warnings and kept quiet! Still, he thought, perhaps a woman couldn't help that sort of thing. Not that Bean knew much about women. This was the first one he had even seen naked.

He gave up on the mush, holding the pannikin to the woman's lips instead. At least she drank a little.

'Won't be long now.' Stepping forward, shouldering Bean aside, Polty ran a finger down the woman's distended belly. A stream of water shot into his face, but Polty only laughed. Without even bothering to wipe his face, he pushed himself up against the chained woman, covering her, as if protectively, with his bearskin coat. But Bean knew what was happening; Polty *would* enjoy his little games of pretend. Couldn't he see that he was only humiliating himself? But no: bending at the knees, as if to find the right place, Polty made obscene motions with his hips, in and out, in and out, under the domed belly.

Bean turned away, but now Polty, he knew, was sweeping back the woman's matted hair, whispering in her ear, but loud enough for his friend to hear, 'Well may you blame others for your fate, my pretty, well may you blame the whole world!' (In and out, in and out.) 'Have you not brought it all upon yourself? This is the punishment of your sin, my pretty.' (In and out, in and out.) 'To think, that once you were the proudest of society belles! Who would have imagined you would be reduced to this? Ran off with young Javey Heva-Harion, didn't you?' (Rut, rut.) 'Found yourself abandoned soon enough, didn't you? (Rut, rut.) 'Ended up in Chokey's, didn't you?' (Rut, rut.) 'Then a little accident, just when we had an opening for a back-up baby! No, you never thought this was where it would lead, did you?

Polty broke away, shouting now. 'Dirty slut, don't you think I remember you prancing up and down at the Ball in Irion, keeping all the fellows hanging on a leash? Who did you think you were, some kind of goddess? Didn't you know you had a horsy face? It was *horsy*, everyone said so!'

Polty pawed the straw with his boot. Holding up his hands, he flung back his head like a rearing steed. He whinnied. 'Oh, it's as well I smashed out your teeth, you ugly bitch! But don't worry, you won't need them any more!' He slapped the woman's face. Her head lolled, sobbing. 'This is where it all ends, Miss Vyella Rextel, this is where it ends!'

Bean clenched his fists. How he longed to intervene! But he dared not, he dared not! Through hot tears he looked away, towards the tied-up child at the other wall, no longer struggling but staring, wide-eyed, at the lurid scene.

Polty turned abruptly. 'Come on, Bean, I'm off to Chokey's.'

Bean gasped. 'Polty, no! Toth said we had to stay down here. We're on duty, Polty!'

Rolling his eyes, Polty gestured to the prisoners. 'And where's *she* going? Where's *he* going? Use your head, Bean! We've done our day's work. What are we, sentries? It's early yet. Come on, we can have a nice evening at Chokey's, then get back here for midnight.'

'But Polty, if Toth finds out—'

'And what's he going to do? Eh, Bean?'

'He's magic, Polty!'

'Magic, and he can't even put Penge back on? How can he expect a man to endure—'

'It must be hard to *do*, Polty, I mean—'

'I'm sick of taking his orders, sick of it, do you hear?' Polty spat into the straw. 'And sick of your whining, too. You just don't *want* to go to Chokey's, do you? Didn't I say I'd help you? Didn't I say I'd give you advice? You're such a girl, Bean!'

Polty grabbed the lantern, striding out of the door. He flung the keys behind him. 'And lock up when you've finished. You can always practise on Vy, she's spread and ready. Just be careful of the back-up baby, we never know when we'll need it. Not that I imagine that's much of a problem – we're not exactly talking *Penge*, are we? Not with you!'

'Polty, wait!' Bean fumbled with the lock as the lantern retreated down the dripping corridor. More than his fear of Toth, Bean at this moment was terrified just of being left in the dark.

'Polty, I'll come to Chokey's, anything! But wait!'

Chapter 29

WOBBLE, WOBBLE

'Oh, Eay ... Oh, Eay ... Oh, Eay...'

For a long time this was all Umbecca said, repeating the syllables until they became a mantra. On a gilt-armed chair beside the sickbed the fat woman creaked from side to side, shuddering in a slow rhythm of grief. From time to time she reached for the little table behind her, fumbling at a multi-tiered, spinning platter piled prodigiously high with her favourite delicacies. Umbecca derived no pleasure from the cream horns, mince pies or individual blueberry cheesecakes she would stuff unthinkingly into her little mouth. Her attention was all for the bed, and the limbless thing that lay there. From time to time she would dab Feval's forehead with a damp cloth, or lean forward, kissing his neck or lips. How could she believe he would not be well again?

'Oh, Eay ... Oh, Eay ... Oh, Eay...'

The Widow had not returned; the others, even the apothecary, were getting ready for the Ball. Umbecca was alone with the torso on the bed. On the covers around it she had laid the four severed limbs, all in correct positions, as if it were only a matter of time before they would be fused again to the cauterised stumps. Perhaps, with the Love of the Lord Agonis, Umbecca could make it happen. Painfully, she slipped to her knees beside the bed, clasping her hands in prayer. What had happened to the faith that once had burned so brightly in her heart? Her eyes roved around the walls, gazing as if for support at the holy icons and the big golden Circle of Agonis. She struggled to remember her litany-lines, but all she could do was mouth the mantra as before.

'Oh, Eay ... Oh, Eay ... Oh, Eay...'

The wind howled and rattled round the Koros Palace; the fire plunged and plopped in the grate. Umbecca thought of the days before she had met her beloved spiritual advisor. Was she not sensible of all she owed him? There she had been, in her provincial fastness, humbly accepting her lowly lot; then came the handsome, urbane Feval, like an emissary from the great world, sent to call her to her destiny. Oh, but how could a woman of such power, such splendour still be filled with such hopeless yearnings? Eay, dear Eay, had given her so much; but never had he given her what she really wanted.

Umbecca ran a hand over a cold, purple arm. How she wished that arm could hold her tight! She kissed it, licking at the encrusted blood, all thought of prayer forgotten now. A rumbling, like a subterranean tremor, began deep within her bloated form. Her caresses moved to the torso. Impatiently she pulled back the blankets; a limb tumbled to the floor, but Umbecca did not care. Her hand ran across the sweaty, hairless chest; the torso gibbered; the hand ran lower. Umbecca moaned like a seal giving birth. She rucked up her skirts, her body juddering like an enormous jelly. Blindly she reached behind her, pawing for the platter, desperate to stuff her mouth with food, more food.

'Will this do, Umbecca?'

Umbecca screamed. Her bladder gave way, soaking her petticoats in acrid cascades.

'*Silas Wolveron!* No, it can't be—'

But the figure was unmistakable. Dressed in his familiar dun-coloured robes, the old man had pushed back his cowl, revealing the empty, gaping holes where his eyes had once been. In one hand he held his gnarled staff; in the other, he extended an oozing cream horn, his mouth parting in a grisly smile.

'What are you doing here? How did you—?' Umbecca struggled to pull herself up from the floor, but all strength had left her. She cowered back against the Lector's bed, her sodden skirts slithering back over her thighs, her mouth sticky with pastry flakes, icing sugar and blood. 'You're … you're *dead*, you—'

The smile became a laugh as the figure before her shifted and blurred, resuming its true shape.

'First Minister! I—'

'You thought I was another?' The white-garbed form moved nearer, taking a bite from the cream horn. 'Or perhaps you would *like* me to be another?'

Cream rimmed his mouth, dripped from his chin. Umbecca rallied. She staggered to her feet. 'Impertinent man, what are you doing here? Are you not aware that this is a lady's bedchamber?'

'Actually, my lady, this chamber is the Lector's. But I am more interested in what *you* are doing here. Should you not be readying yourself for the Ball? How are we to support ourselves through a long and tedious evening if we are not diverted by your delightful Harlequin Owl?'

Umbecca looked confused. 'Ball? What are you talking about? How can I – when…'

'You would attend if Feval could too?'

'Of course I – how can you…'

Tranimel licked his creamy fingers. He looked at the dishevelled bed, then at the carpet around it. 'Dear me,' he murmured, 'here's a leg – just lying on the floor. How careless.' He brought the stiff, purple thing up to his face and smelled it as if it were a piece of game. 'Do you know, I think it's rotting already?'

179

Umbecca watched him, wide-eyed. 'Eay's leg? Never—'

'Unless he had gangrene, did he? No, the heat in here is stifling, that's what's done it. Still, I dare say he's cold with no blanket.' Tranimel stepped towards the bed, prodding the patient. 'Hm, Torso? Will you answer me, Torso? Ho, a cagey fellow, this one—'

'Leave him!' Umbecca gasped. 'He's sick—'

'Sick, on the night of the Bird Ball? What, and he'll get himself thrown out of society? I can't see that happening to *this* fellow, can you? If there was one thing I always said about Lector Feval, it was that this was a man who would stick to society like a limpet. And he has, hasn't he? Lady Cham-Charing tries to banish him for good and what happens? Back he comes, more powerful than ever. Can't keep a good man down, hm? Wouldn't you agree, dear lady?'

As he spoke, the First Minister strutted backwards and forwards with the severed leg, stumping it across the carpet like a walking cane. Now, as he turned back towards the bed, he left the leg behind him; the leg, however, did not topple. Instead, the rotting limb began to jig about a little, as if in readiness for a sprightly dance.

Umbecca clutched a hand to her face.

'But what's one leg without another?' cried the First Minister, flinging out the other leg to join its fellow. Sparks crackled in the air and a disembodied music began to swell as both legs now scissored in and out, keeping time to a merry gavotte. Here and there a stream of fat oozed down the bloody flesh, a chunk of charred meat fell to the floor.

The arms came next; in an instant, all four limbs were working in consort, heels clicking, hands clapping. Umbecca half-swooned, but Tranimel was not finished yet. While the fat woman watched helplessly, he leaned over the bed, picking up the torso with its lolling, drooling head; then, as if it were of no weight at all, he hurled it into the centre of the moving limbs.

Sparks flashed; now the severed parts danced as one, as if held together by the gleaming, fizzing aura. Umbecca gazed, fascinated and horrified, at the dangerous jerkings of Feval's head, at the leech-marked chest and belly, at the obscene flappings and bobbings at the torso's base.

'Go to him, dear lady. Join him in his dance.'

Terror rose in Umbecca's throat, but somehow she could not resist the command. She stumbled forward. Rotting arms embraced her; the gavotte had become a slow, romantic waltz. Round and round the fat woman reeled, aware of her urinous petticoats, of the torso's lolling head, of the strings of drool that swung from its mouth, webbing her breasts with silver trails.

She shuddered, but the music was mounting, swelling into a tidal surge; she closed her eyes and for a moment it seemed that she was really at the Ball, whirling in the arms of the man she loved. Fat bunched in rolls behind her neck as she arched back, searching for the slobbering mouth; she fixed her sticky lips upon it ardently, hungrily, until it flopped away. She shuddered as the drool ran into her mouth.

The dance went on; Umbecca opened her eyes to find Feval, and all his limbs, dressed already in their Pigar Parrot costume. A beaked headpiece covered his face; gazing up into the many-coloured plumes, she realised that she too had magically assumed her own outfit, looking out from behind her huge-eyed Harlequin Owl mask.

Indeed, it was as if they were at the Ball! Joyously the music mounted; the fire in the grate leapt in time; on the walls, holy icons went *wobble, wobble,* just like Umbecca's quivering flesh. In the next moment, she was certain, her beloved would speak to her, spilling forth the words of love he had held in so cruelly, so continently long.

'Oh, Eay ... sweet Eay—'

'Aunt Umbecca?'

The door opened. It was the Queen. Bulkily resplendent in her Silver Swan costume, the girl waddled forward, removing the elaborate, high headpiece which simulated the swan's curvy neck. In the moment of her entrance, the music had stopped abruptly, as if in a game of musical chairs. Her brow furrowed at the sight of the monstrous Harlequin Owl embracing the Pigar Parrot.

But not quite embracing. Looming from the shadows came the First Minister, humming the tune of the departed waltz. Still in his accustomed white garb, he wheeled the bath-chair from beside the bed. Slipping from Umbecca's arms, the enormous parrot lolled into the chair.

Umbecca turned, pulling away her mask. Her face was red and rolling with sweat, like a fatty side of pork in a roasting pan. A crazed look filled her eyes. 'My child—'

Umbecca reached for a cream horn; there was just one left. Then she reached for a gooseberry tart.

Jeli set down the swan's neck on the sofa. She faltered, 'I'm – I'm pleased to see you're ready, Aunt, I thought ... but who's this?' In the gloom, she could not see that Eay Feval's torso had vanished from the bed; besides, the Pigar Parrot had limbs enough. 'But that costume, wasn't it going to be for the—'

Her eyes darted suspiciously round the chamber, but what she suspected, she could not say. The icons on the walls were strangely askew. Still the smell of burned meat hovered in the air; there was something else too, something damp and hot. And what were these sparks, playing about the parrot?

Tranimel, still humming, pushed forward the bath-chair. 'Your Highness, there's someone I'd like you to meet. Or rather, someone *you'd* like to meet ... or rather, meet *again*. How sad he should be a helpless cripple!'

Smiling, as if conferring some blessing on the girl, the First Minister reached out a long hand. Jerking back the lolling head, he pulled away the mask.

A young man smiled at Jeli. His face was lean and angular, surmounted by a prodigious crop of blond, haystack hair. She staggered back. Could these be eyes that she had longed to see again, lips that she had longed to kiss?

A cry caught in her throat. 'Nova ... *Nova?*'

Umbecca, with ballooning cheeks, gorged on blueberry cheesecake. The huge Harlequin Owl had slumped to the carpet, her feathery legs stuck out at angles.

Jeli, more elegantly, sank to the sofa. Only now did she see that the figure in the bath-chair was not, after all, the young man whose love she had spurned. That the costumed Lector was a sight equally strange did not occur to her; she could think only of her vision. Wonderingly, she gazed up at the First Minister. Could that be laughter gleaming in his eyes?

A footman appeared, bowing to Umbecca. 'Excuse me, ma'am, there's a lady here to—'

'Lady? Now?' Crumbs spluttered from Umbecca's little mouth. 'Tell her to go, I'm seeing no one!'

But the lady would not be denied. She blundered past the footman.

'L-Lady Veeldrop, I—'

Lady Margrave faltered. Blinking, she gazed upon the fat woman on the floor, at the lolling cripple, at the sardonically smiling First Minister. And she had thought the situation at Cham-Charing House was alarming! Hoping to throw herself upon the mercy of Lady Umbecca, she had come here to plead for her friend and her friend's unfortunate daughter. Constansia, distraught at Tishy's disappearance, had yet to grasp what might happen if Tishy had not appeared by the time of the Ball. Lady Margrave was only too aware of the threat. Social death! She was in despair. But how was she to put her case?

She saw the Queen and faltered again.

'Y-Your Majesty, I—'

Umbecca cried, 'Footman, take this baggage—'

Now there was a new commotion at the door. It was a party of guards.

'Lady Veeldrop?' a voice barked.

Umbecca struggled back to her feet. She brushed crumbs from the front of her costume.

'What is it now, what's—'

'Let me go, you brutes!' came a voice.

Umbecca turned pale. How many times had she heard that voice? Never had she heard it raised in anger, but that coarse, common Tarn-tone could hardly be mistaken. She lurched to the door, just as the guards dragged forward the struggling, dishevelled figure of her former maid.

'The mistress!' Nirry cried at the sight of what appeared to be a monstrous multi-coloured owl with a fat human head stuck to its body. She gasped, sinking, as the feathery creature bore down upon her. The others could only look on at the furious confrontation; Eay Feval jerked in his chair as wild words burst from Umbecca's mouth.

'Well may you quail, Nirrian Jubb, to look upon the mistress you have betrayed! Like a fool, I made you privy to the secrets of my heart. Like a fool, I permitted you the deepest intimacies. You dressed me, washed me – how I shudder to think of your touch! Wicked, ungrateful girl! With me, you could have risen to the highest pinnacle of a servant's career. You could have been my maid here in Agondon, tending me in the glory of my new station. Instead, you flung back my faith in my face, you trampled on my innocent hopes, running off to be – what, a whore? A *whore*, is that what you are now, Nirry Jubb?'

This was too much for Nirry. For a time she had swooned; now she rallied, struggling again against the flanking guards. 'It's Nirry Olch! I'm a married woman, you fat old cow, and I'll have you know I'm—'

'A rebel!' Umbecca shrieked. She slapped Nirry's face. 'That's right, Nirry Jubb – a rebel and a traitor, that's what you are! Don't you think we know who bombed the Great Temple? Don't you think we know whose life must be the forfeit? Oh, that I harboured you close to my breast! Did I not treat you as I would my own daughter? Think on what you have done, wicked girl, in the short time that is left to you before your execution.'

Umbecca turned away, shaking with passion. 'Guards, take her from my sight! I can no longer bear to look upon this rebel … this traitress … this *murderess*!'

'*Murderess*?' Now, if the guards had not restrained her, Nirry would certainly have attacked Umbecca. Her screams rang out as they dragged her away. '*Me*, a murderess? You lying, evil old bitch! Don't you know why I left you? Don't you know I saw what you did – you, and that viper Feval? *I saw you kill Lord Margrave – I saw you!*'

There was a stunned silence when Nirry was gone. Umbecca sank slowly into a chair. 'Of course, the girl is mad,' she mouthed, 'quite mad…'

'Of course,' the First Minister agreed. 'Is she not condemned to die?'

'That accent,' said Jeli. 'So common – *ugh*!'

Only after a moment did Umbecca note that her quality-visitor had slipped away, without even stating her business. Strange. 'That … that woman, who *was* she? I've seen her before, but—'

The footman hem-hemmed and gave a little bow. 'If I may, ma'am – she gave her name as … Lady Margrave.'

It was then that Eay Feval opened his eyes and laughter rang from his drivelling mouth.

Umbecca blanched.

Chapter 30

CARDS ON THE TABLE

Two sentries.

Not Morven and Crum.

By a low side-door, between two giant buttresses of stone, the fellows stood irritably. One was simply bored, desperate for the long watch to be over. How he longed to be back in his billet, ale-pot in hand! He'd play a few rounds of Orokon Destiny, winning back everything he'd lost last night.

The other's desperation was somewhat more immediate. Stamping, writhing a little, he shifted the burden of the musket on his shoulder.

'By the Lord Agonis, I've got to *go*.'

'Then *go*. What's a doorway for?'

'Not that sort. The other.' A loud report, as if in illustration, sounded from beneath the bearskin coat.

'Eh, not here you don't! Over in them graves.'

'Graves?' Fear came into the fellow's voice. 'Them's quality-folk that's buried there – I mean, that's *blaspher*-something, isn't it? I'll just … hang on.'

This, perhaps, would be difficult to do. A second report came, louder this time. The fellow doubled over; his companion flapped the air. 'Off, I say!'

'But we're not supposed to *move*—'

'And what do you think you're doing, jigging around with an arseload like that? Next thing I know it'll be in your breeches, and I'll be smelling it all night! Off!'

'But they're dead! And it's dark—'

'Coward, I've had a hundred whores behind them vaults—not in this weather, mind. You don't think anything's lurking out there, do you? Not unless it's rebels, come to blow us sky-high!'

'Them's the ones we're watching for—'

'And they ain't here now. Off, off.'

It was Jem's chance. While Polty and Bean were below, the shivering intruder had managed a circuit of the Great Temple, scurrying from one concealment to another amongst the snowy headstones, vaults and trees. If he was on the lookout for a way in, there was none. At every entrance were armed guards; a patrol, too, went round and round. Jem knew he had to keep moving. More than once he longed to huddle down, surrendering himself to the flurrying snow. One thing was certain: he could not hold out much longer.

Now the sentry advanced towards him, hastily, clumsily unbuttoning his bearskin. Jem crouched behind a tall, crumbling vault, shadowed between seepings of bluish moonlight. He curled a shard of masonry in his hand. This had to be quick. If the fellow called his companion, Jem was done for.

The fellow squatted, ripping down his breeches.

Jem leapt, dashing down the chunk of stone.

Moments later, it was Jem who emerged from behind the vault, in Bluejacket uniform, bearskin, musket and all. He kept his head down, drawing his hat low over his eyes as he made his way to the door between the buttresses.

'There, that's better, isn't it?'

Jem gave a grunt.

A grin. 'See any rebels? Reckon your stinking would have seen 'em off, eh? Secret weapon, like.'

Jem managed a muffled guffaw. He braced himself. Surprise, that was the thing. Averting his face, he sank into the shadows as his companion began to expatiate upon the game of Orokon Destiny, and how he would win back what he had lost last night. Every last bit of it, from Rottsy especially – Rottsy and Supp. Those fellows were little more than dirty thieves...

Voices came from behind and the low side-door crashed open. Jem jumped.

'Polty, this really isn't a good idea. Come back!'

'What have I told you, Bean? Don't be such a girl!'

How Jem prayed that Polty would not turn, even for a moment! But his enemy strode forward, Bean scurrying after him, crunching across the drive. Their coach had been taken to the Temple stables; they proceeded on foot.

With a cynical smile, Jem's companion noted the direction. 'Off to Chokey's, I'll bet. Lucky fellows, them Special Agents. But what do they want with them brats in the Temple, eh? Someone said the Great Lector does special blessings at night – sick children, like. But there's no Great Lector *now*, is there? Unless they've got another one, quick smart.' The fellow made a spitty explosion with his lips. 'Reckon they were scraping him off the walls, they do.'

There was a pause. Jem braced himself, waiting for the footsteps on the drive to fade.

He pointed suddenly. 'Look!'

His companion turned, startled. But danger was closer at hand. He gasped, then dropped as a musket-butt slammed into the back of his head.

Jem vanished through the low side-door.

185

'It's just like the crypt—'

'What's that, Bean?'

'Dark and evil. Polty—'

But Polty was not listening. Exclaiming, flinging out his arms, he sailed through the smoky air, eagerly embracing the lizard-like old man who shuffled forward to meet him.

Bean gulped nervously. Screwing up his face, he peered into the clouded vista of low-burning lamps, of Jarvel-pipes, decanters and green baize tables, multiplied endlessly in the looking-glass walls. Of late, Chokey's domain had been expanded, taking in a second capacious basement; to Bean, the place had always suggested infinity.

Nonetheless, there were few patrons tonight.

A footman in a jacket with unravelling braid smiled at Bean unctuously, taking his coat and hat.

'And your ... *musical instrument*, sir?'

'I'll keep it.' Clutching the W'enge-case, Bean followed Polty to a large and well-placed table, reserved for the proprietor's particular favourites.

'Balls!' Chokey was saying. 'How I loathe them! How I despise them! Alas, my dears, we are much depleted ... Ho hum, such are the perils of running an establishment for *quality*-gentlemen ... But Master Veeldrop, surely you are attending? I can hardly believe the Koros Palace is closed to a fellow of *your* connections.'

Polty waved a hand as if to indicate that of course he was free to walk in and out of the Koros Palace as if it were his home; that the Ball, consequently, was hardly of any interest; that he might make the effort later, if he could be bothered, but probably could not be bothered at all.

'Are there not are *other* entertainments?' he grinned.

It was a response Chokey appreciated; the old man, rubbing his wizened hands, permitted himself a remark or two upon the follies of fashionable life, the corruptions of the Court and the superior attractions of his own establishment, before clicking his fingers for Jarvel and Vantage.

'And the ... *entertainments*, Master Veeldrop? Perhaps you mean your friend is to play his instrument? Chokey fixed an eye on the ornate case. 'I've seen him with that thing before. What kind of instrument is it, I wonder? A little gittern? A horn, perhaps? A very *fat* recorder? Would you not treat us to a tune, Master Throsh?'

Polty laughed as if the joke were a good one. 'My side-officer is shy. Actually, old friend, I *was* thinking of a little entertainment. Something along the lines you provided before.'

'A song and dance? There'll be one soon.'

Polty wagged a finger at the lizard-man; Bean sighed, bored with their stupid game. Vantage came, and Jarvel, and he dived for them eagerly. This was not like Bean; but Bean, of late, was often not like Bean.

He lit his Jarvel-pipe. Sucking back on the acrid smoke, he gazed intently upon the squalid old man who stood by Polty's side like an evil, corrupting familiar. Chokey had grown uglier, if that were possible for a man with a mottled, hairless head and a crumpled, reptilian face hanging like a husk above the stinking, stained ruins of an ornate smoking jacket. Some said he broke in all his girls personally. He was said to be an expert in the arts of love, proficient in all the most arcane refinements.

Bean shuddered.

'Nothing *fresh*, I suppose?' Polty was saying, lighting his own pipe. 'Weren't you expecting a young Tiralon?'

'Dead, alas,' said Chokey, as if this were hardly unusual news. 'I'm afraid Reny Bolbarr's crowd got her first – those young chaps *do* get carried away, don't they? Well, at least they took her to the plague pit afterwards.' The lizard-man stroked his chin; magician-like, he produced a deck of cards, flicking it down with an incidental air between the goblets and Jarvel-pipes. 'So, no Tiralon – *wanton*, she was, too.'

Polty looked crestfallen.

'But,' said Chokey, 'there *is* something just in.'

'Young?' Polty perked up.

'Naturally.'

'Pretty?'

'Of course.'

'Innocent?'

'Hah! You'd like to find out?'

'Hah! Old friend, I think I would!'

With that, proprietor and customer slapped palms together, delighted, it seemed, with each other's wit.

'And your side-officer?' added the proprietor. 'I seem to recall he *seldom* partakes.'

'Let him loosen up for a while – eh, Bean? But Chokey, this new girl – you'll have her *prepared* … like last time?'

'Blindfolded? Hands tied? Master Veeldrop, consider it done. Just give me a little time.'

'Not much, I hope. A man becomes eager!'

'Ho, am I not versed in the ways of love? Pretty, pretty,' Chokey added, in a strangely senile murmur, looking again at the W'enge-case with its glittering, inlaid patterns. The wizened hand felt the cool surface, then snapped away. 'But a little time, a little. As I say, the lass is just in, and I must ready her to … *receive* you.'

Smiling at the delicious *double entendre*, Polty poured himself a generous dram of Vantage. Alternately sipping from it, then drawing on his Jarvel, he launched into a paean to the departing Chokey, for all the world as if the fellow were a wise and generous teacher instead of a vicious, cynical businessman, stirring up the worst instincts in young men in order that he might profit from their depravities. The lizard-man was a monster, no doubt about it: Bean knew that, even as he sipped Chokey's Vantage, even as he filled his lungs with Chokey's Jarvel. Revolted, he gazed after the shuffling form with its bent back, its stiffened pyjamas under the smoking jacket.

Particular horror inhered in Chokey's ankles: swollen, empurpled, ringed with sores.

❈   ❈   ❈

But where was Agonis?

Koros, Viana, Theron, Javander...

Shuffle, shuffle. Idly Polty laid out the God-cards, the ones he could find. The dim lights of Chokey's glimmered all around; the amethyst ring glinted on his hand. Again he shuffled. And could it be true, he found himself murmuring, that Chokey was *really* Jorvel Ixiter, Archduke of Irion? Rumour said so, and rumour (said Polty) seldom lied. 'Imagine it, Bean – imagine Chokey, presiding over our own little province, in the days before Governor Veeldrop came. Why, he was a great man!'

What was Bean to say? The Archduke had only one claim to fame, and that was giving up Ejard Red to the Bluejackets. Everyone in the Tarn cursed his memory, especially as he had simply left the province when the Siege of Irion was over. In deserved irony, Jorvel Ixiter had lost his power under the new régime. Like many a decayed princeling or aristocrat, the traitor had fled to Agondon, determined to solace himself in the amusements of the town.

And all *this* was his solace.

Slapping down the Wild Cards (Warlock, Vaga, Harlot, Horseman – where was Harlequin?), Polty spoke fondly of this *greater destiny*, this *finer province* Chokey had found, here in his subterranean domain.

Bean should have protested. Was it not a calumny, a blasphemy, to compare their beautiful, thickly wooded homeland with the province Chokey tended now?

Of course: but the Jarvel had done its work and Bean heard Polty's words from far away. Now his friend entered upon an elaborate metaphor in which Chokey was a gardener, tending to his plants; a fisherman, hauling in his catch; a baker, with a generous basket of loaves – the upshot of it all was that Chokey was a father, that they were his children. And wiping a Jarvelly tear from his eye, Polty blessed the condition of fatherhood, and this finest of fathers he – no, *they* – had known.

Could Polty really wish to be Chokey's son? To be sure, Bean's friend had known other fathers – Goodman Waxwell, Lord Veeldrop – neither of whom he had reason to love. Why should he not prefer Chokey, a father who might encourage him in all his desires, permitting all excesses? His adoptive father, the pious Goodman Waxwell, had beaten Polty viciously,

188

time after time; when Waxwell was killed in a coaching accident, Polty had displayed not even a glimmering of grief.

From Lord Veeldrop, his natural father, Polty had thought he deserved all indulgence. Yet what had Veeldrop brought him but bitterness, with his cruel, unfeeling Last Will and Testament, railing against his son's moral character, leaving him his titles and estates conditional only upon his marriage to Catayane? Thinking the girl the embodiment of innocence – she, a slut if ever there was one – the old fool had imagined she might reclaim his son, leading him back from the brink of depravity. How Polty cursed the senile old hypocrite, who luxuriated in a life of moral turpitude, only to succumb to deathbed piety!

Nor had he done much better with his mothers. His first adoptive mother, Goody Waxwell, had been a pathetic, passive creature, utterly cowed by her monstrous husband; his second, Aunt Umbecca, had seemed at first to love him, but then betrayed him brutally, turning her back on him after her elevation from provincial life.

At least his natural mother had loved him, even if she had never told him he was her son. Wynda Throsh! For a time, Polty had been appalled at the thought that he had sprung from her loins; now he saw Wynda, who had taken him in at her tavern after he left Goodman Waxwell's, as the only woman who had ever treated him well. If he got back to Irion, he would reward her for her goodness. His only concern was that Bean should never find out the truth.

It would hardly do for him to know they were brothers.

Bean gazed into the swirling gloom, into which Chokey had vanished like a sinister apparition. Girls plied their way between sparsely occupied tables, tending to gatherings of officers or civilian gentlemen – gentlemen, Bean surmised, of insufficient quality to receive invitations to the Ball. He saw a grinning mouth, a flash of cards; he heard a chuckle, a chinking of coins, and somewhere, far away, a harpsichord. What was the tune? A bawdy song; but now the tune was picked out softly, as if it were a melancholy ballad.

Bean's eyes roved the looking-glass walls, lighting upon the instrument and its player. Looming like a shadow, the fellow wore a dark cape and a black, many-feathered, hawk-like mask. Bean gulped; for some reason his hand covered the case of his own supposed instrument. In moments, no doubt, he must surrender it to its owner. How he wished he could lose the thing! What did it do but torment Polty? But even if he dropped W'enge into the sewers, Bean imagined the thing coming back to them, clickety-clacking down the cobbled streets as if animated by an evil magic.

He looked across the table at his friend. Alas, even in the flattering lamplight, Polty was no longer a handsome man. His long hair was decidedly lank, quite without its old life and fire; his jaw was jowly, like a

189

ghostly reminder of the fat boy he had been before with the magical arrival of Penge.

Polty had found the Agonis card. Musingly, he held it up. 'This fellow was loved by his father, was he not? Did Orok not favour him over all his children? Did he not vouchsafe him the rarest of the crystals? You see, Bean, fathers *can* love their sons. How I shall love mine, when I hold him in my arms! How I shall caress the downy flames of his hair! Ah, and what pride will swell my heart when he grows up, as he must, to be a great man!'

He smiled sadly. 'Sometimes I'm impatient, I'll admit it. I weary of this life, Bean. When Penge is back in place ... when Cata is my wife ... when my father's titles are mine at last – what happiness shall we know then! (You too, Bean, for shall you not still be my loyal man?) But the greatest happiness, for all of us, will come from my son and heir – Poltiss Junior, that's what we'll call him. (Don't worry, my lanky friend, you'll love him too. Can't I see him jiggety-jogging on your back, all around the nursery and up and down the stairs?)

'Of course, Little Polty will just be the first. Many a time Cata's belly will swell, bringing forth many a brother, many a sister for him too. Why, Bean, I might let you marry one of the plainer ones, how would you like that? – But then, how could there be a plain one, even *one*, when Cata, sweet Cata, is the mould from which they take their stamp? – Ah, Bean, what a *family* shall be ours! (Yours too, I say, for shall you not be the favoured of my domestics? Fondly I see us in our dotage, sitting over a decanter, laughing over the merry adventures of our youth!) But for all our happiness, all our glories, always it will be Little Polty who is our tenderest care. How I long for him! Oh, my son, my son!'

A tear slid down Polty's face; he might have sobbed outright, but just then the footman with unravelling braid appeared by his side, murmuring that a certain young lady was ready for him now.

Struggling, Polty made a bright reply. He winked at Bean, grabbed the W'enge-case and blundered away.

Chapter 31

IN YOUTH IS PLEASURE

'All right, you've had your laugh—'

'Come on, enough—'

'*Please*, Folio—'

Folio Webster restrained himself only with difficulty. Of course he shouldn't be laughing, especially when Bando could hear. The young man was ashamed, but how could he stop himself? Hul and Cata – they looked so silly!

He broke off, wiping his eyes. 'I'm sorry. They're brilliant costumes, splendid, much better than Father's—'

'They're the only ones we could get, as well you know,' Cata said sharply. 'It's not as if we had time to make our *own* or—'

'Original, I'll grant you that,' Folio sailed on. 'A sort of … *crow* with a deformed neck, and a fat brown feathery bundle of—'

Hul sighed. 'Cata, as well you know, is the celebrated Black Swan of Lania Chor. (I think you'd better *carry* the headpiece, my dear – the tunnels are low.)' Hul pushed up his feathery mask. 'And I assume you *do* know what I am, Folio?'

'Festival Turkey?'

Hul was grudging. 'Well, yes—'

'It's unmistakable.' Grinning dangerously, Folio might have been about to laugh again; with a glance at poor Bando, he restrained himself, but still permitted himself to add, with a snort, 'It's as well Father's not here tonight, that's all I can I say. He'd have been envious – really he would.'

'And what *is* your father going as?' asked Cata levelly.

'Tiralon Tiger Gull – just look for the stripes. Or rather, don't. You might draw attention to yourselves if you laugh as much as I did.'

Folio grimaced. Shaking his head, he looked again at Bando. Really, it was unnerving, the way the fellow just sat there, motionless, slumped against the wall. If only there was something they could say to him. In the dim lamplight, the familiar red bandanna circled Bando's head like a cap of dried, purplish blood.

'But Father was *so* proud to be invited – you should have seen him getting ready.' Folio was speaking for the sake of speaking. Quickly he began clearing away barrels and boxes, exposing the crumbling basement wall that led into the bowels of the Royal Ejard Library. 'There are only ever a few places for the trade folk, and he's never been lucky before.'

'Just as well, or we'd be in trouble, wouldn't we?' said Hul. He looked apprehensively above their heads. Echoing down from the coffee house came the tramp-tramp of feet and the murmurous voices of assembled scholars. How Hul wished he could be amongst them, debating the merits of Mercol's edition of Thell or the aphoristic moralisings of Dr Tonson's *Speculator*. Sometimes – but only sometimes – Hul wished he had never heard of Vytoni, the great Zenzan philosopher who had changed his life so dramatically. 'But Folio, I can hardly see your father being quite so pleased about *rebels* using his—'

'Hul, are you sure this is a good idea?' said Cata, squashing her swan's neck under a feathery wing. She shook back her long, dark hair.

Hul was surprised. 'Cata, this isn't like you!'

'I don't mean whether our plan is a good idea – we've hardly got a choice. I mean, should we have changed into our costumes *first*?'

'You want to change in the cross-tunnels?'

'Well, no. But won't we be filthy when we get to the Ball?'

'So will the rest of them. Haven't you ever seen a Ball, Cata? Sweat, dripping wax, running pomade—'

'What about brick-dust, cobwebs and slime?'

'Cata, I could never get this thing on *in* the tunnels!'

'You'll be lucky to get *through* the tunnels in that get-up, I'd have thought,' was the reply.

Then Cata wished she had been silent as Folio looked set to laugh again.

Fortunately Magda Vytoni appeared just then, picking her way down the wooden stepladder in her dainty, spiky shoes. Hul watched the swish of her skirt about her ankles; so did Folio. 'Magda, didn't I tell you to stay up with the others? You know we can't all risk—'

Drawing on a tobarillo, the daughter of the great philosopher-martyr leaned against the stepladder, hand on her hip. 'Ah, but I tire of your friends, Folio – Roly Rextel, Onty Michan, Danny Garvice, what are they? Call themselves revolutionaries! Does even *one* of them have a coherent critique of Imperial Agonist society and its inherent contradictions? On what fundamental principles do they—'

'How about the *principle* that Ejard Blue is a tyrant?' Bando burst out, scowling contemptuously as Hul flapped a hand – or rather, a wing – in an earnest, automatic shushing motion.

'A tyrant indeed, but sometimes I think your masked highwayman is pretty much the same,' said Magda. She eyed Bando coolly. 'Why isn't Master Scarlet going on this mission, hm, if he's *so* intrepid? Like every corrupt ruler, he sends his subordinates. He's not worthy of you, Bando, haven't you ever thought, he's just not—'

'I – I think we'd better be going,' interjected Hul. At another time, he would have found it hard to resist a debate with Magda Vytoni. Not now. 'Bando, you're ready?'

His old friend cursed, but roused himself wearily from the corner where he had sat, shouldering his musket, taking up a swinging, rusty lamp.

'You *are* all right, Bando?' Hul said quietly.

Bando turned towards the hole in the wall, irritated by the show of concern. Hul thought it best to say no more. If their friend had said he could not come with them, neither Hul nor Cata would have demurred, much as they needed their lookout and guide. How Bando – facing the loss, perhaps the death of his son – had managed not to crumple into hopeless despair was astonishing to them both.

'You've got the lamp, Bando?' Hul said, pulling down his turkey-mask again. 'And I've got the map. Don't forget your headpiece, Cata, all right?' There was a forced exuberance in his voice, rather as if they were setting out on a picnic. He cleared his throat nervously. 'Now, let's just go over a few things. This is a vital mission, it's not going to be easy, it's—'

'We *know*. Let's just get going,' said Cata.

Magda ground her tobarillo underfoot. A new expression came over the beautiful, exotic face as she embraced the three friends, lingering longest with Bando, as if she liked him all the more because he had been angry with her. The others watched, startled, as she kissed the Zenzan tenderly.

'Don't despair yet, rebel-man,' she whispered. 'We've all got contacts in the Redjacket League. We'll get back that boy of yours, I swear it, if we've got to tear this city apart, stone by rotten stone.'

Folio cleared his throat. 'J-Just remember, everyone, don't look at Father. Well ... see you back here soon – with the Queen, hm?' He smiled awkwardly as the little party vanished, one by one, through the hole in the wall.

'I'll practise my curtsey,' Magda said wryly, and Bando, as he turned to go, almost smiled.

❋   ❋   ❋

'Hurry up, lovey, hurry up! Haven't you put on your green garters yet? Here, let me—'

'No!' Jilda slapped away the claw-like hand.

'Feisty!' Chokey grinned. 'Well, I dare say that's what this gentleman wants. It has to be said he's developed some *particular* tastes since he got back from foreign parts – isn't that always the way? Still, he pays well – one of my best. Consider yourself privileged, my dear. Just think, it could be Reny Bolbarr!'

The lizard-man rubbed his hands, pacing with peculiar deliberation round the exotic little den of cushions and elaborate hangings that was concealed behind the looking-glass walls. Here there was only one looking-glass, shimmering in the glow of many candles as Jilda, fearful and trembling, resumed her harlot's guise.

With relish, Chokey looked upon the half-naked girl. He loomed close, arranging her gown, pulling here and there at a lacy ruff. Ah yes, she had lost nothing! If anything, the girl's temporary retirement had only increased her charms.

'But what's this? Tears in your eyes? A snivelly nose? Dear little Jilda, don't you know how much we've all missed you? Still, I suppose you're overcome with emotion. How can you be sad, when you're back where you belong? Back home! Back with your *family* ... Oh, I know it seems a bit simple after where you've been, but never mind, we'll find you some pretty things to wear – it's not as if you're shivering out in Redondo Gardens, is it? Didn't I ever tell you, lovey, there're those who like a lady to dress up as the Queen? Well, I've been thinking, who could do it better than little Jilda? Would you like that?

'Oh, I dare say you've seen Her Royal Majesty in one or two *intimate* situations, too? Know the cut of her jib? Just think, what you might whisper in a gentleman's ear! Hm? ... But come, we're nearly ready – now, just let me tie your wrists behind your back ... No lovey, don't shy away! Careful, careful – no kitty-claws ... He's a fine gentleman, I promise you. (Remember, do what he wants or you'll feel the lash!) ... There, there we go, lovey. Ropes too tight? No, I don't think they'll hurt at all – yes, that's right, sit on the couch here ... Now there's just the blindfold – the gentleman has *particular* tastes.'

Chokey had just finished blindfolding the girl when a faint rapping came at the door. Slithering forward, he exchanged a muttered word with the footman, then turned back to Jilda, who slumped, shaking, over the couch.

The old face crumpled into an expectant grin. 'Perk up, lovey, your paramour is here! Which means *I'd* better not be ...' But Chokey made no motion to vacate the chamber, vanishing instead into a hollow in the wall, concealed between two ornate hangings. 'Don't mind me, lovey, but this is one I've *got* to see. There've been rumours about Master Veeldrop, ever since he came back from foreign parts – I'll admit I've grown a little curious ... But don't mind me, don't mind me.'

Jilda, just then, was barely listening, lost in the wilds of her own grief. Could it really be true that this was now her home? Could Chokey really be her father now? Sobbing, she thought back to the time of her innocence, and how suddenly, how violently that innocence had been lost.

Never again had she seen Captain Foys Foxbane, the suave, dark-haired Bluejacket who had ruined her at the end of that fateful Varby season. Of course, she had written to him, many times, at first in hopes that all could not be over, that he might yet return and take her as his bride; in pathetic self-abasement, she had said she loved him still, and blamed herself entirely for all that had passed. Poor Captain Foxbane! What shame he must feel! But how could she have known she would inflame him so grievously with all her silly, teasing ways? Oh, but she had not meant to be cruel! Could he not excuse a foolish, giddy girl, unacquainted with the passions of men?

Later, Jilda's letters had changed, giving way to execrations, curses, demands; in any case, it was all to no avail. From Captain Foxbane there had been no replies; then, at last, came a letter from the chaplain of his supposed regiment, informing her that no such man as Foys Foxbane was registered in the Bluejacket lists. In not unkindly tones (but they cut Jilda to the heart) the chaplain told the girl that she had been deceived, counselling her to pray, and pray hard, seeking salvation in the Love of the Lord Agonis before she was not only ruined for marriage, but wholly abandoned to depravity.

Inevitably, the advice had come too late. From the moment the guards had found her, bleeding and moaning, Jilda Quisto's destiny had been certain. In the grass beside her was a scattering of coins, as if she had been a whore already; the coins, she supposed, had been a portent. And oh, how swiftly that portent had been fulfilled! In the rumour-filled environs of Varby, Jilda's disgrace was impossible to hide. Within a day, she had become a pariah. Her own sister turned from her as from a thing infected; when she went home to her father's house, he cast her on the streets.

Jilda moaned. Could she bear all this again? She rocked back and forth on the couch where soon, no doubt, she would have to endure the pawing hands, the grunting thrusts. She might have sobbed, she might have railed, but why? It would only anger the lizard-man; besides, what he had said was true. Chokey's was her home now, her family, her world.

And now the blindfold girl hears a man's heavy footsteps, pacing around the couch; she hears a low, lustful murmur of approval. A hand touches her cheek; it plays about her throat; it pulls open her bodice, exposing her breasts. Jilda struggles not to flinch, and even smiles; the murmur of approval comes again, then the thud of discarded boots, the swish of breeches slipping down. Almost wearily (but still she smiles) Jilda anticipates what must happen next. Will the man, affecting tenderness, remove her gown, or simply push away her obstructing skirts with crude, rough hands?

But what comes instead is a click, like the opening of a case, then something that sounds like a fumbling with a strap, or jingling belt. Jilda gulps fearfully, wondering exactly what this gentleman's *particular tastes* might be.

Chapter 32

BLACK MASK

'You were right, Hul. We'd never have been able to change here,' Cata
muttered.

Wryly, she looked about the low, arching tunnels. And she had thought
the smell in the library was bad, down amongst the basements! Here it
was entirely vile, a terrible, deathly dankness. The chill cut through her
feathery costume as she picked her way, slithering and stumbling, over a
floor strewn with rubble and dangerous slimy pools. Ahead of her was
Bando, torch in hand; Hul was behind.

'Hul, you must be having a difficult time,' Cata added. 'Can you walk?
Or just waddle?'

'I *am* a Festival Turkey.'

'Hah! My wings keep scraping the walls. I'll be surprised if we've got
any feathers *left* by the time we get to the Ball. And how filthy are we
going to be?'

'You needn't worry. At least you're black.'

'It isn't this narrow *all* the way, is it?'

'Well, we go under the Temple,' Hul said thoughtfully. 'There are the
crypts, and … no, but they're a veritable labyrinth. Straight on through
the Aon tunnels, that's the best way.'

'*Aon* tunnels?' said Cata. 'There are more?'

Hul, with a rustle of parchment, held out his crumpled map. Turning
back, Cata saw a complex web of lines, trembling in the dim glow of
Bando's lamp. Hul's finger traced their route. 'To Temple Cross, where the
lines meet – then a slight bend to your right, do you see?'

'So *many* tunnels! I thought there were five, one for each god.'

'Ah, but there's been a Temple here since time immemorial.'
Awkwardly, they proceeded on their way. 'Cross-tunnels collapsed, new
ones got built; some were closed off, then opened again – at least, that's
what I gather. Luckily for us, no one pays much attention to them any
more.'

'Shouldn't they? If they're escape routes?' said Cata.

'But they're not, not really. They used to be built under every Temple of
Agonis, out from under the altar towards the tombyard perimeter – something about radiating the sacred influence,' Hul explained, the scholarly air
a little incongruous, perhaps, in a man dressed as a turkey. 'The earliest
tunnels were dead ends; it didn't matter if they *went* anywhere. It was only

196

later that some began extending them – that's my theory. Still, between all the different tunnels, I think you can find your way into just about every important building in Agondon – if you've got my map, of course.'

'You're sure about that map?' Bando said dourly.

It was best, thought Hul, not to reply. They crept on, shuddering at the cold, at the cobwebs, at the scurrying rats. A persistent *drip-drip* ran down the walls; ancient stones flared out in the lamplight, lurid with patterns of moss and damp.

Hul's heart pounded hard. So much depended on the mission of this night! He worried that they were in thrall to Agondon's vilest criminals; still more, he worried about their leader. With dread, he thought of the disasters that had befallen them that day. He would like to believe their noble cause would triumph at last. But Hul was no longer sure he could. He had scorned superstition; now it looked as if every dire portent had come crashingly true.

He squinted ahead, straining his eyes through the glow of Bando's lamp. They would be under the Temple soon, wouldn't they? Hul had thought the way was engraved upon his heart; he had made this journey so many times, creeping to the Chamber of Forbidden Texts.

Cata found her thoughts drifting to Jem. Could it be true that her beloved was back? She hardly dared believe it; her joy turned swiftly to an ache of longing. Then came shame: how could she even think of her own happiness? She thought of Raggle; she thought of Nirry. Where Bando's son might be, Cata could not imagine, but she pictured Nirry clearly enough, languishing in a dark cell even at this moment, crushed beneath the burden of her sentence of death.

But no, not crushed. Not Nirry.

The thought of her old friend's bravery and goodness brought tears to Cata's eyes, so she sniffed loudly and said, 'Hul? Did you say this map could take us *anywhere*? How about Oldgate, when we've finished in the palace?'

'Don't even think about it,' said Hul, not unkindly, understanding the question at once. 'I could get us to the Monastery of the White Friars, to Temple College, to the Wrax Opera. But Oldgate? That's one route that was blocked off – oh, epicycles ago.'

'So how did you escape? You *were* caught, weren't you, after you published that Vytoni book?'

'Indeed, but I was never in Oldgate. Nowadays I'd be branded a traitor straight away, but back then I was known as a *rogue scholar*. They charged me under the Statutes of the University – would you believe, Mercol locked me in the library while I awaited my hearing? Thankfully, the old fool never discovered just *how* I'd been getting into the Chamber of Forbidden Texts. Suffice to say I was swiftly free – they called me a traitor *because* I'd escaped.'

'Do you miss your old life?' Cata said, after a moment. 'It must have been hard, hiding out with rebels all these years.'

Hul was silent, as if considering the idea. 'Well,' he sighed at last, 'there were my father and mother – I never saw *them* again … And my younger brother, I missed him terribly. Never could risk getting in touch. Then,' he added shyly, 'there *was* a girl I was going to—'

'Dugs of Viana!' Bando cried as a crash of bricks fell in his path. The lamp swayed precariously in his hands as he steadied himself against the wall. 'You're sure this is the right way, Hul? I don't like the look of this. This floor's getting worse all the time, and it's a lot narrower up ahead, too, by the looks of—'

He took a step forward, just one more.

There came a second crash and Bando, with a wild cry, fell through the floor.

Gasping, Hul and Cata gathered round the jagged hole that had swallowed their friend and guide. For a moment, the light of his lamp flared up, dazzling and auroral, from below. Then the light guttered and all was dark.

'Bando? Bando?'

Only silence came from below.

> *…Lady Fine, Lady Fair,*
> *Ran her fingers through his hair*
> *And smiled and took an eager boy in hand!*

Was that the song?

Bean had become aware of the melody again, tinkling away on the harpsichord. There had been a time when this song, and others like it, had made his cheeks flush scarlet. But was this really the *Lady Fine* song? Perhaps it was some other one … Oh, what did it matter? He glugged down his Vantage; he stuffed more Jarvel into his pipe; he looked blankly at the scattered cards: at Seven of Spires, at King of Swords, at Harlequin and the Lord Agonis, overlapping on the green baize.

The fantasy of the happy family had disturbed Bean profoundly. He thought of his drunken father and his common, crude mother with her hideous wigs and the paint slapped, thick as putty, over her ruined face. Ebenezer Throsh would be a skeleton now, in his ignominious corner of the Irion tombyard; what of Wynda? Was she rotted, too, by death or disease? Or was she still serving in the Lazy Tiger, bawling out her ribaldries to the Bluejackets? In any case, Bean imagined he would never see her again. If he did, would she laugh at him contemptuously, as she had laughed on the day he left home to enlist?

Bean's real family had been The Five, Polty's childhood gang. Even now, Bean could reduce himself to tears thinking of the splendours of their glory days, running through the fields and lanes of Irion in Theron-seasons long gone by. How he missed their old companions, Leny, Vel and Tyl! How swiftly their childhood had slipped from them! With a shudder, Bean recalled the day on Killing Rock when Polty, maddened with envy and spite, had contrived the death of Vel. Bean had tried to save their old friend; it was impossible. On that day, he had known that he was bound to Polty for ever. From the ashes of The Five had emerged The Two.

Often Bean wondered what had become of the two girls, blonde, plump Leny and elfin, dark Tyl. Tyl, long ago, had been Bean's particular friend. How he had sobbed when she left their village, never to return!

'Mind if I join you?' came a voice.

Bean looked up; without waiting for a reply, the owner of the voice took Polty's seat. It was the man in the mask. Bean shifted apprehensively. The mask was not only large, covering all of the fellow's face except the eyes, but elaborate too, its spike-like black feathers fixed in place with innumerable patterned arrangements of tiny jewels. The same patterns were repeated on the fellow's dark tunic, as well as on the backs of his black gloves.

Signalling for Vantage, the fellow swept up the cards and began to deal. Still the bawdy song tinkled from the harpsichord; someone else, evidently, had taken the place of Bean's new companion.

'You looked a bit morose.' The voice was not unfriendly. 'I dare say you haven't been invited to the Ball?'

'I dare say you *have*,' Bean said.

'Indeed,' came the reply. 'It is an admirable costume, is it not? The design is known as *Hawk of Darkness*. But you're familiar with the fashionable world, my friend? – by repute? – by association? Perhaps, then, you will understand why a man might seek a few … diversions, before … the *diversions* of the evening begin. Would you not agree?'

Bean, who was not sure *what* he was agreeing, nodded impassively. The thought occurred to him that this fellow's costume showed not the merest sliver, not the slightest fraction of exposed skin.

Only the eyes: it made Bean uneasy.

'Not partaking of the womenfolk, like your friend?' Hawk of Darkness fanned out his cards; Bean supposed he must do the same. He saw a pile of gold, glinting beside the dark elbow. Bean had little in the way of cash; he hadn't even asked to play this game.

He began, 'We'll have to go soon. We've not much time—'

'That doesn't bother your friend, I think. An ardent fellow? So I've heard – still, there are rumours.'

'Rumours?' Bean's hand was abysmal.

'That he's … not what he was.'

Bean felt a stab of fear. But no, he had his dignity.

'Rumours lie,' he said. 'Don't they *always* lie?'

'Not always. But then, perhaps, we're none of us what we were. You're Special Agents, aren't you?'

Bean looked up sharply.

'Raise you.' The voice was mocking.

For some moments they played in silence. Already Bean was losing, losing badly. Why could he not simply break away?

He picked up a card. It was the Vaga.

The harpsichord had subsided, replaced by the thrummings of a little orchestra; somewhere, in the far reaches of the chamber, a pair of Chokey's girls were beginning a song, their voices intertwining like entangling vines. Bean glimpsed them, floating like phantoms in the looking-glass walls.

Their song, like the last one, was melancholy too, but delivered with a strangely joyous lilt:

> *This is my life,*
> *Slipped away,*
> *Blown and billowed on a windy day:*
> *All in all the promises men make shall soon be broken.*
> *All in all you're lucky if they leave behind a token.*

Bean found himself studying the Vaga-card. Not for the first time, he thought of the Vaga-boy who was Jem Vexing's friend. A slow, steady warmth grew in his heart as he recalled a certain night in Unang Lia. What had it meant, that scene with Rajal at the Sanctum of the Flame? A handclasp on a hot night, that was all, at a time when Bean thought Polty was lost to him.

Yes, but it had been madness – madness, and treachery, with a dirty Vaga! How could anyone replace Polty? Rajal had even called Bean by his real name – Aron, not Bean! Who ever called him *that*, except his mother?

Bean shuddered. He had felt like a different person.

'Raise you.'

The song was coming closer:

> *This is my love,*
> *Torn from me,*
> *Turning, tossing on a stormy sea:*
> *All in all a woman's hopes are sure to be mistaken,*
> *All in all she's lucky if she's not sad and forsaken.*

'You're all right?' said Hawk of Darkness, a little wry.

'I was thinking about … a place,' said Bean, and turned the card over, face down. One thing was certain, Polty must never know about the Vaga, never.

Hawk of Darkness said, 'And this place? Where might it be?'

Why should Bean answer? 'Somewhere … far away.'

'As far as Unang Lia? Raise you.'

Bean gulped. How he wanted to leave! But now the two girls, one dark, one fair, advanced to their table. Converging upon the mortified Bean, they waved silken scarves in the air, draping them round his shoulders and neck. And all the time they continued to sing in their twisty-twiny, mocking voices:

> *This is my heart,*
> *Bleeding red,*
> *Bruised and battered on a dirty bed:*
> *All in all my life, my love was barely worth a token.*
> *Ah, I wonder why my heart was made just to be broken!*

The voices became soft, cooing; fingers curled in Bean's hair and ran caressingly over his chest. Ribaldries, sparser tonight than was usual, rang out of the darkness. Another man would have been stirred to desire; winked, perhaps, and grabbed a girl on his lap, pawing greedily at the breasts that were barely concealed by the wraith-like, shimmery gown.

But Bean was no common man, and tears filled his eyes. Wonderingly, he looked between his two fair tormentors. They were infinitely strange.

One dark. One fair. 'Leny,' he said. 'Tyl.'

He juddered back his chair: '*Leny! Tyl!*'

But the girls didn't know what he was talking about. They skittered off, laughing, to another table, and Bean sank down, defeated.

Eyes glittered behind the black mask.

Just then, there was a commotion by the stairs where the footman with unravelling braid was having difficulties with a visitor of a type not often seen in Chokey's. The visitor was female; worse still, she was elderly, dressed in black, with a Circle of Agonis hanging round her neck.

Heads turned throughout Chokey's as the woman pushed her way contemptuously past. All were astonished, but none more so than Bean. Not since Irion days had he seen this woman with her wizened face, her stick-thin figure, her right arm that ended in a stump.

And never had he seen her behave like this.

He swivelled back to his companion, but Hawk of Darkness had slipped away, leaving not only his hand of cards, but also his pile of gold.

'Out of my way!' cried Widow Waxwell. 'Where's my son? I insist on seeing my son!'

Chapter 33

AFTER SUCH KNOWLEDGE

'Bando? Bando?'

Hul and Cata despaired. Blackness surrounded them and there was no sound from below. With fumbling hands they felt for the hole in the floor, clutching at the jagged rim as if the sheer force of their will could bring Bando back.

'He's fallen to another level,' Hul said at last. 'One of the old tunnels below—'

'He must have passed out—'

'There's a tinder-stick in his pocket. If we can get down there, feel for the lamp, see if it's still—'

'Down there? And how far is the drop?'

'I know, but ... there must be a way—'

'Hul, I'm lightest. If you clutch my hands, perhaps I could sort of ... lower myself, and—'

'Well, we've got to try *something*—'

'Wait! What's that?'

Shining up through the hole in the floor came an unearthly glow. For a moment it was no more than a pale, purplish gleam, dimly illuminating the place where Bando lay. Cata saw that this deeper, rubble-strewn tunnel was not too far below; she had shifted into place, ready to descend, but the strange light had shifted too, forming into clusters of deeper, darker purple.

'What is it?' said Hul. 'I don't understand—'

'Magic! Evil magic—'

The clusters became a swirl. Cata felt heat at her chest, and pulsing through her costume came the green glow of her crystal. She clutched Hul's arm, drawing him back from the hole. By now, the purple light was a spinning shaft of brightness, stabbing up through the rocky portal. Bewildered, Hul gazed between the purple from below and the green, dazzling rays of Cata's crystal. He stumbled back; Cata doubled over, moaning.

Then she snapped. '*Run!* Hul, just *run*—'

The purple light exploded into a flock of birds.

At once, the birds were all about them, throbbing with light, shrieking and clawing, battering wildly at the tunnel walls. Whether they were real, or only bodies of light, Cata could not tell; she knew only that her magical sympathies with all living creatures were of no avail to her here. No, they were not birds at all, these things, but bird-apparitions in the service of evil. Their hideous buffetings, their insane angry cries filled the world.

Cata ran, forgetting Bando, forgetting Hul, forgetting everything in her single desire to escape the birds, the birds.

❈ ❈ ❈

Ah, Penge!

In the single looking-glass that loomed between the hangings, Polty gazed upon his naked form. He screwed up his eyes, but only a little; the dim, flickering candles did the rest. Excitement shuddered through him. He saw himself as a vision of beauty, his hair a tumbling coppery fire, his face unjowled, his belly still firm. As for W'enge, he did not see W'enge at all. Of course not: he saw Penge, jutting upwards in all his glory.

Polty stepped towards the girl, his fingers slipping over her hair, over her throat, over the cheeks beneath her thick blindfold. He raised her from the couch; his lips sought hers; he fondled her breasts, taking each nipple into his mouth. Ah, what ecstasy shuddered through his veins! He clutched her tight, trying not to think of the ropes that bound her arms; his eyes closed and he thrilled to the girl's tremblings as she sensed the hard immensity of W'enge, pressing exultantly into the front of her gown. He pushed back her hair, whispering hotly, his words slithering like poison into her ear:

'Sister, dear sister, we are reunited at last. Can anything separate us again? Nothing, nothing – give me your answer, let your answer be *nothing*! Ah, but do you love me, sister? You must, I know you must. Do you not remember the days of our innocence, when together we ran and tumbled in the Wildwood? What bliss was ours until that wicked boy Jemany came between us! No more – he is dead, and you are mine. Beloved sister, can you not feel my manly pride, burgeoning in the certainty of possession? Can you not feel how I am swollen with seed? The time of your womanly destiny has come. Think of the life that soon shall fill your womb! Think of the son that shall burst from your loins! Ah, how I long to hold him in my arms!'

Jilda's mind reeled. In the sickly madness of the man's words was there not an echo of a voice she knew? No, impossible! But in the corrupted hissing that issued from his lips, still Jilda sensed the ghost of another. Horror filled her as he tightened his grip, forcing her to the couch, smothering her in his flabby bulk. He ripped away what remained of her gown. Jilda braced herself. The man had excited himself so much with his words that she could only hope his actions would be brief. It was certain they would be brutal. Sickened, she felt his probing hands, and the clumsy, harsh proddings of the thing between his thighs.

Oh, let it be brief!

The door burst open.

'My son, where's my son?'

'My lord, I tried to stop her, but—'

Polty reeled round. He saw the hangings on the walls, their patterns leaping in the candlelight; he saw the flustered, stumbling footman; then, shimmering in the looking-glass, he made out the thin, wizened woman. His heart froze; he clambered free from the girl and, looking disbelievingly upon Widow Waxwell, could only force from his lips the single, if not quite accurate word: '*Mother!*'

For a moment, the Widow gazed upon Polty, and Polty upon the Widow. In his bewilderment, he did not even think to cover himself, not until a strap slipped from his wooden appendage. The thing drooped, then fell to the floor with a dull thud. Polty grabbed a cushion, cowering in shame.

'M-My lord, I'm sorry,' the footman sobbed, but his words were not for Polty.

'My poor child,' the Widow burst out; her words were not for Polty either. Appalled, she went to Jilda, kissing the girl, caressing her, pulling back the blindfold. Harshly she commanded the footman to untie the girl's hands. 'Dear child, I wouldn't let them do it to you, I couldn't. I've been so weak, for so long I've stood aside—'

'Oh Widow, Widow—'

'But now I've come to take you away—'

'W-Widow, the Queen—'

'Forget her – there's a way. Now where's my son?'

Polty breathed, 'Mother, this is not what it—'

'Shut up, Poltiss, what else can it be? Don't you think I know all about you?' Jilda's hands were free now and the Widow helped her wrap herself in a blanket. Pushing the hair back from her eyes, the trembling girl let her gaze fall upon the shame-faced Polty.

A strange look came over her face.

'Now where's my *son*?' the Widow said again.

'Mother?' Still Polty did not understand.

Then he did. Standing in the gap between two hangings was Chokey, his lizardy mouth hanging open, astonished.

The Widow assessed him coolly. 'Oh Jorvel, you look like a homeless Reject! When you were born I was a mere girl – I should have known you would be an old man now, but could I have dreamed you would decay so much? Vice has destroyed you, even more than it has destroyed *me*.'

'Vice ... what? But Mother, you're ... *dead*,' Chokey breathed. His voice became stronger; he almost shouted. 'You died of fever on a voyage to Tiralos; I had the letter, you were buried at sea—'

'A story to fool you, no more—'

'But your hand! And Veeldrop, why does he call you—'

'This is mad, insane!' Polty burst out. He had pulled on his breeches now. Swiftly he tugged his tunic over his head. 'Mother, you're Goodman Waxwell's widow, Berthen Waxwell from Irion, how can you—'

The Widow fixed him a withering look. 'Poltiss, call me not by the name of *mother* – let me acknowledge no more than *one* monster as my son. Waxwell was my second husband, isn't it clear?'

It was not; but the Widow had no time for explanations now. Gripping Jilda's hand, she hustled her from the room, but not before the girl suddenly burst back into life, rushing for Polty, pummelling him with her fists.

'It's you, it's *you*, I knew it—'

'She's insane! Get off me, bitch—'

'Jilda, it's no good, come away—'

'Jilda?' said Polty, when the girl was gone. But he was not quite sure who 'Jilda' was.

He looked at Chokey. Both men were dazed, barely believing these astonishing events. Could it be true that Berthen Waxwell and Lady Lolenda, Dowager Archduchess of Irion, were one and the same?

'I don't … understand,' said Polty.

'I … don't understand,' said Chokey.

The footman didn't either, but said nothing.

A new look came into Polty's eyes; it was rather as if, to allay his shame, he felt compelled to goad himself to violence. Menacingly, he stepped towards the brothel-keeper. 'Say, what were you doing, spying on me? Is this how you reward your best customer? You filthy, disgusting pervert!'

Unafraid, Chokey only raised an eyebrow, gesturing towards the fallen W'enge, lying on the floor like a truncheon or club. 'Come, Master Veeldrop, there have been rumours, have there not? I merely wished to ascertain whether they were true. Must I not keep up with the *tastes* of my customers, if I am to give them the service they expect?'

Polty picked up W'enge. He weighed it in his hand.

'Pox, was it?' the old man continued. 'Poor Master Veeldrop, didn't I warn you about those foreign climes? Silly boy, you should have been more careful. How you must have wept as you stood before the surgeon! Still, I'm glad you've found *some* method of gratification – hm, but I'm afraid I might have to *charge* you a little more. After all, that thing could do some damage – more than Reny Bolbarr, I'll be bound.'

'You're … you're mocking me—'

Chokey blinked innocently. 'Master Veeldrop?'

'You're … *mocking* me.' Polty's voice was hoarse.

'Very well, I'm mocking you.' Chokey's eyes narrowed. Suddenly he looked more like a lizard than ever before. 'And why shouldn't I? Don't you think I've had enough of you, coming in here with your superior airs, expecting to be fawned over like the finest quality? Don't you think I've a hundred customers as good as you? Why, better – *far* better! You haven't even got a title! And how dare you call my mother *mother*? I've put up with you for a long time, Veeldrop, but no more. You can take your chunk of wood and go – you're *barred*. This is an establishment for gentlemen, not geldings!'

'You dirty beast!' Polty lunged forward, raising W'enge as a weapon. But the footman was too fast. Rushing to protect his master, he seized Polty's arm. Polty spun round. His fist smashed into the footman's belly. The fellow doubled over, crumpling to the floor. Kicking him in the ribs, Polty coshed him with W'enge, then made again for Chokey.

He seized the old man by the throat.

'Polty! What's going on? What was Widow Waxwell—'

It was Bean. Alarmed, he had searched the side-chambers, looking for the one that contained Polty. He had found his friend not a moment too soon.

'Come in, come in,' Chokey gasped. 'We're just having a fine old chat, the gelding and I—'

'I'm *not* a gelding!' Polty swung back W'enge.

Chokey was nothing if not fearless. 'But I suspect,' he grinned, 'that you shall never father children. At least, never again—'

'Again? What do you mean?'

'Polty—' Bean touched his friend's arm. 'It's getting late. Shouldn't we—'

'Leave me, Bean!' Polty leaned close to the lizard-man's face. 'I said, what do you mean?'

A gurgling came from Chokey's throat; perhaps it was laughter. 'How touching, Master Veeldrop, that a man like you should wish so hard for children. Isn't it touching, Master Throsh? Oh, but they go to the bad, they do – look at my mother, then look at me. Look at my brats, Torvester and Elabeth – rebels the pair of them, traitors to His Majesty. If they weren't dead already, I swear I'd kill them with my own bare hands. You're a sentimentalist, Veeldrop. I just wouldn't have expected it, that's all.'

It was the last long speech Chokey would deliver. Polty tightened his grip on the old man's throat. He slammed him against the wall, swung him back and forth, then hurled him, like a harlot, down on the couch.

'*Tell me what you mean!*' Polty screamed.

Bean danced helplessly behind him. 'Polty, Polty—'

Chokey's head lolled back and forth, as if it were already broken at the neck. His laughter came again, cracked and crazed. 'Remember the night before you sailed for Unang Lia? Of course you don't remember! You were blind, Master Veeldrop! How long ago was it, nine moonlives or more?'

Polty's fists slammed into Chokey.

'Polty, no! Leave him—'

'What are you talking about?'

Chokey only laughed again, bubbles of blood gurgling from his mouth. 'Blind you were, blind! How could you remember who was working that night? How could you remember the lovely Vy? You fool, *Miss Vyella Rextel* is carrying your child!'

'No!' Polty screamed. He struck Chokey again, this time with W'enge, slamming down the cudgel-like thing again and again on the brothel-keeper's head. Blood leapt from the old man's skull, splattering the looking-glass in a savage arc. Brains oozed from the lizard-like head.

W'enge clattered to the floor.

Polty slumped down, spent; Bean, weak with shock, collapsed beside his friend. He held Polty tight, tenderly stroking his sobbing, coppery head.

Chapter 34

THE DEAD COME BACK

Cata collapsed to the rocky floor. For some moments she lay there, breathing deeply, thinking of nothing but the birds and their hideous, unearthly cries.

Only slowly did she realise she could hear their cries no longer; still more slowly did she see that she was no longer in the dank, dark tunnel. A golden softness shone around her. Scrambling up, pushing back her hair, Cata found that she was in a low, circular chamber, illuminated in the centre by a column of blue-tinged light.

At first she thought the light was magic; then she saw that it was the moon, shining down through a shaft in the stone – as the light came from a circle in the ceiling, so it descended through a circle in the floor, penetrating through level after level of the subterranean domain.

Cata realised that she must be directly beneath the Great Temple of Agonis. Five archways opened off from the round chamber. What was it Hul had said? *Temple Cross, where the lines meet.*

But where was *he*? 'Hul? Hul?'

Cata called down the tunnels, each in turn; then she stopped, uneasy. She did not want the birds to come again, or something worse. What would become of Bando, what would become of Hul, she could not guess. Later she would search for them, but there was something she had to do first. Would not Hul and Bando tell her so, if they were here?

Cata was the rebels' last chance.

On the floor beside her lay the long headpiece which formed the head and neck of her Black Swan costume: this, at least, she hadn't lost.

Cata examined it in the moonlight. Bedraggled, but it would have to do. She looked about her carefully. Now which tunnel had she come from? Could she be certain?

Not entirely. But certain enough.

She thought of Hul's directions, and set out quickly.

'Father ... Father?'

Hawk of Darkness crouched over the corpse of Chokey. By the door lay the footman with unravelling braid, his neck a twisted mass of deep, blue bruises.

'Father ... Father!'

Useless, of course, to attempt to revive him; what was there to revive, when the brothel-keeper's brains were splattered bloodily over the looking-glass? Even though Hawk of Darkness might possess mysterious powers, they were by no means strong enough to reverse a death so decisive.

Choking sobs welled from behind his mask.

'Father, bastard I may have been, but was I not still yours? And always my wish was only that you love me! How I longed for you to embrace me before you died, even once! Here, let me put your hands upon my shoulders ... Oh, but how cold they are! Oh, they slip away!'

Slowly, the dark figure removed his bejewelled mask. Raising up his father in his arms, he kissed the cold lips, then gently let the corpse slip back to the floor.

'Ah,' he whispered, 'but I did not foresee this! Never did my master warn me this could happen! Cursed, cursed be Poltiss Veeldrop!'

Rising, he turned to the looking-glass. The visage that confronted him was one of horror. Moving forward in the hazy lamplight, he ran a gloved hand down the cold glass, then turned back to his dead father.

Suddenly, viciously, he kicked the corpse.

'Father,' he cried, 'I'm not a monster! I'm not an animal! What am I but your son, your son?'

Then, again sobbing, 'Cursed be Veeldrop, curse him!'

✵ ✵ ✵

'I can't believe it! I just can't believe it!'

One moment raging, the next sorrowing, Constansia Cham-Charing flung herself about her large, elaborate dressing-room. Sometimes she would cast herself down on a chaise-longue, as if about to give way to tears; immediately she would rise, pacing again and cursing, the train of her gown swishing angrily behind her. Once, with moans of *Poor, poor Tishy* and *How lovely she would have looked*, she even sobbed upon her daughter's sleek white costume, which stood waiting on its dressmaker's dummy.

That silk would mark *so* easily!

'Your Ladyship, please—' Betty, her personal maid, looked on helplessly. There were pins in her mouth. There were plumes in her hands. What was Betty to do? Her Ladyship was half undressed, and appeared determined to go *on* being half undressed until the evening was over.

'Constansia, calm *down*,' said Freddie Chayn in a voice that was not entirely calm itself. Resplendent in an extraordinary puce outfit, the heir to a worthless principality stood amongst the forests of hanging gowns with the awkward air of a man looking for something to lean against – or, perhaps, with the awkward air of a *man*, since he was, after all, in a lady's dressing-room.

Betty was shocked. Propriety seemed to have gone to the winds; but then, she supposed, it wasn't every day that the young mistress ... and then she began to snivel too, stifling herself with a sharp, snorting intake of breath.

Constansia shot the girl an exasperated look, but hardly as exasperated as the one she gave Freddie, which was withering. 'Calm down? Calm *down*? How can I *calm down* when my daughter is dead?'

'You know that's not true,' Freddie sighed. 'Haven't I been back and forth to the Temple all day? They've questioned the witnesses, they've shifted the rubble, they've ...' Breaking off, he went to her. Poor Constansia! Gripping her hand, he said in a gentler tone, 'You silly old stick, they'd have found her if she – if she were ... You *know* she was with us after it happened – we saw her, still in one piece ... She's just ... *missing*, that's all.'

'Yes, kidnapped!' Constansia caught her throat. 'Abducted by – by rebels...'

'No, no – it's impossible, I swear it.'

'Freddie, how can you be so sure?'

'I just ... well, what would *rebels* want with Tishy?'

The withering look returned to Constansia's face. Really! One brought people into one's circle, trusted them intimately, and then what happened? They insulted one to one's face!

She spoke levelly, as if to a child. 'My daughter *is* a young lady of quality, is she not? And am I not a woman of means? Oh, I *know* Tishy may not be Queen – I *know* I am not what I was; I can barely hold a candle to the Bolbarrs and Venturons. But have we not seen enough of these rebels to take their measure? We were separated in the Temple! Tishy was there, and they took her! It's clear!'

'Is it? We've had no ransom demand, have we?'

'They're biding their time. To get us more worried.'

Another voice came. 'Constansia, you could hardly be *more* worried.'

It was Lady Margrave. Constansia's mouth set hard. Her old friend had rallied remarkably. With a Ball to attend, Elsan had called on instincts honed over arduous years of socialising. In a gown fashioned from innumerable speckled feathers, bird-mask held lightly up to her face, she had entered with a flourish. Her mask fell, swinging in her gloved hand – but she might have had another mask fixed firmly over her powdered face.

'Good evening, Freddie. What *is* that costume?'

'Puce Chayn Warbler,' said Freddie, not a little embarrassed. 'Constansia chose it. What's yours?'

'Sparrows of the World – a certain modesty is *becoming* in a woman of my years, I like to think. But Constansia, you're not dressed! Well, barely – where are your feathers? What sort of Blue Plumed Plover are you?

Don't you know we'll have to leave soon? Oh, and your hair! Is your maid as lazy as she looks, or is it you, you senile old baggage?'

What a way to speak to Her Ladyship! Betty gulped, or would have done, had she not realised that her mouth was full of pins. Tentatively she approached Her Ladyship again and was about to fix a plume, just one, when her mistress burst free from her, suddenly angry.

She shook her finger at Lady Margrave. 'Oh, it's all very well for you, Elsan! Is *your* daughter bound and gagged in a rebel stronghold – why, perhaps with unshaven, thuggish brutes threatening, at any moment, to deprive her of her virtue?'

'Of course not! I haven't got a daughter, as well you know.'

'Actually, there *is* another possibility,' said Freddie.

'What?' Constansia turned sharply. So did Elsan.

'We-ell, we're missing someone, aren't we?'

'We know that!' Constansia stamped her foot.

'I *meant* Professor Mercol. He was to come here and don that silly outfit you found for him, wasn't he?'

'Freddie, how dare you! *Silly?*'

Silly or not, the Derkold Bald Eagle costume still stood in the corner. Gazing upon it, Lady Margrave suddenly saw it as sinister – which it was.

The bald, domed headpiece in particular.

'Freddie, what are you saying?'

'I'm saying that he's still not here, as late as this. I didn't want to believe it, but I … I'm afraid Professor Mercol's not *going* to be here. I've sent round to his rooms several times this afternoon, and he's – he's…'

'F-Freddie?' Constansia's voice trembled.

'Well, haven't you noticed him looking at Tishy? And how much time *she* spends with him? Oh, I know he's her tutor, I know she wants to learn, but …' Freddie looked down, flushing. 'I … I think they may have *eloped*.'

Constansia screamed.

Betty swallowed the pins.

As for Lady Margrave, her hand went to her mouth. The bright manner of moments earlier cracked away. Hope against hope, she had told herself that the situation would be saved. Now she knew it was hopeless.

'Oh, but this is appalling,' she gasped. 'Constansia, think of the reprisals! Our party's down by *two*! You'll be banned from the palace! Your career in society – Constansia, it's over, all over! Oh, that selfish, wicked girl!'

Ignored by the others, the maid had slumped to her knees between two racks of especially fine gowns.

'Wicked?' their owner wailed. 'What care I for my social career?' (Constansia had seldom cared for anything else.) 'I'm thinking of my daughter, my poor ruined child … Oh Tishy, and you would have been the belle of the Ball!'

'Well, I wouldn't go *quite* that—'

'Freddie!' Lady Margrave stamped on his foot.

'Damn it, at least the wretched girl's *married* at last, isn't she?' he muttered, flashing her an angry look.

The maid, meanwhile, had collapsed on her side, mouth open in agony. Poor Betty looked as though she would like to scream, but no sound issued forth; still, Constansia made sound enough for both. Desperately she clung to the dressmaker's dummy, which rocked precariously back and forth as she delivered herself of the following monologue:

'Freddie, Freddie, so you were right! Did you not say this was a bad choice? Did you not ask if a mother was wise to dress her daughter as a Zaxon Nightingale? Did you not remind me that a certain notorious lady is known familiarly by the name of that bird? Alas, in the blindness of a mother's love, I thought only that this costume was beautiful, white, and carried a certain bracing suggestion of a bride.'

Fresh wailings burst forth. 'Yes, a bride – for what fond hopes had I but that tonight would secure for my daughter, at last, the splendid match that would lift her from the ignominy of my tottering house, returning her to those heights I thought to be her destiny? But to fling herself away on a lecherous, treacherous old *nobody*! It cannot be! Why did I let that man in my house? Why did I not fling my daughter's books into the fire? Oh Tishy, why would you ever be a learned lady?'

There would have been more, but just then there was an interruption. It was the butler. There were visitors in the drawing room.

'What?' Angrily, Constansia brushed her eyes. 'Visitors, on the night of the Ball? Who—'

With some uneasiness, the butler eyed the inert, blue-faced form of Lady Cham-Charing's personal maid, lying unregarded beneath a rack of gowns; perhaps that was why his voice quavered as he informed his mistress that the older of the two visitors had given her name as Lady Lolenda Ixiter of Irion.

Constansia looked at Elsan. Elsan looked at Constansia.

In the same instant, they both fainted.

Chapter 35

WHAT I DID FOR LOVE

'Aargh!'

  'No—'

  'I wish—'

  'We all *wish*—'

  'But where to *now*?'

  'What *was* that p-place?'

  'I'm certain it was Xorgos—'

  'What? Ejjy, are y-you all right?'

  'Xorgos Island! The prison island—'

  'We blasted it! But why? Why didn't—'

  'That's where all the worst rebel prisoners—'

  'You mean we blasted the *rebels*? B-But why—'

  'Didn't you see? We were setting them *free*, we—'

Careering over the docks, over the bay, and out into the darkness of the Gulf of Ejland, the skyship had made its way to Xorgos Island, where the Bluejackets kept so many of their rebel captives. In a bolt of thunder, the prison walls had cracked and the notorious Pillar of Death, the tower that dominated the island, had crashed to the ground. How many prisoners might escape tonight, finding their way back to the mainland, was impossible to say. But this one magic blast was a rebel outrage more shocking than any there had been before.

  'If only we could control this wretched thing! If Jem—'

  'Yes, if *Jem* were here! Littler, have you noticed—'

  'What, that no one's controlling this? Myla's—'

  'And I wish she weren't! This evil magic—'

  'Don't say it, Raj! B-But where can we—'

  'To Agondon? We're going back—'

  'You can tell? Turn, tumble—'

  'But the lights! See them—'

  'I c-can't! Hey, Ejjy—'

  '*Oof!* L-Littler—'

  'Not again—'

  '*Aargh!*'

  'No!'

'I … I can really see her?'

'You've slopped ale in me mug enough times, Olch, so I suppose I should be kind,' said Figaro Fingers with a black grin, pocketing the recent profits from the Cat & Crown. Holding aloft a smoking lantern, he led the hunched petitioner down a dank passageway.

They stopped before a heavy, grilled door. 'But don't expect more than this, eh? Even this is more than me job's worth. You'll see her for a five, then I opens the door again, eh?'

The turnkey jingled a formidable bunch of keys. 'Still, if you're quick, I dare say you've time to enjoy yourself with your lady-wife? One last time, eh?'

Wiggler Olch was a fellow of no particular courage, no particular gallantry; nonetheless, this insult to his wife would have been enough to stir him to fury at another time; now he barely registered the turnkey's words. Shuddering, he peered into the bleak cell. The stench was vile. Rats scurried through damp straw. But Wiggler saw only the averted form of Nirry, shadowy in a circle of candlelight. In a sackcloth prison shift, his condemned wife knelt before a small, metallic Circle of Agonis, her hands clasped in fervent prayer.

Wiggler's eyes filled with tears. How small she looked! How frail!

'N-Nirry, love? N-Nirry, it's—'

'Wiggler?'

Slowly, Nirry turned. Already she seemed half-lost to the world. Wiggler brushed his eyes. He struggled to smile, but why he should smile he did not know. Even in the weak candlelight, he saw the dark circles under his wife's eyes, black against the pallor of her stricken face.

There was so much they might have said. But then again, only one thing mattered now.

'I … love you, Wiggler.'

'I love you, Nirry.'

They clung together, hearts beating hard, until – much too soon – the turnkey came back.

❊   ❊   ❊

'I can't believe it! I just can't believe it!'

Wind howled in the chimneys of Cham-Charing House and rattled insistently at the drawing-room shutters. Half in her bird costume, half in a shawl, the mistress of the house paced before the fire, barely aware of its lapping heat. She was too restless to sit; Elsan Margrave, in her Sparrows of the World costume, leaned forward in her chair.

Intently the two friends stared at the old woman on the sofa. Would they have recognised this decayed creature, had she not greeted them in the ardent voice of girlhood? *Consy Grace! It's Lolenda Mynes, remember? … Elsan Crispian! And to think you married 'Stick-in-the-mud' Margrave!* It was uncanny, as if the wizened body of this old woman had captured the spirit of a long-dead girl, bearing it within her like a fluttering, frightened starling.

As for the living girl who sat beside her, huddled in a blanket over her tattered gown, Lolenda's old friends barely gave her a glance. Yes, they might have remembered Miss Quisto, a Quick-girl from some years ago; they might have been shocked by her fate; but this could only pall beside their astonishment at Lolenda. Questions crowded their minds. How had she assumed the guise of Widow Waxwell? Whatever had happened to her poor hand?

Freddie, moving awkwardly in his Puce Chayn Warbler garb, returned from the drinks tray, handing out glasses of rum and orandy. Jilda struggled to produce a smile; the others could still only gaze upon Lolenda.

'You ... *faked* your own death?' Lady Margrave shook her head. 'This is almost too much to take in.'

'But to marry a country surgeon! To vanish from society!' Constansia shuddered, despite the heat from the fire at her back. 'Lolenda, I ... I just don't understand you.'

The woman who had been known as Berthen Waxwell looked down sadly. There was much that she must explain; as she launched into her story, the bewilderment of her listeners could only grow. More than once, the friends of her girlhood would be moved to protest, bursting out that this was insane, that this could not be the real Lolenda. Horror mingled in them with sorrow as they heard what had happened to the girl who had once been so much like themselves.

LOLENDA'S STORY

My old friends, you are women of the strictest moral rectitude. There was a time when I, too, enjoyed such a reputation; like you, Elsan, I was known for my loyalty to my husband; like you, Constansia, I was an intimate of the Archmaximate – though I suspect my own intimacy was greater than yours. How could I not be respected and revered? My husband was Archduke of Irion, but like the son who now bears that title, I brought little credit to my noble role.

Ah, but the horror that fills your eyes! – Elsan, turn not away; Constansia, cover not your ears; you cannot pretend you have not heard of my son, nor of that den of iniquity that goes by the name of Chokey's. Is that name not a byword through all Agondon, even amongst its most pious citizenry? If there are those who do not believe the place exists, many are they who know only too well what became of the betrayer of Ejard Red. Since leaving his ruined castle, turning his back upon his

215

native lands, my son has wallowed like a pig in the foulest sty – but such vice was once his mother's, too.

You say this must be false? If only that were so! – Dearest Elsan, dearest Constansia, do you not recall those sweet Theron-seasons of our virgin days? Remember how we would punt across the Riel with Mazy Tarfoot, long before they built Regent's Bridge? Remember how we ran though the daffodils and daisies, scooping at the air with our butterfly nets, where now sprawl the villas of Ollon-Quintal? How we laughed, how we played! My friends, as all this lives in my memory, so there must live those temptations that assailed me after I left those days behind.

But why speak of temptation? I must speak, rather, of yielding – and marriage, I am afraid, did nothing to curb my desires. Many a time did I betray the Archduke, disporting myself like a wanton harlot; many a time it was with gentlemen of the highest *outward* virtue with whom I gratified my depraved lusts. – Constansia, sink not to your knees! Elsan, cover not your face! The truth must be told; for too long have I dissembled ... And yet, I beg you, shun me not as a thing infected; for this Circle of Agonis that hangs at my breast is no badge of hypocrisy. As you are a pious woman, Constansia – as *you* are, Elsan – can you not see that one may suppress one's evil, guided by the love of the Lord Agonis? My friends, I have repented, long and hard, for all the evils of my former life.

What happened was this. After a long course of dissipation, I was at last condignly punished. Again and again I had indulged in *affaires* with young men from Temple College; while *you*, my friends, imagined I came to Agondon for the respectable pleasures of the social round, in truth my greatest joys were in the secrecy of my boudoir, where I rutted like a beast with these ardent, eager boys. How it amused me to corrupt their hearts, to fill their innocent bodies with the burning fevers of lust!

And yet there was one young man I almost loved; one who was more to me than a mere plaything. Perhaps that was why he was my undoing – my *undoing*, I say, for what could I feel but horrified shame when I discovered that my dear, sweet Silas (such was his name), with whom I had indulged in every bestial passion, bore upon his thigh the mark of the Vaga? – Yes, my friends, well may you look appalled! What viler debasement for any woman of Ejland than to give herself to a Vaga-man? At once I saw where my lusts had led me. My heart cracked open; I sobbed like a child, and longed again for the love of the Lord Agonis.

'Alas, my punishment was just beginning. I discovered that I was to bear the Vaga's child. Sickened, I thought I would take my life, even nerved myself to the fatal act; often, since then, I have wished I had accomplished it. But no; in the fervour of my rediscovered faith, I knew I could never commit so grave a sin. Instead, I resolved upon a life of penance. So it was that I arranged reports of my death; then, after my confinement – giving up the spawn of Vaga-lust to the Archmaximate, who

216

promised to dispose of it as he saw fit – I returned in secret to the Valleys of the Tarn, and my husband's seat of Irion. Assuming the name Berthen Spratt, after a servant-girl I had met in Agondon, I took upon myself the guise of a simple, pious widow.

You might wonder that I went back to Irion. I told myself I longed to be close to my husband, that the knowledge of his nearness would spur my penance; I told myself that sometimes I might look upon my son – a handsome creature then, with beautiful blond curls – from beneath the headscarf of my widow's weeds.

If only I had not had a darker motive! That motive, I am afraid, is shameful to reveal; and yet, what can shame me now, after all I have revealed thus far? Suffice to say that my young Vaga-man, suppressing the secret of his tainted blood, was now Lector of Irion. – Yes, Constansia, it is monstrous, I know. A Vaga, taking upon himself the mantle of the faith? Never mind, Silas met his punishment in time, a harsh punishment indeed – but that is another story. I say here only that certain yearnings were not expelled *wholly* from my heart, for all that I had given up my former life … Yet how truly I longed to expel them! Could I but mortify myself still *more*, I imagined I might taste again the purity I had lost.

It was at about this time that my husband died. What fresh despair burst in my heart! Now a widow in truth, I was glad only that the Archduke's death was an occasion for grieving all through the Tarn; at least, I might unburden *some* of my sorrows. My poor husband! How I had betrayed him! Yet still I was aware of the lust that my Vaga-man stirred in my heart; many a time I longed to go to him, casting off my widow's weeds, surrendering once again to his urgent passions.

That was when I met Nathanian Waxwell, who had just come to Irion to practise medicine. To me, he seemed a man of the utmost piety; for a time, I suppose, I even loved him. When he asked me to marry him, like a fool I imagined I was redeemed at last.

But still my punishment had yet to run its course. On the night of our nuptials, Goodman Waxwell asked me to confess the sins of my past. Of course I lied, speaking only of trivial things; and yet, the urge to unburden myself warred in my heart with this instinct of prudence. Perhaps I betrayed myself through a gesture, through a look; in any case, I knew my husband did not believe me. Soon, like an insistent rat, he was gnawing at my resistance, longing to know what sins I concealed; yes, it was a matter of hints, insinuations, but slowly his suspicion and jealousy poisoned any chance of happiness we had.

In his pleadings for the truth, he grew more ardent; once he even came to me begging in tears, insisting that he could see my unhappiness, that he would forgive me, that he longed only to help me as a counsellor and friend. What could I say? His longing was my longing; I told him all.

217

The sequel, of course, is simple enough. Call me a fool; but call me a fool to have married him at all. First he kept me imprisoned in his attic, alternately weeping over me, violating my body and terrorising me with visions of the damnation that would be mine. Then one morning, after a night of fervent prayer, he came to me and declared that he knew the source of my sin. He grabbed my right hand. – Can you guess why, Constansia? Can you guess why, Elsan?

No, I thought not, for I had long contrived to conceal the thin, translucent webbing between the third and fourth fingers. Only to a close observer was it visible, but my husband was nothing if not a close observer.

It was then that I heard a theory he would often voice again, one with which he would justify many cruelties during his long reign as Irion's physician. He declared that my deformity was the source of my evil, an outward manifestation of a diseased spirit. Only through surgery could my Essence be saved; my husband declared there was no other way. How he wept with me! How he prayed!

Then he cut my hand off with an axe.

So began the longest chapter of my sufferings as I endured the terror of my husband's rule. Perhaps you think my fate was deserved, a rightful punishment; or, perhaps, you wonder why I did not escape from him. I can say only that I lived as if paralysed under Waxwell's fearful thrall. All I could do was suffer and suffer, for secretly I believed that I deserved no more.

But all things end in time, perhaps even guilt, and now I see that my own guilt was as nothing to the depravity of my husband; worse still, that Waxwell was a mere child in evil compared to his sometime paramour and pupil, Umbecca Veeldrop, who made me her companion after my husband's death. To think that monster should have taken my place as *grande dame* of Irion! To think that she should now preside in Agondon too! How I cursed my passivity as I sat back and watched her inexorable rise!

I plead only that I was frightened of Umbecca, as I had been frightened of Waxwell before. But that is in the past. Life has broken me, but now I claw together all the shattered pieces of my youthful spirit. My days as Widow Waxwell I put behind me. Tonight I have broken from Umbecca; worse, perhaps, I have defied the Queen, who has grown almost as evil as her aunt, and would have consigned this child you see beside me to the degradation of a harlot's life.

Oh Constansia, oh Elsan, I know you have heard things about this girl; the mills of rumour grind small, and they have ground my poor Jilda Quisto to dust. I beg you not to believe that she is abandoned, any more than you believe that Lady Umbecca is, as she would have us believe, a pious embodiment of virtue. This child is more sinned against than sinning, and I shall be bold enough to say that so am I.

My friends, we have no money; we have no home. We do not expect you to approve of us; perhaps we even disgust you. But as you are women of true piety – and as you loved me once, on those hot, lazy days in Ollon Fields – I beg you not to turn us away.

We throw ourselves upon your protection.

There was a moment of silence when the story was over. Freddie, with burning cheeks, made again for the drinks tray; Jilda, shudderingly, sank into her blanket, while Lady Margrave hunched over, as if in pain.

As for Lady Cham-Charing, she paced across the carpet as the wizened crone who had been Lolenda Mynes struggled slowly, unsteadily to her feet. A cavern of coals crashed in the fire, sending up a cascade of sparks. It might have been a signal. With a guttural cry, Constansia flung herself upon her old friend. They embraced, heaving with sobs; then Lady Margrave joined them too.

Freddie, ludicrous in his Puce Chayn Warbler garb, perched on the arm of Jilda's sofa. Gesturing to the affecting scene, he clinked his glass awkwardly against hers. When the poor girl managed a smile, he was delighted. For all the disorder of her dress – or, perhaps, because of it – Freddie was beginning to see that Miss Quisto was a *very* pretty girl.

She was also much younger than Miss Tilsy Fash.

The butler entered. If the old fellow was still perturbed by Betty's accident, nonetheless he was doing a splendid job in maintaining his demeanour.

He *hem-hemmed* for Her Ladyship.

'What is it, Baines?' said Freddie at last.

'Sir, if I may, the carriage … the carriage still waits.'

Freddie stood with a gasp. 'The Ball!'

Only now did the party remember the catastrophe that hung over them like a sword, ready to descend. With embraces and tears, they had promised to protect Lady Lolenda and the girl she had saved. But what protection would they have to give, if they did not appear at the Ball?

Elsan cried, 'We *must* go, we must—'

'But Tishy,' cried Constansia, 'Professor Mercol—'

'Wait!' It was Freddie who took the lead. 'The Professor's costume would have concealed him completely. Lady Lolenda, you're about the same size. Would you be willing to dress up as a Vantage Bald Eagle?'

Lolenda looked bewildered.

'And … Miss Quisto,' Constansia leapt in, 'I'm … I'm going to ask you to be my daughter. For tonight, at least. You're with us, Miss Quisto? You're with us, Lolenda? Then, tomorrow, we can get you out of Agondon.'

219

'Who … who is it?'

The voice is small, tremulous. How could it be otherwise, in such depths of fear? All around is darkness, stench and the squeakings of rats. Moans come intermittently from the chained, bleeding woman.

And now there is the creak of the door; now, a furtive footstep.

'Who … who are you?' Raggle breathes as a hand rips away the ropes that bind his limbs. 'Have … you come to save me? Have … you come to kill me?'

No reply. The hand wrenches Raggle brutally to his feet, dragging him out through the door. The child struggles, kicks, sure that death has come for him.

But the hand propels him forward. 'Go, child, go—'

'Wh-what?' Raggle lingers. 'But that lady, there's that—'

'Have I not done enough? *Go*—'

Raggle breaks into a run.

Ahead, all is blackness. He blunders into a wall, picks himself up, edges forward, terrified and sobbing. Not once does the small boy look behind him, or see the golden glow that begins to shimmer, like an aura, about the mysterious, caped being who has set him free.

The being smiles. Another move in the game.

Chapter 36

TURN ROUND CLOCKWISE

The birds, the birds.

But gone now? Were they gone now?

Hul whispered, 'Cata ... Cata?'

No reply.

'Cata, can you hear me?'

Still no reply.

Well, *she* was gone. Hul had fallen to the stony floor. For a time he lay there, dazed and spent. And how was he to get up, in his Festival Turkey costume? The scholar was naturally a slender fellow; in this get-up, he was as fat as Lady Umbecca.

Somehow he hauled himself to his feet at last. Awkwardly, he felt for his spectacles. *Hm.* Still in one piece. And much good they did him.

All was darkness.

No, wait. What was this glimmering, somewhere up ahead? Golden ... not purple like those dreadful bird-things. A lantern? Whose lantern?

Dimly Hul recalled the direction in which he had run. Of course, it had been almost automatic, his steps thudding along the old familiar way.

He had come through Vytoni Gap.

That had been Hul's name for that particular hole in the wall, that place where the rock was thin and smashed through. But how extraordinary that the hole should still be here! Evidently, few in latter years had explored the darker recesses of this secret place.

Hul was in the Chamber of Forbidden Texts.

And so, he surmised, was someone else.

Curiosity overcame the scholar. He could hardly return to the labyrinth and its utter darkness. Could he, perhaps, surprise this *someone else*? Could he steal the lamp?

Barely daring to breathe, he squeezed past a teetering set of shelves. One turn, then a turn more, and he might just see who the *someone else* was. There was a rasp of feathers – Hul was surprised he had any left by now – and he stood stock-still for some moments, hoping he had not been heard.

And what could Hul hear?

A turning page. An indrawn breath.

It was rather a *light* breath. *Light?* Yes ... that was the word. He edged forward, wishing he had been dressed as anything but a Festival Turkey. How slowly, how very slowly he moved!

221

Feathers, more feathers rasped away.

He turned the second corner. Now it was Hul who drew in his breath. A *lady* scholar?

The lady had been translating; now, laying down her pen, she leaned back in her chair and, with a critical frown, began to read her work aloud:

FIVE-STAVE TWO

I.

Thus it came to pass that Ondon, Lord Secular of the Children of Agonis, would have them stay unstirring in the green and wooded edge-land: many were the rejoicings of the Children of Agonis, certain now that they had reached their journey's end, and need journey no more.

II.

Yet amongst the Children of Agonis there was a caste of brother-priests, who, in all the days before this journey's end, had been entrusted with a sacred task: these priests were called the Bearers of the Vexing Gem, and from their leader, Father-Priest Ir-Ion, anguished words now came.

III.

For in his devotion to Orok, the dying god, and to Agonis, son of the dying god, Father-Priest Ir-Ion must declare this green and wooded land lay but at the edge of the icy northern realms: further still was the distance they must travel to fulfil the divine destiny.

IV.

So it was that many were the words of counsel Father-Priest Ir-Ion to their leader now set forth: but the case it was that Ondon attended not, for worldly and corrupt had this first of monarchs grown, and no more to the Bearers of the Vexing Gem would heed.

V.

And still his ears were closed when Father-Priest Ir-Ion would offer of his reasons even such as this: that this green and wooded edge-land where Ondon now would dwell had been intended not for the Children of Agonis but rather for the race of Viana, goddess of earth.

Thoughtfully, the lady chewed the end of her pen.

To Hul what she had read was mystic mumbo-jumbo, but what of it? Lady or not, she was a scholar of remarkable promise. Quite remarkable.

'But what *is* this book called?' the lady sighed. '*Something of the Winds.*' She said the title in Juvescial. '*Something*, but what?'

Hul could not help himself. *'Lamasery*, my dear.'

'Wh-what?' Tishy looked up, blinking. Had she really heard a voice?

There was a rasping sound, and a heavy volume crashed to the floor. Flapping his wings, Hul blundered into the light.

Tishy screamed – but then, at once, she laughed. What joke was this? A man dressed as a *turkey*?

The turkey tripped and fell.

'Oh no—' Tishy cried, remembering.

And Hul, turning, saw the sprawled, inert figure that had made him trip.

'Professor Mercol!'

'Damn. Damn.'

Had he been this way already? Jem turned slowly, holding aloft his heavy taper. For how long had he been wandering through this dark labyrinth? Only once before had he ventured beneath the Great Temple. That had been in the company of Lord Empster, and they had entered by quite a different way.

Apprehensively he gazed about the gloomy, sinister chamber that he found himself in now. If he had not been in this one before, he had been in others like it: too many others. Reddish in the taper-light, the tombs and vaults huddled beneath a maze of archways and columns. On one tomb, clouded under thick, draping cobwebs, was a crumbling representation of the Lord Agonis, flanked by the forms of his sister and brother gods. It was a monument of the sort known as a 'Five-God', popular many epicycles ago. As always, the central figure was half-turned, as if about to walk away; the smaller figures of his sisters and brothers reached out their hands, as if imploring him to join them in the Vast.

Jem sighed wearily. Yes, he *had* been here before. He must retrace his steps – and this time, go a different way. Somehow he must find where they had taken Raggle.

Quite what he would do then, Jem was not sure. But he had a Bluejacket uniform. He had a musket.

He turned, and as he turned, he heard a soft flurrying, as of something alive.

A rat? It didn't sound like a rat.

He turned back to see a purplish, translucent form, hovering above the Five-God.

It was a bird, a ghostly bird. For a moment the bird flopped aimlessly, then dived towards Jem, as if to attack.

He lunged out with the torch.

The bird passed through the flame, then was gone.

Then all at once others birds were there, looming from behind the stat-ues, columns and slabs, bathing the chamber in an eerie purple light. They circled evilly through the archways, passing like phantoms between the curtains of cobwebs. Jem backed away, the blue crystal throbbing at his chest. He would turn and run. But run which way?

The birds were everywhere.

That was when the tomb-figure of Lord Agonis began to glow, at first softly, then more brightly, with a rich golden light. At once the birds were flickering, fading. Jem gasped. It might have been an illusion, but the stone Agonis was turning round to face him.

Jem sank to his knees, his burning torch almost falling to the floor. Now his crystal pulsed as if in warning as an ethereal music sounded on the air and the stone Agonis began, grotesquely, to sing.

It was a weird, fluting song, unearthly in its melody. There were three verses, and after each verse the sister and brother gods, glowing with their own particular colours, joined in with a chorus.

THE FIVE-GOD'S SONG

AGONIS: *Young Prince of Ejland, can it really be you?*
All your disguise cannot hide what is true:
So, as was destined, we meet once again
On this fickle stage in the world of men.
   CHORUS: *Turn round clockwise, a fifteenth back:*
   That is your track, that is your track.

AGONIS: *Young Prince Jemany, so you like me not?*
What, you'd prefer it if I die and rot?
Judge me not rashly, you will learn much more
When we at last reach the end of this war.
   CHORUS: *Turn round clockwise, & c.*

AGONIS: *Blue king and red king, red king and blue king:*
Jem-Jem-Jemany, for which do you sing?
Give no quick answer, lest you should be wrong:
Perhaps you might soon sing a different song!
   CHORUS: *Turn round clockwise, &c.*

The chorus, after several repetitions, died away.

Later, Jem would think over the strange verses; for now, he barely understood them. All that made sense was the chorus. Each time they sang, the stone hands of the sister and brother gods would shift, just a little; by the end, they were pointing the way for Jem to go.

Stumbling back to his feet, he tightened his grip on his flickering torch. At his chest, the crystal was cooling; the magic, it seemed, was over. But when Jem looked above his head, he saw that purple birds still lingered here and there like sinister portents, shifting silently amongst the heavy cobwebs.

Deep unease filled him. Almost without willing it, he found himself turning clockwise, then back a fifteenth. He moved forward, crunching over debris, pushing between tombs. Should he go the way the Five-God told him to go? Only with dread could Jem even think of the Lord Agonis now. When the golden god had gone under the guise of Lord Empster, Jem had trusted him, depended upon him; now he knew that his mysterious guardian had been a false guide, a traitor to the quest. But was it really Agonis who had spoken to him? And if not Agonis, who?

Jem thought again of the heat in his crystal, and wondered if he should turn back.

If he had, he might have seen the dark figure that appeared from behind the Five-God. Illuminated briefly in the glow of phantom birds, the figure wore a dark cape. A wide-brimmed hat shadowed its face.

The cape twirled and the figure was gone.

But Jem saw another figure soon enough. It was lying amongst the rubble of fallen masonry, pallid in a covering of chalky dust.

Jem floundered forward. 'Bando! Bando, is it you?'

'M-Morvy?'

'Crum?'

'He'll be all right, won't he?'

How many times? For a moment, Morven was tempted to snap. Weren't they in enough of a mess without worrying about a silly rat? Instead, something stayed him and he said, not unkindly, 'Come on, Crum, of course he will. Was there ever a rat braver than Blenkinsop?'

Crum considered this, furrowed his brow and embarked upon the story – the *tale*, as he punningly put it – of a certain other rat that Zohnny Ryle had found one Viana-season in the curing-shed, whose bravery, all had agreed, was a marvel to behold.

'Why, Morvy, you could write a *book* about Blenkinsop!'

'This *other* one was called Blenkinsop too?'

'Well, most rats *are* called Blenkinsop,' said Crum matter-of-factly. 'The brown ones, I mean. But – but this book, Morvy … just think, I could tell you the story and you could write it down! Put your brains to some use for once! Isn't it the best idea you ever heard? Now, let me just tell you—'

Morven sighed and stopped listening. Just as well there was so much noise from the milling guests and music, otherwise, he would have to tell Crum to shut up. Better, no doubt, just to let him burble on. But perhaps not. Morven was worried. Would they hear the knock from the other side of the wall?

The sentries stood before the painted panels representing the Valleys of the Tarn. Securing their position had been more than a little difficult. Other sentries had been posted here; Morven, insisting that he acted on the orders of Sergeant Bunch, had told them to go elsewhere, sending them off on a fruitless quest. Now he could only hope the imposture would not be exposed. And what of the guests who spilled already into this retiring-chamber? How were Hul and Cata to make their entrance?

Still Crum expatiated on the bravery of a rat; Morven shifted his musket. From the ballroom came a merry sawing of fiddles and the plinkety-plunk of the harpsichord. The clink of glasses came closer at hand, and the trilling of conversations from behind absurd masks.

Idly, Morven listened as a gentleman dressed as a Tiralon Tiger Gull – in fact, he looked more like an enormous bee – exchanged pleasantries with two others, one a Varby Pink Partridge, the other a huge-billed Orandy Duck.

'But how *do* we know who is who?' said Gull.

'I thought the idea,' said Partridge, 'was that we did *not*.'

'Nonsense,' said Duck. 'Do I not know both of you?'

'You do?' said Partridge.

'Come, my friends,' Duck went on (his voice distorted by his protruding beak), 'we are of the commercial classes, are we not? Is that not what draws us together? May I suggest that one of you is the proprietor of a certain well-known coffee house? And the other, Agondon's most celebrated practitioner of the hairdressing arts?'

'Well, I never!' said Partridge – who was, indeed, the hairdresser Mr Carrousel. 'I see I must devote *far* more attention to my costume next time! Alas, so little time remains to me after tending to the coiffures of Agondon's *finest* quality-ladies.'

Gull (Webster Senior) turned to Duck, then away again. It was as if he were considering whether to reveal his ignorance and admit he had no idea who the beaky fellow might be. He thought better of it, and revealed a deeper ignorance instead. 'But how are we to know the King and Queen? Surely we are to know the royals?'

'Of course, and applaud their costumes,' Duck said urbanely. 'When the Ball is far advanced, they will appear to a fanfare – the King as a Wenaya Blue Raven, the Queen as a Silver Swan – and His Imperial Agonist Majesty will select a quality-lady with whom to open the Ball.'

'Odd, isn't it?' Mr Carrousel mused. 'How could it be more *open* than it already is?'

'He does not dance,' asked Webster, 'with the Queen?'

'A formality,' said Duck, in response to both questions. 'Tradition. Ah, but the ways of our rulers are—'

'Look!' Turning, Mr Carrousel flapped a pink wing towards the doorway that led back into the ballroom. 'Now I do know who *that* lady happens to be. Isn't she magnificent? That's Lady Bolbarr, done up to the nines as a Vantage Vulture! I designed that hair, isn't it a treat?'

'Quite,' said Webster. 'But my good Duck—'

'Ooh, and do you know what she told me this afternoon?' the hairdresser sailed on. 'Always good for a goss, is Lady B, and it seems that jumped-up gentlemen's tailor – Japier Quisto, you know the one – well, would you believe his *other* daughter's gone to the bad now, too? That little slut Heka, that's the one. Last I heard, she was all set to marry "Binkie" Urgan-Orandy, if you could credit it. We-ell, Lady B's heard on the most re-*li*-able authority that the little minx already has a bastard brat that she's desperately trying to offload, even to the extent of—'

While Mr Carrousel was speaking – his gaze fixed, all the time, on the admirable Lady Bolbarr – Orandy Duck was removing, with some difficulty, the enormous bill that concealed his face. Throat-clearings from Webster were to no avail, so it was that the hairdresser turned, to find himself staring into the face of Japier Quisto.

The tailor had put up a bold front: now it cracked.

'Mr Carrousel,' he said hoarsely, 'I am afraid my daughter Heka was found *murdered* this morning.'

Morven stared, gulping. Fortunately it was just then that Crum alerted him to a knock, sounding from the other side of the panel.

The panel opened, then closed.

Cata breathed, 'Brush me down, quick—'

'Miss Veeldrop,' Morven hissed, 'but where—'

'Change of plan, boys. Just me. Wish me luck!'

And Morven could only stare as Black Swan of Lania Chor sailed out into the ballroom.

Chapter 37

A PRAYER FOR MY SON

Courtiers, mingling:
  'The sparrow-thing?'
  'Elsan Margrave, I think.'
  'Professor Mercol? Bald Eagle?'
  'I'm certain. And *that*'s the Great Cham.'
  'And the daughter, I dare say? Pathetic creature!'
  'Oh, that's a little harsh. The girl's quite fetching, really.'
  'You think so? You know, there's one thing I've never understood. The Cham's *ancient*, isn't she? Can she really have a daughter of that age?'
  'You haven't heard the story? I *am* surprised.'
  'What story?'
  'Hah, is that eagerness I hear? Quite a good story, actually. Of course, Constansia's tried to hush it up as best she can, but truth *will* out. Would you believe Constansia *did* have a daughter – cycles ago? Went to the bad.'
  'Oh? How bad?'
  'Mother to a Vexing.'
  'No-o! The slut!'
  'My sentiments exactly. Anyway, Tishy – the real daughter was a Tishy too, you see – w-e-ell, she died in childbirth. So there's Lady Cham left to bring up the brat. Some say that's when she started to go funny.'
  'Cham? You think she's funny?'
  'Loopy. Calls the girl Tishy, just like the first one ... forgets the first one ... insists that *this* one's her daughter ... tries to bring up the perfect girl – now there's irony for a start. Tishy, of course, has no idea. But few *do*, nowadays.'
  'Dear me ... you're *sure* this is true?'
  'It's what they say.'
  'Hm. You know, I do recall some rumours about Cham. Wasn't it Cham? Oh, a cycle or so ago. Didn't I hear that *she* was mother to a Vexing?'
  'We-e-ell, in a sense you might say she is. Oh, but she was furious about that little tale! Tried to stop it going any further, but you see she didn't succeed entirely.'
  'Tried to stop a *rumour*? How?'
  'Let's just say a certain fellow – gossiping fool that he was – was *very* sorry.'

'Oh? And who was that?'

'You don't recall? Feval. Eay Feval.'

'Dear me ... I suppose he's even sorrier *now*.'

'Droll, my dear. Very.'

The courtiers mingled some more. Glasses clinked; fans flapped. The heat was stifling, and so was the stench. Steam wheezed through underfloor pipes; wax dripped from blazing chandeliers. Sweltering in their costumes, many amongst the quality-folk envied the footmen, bearing silver trays, who pirouetted so freely through the crowd; those in bulkier masks tilted them back frequently, allowing for the guzzling of Varl-wine or potent Festival punch. Pressure on bladders was soon acute, but still there were wingtips always raised, ardent for the footmen, ardent for the trays.

Courtiers, dancing:

'That's Mistress Quick?'

'Oh, certainly. And Goody Garvice.'

'*Lovers*, I've heard. And look, there's Mandy H-H.'

'That's him? In that get-up?'

'You *are* an innocent, my dear. But you'd do well to recognise Mandy. Almost certain to be next First Minister, don't you know.'

'The *next*?'

'If there is one. Won't there be? Though really, that nephew of his is a trial. Still, I heard some thugs waylaid him last night and he was nearly coshed to death.'

'Javey Heva-Harion? Murdered?'

'Nearly. There's a difference.'

'Droll. But ... who's *that* lady? The Black Swan?'

'What? By the Lord Agonis, I don't know!'

'Never mind. This *is* a masquerade.'

'My dear, but I know everyone!'

'Ooh, diddums!'

And another conversation:

'I say, over there! Isn't that the Prince of Chayn?'

'As Puce Chayn Warbler? Not a lot of *difference*!'

'Not at all. But to dance with that woman – here, in front of everyone!'

'What woman? You know her?'

'Zaxon Nightingale! Who *else* could it be?'

'Of course! Miss Tilsy Fash ... but wait, see what I see? Isn't that *another* Zaxon Nightingale?'

'Yes, and approaching fast!'

'My goodness, what—'

It was the first, and least frightening, of several altercations that were to enliven the evening. Amused, the guests looked on as the celebrated Miss Fash, revealing her fiery Zaxon temperament, ripped the mask from the astonished Freddie Chayn.

The poor fellow might have blurted out excuses, even apologies to his jealous lover, but at once was busy saving his dancing partner – this *other* Zaxon Nightingale – from the wrath of the original. Soon word would spread that the girl in question was one Laetitia Cham-Charing, but before Miss Fash's violence could go further, perhaps revealing the identity of her rival, the dance ended and a fanfare announced the advent of the royals – not a moment too soon.

Courtiers, whispering:

'Oh, but the King! Has he ever—'

'Looked so bad? Worse, sometimes. *But*—'

'What? Be glad he's wearing a mask?'

'*That* can't hide his walk—'

'So who's he going to dance with?'

'Not Her Royal Majesty?'

'Droll. Look, Mandy's choosing.'

'Mandy? Shouldn't that be Tranimel's job?'

'The First Minister, I think, is above such things.'

'Really? Don't they say there was nearly a civil war back in Good Queen Elabeth's time, when she danced with a Venturon instead of a Cham-Charing? These superficial things are the most profound of all, you know. But what's this? Who *is* that lady Mandy's pointing to?'

'Reluctant, whoever she is.'

'Tut-tut. Not sensible of the honour?'

'Dro-oll. Ah, but she doesn't want to make a scene. Here she comes. Sensible girl.'

'Girl? Could be an old hag, under all that.'

'I *don't* think so, somehow. See that nice little arm?'

Sigh. 'To dance with the King! Every girl's dream, hm?'

'Ho ho. But she dances well, doesn't she?'

'Like a dream ... like a dream.'

'But ... how very odd.'

'What's odd?'

'Well, there's Her Royal Majesty got up as Silver Swan. Then here's the King, dancing with Black Swan.'

'Funny. Wonder who she can be?'

'You're sure, Bando? Look, if you lean on me—'

'It's nothing. Well, nothing's *broken*—'

'But you're limping, you're—'

'Leave me! I'm all right!'

The anger in Bando's voice was real. What did he care for his own pain now? Jem's story had banished all other thoughts from his mind. Even Bob Scarlet was neither here nor there. Bando had thought his son was

230

lost, that nothing could bring him back. Now, if there was even a faint chance that Raggle could be saved, that was all that mattered.

The tombs lay behind them. The Five-God's directions had brought them to a narrow, foetid passageway. More than once Jem had felt a strange apprehension, as if there were a purple bird, hovering just beyond the edge of his vision.

'Ugh!' The torch, with a rank sizzling, burned through a curtain of webbing.

Jem brushed a spider from his hair.

'But Jem, you *saw* them?' Bando said again. Jem heard the pain in the old rebel's voice. 'You *saw* them take him? But why bring him here? I've heard that little children are sold into slavery, sent to the colonies—'

'It's worse than that, Bando,' Jem muttered grimly. 'I've seen what goes on under the Great Temple, and—'

'What will they do to him? *Tell me*—'

Jem wished he had said nothing at all. Gently, he replied that this was no time for talking. Let them find Raggle, just find Raggle. What was the use in upsetting Bando more? It was easy to forget that most people, even rebels, knew nothing of the depraved magic that underscored the Bluejacket tyranny.

They edged forward. Questions swirled through Jem's mind. If Bando had been startled by Jem's story, Jem had been almost as startled by Bando's. To think that Cata was here, somewhere in this labyrinth! How close, yet still so far! Where was she now? Where was Hul? And could they really manage to kidnap the Queen?

With a pang, Jem thought of the girl he had known as Jeli Vance, in the days when he went by the name of Nova Empster. There had been a time when he had imagined he was in love with this haughty, cold girl. Perhaps he *had* loved her, a little.

But no, Jem would not think this way.

Bando sighed deeply. 'You're sure it was this Veeldrop?' he began again. 'The red-haired fellow? I knew he was a villain, but I never, I never ...' He swivelled round, grabbing the lapels of Jem's coat. 'Tell me, what *will* they do to my son? Will they torture him, will they—'

'Bando, *shh*!' Staggering back, Jem almost dropped the torch. The light flickered wildly.

'No, *tell* me—'

'Bando, *shh*!' Jem was in earnest. His voice was a whisper. 'I *heard* something, didn't you?'

Cautiously they peered into the gloom ahead. In the glimmering shadows, they saw the dark, cavern-like openings of another passage, crossing with their own. And something, they were certain, was coming down that passage.

Footsteps. Voices.

Jem leaned close to Bando's ear. 'You've got a tinderstick, haven't you? Because I'm going to put out this torch. It's a risk, but I think we've got to take it.'

Waving away the smoke, pressing themselves back against the walls, Jem and Bando waited as the voices came nearer. Jem recognised them soon enough.

And so did Bando.

One voice: 'That old bitch! I'll never forgive her, Bean.'

The other: 'I don't think that's going to bother her much.'

'No, and that's what's wrong! Some mother she is – why, she's even worse than yours.'

'But she's *not* your mother, is she? She's Chokey's.'

'She used to be! Didn't I *think* she was my mother for years and years? And did she show any concern for me at all – even a glimmer of maternal feeling? What does she care about that little tart Jilda? The old bitch is senile.'

'Polty, don't get worked up about her again.'

'*What?*' A pause. 'No, Bean, you're right. What do I care about anything, except my son? How I pray—'

Polty's son? Jem had no time to wonder; he was struggling to hold Bando back. He wrapped a hand round the old rebel's mouth. He pinioned back his arms. In his faintest voice he whispered in Bando's ear, begging him not to give them away.

Not yet, not just yet.

Bean: 'But Polty, you *can't* believe that, can you? Chokey was having you on. He was just trying to upset you, I'm sure he was—'

'Oh? And how would you know? Chokey doesn't joke, not about things like that. It's true, I'm sure of it – the old villain was laughing *because* it was true!'

'But what are you going to *do*, Polty?'

'Save my son, that's what! I'm taking Vy and getting her out of here—'

'But Toth—'

'He's got the *other* one, hasn't he? Let him do what he likes to that swarthy little foreign brat from Flowerdew Lane, and all the other brats just like him, but if he thinks he's taking his carving knife to *my* son—'

With a trudge of heavy boots, with a clink-clink of weapons, Polty and Bean passed the junction of the corridors. The lamp in Bean's hand cast a sickly, searching beam. Jem pulled Bando harder against the wall.

Bean: 'But there's no time. The ceremony—'

Polty: 'What's that? You're not going to help me?'

'N-No, I mean I want to, but they're not going to need the *back-up baby* tonight, are they? You just said, they've got the other one—'

The light passed by, but glimmered back from around the corner. Polty and Bean had stopped. There was a jingling of keys.

'Bean,' Polty was saying, 'can't you understand the feelings of a *father*? Do you think I'll leave my son – *my son* – in this monstrous place for one moment more? How I pray, how I pray that he's come to no harm!'

'Polty, you're the one who doesn't understand.' Bean spoke rapidly, in a voice filled with anguish. 'It's bad enough that we're doing what we're doing. Do you think I like it, snatching these children, sending them to their deaths? It makes me sick, Polty, and I can't pretend it doesn't – not any more. But now we've got a chance to do something good. I'm on your side, I really am. But *think* – if we upset Toth, what will he do? He'll kill us, won't he? Then how can we help Vy – I mean, your *son*?'

It was a fine speech – for Bean – but Polty was barely listening.

Nor was Bando. The old rebel had been in many a dangerous situation, and always he had kept a firm command of himself. But never had his son been about to die. His nerves were frayed. Now they snapped. He wrenched free.

'No, please—' Jem burst out.

It was as well that Polty dropped the keys. The clatter echoed down the corridors. He cursed, picked them up again and fumbled for the right one.

Frustrated, he kicked the door.

'But it's open!' he gasped. 'What the—'

'*Die*, Bluejackets!' Bando cried.

Polty reeled, Bean too. A musket-shot rang out.

Bean shrieked. He collapsed, clutching his shoulder.

Polty grabbed for his own musket. Too late. A chunk of stone crashed down, blasted from the ceiling.

He collapsed too.

'Jem, quick!' said Bando. 'This must be the place—'

Jem raced forward, heart pounding. He cursed his cowardice. Bando had been right, of course he had been right.

They charged through the open door of the cell.

'My son, my son—' Bando cried.

When Bean fell, the lantern had rolled across the corridor. Shadows loomed grotesquely in the guttering light. They peered around the gloomy cell, stench assailing them. Where was Raggle? Where could he be? All they could see was a set of ropes, discarded on the floor.

Then, by the far wall, they saw something else.

Jem stumbled back. At first he thought the bloated, bloodied thing was an animal, then he realised the truth. Astonished, he turned to Bando, as if to confirm that what he saw was real.

The door slammed shut. They were trapped in darkness. From the corridor, they heard Polty's laughter.

A moan came from the woman by the wall.

And Raggle?

Forward, forward through the darkness. But how to escape? He feels the drapings of sticky cobwebs, the viscous drippings of slime. Foulness fills his nostrils. He hears the scuttle of rats; then stranger, unexplained echoings, boomings. Purple, bird-like creatures flap before his eyes.

Terror rises in Raggle. He slips to the floor. Still the purple birds – if birds they are – come clustering, clustering, glimmering and screeching.

Then there is the voice.

'Well, *well*, my little man—'

The figure, illuminated in the purplish light, is one that Raggle knows at once to be evil, though undoubtedly it is garbed in religious robes.

Instinctively, Raggle scrambles back.

'No, my little man, you will come with me—'

And Toth smiles. Yes, another move in the game.

Chapter 38

THE HARLEQUIN'S DANCE

Tishy Cham-Charing sighed.

'I ... I can barely believe it—'

'What's to believe? The rebels—'

'No ... I mean being here, meeting you—'

'Oh, well that's—' Blushing, Hul almost wished he had not removed his mask.

His spectacles glinted in the lamplight; so did Tishy's. With *Lamasery of the Winds* brushed aside, Tishy had thoughts only for *Discourse on Freedom*. Enraptured, she hugged the little book against her gown. 'But to think, you edited this very edition! You ... actually wrote the footnotes!'

'And the introduction,' Hul added shyly.

'Oh, that was marvellous!' Tishy sighed again, leafing through the little book. 'But Mr Hulverside, what are we to do now? What's the plan?'

Hul was flustered. 'The *plan*, Miss Cham-Charing? Why, I'm to get you out of here, and safely back home! With a lamp to light the way, I just think I—'

Tishy's eyes grew wide. 'Mr Hulverside!'

Hul blinked. 'Miss Cham-Charing?'

'Have I not told you of my admiration for – for Mr Vytoni ... of my rebel sympathies ... of my loathing of tyranny in all its forms? All this, and you would *take me back home*? You disappoint me, Mr Hulverside! What is my destiny, but to join your rebel band?'

'You ... you mean it, Miss Cham-Charing?' Hul knew he should have demurred, but somehow he could not. Gulping, he looked into the young, bespectacled face, at once so innocent, yet strangely wise. 'Come, we must find the others.'

Exclaiming, Tishy pushed back her chair. Swiftly she donned her coat again and clutched Mr Vytoni's book like a talisman. Texts for translation she could find anywhere, but Hulverside's Vytoni? She would not be leaving this behind! 'And can we really get out so easily, Mr Hulverside? Here was I, thinking I was trapped! What a fool!'

'No, never a fool, my dear.'

'But wait ... what about the Professor?'

'Hm ... he's still breathing, at any rate. I'll leave a message at Webster's ... but you're ready, Miss Cham-Charing? Vytoni Gap, here we come!'

'Just one thing.' Putting down her book on the cluttered table, Tishy took up a roll of parchment instead. Bending down, she prodded it into Professor Mercol's hand.

Hul's brow furrowed.

'A joke,' Tishy smiled. 'Just a little joke.'

'Really? Old Rabbity was never much of a one for jokes in my day,' said Hul.

'*Rabbity?*' Tishy had to laugh. 'Oh, he *is*, isn't he! Now where's Vytoni Gap?'

And, half-turning, she grabbed her book again.

❋ ❋ ❋

'Up you get, Bean.'

Polty, grinning with triumph, dusted down his coat. With casual contempt he kicked away the heavy stone that had felled him. He reached down, setting the lantern upright and nuzzled at Bean with the toe of his boot. 'Come on, get up.'

'I'm *hurt*, Polty. My shoulder—'

Polty knelt down. 'It's a flesh wound – why, it barely got through your coat. Get *up*, you lanky fool.'

Bean complied reluctantly, stumblingly, a hand fixed to his shoulder. 'S-So what do we do n-now, then?'

A cunning look came to Polty's face. He drew Bean aside, just in case the captives in the cell could hear. His voice trembled with excitement.

'Do you realise who that *was*, Bean?'

'Who *who* was? Some rebel, I suppose—'

'Not him, the other one. *Jem, quick!* – that's what the fellow said, wasn't it? That was the Vexing, friend. Do you know what this means?'

'That Jem Vexing's back on the scene? We knew that.' Bean almost sobbed with pain, leaning heavily against the wall. 'We also know the ceremony will be any moment now, and we've lost the boy from Flowerdew Lane—'

'You're sure you locked the door, Bean?'

'Of course I ... I must have ...' Bean flushed hotly.

At another time, Polty might have burst out in rage. Now he only grinned. 'Friend, it was ordained – because I've *got* him, don't you see? The Vexing: Toth wants him, and I've got him. Oh, Bean, what else matters now? Remember what Toth said? What was tonight *for*, but to lure the Vexing? If Toth doubted our worth before, how can he doubt it now?'

'I'm not sure we did all that much, Polty—'

'*You* didn't do much,' Polty said scornfully. He gripped the lapels of Bean's coat, wrenching his friend upright again. Bean grimaced; Polty smiled. 'As for me, let's just say I can't see Penge languishing in that jar for much longer.'

'What about Vy? Or have you forgotten her now?'

'What do you think I am, Bean? I'm getting Vy out of here right *now*—'

'Well, that's not going to be easy, is it? She's in there with them. *And* they're armed – very well armed,' Bean added ruefully, wiping his bloodied hand on his coat.

'You've no confidence in me, have you, Bean? Do you think I can't disarm the Vexing and some shabby old Redjacket just as quickly as clicking my fingers? Watch me. Now listen: you heard the rebel say *my son*, right?'

Bean, who had been writhing in agony at the time, had not quite taken in this point.

Polty jerked a thumb towards the cell door. 'Get it, Bean? The Flowerdew brat must be the rebel's, right? Can't you just see the Vexing getting involved in some soppy scheme to save a dirty little mongrel like that? It all adds up. And so does my plan.'

Polty leaned closer. His voice became softer.

Listening to the plan, Bean's eyes flickered; he longed only to lie on the floor. Instead, he was compelled to join Polty beside the cell door, his role being to emit, at Polty's direction, a series of high-pitched whinings, after the manner of a cringing dog. Could the plan possibly work? Polty said the Vexing was enough of a fool to make it work a hundred times over.

He rapped on the door with the butt of his musket. 'Can you hear me in there? Can you hear me?'

Jem's voice came back: 'We hear you, Polty—'

'Now listen. I've got the key to this door. And I've got the brat, too. Hear him squeal? He got out, but we found him—'

A cry of rage – Bando's – came from within.

'Shut up and listen!' said Polty. 'I'll let him go, but in return I want Jem Vexing – I want him to give himself up to me. Now I'm going to open this door, just a little, and you're both going to throw out your weapons, do you hear? Then you're going to come out with your hands in the air. Do as I say, and the brat lives. I'll give his father time to get him away, that's how much I'll do for you. Any tricks, and it's curtains for the brat.'

Bean, with a jab from Polty's bayonet, made a particularly loud whimpering.

There was silence from behind the door.

'Do you hear me?' Polty shrieked.

Jem came back, 'How do we *know* you've got the boy?'

'Can't you hear him, you fool? Can't you hear him *cry*?'

'Let me talk to him.' It was Bando's voice. 'Taggle ... *Taggle*, are you all right?'

It was a bluff, of course. Polty struck his musket angrily against the door. 'Do you think you can bargain with me, rebel scum? I've told you my conditions. Now do as I say!'

He grabbed Bean's collar, wrenching him from the door; this time, his friend's howls were authentic.

'Bean,' he hissed, 'musket ready – quick, quick!'

The key clunked in the lock. Polty held his own musket, ready to fire. He had said he would open the door just a little; instead, he kicked it viciously.

'Throw out your weapons! Now!' said Polty.

There was a pause, but not for long. Two muskets clattered out. Polty kicked them down the corridor, past Bean. 'Now you're coming out with your hands up, do you hear?'

Another pause; it lengthened.

'And what if we don't?' came Jem's voice at last. 'It's lighter in here with the door open, Polty – thanks for that. We can see things we couldn't before – do you know, I can see Bando over by the wall? He may not have his musket, but he's got a knife ... Weren't you saying something about your *son*, Polty? I didn't understand before. Now I do.'

Polty faltered, 'What are you talking about?'

'You're the one who's going to throw down his weapons now, Polty. You and Bean, all right? I *think* you understand me. Don't you?'

It was a still more desperate bluff than before; Bean recognised it at once for what it was. But Polty, like all villains, judged the hearts of others by his own.

Panic filled him. His son! Not his son!

He burst recklessly into the cell, firing in the direction of Jem's voice.

The shot missed. Jem lunged forward, Bando too.

There was a struggle. 'Bean, help me—'

But Bean had doubled over, clutching his shoulder. Polty staggered, pummelled by a rock-like fist.

Someone kicked the lantern. There was blackness.

'Bando, run!'

'Torso, Torso!'

'Ha-*ha*, ha-*ha*!'

Where did it come from, the dead man's voice? Whirling to a gay Strossini waltz, Umbecca and Torso took to the floor. Space cleared around them, as well it might for a woman so monstrous – and so powerful. For who could doubt who she was, this huge Harlequin Owl? Gossip could wonder only at her paramour, whose Pigar Parrot outfit, some were sure, had been intended for Lector Feval.

Round and round they went.

'Torso, I have spoken to the Archmaximate! Did I tell you I would speak to him tonight? It's all arranged, my darling – your canonisation!'

Whirling, twirling.

'Ah, how they envy us, the crowd! But who is that lady who looks so intently? An *old* lady, don't you think? I feel her eyes burning through her mask!'

Da-*da*-dada-*dum*, da-*dum*—

'She's making me uneasy! I declare, that costume could have been made from all the Sparrows of the World! But come, Torso, speak again! Won't you speak?'

Poor Umbecca! She would regret this request.

Until now, the voice that issued from the Pigar Parrot's beak had given her only compliments, pleasantries, little fritterings of tittle-tattle; the fat woman, squired by this noble paramour, had felt herself enfolded in transcendent bliss.

Now came a voice again, but not Eay Feval's. A voice from afar, sounding through his beak. Could it be Tranimel? But where was Tranimel? Her mind reeled, but all she could do was dance, dance, dragging her fat form round and round, trapped in the arms of the wheeling, jerking puppet.

The voice was audible only to Umbecca. Dissonantly, grotesquely, it rose and fell in time with the surge of Strossini's waltz. 'That's right, Torso, hold her in your arms! Ah, but do you think she loves you, Torso? Umbecca, do you think you're in love with *him*? What has he ever been but a substitute? Poor lady, hankering after a cold and passionless half-man – for was he not *half* a man, even when he was whole? A dandy-fellow who knew the cut of a dress, the hang of a curtain, but never the throbbings of a lady's heart – who knew the price of a tea service, but not the value of the love he spurned!'

'No, you can't say that – no, no ...' Umbecca sank, sobbing, on Torso's chest.

On and on the puppet danced.

'Umbecca, you gossiped with him about the great world, dreaming of your conquest of society – but all the time, did not your thighs chafe with *other* longings? Was it really this half-man you desired, this capon in all but fact? It was Wolveron, wasn't it – Silas Wolveron? Yes, he was the one for whom your heart always burned! When he was Lector of Irion, you would have been his wife; when he went mad, you would have nursed him; even when he ran off with your cousin Yane Rench, living in the Wildwood like a beast in a cave, still you would have gone to him, forgetting all else, if only he would fling you to the forest floor, goring your thighs with his boiling lust!'

'It's not true – not true ...' Helplessly, Umbecca tried to break from the puppet-man, from the beaky mask, from the pitiless words that pierced her breast like arrows; she muttered prayers, calling upon the Love of the Lord Agonis.

But no help came. Da-*da*-dada-*dum*—

239

'Ah yes,' the voice went on, 'what would that have been but the climax of your fate, to moan in ecstasy on the forest floor, pinioned beneath a Vaga-man in filthy robes? But you were not pretty little Yane Rench, were you? No, you were not worthy of love, even the love of a depraved, crazy renegade! You failed in love, Umbecca, and in your shame, in your humiliation, you could only turn to vengeance. And such a vengeance! Remember how you denounced him, telling the Bluejackets he was an enemy agent? Remember how Veeldrop seared out his eyes? What shuddering pleasure filled your body, the deepest pleasure you were ever to know!'

'Please,' Umbecca sobbed, 'mercy, mercy—'

By now, her distress was obvious to all. A path had cleared for the jerking, writhing couple; courtiers stared, pointed. Why, the fat woman would give herself a seizure! Who *was* he, this fellow who trapped her in his arms?

The waltz went into its final flourish.

'Ah, but even then your lust was not allayed! If he wanted you – the reeking old Vaga with his lice and pustular sores – would you not have him even now, flinging aside your position and place, forgetting all pretences of piety and virtue? Poor Umbecca, tragic Umbecca! To have worked so hard, to have plotted and schemed, all for so little! Dance in the arms of this impotent puppet, but think of the one man you really wanted! Dear lady, shall you ever see him again? What would you not give to see him again?'

'You're mad ... Silas ... he's dead—'

'Lady, are you sure? You're really so sure?'

The waltz ended at last. Umbecca slipped from the puppet's arms, collapsing to the floor. The commotion around her – the alarmed figures, the rushing footmen – was the merest blur. But who was this she saw through her tears, this one figure who was almost clear?

Wolveron? Silas Wolveron?

Like a portent he stood in the centre of the ballroom, staff in hand, cowl about his head. With gnarled hands he pulled the cowl back, revealing the pits where his eyes had been.

Umbecca screamed. She flung away her mask.

Already the Feval-puppet had jerked away, reeling back through the parting crowd. But still Umbecca heard the cruel words, booming inside her skull.

'Lady, he's here! Your beloved is here! Ah, but does he love you? Has he ever loved you? No, it is another who has known his love – moaned beneath him a hundred times, and borne his bastard, too! Another, and one close to you! Who but the woman once known as Lady Lolenda – the woman known to you as *Berthen Waxwell*—'

'You're mad; I won't listen, I won't—'

'And the bastard son? Never knowing the secret of his parentage, put out to a foster-mother by the Archmaximate, while his real mother mortified herself in a marriage of torture, who could it be, this half-Vaga bastard, but our dear, beloved *Eay Feval*? The irony, Umbecca, the irony—'

Wild, crazed laughter rang in her ears. But Umbecca, by now, could take in no more. She hauled her bulk upright, dashing away her tears, looking only for Silas, Silas. Now she would have flung herself upon him – to embrace him, perhaps, or tear him apart with her own hands.

But where was he? *Silas? Silas?*

'Good lady, you're unwell, come, come—'

Umbecca knocked the footmen from her path. Trays crashed to the floor.

There were guards here, too. 'Your Ladyship—'

But who would dare to grab her, to pinion her arm?

Her lover, her lover. 'Silas, come to me—'

Instead, another figure burst from the crowd. It was Sparrows of the World, her mask flung aside. Puce Chayn Warbler, then Derkold Bald Eagle, tried to her hold her back. Blue Plumed Plover screamed, covering her eyes. But Elsan Margrave rushed forward, murderous.

'*You killed him, you killed my husband*—' Enraged hands circled Umbecca's neck. But it was too late for justice now.

Shots rang out and Lady Margrave fell.

Chapter 39

FOR WHOM THE BELL TOLLS

Courtiers, puzzled:

'Nastier and nastier—'

'Where's the fat woman now?'

'I don't know, but see the First Minister?'

'Indeed. And why isn't *he* dressed up as a bird?'

'Can you imagine it? But look at that evil little smile on his lips! Look how his eyes blaze! I declare, he's quite interested in Lady Cham, isn't he?'

'Poor lady! Sobbing in a corner, at the Ball!'

'Stupid old bitch! Doesn't she deserve it, after lording it over us all for so many years?'

'But to see her best friend *killed*—'

'I know, I know. If only we were allowed to *leave* this wretched gathering!'

'Well, it's midnight soon—'

'Midnight? They'll keep us till dawn!'

'I say, that daughter of hers looks intimate with Freddie Chayn, doesn't she? Think she's had a change of heart?'

'The *other* Zaxon Nightingale? Wait, but where's she going now? (Footman, more punch!) Ah, there's more than one that's sobbing in a corner! See, she's going over to him – the Orandy Duck, see?'

'She's trying to comfort him? But who's *he*?'

'Do you know, I think it's the tailor – Quisto?'

'What? How odd! Her gestures, it's as if … as if the girl's just heard something *terrible*. But look, he's turning on her – waving her away! I say, he's really angry!'

'Ah! The bells—'

It was midnight at last, tolling above the hubbub of the Ball. In a moment, much was different. The orchestra left off its sawings and plunkings; raggedly, the couples on the floor retired. Around the hot chamber, glasses were charged; masks were removed.

All knew the significance of Festival midnight. This was time for the monarch's address – time, on the brink of the god-days, for their god's representative in the Realm of Being to speak to his peoples. Last year, His Imperial Agonist Majesty had blurted just a few drunken phrases before collapsing amongst the gitterns and viols. This year would be different. A strange animation filled the royal face, an animation few had seen before.

Courtiers, behind their hands:

'Ugh, this wax is dripping in my hair! But I say—'

'Who's propping the old bugger up? By the Lord Agonis, he almost looks alive!'

'You think so? No, like a puppet, jerking on wires—'

'Ah, but what has he *ever* been but a puppet?'

'No, listen to him! Such oratory! I never—'

'Wh-what's he on about? My hearing's not quite—'

'About the rebels, how we'll defeat them! About the war that's to come, the war to end wars! I say, I never thought he had it in him! Where's the First Minister? I do believe he's nowhere to be seen!'

'You're sure? Not egging him on?'

'Can't see him. But look off to the side!'

'The swans? Wh-what's happening?'

'Silver Swan, that's the Queen … Who *is* that other lady? Still in her mask—'

'I saw her with the Queen before—'

'It's as if … as if she were *teasing* her—'

'Trying to make her come away—'

'Come away? I see, to that retiring-room—'

'In the Festival speech? Why, it's as if she'd *show* her something. As if she's *imploring*—'

On the podium, His Imperial Agonist Majesty flings out his arms, reaching for his rousing peroration. He speaks of triumph, he speaks of power, he speaks of the empire of the Agonists and how its glory will spread throughout the world.

Then, from above, comes a shattering of glass and, swinging down from a chandelier, comes a bird none had believed could appear at this Ball.

Courtiers, screaming. Chaos breaks out. Shots.

A pistol spins. Guards fall; blood spurts out.

'Look, he's leapt down to the podium—'

'Bob Scarlet! I don't believe it, but—'

'He's … knocked out the King—'

'He's ripping off his mask—'

'No, I *can't* believe it—'

'He's … *Ejard Red*!'

'Flee, the rebels!'

'Flee, flee—'

'*Aaargh!*'

Ejard Red flings back his head, laughing wildly.

'Can this be destiny?' one courtier gasps.

'Can this be the end?' another cries.

'But he's dead, he was *killed*—'

'What's that he's throwing?'

'I declare, it's a *rodent*—'

'Look, that sentry—'

'He's caught it!'

'But what—'

'Why—?'

Triumphant, the deposed King surveys his peoples.

❊   ❊   ❊

'Ah my love, how could you think I had abandoned you? Could you really think I would be untrue? Silly girl, to think I would leave you in that dungeon ... Why, if I'd had my way, none of this would have happened! It was Toth, the evil Toth who made us keep you here ... Wasn't it, Bean?'

Bean gulped, holding the lantern aloft. They made their way through the dank, winding passageways. What they would do when they escaped, he did not know. All he knew was that they must leave this place, and leave it now.

Polty supported the foundering Miss Rextel. Viciously, almost shouting, he repeated his question.

'Wasn't it, Bean? *Wasn't it?*'

'I ... of course, Polty. It was Toth—'

'Hear that, my darling?' With a fond hand, Polty smoothed the girl's enormous belly. 'What a lucky thing you are – saved, in the nick of time! Don't worry, those scratches and bruises will heal soon enough. A pity your pearly little teeth are smashed, but never mind, there are plenty of girls with teeth to sell ... Darling, think of the happiness before us! You, me and little Polty! Eh, Vy? Eh, Bean?'

Since Miss Rextel could only loll her head, it was up to Bean to offer a suitable reply. And he would have done – just then, he was composing a veritable eulogy to family life, to domestic bliss – but for the looming figure that appeared, at that moment, in the light of the lamp.

'Eh, Bean? Eh?' Polty repeated.

Bean gasped. 'P-Polty, *look*—'

Purple birds clustered round the white-garbed figure.

'Well, well,' said Toth, 'if it's not my favourite assistants, I declare, and my favourite *baby*, too. But come, friends, I do believe you're going the wrong way.'

❊   ❊   ❊

They ran in darkness.

Then there was light.

Jem staggered. 'The Hornlight Focus—'

'The what—?' Bando clutched at a stitch in his side.

244

'It comes from the pinnacle of the spire,' murmured Jem, remembering what his guardian had told him long ago. 'Down through the great central column – down, down, through level after level...'

'We're underneath the Temple?'

'Right underneath.' Jem gazed upon the crypt around them. He saw the lines of pillars, as in a cloister; he saw dark pews before a raised altar. He took in the familiar stone slab, stained thickly with blood, and the sinister curtains hanging behind. 'But this place was destroyed – I *saw* it destroyed...'

Bando snapped, 'Never mind that, where's my son?'

They would have blundered on, but something about the Hornlight Focus made them linger.

'It looks like Raggle's escaped,' said Jem.

'Ah, Raggle! Didn't I know he'd be as brave as his father?'

'But we'd better be careful.' Jem motioned to move on. 'We gave Polty a pummelling, but I wouldn't be surprised if he's after us already. And *we've* lost our weapons—'

There was a commotion. Two figures burst into the crypt from the other side.

Bando exclaimed joyously, 'Hul, but where have you been? And who—'

For a moment, Jem had to laugh at the sight of Hul's costume. Then he forgot the Festival Turkey, thinking only of the man inside.

How splendid to be back with Hul!

But who was this girl? As she swept into view, Jem had first thought she was Cata. Now he could barely hide his disappointment. This girl could hardly be more different, with her horn-rimmed spectacles and tied-back hair.

Clutched against her breasts, like a talisman, was a book.

'This is Miss Laetitia Cham-Charing,' Hul said breathlessly. 'Oh Jem, I was sure it was you! We rushed to catch you ... But poor Miss Cham-Charing, she's been locked in the Chamber of—'

'Lady Cham-Charing's daughter?' Jem blurted.

Questions burst in his brain, but Hul enfolded him in a feathery embrace.

It was left to Bando to ask about Cata.

'We were separated,' Hul said. 'Purple birds—'

Despairing, Jem clutched a hand to his forehead. Was he fated never to see Cata again?

He struggled to recover himself. 'You're all right, Miss Cham-Charing?'

'Oh yes,' said Tishy, with a smile for Hul.

'Miss Cham-Charing's a rebel, just like us—' Hul began.

He could go no further. A thunderous booming came from above. They staggered back, covering their ears. It was the Temple bells, echoing down through the Hornlight Focus. Everything around them – the altar, the curtain, the light itself – resonated in time with the cold, metallic clanging.

It was midnight. Fear gripped Jem, and he thought of the last time he had heard these bells.

That had been in this crypt too.

Now, as if the memory were becoming real, phantom figures formed around him, black-caped, cowled, filling every place in the sinister pews. Jem's mind reeled. Could these be illusions?

Bando cried out. Tishy screamed.

'What are they?' Hul shouted. 'Where do they—'

They might have run, plunging down a corridor, any corridor that led away from the scene. Too late. A white figure shimmered at the altar; then the black figures shimmered no more.

Jem's crystal burned at his chest. Rapidly he ushered the others into the shadows beyond the pillars. On and on went the tollings of the bells – *four, five, six, seven.*

'Are they ghosts?' cried Bando. 'Are they men?'

'Bando, *shh*! They mustn't know we're here—'

'Jem, your chest!' said Hul. 'What's happening?'

'That man in white!' Tishy burst out. 'But that's—'

'Hul, *shh*! – Miss Cham-Charing, *shh*! – If Toth … if Tranimel sees us, he'll kill us all.' Jem hunched over the crystal. How could it shine even through his coat? 'I … I can't explain anything now, but listen, all of you: don't cry out, don't even stir once the bells stop ringing. Something's going to happen here and it's going to be gruesome – frightening – the most horrible thing you've ever seen. But there's nothing we can do – not yet, not now.'

But what, Jem wondered, could Toth do? He was aware of the birds again, clustering above the pillars, shifting as if in anticipation. He gulped, peering carefully over the pews. Still the bells tolled – *ten, eleven.* Now the cowled Brothers looked very real and Toth flickered into being too, presiding over the altar with arms outstretched. Flinging back his head, he gazed as if in rapture into the Hornlight Focus.

Then, as the tollings neared their end – *twelve, thirteen* – Jem saw the lanky form of Bean, reeling towards the altar as if compelled by a force beyond his control. Gasping out excuses, he bowed, scraping the floor; wretchedly, Polty stumbled behind, leading the mysterious girl from the cell. The girl was limping, trailing blood; draped round her shoulders was Polty's jacket and he held her firmly in a protective arm.

Bando and Hul exchanged solemn glances.

Tishy clutched her throat, aghast.

Polty began to shout at Toth, to plead with him, but all that issued forth were inarticulate cries. Now came the last tollings – *fourteen, fifteen* – and

Toth, in dumb show, dismissed his hapless servants. Powerless, they blundered to the back of the altar, off to the side of the dark curtain.

Through what followed, Bean would look on in fear and trembling; Polty, by contrast, would be almost oblivious, often on the brink of sinking down, remaining with his arms clasped about the girl. Sometimes he would lean close to her ear, like a lover mouthing endearments; sometimes, his face flushed with pride, he would stroke her belly's fecund dome.

The girl only shuddered, crazed and lost. Her hair was matted, her face bruised; but a strange certainty came to Jem that he had seen this girl before tonight. What was it an old buck with a wooden nose had said to him once, at a provincial ball? *But look you, boy, feast your eye, feast your eye on the luscious Vy...*

Chapter 40

UNTIMELY RIPPED

But now the Black Canonical begins.

The tollings fade. Toth stares, exultant, at the Brotherhood. At once, as if compelled by the force of his will, the cowled figures burst into evil chanting. Feet stamp the floor; voices rise as one, booming and crashing round the subterranean domain.

Sickened, Jem hears the mantra. All is so familiar; he thinks that he has heard these chantings not once but many times, echoing again and again in his dreams. But this time, the words are new.

> *Unbeing Bird, mighty bird of fire,*
> *Come to us, come to us, fill our desire:*
> *Come to us, come to us, fuel our desire!*
> *Unbeing Bird, mighty bird of flood*
> *Come to us, come to us, bathe us in blood!*
> TOTH *who is Sassoroch waits now for you,*
> TOTH *who is Chorassos will fly with you!*
>
> *Unbeing Bird, mighty bird of ice,*
> *Come, let us offer up our sacrifice!*
> *Unbeing Bird, mighty bird of snow.*
> *Come to us, take us where the saved must go:*
> *Take us to the mountains of the ice and snow!*
> TOTH *who is Chorassos waits now for you,*
> TOTH *who is Sassoroch will fly with you!*

At the ceiling, the purple things shift and caw.

Round and round goes the chant; then it stops, and Toth begins to speak. Bathed in the dazzle of the Hornlight Focus, his face a blur of white and harsh, black shadows, he wrenches his words explosively from the First Minister's frame.

'Brothers, again I summon you!' he cries. 'While your secondary forms remain present at the Ball, garbed in the costumes of oafish revelry, in the reality of your beings I draw you here – here, where only truth reigns – here, where all illusion fades – here, where tonight, you are to witness the event that heralds, at last, our certain triumph!

'Yes, Brothers, let your hearts swell with pride, for soon the Time of

Dominion will be upon us! While the fools in the world above parade as birds, little do they dream what great and mighty bird my powers are about to unleash over this city!

'Even now, as I address you here, my puppet that goes by the name of King jerks upon his wires before the revellers, his mouth opening and shutting with a music even hollower than the waltzes, the mazurkas, the reels he has displaced. He speaks of wars, of reprisals, of the rout of rebels; here, I speak of our true destiny, the destiny that will come when Chorassos flies!'

He gestures to the clustering, shifting purple birds. 'Mauvers, how eagerly you await your master! My pretties, tonight your wait is over. And what then? For five days, in a great spiralling wheel, the mighty Unbeing Bird will circle this kingdom, invisible to the eyes of those untouched by magic. Yes, Brothers, pity the fools in the world above, benighted in the belief that this Year of Our Atonement is the one that is numbered 999d – an ancient error in their paltry calendar, working to our advantage. The fools, the fools! In five days, the truth will be known to them when the Unbeing Bird reveals itself! Then, at last, The Atonement ends! Then the time of our power is at hand!'

Toth flings back his head and laughs; behind the pillars, Jem and his companions look on in horror. Still Jem struggles to conceal his crystal.

'But what does he mean,' he murmurs, 'about the *year*?'

'It's 999e – now?' says Hul. 'But this is extraordinary!'

'The calendar's *wrong*?' Tishy breathes. 'So after today, there are only the Meditations? Then the Thousandth Cycle begins?'

Jem gasps. Can this be true?

'Brothers, but what of the Crystals of Orok? Does this question not gnaw at your minds? Does my power not need the five mystic crystals if it is to endure, if it is to grow? For what did I rage, in the torments of Unbeing? Ah yes, only with the crystals shall I rule, and rule for ever! But think you that I have failed? Think you that I am ... *vexed* at every turn?'

Jem shudders at the ironic words. A smile comes across the First Minister's face, then the face flickers, as if a curtain has flapped back momentarily, exposing a visage of rotted flesh, hanging from a grinning skull.

And the black curtains behind him billow and bulge.

'But no more of vexing – or of *Jemany* Vexing!' Toth's next words echo triumphantly: 'For what is Chorassos but the ultimate weapon, the weapon that will bring the crystals to me? Prodigal of all the powers at my command, from the depths of Unbeing have I summoned this creature, whose mighty rays of psychic force will at last thwart the Vexing and his companions, spiriting the crystals into my grasp!'

Jem's eyes widen in fear. By now, his crystal is searing his chest.

Toth leans forward, and again it appears that a mask has been stripped from his face, revealing the hideous, decomposing being that once shrieked from a magic mirror.

'Is this not the *last* day of the *last* moonlife of the *last* year of Atonement? All through this moonlife, for night after night, we have sacrificed to Chorassos. Now comes the night of our final offering; now, before Atonement ends, only the Meditations are to come. Yes, only the god-days of Orok's five children – of loathsome Koros, Viana, Theron, Javander ... of Agonis, most hated of all!

'Brothers, what are these days but the ultimate negation of Orok's children, of all they stand for, of all their power? For on each of these days – with each mighty circuit of the Unbeing Bird – a crystal, Brothers, will come to me! The Key to the Orokon thinks he has triumphed, but his final defeat is nigh! Yes, I will crush him like an insect underfoot, seizing all the powers of the Crystals Five! Brothers, it is ordained! Our plan cannot fail!'

Toth's laughter bursts like thunder round the crypt. Jem, in his concealment, doubles over in agony, clutching his blue, glowing crystal as if already the anti-god reaches for it, hungry to clutch it. In urgent voices his companions hiss, *Jem, what's wrong?* and *Jem, are you all right?*, but Jem cannot speak. Images of the crystals fill his mind, whirling round in a blaze of colour; through the circle they make he sees Toth, his face rotting, flung back and laughing. It seems to Jem that time itself is collapsing, that no more time remains, that already Toth's crazed plans have come to pass.

Now the chanting resumes, but wilder; now the curtains tear away. In the looking-glass is the image of a dragon-like creature, half-serpent, half-bird, shimmering with an evil, greyish phosphorescence. Waves of force stream from the glass, sending the Brothers, and the intruders too, reeling back as if from a physical blow.

Energy is rising, higher and higher. Still the chanting resounds; still the anti-god cackles with laughter. Round and round flurry the Mauvers, crashing and colliding above the cowled assembly, frenzied as if in anticipation that soon their master will be amongst them.

The time has come.

'Now,' shrieks Toth, 'the sacrifice!'

'No,' cries Jem, 'he *can't*—'

'N-No ... please—' Polty sinks down, despairing, clutching the naked girl in his arms.

Toth only laughs at Polty's fears. How it amuses him to terrify his servant! But no, he has no call for Miss Vyella Rextel's burden. He flings back his hands. Rays fizz from his fingers and on the slab before him there materialises a squirming, naked boy-child, bound and gagged. Toth whips a knife from beneath his white robes.

'*Raggle!*' Bando rushes forward. 'My son, my son—'

'Treachery!' Toth's eyes blaze. A bolt of force leaps from his hand and the old rebel crumples, agonised, to the floor.

All is chaos. Still the power builds and builds. Now, at this moment, the sacrifice must be made; now, at this moment, Chorassos must come. Desperately the Mauvers shriek and swoop. Still the Brothers stamp and chant; the Hornlight Focus flashes on and off.

But now Jem, too, has burst from concealment, the blue crystal blazing at his chest. Hul and Tishy race towards Bando.

'The Crystal of Javander!' Toth cries, exultant, as if he already clutches it in his hands. Rays shoot forth; Jem hurtles into the air, fixed in a spinning field of force.

'Key to the Orokon, you shall not defy me!'

Toth clutches the squirming, naked Raggle. Now he will slash open the child's torso. Now he will hold aloft the glittering, bleeding heart.

Back, back sweeps the knife through the air.

'N-No ... *no!*' Bean rushes forward, seizing Toth's arm.

Toth swats him aside like an insect.

Back, back swings the knife again.

All at once, Jem knows what to do. He thinks of the night when it was Myla on the slab. He thinks of a shattering, of a surge of energy, counter-acting – for a crucial moment – Toth's evil energies. Whether the ploy will work again, he cannot know. Perhaps he will only be surrendering his crystal; perhaps he will be surrendering the quest itself. But if Jem is taking a chance, it is a chance he has to take.

He rips the glowing crystal from his chest, flinging it into the magic glass.

An explosion rocks the crypt.

Glass bursts everywhere. Toth shrieks; the knife drops from his hand and Raggle hurtles forward, rolling and tumbling into Bando's arms.

Gasping, Bando clutches his child. Tishy and Hul exclaim in joy. But still Jem whirls round and round in the air. Still the power is building and building, surging from the smashed glass in cataclysmic waves.

At the altar, Toth points desperately to the intruders. 'Brothers, seize them!'

But only one of the Brothers steps forth. Something, some new force, holds the others away.

Time is arrested. A cowl sips back. 'Fear not, Jemany, your destiny is nigh—'

'Lord Empster!' Jem cries, astonished, as his guardian, swathed in mystic power, reaches forth a long hand, holding out the Crystal of Javander.

'Quick, Jemany, take it, take it back—'

Toth cries, 'Agonis, you will not defeat me! Agonis, *no*—'

Exulting, Jem seizes the stone. Its light blazes up; then time is rushing faster and faster; Jem spins faster and faster, too. As rival energies contend in the crypt, the very walls, the columns, the floor and ceiling are distorting, distending. Cacophonous sounds crash all around and the Mauvers are everywhere, soaring and plunging.

Jem's friends reach for him, to no avail. Tishy grabs his hand. Round and round swirl the crystal's stabbing rays. And suddenly Tishy, who has clutched her book all this while, is wrenched up from the floor – fused, fixed to Jem's grasping hand.

Hul struggles to save her, but now Jem, and Tishy too, are rising higher and higher. Inexorably, they are drawn to the Hornlight Focus, spinning towards the gaping vent. Still the light blazes with impossible brightness, then flickers weirdly into deepest black.

Just before they vanish into the vent, Jem sees his lost guardian sweeping back a capacious cloak, enfolding Bando, Raggle and the struggling, distraught Hul. There is a flash and Agonis is gone, bearing Jem's friends from the dangerous scene.

Meanwhile, the creature called Chorassos remains visible in the cracked glass, pushing and pummelling at the walls of Being. Toth flings Polty out of the way. He strikes Bean. Clumsily he seizes Miss Vyella Rextel, flinging the naked girl across the altar.

This time, there will be no delay. The girl struggles, screams, but Toth stabs her throat. The knife swings back, then plunges down again.

Tishy screams helplessly.

Jem cries, 'No! *No*—'

The Brothers cheer, stamp. Blood spurts in geysers from the dome-like belly. Toth's robes are scarlet. With bare hands, he rips back the girl's flesh, triumphantly digging out a dripping, bloodied boy-child.

The umbilical cord throbs savagely.

'My son, my son—' The words come again. This time, they are Polty's, but a force holds him back. His struggles are useless.

No, this time there will be no delay!

'Chorassos, come to me! Chorassos, come!'

The child screams, its only scream. For now, even as the navel-string still pounds, Toth slashes open the new-born torso, gouging out the tiny heart. A roar fills the crypt. Through the shattered looking-glass Chorassos bursts, its mighty form half-phantom, half-real, and too vast by far to be contained in the crypt.

Up, up, soars the creature through the ceiling, passing through layer after subterranean layer.

And at the Ball?

The terror of moments earlier has taken on a new, wilder form. A rumbling, like an earthquake, rocks the Koros Palace. Chandeliers crash down; there is a rush of mighty wings, then all is dark. Can this be another rebel outrage? All realise it is more, much more. As if evil is suddenly bursting into being, a vast purple phantom passes through the darkness.

Swiftly Ejard Red makes his escape. Cata, clawing at the terrified Queen, struggles to hustle her to the panel in the wall. This is her chance, her last chance. Screams, cries fill the ballroom. But Cata's mission is doomed to fail.

When the vision has gone, all are stunned, disbelieving. Many are injured. Some are dead. And Cata, losing her grip on the Queen, finds herself suddenly rushing upwards, borne up on a fizzing, blue beam of force while Morven and Crum look on, goggling.

Upwards, ever upwards Cata spins, passing through the ceiling as the Unbeing Bird has done. Arms wheeling, she bursts into the sky, just in time to see the vast, purple, phosphorescent creature swooping away into the dark clouds. But Cata has no wings to fly. Down, down she is about to plummet – when suddenly, from the clouds, there soars the skyship!

She gasps. A panel opens.

Cata tumbles inside.

And meanwhile Jem, clutching Tishy, is soaring upwards too, whipping round and round, rushing up through the Hornlight Focus.

They burst out into the night.

Jem's crystal blazes.

They turn slowly, magically in the sky. Horror fills their minds at all that has passed, at all that still must pass with the Unbeing Bird free. But neither Jem nor Tishy has time to think further on these things.

'The crystal,' Jem gasps, 'it's fading—'

Tishy begins, 'Does that mean—'

They plummet. But then the skyship comes.

END OF PART THREE

PART FOUR

To the Crystal Sky

Chapter 41

COME TOMORROW

All over Agondon, when the Bird Ball was over, there were many who spent restless nights staring through dark cracks between curtains or into the embers of dying fires, hoping, praying, that the horrors of the night would fade like phantoms born of fevered brains.

There is a mercy in darkness, shrouding the world in its black veil. In darkness, terrible things may come, yet seem strangely unreal, like dreams. Time, and all that time brings, appears suspended, hovering on the brink of reality as if about to vanish with the dawn. But truth, when dawn comes, will not be denied; and though the night was long, dawn came at last.

It was the Meditation of Koros, first of the god-days that end the year. That day, few except for servants ventured out of doors, hurrying through the white world on necessary errands.

Servants – and Bluejacket guards.

But not all Bluejackets served Ejard Blue. Not any more. In the Koros Palace, buttoning their bearskins, two young recruits crept downstairs. It was long before they were meant to be on duty again, but this was duty of a different sort. Stumbling, they scurried across empty courtyards where ice in pools glimmered greyly, like looking-glasses shattered on the cold stones. More than once the fellows stopped, whispering nervously.

'M-Morvy, are we doing the right thing?'

'You know we are, Crum. Think of Blenkinsop. Doesn't *he* know?'

Fondly, Crum cupped the squirming little burden in his tunic. Who could have believed that Blenkinsop would be returned to him, safe and sound?

Oh yes, they were doing the right thing!

In the night there had been many whisperings, spreading between the soldiers like passwords between members of a secret sect. Now it was time for the sect to act. The recruits came to an unfamiliar yard. Others were there already; there were nervous noddings. A chill wind rattled at stable doors; a horse whinnied.

Elsewhere, other deserters readied themselves. At sentry posts, men exchanged glances; then, as if glances were vows, they left their posts. Trudging patrols made their way down the streets and one man, then another, slipped away. If they were caught, they could expect no mercy. But there comes a time when there are things men fear more than firing squads.

The figures moved, furtive but certain, towards their destiny in the Agondon Hills.

※　　※　　※　　※

In Corvey Cottage, the rebels held a council of war. Their situation, on the face of it, was desperate. The climax was upon them, and all their plans had failed. They did not have the Queen. But they had the King. The real King.

The first deserters came soon after dawn.

'Bluejackets!' A rebel sentry gave the cry.

There was a flurry in the farmhouse. But the Bluejackets cast down their muskets in the snow. They kneeled, snatched off their hats, bowed their heads. Astonished, the sentry looked on as his red-garbed master emerged from within.

There would be no more despair in Corvey Cottage, not today. Times come in history when the tide of events turns suddenly in a new direction.

The man who had been known as Bob Scarlet trudged forward, towards the first of the kneeling figures. His hand reached out, touching the crown of the soldier's head; while his fingers lingered there only for a moment, the touch might have been a benediction. The solider looked up, staring in astonishment into the regal face, concealed no longer by its black mask.

The soldier, as it happened, was Recruit Crum; but even Crum, as if guided by instinct, knew what to say.

'Y-Your Majesty,' he gulped, 'my royal liege—'

In Crum's uniform, Blenkinsop squirmed happily.

Ejard Red smiled. Yes, the tide had turned his way.

※　　※　　※　　※

Still, there were other Bluejackets who remained strictly loyal.

On the Riel Embankment, heavy boots thudded towards Cham-Charing House. A gloved fist battered at a door. There was a pause; the fist battered again, then the butler appeared, opening the door just a crack. It was enough; the fist became an outstretched palm, pushing back the heavy slab of oak. Terrified, the butler fell to the floor. He heard the barking of a harsh voice; the hand shoved a warrant under his nose.

Picking himself up, the old man scurried to his lady's chamber. How was he to tell her the terrible news? Already troops were massing in the hall. They were bringing in boxes, sandbags, sacks, even a rumbling artillery gun. Slushy boots trailed across the carpets; the terrible words, like a knell of doom, echoed in the butler's brain. *In the name of His Imperial Agonist Majesty, King Ejard of the Blue Cloth ... May the Lord Agonis save the King...*

Could it be true? Could Cham-Charing House, seat of the Cham-Charings for epicycles, be commandeered for the Bluejacket army? But already the butler knew the answer was yes, a thousand times yes!

In moments Her Ladyship would be sobbing in despair.

❋　❋　❋　❋

'Oh, Torso … sweet Torso…'

In the Koros Palace, another noble lady knew a different despair. Umbecca, lowing and rocking, slumped once more by her beloved's bed. Only the Pigar Parrot costume, discarded in a corner, remained as a reminder of the Ball. Barely breathing, the body lay naked on the bed again, its severed limbs arranged around it, reeking in the heat of the fire.

'Dear lady, come away. There's no more you can do.' Franz Waxwell hovered unctuously, wringing his hands. For some time he had been urging Lady Umbecca to repair to her own chamber; she barely heeded his words. Gropingly, she reached behind her, grabbing a prodigious seed cake from the multi-tiered platter. Breaking off a chunk, she sopped it in a dish of milk, then held it, crumbling, to her beloved's mouth. She leaned against his ear, whispering sweet words.

Would Torso not eat? Would Torso waste to nothing?

Torso only drooled and moaned. Umbecca sighed. The seed cake, perhaps, was a little too bland. Stuffing the portion into her own mouth, she decided that yes, it probably was, and ate the rest of it just to make sure.

She reached behind her again. Profiteroles? Torso had never much liked them; impatiently, the fat woman polished them off … But this? Redforest gateau with kirsch and cream? Had she not shared such a gateau with Torso, one happy morning but a short time ago? Indeed; with arched eyebrow, with pursed lips, the beloved man had sat on a chair beside her bed, legs crossed at the knees, fork poised elegantly, regaling her with gossip about sluttish Sonia Silverby, about mad Louisa Bolbarr, about that stuck-up old bitch, Constansia Cham-Charing.

If only those halcyon days could return! Again Umbecca thought of Nirry Jubb, that monster in woman's form, that cruel, wanton destroyer of her happiness. To think, after all she had done for that girl! To think how the trollop had repaid her! Anger filled Umbecca's heart, then despair. Sobbing, she might have flung herself upon the naked Torso; instead, she devoured the Redforest gateau.

The apothecary had endeavoured several times to intervene. He had crept progressively closer to the bed; he had tried to catch the lady's eye; he had let forth a little *hem-hem!*, all to no avail. Now, perhaps, he should be more decisive. With a louder *ahem!*, he begged the lady to consider – for all the lavishness of her womanly care – whether his *professional* attentions should be delayed any longer. Had not the time come for further medication? (Dear Torso *did* seem to be turning blue.)

Poor Franz Waxwell! The morning light pressed behind the curtains; the clock on the mantelpiece ticked away, but still he had entered not a single item into his account book. It made him uneasy. He was, after all, a man of strictest probity; not for Franz Waxwell the practices of certain of his colleagues, who thought nothing of a little shameless supererogation, here and there.

Distastefully, he eyed the *almost*-corpse. What a sight it was, with the leech-welts on its chest, with its cauterised stumps, with its rotting arms and legs splayed around it! Without doubt, the thing would be dead soon; to the apothecary, it was imperative that he deploy his arts to the utmost before that sad event came to pass.

He stepped a little closer, venturing a hand towards Umbecca's fat shoulder. The lady, too, required his attention. Chocolate rimmed her mouth; cream spattered her front, dripping from the golden Circle of Agonis she wore, once again, around her neck.

The apothecary smiled. Some time ago, gesturing contemptuously towards the tiered platter, he had urged upon the lady the importance of her accustomed morning meal. Must not a lady keep up her strength? What were these stale pastries to the superior charms of a full Ejland breakfast? With admirable aplomb, he had spoken of the porridge, the sausages, the venison, the kidneys, the cream-drenched scrambled eggs and glistening, oozing bacon that awaited her in her own apartments.

Now Waxwell intimated a graver concern. The lady's humours, he was certain, were decidedly out of balance. Medication was imperative; indeed, the apothecary grew bolder, insinuating the necessity of a procedure he had never before thought it desirable to perform upon this lady – as opposed to, say, the Queen.

Umbecca was unmoved. 'Cruel apothecary, would you take me for one of your idle, flighty women of society, concerned only for her own petty ailments, when the beloved of her heart languishes in need of a nurse's care? Yes, *beloved*, I say, for was it not dear Torso I loved, even as I exchanged my vows of wedlock? Call me blasphemer, call me what you will, but no longer can I deny my love! Where must I be but by his side, so long as he should need me?'

Umbecca snatched up a severed leg. She clutched it in her arms, kissed it, stroked it. 'Dear, sweet Torso, fear not that I shall leave you. What are you to me but life itself? What should I be if you were with me no more?'

Waxwell reached for the leg – which happened to be dripping thick, golden pus down the lady's gown. 'Lady Veeldrop, your humours! Come, let me—'

She slapped him away.

'Dear lady, you're overwrought—'

'Cruel man, wicked man, go from me, go—'

Umbecca might have screamed. Fortunately a footman came to the door.

He announced the Archmaximate.

'You wished to see me, ma'am?' The great man stood there in his elaborate robes. If he was startled by the scene before him, he managed not to betray it; in long years in public life, he had seen much.

It was Umbecca who was startled. A memory of the Ball came back to her and she recalled why she had summoned this functionary. Like a proud mother she shuffled forward, bearing her mottled, bloodied burden.

But a tremulous confusion was evident in her voice. 'His ... canonisation,' she murmured, 'his ... sainthood—'

'That is the Lector's ... *leg*?' said the Archmaximate, raising an eyebrow.

Yes, he had seen much, but so high a dignitary of the Order of Agonis was hardly accustomed to the stench of rotting flesh. His eyes slid from Lady Veeldrop, flickering over the hissing lamps, the drawn curtains, the flames flashing on the holy icons. He looked upon the blue, mutilated thing lying naked on the bed. Should he offer up a prayer?

'A tragic end,' he said piously, 'for one so ... promising.'

'Dead? Torso, *dead*?' Umbecca laughed gaily, then a little hysterically; troubled, the Archmaximate turned to the apothecary.

Waxwell bowed graciously. Amongst gentlemen of his profession it was well known that the Archmaximate suffered from gout, indigestion, bronchial inflammation, indeed all the customary infirmities of age; well known, too, that his private physician was a doddering old fool. The apothecary's mouth twisted into a smile; alas, the great man did not return it.

The lady recovered from her fit of laughter. 'But he *shall* be sainted?'

'A saint, ma'am, is dead,' the Archmaximate said gently, endeavouring not to breathe too hard.

'Or living eternally?' The fat woman disported herself upon a chaise longue. Signalling to the apothecary for water and a sponge, she began the task of bathing the leg. One almost expected her to wrench open her gown, offering a breast for the leg to suckle; fortunately, the lady only hummed a little lullaby and tut-tutted over the pus and dried blood.

The gentlemen looked on nervously; the Archmaximate, affecting a touch of catarrh, had reached into his robes for a handkerchief. Holding it over his nose and mouth, he observed that Lector Feval would, of course, be buried with all due ceremony, as befitted so esteemed an officer of the Order of Agonis.

'Buried?' Umbecca's eyes flashed.

'But ma'am, you speak of sainthood.' The great man endeavoured to take her hand; still the lady dabbed with her sponge. Poor Torso! Look on this thigh, this angry red mark! Obscured before by encrusted blood, the red mark now flamed out with startling intensity; the colour, it appeared, was embedded in the skin.

Again the Archmaximate glanced at Waxwell. If only the fellow would leave them now! Should the great man have bustled him from the chamber? Perhaps he should seize the Lector's limb, flinging the vile thing into the fire.

A weariness overcame him, and he slumped beside the lady.

He struggled to speak, hoping to distract her. 'Already, ma'am, there are reports of the rebels—'

'Hm. Hm.' Then: 'Torvester? Not my sweet Tor?'

What was she talking about? (Still she dabbed at the spot.) To the Archmaximate, the prospect that Lady Umbecca had lost her mind was at once enthralling and alarming. Her influence over the young Queen was a baleful one, he was certain; her elevation of Feval, whom he had once banished, filled the great man with horror and shame. But if one so formidable was to collapse into madness, what security might others feel? What did this portend for the Bluejacket régime?

He attempted, 'Your ex-maid, the traitress ... was it not fortunate they captured her?'

This would stir her, would it not? The girl, he had heard, was to be executed on the morrow, hanged by the neck from the Erdon Tree. Already there were reports of rebel movements. Some spoke of desertions in Bluejacket ranks. The great man was frightened. Could it really be Ejard Red who had returned, seeking vengeance?

It was a prospect too horrible to contemplate.

The apothecary contemplated prospects of his own. Surely now he might seek the Queen's permission to confine the stricken lady? Like a heavy-laden ship, bound for remote, perilous waters, Lady Umbecca was embarking, it was clear, upon a long, perhaps endless voyage of mental turmoil. Sleepy-treacle, in regular doses, would certainly be required, not to mention other, more exotic potions; no remedy, indeed, could be overlooked, not for so valuable an ornament to the Court.

As for the Archmaximate, his humours were in a parlous state – why, that private physician of his must be useless! Some cordial, at the least, was necessary now; the great man, if anything, was even more important to this imperilled city than the lady. Should he not have the finest ministrations?

On and on he droned about a maid condemned to die. 'This execution, they say, is the most significant in a cycle – nay, in a gen. What is it but an example, a warning, to those who would betray our noble cause? But to *you*, dear lady, shall not the gratification be so much more?'

Dab, dab, went the sponge; furtively, the great man glanced at the apothecary. The fellow, he thought, appeared to be transfixed, gazing in a kind of rapture on the madness around him. But could he, in truth, be gazing upon the thigh? Sternly, the Archmaximate gestured towards the bed. Was the patient breathing freely? Was he breathing at all? Was it not incumbent upon the apothecary to know?

Dab, dab – the great man sighed. He was not an evil man; at least, he did not think of himself as one. Had he not lived only for the love of the Lord Agonis? But somehow, as his career unfolded, the fervour of his faith had faded, then died, tarnished by favours, compromise, betrayal. To the world, he was a man of the cloth, the greatest such man there could be; really, he was only a politician, with all a politician's moral shabbiness.

Again, he looked at the thigh. What was it but a symbol of his failure? He thought, as he often thought, of a young man called Silas, and a beautiful lady called Lolenda. He thought of a baby he had put out for adoption, long years ago.

Dab, went the dripping sponge, *dab, dab*. Ah, how immutably the red spot flamed! Ah, how carefully Feval must have concealed it, all through his years in the Order of Agonis!

Despair filled the Archmaximate's heart. If only he could have denounced this evil man! There are truths that should never be brought to light, but somehow, nonetheless, they force themselves to the surface. Even now, the revelation rose like vomit in the great man's throat. Should he tell Lady Umbecca – tell this deluded old bitch what Feval had been, whisper it in her ear like a lover's secret? A surge of cruelty filled his heart; he longed to see the lady crushed and broken, weeping, pleading that this shame could not be so.

The apothecary turned. 'He's dead ... dead.'

The words cut like a knife through the gloom. The lady looked up. Realisation came slowly to her face; slowly the leg slipped from her arms.

'Eay! Not my Eay—' Tears burst from her; on the walls, holy icons shimmered and flashed as the Archmaximate – awkwardly, hopelessly – embraced the stricken woman. What different impulse was it that seized him now, compelling him only to mercy, love, compassion?

'Dear lady, fear not ... he shall have his sainthood.'

The apothecary, for his part, took out his little book. He smiled; then his smile became a frown.

Again he looked at the leg. What *was* that mark?

Chapter 42

BOOK OF REVELATION

'I don't like it.'

'It can't go on.'

'But what can we do?'

The speakers were Jem, Cata and Rajal. Huddled in blankets in the jud-dering skyship, they gazed at the mysterious, transfigured form of Myla, hovering like a phantom against the padded ceiling. Still the strange music flowed from her lips and her skin glowed with unearthly light. Through the metal hull they heard the howling of the wind. Snow pelted against the portholes and the curving glass screen in the skyship's prow.

'What I want to know,' said Cata, 'is—'

'Where we're going?' Jem smiled.

'All right, I've said it before. Can I say it again?'

'Of course. And I can say again that I've got an idea. At least, I think I have.'

'Still the same one?'

Jem toyed with Cata's hand. 'We're heading north, aren't we? It's get-ting colder, too. I wonder, are we bound for this Lamasery of the Winds?'

'And the Crystal of Agonis? Depends on the magic.'

Jem raised her hand to his lips, marvelling to be with her again. If only this adventure were far behind them! 'Five days,' he murmured,' to save the world ... But if it's going to end, at least we'll be together.'

'That's a big *at least*,' said Cata.

'I know,' said Jem, 'I know.'

They sighed; Rajal, a little apart from them, sighed too, for a different reason. His dark eyes were fixed upon Myla. How much magic had she used to get them here? She looked no older than before. But for how much longer?

It was late in the morning, but still the exhausted Littler slept on a padded couch, an arm round the purring Ejard Orange; on an opposite couch, dozing lightly, was Tishy Cham-Charing, head on one side, horn-rimmed spectacles slipping down her nose. Open on her knee lay a mouldering book.

Jem reached for it. 'Some people can read anywhere.'

'At home in bed would be the best place for her,' muttered Cata. 'Why here?'

'She could hardly help it,' said Jem.

Cata scowled. How many Tishy jokes had she heard at Mistress Quick's? The girl was notorious, and for all the wrong reasons.

Jem, from his society days, knew something of her too. 'Come on, Cata, she's not so bad. I thought you'd like an unconventional girl.'

'You're comparing me with her? Didn't you ever hear that ditty, *Tishy, Tishy, all fall down* – about the time she danced with Ejard Blue at the First Moonlife Ball? She's not unconventional, she's just *wet* – a girly-girl, who's not even any good at being a girly-girl. How long did it take us to calm her down once she found out she was flying in the air? I had to slap her face!'

'It's not as if she's used to magic,' said Jem, 'not like us.'

'She'll be trouble when we get where we're going.'

Rajal, hearing this exchange, felt himself smiling for the first time that night. Hadn't Cata slapped Tishy a *little* harder than was necessary?

In Jem's hand, unregarded, lay Tishy's book.

'What is it, anyway?' said Cata. 'Some romantic falderal, I suppose – I've noticed that *plain* girls tend to like that sort of—'

Tishy opened her eyes. 'Actually, it's a rare work of ancient theology. I stole it from the Chamber of Forbidden Texts.'

Rajal could not help himself. He laughed aloud.

Cata flushed. 'R-Really? How interesting, Tishy—'

'I meant to take *Discourse on Freedom*, by Mr Vytoni. I'll admit, I picked up this one by accident. At first I was disappointed, but I begin to think it really is fascinating, and a great scholarly challenge. It's called *Lamasery of the Winds: A Prophecy*, and it's—'

'*What?*' Rajal stopped laughing.

Jem looked down, startled, at the book. Recklessly, he leafed through the crumbling pages. 'But it's … I mean, it's—'

Tishy scrambled up. 'Careful! It's Juvescial, and—'

'You're sure?' said Jem. 'I had to study that stuff when I was learning to be a gentleman, and this writing looks quite different. Anyway, girls don't—'

'*Girls don't, girls don't!* How many times have I heard that?' Tishy sniffed, pushing her spectacles back up her nose. 'For your information, it's in Juvescial Aros, what they call the Tongue of Agonis, not that Juvescial Standard stuff they teach the likes of you – I'm still learning how to read it, and it's hard. But at least I'm past the *basics*.'

Gulping, Jem handed back the book. 'I'm sorry, Tishy, I … I didn't mean anything, really. Neither did Cata – did you, Cata?'

Cata remained silent, but shook her head.

'This book,' Jem urged, 'what does it *say*?'

A faraway look came into Tishy's eyes. It was a dangerous moment. She might have launched into a learned disquisition, full of arcane discussion of textual transmission and cruxes of translation; fortunately, being young in her scholarly life, she had consideration enough for her audience simply to explain that the book, so far as she could make out, was about the earliest days of Atonement, when Agonists first settled in the Realm of Ejland.

'That doesn't sound very exciting,' said Cata. 'Why was this book forbidden, if that's all it's about?'

'And this ... lamasery?' Jem urged.

'Lama-what?' yawned Littler, whose eyes had opened again. Ruefully he gazed about the moving skyship and the hovering figure of Myla. Still the music issued from her lips, winding its sweet, strange tendrils round the harshly howling winds.

'A lamasery? Sort of a religious house, isn't it?' said Cata.

Despite herself, she looked to Tishy for confirmation.

'In legends, or foreign parts, they're sometimes called that.' Tishy indicated the book. 'But I haven't found one in here yet. Still, there might be one – after all, I haven't puzzled out much of it yet. There's something about the Kolkos Aros, I note.'

'The Crystal Sky?' Cata looked at Jem. With trepidation they both thought of the white mountains that had loomed above their childhood home in the Valleys of the Tarn. Hovering against the horizon like a ghostly backdrop, the Kolkos Aros had never seemed quite real. Some said the mountains were indeed only an illusion; everyone said they were impossible to climb. Could this be where they were headed now?

'But this book,' said Jem, 'why *was* it forbidden?'

Tishy looked thoughtful. 'When the Children of Agonis left the Vale of Orok,' she mused, 'that's where they were supposed to go – up into the mountains.'

'Not *into* them,' said Jem, remembering his religious lessons, 'just near them. That's why we came to live in these northern lands, as opposed to—'

'No, *into* them,' said Tishy. 'That's what the Ur-God told us to do – I mean,' she added with an emancipated air, 'if you take what's called the Literalist line. Of course, theologians have said that virtually everything in the El-Orokon's just a metaphor, so we don't have to take it all seriously—'

'So we can just do what we like?' said Cata.

'That's right,' said Tishy. 'But I suspect this old book's more than a little too Literalist – thereby censuring, at least implicitly, the theo-ideology of the current régime. I'd guess it was banned around the time of the Great Schism, or perhaps in the aftermath to the Counter-Schism, early in the reign of Elabeth I...'

Since none of the others could dispute this, there was silence. Cata wondered just how to take so learned a lady; Rajal wanted to ask about this business of the Agonists going up to the mountains, while Littler was

266

playing a game with Ejard Orange, somewhat to the annoyance of Ejard Orange.

> *Uncurl the tail:*
> *Curl it up again.*
> *Uncurl the tail:*
> *Curl it up again,*

Littler chanted under his breath; then, growing bored, he looked towards the wicker hamper which contained their remaining provisions.

Ejard Orange looked at it, too; then both Littler and Ejard Orange registered disappointment as Jem, with sudden enthusiasm, asked Tishy if she could read them any of the book.

'Is it a *story*?' said Littler between clenched teeth, flicking one of Ejard Orange's ears.

'Oh yes,' said Tishy, 'though hardly the sort you'd have heard before. Now, I'd just managed to puzzle out another five-stave ... let me see.'

She read in a slow, flat voice, stumbling more than once over points of translation; nonetheless, by the intentness with which the little group listened, Miss Laetitia Cham-Charing might have been a mistress of the storyteller's art.

This is what she read:

FIVE-STAVE THREE

I.

So it was that Ondon, first of the green and wooded edge-land's many Kings, rejected all the counsel of Father-Priest Ir-Ion, and thus, too, the will of Orok the Almighty: never, so declared the proud and boastful King, would his peoples leave this edge-land where they really should not be.

II.

And the remonstrations of the Father-Priest were made to no avail: for long had Orok slept in the darkness of his death, and long had Orok's children been away; then, too, the Vexing Gem had long lain inert, a symbol and no more, unglowing with the sacred light of faith.

III.

And yet it was that Ondon, in the palace he now had made, still found a place for Ir-Ion and all his brother-priests: for though King Ondon ruled but by the standards of the world, he would that as a man of faith he should be seen by all, as worthiest of all the Bearers of the Vexing Gem.

267

IV.

Thus it was he reasoned: that though the common people would much celebrate their King, and nowhere else would live but in this edge-land they had found, still with the thrall of faith they could not break, and would have it they were sanctioned by will of the divine.

V.

This then was the task to which Ondon set his priests, for he would have them by him as an instrument of state: though silent the gods might be, the monarch, like all human monarchs, yet would have it that they spoke, and spoke in a voice that was like unto his own.

Curious. Very curious.

Several times as Tishy read, Jem and Cata, Littler and Rajal had found themselves exchanging glances. To some, perhaps, the contents of the five-stave might have been cryptic, hardly sensational; but to the foursome that listened to Tishy now, the implications of what she read were clear. When she paused, they all burst into exclamation.

'So the Agonists,' said Rajal, 'don't belong in Ejland? And for all these years they've been trying to toss out us Vagas!'

'These Bearers,' said Littler, 'where are they now?'

'The *Vexing Gem*?' said Cata. 'What do they mean?'

'It must be the Crystal of Agonis,' said Jem, 'but—'

Eager to unravel the ancient mystery, he was about to urge Tishy to translate some more when a mighty buffeting shook the skyship. Ejard Orange leapt up, hissing, bright fur standing on end. Jem and Cata, Rajal, Littler and Tishy all went sprawling. For a moment Myla's song ceased and her eerie light guttered.

'Wh-what happened?' said Tishy, wide-eyed.

'L-Look!' said Cata. 'Through the portholes!'

The purple gleam filled the sky.

'Mauvers,' Jem gulped. 'They're all around us.'

Chapter 43

THE WHITE MOUNTAINS

On and on the skyship howled through the cold brightness of the morning, lurching as if it were a real ship, pitching and tossing on a stormy sea. But the sky, though clouded heavily, was calm; even the flurryings of the snow had abated. The tumult came from the Mauvers, buffeting the metallic hull. Ominously, the creatures would cluster about the portholes, filling the interior with eerie light; then, for no reason Jem or his friends could see, they would veer away sharply, cackling and cawing like unearthly gulls, until suddenly, violently, they converged again.

For now, they had scattered. A pallor of whiteness filled the skyship.

'If only I could snap her out of it,' murmured Rajal, gazing up at his entranced, hovering sister.

'Yes,' said Littler, 'and the skyship would plummet.'

'That's not what I mean.' Rajal shifted uncomfortably. 'But what *do* I mean?'

'That you want her back? Like before?' Littler felt the same, thinking again of the dark-eyed little girl he had encountered in a secret garden during the course of their last adventure. Sad-eyed, renewing an old campaign, he urged Rajal to tell him more about Myla as she had been before – the *real* Myla – back in the days when Rajal and Jem, the Great Mother and Zady had travelled with her in the Vaga-van.

Rajal tried to think, but sorrow ached behind his eyes. His gaze wandered to Jem and Cata. Hands clasped, heads together, the lovers sat before the curving screen, looking intently at the scene below.

Jem pointed. 'I was right, I knew it—'

'The Tarn?' breathed Cata. 'The Wildwood? Oh, how strange to see it from on high—'

'Look, there's Irion—'

Rajal and Littler gathered round, too; Ejard Orange bounded up on the ledge before the screen. Only Tishy hung back, burying her nose deeper into her book.

'Jem, is this where you came from?' said Littler.

'See down in the middle?' said Jem. 'That snowy circle? That's the village green under all that. And look, that building over there—'

'The big one? With the columns?'

'The Temple of Irion. Would you believe Cata and I met on those steps?'

Cata was solemn. Wonderingly, she looked at the white world. When, in the many nights of her exile, she had dreamed of her first home, she had seen it as it was in the Season of Viana, with the birds coming back and the opening flowers, with the quickening river and the burgeoning shoots; or in the Season of Theron, sticky with incense and honeyed light, rippling with joyous songs of ragged, wild choirs.

A memory came back to her from earliest childhood. At what time of the year she had been born, Cata could not be sure, but consciousness must have come to her in Theron-season, for when she had first known the cold, she had sobbed, thinking the warm world was gone for ever, and the leaves were falling, never to return.

Silly, of course; but now this first sadness welled in her again, strangely real. Below, there was barely a glimpse of green, and Cata was afraid, as if it were a portent.

Ejard Orange clawed at the screen. Jem, watching him, might have wondered why, but just then he gasped as a haze of cloud cleared away to reveal a vast edifice, towering above the village upon a high, rocky outcrop.

'Littler, look – the castle! That's where I grew up. When I was your age, it was just a ruin – well, the whole village was a ruin, compared to today—'

'Did time go in reverse? Like in Kal-Theron?'

'Not quite, Littler. The Bluejackets came.'

For a moment, Jem was silent; Rajal had been silent for some time. Screwing up his eyes, he could just make out the hill, to the west of the village, where the conquering forces had corralled all the Vagas into a squalid camp.

'Did you live here too, Raj?' said Littler. 'And Myla?'

'If you call it living,' Rajal said softly. 'Luckily, we escaped.'

Ejard Orange cuffed a paw at the screen, letting out a plaintive *miaow*.

Jem smoothed the cat's furry neck. 'What's wrong, Ejjy?'

'He's hungry,' said Cata. 'As usual.'

'This is your animal-telepathy?' said Rajal.

'Just a good guess. He hasn't had any breakfast.'

'Neither have we,' Littler moaned. Expectantly he turned towards the hamper that had accompanied them all the way from Wenaya. 'Couldn't we have just a *little* something?'

'It'll certainly be a *little*,' said Jem. 'Remember, there's been nothing new in that hamper since we left Inorchis.'

'Isn't there still some chicken?' said Littler. 'And tongue-and-yam pie? And an urn of lemonade?'

Jem had to laugh, but at once was sombre again. 'You're right, Littler, but we'd better go easy. Let's see where we're headed.'

'I'd have thought *that* was clear.' Cata looked ahead. Already the Tarn was retreating behind them and the icy mountains loomed. She pulled her coat tighter around her, shivering, but not just from the cold.

Littler said glumly, 'At least we've got coats this time.'

Jem nodded. It was something; but they would need more than coats in the Crystal Sky. Much more.

A new, violent lurching shook the skyship. Ejard Orange hissed.

'The Mauvers,' said Cata. 'They're back.'

Jem looked at her curiously, then at Ejard Orange. There were no Mauvers at the portholes; there were none at the screen.

'They're ... settling on top of us – clustering,' said Cata. She was whispering, and a strange look had come into her eyes. Distractedly she reached for the marmalade cat, smoothing his hunched back, his agitated fur.

Jem said, 'You can sense them? But they're ... phantoms.'

'Phantoms,' said Rajal, 'that can rock the ship.'

'You mean ... they're *real*?' said Littler.

'Not quite,' said Cata. 'Something in between—'

Littler looked questioningly at Ejard Orange. 'That wasn't just about your breakfast, then? Before?'

'He sensed them before me,' said Cata. 'And something else. I'm sure there's something else.'

Again she looked down at the white world, her trepidation increasing. The valleys were slipping away; soon the ship would be flying between mighty mountain peaks. Looming into view came vast forbidding gorges and rocky outcrops, ravines, escarpments, plateaux. If the mountains, from a distance, were a fluttering scrim, a gauzy pallor against the sky, at closer quarters the great craggy ramparts were all too real, the rocks forbiddingly dark against the whiteness.

Fresh snow pattered at the screen, and once again the skyship rocked.

'Tishy, are you all right?' said Jem.

'I ... I've got another five-stave,' said the scholarly young lady. She had turned a little green.

'You've worked it out? Can ... can we hear it?'

This was hardly the time. Mauvers thudded, screeching, against the hull; one porthole, then another, shone with purple light. Soon the rockings were regular, growing more extreme; still Myla's light shone and the song poured from her lips. Ejard Orange howled, racing about the cabin; the others clung to the couches, the pylons, the useless control panel.

Littler cried, 'If only I had my orb! We c-couldn't c-*crash* into these mountains, could we?'

'I don't see why not,' said Rajal. 'Amulet, are you listening?'

'You'd better hope it is,' Littler said grimly. 'We'd all better—'

'Come on, we're always crashing,' Jem snapped. 'Surely we'll be lucky *this* time? Besides, we've got Myla now – she's brought us this far, hasn't she?'

'It's not Myla I'm worried about,' said Rajal. 'I mean ... well, I *am*, but you know what I—'

'Won't someone shut that *cat* up?' said Tishy.

'Look!'

It was Littler who cried out first. His eyes grew wide. His hand went to his mouth. Across the snowy fields below, a vast shadow moved.

It was the shadow of a bird, an immense bird.

❋   ❋   ❋   ❋

Jem was cold with horror.

Pressing his face against the screen, he strained to see the sky above. Already the Mauvers blocked his view, but just for a moment, dark against a dazzle of whiteness and grey, he made out the flying shape that arced across the sky.

'The Unbeing Bird,' he breathed.

Then it happened. Cata screamed. She fell to the floor, clutching her head, and the skyship began to spin. Jem and his friends were thrown this way and that. Ejard Orange was frantic, leaping, hissing, scratching. Myla's song became a wild cry and her light began to gutter.

'Myla, no—' cried Rajal. 'Myla—'

Still Cata screamed. Jem grabbed a pylon. Terrible pain exploded in his mind and the blue crystal at his chest burned like fire as the Unbeing Bird made its mighty circuit. Round and round the skyship whirled; now the Mauvers were pushing past the hull, forcing their way through the metal and the glass, beating and battering at the air inside.

Time distorted, fractured.

Jem's crystal burned and burned; so did Rajal's, Cata's, Littler's; while searing all around them like a tangible force was Toth's depravity. It might have been a slow, purple explosion, bursting endlessly outwards and outwards, and all Jem could feel was the burning crystal; all he could hear was screaming; all he could see, as in a vision, was the dark and terrible Unbeing Bird, scything through the sky like a promise that evil, and only evil, would reign in this world and reign for ever. The world was the bird. The bird was the world.

Then the bird passed. And the skyship was falling.

Chapter 44

THE HAWK UNMASKED

And then? What did you do?

'Didn't I say? We held out the child to its proud mother. What happiness burst across her flushed, sweaty features, transfiguring the countenance that, moments earlier, had strained and twisted in the travails of birth—'

But then? What did you do?

'Did we not swathe her in praises, lauding the beauty of her fair prize? Fondly we gazed upon Little Polty; fondly, too, I gazed upon the father. How I envied him the happiness of his lot! Indeed, I too longed to know such ... such – I was going to say, *emotion*—'

Your feelings, then, were stirred?

'Very, but ... of course they were!' Bean faltered. 'It could have been darkest night. Instead, it was brightest day ... How merrily the sun sparkled on the waters! The mallard ducks, how happily they swam, quack-quacking between the soft, spiky reeds, and—'

Aron, you were speaking of the child.

'The child?' A faltering, again. 'Yes, the child – how could I not be happy? How could you wonder? After all, it's not every day that a child is—'

Born? I would have thought it was a frequent occurrence.

'Yes, but – not Polty's ... Oh, and such a child! At once, we saw his resemblance to his sire. Polty laughed; I laughed; Miss Rextel was in ecstasies. How we relished the baby's sturdy legs, kicking energetically into the air; how we marvelled at his plump hands, curling round first his father's finger, then his dear mother's! His infant cries were the sweetest music – and was he not delighted by the mallard ducks? Naturally, we dribbled his forehead with the customary Vantage, affirming the luck that surely must accompany so special a child through all his life. And how fondly we stroked his flaming down!'

His hair was red? said the phantom. *Like a flame?*

'Like blood – n-no, not blood.' For a third time, Bean faltered. 'Why ... why did I say that?'

He knew he was dreaming. But how real the dream! His heart hammered painfully in his chest as he gazed once again on the billowing entity in its striped robes of black, white and grey, radiating light from where its face should be. The voice came again – smooth, caressing – and now Bean felt something crumbling within him. Terror gripped him, but still he could only stare, transfixed and trembling.

Blood, came the whisper, *there* must *have been blood. Come, was there not blood, blood?*

'At a birth?' said Bean. He sensed something burning behind his lips, like a secret longing to burst into the world. No more could he restrain himself. 'Blood,' he blurted, 'and darkest night, and chanted prayers, and cries, and a knife, glittering, plunging down—'

Yes, and the blood, the blood! the phantom hissed. *Remember it splattering, remember it gushing in wild cascades—*

'No, I – no … Empress, what are you saying?'

Bean felt as if his heart would explode. *Empress?* Why was he calling this phantom *Empress?*

Remember, she intoned. *Aron, remember.*

'Never.' It was another voice. 'Never, never.'

❋ ❋ ❋ ❋

Bean woke. Was he in his own chamber? On his own bed? Daylight pressed, purple, behind the drawn curtains. Yes, he was back in Polty's quarters; but how he had got there, Bean did not know. He felt as if he had been hit, and hit hard. He moaned, clutching his face.

'Never, never,' came the voice again.

'P-Polty?' Bean's voice was reedy, like a child's.

His friend stood in silhouette, turning slowly in the middle of the dis-ordered chamber. Something glinted in his hand, a Vantage bottle; he swigged from it contemptuously, then flung it down.

'P-Polty? Polty?'

Polty turned. He was shivering, and no wonder: he wore only a shirt; there was no fire in the grate. Oh, but this was unprecedented – Polty awake, Bean still in bed? Appalled, mouthing apologies, the hapless side-officer scrambled up as if about to embark on his accustomed duties.

Polty grabbed his arm. 'It's all over, Bean.'

'P-Polty, what do you mean?' Bean's teeth chattered. A harsh wind whistled in the chimney; snowflakes struck insistently at the windows; but Bean was possessed by a deeper chill. Of course he had known that nothing could be the same. How could it? But even now, he was terrified at the thought of change.

Polty's voice came hollowly. Dark circles ringed his eyes. 'Do you think I can go on serving him? Carry on, after all that he's done? Don't you see, Bean? I've been a fool … a fool, and now he's killed my son—'

'Polty, I'm so sorry … Polty, I—'

'He's been using me, that's all.' Still the voice was hollow, like an echo from a well. 'I suppose you knew that all along, didn't you, Bean? Did you ever believe he would make me whole again? Hah! It would be laughable, wouldn't it, if only, if only—'

Polty broke off. Longing stirred in Bean's heart. He moved closer, thinking that now, perhaps, he must clutch his friend, hold him tight, comfort him as he sobbed for the ruin of his body, for his dead son, for everything.

Instead, Polty turned sharply. Briskly he strode across the squalid chamber, kicking from his path a discarded coat, a plate, a chamber-pot that sloshed and clanged. He clasped his hands behind his back; his shirt flapped about his wobbling thighs.

'I see what we must do – don't *you*, Bean?' Polty's voice was different now; gone, all at once, was the blankness of his grief, replaced by a febrile excitement. He stood by the windows. He wrenched open the curtains. 'We'll leave him,' he said, 'just go – you and me, Bean. And you know where we'll go?'

'Polty, where?' Now Bean was excited too.

'I've been thinking about Cata,' said Polty. He turned again, shadowy against the white window. 'Oh, I'm always thinking about her, it's true, but now I understand what I didn't before. I know where she's hiding; all I wonder is why I never saw it.' He grinned. 'Oh Bean, come on! Can't you guess? Isn't it obvious?'

Not to Bean. 'I ... I—'

'Irion!' Triumph shone in Polty's eyes. 'Bean, I'm sure of it. What is Cata, what is she in her heart but a simple child of nature? She's gone home, I know it, back to that crazy old father of hers—'

'But Jem Vexing? Isn't she, wasn't she with—'

Polty waved an impatient hand. 'Bean, what does my heart-sister care for him? Cata never loved the crippler-boy, not for a moment. She was teasing me, that's all, just pretending. Wouldn't she want to make me jealous? Wouldn't she want to test my love? When you understand women as I do, Bean, you'll get used to their flighty ways ... Still, what's the chase, but part of the pleasure?' Polty had to laugh. 'Poor Bean, you're such an innocent! Loved the crippler? Cata? Never!'

He paced again. 'But Eyeless Silas? That crazy old half-Vaga? Wouldn't she want to take care of *him*?'

Bean was puzzled. 'Can he still be alive?'

Polty rolled his eyes. 'Bean, I tell you, Cata's back in Irion – and that's where *we're* going, too. We're leaving today. Oh Bean, I can see it all now, can't you? The castle, the temple, the Lazy Tiger ... the village green, the Wildwood, the river—'

'Mallard ducks? Will there be mallard ducks?'

'What's that? Oh, hundreds. But Bean, what do you think has become of your old whore of a mother? Wynda must still be thriving, mustn't she? She'll hide us out, I'm sure of it ... And Old Wolveron? Ah, I always had a fondness for that wily old rogue—'

'You *did*, Polty?'

'Of course! Isn't he Cata's father? Oh, he always *knew* I was on his side – he's an enchanter, isn't he? No, Bean, none of your doubts. Didn't he make the Vexing walk? He must have done – and if he can make a crippler *walk*, don't you think he could put back Penge? Mere child's play for Eyeless Silas—'

Bean goggled. 'Do you think he will, Polty?

'When he knows I've come to marry his daughter? Bean, don't be such a fool! Oh, how I long to clutch her in my arms again! But she, *she* must be longing for it as much. How the love will come flooding back to her heart when she sees me striding into her father's cave! Bean, think of all the sons we'll have – sons, and daughters, too! Enough of this wretched life … Home, Bean! We're going home.'

Bean nodded tearfully. As Polty spoke, the lanky fellow had sunk to his knees as if in worship. Visions of Irion filled his mind. He swooned, forgetting Toth, forgetting all that had happened last night. Oh, to go home! Oh, to go home with dear, dear Polty!

'Quickly, we must pack!' Polty snapped into life. 'We've a long journey ahead, and it's going to be hard. We'll be deserters; we'll have to lie low. Now, where're my breeches? Where's Penge? Quickly, Bean, quickly!'

Bean needed no encouragement. Already he was bustling round the squalid apartment, collecting up random items they might need, jackets and coats, tooth-powder and razors, handkerchiefs, hip-flasks. Clumsily, Polty struggled into his breeches. He grabbed Penge, clutching the sloshing jar. Good old Penge! To think he would soon be back in his rightful place, fit and well and ready for his wedding day!

'Come on, Bean, no more dawdling—'

Bean stuffed linen into a holdall. 'But Polty, just a moment, where are we going?'

'*Irion*, Bean, *Irion*—'

'But first? Before we—'

'Bean, come on!' Polty strode to the door. What about his coat? What about his boots?

Bean had to laugh. 'Oh Polty, Polty—'

A thudding came at the door.

'Who can that be?' Polty turned, annoyed. 'Get rid of them, Bean. Quickly.'

Bean opened the door. He gasped; he might even have closed it again at once, but already the figure in the corridor had pushed past him, advancing into the apartment.

Alarm filled Polty's face. 'Bean, who is it? Who *is* this?'

The new arrival wore a black costume that showed not the slightest sliver of skin. Hanging behind him, billowing as he walked, was a bifurcated cape like a pair of wings; spiky feathers covered his mask. Tiny jewels, in patterned arrangements, glittered all over his sleek, elaborate garb.

'It's ... it's Hawk of Darkness,' Bean said, gulping. 'He's from Chokey's ... I mean, he was there last night. This was ... this was his costume for the Bird Ball.'

Polty struggled to conceal his fear. But why should he be afraid? Exasperated, he would have flung the intruder out, but the fellow looked nothing if not formidable.

'So? What do you want?' Polty demanded.

The voice was wry. 'It's our *master* who wants you, Polty.'

'Our ... m-master?' Polty stepped back. 'You're ... you're a servant of Toth?'

'Of course I am, Polty. I'll admit, I haven't been in his service for *quite* as long as you – or our lanky friend here. For a long time, I didn't even understand who he was – I certainly didn't know about *you* and him. But then, I always was slow, wasn't I? Always slow, compared to you? But what do they say about the race not always going to the fleetest of foot? Isn't there something about that in the Adages of Imral? You know, that book the Unangs were always going on about? Got tiresome, didn't it?'

As he spoke, the fellow paced around the apartment, the eyes behind the mask flick-flicking here and there. Polty found himself trembling; Bean sank into a chair. The voice, he realised, was really rather familiar. And not just from last night.

'You s-seem,' stammered Polty, 'to know me well. I suppose ... I suppose Toth's told you—'

'Oh, Toth didn't have to tell me much. Aren't we friends, Polty? Aren't we *old* friends?'

'Polty,' cried Bean, 'that voice, it's—'

But Polty had already darted out a hand, snatching away the feathery mask.

He stumbled back, gasping.

Behind the mask was a twisted, sickening mass of burned, scarred flesh. The eyes glittered; the lipless mouth parted in a grotesque grin as the creature turned to Bean, then back to Polty.

'What's the matter, my friends, don't recognise me? Don't recognise old "Jac" Burgrove, handsomest bachelor in Varby? Oh, but I suppose you hardly could. This is the kind of thing that happens when a fellow's been left to burn alive!'

Polty gasped, 'Jac, I didn't ... Jac, I thought—'

Mr Burgrove spoke calmly. 'You left me to *die* in Unang Lia, Polty. You left me in that distemper cell in Qatani, under the Khan of the Crescent Moon – left me there as the fire raged. You saved yourself, you even saved Bean – but you didn't save your old friend Jac.'

Polty could not think to defend himself. Appalled, he turned away, clutching Penge tightly in the green, sloshing bottle. Mr Burgrove went to him, his voice light, almost conversational.

'I suppose it was just as well I met Toth, wasn't it? Oh, I was a mess after the fire. The guards who found me thought I didn't stand a chance. Somehow I managed to pull through; somehow I got a passage back from Unang Lia, skulking deep in the ship's hold so no one would see me and cry out in terror. Does your heart not pine for me, Polty? What a fate for old Jac! Remember how the ladies' heads used to turn in Varby every time he walked by? I suppose you envied him, didn't you, Polty?'

'Jac, I—' Polty's throat was dry.

'Oh, don't let it *bother* you, old friend!' The lipless mouth laughed. 'We all make mistakes when we're young, don't we? And aren't we quits now?'

'Quits? What do you mean?'

Mr Burgrove indicated Penge. 'I mean, Polty, that we've both been punished for all the wickedness of our old lives. And I mean that now we're both waiting to be ... *restored*. That'll be our reward, won't it? And soon? Remember, the time of our master's supremacy is at hand!'

'I—' Desperation consumed Polty. 'Jac, you can't believe him! Jac, don't you see—'

'We're his servants, Polty! There's no escape!'

'No—' Quite what Polty meant to do next, he could not have said. Perhaps he would have launched into a new, impassioned plea; perhaps he would have lunged forward, overpowering Mr Burgrove, imagining that he could escape Toth so easily.

He stumbled and the Penge-jar slipped from under his arm.

'No!' cried Bean, Polty too; at once, both were on their knees, scrambling amongst the liquid and broken glass. A foul stench filled the air.

Where was Penge?

There was a curt laugh. They looked up, horrified. Mr Burgrove had not squatted or stooped; how, then, could this be? The precious thing that had lodged within the jar now hung, pendulous and dripping, from their old friend's hand, the long foreskin – stretched, almost translucent – pinched between his fingers.

Polty reached up, grabbing, but glass stuck in his knee.

He cried out, buckling.

And now, sickeningly, the foreskin began to tear; Mr Burgrove only smiled and gripped the organ instead by its severed root. Whimpering sobs came from Polty's lips; Bean looked on, astonished, as the ruined face now tilted back, as the gloved hand rose.

Like a thick, slimy eel, Penge hung suspended over the lipless mouth.

'So,' Mr Burgrove murmured dreamily, 'he leaves his old friend to die in a fire ... Then, as if that's not enough, he batters to death his old friend's father—'

'Father? Jac, what do you—'

'What, forgotten him already? Forgotten Chokey?'

'*Chokey* is your—? But Jac, if I'd only—'

'Dear me, what a memory,' Mr Burgrove went on. 'Still, I dare say you've never forgotten *this* thing, have you? And never will.'

The eel-thing slipped closer, closer to his lips.

'Ah Polty, how proud you were of this cylinder of flesh, how inordinately, maddeningly proud—'

'No—' Polty whimpered.

But already Penge had slipped from the gloved fingers, vanishing in a single, slithering movement down Mr Burgrove's throat.

Chapter 45

TOTH ATTACKS

Silence. But not quite.

There was the wind, cold as ice, whistling across the snow; and twining around the wind, colder than the wind, a mysterious, taunting music. Rajal opened his eyes. He staggered; standing in the snow, he was not quite sure how he came to be there. Entranced by the music, he gazed up, staring at mountain after cold mountain. Where were the others? Where was the skyship?

He turned. Mountains, only mountains: ah, but was there not one in particular? Like the elegant arch of a temple window, its peak was perfect in its symmetry, but possessed too, of an ominous power...

And now the feeling stole across Rajal that all this was only a vision, a dream; no, this was not the waking world at all. His eyes blurred; the eerie music twisted and distorted: the perfect mountain was calling him, summoning him with a clear, cold voice. Alarmed, Rajal would have run away and hidden, as if the mountain were sentient and could see him; instead, he felt the Crystal of Koros, pulsing unbidden beneath his thick furs.

It was answering the call. The purple light was burning through the furs, stabbing its rays into the snowy whiteness. Rajal gasped, twisting with pain, pain that was real, even if this scene were not. Uselessly, he beat out with his hands, aware of the Mauvers clustering around him, clamorous, crying. He fell to his knees.

And that was when he saw, through the flurrying Mauvers, through the snow that all at once was whirling thickly, coming towards him, the figure of a man. A welling fear filled Rajal, a fear worse than the pain. It was as if he knew what was about to happen, knew it with a certainty that could not be denied. But how could this be?

Only a vision. Only a dream.

But now the figure was clearer. The Mauvers had vanished; rustling, shimmering like a purple ghost, the figure might indeed have been compounded of the sinister bird-things, fused into a single embodiment of evil.

The hand reached out, fluttering, fluttering. And Rajal knew he could not resist. Once, twice, he tried to knock the hand away, but it was as if all strength had left his limbs. He moaned, sobbed. Still the strange music whistled and twined; now, beneath the music, came a teasing *Rajal, Rajal ... Rajal, Rajal—*

This time, the hand would not be denied.

Fluttering, fluttering … Rajal felt the half-phantom fingers, scratching and clawing through his thick coat. The wrenching, the tearing. He cried out. Laughter played softly on the air around him, and still, beneath the laughter and the music too, came the taunting *Rajal, Rajal…*

Then the voice was different: *Raj, Raj—*

Mmm. Mmm—

When would this stop?

The War Lords ignored the noise. Or pretended to.

'A handsome chamber? Oh, indeed.' Baron-Admiral Aynell turned with a sigh, taking in the thick, swirling carpets, the purple leather, the curtains drawn against the cold daylight. 'When first I called upon my lady wife – before, of course, she *was* my lady wife – she received me, so I recall, in just such an apartment.'

'In a Privy Chamber?' enquired the Prince-Elector.

'In a privy? Sir, what are you suggesting?'

Mmm, continued the First Minister.

Really, how much longer?

Oblivious, with an urbane laugh, the Prince-Elector stroked his famous moustaches. Hitherto he had observed the conventions of politeness; now, bored, he found himself giving way to mischief. Just a little.

'Admiral,' he returned, as if speaking to a child, 'I refer not to a latrine, but to such a place as this – a chamber of withdrawing for the powerful and great. And was not your lady a daughter of greatness?'

Aynell's eyebrows knitted. As a simple tar – so he would deprecatingly refer to himself – he had never quite accustomed himself to the wit of the town; nor, he would add, had he wished to do so. But what could this mean? Talk that he owed his status to a fortunate marriage had never been uncommon; the talk was true, but Aynell, not unnaturally, regarded it as a calumny. Had he been elsewhere than in the First Minister's withdrawing room, he should certainly have called the Prince-Elector to account. The fellow – his moustaches curled, so legend said, by a musket-shot at the Battle of Bajari – was a disreputable fop, and Aynell had always despised him.

He snorted; the Prince-Elector smirked. Gesturing to the painting over the mantelpiece, he might have asked if such a work, with its seething lizards, serpents, tortoise-spiders, beetle-giraffes and other assorted *abortions* – yes, that was the word – were quite to the taste of pink, yielding Baroness Aynell. But no; a weariness descended upon the Prince-Elector and he directed his attention, as if with a dying fall, to the world-globe in the corner, setting it spinning with a long, gloved finger.

Mmm, hummed the First Minister.

How much longer?

The Olton-clock ticked. Lamps hissed; the fire crackled. By the window, General-Lord Gorgol peered out through the curtains, screwing up his shaggy-browed eyes against the snow; by the bookcases, monocled Varby & Holluch (one man, not two) leafed idly through the statute-books. Did he note that pages had been torn away? He did, and adjusted his monocle; at another time, the matter might have alarmed him more.

Now there were other reasons to feel alarm. Solemnly, he lowered the heavy tome. Might they not, he was about to suggest, make another attempt upon the First Minister? They had agreed to wait; could they wait any more?

Varby & Holluch had no need to speak. There was a thumping of boots on the stairs outside. The door swung open; a sentry's heels clicked and Major-General Heva-Harion appeared at last.

Prince-Elector Jarel raised an eyebrow. In his lateness, Mander Heva-Harion had lost a little – more than a little – of his accustomed calm.

He was not to regain it. Adjusting his wig, mopping his brow, the fellow might have been expected to fall into breathless apologies, expatiating, as others had done, on the delays which had beset him, the disruptions in the streets, the confusion that reigned throughout the city. There was none of this. Instead, the Major-General's eyes, and his mouth too, opened wide in astonishment.

Bemused, the Prince-Elector watched as his tardy colleague took in the scene before him, his gaze travelling between the War Lords, standing awkwardly, and the First Minister in his white robes, cross-legged by the fire, motionless, idol-like, long fingers pressed against his shaven skull.

'Is … is he all right?' whispered the Major-General.

Shrugging, the Prince-Elector did not whisper at all. 'He's been like this since we got here. It's beginning to be *dull*.'

'But … we must do something!' was the reply.

'What *can* we do?' blurted Aynell, irate.

'Why, he must listen to us, and listen now!' cried Gorgol in his guttural Derkold voice, which gave the impression that his throat was clogged with phlegm. Bear-like, he reared over their cross-legged master. 'Your Excellency, don't you understand? The rebels are massing, our men are deserting … Ejard Red, if it really is he, demands that we parley – or Agondon, he says, will be razed to the ground! The future of our city – nay, of our very empire – hangs in the balance!'

Gorgol might have gone on, but it was useless. Never even flinching against the onslaught, never even opening his eyes, the First Minister still only hummed tunelessly, breathing out an interminable *Mmm—*

'Enough of this,' snapped Varby & Holluch. He moved to the door. 'What are we to think but that Tranimel is mad? What are we to think but that his reign is out? Where's the King? We must speak to the King—'

282

'Come back, you fool!' Gorgol burst out. 'We are the War Lords, are we not? Is it not upon us, *us*, that the security of this realm depends? What thought must we have of other authority? Forget the First Minister! Forget the King! Cowards amongst our ranks might have gone to the rebels, but still we stand at the head of a formidable army. Think of the Battle of Wrax! The Green Pretender! What can rebels do against Bluejacket might? I say we attack, and attack now!'

Heva-Harion's face had turned the colour of beetroot. 'Gorgol, it is you who is the fool! Are we to rain down devastation on our city and the fertile hills that surround it? To attack now would be to acknowledge the rebel threat. Can we believe they will cast the first stone? I've said it before, and I'll say it again: working by stealth, we must seize this so-called Ejard Red, seize him and expose him for the impostor that he is. It is a task for Special Agents. We must parley, or at least appear willing to parley.'

'And, perhaps,' Prince-Elector Jarel said slyly, 'to hand over His Imperial Agonist Majesty?'

'The King? But this is treason!' Aynell exploded.

The Prince-Elector rolled his eyes. 'Really, can we not discuss prospects, possibilities? Calm yourself, Rear-Admiral—'

Aynell blistered, '*Baron*-Admiral—'

'Indeed, indeed. But perhaps your earlier title was *even more* appropriate?'

'Why, you prancing ninny—'

'Gentlemen, gentlemen,' said Varby & Holluch.

Heva-Harion cried out: 'Look!'

The War Lords gazed upon their white-garbed leader, if leader he still were. All this time, Tranimel had continued his humming, *Mmm, mmm* … It was maddening. But now there was something more. The cross-legged figure was rising from the floor, ascending slowly but steadily into the air.

'I … I don't believe it!' blustered Gorgol.

Varby & Holluch gulped, 'He's … he's turning!'

The War Lords stumbled back, cowering against the bookcases as Tranimel revolved towards them, eyes open now and blazing with unearthly light. Behind him, the fire in the grate leapt madly, strangely; the lamps guttered and plopped and the curtains billowed.

Then there was the picture over the mantelpiece. Almost bursting from the frame, the hideous creatures squirmed and seethed, flapped and festered with depraved life. Terrified, the Prince-Elector slithered to his knees. Varby & Holluch tried to make it to the door, but fell, clutching his chest. Bellowing, Gorgol might have rushed upon Tranimel, but an unknown force held him back.

Mmm, mmm. The humming was louder now, booming explosively. And now, though still the humming went on, Tranimel began to speak. His eyes flashed. The chamber rocked. Fluttering around him, screeching and crying, came phantom bird-creatures, translucent, glowing purple. Then there was the shadow of another creature, something immense, passing impossibly through the chamber with a thunder of mighty wings.

The War Lords cringed and cowered.

'Ah yes, the time is upon us!' came the evil voice. 'Ah, my pretty, I am with you now! Fly, my pretty, fly towards the mystic mountain! Ah, and do you see him, there in the whiteness? Does the Vaga-boy stagger? Does the Vaga-boy fall? He must, he must! Fool, Vaga-boy, to think that fate could grant you the prize that was rightfully mine – *mine*, I say! For what were you, Vaga-boy, what could you ever be, but a lowly steward in the service of my glory? For a time I let you believe that the purple stone was yours – but only for a time, and now that time has passed! Ah yes, I see you in the snow! And now, as my pretty cleaves the skies above, so too I reach out this imagined hand ... But imagined, do I say? No, for I imagine no longer!'

He reached out, clawing, clutching at the air. Ecstatically he flung back his head, moaning out the name *Rajal*, *Rajal* as a chaos of music crashed around him; purple light enveloped him and there was a blinding flash.

Then came silence, or almost silence – but for the fire, and the hissing lamps, and the soft tick-tick of the Olton-clock.

When the War Lords looked up, they saw their leader – for indeed, they knew now that he was still their leader – stretching down his legs to meet the floor. A thin smile crinkled his ascetic face and in his hand he held a purplish crystal.

The lords looked on, intrigued. Just for a moment, the crystal glowed, as if with a light of its own; then the light subsided and the crystal became only a dull, dark stone.

Insouciantly, the First Minister secreted it beneath his robes. He turned to the picture over the mantelpiece where the monsters once again were arrested in stillness. Almost sadly, he gazed upon the vulture-bat, the tortoise-spider, the many-headed wolf. When he spoke, his words were distant, even ironic, but the words were enough to compel obedience from his astonished servants. After all, they were the words they had craved, all the time they had waited here.

'Come, my lords, must I not wonder why you tarry? Are you not men, and Ejlanders? Is there not a war to be won? Make haste, and ready for battle. A great victory is to be won, and I am sure it is to be ours – oh yes, most certainly ours.'

'Raj, wake up!'

This time, Rajal's eyes really opened. He was lying, curled on his side, in the snow. 'Jem! B-But of course ... it was just a vision – a dream...'

He struggled upright, shaking his head. 'Wh-where are we? What happened?'

'Remember, just before we went down? I opened the hatch. I said jump – and you did, remember? You and Littler? Well, I just about had to throw *him* out.'

'L-Littler?' Rajal's face was blank. Automatically he clutched his chest, feeling for the crystal beneath his furs. He turned, horrified, concealing the fear that filled his eyes. The dream! No, it could not be real, it could not!

'And I was still in the skyship,' Jem went on. 'Narrow escape, Raj – lucky we only ploughed into a snowdrift. If we'd gone into some of these *rocks* ... well, it's not worth thinking about, is it?'

Rajal nodded. A terrible guilt filled him, and he longed only to hide it. He looked about him, this way and that. He saw Littler, wide-eyed and shivering, clutching Ejard Orange in his arms, and Tishy Cham-Charing, struggling to her feet, still triumphantly clutching her book. Wedging the little volume beneath her arm, she searched in a pocket for a pair of gloves. Beyond her, almost buried in a snowy mound, the skyship lay on its side.

Lightly, Jem touched Rajal's arm. 'Raj, about Myla—'

Rajal swivelled back, all else forgotten. 'Myla? Wh-what about Myla?'

Jem breathed, 'Raj, she's—'

'Myla!' Desperately, Rajal floundered towards the ship.

Jem started after him, but Cata appeared beside him. 'Let him go, Jem. He's got to find out.'

Rajal disappeared through the ruined hatch. For a moment Jem expected a cry of pain, perhaps a scream; instead, there was only silence from within.

Perhaps that was worse.

'At least he remembers,' Jem sighed. 'I was worried there for a moment.'

'He was out cold, wasn't he?'

'Seemed like it. But Cata, what happened to *you*?'

'The screaming? Up in the air?' A pained look crossed Cata's face. 'I don't know, but the Unbeing Bird ... it was as if it was – inside my head.'

'Like other animals? The way they ... talk to you?'

'Yes, but ... oh, but this was horrible, violent, filled with death.' Cata shuddered and Jem embraced her, awkward in his thick furs. 'It was agony,' she murmured, 'and I couldn't resist. The power of that creature ... it's overwhelming.'

'I know, I know ... at least it's gone now.'

'Gone, yes – but for how long?'

'Oh Cata, what are we going to do?'

Cata pulled away. 'We'll find this lamasery, Jem – what else?'

Ejard Orange gave a plaintive *miaow*, struggling down from Littler's arms.

'He'll be looking for the hamper, won't he?' Jem said kindly. He squatted beside Littler. Still the child was shivering, and his face was fixed in horror. Jem was not surprised: it had been Littler, after all, who had been the first to see what had happened to Myla.

Jem caught the small, gloved hands in his own, struggling to think of comforting words. What could he say?

He glanced round. 'Where's Ejjy going?'

The big cat padded off around a rocky, snow-draped outcrop, as if he were on the scent of something.

Jem glanced at Cata. With a dutiful air, she had been attending to Tishy; now she turned, puzzled, in the direction that Ejard Orange had gone. Jem followed her, Littler too. Wonderingly, they rounded the rock. Ejard Orange miaowed again.

That was when they caught their first glimpse of the strangely perfect mountain peak, hovering far off across the frozen wastes. Fleetingly – but no, it was a trick of the wind – a mysterious music seemed to filled the air.

Cata put a hand to her head. 'That mountain, it's as if...'

'It's calling,' Jem said, 'calling us to come...'

'My crystal,' said Littler, 'I can feel it throbbing...'

Cata looked at Jem. Jem looked at Cata. Beneath their coats, both of them could feel their crystals stirring too. Excitement filled their faces.

'What *are* you all grinning about?' said Tishy, confused.

They ignored her.

'But it's *so* far away,' said Jem.

'And the Mauvers,' said Cata, 'they'll be back—'

'And the Unbeing Bird? Five circuits—'

'Then it means we've got to hurry—'

'And Myla? What about Myla?'

It had been Jem who said Myla's name. Littler let out an anguished cry. He slumped down in the snow. For a moment he had thought only of the adventure ahead; now he thought only of his poor friend's fate.

Jem comforted the little boy while Cata went back to see to Rajal. He would need all his strength; they all would. But when she saw him clutching his sister, gulping and crying, Cata could not help from breaking down, too.

Slumped and inert, her magic gone, Myla was now an old, old woman.

Chapter 46

NIGHT CLOSES IN

'Storytime, Tishy?'

Cata tried to keep the sarcasm out of her voice. Snow fluttered down over the white hillside. Making their way towards the mysterious mountain, the little party had paused beneath a rocky ledge, eking out the remaining provisions which they had transferred from the hamper into an alarmingly small sack. Littler gnawed at a chicken leg; Cata ate a banana which was almost frozen; Jem swigged miserably from the urn of lemonade. Rajal managed only to pick at some nuts.

Tishy, nibbling at a biscuit, eagerly opened her book.

FIVE-STAVE FOUR

I.

So it was that Father-Priest Ir-Ion, and all the Bearers of the Vexing Gem, had to lodge as if imprisoned in the palace of their ruler, pretending blindness to his heresies: sanction must they give to all he would do, though much there was that could never be sanctioned.

II.

And of these things that could never be sanctioned, greatest was the war that Ondon now declared: for as unto himself this mightiest of rulers had taken all the green and wooded edge-lands, by the dying god intended for the peoples of Viana, so he would destroy Viana's people.

III.

With pride it was that Ondon's race, still falsely called the Children of Agonis, now fell to fearsome strivings against their enemies: long and bloody were the battles in these edge-lands, as viciously they beat back the Children of Viana into the lands that lay far to the east.

IV.

Thus, deeply troubled was Father-Priest Ir-Ion: long and hard he prayed to his silent, vanished gods, and there came to him a sign as from above: the Vexing Gem now glowed and in its sacred golden light it seemed to him that all he now must do was clear.

V.

*Now from false Ondon the Father-Priest would break and take his
sorrowing Bearers and the Vexing Gem away: while still their evil
monarch pursued his course of war, thus they did escape upon a long
and perilous journey, bound, as once had been intended, towards the
Crystal Sky.*

'That's it?' Cata arched an eyebrow.

'Well, as far as I'd got,' said Tishy, 'before the skyship came down. I'll
need time to translate more. But I'll try—'

Much as he admired Tishy's talents, Jem had to admit that he was disappointed. It seemed churlish to say so, but Cata had no qualms. She took
the urn.

'Not exactly telling us anything we *don't* know, are you?'

Tishy sniffed. 'I … I'd never heard of this Ondon fellow, had you? Or
Father-Priest Ir-Ion?'

Cata remained unimpressed. 'Very interesting, I'm sure.' She grimaced,
deciding, like everyone else, that flat, half-frozen Wenayan lemonade was
hardly the thing for the Kolkos Aros. 'But we *knew* the crystal was up in
these mountains, didn't we?' she went on. 'Why else are we here?'

'The next five-stave might tell us more,' said Jem, a little to Cata's
annoyance. 'Don't be discouraged, Tishy. We might know where we're
going, but we don't know much more, do we?'

'What else is there to know?' said Rajal, leaning sadly over the
withered, silent Myla.

'What we'll find when we get there?' said Jem.

'Whether we'll get there *at all*?' said Littler. The young Unang boy was
shivering more than the others, and very glum. Throwing down his chick-
en bone, he reached for Ejard Orange. If the big cat looked regretfully at
the bone, still he did not struggle in Littler's arms. At least they could
keep each other warm.

Wearily, the party prepared to move on.

'We'll get there, we'll get there,' Jem murmured. But he wished he
could be sure. Grimly, he gazed towards the mysterious mountain.
With a makeshift stretcher for Myla, with a coil of rope, with a tinderstick
and their few remaining provisions stuffed into a bag, by now they had
left the skyship far behind. Already the darkness was drawing in and the
strangely shaped mountain looked no nearer.

'It's shifting,' shivered Littler, 'I'm sure of it.'

'Don't even think about it,' said Jem, reaching for his end of the
stretcher. The frail old woman that had once been young Myla was, alas,
surprisingly heavy. 'Ready, Raj?'

'Jem, shouldn't it be *my* turn now?' Littler said earnestly.

'Don't be stupid,' Rajal snapped. 'You're too little.'

Littler was crestfallen. From the first, he had wanted to carry the stretcher. 'Don't be mean, Raj. She may be your sister, but she's my friend.'

'What do you know about her, you snivelling brat?' said Rajal. 'Just shut up, why don't you?'

'Why don't *you*?' said Cata.

'They can both shut up,' Jem said grimly. 'He's just trying to help, Raj. And come on, Littler, you've got to take care of Ejard Orange. That's quite enough responsibility, isn't it?'

❊   ❊   ❊   ❊

They trudged on, cold chilling them through their furs. From time to time the carriers of the crystals would feel renewed throbbings from the mystic stones, but these were intermittent, and weaker than before.

As darkness descended, their spirits sank. Their destination, it was clear, was far more than just a day's march away. Soon they would have to stop for the night. Jem thought of the tinderstick. Here and there were a few windblown fir-trees, their branches laden heavily with snow. He supposed they could try and make a fire. But he wouldn't like to bet on their chances.

'I hope it's warm in that lamasery,' Littler said ruefully.

'And friendly,' said Jem. 'That's important, too.'

'I just hope they let us in at all,' said Cata.

'We're sure it's even … *there*?' said Rajal, struggling by now to bear his burden. 'How do we know there *is* a lamasery?'

'The harlequin doesn't lie,' said Jem.

'I'm sure my book will help us,' Tishy said brightly. 'If I could just get another five-stave translated, I know we'd learn *something*.'

'Oh yes,' said Cata, 'something of great historical interest, no doubt. I'd rather know just where this lamasery might be. What do you think, Jem? Nestling at the foot of the mountain? Or halfway up the side? Raj has a point, you know. How can we be sure it's there at all?'

'Didn't I say the harlequin doesn't lie?'

'You're sure it was the harlequin?'

'Cata, what are you saying?'

Cata did not reply. They trudged slowly uphill, weaving their way between snowy boulders. Far ahead, the mystic mountain was fading, sinking back into a precarious snowscape of gorges, ravines and high rocky outcrops, empurpled eerily in the evening light.

Jem shuddered, thinking of the Mauvers. With each weary step, his thoughts were growing bleaker. By now he shared Cata's doubts, and Rajal's too; he even had new concerns of his own. Cata carried the food-sack, slung across her shoulder. Jem suspected it was alarmingly light. And where were they going to shelter in the dark?

'I wish we could still see the Tarn,' said Cata.

Jem did too. Back near the skyship, they had been able to look down towards the valleys below. It had been a comfort, however forlorn. Now they were lost in a snowy labyrinth, with only the mystic mountain to guide their way.

'Have you thought,' gasped Rajal, 'that this is … just the *easy* bit? Sooner or later, I'll bet we have to climb … *really* climb. And then what will we do about Myla?'

It was the last thing Jem wanted to think about. 'I don't know, we could be lucky—'

Cata gave a hollow laugh. 'Jem, is that meant to be a *convincing* voice?'

'At least I'm looking on the bright side,' was the glum reply. '(Littler, don't dawdle.) Do I have to remind you all that there *is* one? We've got the crystals, haven't we? No fewer than four? *And* we're on the trail of the fifth. Come on, things could be a *lot* worse. Besides, we've escaped Toth, haven't we?'

'For now,' Rajal could not resist adding.

Jem ignored him. 'Well, which way?'

They had proceeded, for some time, between monstrous, snowy boulders. Now they came to a forking of the path.

Littler pointed to the right. 'This way.'

'That way,' said Cata, and pointed to the left.

Jem's brow furrowed. Adjusting the weight of the stretcher in his hands, he turned just a little, this way and that. 'I'm not sure, but I think … I think Littler's right. My crystal's stirring when I turn *this* way.'

Cata groaned. 'And mine is,' she said, 'when I turn *that* way. What about yours, Raj?'

Rajal's voice was flat. 'I don't know, what does it matter?'

'Quite a lot, actually,' Jem said, startled. 'I vote this way. Cata?'

'Well, perhaps you're right. But Raj, which way?'

'All right, Jem's way,' Rajal muttered, as if he didn't care at all. Gulping, Littler would have raised his voice in protest, but somehow he forced himself to say nothing.

Only Myla mattered, only Myla.

They went on in strained silence. A white field, steeply sloping, opened to one side of the narrow path, dappled darkly by clouds and purple light. Snow fell more thickly. By now the mystic mountain had vanished entirely, obscured beneath clouds and the gathering darkness.

'Oh dear, I'll strain my eyes soon,' sighed Tishy, who had been attempting to translate another five-stave as they trudged along. 'I suppose I'd better give up for now. But really, this next one *does* look interesting.'

'I think we'd all better give up soon. For now, at least,' said Jem. He paused, lowering the stretcher; blankly, Rajal did the same. 'Let's just hope we can light a fire. (Littler, don't dawdle.)'

Littler scurried after them. 'Perhaps we could heat up the tongue-and-yam pie,' he shrilled, with forced optimism.

'I said there was a bright side,' returned Jem, in a similar voice. 'We're even going the right way, aren't we? My crystal's still glowing. What about yours, Raj?'

Rajal turned away.

'Cata?' said Jem. 'Littler?'

They both nodded, but Cata's face was grave. 'Are you really sure you trust these crystals, Jem? Remember, they glow for more than *one* reason.'

'What was that about the bright side?' Jem groaned. 'Really, you lot – Littler, didn't I tell you to stop dawdling?'

'Perhaps they're just getting ready,' Littler piped up.

Jem's voice was sharp. 'Ready for what?'

'For the Unbeing Bird to come round again – he will, you know, Jem. I … I saw some Mauvers back along the path, I'm sure I did – Ejjy did, too, didn't you, Ejjy?'

'It's the twilight,' said Jem, 'it's just—'

'Oh, what's the use?' Rajal burst out. His hands darted up, clutching his forehead, as if his head were racked by sudden, searing pains. His next words came in an anguished shriek. 'You fools, fools! Don't you understand, it's all over? Don't you understand, we've lost already?'

Jem cried, 'Raj, what are you talking about?'

But Rajal had turned and flailed away, skidding down over the snowy, sloping field.

Jem pursued him, arms wheeling. 'Raj! Raj—'

'Should … should we go after them?' said Tishy.

'Oh, leave them, just leave them,' said Cata, almost bitterly.

She looked ahead. They must stop for the night. But where?

❉   ❉   ❉   ❉

'Raj, Raj—'

Down in the field, Jem wrestled the runaway to the ground. Troubled feelings burst in his mind. What madness could this be? He might have slapped his friend, punched him, but all he could do was hold Rajal's arms, tight as he could.

Breathing heavily, Jem gazed into the twisted, cold face. 'Raj, what is it? Raj, what's *wrong*—?'

Rajal let out a heaving sob. 'It's over—'

'I don't understand. Tell me *why*—'

'Can't you see? When the Unbeing Bird came—'

'Came, and went again—'

'Feel, Jem. Just *feel*—'

Clumsily, roughly, Rajal guided Jem's hand. Horrified, Jem felt his gloved, unfeeling fingers pulled between the parting furs.

'I … I thought it was a vision,' Rajal stammered, 'a dream. But Jem – oh, Jem, when the Unbeing Bird came…'

'No—' Jem broke away. Pain filled his mind; purple, ever deeper, swung down through the sky.

'Do you hate me, Jem?' Rajal's teeth chattered. 'Jem, I didn't—'

Now, more than before, Jem could have struck him. But why? This was mad, it had to be. *Like a dream. Like a vision.* Ah, but how much, in that visionary moment, it felt as if Toth were all around them, teasing them, taunting them! They must not give in, they must not!

Jem muttered, 'Raj, you're the one who doesn't see. This isn't the end, how can it be? Toth's got one crystal – all right, *one*, but we've got the rest—'

'And the bird's coming back—'

Jem gritted his teeth. '*And we're going to get the last.*' Almost sobbing now, he grabbed Rajal's shoulders: shook him, shook him. 'Do you hear me, Raj? We're going to get it, I swear we will. You've got to believe it: believe it, Raj.'

Rajal whimpered. There was snow on his face, snow slipping inexorably beneath his furs. How he despised himself! He broke from Jem's grip, rolling away in the powdery whiteness.

'I … I believe you.' His voice lacked all conviction.

Jem breathed deeply. He scrambled to his feet, reached out a hand. 'Come on,' he said quietly, 'let's go back to the others. And Raj? Tell them nothing. Just get up, come back with me – come on, come on.'

Slowly, reluctantly, Rajal complied. The way back was hard, and further than they thought; often they stumbled in the precarious twilight.

'Jem, Jem—' It was Littler, bursting back round a bend in the path. Ejard Orange frisked around his feet. 'Jem, you won't believe it, Ejjy's found a cave, isn't it marvellous? There're trees, we can make a fire, can't we? You've got the tinderstick, haven't you – Jem?'

At once, Jem was laughing. And Rajal tried to smile.

Chapter 47

CARNEY TO THE RESCUE

'You're all right, Baines?'

'I ... I don't know about this, Miss Landa. Begging your pardon, but Goody Olch has always been a pious Agonist woman, she has, never a one for any sort of *heathen* palaver – I mean, begging your pardon...'

'You're sure, Baines?' With a sad smile, Landa recalled a time when a bewildered Nirry had accompanied her in worship, pleading with the goddess to return the lost Cata. That had been in greener woods, on a warmer day, in a time already lost in the past.

'I'm ... not sure what you mean, Miss Landa.' Tears danced in Baines's single eye. 'I just want to do right by Goody Olch, that's all, and if there's anything, anything...'

Landa squeezed Baines's arm. Trudging through the hills, wrapped heavily in furs, they made a strange pair, this beautiful, statuesque Priestess of Viana and the one-eyed old servant who had not been quite careful enough, in the depths of her distress, to make sure her coat-buttons were in the right holes. Already she was shivering, and she shivered all the more when they came upon a barren, ancient yew, tilting precariously on a snowy rise.

'Th-this is the one, Miss Landa? B-Begging your pardon, but that looks like it's fit only for firewood.'

This time, Landa did not smile. 'The power is weak here, far from Viana's woods. This is the oldest of trees in these hills, and the only one where I feel my prayers are heard. Here, each day, I have begged the goddess for strength; I have prayed for our leader; for Master Jem; for Miss Cata. I have prayed for Goody Olch, and Goodman Olch, and you too, Baines. Soon, I am certain, destiny will be revealed to us. But I need your help.'

'I ... I thought it was something only you heathens—'

'Baines, if I knew where Miss Cata was, I'd ... but you're my best hope, don't you see? You're a *link*.'

'I'm ... a what?'

'Never mind, just do as I say.' To Baines's surprise, Priestess Landa pulled her furry hat from her head, letting her long auburn hair fall free. 'I know it's cold, so we'll be quick. Just do all that I do. And think of Goody Olch. Whatever you do, think of Goody Olch.'

Baines nodded. That part, at least, would be easy. She despaired, thinking of her employer in that bleak cell. Lying in the snow beside the Priestess, prostrated before the ancient tree, the old servant could only be glad that Goody Olch could not see them. What would she say about such foolishness? Right now, she would berate her servant, and her husband too, for neglecting the Cat & Crown.

Last night, Goodman Olch had told Baines all about his visit to Oldgate. In the cell before he left her, he had promised his wife that, even if the worst should happen, he would carry on with the business, that he would never let all her hard work go to waste; sobbing, he had agreed to keep that useless Baines in line (how Baines, through her own tears, smiled at these words!) and never, on any account, have anything to do with those sluts from the wrong side of Redondo Gardens. The Cat & Crown, he had agreed, would be a tavern fit for quality-folk, just as his Nirry had always planned.

Now only a day had passed and the Cat & Crown was boarded shut, Wiggler lay in a sickbed in Corvey Cottage, and here was Baines carrying on like a heathen out in the snow, and catching her death to boot!

'Ul-ul-ul-ul-ul!'

Like sharp, sudden birdsong, Landa's cry rang through the air; Baines's, which followed, was a hoarse, uncertain croak. The Priestess clawed at the roots of the tree, then swayed upright in a serpentine motion, powdery snow falling from her furs; stumbling, Baines did her best to follow her, as awkward in her bulky garb as Landa was not. Already the Priestess appeared to be in a trance, moving to embrace the icy, cracking bark. Oh, it was heathen blasphemy, it was!

'Daughter of Orok, see your supplicant. Sister of Koros, hear her words. Most sacred Viana, soft as leaves, come to me now in this woodland place, where I bring before you a sister who has stumbled in darkness, lost alike to knowledge of your majesty and your mercy. By what design, goddess, you have left her so benighted, I do not pretend to say; I know only that she is a woman of goodness, and would have her spirit fuel my spiritual fires, as I implore you now to aid her beloved mistress, imprisoned unjustly by the men of evil. Daughter of Orok, see your supplicant. Sister of Koros, hear her words...'

Now Landa moved into a complex chant, which Baines struggled ineptly to imitate. There was even dancing – dancing, of all things, under a dead tree in the snow!

At least Miss Landa's heart was in the right place; besides, the efforts the others had made on behalf of Goody Olch were by no means impressive. Until now, Baines had admired the highwayman Bob Scarlet; the discovery that he was really the deposed King of Ejland had filled her, at first, with an excitement so great that she thought her heart would burst.

What was she to think now? The efforts mustered to seize the Queen were not in evidence on behalf of Goody Olch. Some said there was no chance she would be executed; the rebels, they were sure, would have taken the city by then. Yes, others agreed, prisoners languished in Oldgate for an eternity before anything actually happened to them – as if a day in that foul place were not too long for a woman like Goody Olch!

Baines was growing breathless.

'Viana-Vianu, Viana-Vianu—'

'Goddess of the living, consume me like a fire—'

'In the greenwood let me lie, let me live and—'

Hul and Bando might have done something, but their leader had sent them off on a reconnaissance mission that morning; Morven and Crum were eager to help, but Baines could not place much confidence in *them*. If only Miss Cata had not disappeared again! And what had become of Master Jem and his friends, so soon after they had returned to Agondon?

It was a rum do, a very rum do. And so was this.

'Let no axe fall in the hills of Wrax—'

'Ooh, goddess, please save Goody Olch!'

Ho, very likely! Did Miss Landa think she would stir up heathen magic, sufficient for Goody Olch to burst free from her cell? Or were they supposed to receive some godly visitation, some vision that would tell them what to do?

On and on went the chant, the dance.

'Let me live and let me die—'

'Goddess of the dying, grant me my desire—'

'Viana-Vianu, Viana-Vianu—'

By now, Baines was thoroughly exhausted. She had to admit she was no longer cold. But was there even a hint of magic? There certainly was not, and she was ready to drop out, pleading her poor lungs, when she spied a figure in furs, struggling towards them over the snowy hillside.

A voice called, 'Miss Landa … Baines!'

Baines broke free. 'Wiggler, up from his sickbed? What can have happened?'

Only one thing was certain, that the fellow was distraught. Flailing behind him came the Bluejacket deserters, Morven and Crum, evidently trying to keep up with him, perhaps to restrain him.

Baines gasped, 'Goodman Olch—'

Sobbing, Wiggler fell into her arms and it was left to the soldier called Morven, his throat-apple bobbing painfully, to blather out the terrible news. Word from Agondon had reached Corvey Cottage. The Great Temple Bomber – Miss Nirrian Jubb, as they called her – was to be hanged that afternoon.

Landa joined them. Wrenched too suddenly from her mystic trance, it took the Priestess a moment to take in what had happened.

'*Executed?*' she breathed. 'But—'

Morven gulped. 'Hanged by the neck—'

'This afternoon,' said Crum, 'at the Erdon Tree—'

'No! By Viana, no—' Sweeping back her auburn hair, Landa looked back at the barren place where she had struggled to summon sacred forces. Her faith, it appeared, was useless. But there was more than faith. Decisively she gazed between her companions. 'Baines, look after Wiggler. Morven, Crum – saddle some horses. And get a cart. I'm off to see Ejard Red. We're going to need reinforcements.'

Quickly, she strode back towards the cottage.

❊   ❊   ❊   ❊

'More ale, slut!'

'Eh, who you calling a slut?'

'Your daughter, Offero!' said 'Scars' Majesta. 'Don't we all know you've put her out in Redondo Gardens? And a fine addition to Agondon's ladies of the night she is,' he added gallantly, and would have attempted a bow, but Offero the Mole, outraged, cuffed his fellow villain on the side of his head.

Shammy the Hood sniggered, spearing a cut of turkey from Offero's plate.

'The Gardens, indeed!' cried Offero. 'And why, Majesta, is my lovely, virtuous daughter here, right now, slopping Ejland's Finest into your unworthy goblet? And yours, Fingers? Impalini? Molly?'

Majesta sniffed. 'Didn't I say she was a lady of the night? It's broad daylight, Offero.'

'Boys, boys,' said Molly the Cut. Gripping the skivvy's thin, dirty wrist, she flashed the girl a gap-toothed smile. 'Don't let them worry you, lovey. None of this lot would even sniff a piece of skirt if they didn't have to pay for it. Ignore all their holier-than-thous. Make all you can while your bloom lasts, that's what I advise. You're a good sort. When Redondo's done with you, there'll be a place for you in my all-girl gang.'

Snivelling, the girl thanked her kind benefactress.

'Slut! More ale!' cried Offero the Mole.

The scene took place in Oldgate Prison, where Agondon's most notorious underworld leaders were enjoying luncheon in the lushly appointed quarters of the turnkey, Figaro Fingers. Velvet and silk, ivory, gold, silver and innumerable precious stones – all courtesy of Agondon's best ruined gentlefolk – glimmered in a slant of mellow sunlight.

It was no ordinary Festival gathering. Battle plans had been agreed that morning, and the villains-in-chief, whose underlings would take care of any necessary fighting, let alone dying, were already celebrating the Redjacket Restoration.

Undoubtedly they were at the dawn of a golden age.

296

'Can we really corner the Jarvel trade?' grinned Peter Impalini.

'If the docks are in our power,' said 'Scars' Majesta.

'And the customs-houses,' said Offero the Mole.

'What about the harlots?' sniggered Shammy the Hood.

'Harlots?' Molly the Cut rolled her eyes. 'Don't you boys think of anything else? Now, government bribes, there's a respectable calling. I've always fancied ending my days as a fine lady, and I've a feeling I might just become one, once Bob Scarlet's on the throne.'

Fingers leaned back, stuffing a pipe. 'Boys – that includes you, Molly – *I've* a feeling that the sky's the limit for the gentlemen of our profession. Good old Bob! Did anyone ever meet such a villain?'

'Can he *really* be Ejard Red?' said Peter Impalini.

'Hah! It's just another of Bob's tricks,' said Offero the Mole. 'But what a trick! What I'd have given to be at that Ball!'

'Trick?' bristled 'Scars' Majesta, always the staunchest of Redjacket loyalists. 'What do you mean, *trick*?'

There might have been a new altercation, but just then there was a thumping at the door. Alarm flickered over several faces when the skivvy, smudging her forearm over her nose, announced, in the sing-song snivel of a child reciting litany-lines, that Sergeant Carnelian Floss of the Fifth Royal Fusiliers of the Tarn awaited attendance on Goodman Fingers.

'Bluejackets! Treachery—' Knife in hand, Peter Impalini blundered up from the table.

'Down, you drunken fool!' hissed Offero the Mole. 'This is Oldgate, remember? Prison business, eh, Fingers?'

Fingers, who hoped so, stepped out into the corridor.

The turnkey's eyebrows knitted. He had been expecting a Bluejacket, but not one quite like this. The fellow was dishevelled and sweating, and round his head was a bandage, stained purple with dried blood.

His voice was a rasp. 'Give ... give her to me—'

'You've come for the Bomber?' said Fingers.

An eager nod. 'For Nirry ... to take her ... take her—'

'Yes, yes, to the Erdon Tree, where else?' The turnkey was impatient, eager to get back to his criminal cronies. Jingling a set of keys, he shambled off down the corridor, pipe-smoke clouding the air behind him, quite unconcerned about the fate of a woman he might have been expected to help. But Figaro Fingers would risk his neck for no one. 'This way, this way ... That Lector fellow's with her now, you know, been there all morning ... the *new* Lector, of course!' The turnkey guffawed. 'Say, mate, you don't look well. Not *worried* about these rebels, eh? Or perhaps you was on the piss a bit late last night? That's it, I'll bet ... I know you soldier blokes!'

'I've ... I've lived a ramshackly sort of life,' was the reply. 'Oh, I tell myself I'm not so bad, but there's none would call me ... none would call me a *good* man. Still, old Carney Floss has got a heart, he has, and before he goes, he'd like to do just one thing that was good ... just one thing—'

'What's that, mate? You're mumbling ... Eh, mind that slop-hole in the corner there – that's straight down into the sewers, if you fall down that!' They were outside Nirry's cell. Guffawing again, Fingers fumbled with his keys. Through the grilled door came a pompous clerical voice, intoning prayers over the condemned prisoner.

'Left your mates outside, did you – the others?' said Fingers. The pipe-stem wagged in his mouth as he spoke. 'Can't be just *you* guarding this one, can it? They say she's the most important rebel they've ever hanged ... some say it might spark a revolution, how about that? Just another tart, if you ask me ... bag over their heads and they're all the same, eh?'

The third guffaw was the loudest. Fingers turned away, the better to peer at the keys in the light. 'Go and see the fun myself, I would, but I'm having a little Festival gathering with a few business colleagues, and ... well, I've never much liked crowds, and anyway, a death's a—'

'*Death*,' hissed Carney Floss, plunging a knife into the villain's neck.

The pipe clattered to the floor, then the keys. Floss seized them. His heart racing, he shoved the turnkey's body down the slop-hole and turned back impatiently to the cell door.

The prayers had ceased and there were softer voices. The first was Nirry's, and was filled with kindness.

'I'm ... I'm glad it was you, Canon Flonce—'

Sternly: '*Lector* Flonce, my child, *Lector* now—'

Abashed: 'I ... of course! I always said *you* should—'

'Oh, corruption! You don't mean to say that *that's* why you did what you—'

'B-But Lector, I *didn't* do it! I j-just meant—'

'What! I have prayed with you all morning, yet *still* you deny your guilt? Was there ever such wickedness? I declare, Nirrian Jubb, you are a depraved creature, beyond the Love of the Lord Agonis! When your neck snaps, it's straight to the Realm of Unbeing with you, without so much as a—'

'Die, pig!' The door burst open. A knife stabbed.

Moments later, with Lector Flonce consigned to the sewers, Carney Floss held in his arms the shuddering Nirry, who had been too shocked even to scream.

'Oh Carney, Carney, what have you—'

The sergeant stopped her mouth with a kiss.

At another time, Nirry would have remonstrated. For now, she sank into her deliverer's embrace. She could have stayed there for eternity, feeling the comfort of his enveloping warmth. But already Carney was breaking away, telling her they must hurry, hurry; and already there came an ominous tramp of feet, echoing down the corridor outside.

Carney spun around. 'What's—'

'Ah, Sergeant, she's ready?' It was Major General Heva-Harion. Standing behind him was a patrol, six men strong, perhaps eight. 'Now, what can have become of that turnkey, I wonder? Useless fellow ... But come, man, bind her hands. And her blindfold? Where's her blindfold? You're her personal guard, are you?'

Carney gulped. 'Y-Yes, sir.'

'Then remember, this is a dangerous murderess. Not so much a woman as a monster in woman's form. This execution is vital. Should anything happen to her, I hold you personally responsible. You understand? Understand, Sergeant?'

The gulp again. 'Y-Yes ... yes, sir.'

Chapter 48

NIRRY'S FATE IS SEALED

'Mort-y, Y'Lediship?'

Constansia nodded curtly. What had become of her beautiful tea service? What had become of her own servants? Who were these foreign maids in vulgar, frilly uniforms? Her cup jittered on the ugly saucer as she raised it, looking again through alarmed eyes at the richly papered walls with their streaky looking-glasses, gaudy hangings and innumerable cluttered paintings, etchings and cameos of this creature who called herself the Zaxon Nightingale.

Everything was vulgar. Nothing was clean.

'A bordello,' she said aloud. 'The place is a bordello.'

'*Shh*, Constansia.' A hand touched her arm and Lady Cham-Charing remembered the presence of Lolenda Mynes, sitting just beside her.

How shrivelled, how mottled was that single hand!

'Sweet Lolenda, what became of our virgin days? Remember when we punted across the Riel with Mazy Tarfoot, before they ever built Regent's Bridge? Remember how we ran though the daisies and daffodils, scooping at the air with our butterfly nets? How we played, how we laughed...'

'*Shh*, Constansia. You're safe now.'

'Safe?' Again the cup jittered and Lady Cham-Charing looked across the chamber (undoubtedly a bordello) to the sofa opposite, where Miss Tilsy Fash, in extravagant finery quite inappropriate for a modest woman, perched beside Freddie and that Quisto girl (the one who had been ruined, by all accounts).

And Freddie a royal! In such company!

Miss Fash, whose fingernails were long and red, rested a hand on his knee. 'You *have* forgiven me, haven't you, Freddikins?' She spoke in a husky, laughing voice. 'I am a jealous woman, as you know, and – absurd, I agree – I imagined you were having an *affaire* with poor little Miss Quisto.'

Freddie flushed; the girl looked down. Leaping up, Miss Fash swished back and forth as if showing off her gown, and fixed a tobarillo into an ivory holder.

Smoke clouded the air behind her.

'But what is a public scene, from time to time, if not the *spice* that a woman craves? (I speak, of course, of a woman of spirit.) Ah, Freddie, but your charitable work delights me. I myself have performed in aid of reformed harlots (in the southlands, of course, where morals are more lax).'

The perfumed creature reached across Freddie, almost pressing her breasts into his face. With the back of her hand, she stroked Miss Quisto's cheek.

'Poor darling, should you like to work for me? I'm always in need of another dresser. And my cook? My cook is a slut. But then, I dine out every night, so what practice does she get? You know, my dears, I believe she receives gentleman callers? But here, perhaps, is a caller of my own.'

This last remark, delivered with a tinkling laugh, referred to a sudden rapping at the door. Constansia could hardly believe it. In Cham-Charing House, her butler announced any intruder, and then only when Her Ladyship was At Home; Miss Fash, without even waiting for a servant, launched towards the door and opened it herself.

Leaning in the doorframe, she stood talking in a low voice, apparently to a gentleman. But his tone was hardly that of a gentleman of breeding.

Constansia's teacup rattled again. 'What *is* this place?'

Lady Lolenda took the cup away, resting it, a little precariously, on the edge of the table. Her voice was tender. 'Poor Constansia, you don't remember? We had to flee, didn't we? Miss Fash is Freddie's ... *friend*. She took us in when no one else would. You remember, of course you do.'

'N-No one?' said Constansia. She raised her voice. 'But ... I want to go back to Cham-Charing House. When can we go back to Cham-Charing House?'

Concerned looks came from the other sofa. Freddie was embarrassed, but Jilda's face crumpled with compassion and she rushed towards the stricken old lady.

'Lady Cham-Charing, you've been so good to me. You'll have your house back, I swear it. Freddie says we're certain to win! Already the rebels are massing.' She glanced to the door, where Miss Fash nodded, laughed and blew out a long stream of smoke. 'Why, there may be more news now. But it's certain, it has to be! A Redjacket victory.'

'R-Rebels?' said Lady Cham-Charing. 'R-Redjackets?'

Miss Fash slammed the door, reeling back to her companions with a triumphant *Hah-hah!* 'A messenger from Danny Garvice. We've got them now. By tomorrow, the Island will be surrounded! *And* a certain little event of this afternoon,' she added mysteriously, 'will certainly turn all the doubters our way. Oh, those Blues have done it now!' She skittered towards Freddie, kissing him fulsomely. 'Silly Freddie! Did you really think I could play both sides? What have I ever been but a rebel in my heart?'

There was a crash as Lady Cham-Charing, rising to her feet, brushed against the precarious cup and saucer. Her head trembled violently.

She could barely speak. 'F-Freddie, you mean you *knew* about this, you … and to think, I would have married you to Tishy, I really might have—'

'Come, Lady Cham,' Miss Fash said kindly, 'you *know* the injustices of the Bluejacket régime—'

'The Bluejackets,' said Jilda, 'who took your house—'

'The Bluejackets,' said Lolenda, 'who killed poor—'

'I … I know the government. I know the law!'

'The law, Constansia, that dispossessed you—'

'The law that executes innocent women—'

'But … but *rebels*? It's not right, it's not … Lolenda, not you, too?' Constansia clutched her forehead. She looked this way and that. 'Oh, but where's Elsan? Where's Lady Margrave, she would understand, she would—'

'*Shh*, you know poor Lady Margrave—'

And Constansia, with a piteous keening, sank to the floor. The women rallied round her while Freddie, his cheeks crimson, peered into his teacup.

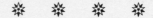

'Faster, Bando—'

The whip cracked.

'If only—' Hunched on the box on the passenger side, Hul tore strips from his fingernails. The blue carriage hurtled down the Wrax Road, bound for the Erdon Tree. 'Oh, but what are we doing? We can't save her, can we? What can we do but sit and watch while—'

'While the revolution begins!' Bando cried. 'I swear, old friend, the Bluejackets will not survive this! This is the last straw, the very last act of—'

'Bando, no! You make it sound a *good* thing—'

'Never! I … oh Hul, I—'

Abashed, Bando fell silent and only looked ahead down the slushy road. On reconnaissance in Agondon, the two friends had been appalled to learn the news that was buzzing all over the city. At once, forgetting all else, they had raced towards the scene of the execution. But what could they do? Already the crowds were in view – some rich, some ragged, some in fine carriages, some in carts, on horseback, on foot – spilling over the vast field where the Erdon Tree stood.

Here, for as long as anyone could remember, murderers, thieves, rebels and indigents had met their fate, to the entertainment of a vast public. A hanging was always a rowdy affair. Hawkers weaved their way through the crowd and there would be stalls selling ale, roast chestnuts and rock-cakes, not to mention souvenir plates, mugs, linen, ballad-sheets and pamphlets. By the Erdon Tree justice was served and debts paid to society, to the accompaniment of bawdy songs, drunken revelry, shrieking, baying, and liberal hurlings of eggs, rotten apples and tomatoes.

That, at least, was how it usually was.

Bando's moustaches twitched. 'It's strangely quiet.'

'Do you really think there could be a revolt?'

'Don't bet on it, old friend. Look at all those Bluejackets. Remember, they're doing this to demonstrate their power. Anyone steps out of line, there'll be savage reprisals. What does Ejard Blue care if he kills his own people?'

Hul shuddered. 'You mean Tranimel. Or Toth.'

'Don't remind me.' Even now, Bando could barely take in the terrible evil he had witnessed on the night of the Ball. Secretly, he had begun to think their long campaign was hopeless. They had thought they were fighting human evil; the truth was worse than anything he could have imagined. But Bando Riga was a brave man; he had come so far, and would go on. To the end. Whatever the end might be.

'It's a big crowd, Hul.' With a laugh, he gestured to their blue carriage, to their army bearskins. 'I wouldn't much fancy our chances if things turned bad, would you?'

'You think we should disguise ourselves?'

'Or *not* disguise ourselves.' The road forked up ahead. 'We'll take the back road. We can hide the carriage up in the woods and change into our own furs.'

Hul nodded. 'Oh, but to be thinking of *our* safety!'

'I know, old friend, I know. But there's not much we can do for poor Goody Olch, not now. I fear she'll be hanging by the neck soon enough, as cheers rise to the glory of Ejard Blue!'

'Cursed be Ejard Blue, curse him!'

'Cursed be Ejard Red, curse him!'

'What's that, Miss Landa?' said Baines.

'Nothing, nothing.' Again Landa restrained herself. What was the good of telling the others? Still they all thought they were just the advance party, that reinforcements would soon be on the way. How could they believe that their valiant leader, hearing about Nirry, had only stroked his upper lip and smiled? What, was he to bring forward his battle plans? Send rebel forces to the Erdon Tree? The time, he had said, was not yet ripe. But afterwards? A helpless woman, hanged on trumped-up charges: ah yes, they must make sure that everyone knew the truth. Then the time would be ripe, very ripe indeed.

Still Landa shook when she thought of his smile.

'Nearly there,' she called back. 'Let's get a bit closer.'

'Closer? We're nearly crushed already,' said Baines, then admonished herself. What was her discomfort against the sufferings of Goody Olch? If only the rebel raid would succeed! Tightly the old servant clung to Wiggler's hand and looked round for the others. No one, at least, was lost. Morven and Crum scrambled behind them, disguised as peasants. Snow was falling again. And everyone, it was true, was strangely subdued.

Horns rang out, breaking the silence. Then came a thudding of military drums. Terrified, they gazed over furry-hatted heads towards the ominous scaffold, rising in the shadow of the Erdon Tree.

Wiggler gulped. 'Oh, Nirry! My poor, poor Nirry!'

'We're really going to save her, Miss Landa?' said Baines.

Landa's tone was distant. 'Even now, I feel the green force, surging inside me like a tide ready to burst. To think, I thought the goddess was ignoring me! It's true, her powers are weaker here, this far from Viana's woods. But *my* powers are stronger. I can save Goody Olch, I'd stake my life on it.'

'If you say so, Miss Landa,' said Baines, who had rather assumed that Bob Scarlet would come swinging down from somewhere – from where, she was not quite sure – and save the day.

Not all this magic nonsense again!

Already Landa sounded half in trance. Her gloved fingers pressed at her forehead. 'When I unleash the green force, the men of evil will be helpless.' *Confidence, that was the way.* For now, Landa had to believe she could do it. Even if she could not. 'Then we just have to get Goody Olch away from here.'

'That's where the reinforcements come in,' blinked Morven, wiping his spectacles. Like Crum, he concealed his musket under his coat. The two of them could hardly do much against the massed ranks of Bluejackets. They needed a rebel army. And they would have one, wouldn't they?

'My poor Nirry!' Wiggler gasped.

For now came the prisoner's escort, leading Nirry up the scaffold steps. From a branch of the Erdon Tree hung the noose, ready and waiting; the executioner, in ceremonial black, was ready too. The horns left off, and the drumbeats; a man of the cloth stepped to the fore, raising a small El-Orokon bound in black. The fellow looked a little harried, as if not quite prepared for the occasion. Awkwardly he adjusted his collar, like a man who had thrown on his clothes too quickly, and now, belatedly, tried to make amends.

Delivering the Litany of the Dying, he stumbled over his words several times.

'Isn't that … Chaplain Etravers?' hissed Baines. 'And I heard Canon Flonce was the new Great Lector! Surely they'd send *him* to an execution so important? It's an insult to the mistress, that's what it—'

Baines would have gone on, but Wiggler grabbed her arm. His voice trembled, cracked. 'I ... I don't believe it! That fellow behind my Nirry, see him? That's ... that's Carney Floss! Oh, who'd have thought he'd ever—'

Wiggler could say no more, falling into Baines's arms and breaking down in helpless tears. With Nirry, the simple fellow had known a happiness greater than any he could have imagined; now, after so short a time, his happiness was over, and the sadness would be greater by far, and last for the rest of his life.

The end came soon enough.

The drumbeats sounded, and the horns; the man of the cloth stepped back, his duties done, and the executioner took his place, draping the noose round Nirry's neck. Snow fell more thickly, and the barren branches of the Erdon Tree stood out, black and stark, against the whiteness.

Silence. In moments, the trap would fall.

'*No!*'

It was Carney Floss. Reeling suddenly, he stabbed the executioner, then the chaplain. A roar erupted from the crowd. Ripping the noose from Nirry's neck, the renegade sergeant leapt with her from the scaffold just as a mighty burst of force exploded from the skies, consuming the Erdon Tree in a ball of green fire.

At once, all was chaos.

Landa cried, 'Quick, we've got to get to them!'

She cut through the crowd, green lightning fizzing from her hands. The others raced behind her. Already the Bluejackets were rallying.

Shots rang out. Morven and Crum fired back.

'Nirry, Nirry—' Landa ripped the blindfold away.

Nirry swivelled round. '*Carney—!*'

For what happened next, time would allow only a single, pitiless moment.

It was a moment Nirry would never forget.

Into the slush, spurting blood, fell Carney Floss.

Oblivious of the cries, the shots, the chaos, Nirry sank beside him in the bloodied snow. Only now, all the day's emotion burst from her eyes.

'Carney ... Carney, *no*—'

His rough hand touched her cheek. 'Dear Nirry ... sweet Nirry, how I've loved you!'

Then the moment was over.

And Nirry, lost between despair, terror and joy, looked up to see Wiggler and Baines, Landa, Morven and Crum – then Hul and Bando, bursting amongst them, urging them desperately to come this way, come this way.

Chapter 49

TOTH ATTACKS AGAIN

'How much longer?' Cata sighed.

Whether she was referring to their journey, or to Tishy's translations, was not quite clear. With ropes around their waists, linking them together, the little party edged their way up a narrow, slushy track. Cata went first; then Jem and Rajal, with Myla on the stretcher; then Tishy; then Littler. Ejard Orange prowled between them, sometimes padding ahead, sometimes falling behind.

And Tishy kept her book open, struggling to translate.

FIVE-STAVE FIVE

I.

Now mighty was the rage of Ondon when he found that Father-Priest Ir-Ion and his followers had fled, taking with them the precious jewel that might have guaranteed his reign: thus Ondon called them traitors, and would track them down, the treacherous Bearers of the Vexing Gem.

Jem groaned. 'Bearers of the Vexing Gem, indeed!'

'You're wishing there was a Bearer of the Jem Vexing?' Cata smiled.

'*Prince Jemany*, if you please,' said Jem, with mock formality, and Cata made an awkward bow. Both laughed, but this was hardly a time for jokes. On one side of them was a sheer, rising wall of rock; on the other, a deep ravine. All that morning, the journey had become ever more dangerous.

Rajal looked down anxiously at Myla's stretcher. 'I'm rather wondering about this track,' he said. 'Does it just *happen* to be here? Or did someone make it?'

'Like who?' said Cata. 'No one lives in the Crystal Sky.'

'What about in this … lamasery?' said Jem.

'Well, except for them. If they exist,' Cata had to add.

'Of course they do,' said Jem. 'Just think, perhaps this track means we're getting closer. Let's hope so.'

They trudged on. Tishy read another verse.

So, while still the war convulsed the green and wooded edge-land, Ondon
raised a band of his most trusted minions: and riding off in haste after
those who had betrayed him, Ondon said that Father-Priest Ir-Ion would
he kill, as in triumph he seized back the Vexing Gem.

'I wish *we* could ride off in haste,' Rajal said wryly.

'Do we *have* to have this story?' Cata complained. 'How about a song to
cheer us up? Raj, how about one of your old favourites?'

'*King and Queen of Swords*?'

'Not likely,' said Jem. 'Keep going, Tishy. If you can.'

'I told you this was a remarkably interesting five-stave,' Tishy said
defensively.

Cata rolled her eyes, hearing the rustle of a turning page. Really, it was
ridiculous! But Tishy would be too frightened to venture up the narrow
track at all unless she could glance, between every step, at the mouldering pages of her book. Cata began to hum to herself. She was thoroughly
sick of the dull story, and sick of Tishy, too. If only Landa could have come
with them instead!

The next verse, thought Cata, was just as dull as the rest.

III.

But alas it was that journeys long and perilous lay before the raging
monarch and his men: for treacherous were all the northern regions;
elusive proved the priests that they pursued; and long years passed
and still they were not found, as if a secret magic had helped them in
their flight.

'Perilous journeys?' said Cata. 'There's a cheering thought.'

'Not to mention *long years*,' said Rajal.

'Which we haven't got,' said Jem. 'Five days, remember?'

Rajal laughed mirthlessly. 'You think we've forgotten?'

The thought weighed heavily on all their minds. By now their way was
tough, and getting tougher. Dark clouds obscured the mystic mountain;
the day was at its height, but deeply shadowed, and the crystals throbbed
only fleetingly. All the friends knew was that they were climbing higher.
There was no turning back, time was running out, and all their provisions
would soon be gone.

'I suppose it might be lunchtime soon,' Littler said hopefully, still
aggrieved that breakfast had been so meagre. And after such a long night,
too, huddled in that miserable, smoky cave!

Jem, with a sigh, was about to begin a lecture, and not his first one, on
the need to conserve their resources. By now the food supply was very
low indeed. Ruefully he eyed the jogging sack that Cata had slung, far too
easily, over her shoulder. He steeled himself to begin.

But already Littler was distracted.

'What's wrong. Ejjy? What is it?'

As it happened, Littler would answer his own question. Gulping, he pointed above, then below.

Mauvers were clustering.

With a catch in her throat, Tishy launched at once into a fresh verse.

IV.

But never would the monarch cease his long pursuit, though his many minions died and great he grew with age: tales he had heard of a golden citadel, and though his path was mazy, it happened that in time he came upon the mountains that are called the Crystal—

'Wh-what are we going to do?' Rajal burst out.

'Do? There's nothing *to* do,' cried Cata. She strode ahead, tugging on the rope that tethered her to her companions. 'So Toth's on our trail! Did we expect otherwise? We've all got our crystals, haven't we?'

Rajal began, 'Well, actually—'

'Raj, shut up!' said Jem.

'What's going on?' Cata turned sharply. They had paused on the path, lowering Myla's stretcher to the ground. Above, the Mauvers were cawing, swooping closer; still Tishy studied her book. Her spectacles were misting; she wiped them angrily.

'There's a revelation here, I'm sure of it,' she muttered.

Cata was saying, 'Raj, what are you talking about? Jem, don't you trust me? Don't you think I can *sense* something, both of you? Don't you—'

But what Cata sensed next was nothing to do with her friends. Ejard Orange let out a shriek. A vast shadow passed above.

Cata cried out, stumbling back.

'No, no—' Jem floundered towards her, cursing the ropes that held him back.

It happened so quickly. First Cata was screaming, then she slipped from the path. Jem braced himself, tugging at the rope that circled her waist.

'My hand, reach for my hand—'

His pleas were useless. Cata was convulsing; the rope jerked and twitched. Desperately, the others struggled not to fall. Tishy's book fell from her hands, wheeling down into the deep ravine; pages detached themselves, scattering to the winds.

And still the Mauvers shrieked and clawed. Still the Unbeing Bird described its great arc, turning back towards the blighted Realm of Ejland.

And Cata could only scream and scream.

Jem screamed too. 'Oh, Cata! Cata, please—'

Could he reach her hand? Or would she wrench him down? If Jem fell, the rest of them would be dragged down too.

'Cata! Oh please, Cata—'

Could she hear him at all? Her eyes had rolled up into her head; her face was a rictus of agony. No, she could not hear him: there was only the Unbeing Bird, possessing her in all its terrible psychic force.

Then came the laughter, bursting all around her.

Jem gasped, 'Please! Oh Cata, Cata—'

'Cata, come on—' Littler urged.

The wind whipped around them on the slithering ledge. Precariously, Ejard Orange leapt and danced; Myla lay inert, wizened and drained, while Tishy could only murmur and murmur, as if in the grip of some vision of her own.

'Jem, can you reach?' Rajal slithered forward.

'Her wrists, just grab her wrists—'

They reached, reached; but another hand, a phantom hand, was reaching too. It would not be denied. Triumphant laughter burst in Cata's ears. Then she heard Jem, sobbing and gasping, dragging her back to the perilous path, just as the Unbeing Bird vanished again.

Just as Toth's laughter died away.

'Cata, are you all right? Cata, speak!'

She murmured, 'It's over, Jem, over—'

'No!' Jem burst out. 'I won't believe it!'

But it was then that Tishy's murmurings, which had gone on all the while, became a sudden, strident declamation. It was the last verse of the five-stave, the verse she had translated just in time.

V.

And it was there he came upon the golden citadel, the place where he was certain that his enemies must dwell: and dying, he stumbled forth to demand the Vexing Gem: but as he rapped upon the gates an avalanche swept down, destroying both the seeker and the golden citadel.

What strange, hideous triumph filled her voice! Laughing, crazed, she might have repeated the verse again, had Rajal not swivelled back and slapped her face.

She sank back, abashed. 'I ... I'm sorry.'

'The lamasery?' breathed Jem. 'You mean it's gone ... destroyed?'

Tishy nodded slowly. Jem clutched his face in his hands.

Two crystals gone.

No way home.

And nowhere to go.

'Harlequin,' he murmured, 'how could you lie?'

The quest looked hopeless. If they knew anything, it was only that the Unbeing Bird would come back, and back, and that they had no way to resist its powers.

Three days, and the world would be Toth's.

❋   ❋   ❋   ❋

It was Littler, in the end, who broke the silence. 'L-Look,' he gulped. 'Up ahead.'

They turned slowly; through the haze of the snow they could just make out the figure on the path. It was a man, or appeared to be a man, dressed in skins, furs and a long, trailing cape of thickly spun wool, dyed in strange geometric designs. Planting a thick staff carefully before him, the man made his way towards the stricken travellers.

Trembling, Jem rose to greet him. Beneath the man's furry hood, he made out a reddish-brown, weather-beaten face. Jem faltered, wondering what to say. Might the stranger be hostile? Impossible to tell; levelly, he gazed upon the travellers.

Then the man spoke, and Jem's brow furrowed. 'I ... 'I'm sorry, I don't understand.'

'And I don't believe it,' Tishy breathed. 'Can't you recognise it? He's speaking Juvescial – the Tongue of Agonis! He's ... he's *welcoming* us, Jem.'

The stranger turned, beckoning them to follow.

Chapter 50

FOREIGN TONGUE

There are several annoying things about foreign tongues, especially if you happen to be peevish, tired or frightened. There is the opportunity they give for those who speak them to appear superior to those who do not; Cata was conscious of this. There is the puzzlement they create in others, even when the words are translated; Jem, at this time, was very puzzled indeed. And there is the ugliness of the sounds to alien ears; Rajal, whose ears were sensitive, was looking a little pained.

Littler, for his part, could only wonder where the stranger's house might be, and what sort of food he would serve them when they reached it.

'I wish she'd tell us what they're talking about,' said Cata, gesturing resentfully at Tishy and the stranger. The two Juvescial speakers had gone ahead, trudging energetically up the crisp hillside. 'He must have said more than *she*'s told us. Much more.'

'Oh, it probably takes twice as long to say anything in that dreadful language,' said Rajal. 'Fancy talking like that all the time! I can't help thinking he's putting it on.'

'Raj, you're sounding like Captain Porlo,' said Jem. 'You'll be going on about *bloody foreigners* next.'

'I'm a Vaga, aren't I? Still, there're foreigners and foreigners.'

Littler interjected, 'But what sort of *food* do you think he'll have?'

'Really, the pair of you!' Cata had to laugh, but just for a moment. She looked at Myla's withered face, lolling back and forth on the stretcher. By now, Myla was barely breathing; alarmed, Cata snapped her eyes away. To distract herself she asked, perhaps for the third time, what Tishy had said the stranger's name was.

'Starzok,' said Rajal, who could not look upon the stretcher either. 'But where does he come from?'

'From the lamasery, of course,' Jem said, too quickly.

'Then he's a ghost? Didn't Tishy tell us the place had been destroyed?'

'You believe that, Raj? It's a legend.'

'So was the Sisterhood of the Blue Storm.'

Jem thought it best not to reply. He jerked his head towards Ejard Orange. The big cat had been restless, darting and hissing here and there, ever since they had taken up with the stranger. 'He's still not calmed down. What's up with him, Littler?'

'It's snowing. He hasn't got a coat.'

311

'He's got fur,' said Jem.

'I wish we had,' said Rajal. '*And* coats, too.'

Cata knelt in the snow, smoothing the big cat's icy pelt. Her brow furrowed. 'Something's worrying him, and it's more than the cold.'

Jem said, 'Let's just hope it isn't Starzok.'

'Could be,' said Rajal. 'There's something funny about him, I'm sure of it. I mean, he's not very *curious*, is he? I can hardly believe he gets visitors every day. Come to think of it, he wasn't exactly surprised to see us.'

Cata shuddered. 'Perhaps he was expecting us. Really, why can't that wretched girl tell us more?'

'She will,' said Jem. 'Think about something else.'

'Shelter? Rest? Food?'

'Especially that,' said Littler.

Rajal grimaced. 'Shut up about food!'

'But I'm *worried*,' said Littler. 'Myla must be starving.'

At this, Rajal went quiet.

They trudged on.

The mountain got steeper; still the snow kept falling. By now, all that guided their way was the shifting pennant of Starzok's cape, far up ahead, with its emblazoned riot of geometric shapes. They were all exhausted. For a time Cata took turns with the stretcher, taking first Jem's end, then Rajal's; Littler would have helped too, but Jem told him again to keep an eye on Ejard Orange. Besides, Cata added with a glance towards Tishy, there were *others* who should have been taking their turns.

'Looks like she's really getting on with our new friend, doesn't it?' said Jem.

'If friend he is,' Rajal added ominously.

Following Starzok over a final powdery bluff, Jem and his companions found themselves on a shelf of flat ground that stretched before a backdrop of conifers and rising walls of rock. Snow filled the air in a dancing haze, but Jem could just make out a cluster of dwellings, emerging like grey phantoms from the whiteness.

'Huts,' he said. 'Wooden huts.'

'Not all wooden. Not all huts,' said Cata.

'You're right, they're substantial. Especially that one in the middle. Look at that portico. That verandah.'

'See those carvings?' Rajal jerked his head. 'In that stone? Just like the designs on Starzok's cape. What is this place?'

'His village?' Cata replied. 'A wild guess, I know.'

'At least there'll be food,' said Littler, squelching ahead. Peering into the verandah of one of the smaller houses, he called back, 'They keep the food right out here!'

Jem made out a large furry shape, hanging on a hook. 'What do you think that is, Cata?'

'I'd say it was a dead bear. Or a wolf.'

'You know, I'm not sure I like this place.' Jem trudged towards Tishy, who stood by smilingly while Starzok, babbling in his strange language, gestured proudly at the dwellings around them. 'Tishy?'

Jem said her name again before she turned. Her eyes were bright behind her spectacles, and colour rode high in her windburned face. 'Do you know, this is really *most* remarkable? Not only a Juvescial speaker, in this day and age – but one who speaks in the Tongue of Agonis! Think of the scholarly papers I could write! Oh, if only I could stay with him for ever.'

'Perhaps that's what he's got in mind,' said Cata, joining them. 'You'd better hope he's got a wife.'

'Wh-what?' said Tishy.

Rajal interrupted. 'I can hear music.'

'He's right,' said Jem. 'A tabor? A recorder?'

Where did they come from, these soft drumbeats, these low ululations? Jem looked one way, Rajal the other, but it was Littler who pointed out the two old men, garbed like Starzok, emerging from one of the smaller houses. High-stepping, kicking at the powdery snow, the men made their way forward, performing their solemn music; Jem would have asked Tishy what was happening, but almost at once there were more villagers, filling the white scene with their colourful, patterned costumes. Two boys hurled snowballs at each other, ducking, weaving, laughing; there were other men, younger than Starzok or the musicians; there were women and girls, shapeless in their thick furs, some of them with swaddled infants in their arms.

Slowly they clustered round the new arrivals.

'Friendly, aren't they?' said Jem. 'Quite a sight.'

'Not to mention *smell*,' Rajal muttered; Tishy hushed him, but Rajal merely repeated the charge more loudly, and in ruder words, as if to point out that the villagers would hardly understand.

Luckily, they did not. By now there were perhaps thirty of them, pressing in eagerly upon the strangers, grinning and fondling. One of the boys grabbed Ejard Orange, picking him up roughly by the neck. The cat howled and Littler snatched him back, fearful lest his marmalade friend should meet the same fate as the wolves and bears.

The old women peered down at Myla. Some of them touched her, and the stretcher rocked; others, old and young alike, were curious about Cata. Gently but firmly, Cata pushed away the probing hands. Instinctively, she drew her hood across her face. Jem was becoming alarmed; so was Rajal. He gathered up his sister's inert, aged form, shielding her in his arms.

313

Starzok raised his staff, and his voice too, addressing the villagers in tones which might have had in them an element of pleading.

'What's he talking about?' Jem called to Tishy.

Tishy had to raise her voice. '*People of the Below*,' she translated roughly, '*never have* ... something about *such fine supplicants*, how they've never had finer before, come to wait before the Kolkon Vera Kion—'

'The what?' said Rajal, but Tishy could not hear.

She went on, '*Always* ... there have always been those who sought admission, there have always been those who – something like *withered and wasted*, but this time, he's certain, these supplicants ... oh, but the grammar, it's simply fascinating, such curious declensions of the—'

Tishy could have gone on, but the attentions of the villagers were growing more insistent. Littler clutched Ejard Orange harder; Rajal struggled with Myla, but now it was Cata who received the most attention. Jem tried to push the villagers away. They would not be deterred. Reddish hands reached up, grabbing Cata's coat, clawing at her hood. It pulled away and her dark hair flowed free, twisting and twining in the flurrying wind.

Starzok's speech was forgotten. A woman screamed. Then a man. Then a child. The villagers surged back. Some abased themselves; some collapsed, wailing, into the snow. At once, both fear and anger consumed the crowd.

'What is it, what is it?' Jem burst out. He pushed forward, clutching Cata in his arms.

'They're saying it's ... the *Empress*!' Tishy cried.

'What, can they see the future?' said Rajal. 'Jem's not even on the throne yet, and—'

'Not ... Empress of Ejland,' Tishy gasped, jostled by villagers. 'Something about the Empress of the ... *Dream*, the Unending *Dream*—'

'*Endless* Dream?' Cata was aghast.

The clamour would have gone on, but Starzok, just a little tardily, lashed out with his staff. This time his voice was commanding, imperious; abashed, like whipped dogs, the villagers retreated.

'Fools!' Tishy translated. '*They are supplicants like the others. This girl is one of them. They're all only supplicants, can't you see? Leave us now; leave off your folly. The strangers will be here but for this night. Tomorrow, I guide them to the Kolkon Vera Kion.*'

With that, Starzok indicated the largest of the dwellings, the one with carvings over the portico. Several times he turned back, beckoning, and Jem, for the first time, saw the old man smile. His teeth were a deep, yellowish brown.

Chapter 51

RIMMED WITH BLUBBER

'Supplicants?'

'But why is he helping us?'

'Who *is* this Starzok?'

'Kolkon *what*?'

Still the questions buzzed between the guests as they looked around the mountain-man's crowded, shabby dwelling. Braziers, placed here and there, filled the cave-like interior with a burnished glow. In the centre of the chamber was a long, slab-like table, lined with high-backed chairs; skins, furs and carcasses hung from the rafters, while dishevelled bedding lay about the floor.

Jem and Rajal set down Myla's stretcher.

'This smoke's going to hurt my eyes,' said Jem.

'Smoke?' said Rajal. 'What about the stench?'

'Some of us don't seem to mind,' said Cata, glancing at Tishy. Between the curtaining furs was a shelf of disorderly scrolls and crumbling, leatherbound books. While their host bustled in the background, Tishy made for the shelf at once, barely able to contain her excitement.

From outside came renewed sounds of tabors and recorders. There were murmurings, too; the villagers appeared to be clustering on the verandah, eager just to be close to the strangers.

'They must be cold!' Cata shuddered, drawing her coat tighter around her. 'I'm cold, even in here.'

Littler shuddered too, for a different reason. Uneasily he clung to Ejard Orange, surveying the hanging skins and furs. 'I don't *think* I see any cats. No marmalade ones, at least.'

'Who's that boy, I wonder?' Jem gestured.

By the fire, a large, unidentifiable side of meat sizzled and dripped on a squeaking spit, turned by a crook-backed youth. Furtively, the youth glanced at the newcomers; Starzok, with a cry, struck the youth's head, evidently commanding him to return to his duties.

The old man turned back, smiling, to his guests.

'Looks like he wants us to sit,' said Cata. 'Shall we?'

Dubiously, Jem and Littler complied; Rajal, for his part, lingered over Myla. Perhaps it was the shadowy light, but her face looked even more wizened than before.

He turned away sadly, pulling out a chair from the table. The chair, though shabby, was extraordinarily ornate, patterned with elaborate carvings. Further carvings covered the table and the dark beams above; golden icons shone dimly from the walls, obscured in the gloom between the braziers.

But this village was so mean, so paltry! Could it be a remnant, a last surviving outpost, of a once-fine civilisation?

With a martyred air, the serving-youth brought forth silver goblets, similarly ornate, filling them from a heavy decanter. The foursome at the table sniffed uneasily, first at the youth's pungent, foul smell, then at the greyish, watery liquor he served. Reluctantly, Tishy took her place at the table, bringing a scroll or two and some books from the shelf.

'You *are* going to talk to us, aren't you?' said Cata.

'What I want to know,' said Jem, 'is who these people are.'

'The boy's called Blayzil,' said Tishy. 'Starzok's son – his only son, and a shame to him. Well, that's what the old man said.'

'What about the rest of them?'

With a scholarly air, Tishy swirled the liquor in her goblet, took a sip – and gagged.

Cata had to smirk.

'That's right,' she said quickly, 'all those villagers?'

'The People of the Below,' Tishy spluttered, red-faced. 'That's what they call themselves.'

'Below what?' said Littler, eyeing his goblet.

'This Kolkon thing?' said Cata.

Blayzil brought plates and dirty-looking cutlery. If his mouth was sullen, his eyes were eager; had he not been careful of his father's wrath, the youth might have lingered, dog-like, about the guests. Glad that he did not, Cata treated him to a strained smile, surreptitiously breathing through her teeth; Ejard Orange, less diplomatically, struggled out of Littler's arms. Angrily, the big cat swished about the carpet.

Jem screwed up his forehead. 'Kolkon Vera Kion … *Mountain of the Real*?'

'You *did* learn something!' said Tishy, impressed.

'But Tishy, what about you?' said Rajal. 'Or rather, what about Starzok? Have you found out why he's helping us? Come on, he must have told you something.'

Tishy grimaced. 'You'd be surprised how little.'

Blayzil returned, this time with the dripping side of meat. At once, Ejard Orange forgot his disgust. With a *miaow*, the big cat leapt back up to the table, ready to share from Littler's plate; a high, strained keening, as if in counterpoint, sounded from outside.

Anger came again to Starzok's face and he strode to the door. Opening it, he shouted into the flurrying darkness. There was a sound like a slap. Voices ceased, music too; then came the clatterings of fleeing feet.

316

Starzok turned back. Taking his place at the head of the table, the old man carved the sizzling meat. Jem and his friends tried to look grateful, but it was difficult. Blubbery borders of fat cushioned each slice, and white circles marbled the brown, slimy flesh.

Smiling, Starzok gestured to Littler.

'He wants you to sit beside him,' said Tishy.

'You're sure he doesn't want Ejjy?' Rajal murmured. 'As a first course, perhaps?'

❋　❋　❋　❋

For a time the meal proceeded in silence, or rather, in an absence of speech. There was the fire, plopping in the grate, and the crackling braziers; there was the wind, clattering at the shuttered windows; there was the reluctant scrape of cutlery from the guests, and the juicy grindings of Starzok's jaws. Abandoning pretences of politeness, the mountain-man had rapidly discarded his knife and fork, ripping at the meat with dirty hands, slurping and grunting as he shoved it into his mouth. Grinning, he would pause only to paw at Littler, pinching the little boy's cheeks, patting him and stroking him, urging him with merry gestures to eat, eat.

Meanwhile, Blayzil hunched in a corner, whimpering and cowering like a whipped dog. Once, muttering irritably, Starzok flung him a strip of fat.

'He says ... he says he wishes he still had his daughter, rather than this useless son,' translated Tishy.

'Daughter?' said Jem. 'What happened to her?'

'Died of hunger, if he treated her like the son,' said Rajal. 'Unless, of course, he treated her like Littler.'

'No wonder she ran off,' said Cata. 'Bearing up, Littler?'

'Better than being outside, isn't it?' Jem said, not quite convincingly, making an attempt at the greyish liquor. Surprisingly fiery, it served, at any rate, to quell the taste of the bear-meat, wolf-meat, or whatever it might be. 'But Tishy, can't you try and find out more? You had him talking earlier.'

'About grammar, wasn't it?' Cata said tartly.

Tishy flushed, but just then there was a renewal of music from outside. Tabors thudded, recorders shrilled. Starzok looked up sharply, but this time it was Blayzil who burst into life, leaping forward and grinning, breaking into a clodhopping dance. At once he began to sing, his cracking voice riding crazily over the music.

'What's he doing?' Alarmed, Jem thought Starzok would beat the boy viciously. Instead, the old man was strangely fixed in place, even when the boy reeled across the chamber, singing all the while, and flung open the door. There was a burst of cold wind, braziers blew out, and the villagers stomped in a circle round the table, filling the firelit gloom with their wild, strange music.

317

And Starzok, all the while, laughed and clapped.

'He's had a change of heart,' said Rajal.

Cata said, 'Tishy, this song! What's it about?'

'The melody,' said Jem, 'I've heard it before—'

Tishy struggled to make out the words. 'This ... Empress, it's about this ... Empress—'

'Empress of the Endless Dream?' said Cata.

'But who is she? What is she?' said Rajal.

They were shouting over the cacophony. Then the song was over, as suddenly as it had begun, and the villagers had stomped outside again, slamming the door behind them. Only Blayzil remained, grinning and bowing as his father applauded.

Jem and his friends could only join in the applause. Bewildered, they gazed at Blayzil, then at Starzok, then at each other in the dim, red glow from the leaping fire.

Starzok gabbled rapidly, almost muttering.

'He says ... he says he knew they'd *get* him,' said Tishy. 'It looks like that song is some kind of ritual. Once started, it can't be stopped.'

'But what's it *for*?' Jem urged.

'Yes,' said Rajal, 'what does it *mean*?'

Shrugging, Tishy gestured to the scrolls and books that still lay about her on the dark table. To her disappointment, Starzok seemed happy in the gloom, making no move to light the braziers again. He hacked off fresh chunks of meat, serving Littler, then Tishy, with especial generosity. He gulped from his goblet, called back Blayzil to fill it again, and gestured to the others to resume their meal. None of the guests had much appetite by now, though Rajal found himself becoming fond of the grey, fiery liquor.

No answers, it appeared, would be forthcoming that night. But when Starzok finished his meal at last, he leaned back, goblet in hand, becoming expansive. He pulled Littler close to him, squeezing and fondling.

'He says he's a good boy,' said Tishy, 'a very good boy.'

'Really?' said Rajal. 'How does he know?'

'He says he'd like Littler, not Blayzil, for his son.'

Littler squirmed in the old man's smelly grasp. Jem and the others were embarrassed, disgusted too; but a curious fear prevented them from intervening. Besides, by now they had all partaken of the crude, greyish liquor. To their dulled eyes, the chamber seemed to shift a little, the carved patterns to jostle and bulge.

And Starzok began to speak about the Empress.

Tishy translated. 'She is the one who calls from beyond ... She is the one who calls ... She is the one—'

'Well, that explains it, then!' Rajal burst out.

Jem held up a hand. 'Raj, shh—'

'This *is* fascinating,' Tishy murmured after the old man had spoken for several moments more. 'To think, a whole *ancient mythology*, lost to scholarship! Oh, if only I could study these scrolls, these books – who knows what treasures they contain?'

Cata was impatient. 'But Tishy, what does he *say*?'

Tishy adjusted her spectacles. 'I'm afraid it's all rather vague. This Empress, you see, was – well, he says *is*, but I don't trust his tenses, they're all over the place, quite without system, for all the world as if past and present—'

'Get on with it, girl!' Cata snapped.

Tishy was flustered. 'Well … it seems she was – is, was – a kind of ghost, but not *really* a ghost, a sort of … *spirit*, I suppose, that manifested itself from the Vast, a kind of … *summoner* who seeks out the ones, or *the one* – he's vague on number too … really, the language *has* fallen into decline, it just goes to show what happens without proper, systematised, formal teaching—'

'Tishy!' snapped Rajal. 'The ones who *what*?'

'The ones who'll go to the lamasery, of course.'

Jem was startled. 'What? But we—'

Cata murmured, 'I have, I'm sure I—'

'Cata? What are you saying?' Jem turned to her, but just then Starzok began to speak more rapidly and Tishy had to struggle to keep up with his words. Anguish blazed in the old man's eyes and he gestured floridly.

'He's speaking of his daughter, his lost daughter,' said Tishy. 'Her name was Mishja, sweet little Mishja, and never was there a finer child, never a happier father – until the summons came, and Mishja went away … Ah, but the summons was all in her mind! Like many before her, dazzled by a phantom in the snow, poor little Mishja, crazed little Mishja had obeyed what she thought to be a sacred summons, little realising that the summons was deceptive. To think, that any common village child could count herself one of the Summoned Five, and think they would receive her in the lamasery!'

'Wait,' said Rajal, 'this lamasery – *is* it here, or gone?'

'Real, or just illusion?' Cata jumped in.

'What about the avalanche?' said Jem.

Starzok had fallen silent, tearfully squeezing the squirming Littler. Earnestly Tishy plied the old man with questions, and through his cracked replies began to piece together, at last, the answers Jem and his friends had sought. Astonished, they learnt that the lamasery, aeons ago, had indeed been destroyed in an avalanche; but this, Starzok claimed, was not the end of its story. Rather, at the end of every five-cycle, the lamasery would reappear. It was then, defying the cold, that supplicants would come, eager for admission into its sacred portals.

Littler squirmed. 'But why? What for?'

'Come from where?' said Jem. 'From this village?'

'From here,' said Tishy, 'and far away. Starzok says that somehow, secretly, the legend spread, far into the world beyond these high mountains. (That must be true, mustn't it? Think of the book I lost today.) Always, he said, there would be those who thought themselves summoned, and had no choice but to obey; always they would be few in number, but always they would come, chancing all on what seemed, but only seemed, a prospect of eternal bliss, with those he calls the Accepted ... that's right, the Accepted.'

'I'm not sure I like the sound of this,' said Cata.

'What does he mean,' said Jem, *only seemed?*'

Starzok laughed, almost as if he had understood the question. But when Tishy translated his next words, he might have been thinking of something else entirely.

'But you,' he says, 'are The Five. Yes, you are certainly The Five.'

Still the old man kept grinning, and squeezed Littler with particular enthusiasm.

Littler's eyes popped.

'Uh ... there're six of us,' said Rajal, glancing ruefully towards the inert Myla. Starzok had barely been interested in her at all. This, to her brother, was more than a little strange. He clutched his forehead, wishing now he had drunk less of the greyish liquor.

Jem wished the same. 'That's right, six,' he said slowly.

'Seven,' said Littler,' if you include Ejjy.'

An ominous look came into Starzok's eyes.

Tishy translated, *'But you think of yourself as the chosen ones, do you not? Most certainly you do, and glad you must be that the call you have heard is true, not false. Alas, that my poor Mishja once thought the same! So beautiful she was, like dawn against the darkness, that when she gathered her followers around her, they were all only too eager to follow her, in certainty that they would pass through the sacred portals. There was Ekik, her betrothed; there was Lanzik, his best friend; there was Jamaja, my wife, and my little son Blayzil.*

'Ah, I did all in my power to make them stay! To what avail? Go they would, but like all false seekers, disaster lay in wait for them before they reached the lamasery. It was a day of dark skies and swirling snow, and the way was harder than at any other time in the cycle of the seasons. Fools, fools! On Gijok's Ridge they took their fatal steps. The perilous gorge claimed them – my daughter, her betrothed, his friend, my wife – and only Blayzil, saved as if by a miracle, returned to me to tell the tale. Only Blayzil, accursed Blayzil!

'Ah, but if only it had been another!'

Starzok was overcome by emotion. Almost brutally he pushed Littler away, juddered back his chair and stood, rearing over his guests like a shabby, angry god. For a moment they were afraid, as if the old man might do some violence, perhaps to them, perhaps to Blayzil – even, perhaps, to himself.

Instead, he shuffled away, muttering.

'Charming,' said Rajal. 'Now there's a host for you.'

'Raj, shh! Tishy, what's he saying now?' said Jem.

'That we must sleep,' said Tishy, 'we must all sleep. At first light, he will guide us to the lamasery.'

'Simple as that?' Gulping, Jem watched Starzok's retreating back, dark against the flickering redness of the fire.

Chapter 52

THE KICK INSIDE

'You're all right, Littler?' Jem whispered.

'Now I'm not *squashed*,' Littler whispered back.

Jem smiled. Littler had been annoyed by Starzok's fondlings; it had been left to the others to find them more disturbing.

The old man had vanished for the night. Taking himself off to an inner chamber, he had left his guests with the shabby furs and blankets that lay in heaps all round the edges of the dining hall. Blayzil would have lingered, grinning eagerly, but Starzok had cuffed the youth around the head and sent him off, howling, to his own quarters.

Fresh logs crackled in the fireplace.

'You're sure you're not cold, Littler?' Jem went on.

'It never got cold like this in Unang, I'll say that much. Even when it *was* cold, I mean. But I've got Ejjy, haven't I? He's better than blankets.'

'Of course he is.' Jem scratched the big cat's ears, which were just visible above Littler's bedding. He turned away. 'Now try and get some sleep, hm?'

Littler yawned. 'Ejjy's sleeping.'

'I mean the pair of you.'

'Jem?' Jem turned back. 'Do you really believe it? About this lamasery, and everything? Will we really get inside?'

'Oh, I believe it,' Jem whispered. 'We've got to.'

But secretly, he was filled with doubt. What had Starzok meant, speaking of The Five? Dubiously, Jem peered through the firelit darkness to where Rajal had made a bed for himself beside the comatose Myla. From Starzok's account, the journey that lay before them would be a treacherous one. Would they be able to take Myla? What would they do if they could not? He felt helpless – he hated their dependency on Starzok.

But this, thought Jem, was ungrateful. Where would they be without the old man?

Or without Tishy?

As he found his way back to his own makeshift bed, Jem passed the hunched, dark form of the young scholar, who had fallen with surprising ease into a noisy, snorting sleep.

The grey liquor, no doubt. Eager to quell the taste of the meat, they had all partaken a little too much of it, even Littler. Only now did Jem wish

322

they had not. More than once he had felt a heaviness in his limbs, then a strange lurching, as if the chamber were turning.

He settled down next to Cata, wrapping his arms around her with an eager shudder. If only they were alone!

His lips sought her ear. 'Not sleeping yet?'

'I think there might be fleas in this bedding.'

Jem laughed softly. 'They haven't bothered Tishy.'

'They wouldn't go for her. No blood.'

'Hah! I'll bet you wish you'd studied Juvescial too.'

'You're saying I'm jealous?' Cata rolled over, pressing herself against Jem. Through their thick furs, they could barely feel the shapes of their bodies. 'Still, it'd be better than some things I've done.'

'I can think of better things.'

'And you're only going to think of them. Put it down.'

'How can you tell? Anyway, I can't help it.'

'That's what they all say.' They kissed, several times, then Cata broke away. 'Enough of that. That's what got me into this trouble in the first place.'

'Trouble?' For a moment, Jem did not understand.

Since being with Jem again, Cata had often been on the brink of telling him about their child, but she told herself that the time was not yet ripe; that there was no point in worrying him; that she would wait until this adventure was over. Now, unexpectedly, the words came from her.

'Remember that night in Unang Lia? And if you ask which one, you'll be getting a swift kick where it hurts ... Well, let's just say that someone should have taught you how to be careful.'

Jem sat up abruptly. At once he was bewildered, delighted, frightened. He wanted to laugh, to cry, to whoop and punch the air. As it was, he only grabbed Cata's hands, his voice bursting from him in a thick gasp. 'Oh Cata, Cata! But ... you silly girl, you've been running around like a mad thing, you've been climbing, you've been—'

'*Shh*, Jem, you're as bad as Nirry! I'm hardly like the side of a barn yet, am I? Come on, I'm made of stern stuff. You must know that, if nothing else.'

'But ... you've faced this alone?'

'I haven't, I've had Nirry ...' Cata had to smile. 'Of course, *she* knew at once. First time I threw up in the morning, there was Nirry eyeing me beadily! She's a little bit shocked, but I told her we were married ... We *are*, aren't we, Jem?'

Jem thought of the strange ceremony in Unang Lia, on the steps of the Sanctum of the Flame. 'We-ell, you were impersonating a foreign princess at the time.'

'And you a foreign prince. *They* were married. So?'

Jem laughed. 'Shall we do it again?'

'What, in an Agonist temple?'

'We'd better. After all, when I'm King, you'll be my Queen.'

Marvelling, Jem moved a hand to Cata's belly, as if he expected it already to be a taut, ballooning mound. 'I can hardly believe it. What shall we call him, our son and heir?'

'*Son?* Typical. It might be a girl.'

'Cata, I felt him kick!'

'You did not! It's too early.'

Jem would not dispute it. Happily, he sank into Cata's arms again. 'Oh Cata, I love you so much.'

For a time they lay there, entirely content, as if they had been translated into another sphere, far beyond this strange cold place. No danger disturbed them; their enemies, even their friends seemed not quite real. It was as if this adventure lay far in the past, like a dream from which they had woken, and already they found themselves in a bright, happy future.

Cata was the first to break the spell. She shifted restlessly. 'But Jem, what are we to going *do*? I mean, here? Now? I've tried to be brave, but this is too much. Raj has lost his crystal … mine's gone too. That means Littler's next, doesn't it, next time the Unbeing Bird comes round?'

Reluctantly, Jem forced himself to face their situation. 'I know, Cata. That's why we've got to get to the lamasery as soon as we can. First light, Starzok said.'

'And you trust Starzok? I don't, not one bit. Why should he be helping us? Why's he so fond of Littler, when he hates his own son? And he doesn't care that his *wife* is dead, does he? Did you pick up on that?'

Jem murmured a miserable assent. But what could they do now? He kissed Cata and stroked her hair, urging her gently to sleep; but after some moments, she resumed her whisperings. 'And how often do you think he has guests? This bedding was all laid out when we got here, wasn't it, just ready and waiting?'

'Cata, *shh.*' Jem would have kissed her again, but broke off, feeling the lurching he had felt before. How he wished he had left the grey liquor alone!

A log settled, sparking, in the fire.

❄   ❄   ❄   ❄

Later, Jem would suppose that he had slept for some time. He stirred, aware of an ache in his side. The hardness of the floor pressed up through the bedding and he felt a chill creeping over his limbs.

He stared into the darkness, wondering if he could bring himself to rise, blunder across the chamber, feed the fire … No, he would press himself against Cata … Shapes churned in the distant, purplish glow. Yes, Cata … Instead, Jem closed his eyes again, thinking of the Mauvers, imagining them here in Starzok's chamber. Could they be hiding behind the hanging skins, hovering above the criss-crossing beams? In his mind, he saw them fluttering forth, stealing down towards the sleeping guests; he saw the separate, bird-like creatures gathering into the shape of a man, and the shimmering man rising above him, reaching out a hand for the hidden crystal...

He woke with a start. A dream, only a dream.

'Oh Cata, Cata ...' That was when Jem felt real fear. He reached for Cata.

She was gone.

By now, the firelight had faded entirely and he could see only a deep, velvety darkness. He shuddered, rubbing his arms against the cold. There were sounds of breathing, regular and slow, and the harsh whistlings of the winds outside.

Then there was something else, too. Drifting above the winds came a sound of music, a soft, high wailing, softer than the breathing of Jem's friends, higher than the keenings they had heard before.

He turned, peering uselessly. It was coming from outside. Had the villagers come back? A window rattled in the wind and Jem thought he saw a shaft of colour, a purplish glow, seeping thinly through a crack in the shutter.

Flinging back his bedding, Jem groped for his boots. He crept to the door, blundering like a blind man; the chamber behind him might have been a void, a desolate emptiness of velvet black.

The glow came again, purple then green. Jem felt something buffing at his calves and looked down to see golden, glowing eyes.

Ejard Orange miaowed.

Relief flooded Jem, but only for a moment. The cat, with a cuffing paw, directed him to the doorway. Through the shutter, the light came red, then blue.

What *was* that music? What *was* that song?

> Come, meet the Empress of the Endless Dream!
> Now nothing will seem the way it seemed to seem:
> > Gold will gleam,
> > Time will stream
> When you meet the Empress of the Endless—

Foreboding thudded in Jem's heart. Wrenching the door open, he staggered back, blasted by winds. Snow flurried in his face and he held a hand to his eyes, but through the blur he made out a startling scene. Aghast, he struggled across the icy verandah.

'Cata! Cata, what are you doing?'

> Ah, see the Sister of the Sacred Night
> Who looks upon your face with blinding sight:

> Endless light,
> Timeless flight
> Is yours with the Sister of the Sacred—

Barefoot, her furs littering the ground, Cata danced naked in the snow. Through powdery, heaping drifts she strode and leapt, whirled and reeled with impossible elegance, her skin glowing with rainbow colours.

Jem stumbled down the steps, mouthing her name.

> Look to the Mistress of the Mystic Quest
> Who longs to take you to her sacred breast:
> East or west,
> Final rest
> Awaits you with the Mistress of the Mystic—

He knew he must stop her, but what could he do? All the while a second, phantom figure hovered above her like a puppet master – a female figure in striped robes, with only light where her face should have been.

'Cata!' Jem cried. But of course, she could not hear him.

> Embrace the Daughter of the Damned and Saved
> Who always waited on each road you braved:
> You roared, you raved
> Like those enslaved
> Still, you loved the Daughter of the Damned and—

Cata was entranced, and Jem, watching her, was soon entranced too, translated into a dimension of mysterious magic, oblivious to the snow and cold. Magic enfolded him, as if he were on the brink of transcending this world.

'Oh Cata, Cata—' She pirouetted. She whirled.

> Can this really be the Empress of the Endless Dream?
> Can nothing still seem the way it seemed to seem?
> Ah, yet light will beam,
> Love will teem
> Between you and the Empress of the—

Miaowing, Ejard Orange tried to break the spell. The big cat leapt forward, pouncing upon the phantom, but only passed through it. The dance might have gone on, endlessly reeling, until Cata had slumped down, frozen, spent.

Instead, something happened. From the flurrying darkness burst a new figure, shapeless in furs, hurtling towards Cata. The figure cried out. It struck her, knocked her sprawling.

Then the figure was gone. And so was the phantom.

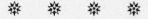

326

Pallid moonlight fluttered through the snow.

With Ejard Orange capering around her, Cata lay motionless, face down. Jem flailed towards her, gathering up the discarded furs, bundling them clumsily about her limbs. He had no gloves and could barely feel his hands.

'Cata, are you all right? Cata, lean on me—'

The wind cut through him and his teeth chattered. Jem tried to lift Cata, but slipped and fell. He gasped. Should he call out? Would anyone help? Would anyone even hear? On the verandah, Starzok's door banged back and forth.

Then someone was there, hands reaching out.

Only after a moment did Jem see the face. 'Blayzil!'

Together, Jem and the strange youth hauled the unconscious Cata back into the house. Soon the others were stirring, wondering what had happened. Blayzil made up the fire again and Jem slumped before it, embracing Cata, whispering to her, rubbing her limbs.

A voice said, 'She all right – she all right now.'

It was Blayzil who had spoken. Startled, Jem looked upon the shapeless, fur-clad form and thought again of the figure who had knocked Cata down. He had thought it must be one of the villagers. Had that been Blayzil too?

Ejard Orange miaowed.

'Say,' yawned Rajal, 'where's Littler?'

'He's not ... not with Starzok?' Tishy shuddered.

Distantly, Jem registered the words. Alarm shook him, but now Cata's eyes flickered open and all he could think of was her cold, beautiful face.

'She wants me, Jem ... Jem, she's waiting for me.'

'Cata, who ... what do you mean?'

'The Empress,' Cata murmured, 'of the Endless Dream...'

Chapter 53

ANOTHER FOREIGN TONGUE

The whiteness was dazzling.

That morning, even the wind had dropped and the scene was strangely static, crisp and keen as if the air itself were freezing. High over the mountains the sun flamed coldly, illuminating every crevasse, every crag and rise with a desolate, sharp flatness. Jem and his friends had to screw up their eyes. Often they walked with their heads down, and if they looked ahead they would bring their hands up to their brows like visors. Only Starzok strode confidently, planting his staff in the snow with a calm, dogged certainty.

From the beginning of the journey, Jem had a sense that time was suspended. Uncertainly he held Cata's hand, while Tishy took a turn with Myla's stretcher. In the bright dawn, as they had gathered before Starzok's house, the events of last night had seemed like a dream. Littler scuffed merrily in the snow, back amongst them, quite unharmed. Cata could hardly believe she had danced in the snow. Villagers milled around, smiling and singing, as if already celebrating the triumphant conclusion of a quest they could hardly have understood. Only Blayzil had been subdued. More than once, Jem had tried to talk to the youth; Tishy had too, but Blayzil had been shy, and frightened of his father. When Blayzil had motioned to accompany the expedition, the old man pushed him angrily away.

They trudged in silence.

Jem and Cata fell back behind the others. Still the way before them was level and wide, the uphill slope barely steep at all. Filling the sky was the mystic mountain, its tapering peak a vision of ethereal, cold splendour, apparently neither more real nor any closer than before.

'Was it the grey liquor?' said Cata. 'Was that what's making us feel this way?'

'Perhaps. But there's something about this place.'

'There was something about it last night.'

Silence again. 'But now she's gone? You're sure?'

'Jem, I'm sure of nothing. All I know is that she was there last night, all around me like water. Like air.' Cata turned away. 'There was nothing I could do. But then, there was nothing I wanted to do.'

Jem expelled a whistling breath. He would have said more, but his thoughts were as cloudy as the air from his lungs. Great walls of rock, silver-grey with ice, rose ahead. The white way was narrowing, growing steeper. Solemnly he gazed upon their companions, on Rajal and Tishy with the burden of Myla, on Littler, with Ejard Orange in his arms, up ahead with Starzok, flailing along beside the old man. Starzok reached down, fluffing the little boy's furry hat.

'What about Tishy?' Jem said. 'Doesn't look like he's got time for her now.'

'He got bored,' said Cata. 'Most people do.'

Jem laughed, but stopped himself. 'This thing with Littler, I don't like it.'

Cata said, 'But what happened last night? Did Littler really end up in Starzok's chamber?'

'You saw him come out of there this morning, didn't you?'

'Jem, he'd only been sleeping! Starzok must have picked him up and carried him. What was it he said to Tishy? Something about being worried about the boy?'

'Huh! He should be worried about Blayzil.'

They trudged on. There was a powdery crash, somewhere behind them. In the white morning it sounded unreal, a dreamy susurrus against the vast mountains.

Cata said, 'Perhaps it was to do with the grey liquor. Didn't Littler drink it too?'

'Why, I wonder? Why did any of us?'

'Perhaps Starzok's got some kind of power. Perhaps the liquor only *looked* grey in that light. Perhaps it was purple, Jem – purple like the Mauvers.'

'What are you saying?'

Cata fell silent. Then she said, too late, 'That crash. What was that crash?'

Jem said, 'Falling snow. Just falling snow.'

Jem and Cata fell further behind. They floundered, struggling to catch up with the others.

Jem said, 'Tishy's tired. I should go back to Myla.'

'Don't. Wait, we could take a turn together.'

'You're up for it? It's going to get harder soon.'

'Of course I'm up for it!' Cata snorted. But she paused. Clutching Jem's gloves tightly in her own, she turned her cold face full against his. 'How much longer?'

'It's early yet, still early—'

'The Unbeing Bird—'

'It's coming, I know—'

'And Littler's crystal—'

'It's next, I know—'

'Wait – Jem, what if I ... what if *you* were to take his crystal? Mind it, I mean?'

'Cata, I can't explain, but the crystals … they don't work that way. And there's nothing I could do that Littler couldn't. The red crystal may have been mine once, but it's *his* now … *his*, like yours is—'

Roughly, Cata broke away. 'Was, *was*—'

Jem blundered, 'I'm sorry—'

At once, Cata turned back. They embraced, holding each other with fierce longing. 'I can't help it, Jem. So many times I've been strong, but this time I'm frightened, really frightened—'

'Cata, so am I—'

'Oh, how much longer?'

'Till the lamasery? It has to be soon—'

'No, Jem. Till the Unbeing Bird—'

To Jem, Cata's words were icy as the air, and he shuddered, even as he embraced her. Nuzzling into her coat, he closed his eyes, the better to sink into her dark, compelling warmth; instead, he visualised the mighty Creature of Evil that Toth had unleashed, arcing through the third day of its terrible, circling flight. Midnight over Agondon. Midday over the mountains. Oh, but it was early yet, wasn't it early still?

Ahead, Starzok had turned back, raising his staff. Quickly, Jem and Cata caught up with their friends. With gestures, they offered to take the stretcher, Cata at Rajal's end, Jem at Tishy's. Rajal demurred, shaking his head; Tishy, exhausted, relinquished her burden with evident relief. Wiping her spectacles, she squinted into the blazing white as Starzok began to speak.

Cata fell in beside her. 'What's he saying now?'

While Tishy listened intently, Jem was not listening at all. Sadly he stared at Myla's ruined face. Her mouth was open and drivel ran down; her gums had withered and her teeth were blackened, twisted, like rotted fruit ready to fall. To be sure, she must die soon … Jem bit his lower lip. No, he must not think this way, he must not. When Rajal turned to him, Jem avoided his friend's eyes.

'From here,' Tishy was saying, 'the way gets harder. There's a path called … Jamantis Way – very steep and winding; then a plateau called … Horizon Achieved, or … no, Found Horizon—'

Cata rolled her eyes. 'Does he say how long it takes?'

'Wouldn't matter if he did,' said Tishy, settling her spectacles back on her nose. She was a little affronted. 'Their time's *very* different from ours, you know.'

'What?' said Rajal, overhearing. 'Their standards of hygiene I can understand, but their *time*?'

'Raj, shh—' Cata put a finger to his lips.

Jem heard the exchange as if from afar. Again, in these moments of idleness, a familiar strangeness pressed upon him. Time, a different time? Yes, he understood. And how could Rajal not understand, when

Myla's time had run ahead so catastrophically, consuming a lifetime in a matter of days? For the others, time remained suspended, silvery and frozen like the ice and snow. But soon, Jem was certain, it was going to shatter.

'And in the end,' Tishy went on, 'comes Gijok's Ridge—'

'Isn't that where his daughter—?' Cata began.

'Best,' Tishy muttered, 'not to mention *her*.'

Rajal said, 'It's not as if *he* can understand, is it?'

'Don't anyway,' said Tishy. 'It might be bad luck.'

Since this had been just what Cata was thinking, she found herself softening towards the young scholar. A little sheepishly, she touched Tishy's arm. 'Tishy, I don't know where we'd be without you. How would we ever have got this far?'

At another time, Tishy might have flushed with pleasure. Now she could only shiver. Starzok's speech had been laden with warnings, and she had translated only the facts, the names. Blank-faced, she said that they were not there yet.

It was Cata who flushed, turning angrily.

'Polty?'

Polty stirred. For how long had he lain there, shuddering and moaning? It might have been for eternity. Illusions churned in his eyes; phantom-birds, phosphorescent, shifted restlessly in the corners of his chamber. Once he thought he saw the giant giraffe-beetle scuttle across the carpet, vanishing under his bed with a downward swoop of its neck. Sometimes he sobbed; sometimes he would scream, lashing out, but his strength was gone. Sweat ran unendingly over his softening body and acrid jets squirted, uncontrolled, from the scarred hole where Penge should have been. Poor Penge! Again and again, Polty saw Burgrove's ruined face, and the lipless mouth yawning wide.

A hand shook him. 'Polty? Polty!'

'B-Bean? Where ... what?' Pain beat behind Polty's eyes as he took in his familiar apartment, its panelling, its fireplace, its moulded ceiling, looming above him impassively. Through a crack in the curtains, light cut the carpet in a long, pale sliver. 'But the birds ... the beetle? Bean, where have they gone?

'They've gone.' Breathing carefully, Bean looked down on his friend with sad, desperate eyes. 'Oh Polty, you've been sick. But it's over now. No more fever, no more shaking.'

'Fever?' Polty pushed back his blankets, running a hand over his sticky, naked chest. 'I've been delirious, haven't I? Oh Bean, Bean! Can you believe I saw the wolf with many heads, slavering over me with its multiple jaws? How they reeked, how they dripped!'

'Hush, Polty, there was no wolf.' Bean forced a smile. 'Unless you mean me. I've been sponging your forehead. And your chest. Even tried to change the bedsheets once, but you were a bit too heavy to shift. Just a bit.'

'I … I've pissed myself, haven't I?'

'And worse. But you're better now, aren't you? Polty, do you know what this means?'

'Means? What does anything mean?'

Bean's voice cracked. 'We're going home. Remember, we were just setting out when … when you got sick? But I packed our bags, didn't I? We'll go now, won't we? To Irion? To the river? To the mallard ducks?'

Polty flopped back. 'What ducks, Bean?'

'We'll meet them when we get there.' Tears burst from Bean's eyes. He flung himself across his friend. 'Oh Polty, how happy we're going to be!'

'What? Get off me, get off!'

'A touching scene.' It was another voice.

'Burgrove!' Polty jerked upright. Bean fell to the floor with a thud.

'Or Hawk of Darkness, if you prefer.' Glittering, the black-garbed figure stood in the sliver of light. Again the mask covered his face. 'Yes, very touching indeed. But I don't think you fellows will be going home *just* yet. We've been keeping you here, can't you see?'

Bean scrambled up. 'Leave him, you—'

It was useless. If Bean hurled himself at the dark figure, it was only to be sent sprawling again with the flick of a gloved hand.

'*You monster*?' Burgrove said wryly. 'Is that what you were going to say, Bean? And I thought you were *so* intimate with our friend Polty. Is he not a monster, too? And what of the lickspittle who has served him so well, aiding him eagerly in all his depravities? You're a sentimental fool, Bean. By the standards of this world, we're all monsters. But now this world is ending and a new time is upon us.'

Polty sat up slowly, covering his nakedness with a soiled blanket.

'New … *time*?' he said, expressionless.

'Didn't I say we'd been keeping you, Polty? Yes, keeping you, until we wanted you.' A gloved hand waved. 'Never you mind, Bean, you'll be coming too. Our master has a mission. A mission for you both.'

Bean's voice was sullen. 'We're … going home.'

'Yes,' said Polty. 'Home.'

Burgrove laughed. 'Ah my friends, perhaps you are!'

And crossing to the windows, he touched the curtains lightly. They fell away, filling the chamber with a pallid glare. In the snowlight, the clutter, the cobwebs, the dust and stains quivered into a harsh focus.

'The light,' said Burgrove, 'the truth. In the light, we may see things as they are. Should you like to see things as they *are*? Hm, Polty? Hm, Bean?'

Casually, Burgrove pushed up his feathery mask. With thudding dread, Polty and Bean gazed upon the scarred, twisted face that once had been the visage of Varby's handsomest bachelor. Burgrove opened his lipless, grinning mouth. He spread his arms wide and a loud, repellent retching erupted from his throat.

Bean quailed. 'What's ... what's he doing?'

The sound rose in pitch as something fleshy, something bloodied – it was not Burgrove's tongue – began to emerge from the yawning jaws. Polty gasped. Oh, how could he mistake that thick, glistening mushroom of pink?

'Penge!' He rushed forward, tripping on his blanket.

Would he have grabbed the end of the thing, pulling it out? He was not to have the chance. Burgrove stood upright with a snapping motion, drawing the cylinder of flesh back into his mouth as if indeed it had been a deformed tongue.

'I'm keeping him for you, my friend.' He draped an arm round Polty's shoulder. 'Keeping him here, safe inside me, until you deserve your reward. And you'll deserve it, shan't you? Yes, of course you shall.'

Burgrove's voice rose. 'But come, our mission awaits.'

With that, he enfolded Bean, too, into a grip like an embrace, and swung his companions in a half-circle, marching them towards the panelling. Light fizzed around them and they stepped through the wall.

They emerged in the apartments of the First Minister, far away on the other side of the palace.

Chapter 54

OBVIOUSLY FIVE BELIEVERS

'Elsan? Where are you?'

The whimper brought no reply.

'You're not keeping up!'

This time, the voice was hoarse.

'Oh, why did I bring you?' Huddled in furs, Lady Cham-Charing peered through the snow. 'I'm warning you, Elsan, I'll leave you behind—'

Of course it was only a game, just a game to keep up her spirits. Slipping from doorway to doorway in the cold, empty morning, Constansia knew she was really alone. She wasn't mad, was she? Never! As sure as she knew this was the Meditation of Theron, AC999*d*, Constansia knew that Elsan was dead, murdered by the rebels. And how narrowly Constansia had escaped their evil clutches! They were certain to have gone for her next. Oh yes, they had Freddie on side, even Lolenda; but the rebels knew a Cham-Charing would never turn traitor. No doubt they had done away with poor Tishy already; yes, that must have been what had happened to her.

Constansia shuddered. 'Come, Elsan, it can't be far now. Didn't they say the streets were thronged with Bluejackets? We must throw ourselves into their protection. We must denounce these rebels.'

Snow howled in the old woman's face as she hobbled along in the white, deathly silence.

Only with difficulty had Constansia escaped from Miss Tilsy Fash and her evil minions. The woman kept a large establishment, with numerous slovenly servants, and a great many personages of indeterminate class or status, presumably guests or hangers-on – rebel types, in any case. And everyone would fuss over Constansia so, trying to make her rest, trying to give her medicines.

Medicines, indeed! Clearly they would use poison when they murdered her, something to make it look as if she had died naturally. After all, there would certainly be an enquiry; there must be soldiers combing the city for her, even now; news of her disappearance, Constansia was certain, would be the one topic of conversation in Agondon society.

It was the medicines, in the end, that had given Constansia her chance. Pretending to swallow some vile potion proffered by the treacherous Miss Quisto, she had feigned sleep, and the little fool had left her alone, no doubt waiting for the poison to accomplish its fell work. Fortunately, the girl had neglected to lock the chamber door. At once, Constansia was on her feet, rifling through her box for her warmest clothes; in a trice, she had slipped down the stairs. And suddenly the old woman was in the street, alone, for the first time in her life.

Something nuzzled at her heels. Constansia looked down, alarmed, but her alarm turned to surprise when she saw that it was only a small, wiry-haired terrier, of the type some ladies would keep as lap-dogs. The dog was shivering, dishevelled and very dirty. At another time Constansia would have recoiled, disgusted; now, bending stiffly, she scooped up the little creature, hugging it under her furs.

She dragged herself onwards, resting frequently. The whiteness was dazzling. The snow stung her face. But where could she be? Constansia, whose knowledge of the city in which she had spent her life was limited to a few select areas, was by no means familiar with this part of the Island – an area, apparently, for theatrical types which, if not as squalid as she might have expected, was by no means what *she* would define as respectable.

Oh, but surely she would find the soldiers soon? Constansia voiced the question in a whisper, no longer to an imaginary Elsan Margrave but rather to the lap-dog she instinctively, and inaccurately, referred to as 'Pug'. Poor Elsan had once had a dog called Pug; but then, hers had been an actual pug-dog, as opposed to a Vantage terrier.

'You've chosen a bad day to be out, haven't you, Pug? But did you choose it? Or are you houseless, like me? Houseless, cold and hungry, that's right! I dare say you've an evil mistress who's gone over to the rebels and lost all care and concern for you! Ah, it's a terrible thing when rebellions come. But can we believe our brave Bluejackets will let anything happen? I don't believe it, Pug, do you?'

It was just then that Constansia, turning a corner, spied a two-man patrol. Relief overspread her frozen face and she scurried forward, as best she could, fearful lest her deliverers should fail to see her. She raised her voice, or tried to, but to speak above a whisper was painful. She reached out, clawing at a bearskinned arm.

'Corporal, please—'

'Be off with you, crone!'

Corporal Supp guffawed; his companion, Soldier Rotts, made a coarse gesture. Constansia's mind reeled. Didn't these fellows know who she was?

'I ... I—' Her words caught in her throat.

'Back to the Gardens with you, lady—'

'Lady ... yes, that's right, I'm Lady ... Lady—'

'Bit past it for the Gardens, isn't she? Stones of Agonis, I'd choose my fist any day over this wizened old twat! What do you say, Suppy, shall we take her to Oldgate?'

'Leave her, Rottsy. What time have we got for Rejects, with Redjackets rimming the city like ringworm? Off with you, crone, and count yourself lucky!'

'No ... good Corporal, please—'

Constansia would have caught at the fellow's arm again, but Supp struck her with his musket-butt. She crumpled to the ground.

Yelping, the terrier fell from her coat.

'Crazy old Reject!' Supp laughed, kicking the dog for good measure; Rotts, for his part, spat on the old woman, then kicked her too.

The soldiers trudged on.

'Reject?' said Rotts. 'Did you see that coat? That one's earned a few coppers in her time.'

'And a long time ago it must have been!'

They laughed again, vanishing into the snow.

Meanwhile, the injured little dog crept back to Constansia's stricken form, nuzzling into her coat again as best he could. He lay there, whimpering.

Constansia did not stir.

How much longer?

Rocky walls closed around them as they began their journey through the Jamantis Way. Steeper, narrower grew the snowy path. Sharp alternations of sunlight and shadow stabbed down jaggedly as the path turned and twisted. Often they stumbled, and soon they had no choice but to go single file. Sound came only from their rasping breath, their feet. Once or twice there was a distant crash of snow; once there was a rat-like scurrying of stones.

Cata said, 'Ejjy ... why are you here?'

The big orange creature looked up at her, miaowing, twitching his ears and upright tail. At that time, Cata lagged at the end of their procession. Not until she rounded a rocky angle did she make out, through squinting eyes, what had happened up ahead. Starzok had hoisted Littler on to his shoulders. Like a proud sentinel, or the figurehead of a ship, the little boy gazed forward imperiously. Ejard Orange, by the looks of it, was forgotten.

'Poor Ejjy—' Cata scooped him into her arms. As she trudged on, she pressed him against her cold cheek, feeling the warmth of his furry muzzle. Slowly, gummily, his golden eyes blinked; inevitably, she found herself attuning to his thoughts. Ah, but Ejard Orange was not only angry! He was worried, very worried, as if he sensed something, *something*, would be happening soon ... Cata believed it. She thought of Littler, of Starzok. Then she thought of the Unbeing Bird. How much longer?

It was Jem's question too, but his answer would have been different. Bearing his end of the heavy stretcher, he felt himself juddering into a dulled, trance-like state. Idly, his gaze slid between Myla's lolling face and Rajal, ahead of him, with his bowed back and hunched shoulders, straining beneath his thick furs. Brighter grew the whiteness where the sun flowed down; darker grew the shadows from the overhanging rocks. Jem felt himself filling with a deep, calm solemnity. How much longer? It might have been for ever.

Then they were scrambling up an icy slope. Cata was cursing; Rajal's words were tender. As in a dream, Jem watched his friend gather Myla into his arms, slinging her, sack-like, over his shoulder.

Left with the stretcher, Jem bundled it under his arm. He scrambled up after Rajal, aware of Myla's face suspended just above him like a hanging, ruinous moon, strangely visible against the bright sky. Jem sighed, wishing he could sleep. Then the face was gone and brightness filled his eyes. It was a kind of blindness, a blindness of white. Jem gazed into the crystalline sky.

He heard voices. Exclamations. Oh, but he was falling … falling behind. Cata reached down. 'Quick! Come and see—'

Jem's trance vanished and the stretcher fell as he made it up to the slithery plateau. Could this be the place called Found Horizon? Shielding his eyes, he saw an astonishing vision.

All through their journey to the Kolkon Vera Kion, Jem and his friends had thought they were making for a single indivisible peak, rising in tapering, imperious perfection above the lesser, jagged peaks that surrounded it. Now, gazing across a mighty chasm, they saw they had been deceived. There were two peaks, not one; one must previously have been hidden behind the other, and each was quite as perfect as the imagined single peak.

But if this was striking enough, a vision to fill any but the dullest heart with awe, what was most amazing was the mysterious edifice that lodged, as if suspended in the silvery air, on a glacier in the cleft between the peaks.

The lamasery!

To Jem, at first it was only a dazzle of gold; then, as he stared, the dazzle resolved itself into something more. He had seen many strange places, but this was one of the strangest. Constructed upon the glacial ice, the lamasery was a collection of slab-like jutting rectangles, stacked one atop the other with the haphazard, precarious ease of a child's blocks. From a distance only the shape could be seen, and the brightness of the gold; not until later would Jem make out the elaborate, almost alarming ornamentations, writhing and twisting in mysterious curlicues, covering every surface of the sacred walls.

No matter: from the first, he sensed the power, pulsing from the lamasery with every stabbing arrow of light against the gold. He stumbled forward, forgetting his companions. Words – no, only sounds – escaped Jem's lips and he crashed to his knees in the powdery snow. He screwed up his eyes against the painful glare; he clutched the crystal through his enveloping furs, feeling it pulse, feeling it burn.

Jem almost sobbed, though he was not sure why. And distantly, eternally, he heard the sound of laughter. Was it Starzok? Or another?

'Jem? Can you hear me?' Cata touched his shoulder.

'The quest,' he said, 'it's come to an end.'

Cata nodded, her face strangely sad.

In a great semi-circle like a tenuous ribbon, Gijok's Ridge ran through the air, crossing the ravine between Found Horizon and their mysterious golden destination. Starzok held up his staff, gesturing; obediently, like cowed children, first Tishy, then Cata, then Rajal, then Jem tied themselves together with linking ropes. By now, all of them were desperately tired, numbed as much by anticipation as by the whiteness, the cold and their trudging, relentless journey.

They went on. Only Jem lingered, before the tugging of the rope compelled him forward. In the silence, he heard again the sound of something falling, echoing this time in the deep ravine. Instinct made him turn. Could that be a figure he saw behind them, staring down at them from a rocky outcrop?

Blayzil. He was sure it was Blayzil.

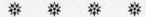

'Wh-where is he?'

Tremulous, Polty looked this way and that, drawing the blanket more tightly round his shoulders. Flames leapt in the several fireplaces, but a chill clamminess clung to the air. For a moment, he thought his fever had returned. A Mauver flapped past his eyes, and he heard something that might have been the hiss of a serpent. He blinked. Dappled in the light through the tattered curtains was the familiar rubble of bricks, plaster, splintered timbers. The stench was foul. Rats scurried; dust rose; remnants of a looking-glass sparkled jaggedly.

'Is he … is he here?' said Bean. He glanced behind him. Glitterings, like the glitterings of Burgrove's costume, played against the wall where they had stepped through.

A thumping came at the door.

'You'll excuse me?' said Burgrove with absurd politeness, releasing his companions from his dark embrace. Striding to the door, he could be heard exchanging low, muttered words with a petitioner who appeared to be Baron-Admiral Aynell.

Bewildered, Polty and Bean stumbled through the rubble. With a clatter, Bean knocked over a silver candelabra, stuck thick with arrested, waxy cascades; Polty, with a bare foot, kicked something soft, and did not

dare look down to see what it might be. His blanket snagged on something, almost pulling away. He jerked it back, shuddering. Thick columns,
sagging askew, rose towards the ceiling; jutting up at an odd angle was a
sleek, ornate screen. Polty ran a hand along the cool, thrilling surface. But
what was this *cooing* he could hear?

He peered around the screen and gasped.

'Aunt Umbecca!'

Squatting on a heap of fallen masonry, the fat woman rocked back and
forth like a wet-nurse, holding something bulky and cylindrical in her
arms. The stench was abominable. Bean recoiled; Polty clutched a hand to
his mouth. Horrorstruck, he thought of his dead son, and not until a
moment had passed did he realise that Umbecca's burden was a decomposing human leg. Looking up, round-eyed and smiling, she held out the
vile, suppurating thing, as if for admiration.

'My baby,' she breathed in a little-girl voice.

'P-Polty, what's wrong with her?' Bean burst out.

'She's ... she's mad!' Stumbling, Polty backed away.

Meanwhile, Burgrove's exchange rose in volume; Aynell, it was clear,
had been joined by Varby & Holluch, perhaps even by Heva-Harion.
There were angry bellowings. Burgrove slammed the door. 'Really, these
War Lords are useless! Can they not make their own battle plans without
recourse to the First Minister?'

But where, Bean wondered, *was* the First Minister?

Or rather, Toth?

From behind the door came muffled cries; then there was another cry,
muffled too, but closer. Bean peered into the dappled light. On a heap of
rubble, bound against a column like a victim at a stake, was a young
woman in a lush, trailing gown. A gag filled her mouth and she tugged
against her bonds.

'Come, child, are you to exhaust yourself?' said Burgrove, turning back.
'Did I not say that a splendid adventure, the greatest of your life, was
about to unfold? I'm sure I must have *mentioned* it. Save your strength,
child, save it, for what lies ahead.'

Polty began, 'But that's ... that's—'

'The Queen?' said Burgrove. 'And is she not as necessary to this mission
as the others I have assembled? Ah, but if only she were as compliant as
her dear husband. He's *much* less trouble.'

'Her ... husband?' said Bean.

With a black arm that flashed in the light, Burgrove waved towards the
tattered curtains. In a shadowy corner, slumped and disconsolate, peering
over the window-ledge, was a figure swathed in ermine and rumpled
blue velvet. Stirring, the figure rose, shambling unregally towards them,
his furs catching in the rubble. Should they have bowed? Cringingly, Bean
would have done so, but Burgrove merely laughed.

The King stooped forward, confused, pointing back to the windows with his mutilated hand. Was he speaking to Burgrove? To Polty? To Bean? It was hard to tell. In any case, his voice was strained and fluting. 'But what's … what's happening? The streets of my city … why are they empty? Why are there armies, massing on my hills?'

Renewed poundings came at the door and Burgrove started for it impatiently. Now Gorgol and the Prince-Elector, perhaps Heva-Harion too, pleaded for an audience with the First Minister. They were not to have it. Burgrove's words were curt, and the War Lords quickly angered. They might have pushed past him, blundering into the apartment; instead there was the sound of a sharp, harsh fizzing, followed by screams.

The door slammed again. 'Curse those War Lords,' said Burgrove. 'Can't they see their battles will soon be meaningless? Let them win, let them lose, what does it matter now? Oh my master, our time has come!'

Bean clutched at him. 'Burgrove! What do you mean?'

But the King was to provide a further distraction. Eyes bulging, Orok's representative in the Realm of Being had hummed a little tune and danced a little jig as Burgrove attended to the irksome lords. Now, unexpectedly, he clapped his hands. 'But of course, it's my victory, playing out again! That's what's happening, isn't it? The victory of Ejard Blue! A celebration, a pageant! But how many years? Tell me, Hawk of Darkness, how many years? How long now, since we destroyed my hated brother?'

Burgrove slipped an arm round the ermine shoulders. 'There there, Your Imperial Agonist Majesty, there's no need to worry about Ejard Red now – no need to worry about anything at all. Soon you'll be far from Agondon, embarking upon a new and enthralling life.'

The King gibbered, alarm spreading over his fleshy face. 'Far from Agondon? No, not far from Agondon! But where's … where's my First Minister? Surely he couldn't … he couldn't! Tranimel … Tranimel, where are you?'

Such, perhaps, is the power of a monarch that the question was answered at once. There was a murmur of phantoms; then, in the upper reaches of the chamber, came a mysterious, shimmering light. Astonished, the figures in the rubble looked up to see the First Minister, evidently deep in meditation, revolving cross-legged in the air. As the figure turned, his robes and shaven head glowed purple, then green, played upon by the gemstones that slowly spun above him like tiny, gleaming planets.

Bean cowered. Polty stumbled, colliding with the King; the Queen, at her column, renewed her thrashings. Only Umbecca remained oblivious. Still she sat behind her screen, cooing and crying over the severed leg.

Burgrove sank down. 'Master! Master, *now*!'

Thunder crashed from nowhere. Monsters writhed, and a mighty, whirling wind suddenly filled the apartment.

Chapter 55

HERE WE ARE

The way had always been hard; now it was harder, much harder. The pathway narrowed. More than once they slithered, almost slipped; then, cutting through the stillness, came buffeting, frozen winds. They gritted their teeth; they willed themselves forward, left foot, right foot, lungs straining in the thin, icy air.

Trudge, trudge. Up-down, up-down went Littler on Starzok's shoulders; back and forth, back and forth swung Myla's hanging head. How much longer? The question was every bit as compelling as before; and yet, strangely, not compelling at all. The lamasery was so near. The lamasery was so far. Perhaps it would always loom ahead, ahead, ahead, flashing in the painful light.

Trudge, trudge. Up-down. Back and forth.

And all the time Jem watched Myla's face, swinging like a pendulum before his eyes – back-forth, back-forth, with every breath he exhaled. It was entrancing – and more entrancing still was the change that Jem saw slowly coming over the ruinous, ancient visage.

The wrinkles were smoothing. The sagging flesh grew firmer. As they neared the lamasery, Myla was growing younger. Jem might have cried out, shouted joyously to Rajal. But the trance held him.

And then the climax came.

They struggled up the last precarious ribbon of rock. Until now, the lamasery had remained a blur, a dazzle; then, with a clarity that came in a rush, they made out scrolls, curlicues, gargoyles fashioned in gold. There were jutting, snow-clad eaves; there were high, strange windows; there was a mighty portal – a drawbridge, shut fast, that would descend, when it descended, over a moat of ice.

Littler pointed excitedly, bouncing on Starzok's shoulders. An ululation, like a summons, broke from the old man's throat. Exhausted, ready to slump down, the party had only to make it over a last icy bluff.

And then came the Mauvers.

The horror happened in a sudden, dream-like transition. All at once, borne on a mighty wind, the evil entities were upon them, beating around them in the fractured light. Thunderous wings filled the air; there were boomings, screechings, cawings. Snow whirled. The sky was purple.

341

Cata sank down, clutching her head; hissing, Ejard Orange twisted from her arms. Starzok collapsed; Littler crashed on top of him. Tishy slithered dangerously; Rajal struggled with Myla.

Then came another change, and he struggled no more.

It was Jem who saw it first. Floundering, staring through Mauvers, still he saw Myla's transfigured face. Then the face was rising, open-eyed, and Rajal was turning, crying out, as his sister, in the form of a young, beautiful woman, rose into the air, scattering the screeching, purple half-phantoms. Song burst from her lips and she whirled round, arms raised.

Jem writhed, crystal-light bursting from his chest. Screaming, he rolled to the edge of the ridge, his rope tugging, pulling at Rajal, at Cata. He clawed at rock. The chasm yawned immensely beneath him. He was on his belly, crystal-heat burning through his furs; Mauvers rushed back, crying out defiance, and as if a force possessed him, he flipped over violently, bashing down on his back, and the light from his chest streamed upwards, unobstructed, in a blue, fluorescing beam.

And still Myla sang, still Myla spun.

Then Jem saw a red beam too, arcing across his own. It was Littler's crystal, its light, like the blue light, darting this way and that way through the Mauver-filled air.

Chaos crashed around them; echoes boomed up from the emptiness below. There were the Mauvers, there were the crystal-beams, there was spinning Myla; then, looming over all, was the terrible shadow of the Unbeing Bird. Its wings beat, gigantic. Only Myla held it back. Crystal-beams, dazzling, crossed and crossed.

Meanwhile, Mauvers surrounded Starzok, zapping purple rays into his fallen form. He rose up, glowing with dark luminescence. Shrieking the name of his dead daughter, the old man loomed over Littler. Twisted evil filled his face. His eyes glowed, inhuman, and his hand lunged out, greedily thrusting into the crystal light.

'Mishja ... Mishja—' Starzok cried.

'Toth ... it's *Toth*—' cried Jem, unheard.

Thunderous, from the chasm below, came a mighty, churning ball of purple haze, drawn up by the force of the Unbeing Bird. Zigzag lightning rushed and zapped as the great ball rumbled higher and higher, nearer and nearer, as if it would sear away all in its path.

On the ridge, Ejard Orange sprang upon Starzok. The old man reeled, searing with his borrowed, evil energy. Enraged, he ripped the cat from his shoulder. Scrambling, hissing, Ejard Orange attacked again, claws ripping, razor-like, at the contorted face. Littler, desperate, tried to scramble away, but could barely move, pinioned by the force of his crystal.

'Littler ... Littler—' Jem struggled to rise, but his crystal trapped him too. Rajal, on his knees, reached imploringly to Myla. Tishy slithered, sobbing; Cata writhed and screamed, battered by waves of crazed psychic force.

Blundering back and forth, scrambling, almost falling, Starzok ripped Ejard Orange from his face. He flung the cat away. Spiralling, spread-eagled, Ejard Orange plunged down and down, cries unheard, fizzing into the rising, sizzling haze.

'No—' A new cry, unheard too.

It was Blayzil, leaping from the rocks above.

The boy charged, infuriated, at his transfigured father. Purple light zapped, but the boy charged again. They struggled; Blayzil flailed. Starzok roared, rearing down. Blood streamed from his face, soaking his beard and robes. He beat at his son, slapped him, almost flung him from the ridge.

Blayzil rallied. Back he came, and back again, but Starzok was too strong.

Still the mighty bird loomed.

Blayzil lay gasping. The old man seized a rock. Now, hurling back his arms, he would bring down the rock, battering out his son's brains.

And still Myla spun. Still the crystal-lights crashed, collided. Rapidly, her spinning form began to flash, pulsing like a beacon in the tormented air.

The rock came down. Twisting away, Blayzil saw Starzok's staff, lying in the snow. He scrambled up, grabbed it: turned, lunged, running on his father as if with a spear.

Starzok doubled over, gasping. The old man teetered on the edge, ready to fall. Then, suddenly, his hand darted forward, clawing again for Littler, for the crystal. His hand plunged through the red beam. The light streamed through his hand. Triumphantly, he pulled Littler forward.

In the last moment, Blayzil snatched Littler back. But even as he flung the little boy behind him, the youth overbalanced, falling with his father.

Blayzil had saved Littler. But not the crystal. As the old man fell, the crystal blazed in his hand. But it was then that the blue beam of Jem's crystal and the red beam of Littler's fused together, striking the spinning, flashing form of Myla.

An explosion filled the world and Starzok, like a leaf in a fire, whirled up, helpless, crystal in hand, into the immensity of the Unbeing Bird. From below, the purple haze rushed up after him. There was a flash; the evil creature was gone, and icy, silent brightness reigned again on the ridge before the Kolkon Vera Kion.

It was over. But not quite.

Blazing light filled the First Minister's apartments; in the winds, the tattered curtains had torn away. Bean moaned, rising up, looking round

343

anxiously. In the chaos, wild images had filled his mind, images of white, dazzling mountains and a terrible bird-creature descending, as if for the kill, upon a hapless party of climbers.

But not any climbers. He had known who they were.

'Raj,' he breathed, 'Raj … are you all right?'

But it was Polty that Bean floundered towards.

By the column, the King clung to his bride, as he had clung to her all through the wild, terrible magic. For a time she had struggled; now she slumped down.

Umbecca emerged, keening, the severed leg forgotten.

And now came Burgrove moving amongst them, drawing them to him with mysterious, silent force. He raised a hand and the Queen's bonds fell away; she staggered into a circle with her four hapless companions. Far above them, invisible in the brightness, the anti-god still revolved. But now, circling his head, were three crystals, not two.

'What's … what's happening?' Bean moaned.

'With each crystal, my power has grown,' came a voice, not quite in answer, from behind Burgrove's mask. *'With the first, I could see my enemies as if they stood before me; with the second, I could see into their very minds. Now, with three crystals, the power has tilted towards me; to take the fourth, tomorrow, will be child's play. My victory is certain. And you, my friends, shall be the agents of my victory, the five believers who go forth to claim my greatest prize. Come, believers, come.'*

With that, Burgrove raised his mask again and his face, in that moment, was the face of the First Minister. Crystal-light flashed redly from his eyes as he gazed upon his prisoners, one by one. Now he stood aside and there before them, filling their eyes, was the vision – but it was more than a vision – of a vast golden drawbridge, descending towards them in a landscape of ice. Light shimmered around them.

They stepped forward, entranced.

It was at that moment that a ragged party of five – Jem, Cata, Rajal, Tishy and Littler – scrambled over the last rise before the lamasery. Exhausted, wanting only to slump down, senseless, they were just in time to see the great golden drawbridge descend majestically over the moat of ice, welcoming the supplicants who suddenly appeared, shimmering by magic out of the cold brightness. There they were, the fortunate five, resplendent in their courtly costumes, ready to be received.

Polty. Bean. Umbecca. Jeli. Ejard Blue.

They crossed the drawbridge and it closed behind them.

END OF PART FOUR

PART FIVE

Revelation of the Orokon

Chapter 56

LITTLE STAR

Reader, we have arrived at the final stage of our journey. We have travelled together for a long time, and soon must part; this may be our last chance to say goodbye. What we have shared has been a species of dream, a billowing illusion and no more. Yet dreams are neither trivial nor false. We imagine, beyond the fancies of our minds, a world solid and implacable as a stone that we might kick; this, too, is illusion. Our dreams are shimmering curtains, caught on the breeze: but so is life.

After the deceptive languor of its beginnings, life begins to hasten, and the knowledge comes to us that soon we will be dead. When I was a child, my death was like the little star that children wish on when the night draws in; time lay before me like an infinite land that one day, at my leisure, I would conquer and explore. Now I find myself upon a shrunken island, where the tide laps hungrily at receding sands. To be born, a man once said, is to be wrecked upon an island; we come to death like shipwrecked sailors too, realising only then that the world we thought so wide was really this little circle all the while.

So short a time ago I was beginning everything. Pride was strong in me; I was young; I stood upon a hill and thought the world was all before me. In my turn, as everyone must do, I imagined that time, which stops for no one, would stop for me, letting me linger in eternal moments. But time is not so kind; soon we see that life only bears us backwards, in a long going-away from all that we have been. We delude ourselves with dreams of power, but have no power when all that we love can be swept from us so easily. Oftentimes we laugh at death, but death will not be allayed. My death has become a spreading tree, shading me darkly whichever way I turn.

As death closes in, inevitably there is panic at the thought of all we have not done: so little wisdom gained; so much love ungiven; our best things squandered or left in disarray. The world, it has been said, is a comedy to those that think, a tragedy to those that feel; the source of the comedy and the tragedy is the same. Life is wanting, a relentless wanting. If, at the end, our desires burn away, perhaps for the first time we will see with clear eyes, looking back bewildered on all our pride, all our presumption, all our paths of glory that have led but to the grave. We are dust in a shaft of sunlight, floating down and down; the sun catches us, and makes a little star: and this is life.

The scrim billows, restlessly stirring. I will soon be dead and so will you. We must be careful of each other, and kind. When I am dead, perhaps you will think of me, and remember that once I was alive like you.

✳   ✳   ✳   ✳   ✳

For a time, her vision was hazy.

When it cleared, she found herself in a small, clean chamber of the utmost simplicity, the sort which might have belonged to a respectable servant. Only the incense that wafted in the air and a string of coloured beads in the window, sparkling in the cold light, hinted that it might be somewhere more exotic.

How she had got here, Constansia Cham-Charing could neither know nor guess. If she was not frightened, it must have been because of the soothing voices she had heard, many times before her vision came back; then, too, there was the knowledge that Pug was with her, nestling warmly in the bed beside her. The little dog was very much cleaner and sweeter-smelling than he had been before.

Slowly, Constansia became aware of the three extraordinary figures who loomed over her bed. These, she knew at once, were the owners of the voices. All were elderly, just like her, and all were very kind. Two were gentlemen, and one a lady. But what strange gentlemen! And what a strange lady!

Not until some time had passed would Constansia realise that the gentlemen were known to her. Of course, in the old days she had never seen them without their accustomed theatrical attire. One, who called himself Harlequin, had always worn a mask; the other, known as Clown, had painted his face white. How fondly she recalled their splendid performances in the glory days of Cham-Charing House!

For a long time they sat with her, reminiscing.

As for the lady, Constansia had never seen her before, but knew her at once to be a distinguished personage. Long after Harlequin and Clown had left her, the lady remained, speaking little, but several times offering her a curious sweet potion, urging her to drink. Dimly, Constansia supposed that this was a drug, but whatever drug it was, it was no rebel poison. This was something good, something healing.

On her head, the lady wore a curious arrangement of cloth, inset with a flashing stone. Constansia became fascinated with this stone, and gazed and gazed upon it. If she thought that the lady, like Harlequin and Clown, was a Vaga, it perturbed her less than it no doubt should have done; if she was aware that none of them addressed her by her title, she did not care.

This little room, Constansia sensed, was a special place, severed from the world outside; these friends who had saved her were special people.

Or, perhaps, more than people.

'Are you gods?' she asked at last.

348

'Not gods,' smiled the old lady, 'but those who help gods on their way. After all, the gods are much in need of help, when the forces of the anti-god are ranged so strongly.'

'Anti-god?'

Still Constansia was puzzled, but the old lady did not explain further. Instead, she spoke fondly of her great-children, and how much she would like to see them again before she died – a prospect which did not otherwise seem to alarm her much.

'My powers are weak now, my time nearing its end: but ah, how I long for my Rajal and my Myla! As you, my friend, long for your own dear great-child.'

Constansia blinked. 'Great-child? No, there is some mistake. I have a *child*. A daughter.'

'My friend, I fear that is hardly possible. Hush, there can be no pretences with me. I know what you have done and I know what you will do. You are a foolish, errant woman, but not a bad one in your heart. I forgive you, as your great-child must forgive you – and as you must forgive your great-child. And your daughter.'

'Forgive? I don't understand.'

'My friend, I hardly expected that you would. But trouble yourself not; you have suffered much, but your sufferings will not last. Mysterious and winding are the ways of fate, but much that you have lost will be restored to you. Including, I suspect, your missing great-child.'

'Tishy?' Abruptly, Constansia sat up in bed. 'Tishy's coming back? But how can you know? How can you be certain? And … and who are you?'

Snowlight danced on the beads in the window. A hand reached for Constansia's hand; a hand very much more gnarled than her own.

'There are those who call me the Great Mother. There are those who call me Xal. Yet what am I, really, but an old woman like you – sheltering, like you, in a time of storm? Let us be glad that we have found each other, and the hospitality of Harlequin and Clown. Without doubt, our acquaintance will be brief; when the storm has passed, we shall return you to your friends. In the years that remain to you, perhaps you will think of us from time to time, as one might think of an unsettling, but not unpleasant dream.'

'What … what do you mean?' Later, Constansia could never have explained the extraordinary sensation these words induced in her; she would know only that she had been moved, moved almost more deeply than she could bear.

Tears slid down her wrinkled face and she drew the warm Pug closer beside her.

'Great Mother—' she began.

But what she had meant to say, Constansia had forgotten already. Instead she said, 'Your great-children … what did you say their names were?'

'The boy is Rajal. The girl is Myla.'

'They are strange names,' said Constansia.

The Great Mother only smiled again, sadly this time, and kissed Constansia's cheek.

❊　❊　❊　❊　❊

Jem's eyes were the narrowest of slits. His face burned with cold. Through the snow, he saw only a golden haze, shimmering across the moat of ice. Could it be that the lamasery was vanishing, fading already out of Being now that the drawbridge had opened and closed, receiving the five?

Despair filled him. Again his hands, numbed and fumbling, tore at the crystal beneath his furs. Shivering, he sank to his knees. *No, it cannot be. No, it cannot be.* While one crystal was free, how could Toth have triumphed?

For now, Jem's crystal was cold, impassive. He cursed, moaned. How brightly the crystal had blazed before! Why would it not sear like fire, bringing down the lamasery walls, destroying Polty and his accomplices in a surge of mystic power?

Jem heard a footfall. There was a puff of powdery snow and a glove reached down, clutching his arm.

He held up the crystal. 'It's dead – *dead*, Cata.'

'Jem, it's not the time. You know that, don't you? Come back to the cave. You've got to help me cheer up Littler. He's so upset about the loss of Ejard Orange – not to mention Myla. As for Raj—'

Half reluctant, Jem rose again, letting Cata lead him across the snowy bluff. They had found shelter in a rocky outcrop, sufficient to protect them from the wind and snow, but barely from the cold. There was no way to make a fire and already darkness was falling.

'What are we waiting for?' Jem murmured. 'What's the point? Why this vigil?'

'Would you turn and go?' Cata squeezed his arm. 'Jem, something's got to happen. This is Toth's trick, but how can it work? They'll know that Polty's not – and Aunt Umbecca, and … They'll *know*, won't they?'

'Cata, who will know?'

'Why, the Bearers of the Vexing Gem.'

'Yes, but who are they? Who *are* they, really?'

Cata fell silent. Miserably they huddled in the curtain of rock that it was, no doubt, generous to describe as a cave. Littler looked down, shivering, and Jem hugged him close. He tried to smile at Rajal, but could not quite manage it.

'They're … just what they always were,' said Tishy, after a moment.

Jem turned to her. 'What?'

'The Bearers. All through The Atonement, they've been the same. Worshipping. Waiting. And now they'll think their time has come.'

Cata was doubtful. 'How do you know this?'

'There was more in that book than I read out. A lot more.'

Jem urged, 'Like what? What do you know?'

'That the Bearers are Tethered, not Transcendent—'

'Very helpful, I'm sure,' Cata said sharply.

'Cata, *shh*—' said Jem.

'That the twin peaks of the Mountain of Truth are known, and must be known, as Confrontation and Contemplation—'

Cata could not resist. 'Oh? And which is which?'

Tishy only went on, 'And I know that the Bearers, like the mountain, are divided. And that their god is divided, too.'

'Agonis?' Jem blinked. 'Divided, how?'

'She's raving, Jem,' said Cata. 'Her eyes are glazed, she's blue with cold ... Tishy, snap out of it! Think of the day when you'll be back amongst your books. Your books, Tishy! Your library! Think of it, and believe it.'

Littler said, 'What about ... Ejard Orange?'

'The cat?' said Rajal. 'What about ... Bean?'

'*Bean?*' Cata was incredulous. 'Raj, I thought you were going to say *Myla*—'

Littler murmured, 'So ... so did I.'

Troubled, Cata studied the faces of her companions. She would have spoken again, but her words froze. The wind howled round the curtain of rock. Darkness fell, and the little party felt an ominous numbness creeping across their limbs. Was there nothing they could do? Cata imagined skidding over the icy moat, storming the walls of the lamasery with sudden, impossible power.

No. Absurd. She shivered, thinking of her lost crystal, thinking of the shadow of the Unbeing Bird.

Time passed. Silence thickened between the five travellers, until light crept mysteriously into the stormswept dark. There was a glow of purple, then a glow of gold, playing about the lamasery; there were swirling, ghostly patterns, and then there was music, twining around the howling wind.

And Jem and his friends were held in stasis, unfrozen, but unmoving too. Perhaps it was the backwash of Toth's magic, lingering mockingly; but perhaps it was another magic, readying itself to claim them.

It was Cata who heard the call, when the call came. In a reverie she stumbled to her feet, moving towards a moving light; in a blaze of gold, the light enfolded her, then retreated, shrinking across the moat of ice into the walls of the lamasery.

Time passed; then it was Jem who stirred to consciousness, registering with strange calmness that Cata had gone. He rose, moving forward into the churning air, into the music of the wind and snow and the other, eerie music beneath it. Turning back to his companions, he saw them only as cold statues, glazed in ice. He clutched the crystal and this time it glowed; he looked towards the lamasery, illuminated in the enchanted lights.

A voice came from behind him. 'Jem, this trial will be over soon.'

The harlequin? Could it be?

This time, Jem did not turn. As if at the lifting of a veil it was morning, and Jem saw Cata coming towards him, gliding ethereally over the ice and snow. Beside her, gliding too, was a tall, cowled figure, dressed in trailing robes of gold.

Only now was Jem astonished. Behind him, he knew his friends had gathered, the ice cracked and slipping from their frozen faces.

Rajal. Littler. Tishy.

But Jem could not turn; he could gaze only at Cata. *Transfigured. But how?*

She smiled, pressing close against the golden stranger. And Jem thought that this stranger, whose face he could not see, was no stranger at all.

'Jem,' said Cata, 'it's all right. Really, it's all right.'

The stranger raised a golden arm.

When Jem awoke, he found himself in the lamasery.

Chapter 57

PATHS OF GLORY

The Siege of Agondon, which ended the reign of Ejard Blue, did not last for long; compared with the Siege of Irion, which had put the Blue King on the throne, it was the mere flickering of an eye. But time in war is not the same as ordinary time. For those who took part in the Siege of Agondon it was too long by far, and the suffering it left in its wake would last for many a year.

By the Meditation of Koros, rebel attacks on Bluejacket posts had become too frequent to be put down, like brushfires bursting again and again from the undergrowth. Compared with the mighty army that opposed them, the rebels were ragged and ill-disciplined; they were also entirely ruthless, unfettered by the lumbering chain of command that hobbled their enemies, from the War Lords in their plush chambers to the raw recruits in slushy streets and fields, ill-fed, frightened, and no longer sure what they were fighting to preserve. Trained for marching, stiff manoeuvres and the unthinking following of orders, the Blues hardly knew what to make of their ragged enemies with their sudden dartings and flurryings and wild, opportunistic raids. Stealth and surprise were the Redjacket way; in years to come, with a new King on the throne, the armies of Ejland would learn much from the events of those bleak, desperate days.

By the Meditation of Viana, conflagration loomed. Orders flowed from the War Lords, but nothing could allay the fervour that had swept the city with the news that the rightful King had come back at last to seize his crown. The failed execution of the Great Temple Bomber only added fuel to the fire. To simple folk, the lightning that consumed the Erdon Tree was a sign of divine displeasure with the Bluejacket régime. The Bluejackets were put to rout. Many a deserter crossed enemy lines, eagerly wrapping a red cloth round his forehead; one after another, posts were abandoned; all through the outlying precincts, patrols were forced from the streets. By now, escapees from Xorgos Island swelled the rebel numbers, exciting the people with stories of their own extraordinary deliverance.

The next day would be decisive.

At dawn on the Meditation of Theron, the Agondon Hills were entirely in Redjacket hands. By midday, rebels controlled the docks, and all the land routes into the city. That afternoon, breaking through the barricades along the Bolbarr Road, an intrepid band under the command of Danny

353

Garvice overran the merchant precincts of Ollon Fields, staining red the ground where Lady Cham-Charing and the friends of her youth had run and laughed with their butterfly nets, so many years before. As night fell, the 'Thieves' Armies' of 'Scars' Majesta and Shammy the Hood sacked Ollon Barracks.

And that, as many said, was when it was all over. That night, a ragged red army under the man once known as Bob Scarlet marched in triumph through the plush streets and squares of Agondon New Town. The Island was the last remaining Bluejacket stronghold. Parleys went back and forth. The War Lords refused to yield. And all the time the First Minister, locked in his hot, ruinous chamber, offered them neither advice nor help.

The great battle would take place on the morrow.

'Are you proud, Morvy? Blenkinsop's proud.'

'Crum, you haven't brought that rat with you?'

'Of course not! No, I gave him to Raggle and Taggle to look after. Good old Blenkinsop's down at Corvey Cottage, all warm and cosy by the fire.'

'Or whizzing round by the tail.'

'You're muttering, Morvy. What's that?'

'Nothing, Crum. I said that was *kind* of you.'

'Well, I suppose I'm a bit old for him. I mean, he's rather a *small* pet, isn't he?' Crum fell silent, considering. 'Did I ever tell you about the time when Zohnny Ryle gave away Blenkinsop to Cousin Binty?'

'This is *his* Blenkinsop?'

'Of course, Morvy! Really, you can be ignorant. And not only about rats. But Blenkinsop's proud of you all the same,' Crum added kindly.

'Proud for what, Crum?'

'For being here. For fighting, Morvy.'

Morven gulped. Fortunately, they were not fighting yet. It was night on the Meditation of Theron. With red cloth tied round the arms of their bearskins, the two young recruits were on sentry-duty, standing outside a house in Davalon Street, Agondon New Town, with golden scrolls above the windows and doors. Commandeered for the Redjacket invaders, the house was the headquarters of the man who called himself His Imperial Agonist Majesty, King Ejard Redjacket. Within, the King and his generals plotted the strategies of the morrow; without, braziers burned, bright against the snow; drunken rebels reeled down the street and harlots clustered expectantly. Drums thudded somewhere, perhaps across the river.

Crum said, 'We're going to win, aren't we, Morvy?'

'Our side? Well, we're going to attack. In the morning.'

'Morvy? Remember the Battle of Wrax?'

Morven did. The two friends had spent it in the Wrax Infirmary, after an unfortunate accident the night before. On the one occasion when they

354

had meant to be in battle, they had instead experienced lumpy beds, shrewish nurses and awful food. It was a fair trade.

Crum said, 'Morvy? We're not going to get out of it this time, are we?'

Morven would have liked to speak in elevated tones of heroism, justice and the struggle for freedom. Instead he said hoarsely, 'No, Crum, we're not.'

'You'll keep your head down, won't you, Morvy?'

'I'll do my best, Crum. And you will too?'

At that moment there was a curious altercation just below the steps of the House of Golden Scrolls. Unregarded, a cart had been rumbling down the street; now a familiar female figure leapt down from the cart, accompanied by an anxious fellow, struggling to restrain her. Leering soldiers converged upon the lady, but her harsh tongue scattered them at once.

Morven and Crum goggled. It was Nirry.

Enraged, she flung herself up the steps of Ejard Red's headquarters.

'Where is he? Where is the traitor?'

'Goody Olch, please—' Her male companion fluttered behind her. It was the Friar, unfamiliar in a thick coat, his tonsure concealed beneath a furry hat.

'Let me see him—' Nirry blustered.

'She wants ... the King,' gasped the Friar.

'His ... Imperial Agonist Majesty?' said Morven.

'That's right, and you'll let me pass!' Nirry's eyes blazed.

'B-But Goody Olch, we thought you were safe at Corvey Cottage, with Baines, and Raggle and Taggle and—'

'And my *Wiggler*!' Nirry shrieked. 'Where is he? Ooh, I knew the silly man wasn't to be trusted! Was it you, his old cronies, who told him to fight? You egged him on, didn't you, I'll bet you did!'

'Fight? Goody Olch, I don't—'

'Wiggler, fight? But Wiggler's not—'

'Not even in the army, that's right! But he's gone and joined them rebels, hasn't he? Joined them rebels, after I spent my hard-earned savings to buy him out of the Blues! That wretched King of yours promised me, and now—'

'G-Goody Olch, please—'

'Out of my way—'

With that, Nirry pushed Crum aside, stamped on Morven's foot and blundered through the door.

The Friar leaned, exhausted, in the elaborate portico, while the whimpering sentries nursed the wounds which, if damaging, were not quite damaging enough to keep them out of the morrow's fighting.

'Dear me,' gasped the Friar, 'I tried to stop her. Instead, she forced me to drive her into the city ... She says, *What manner of man are you? Are you going to let a defenceless woman go off alone, on the night before a battle?*

Defenceless woman, indeed! Oh, it's far too much excitement for an inno-cent man of god ... I say, you fellows, you don't know where a poor friar might find a bite to *eat*, do you?'

Meanwhile, the formidable mistress of the Cat & Crown, defying sentry after sentry, had burst her way into the elaborate drawing room where Ejard Red paced before his rebel chiefs. Shammy the Hood was there, and 'Scars' Majesta; there was Offero the Mole, Peter Impalini and Molly the Cut; there was Folio Webster, Roly Rextel, Onty Michan, Danny Garvice and Magda Vytoni; not to mention Hul, Bando and Landa.

The King had been speaking of the destiny that was at hand, the glory of the battle to come, the victory that was certain; magnificently, the fine phrases flowed from his lips, when suddenly they were quelled by the irruption of Nirry.

All were astonished at what happened next.

Charging to the King, Nirry beat at him with her fists. 'Traitor, rotten traitor! Look at you, puffed up with pride like a great big puffer-toad! I let you use my tavern, and this is the reward I get! You promised my Wiggler wouldn't have to fight! Give you the Cat & Crown, you said, and Wiggler would be safe! Now he's run off with your rebels, and your rebels have taken him! Where is he? Give him back to me, give him back to me! Rotten, lying rebel scum—'

It was Landa, in the end, who managed to restrain Nirry, embracing the distraught tavern-mistress as she collapsed, at last, into helpless tears. With a glance for Hul and Bando, Landa indicated that she would make sure that Nirry was all right. Coarse, belated laughter rang behind the two women as they made their way from the meeting.

Out in the hall, they sat on the stairs. Tenderly, Landa rocked Nirry in her arms, explaining that the King knew nothing of Wiggler's where-abouts; the rebel forces, after all, consisted by now of thousands upon thousands of men. Wiggler could be anywhere. It was not the King's fault.

But Landa felt hollow as she mouthed the words.

'He said my Wiggler would be safe. He promised me.'

'Nirry, I'll ... we'll do all we can to try and find him, I promise. As soon as the battle's over.'

But Nirry had ceased to listen. She wiped her eyes roughly. 'Look at the mess they've made of this lovely house! Snow and slush tramped every-where, ornaments broken, pictures all crooked, filthy black handprints on the walls – everything that was nice all dirty and spoiled. That's men for you, Miss Landa, that's what men do!'

Rallying, Nirry sprang up. 'Ooh, how can I have spent even a moment away from the Cat & Crown, at a time like this? I've got to get back there, I've got to! Miss Landa, if you think I'll let these wretched men ruin my tavern, you've got another think coming, let me tell you—'

Landa gasped. 'But Nirry, you're overwrought. Remember, we're in Agondon New Town ... the tavern's on the Island, behind enemy lines. Oh, you can't ... Come, Nirry, Wiggler's Wiggler, but a tavern's just a—'

Nirry reeled as if she had been struck. 'Just a tavern! I've put my life's savings into that place! Do you think I'm going back into service because a lot of useless rebels have smashed up all my hard work? I'm getting over there. Blues or no Blues, Reds or no Reds, I've got something of my own to defend, and I'll defend it come what may. Ooh, I know it won't be easy, but you're magic, aren't you, Miss Landa? Are you with me?'

Landa's mouth hung open. But before she could answer there was another voice, behind her.

'Don't worry, Goody Olch, *I'm* with you.'

Nirry turned sharply. 'Baines! But I told you—'

And not only Baines was there, but Raggle and Taggle, one little boy leapfrogging over the other.

'Biddy-biddy-bobble!'

'Diddy-on-the-double!'

'I'm sorry, Goody Olch,' Baines explained, 'but I couldn't let you go off alone, could I? Did you think I could wait while you were in danger? And as for keeping *these* two back—'

Puffing, the Friar lurched behind them. 'We're off to the tavern? Oh, I say—'

Landa could only laugh.

So it was that, later that night, she led an intrepid little party over the ice. Scaling the Embankment was hard, especially for the fat little Friar, not to mention the ladylike Baines; still, Landa had just enough magic remaining from her last call on the goddess to make sure that all of them made it back safely to the Cat & Crown.

Chapter 58

THE OTHER SIDE OF THE HEDGE

'C-Cata? Where's Cata? Where are my friends?'

First Jem was aware of a spreading warmth, then a pungent incense hovering in the air. At another time, he might have started awake; this time he only raised his head slowly, finding himself in a small stone chamber, lying on a narrow cot.

There was no other furniture, no decoration. Pale light seeped through a grilled door and, crouched at the end of the cot, was a golden-garbed acolyte, eyes down, massaging Jem's feet with a thick, smooth unguent. Troubled, Jem squinted at the youth; the youth looked up, aware of the scrutiny.

Now Jem might have started. Unlike the tall, stooped figure from the night before, the youth wore no cowl, and his flat, coppery face was familiar.

'Blayzil?' Jem breathed. 'But I saw you die … I—'

The youth showed no sign of understanding, but rose, gesturing towards the grilled door. Jem had thought himself a prisoner; if so, it seemed he was not to be confined to this cell.

He stood uncertainly, realising that he was dressed as the youth was dressed, in a loose robe, but a robe of black rather than gold; Jem also wore a sash from shoulder to hip, striped in the hues of the Orokon. He felt for his chest. Did he still have the crystal? But yes … yes. His feet touched the floor and he felt a soft burning, spreading up like sap from his moistened soles.

The youth opened the door. Following him, Jem found himself in a long stone corridor. Down one side ran a series of further doors, identical to the one from which they had emerged; on the other, light spilled in lemony stripes through high slit windows. Dimly Jem had wondered how he could be so warm, when the world outside these walls was a desert of ice and snow. The unguent, no doubt, had something to do with it; but now, passing through the stripes of sunlight, Jem knew the warmth had a second source. Curiosity filled him as they reached the end of the corridor and the youth led him out into a brighter light.

Jem closed his eyes; when he opened them, he gazed upon a green valley. Dazzled, he took in exotic boughs, draping leaves and bright flowers; luxurious arbours, grottoes, fragrant walks. Perfumes wafted on the air and the sun spilt down; only the distant whistle of winds and the pallid peaks of mountains hinted at the cold beyond this strange, enchanted domain.

'But how ... what is this place?' Jem turned to his companion, but the youth had gone.

He turned again. There was silence; even the wind had fallen into abeyance. A butterfly fluttered through the fragrant air, almost colliding with Jem's eyes. He blinked it away; then, as if a force urged him on, he found himself descending a set of mossy steps, making his way into the depths of the gardens. Warm, winding pathways extended before him.

Marvelling, Jem passed between lush, heady burgeonings of tropical trees and flowers. Sometimes he would reach out, clutching this or that leaf or petal or stalk; perhaps he was trying to prove that it was real.

Still the sun caressed him, insisting its way through dappling leaves. There were birds; there were butterflies now in abundance.

But where were his friends? Where was Cata?

He had entered a maze.

Time distended strangely as Jem made his way between curving, high hedges. The thought disturbed him; the maze went on and on, until finding his way back became a difficult prospect. But why should he want to find his way back? Again he reached for his crystal, wondering if it would glow; touching it, he became aware of something stirring, just behind him.

'Blayzil? I mean—'

It was not the youth. There was a swish, a hiss, and Jem saw a marmalade tail disappearing into the foliage. Ejard Orange? But he had vanished out in the snows with Blayzil, with Myla! Calling out, Jem blundered after the big cat, pushing his way through a fecund hedge. Shadows flickered thickly and dark pungencies of rotting leaves welled up as if to assail him. In a moment, Jem was trapped in a mesh of branches and leaves.

It was then that he heard a struggle on the other side of the hedge – a struggle, and voices too. He dashed leaves from his eyes, trying to make out the owners of the voices.

But there was no doubt.

'Bitch! I told you, I'll never let you go—'

'You're mad! I'll never marry you, not if you—'

'Cata, I love you! Don't you understand, I'll always—'

There were slappings, cries; then Jem cried out too, feeling the blue crystal searing his chest. He gasped, straining against the branches and leaves. Through the green mesh he saw a carroty head, like fire in the sun, then a swinging hank of longer, darker hair. He glimpsed Cata's face,

Polty's too, then a blur of black, then white; Cata and Polty were dressed as Jem was dressed, complete with rainbow sashes.

But while Cata's robes were black, Polty's were white.

Jem called to Cata; he wrenched himself free, bursting blackly through the other side of the hedge.

'The Vexing!' cried Polty.

Cata covered her mouth. 'Jem, are you real?'

Jem staggered. There was a flapping at his shoulder where he had torn his robes; his crystal was exposed, blue rays dancing. But where could he be? The place looked like a bower, an arbour, surrounded by roses. The scent was overwhelming, and so was Cata. He flung open his arms for her, but Polty dashed her aside. The amethyst ring on his finger flashed.

'Leave him to me, bitch!'

Polty's fist swung. Jem ducked. He staggered back; he rallied, charging forward, but Cata was ahead of him, seizing a stone from the ground, hurling it at Polty's head.

Now Polty ducked, staggered; but he rallied too. He lunged, clutching Jem's crystal.

Jem gasped, choking.

Again Cata intervened; Polty slammed her aside. She lay in a heap; then Jem was on the ground, Polty pinning him down, desperate to tear away the searing crystal. Jem battered at the fumbling hands.

'Fool, Vexing! Do you think you'll triumph? Do you think you'll have the crystal? Do you think you'll have *her*?' Polty's fist swung back, ready to strike. 'I'm the winner, and I'm winning now!'

His words were rash. Cata lurched up and hurled herself at Polty. They rolled together, kicking, clawing.

Someone said, 'Well, *really*—'

The voice was high, braying. And familiar.

It was Jem who looked up first. Looming over the bedraggled trio was a figure dressed, like Polty, in robes of white, but so capacious that they might, in their glaring pallor, have rivalled the sun. Astonishment filled Jem.

'Aunt Umbecca! Are you ... real?'

Umbecca sniffed. 'You might with more pertinence ask that of yourself, Jemany, since I know that *you* should have been killed in a storm with Goodman Waxwell, quite some time ago.'

'Should have been?' Jem breathed. 'Waxwell ... he was going to cut my legs off. You didn't want that, did you, Aunt? You *said* you didn't. You cried out as they dragged me away, I heard you.'

The fat woman adjusted her rainbow sash. 'In those days, Jemany, there was much that I did not understand. My dear Torso taught me a great deal; lately, Toth has taught me more. How was I, an innocent and virtuous woman, to understand the depths of your evil? Yes, evil I say, for how else could you have escaped your inevitable fate without evil magic?'

'There's good magic too, Aunt.'

'Of that I have no doubt, for what else has brought me here? But Jem – oh Jem, how did you come to this? Think of the sweet life that could have been yours, had you but accepted the wisdom of Goodman Waxwell! Think how we might have laughed together as I pushed you in your bath-chair through these fragrant gardens! Why, I would have ruffled your hair, Jem, and fed you sweetmeats. Instead, you wallow in a sty of corruption, and assuredly soon must meet your death. And yet I see you are grovelling on the ground: might I hope that you have, just in time, become a cripple again? Then, only then, might there be hope for you.'

Defiantly, Jem scrambled to his feet. Cata and Polty, their struggles in abeyance, sat sheepishly on the ground, cowed before the formidable woman; Jem, almost roughly, grabbed Cata's hand, pulling her up to stand beside him.

'I thought she'd be surprised to see *you*,' he murmured.

'I've seen her already in these gardens,' said Cata. 'I was trying to get away from *her* when I ran into Polty. Rest assured, she's said everything – my betrayal, my ingratitude, my certain damnation. What do I care? Leave her to Jeli. That's who she deserves.'

'Mumbling are we, Catayane?' Umbecca glared. 'Didn't anyone tell you that was ill-bred?'

'Yes, Aunt – you did. Time and again.'

'Hmph!' The fat woman turned away, disgusted. 'To think, that I believed you could be made into a lady – *you*, the spawn of a Vaga and a whore!'

'She … she *is* a lady,' Polty blustered. 'Heart-mother, you forget yourself. You're speaking of the woman who … who will be my wife!'

Polty would have moved, clumsily, to embrace Cata, but Cata glared at him.

Aunt Umbecca rolled her eyes. 'Come, should we not join the others? Might we not conduct ourselves in a civilised manner while we wait for the inevitable End of Atonement? It's soon now, children – and soon all these paltry concerns shall be as mere chaff.'

'Others?' said Jem. 'They're all here?'

He was soon to know the answer; but first, Cata murmured again beneath her breath.

'What did you say, child?' Umbecca boomed.

'I said,' Cata returned bitterly, 'that you don't know what you're saying. Aunt, I know we hate each other, but you're right about one thing – that it doesn't matter now. What matters is Jem's quest. What matters is defeating Toth. Can't you see the anti-god's controlling you? Can't you see he's a puppet master, mouthing the very words that spill from your lips?'

In sudden ardour, Cata seized Umbecca's arm; the fat woman flung her off, outraged.

'Aunt, won't you just listen?' Cata pursued.

'Preposterous girl!' Umbecca, billowing like a wind-plumped sail, forged her way imperiously out of the bower; Jem, Cata and Polty, like dutiful children, followed.

'Cata, leave it,' Jem muttered. 'There was good in her once, but that was long ago. She's nothing now but a great, fat, suppurating mound of evil.'

'I heard that,' Polty leered. 'I'll tell her.'

Again, with jealous cunning, he eyed Jem's crystal; Jem drew his torn garment back around his shoulders, anchoring it with the rainbow sash. He wondered what restrained Polty, what held him back from another assault. Was it only Umbecca? And why was Jem in black, and why was Cata, when Polty and Umbecca – of all people – wore white?

Jem knew he was involved in a terrible game; exactly what that game was, he did not yet understand.

Chapter 59

SPINNING IN COFFINS

'The others,' Jem murmured.

Round the corners of the bower was a sunny glade, a pleasant place of butterflies, bees and many-coloured birds. Somewhere a brook burbled; then there was laughter, ringing from the branches of a broad-boughed yew. Peering into the branches, Jem saw a familiar, squatting figure – in white robes, of course, and rainbow sash – clutching a glittering amphora that he put to his lips, swigging lustily. Cata, Polty, even Umbecca appeared to take the sight for granted; Jem could not help feeling both astonishment and alarm.

The figure laughed again, then gave forth a snatch of spluttering song, waving a hand like a conductor. The hand, Jem noticed, was missing a finger.

He had to ask, 'What *is* the King doing?'

'Serenading the morning,' said Cata. 'What else?'

Umbecca sailed on, swishing through the grasses; her destination was an immense chequered picnic-cloth, laden generously with dishes. The dishes flashed, almost pulsed in the sun; Jem saw the flashing of the brook too. But now he was distracted by another voice, then another, issuing from a fragrant, flowery glade.

'*The ways of fate,*' said the first voice, '*are mysterious, and it is not for us, mere pawns in its unknowable hands (as we are and must* inevitably *be!) to question its intricate and inexplicable designs. But even though only the torments of Unbeing can punish the base deceiver Porlond—*'

'A little slower, Cham-Charing. Really, you are barely articulate!'

'I-I'm sorry, Your Majesty. Shall I begin again?'

'No, go on. But who did Becca marry? I *am* confused.'

The Queen, in white, lay on her back in the grass, a stalk between her teeth, a foot crossed jauntily over her upraised knee. It was hardly the posture of a lady; but then, her status was confirmed by the harried, black-garbed figure she had succeeded in co-opting as her servant.

'B-Becca's not *in* this one,' Tishy ventured, holding up the small, leather-bound book. 'This is *A Beauty of the Valleys* – the last of the "Miss R—" novels.'

'No wonder. How dull can a book be? Dull, dull! Wasn't there anything better in that library? Oh, if only we had *The Horror from Unbeing* – or *Mysteries of the Haunted Abbey*!'

'Those are not … *improving* books, Your Majesty.'

'You want me to be improved, Cham-Charing?' Jeli laughed, rolling in the grass. 'Silly girl, I want to be excited … excited!'

'Jeli hasn't changed,' Cata said darkly.

'Poor Tishy! Can't she escape?' Jem was tempted to assist the escape, not least of all by advancing towards Her Royal Majesty and giving her a swift kick. He restrained himself. 'But what's this?'

Deeper into the glade, close to the brook, they had come upon sounds of a struggle. Umbecca, oblivious, made for the picnic-cloth; Polty looked on with sudden alarm. 'The fool, what's he playing at?'

It was Bean – and yes, in white – rolling and tumbling in the reeds by the brook. Could he be … *wrestling*? Moments passed before Jem realised that Bean's opponent – in robes of black – was Rajal, or that Rajal, all the while, was half-shouting, half-muttering, telling Bean to break free, break free.

Polty's face turned crimson. Floundering through the grass towards his side-officer, he looked, perhaps for the first time, like a proper military man.

'Stop that!' he bellowed. 'Stop that at once!'

Mallard ducks floated on the brook.

Jem turned to Cata, smiling uncertainly. Some distance away, their fat aunt had plumped herself down on the chequered cloth, gorging herself on an enormous pie. 'This *does* have to be an illusion, doesn't it?' he said. 'A sort of dream?'

'You're so sure?' said Cata. 'I'm wide awake.'

'But what are they playing at, these Bearers? And … well, where *are* they?'

The question would soon be answered. But first Jem turned again, delighted, as a small figure in fluttering black came running towards him.

'Littler!' He swept the boy into his arms.

'Hey! Put me down, put me down!'

'Not till you tell me *you're* real, at least!'

'Of course I'm real. What do you think I am?'

'But Littler, where's Ejard Orange? I've seen him twice this morning. He ran away from me, but I don't think he'd run from *you* – would he?'

Littler's face fell. 'Ejjy? He's not here. How … how could he be?'

'He's dead, Jem,' Cata said gently.

'Like … Myla,' said Littler.

'Myla?' Memories of yesterday played in Jem's mind. How distant it all seemed now!

Cata said, 'Here, let me take Littler.'

'No one needs to *take* me,' Littler protested, and would have leapt to the ground, but Cata was insistent and the little boy, with a sigh half of resignation, half of pleasure, let himself rest in Cata's arms. He even let her stroke his hair, but it lasted for only a moment.

Cata doubled over. Littler slipped to the ground.

'Cata?' said Jem. 'What is it, are you all right?'

'Of ... of course,' said Cata. 'A cramp, that's all.'

Littler looked up at her disbelievingly; Jem looked down. Irritably, Cata swept back her hair.

'You're very pale,' said Jem.

'Not as pale as you,' Cata snapped.

They would have said more, but Jem was aware of a stirring on the air, something that was not just a rustling of leaves, not just a gust of warm winds. He looked towards the trees, bordering the edges of the fragrant domain.

In a flash of gold, the Blayzil-youth returned; whether he had emerged from the foliage or materialised from the air, Jem could not be sure. In any case, the youth did not advance towards them, but only stood staring.

'What's he doing?' said Jem.

'I don't know, but there's another one,' said Littler.

'Another?' Turning, Jem saw, on the opposite side of the glade, that a second youth had appeared; this time, he was sure that the figure had simply emerged from the air, suddenly present, suddenly gold.

Then came another, then another. They were surrounded. Tishy, some-where behind them, gave an earnest cry; there was a confused bellowing from His Imperial Agonist Majesty, still up in his tree.

Only Umbecca appeared unconcerned; but then, she had stuffed her mouth with a huge drumstick.

In unison, the golden figures raised their arms; they crossed them at the wrists and there was a slow flash, consuming the glade.

When it subsided, Jem and his companions found themselves in a quite different scene.

❋　❋　❋　❋　❋

Jem clutched Cata's hand, Littler's too. They looked about them uncertainly. In a ragged group with the others, the black-garbed and the white, they clustered in the centre of an immense circular hall. Light streamed in streaks through a high glass dome. In serried ranks around the walls were golden figures, immeasurable in number, standing cowled and impassive.

Only the acolytes were bare of face; whether they were boys or girls was unclear, but all looked like Blayzil. They moved forward now, ten of them, one for each of the guests – or prisoners. Jem resisted, but only for a moment, as a Blayzil-youth detached him gently from his friends, guiding him to one of a series of slab-like tall boxes like vertical coffins that had slid up silently from the stone floor.

The box opened; unresisting, but he could not have said why, Jem stepped in. Wonderingly he saw his nine companions similarly placed; he saw Cata, still pale, stumbling a little, and the drumstick dropping from Umbecca's hand. Ejard Blue gibbered, looking around for his lost amphora; Rajal protested as they separated him from Bean, but all complied, and complied again as the acolytes held up golden goblets, inviting the prisoners – or guests – to drink.

The King was first, guzzling greedily. Jeli wrinkled her nose. Polty snorted. Incuriously, Jem looked into the cool, wine-like potation. He knew it was a drug; knew, too, that he must drink it. Music crept around the coffins, if coffins they were; it was a solemn, chant-like dirge. Then the coffins closed. And then they began to spin.

In what followed, Jem passed through an age of time. A wild fantasia filled his mind, visions of many-coloured swirling shapes, shifting and pulsing in an arabesque dance. Nothing was clear, nothing was real, only the sense of turning, turning, as the closed, coffin-like box revolved; and yet, as if from a world away, the music still came, the chanting and the dirge, resolving itself into words that Jem, in that aeon of strangeness, could barely understand.

This is what he heard.

> *Cleave to us and come to us,*
> *Agonis-in-the-Vast:*
> *Look on us with love for us,*
> *Agonis-in-the-Vast:*
> > *Vex us with the Vexing Gem,*
> > *Yield to us the crystal:*
> > *Vex us with the Vexing Gem,*
> > *Keep us from the crystal.*
> > > *Agonis-in-the-Vast*
> > > *Through Confrontation, come:*
> > > *Agonis-in-the-Vast*
> > > *Through Contemplation, come.*

> *Purify these postulants,*
> *Agonis-in-the-Vast:*
> *Wither them to worthiness,*
> *Agonis-in-the-Vast:*
> > *Vex us with the Vexing Gem,*
> > *Keep us from the crystal:*
> > *Vex us with the Vexing Gem,*
> > *Yield to us the crystal.*
> > > *Agonis-in-the-Vast,*
> > > *Through Confrontation, come:*
> > > *Agonis-in-the-Vast,*
> > > *Through Contemplation—*

It went on, passing through myriad variations, gathering up the cowled

366

figures into an ecstasy of worship, filling the circular chamber with a spiritual force so powerful that it might have consumed the world. Round and round went Jem's mind; round and round went the coffins; round and round went the litany to Agonis-in-the-Vast.

All that Jem knew, as the revolving ceased and he staggered from the coffin, was that never before had he felt so sick. He doubled over, lurching, but at once a Blayzil-youth was beside him, steadying him, urging him to look up, up. The coffins sank into the floor again; the acolytes melted away. Tremulous in a circle, the prisoners – for assuredly they were prisoners – faced their captors. Around them, the chamber had darkened; light came only from the golden robes, glinting and shifting in soft waves.

Then came a voice, but from which of the cowled figures it issued, neither Jem nor any of the others could be certain. Rather, it seemed to come from all, yet from none.

This was what the voice said:

'PEOPLE OF THE BELOW, WE HAVE GATHERED YOU INTO THIS PLACE; NEVER SHALL YOU LEAVE UNTIL A CHANGE HAS COME. THE CHALLENGES, THE DISCORDS BETWEEN YOU ARE OF NO MOMENT NOW. PROPHECY HAS TOLD OF FIVE; TEN NOW STAND BEFORE US, BUT ONLY FIVE OF YOU ARE THE LIBERATORS WE AWAIT. THE PARTY IN BLACK, THE PARTY IN WHITE, EITHER MAY BE THE ONES; EITHER MAY HARBOUR THE ONE WHO IS TO TAKE THE GOLDEN CRYSTAL. AGAIN, I SAY IT IS OF NO MOMENT; IT MATTERS ONLY THAT WE ESCAPE A THRALDOM OF AEONS. LIBERATION IS ALL, AND ASSUREDLY IT WILL COME. THE MORROW IS THE DAY KNOWN THROUGH ALL EJLAND AS THE MEDITATION OF AGONIS. ON THAT DAY, ALL SHALL BE DETERMINED. PEOPLE OF THE BELOW, THERE IS NO MORE TO SAY.'

'No *more*?' Jem murmured. A hundred questions struggled inside him. The Bearers of the Vexing Gem, he had believed, were the true servants of Agonis; did they not *care* who took the crystal? And how could there be doubt? Did ... did they mean that *Toth* could win? Jem bared his chest. Was he not Key to the Orokon, foretold in ancient prophecy?

He clutched the crystal, feeling it pulse.

Polty lunged. 'Vexing, give it here!'

There were cries. Jem reeled, striking his assailant; Polty came back stronger, clutching eagerly, greedily. Colour pulsed in his amethyst ring, throbbing in time with the mystic crystal. He grabbed it.

He tugged, grimacing, slavering.

But now the mysterious figures raised their golden arms, as the acolytes had done in the glade before; then, inevitably, came the slow, spreading flash.

And the scene changed again.

Chapter 60

GARDEN PARTY

Alone, the crystal at his chest subsiding, Jem found himself outdoors again, seated at a long, white-clothed table, laid out as if for a garden party. Only the season was wrong. The trees were bare, the brook frozen; snow lay thick on the ground. Yet Jem felt quite warm, as if the cold were on the other side of a dividing glass wall. He looked towards the yew-tree where he had seen the King. What was this? A streak of colour, high in the branches? A crouching? A leap? Ejard Orange?

Jem pushed back his tousled hair. Spaced at several points down the table were golden candelabra, ornate and five-branched. In every branch burned a candle, even though it was daylight. He breathed slowly, and as he breathed he was joined by others; one by one they shimmered into being, filling the vacant seats. On Jem's side of the table came his companions in black, Cata and Rajal to his left hand, Tishy and Littler (his seat built up with a special box) to his right; opposite, in a line of white, were Bean, Umbecca, Polty, Jeli and the King.

Then, at the head and foot of the table, came two of the cowled strangers. The one at the head of the table pulled back his cowl, revealing a hairless, wizened head; his companion at the other end kept his features concealed. Acolytes moved round the table, serving the guests – for guests they must be – with admirable finesse.

The first course was lavish, and Umbecca exclaimed; the King reached eagerly for a bejewelled goblet, while Polty, unimpressed, glared through the candelabra with ominous resignation.

There was a gust of wind, but the flames did not stir.

'*Some* of us aren't hungry,' said Jem, gesturing towards the golden-garbed figures, neither of whom were partaking of the meal. The uncowled fellow blinked impassively; had his eyes not been open, one might have thought him deep in meditation. Meanwhile, the cowled fellow kept his hands before him on the table, as if at any moment he was about to rise; Jem saw that the hands were gnarled and ancient. He recalled the old man from last night and wondered if Cowl were the same man.

'Well, I don't feel much like eating either,' said Tishy, eyeing the curious concoction which had appeared on their plates, a medley of salmon, lobster and starfish in a port-wine sauce, garnished liberally with candied fruits.

'Actually, I'm ravenous,' Cata confessed.

'For this?' Jem said doubtfully, as she began to prove her claim. 'You're still pale. Are you sure you're all right?'

'What I want to know,' said Rajal, 'is where all this comes from. Seafood? Wine? Fruits? Up *here*?'

Polty rolled his eyes. 'It's magic, isn't it? And how I love magic!' Fondly he gazed upon his beloved Cata. 'My darling, if only you knew what I was keeping for you!'

'Mr Burgrove's keeping it, actually,' said Bean.

'No magic better than wine,' mumbled the King.

'So, what's it *like* being a King?' Littler asked perkily.

Morosely, the King guzzled his wine; once, with a leer, he groped the Queen's breast, but she slapped him away with automatic disgust.

'Prince Jemany, you'll have some chutney?' she asked with a winning smile, gesturing to Tishy to pass the dish.

Cata scowled at Tishy, but Jem had no chance to receive the royal gift; Umbecca's plump hand shot out. In the next moment, she had heaped all the chutney on the side of her own plate.

Wisps of snow fell steadily, melting over the food.

'Cham-Charing, fill my goblet,' said the Queen.

'Aren't there servants to do that?' said Jem.

There were; already they were serving the second course.

Jeli smiled at Jem with apparent grace. 'A Queen does require *personal* service.' Her face went frosty. 'Cham-Charing! My goblet!'

'Do it yourself,' said Cata. 'Honestly, Jeli! To think that we could ever have been friends!'

'Yes, before I knew what you were. Deceiving minx! And I thought you were a respectable girl!'

'I thought the same of you, bitch!'

'Come, no catfights,' Polty intervened, casually twisting his amethyst ring. He leaned across the table, fixing Jem in the eye, and his voice dropped to a whisper. '*You'll never have her, you know.*'

'You're insane!' said Jem.

Jeli, meanwhile, had leaned towards Cata; her words, to Cata's astonishment, were almost the same as Polty's. '*You'll never have him, do you hear?*'

'Polty?' Cata said disbelievingly. 'You think I—'

'Oh, I'm not talking about Polty,' smiled Jeli.

Littler piped up, 'Ejjy! Look, I saw Ejjy!'

But no one was listening.

❋　　❋　　❋　　❋　　❋

The second course comprised an immense unidentifiable side of meat which the acolytes placed in the centre of the table; to Jem's party, it looked more than a little similar to Starzok's unfortunate fare. Still, there were numerous side-dishes, sauce-boats, condiments; steam rose copiously in the cold air, but only Umbecca tucked in.

Polty's carroty hair was bright against the whiteness. Still he fixed his eyes upon Jem; still he twisted the amethyst ring. Jem's robe had slipped again, and the crystal was in view. Was it glowing, just a little? Or was it just the light? Polty looked between Uncowl and Cowl. To be sure, he was considering another attack.

'You've got to listen to me,' Rajal was whispering, leaning towards Bean. 'Aron, *please*—'

'If only I understood,' sighed Jem, waving away one of the Blayzil-youths. 'What was all that about Agonis-in-the-Vast? Agonis isn't *in* the Vast. We've met him, he was Lord Empster ... And what did they mean about *escape*? What do this lot need to escape from? We're the prisoners – we're the ones who have to *escape*.'

'What, and never find the crystal?' said Cata.

'We're trapped,' said Tishy, 'but so are they. They—'

Jeli's eyes flashed. 'Cham-Charing, shut up! Haven't you faced the truth yet? Any sane girl would be thanking the gods to be taken into such reputable service! But you? Remember, your mother is *no one* in Agondon any more, just *no one*. Who are you even to speak to Prince Jemany?'

'Child, haven't I told you?' blurted Umbecca, spraying meat from her full mouth. 'Jemany's no prince, he's only a wicked boy. My niece's Vexing, that's all he is.'

At this, Cata might have flared up again; instead, she just looked nauseous. Jem turned to her; but then there was a new voice, a voice wry, sad – and familiar.

'Whoever her mother may be, Miss Laetitia is right.'

It was Cowl. Cata brightened, eyes widening.

'My friends,' the speaker continued, 'there is a story to tell. You all know that, do you not? Even you, Umbecca, though you appear to be concerned only with that meat. It's whale, by the way – blubbery, I'm told, too blubbery by far. But perhaps that's why *you* like it.'

'What ... who?' Sauce rolled over Umbecca's chins.

At the far end of the table, Uncowl closed his eyes; now the meditation was real. But no, there was a deck of cards before him, arranged in two piles. Blindly, Uncowl picked up a card, turned it in his hand, then placed it languidly on the other pile.

'You will recall, my friends,' said Cowl, 'why the Bearers of the Vexing Gem came to this Kolkos Aros, or Crystal Sky—'

'Sheer perversity,' said Polty. 'To live here, when one could live in Agondon—'

'Indeed, heart-son,' slurred Umbecca, through the blubber, 'I am glad to see us in agreement. Picturesque these mountains may be, but they are undoubtedly *provincial*. It is as well my dear Torso cannot see me now.'

'Didn't the Ur-God make them come here?' said Jem, ignoring his fat aunt. 'Come on, Tishy, you can tell us.'

'Cham-Charing, hold your peace,' commanded Jeli.

It was to no avail. Tishy said shyly, 'The Bearers broke from the thrall of Ondon, the Warrior-King, to find this mountain fastness. Humbly they would live in accord with the commands of Orok, eking out the vigil of aeons that has been called the Time of Atonement. So at least say the ancient texts,' the girl added, gaining confidence, 'though of course there may be dispute as to matters of—'

'Yes!' Cowl slammed down a palm on the tablecloth. 'Dispute, and there must be! In worldly life I doubted all I had been taught; since my return here, I have seen that I was right, only too right, to do so.'

He leaned forward. 'Has it not occurred to you, my friends, that Orok, in the Vast, was but one of *many* gods? That there, too, he was by no means omnipotent? What does the first *page* of the El-Orokon say, but that there was warmaking in the Vast, that Orok was wounded, that he withdrew to a far wilderness? Ah yes, there were gods other than Orok; in the Vast, all do not live beneath his sway. And had not this thought possessed Father-Priest Ir-Ion, in his long meditations on the Vexing Gem?'

'He wanted to escape from *Orok*?' said Jem. 'Not just from Ondon?'

'Wait,' said Rajal, 'that doesn't make sense—'

'Doesn't it?' Cowl's voice was playful. 'The Crystal of Agonis has powers far greater than those of lesser crystals. Staring, like lovers, upon the golden stone, Ir-Ion and his sister and brother Bearers had acquired the ability to see beyond the mere appearance of things. They saw that there were places where the dimensional walls were thin. Such a place was the Kolkos Aros; there, concentrating their crystal-stirred powers, the Bearers might transcend the bondage of this world, releasing themselves into the Vast. No longer Creatures of Orok would they be, grovelling in the degradation of Atonement; rather, they would be free—'

Jeli yawned. 'What are *dimensional walls* anyway?'

'Wine, boy, wine –' The King signalled an acolyte.

Jem hunched forward, as if to stare into Cowl's shrouded face. 'But this is astonishing. You mean the Bearers … you mean *you* … were never really servants of Orok? Or Agonis?'

'Ah, but we are getting ahead of ourselves,' said Cowl. 'You know, do you not, of Ir-Ion's escape from Ondon?'

'Tishy told us all about it,' piped up Littler. 'Ondon wasn't going to the Crystal Sky – and he wouldn't let the Bearers go. They ran away, but Ondon went after them. That's right, isn't it, Tishy? And in the end, Ondon came here. But when he knocked on the portals, there was the avalanche.'

'Must have been some *knock*,' said Rajal.

'Of course it was,' said Cowl. 'Coming to these mountains, we assembled this citadel as a carapace around us, confident that soon it would be the container in which, at last, we would transcend into the Vast.'

'Then it's *really* not real?' Bean said, wide-eyed.

'Shut up, Bean,' said Polty. 'It's all made of spiritual energies, don't you remember? This old beggar's not telling us anything Toth hasn't told us already.'

'Has he told you you're going to lose tomorrow?' said Jem.

Cowl sighed, oblivious. 'Transcendence drew near. We were ready, our energies focused. If only we had attained our goal before Ondon came for us!'

Jem urged, 'But what did it matter? What could he do?'

'Alas,' said Cowl, 'that Ondon, in the long cycles of his wanderings, had increased his own powers. Had he not, like all our race, once been a Bearer of the Vexing Gem? He, too, had been exposed to its power. The fool! He thought he could reject his destiny, cast it aside like chaff in the wind; instead, a negative counter-force built and built inside him, rising to a pitch of intensity as he approached our secret citadel.

'Picture it. He slithered across the frozen moat, merely tapping, merely clawing at our mighty portal just in the instant when we were to leave this world. It was enough: the force exploded around him, and around us too. The avalanche descended.'

'But you're still *here*,' said Littler. 'Aren't you?'

'It depends,' said Cowl, 'what you mean by *here*. No, the avalanche did not destroy us, but it left us in limbo. Transcendence was impossible; we were trapped in a place between dimensions, neither quite in the Earth made by Orok, nor quite in the Vast. Thus it was that our citadel would appear and disappear; thus it was that we would draw forth postulants, petitioners from Orokon Earth, seeking those in whom the spirit burned strong, in a restless quest to augment our energies. But then, my friends, you must know all that. You especially, Jemany. Who are you, Key to the Orokon, but the greatest of our postulants, our petitioners?'

Jem could not suppress a surge of pride. Polty scowled, and only the fussings of the Blayzil-youths, who were busy serving an elaborate dessert, prevented him from launching into some crude, sudden violence. It was just as well. Umbecca would never have forgiven him if he had squashed the raspberry cheesecake.

Now Jem's brow furrowed. 'Good sir ... *sirs*, there's one thing I don't understand—'

'Only *one*?' said Rajal.

'Well, one of many.' Jem looked between Cowl and Uncowl. The snow was falling harder; the wind rose as if at the beginning of a blizzard, but still the candles steadily burned. 'You lot are stuck, right? And all through the Time of Atonement, you've been trying to get ... well, *unstuck*. Building up. Waiting. But you're not still the *same* lot, are you? I mean, as in the beginning? I mean, are you ... immortal?'

Uncowl turned a card in his hands. For a moment it looked as if he was about to speak; in the event, it was Cowl who replied. 'Would it surprise you to know that we are, in a sense, both mortal *and* immortal? Of those who travelled with Father-Priest Ir-Ion, each one has been through countless incarnations. Nor were these confined to this mountainous realm. Seeking new resources of the spirit, often we have directed our energies beyond, assuming many a guise amongst the women and men of Orokon Earth. Why, who am I but a returning pilgrim from the green valleys below?'

'You've lived amongst us?' said Littler.

'Indeed,' Cowl replied. 'Already the last of my worldly lives is fading, but still I recall much of that incarnation. If only I had known what I really was! How much better might I have husbanded my powers! But inevitably, as a mortal must be, I was benighted; not until the time of my worldly death, when a brother Bearer came to retrieve me, did I understand who I had once been, and who I would be again.'

And who was that? The question hung on Jem's lips, but first he looked at Cata and saw that she was trembling. Could she feel the cold to which the others were immune? He slipped an arm round her shoulders, drawing her close.

Meanwhile, several of the diners had been looking with interest upon the raspberry cheesecake. Alas, all but one was to be disappointed. Helpless before Umbecca's commands, an acolyte had replaced several cut slices, then set down the entire cake before the fat woman. Again and again her spoon descended; rich, runny cream rimmed her mouth. Littler looked on longingly; so did Bean. They would have to content themselves with coffee and mints.

Cowl sighed, raising empty hands. 'But of what moment is all this now? Through this long Atonement we have sought Transcendence. But all along, did we not know the truth? Only with the ordained End could our freedom come; only when the Orokon was assembled again, and the Lord Agonis at last clutched to his heart the Lady Imagenta.'

'Blessed be the Lord Agonis,' murmured Umbecca. She had reason to bless: the cheesecake was the finest she had ever tasted. How she longed for another just like it!

Jem was saying, puzzled, 'Agonis ... Imagenta?'

'What, you don't follow?' said Cowl, surprised. 'Prince, I have told you a story. What is a story but a surface, a screen? And who, all the time, has been sequestered behind the screen? Who, indeed, but the Lord Agonis?'

'You'll have to go slower for us,' said Rajal. 'We're not all as smart as Tishy, you know – and even *she's* looking confused right now.'

Tishy coloured. 'You speak, sir, of Agonis-in-the-Vast—'

'That's it!' said Rajal. 'Agonis *isn't* in the Vast, is he? We've met him, and—'

'Raj, *shh*,' said Jem. 'But ... but Lord Empster—'

Uncowl produced a pipe. He leaned forward, lighting it from a candle, then sat back, smirking faintly. Could it be that he was about to speak?

Chapter 61

FOURTH TIME AROUND

In the event, it was Cowl who told the story.

'Legend – or rather, the El-Orokon – tells how Agonis gazed upon a glass, besotted with the image of Toth's fair daughter. But the El-Orokon does not tell all. That glass, given to Agonis by the anti-god, was a portal into the Realm of Unbeing. And the lady, I am afraid, was more than merely a passive creature.

'Ah, she had power! Through Imagenta, the fair god was divided, his Essence spirited into Unbeing; only his corporeal self was left to wander this world, fruitlessly seeking a beloved who was not, in truth, to be found in this world at all. Yes, this Agonis-on-the-Earth, this Empster, is a hollow man, longing to assuage the emptiness that tolls in him relentlessly like the iron tongue of a bell.'

Uncowl snorted. Smoke, by now, shrouded his face.

'But this Agonis-in-the-Vast—' Rajal began, exasperated.

'We speak of Agonis in his ideal form, as he will be after the Ritual of Restoration.'

'The what?' The question, this time, was Jem's.

'The ceremony, if ceremony it can be called, when the golden crystal is claimed, when the Orokon is assembled, when Transcendence, so long delayed, will come. My friends, I have spoken of Father-Priest Ir-Ion; but never, in truth, was Ir-Ion the true director of our destiny. No, it was Agonis, Agonis-of-the-Essence, reaching from his captivity, searing into our awareness through the golden crystal. As Agonis-on-the-Earth pursued his fruitless quest, so the real Agonis, if we might call him such, has urged us on. But of course, he must. For when we achieve Transcendence, so will he.'

Tishy was thinking hard. 'But ... this is extraordinary! The theological implications alone, I can barely ... you mean Agonis, too, longs to *escape from Orok*? But ... Agonis was so good, so dutiful to his father—'

This time, it was Rajal who answered. 'No, I never believed all that. Agonis longs only for Imagenta, doesn't he? And he'll have her, won't he? When the Seeker comes? When the crystal is taken? When the Orokon is restored?'

'Everything,' Cowl said solemnly, 'depends on the Restoration.'

'But how does it *work*?' Rajal urged. 'I can follow this up to a point. There's a crystal round here, right? (Though if you could hurry up and bring it out, we'd appreciate it.) Anyway, Jem's going to grab it, as per usual, and ... but what about the other crystals? Don't we need *all five*? And don't we need the Rock of Unbeing and Being, or whatever it's called? The crystals all have to be shoved into *that*, don't they, and then ... and then what?'

He trailed off, shivering for the first time that day. Beyond the enchanted table, a blizzard raged.

It was Jem who spoke next. 'What I want to know is this. You've been waiting for Transcendence all this time. But in the place we were before – that temple – when all the Bearers were there, they said it didn't matter who triumphed tomorrow. So tell me this: how could it not matter? How could it *not* matter?'

There was silence. Ejard Orange padded round the table; no one saw him. Jem trembled. His eyes blazed, and blazed all the more when Cowl permitted himself a short, wheezing laugh.

'My poor Jemany, I see you remain in the thrall of old beliefs. Have you not learned that everything is different here? To me – oh yes, to me – it is vital that you should prevail. But to my sister and brother Bearers? What do they care but that the crystal is found, the Orokon restored? You were the Key to the Orokon, but Toth's powers, by now, are greater than yours. And if Toth is the agent of Transcendence, what of it? *Why not?*'

Rajal burst out, 'But it doesn't make sense! If Toth gets the Orokon, he'll ... he'll destroy the world!'

'A world,' said Cowl, 'in which my sisters and brothers will have no part. And what does it mean, *destruction*? Orokon Earth is but one of many worlds, whirling through the vortex of Being and Unbeing ... And perhaps this world must be destroyed, that another might be born.'

'No,' cried Jem, 'Toth *can't* win, he just *can't*—'

'He *won't*,' said Cata. 'Jem, you've got to believe it!'

'I did.' Jem slumped forward. 'Always, until now—'

A playing-card, flung from a hand, arced slowly down the table. Cowl plucked it from the air.

He held it out to Jem. It was the harlequin.

'You had to tell that story, didn't you?' Uncowl, astonishingly, was speaking now. Coolly, through the pipe-smoke shrouding his face, he stared down the table to his cowled compatriot.

Cowl let the card fall. 'You didn't try to stop me.'

'I couldn't have stopped you. But poor Prince Jemany! I thought you were his protector. Here you are, crushing the boy's confidence—'

Jem looked sharply, questioningly, at the speaker. How many times had he heard that voice? With a pang, he remembered when the shrouded face was handsome, when its owner was a great man in the fashionable world. But then, too, there had been the wide-brimmed hat that always, with the smoke, rendered his visage strangely indistinct.

A rasp came from Jem's throat. 'My guardian—'

'But he had to know—' Still Uncowl looked steadily down the table. Cowl, too, had now risen to his feet; as they faced each other, it was as if neither Jem and his companions, nor Polty and his companions really existed at all.

'Yet what does it matter?' Now Uncowl – Lord Empster – picked up the cards and flung them, all of them, into the air. They vanished before they could fall. 'What matters but that you can still be free?'

'I annoyed you,' Cowl said, 'didn't I?'

'Of course! To be called a hollow man? An empty, tolling bell? Yet all your words are true. Do not think me divided wholly from my Emanation that lodges in Unbeing with my lady. It is I, not only he, who has urged you on, in the long, tormented aeons of our quest. But on the morrow, all division is over at last. Goodbye, Father-Priest Ir-Ion. Or would you prefer,' he added wryly, 'that I called you by the name of your last incarnation?'

Empster – Agonis-on-the-Earth – did not wait for an answer. As he spoke, the gold of his robes had appeared to spill strangely free, running over his face and hands until his fleshly form assumed a gilded, statue-like splendour. The pipe and the smoke vanished; there was only a golden haze.

And the god, or half-god, had vanished too.

'Wh-where's the fellow gone?' said the King.

'They'll never believe it at Temple College,' said Tishy.

'Well I never,' said Umbecca, who had been licking crumbs from the cheesecake plate. 'If you ask me, that sort of exhibition is hardly *polite*.'

Jem could only gaze at Cowl. 'You're Father-Priest Ir-Ion? But I thought—'

'My child, perhaps your thoughts are true. Did I not speak of incarnations? Look to my daughter. My daughter knows.'

Beside Jem, Cata was smiling; then she began to sob as the old man peeled back his cowl, revealing the mutilated face beneath.

Bean breathed, 'Eyeless Silas—'

'No—' The plate fell from Umbecca's hands. She moaned, lowing like a cow in pain.

Old Wolveron? Silas Wolveron? Lector of Irion?

'Papa – oh, Papa … I knew, of course I knew—' Cata went to the old man, embracing him.

But now Polty rose, pushing back his chair. 'All this is very touching, I'm sure, but—'

'Shut up, you viper—' Jem began.

'Oh, not a viper,' Polty said mockingly. 'Not quite a viper. Look around you, Vexing. You're not very observant. Why don't you just *look around you*?'

377

'Wh-what?' Jem's gaze travelled over the debris of dishes, over the candles, over the faces of his companions. The acolytes had melted away; the candlelit table was a frail oasis of light, marooned beneath the lowerings of a hostile sky. He looked out into the blizzard. Now he saw that there were purple glowings, shimmering through the snow. Heat flooded from his crystal; a shadow passed above and the candles flickered out.

Polty leered; the scene around them was dissolving. Ejard Orange leapt up on the table. Littler exclaimed; but then Littler, Ejard Orange and the table were gone.

Jem clutched at Cata. Instead, he felt Old Wolveron's hand upon his shoulder. 'I'm sorry, my child, it has to be. You will prevail, or not prevail, as the winds of time decree.'

'Old Wolveron, what do you mean?'

But the old man was gone and Jem found himself alone with Polty, with the Mauvers, with the wheeling shadow of the Unbeing Bird, making its circuit for the fourth time.

The blizzard raged, raged; Jem's crystal burned, searing through the fabric of his black robes.

'You, prevail? *You*, crippler-boy?'

Polty stepped forward, dazzling, white; looming behind him, like a puppet master, was a purple shadow. Jem knew it was the shadow of Toth, and that this shadow had always been there, always lurking in secret, even an aeon ago in Irion, as one boy, fat and flame-haired, tormented another boy with useless, buckled legs.

Polty laughed. 'Yes, crippler, all this time I've just been toying with you. Did you think I *had* to delay? Useless, foolish crippler—'

'I'm not—' Jem held up a hand, as if to ward off a blow. No blow came, but none was needed. His legs skewed beneath him and he grovelled in the snow, broken, like the cat that Polty had crippled once, snapping its spine with a sharp jerk. All volition left Jem, all desire. He thought of all he had done to find the crystals. Only with violence, only with terror had Toth taken the others. Rajal, Cata, Littler – all had struggled to resist.

But Jem's crystal? That was easy.

Mauvers shrieked. The shadow darkened. Polty laughed again and his hand reached down; Jem saw the flash of the amethyst ring and consciousness abandoned him.

When he awoke, he was back in his cell.

And his legs would not move.

Chapter 62

JOYOUS INVASION

The Meditation of Javander dawned over Agondon with cold clarity. No snow fell and the sky was unclouded, fixed behind the city like a backdrop of metal that would clang hollowly if struck by a stone.

All along the Embankment, surrounding the great mound of the Island like a collar, Bluejacket forces were primed and ready; ranged across the frozen Riel were the Redjackets, ready too, and certain of victory. In the harsh morning light, the Island stood out like an exposed jewel of great price, ready to be plucked by greedy hands. The sight was almost forlorn. Agondon Bridge and Regent's Bridge had been destroyed the day before, blown up by the Bluejackets to keep the rebels at bay. Nothing could keep them at bay any more.

When the first shots rang out, ragged armies swarmed like locusts over the cracking river. To Ejard Red and his generals, it seemed at first that victory would come swiftly. But men besieged on an island have a certain desperation. Many feared what would become of them should they fall into rebel hands; then, too, many a common soldier was prone to superstition, and said the auspices of the day were good. The day before, when the Reds had made such gains, had been the Meditation of Theron, red god of fire; today was the day of Javander, blue goddess of the seas. It had to be an omen.

The Bluejackets fought harder than their enemies had expected, and the defences of the Island were hard to breach. From time immemorial, this little rocky circle had been Ejland's last stronghold. Cannons bristled from the high-built Embankment; everywhere there were ramparts, bastions, gun-sights.

Redjacket losses were heavy. Folio Webster was amongst those who fell, taking a musket-ball full in the chest; Magda Vytoni was blown up by a bomb just as she was about to scale the Embankment, punching the air with a cry of *Freedom!* Another victim was Peter Impalini. Unlike his fellow underworld leaders, Impalini became too excitable to remain behind the lines; he was run through by a bayonet out on the ice below Cham-Charing House. Innumerable were the nameless ones who also fell that day.

But the Blue army could not hold out for ever; the breach in the walls, when it came, was catastrophic. Danny Garvice's bombs did their work almost too well. Much of the Riel Embankment caved in on the Ollon side and a great many of the contenders of that day, Reds and Blues alike, were swept away in the icy deluge that burst forth as mighty stones smashed through the frozen river. From then on there was only a frenzy of violence, with no clear lines of battle remaining. Redjackets surged into the Island, screaming like banshees through the slithery cobbled streets. The air was a rain of shells and musket shots. Men grappled hand to hand. Bayonets stabbed. Blood stained the snow.

Somewhere in it all were Morven and Crum, doing their best to keep their heads down. The two friends had been separated early in the battle; each thought the other was lost, though seldom were they ever really far apart. Terrified, the hapless recruits only breached the Island with the others because they could hardly help being carried forward; there was no way back across the smashed ice.

Once on the Island, both were lucky. Running from an irate Bluejacket with a bayonet, Morven stumbled into Cham-Charing House, where he had the good fortune to hide himself in the library. He locked the door. To his delight, he found that the book-lined walls admirably muffled the commotion outside. Hoping no ruffian would think to burst in here, he settled down to wait out the battle.

At a time so momentous, Morven thought he should perhaps read Vytoni's *Discourse on Freedom*; unfortunately, his copy had fallen out of his pocket in the mêlée and he was hardly going to find another one here. He thought of the Aon Fellowship, which he so richly deserved, and wondered if he should embark upon some appropriate study. This respectable library no doubt had a great many fine editions of the classics, probably with uncut pages and uncracked spines. But suddenly Morven felt very tired, and contented himself with a book called *Becca's First Ball*, which he had never read before, and which he found surprisingly diverting.

Meanwhile, Crum had chanced upon a secluded courtyard, one of many in the labyrinth that was Old Agondon, where he hid from the battle with a tallow-chandler, the tallow-chandler's daughter, their three dogs, their one-eyed cat, their pigeon and their parrot. If Crum was worried about Morven – rather more so, it must be admitted, than Morven was about Crum – nonetheless he spent a pleasant afternoon. The tallow-chandler was remarkably gracious with his guest, as was the daughter; when Crum left, both urged him to visit again.

Crum, it must be admitted, was particularly fond of the daughter, who reminded him of Zohnny Ryle's sister. She had greatly enjoyed his stories about farm life, and his speculations about what might have happened if Blenkinsop had met the one-eyed cat.

✳ ✳ ✳ ✳ ✳

Wiggler was also to be found on the Island that day, though he displayed rather more bravery than either Morven or Crum. Quite how much was difficult to determine. In years to come, his tales of his heroism would expand in a ratio similar to that of his waistline with Nirry's good cooking, but undoubtedly he fired a shot or two, and perhaps even attempted a bayonet-charge. His principal role that day, however, was the one he played in his wife's imagination.

In late afternoon, as the battle reached its climax, thunderous fighting filled Redondo Gardens. In the Cat & Crown, Nirry peered through the shutters, wringing her hands. Behind her, Raggle and Taggle alternately gazed round her skirts, wide-eyed, at the fighting, or played excitable games of *Biddy-biddy-bobble*; the Friar, who had partaken liberally of the provisions, slept obliviously, his plump fingers laced over his stomach, while Baines fussed with housework, often pausing to curse the dust, and wipe her single eye.

Nirry sank deeper and deeper into despair. Getting back to the tavern had been bad enough, but the battle raging now was worse by far. And where was Wiggler? To Nirry, he had met with every imaginable form of death or disability; time and again, Baines had consoled her, all to no avail.

In justice, Nirry might have been more concerned for Miss Landa, who was certainly braver than Wiggler, and had insisted on returning to the rebels after getting her friends back to the Cat & Crown. But a secret guilt gnawed at Nirry's heart. Her fear was that Wiggler might be taken from her in punishment for her dalliance with Carney Floss. Could the Lord Agonis be so cruel? Frequently Nirry would close her eyes, praying for forgiveness of her sinful heart. If only her husband could be spared from violence, Nirry vowed that first she would beat him black and blue, then be a good, faithful and subservient wife to him all the rest of their born days.

It was as she stood at the window, revolving these thoughts, that Nirry thought she saw a familiar set of ears out amongst the crush of contending armies. Whether it was Wiggler, who could say? But Nirry was convinced that it was. Outraged, she shrieked her husband's name. She seized a broom, ready to beat him; ignoring the cries of Baines, she rushed into the hall, flinging away the chairs and tables that barricaded the doors.

Undoubtedly Nirry intended only to stand in her doorway, calling Wiggler to heel, confident that her familiar, piercing cry would bring him back at once. Alas, it was not so simple; already, the familiar ears were lost from sight, and Nirry edged precariously beyond her well-scrubbed doorstep just as a rebel platoon surged past. Her broom went flying and the ragged tide of men bore her away. Shots whizzed around her. Screaming filled the air.

Nirry feared she would be trampled underfoot; only her anger at the thought of so absurd and undignified a fate filled her with a preternatural strength. She pushed against the marauding men, wishing she still had her broom to beat them back; she had no choice but to go with the tide. Nirry was about to stumble and fall when she felt a hand suddenly grasping her, wrenching her from the fray.

She reeled, astonished. 'Bando!'

They could not speak, nor even shout, so loud were the shellings and cries. Nirry tugged towards the Cat & Crown; Bando tugged her the other way. He had to get her to shelter, the nearest shelter he could. Already they were some distance from the Gardens, borne up towards the Koros Palace. It was the last push, when the rebels hoped to take the final Bluejacket stronghold. Forward they rushed, ever forward, Bando gripping Nirry's hand all the while.

The rest of that day was a blur to Nirry. All at once they were inside the Koros Palace, leaping through a breach in the walls. The noise was deafening. Windows exploded; walls crashed down. She thundered up a staircase with Bando, down another, up another. Scenes of a luxury she had never seen before flashed past her eyes, then vanished. They skidded past suits of armour and ancestral portraits, battered their way into marble halls. Chandeliers crashed. Plaster rained down.

Suddenly there was a voice: 'Bando, this way!'

And through the powdery haze Nirry saw Miss Landa, with Hul and Ejard Red. To her alarm, the Red King brandished a mighty, ancient battleaxe, wrenched from the metal hands of one of the suits of armour.

Miss Landa gasped, 'Nirry, what the—'

There was no time. The five of them were tearing down a corridor.

'This is the way!' cried Ejard Red. 'He'll be holed up in here, I know it! I'll kill him, I'll kill him!'

He smashed through a doorway with the axe.

'S-Sire,' gasped Hul, 'are you sure—'

'I'm sure,' smiled Ejard Red, motioning with the axe for the others to follow. Inside, the noise of battle was distant, yet all within was devastation, ruins, heaps of rubble cluttering what remained of an ancient, luxurious chamber. Curtains had been torn from a window and there was a single shaft of sunlight, cutting through an otherwise deep gloom. In several fireplaces, fires leapt and danced. The heat was stifling.

At once, Nirry felt very strange.

'Wh-what is this place?' She clutched Miss Landa.

'Brother! Brother, show yourself!'

The King's words echoed round the chamber.

Bando gulped, 'The purple birds—'

Nirry saw them too, these strange half-phantoms; then there were other creatures too, things she could not quite make out, rustling and shifting and loping in the gloom. Terror filled her and she would have run, but something kept her fixed in place.

'Sire, this is Tranimel's doing,' said Hul.

'The First Minister?' The Red King's voice was distant. 'A man with no blood, no breeding? What do I care for that functionary, when my brother goes free?'

'S-Sire,' Hul went on, 'I've tried to tell you, Tranimel is rather more ... rather *more* than he used to be.'

But the King was not listening.

Strange music insinuated its way into the chamber, mounting in intensity. Fearfully, Nirry peered around her. On the far wall, she saw an enormous mural, depicting a landscape of snow and ice. Only later would she realise that it was not merely a painting, but a portal into a distant place.

The King strode through the gloom, kicking rubble from his way, calling for his coward of a brother to show himself, to come forward like a man to meet his death.

From the upper reaches of the purplish air came a wild, crazed cry. 'Triumph! Triumph is mine!'

Nirry screamed; Bando whirled, stumbling. That was when they saw the thing that had occupied the body of the First Minister, revolving, cross-legged, high in the air. Three glowing crystals – purple, green, red – circled the First Minister's shaven head; a fourth crystal, coloured blue, had appeared in his hands.

The light was dazzling.

Then there was another voice.

'So, it seems our guests have arrived. But how can I be so inconsiderate, to offer them no refreshments?' Stepping from behind a ruinous, teetering screen, the speaker was a figure all in black, his face concealed behind a hawk-like mask. Glittering evilly in the crystal-light, the dark figure raised his hand as if to cast a spell over the five astonished intruders. 'So, you think you have won this day? My master would bid you think again; all that has passed has been a charade, the better to amuse him before he shows his hand. Red King, you will never rule this empire again.'

And the hawk-man laughed. Did he think Toth's magic made him safe? If so, the thing that had once been the handsomest bachelor in Varby placed too much confidence in his evil master. As with all servants of evil, his own role, in the end, had been a charade too.

Now the charade was over.

'*No*—' The King swung back his axe. He struck; the head flew from Burgrove's body. Horrified, the King's companions reeled back, but their horror could only grow as the headless man collapsed and a bloodied, eel-like thing emerged, slithering and writhing, from the severed oesophagus.

Down came the axe again, chopping Penge to bits. The bits wriggled; the King stamped on them. In the air, the First Minister revolved, oblivious, but now he was turning faster and faster, flashing in the weird refulgence of the crystals. Still came the strange music, cacophonous now. Timpani rumbled. Horns blasted. Cymbals crashed.

Nirry struggled to escape, not caring where. Breaking from Miss Landa, she ran a few steps, then turned her ankle, falling into the debris.

A mighty wind filled the ruined chamber, flinging the intruders against one wall, then another, then another. Hul, Nirry, Bando, Landa, Ejard Red, all reeled and whirled, crashing and colliding. The axe ripped from the King's hand, flying past Nirry, almost striking her; Mauvers flapped and flurried all around them; phantom monsters soared and lunged. Round and round in the air they flew, in the dazzle of the crystals, in the violence of the storm. Then all at once, as into a dizzying vortex, they found themselves sucked into a landscape of white.

Suddenly there was silence. Silence, and cold.

And there, before them, was the Lamasery of the Winds.

Chapter 63

IN THE MAZY DANCE

No, crippler-boy. Oh no, crippler-boy.

Why ... why are you calling me crippler-boy?

Because that's what you are. That's all you are.

But ... I'm a hero. The world's only hope.

If you're a hero, there can be no hope.

I found the crystals. One by one, I found them.

Yes, and then you lost them again.

Not all. There's ... one more.

But you haven't got that one.

I say I'll get it. What if I get it?

Without the others?

In his dreams, Jem tried to push away this voice that buzzed about him. But what was the good of pushing it away? When the voice was there, he saw only patterns of dark, swirling colours; when the voice was gone, the patterns turned into shapes of clouds, and when the clouds parted he looked down, as if from on high, upon a devastated city. It was a place of drifting smoke, of buildings blackened by fire or crumbling into rubble. Down, down he went towards the streets, the slush, the mud; he saw a pool of red, and a dead-cart overturned. A rat clambered over a corpse's face, gnawing at the eyes. And Jem cried out that this could not be, that this could not be Agondon. He would save his city—

Oh no, crippler-boy. No, little crippler.

Why say no? How ... how can you?

How can you say you'll have the crystal?

I'm Key to the Orokon. It was ordained.

Things happen, crippler-boy. Nothing's ordained.

I can't believe that. Life would be a mockery.

Silly boy! Life is a mockery.

You ... you can't believe that.

A dance, that's what it is. A jig, by a clown.

A clown? What do you mean, a clown?

How about a harlequin?

How many times did Jem hear those words? But each time he escaped from the tormenting voice, he would find himself in Agondon again, hovering like a ghost above the ruined city. He found himself in a black, reeking alley. In a doorway that yawned like a carious mouth an old man leered at him, holding up stumps where his hands should have been. Jem turned away, only to be confronted by new horrors. There was a naked child with filmy, sightless eyes; a dead dog, guts strewn on the cobblestones. Then Jem saw a starved orange cat, miaowing piteously; the cat led him forward. There was the wheeze of a hurdy-gurdy. Upon a pile of rubble, shadowy but unmistakable, the harlequin was there, pirouetting with impossible slowness. And laughing, laughing ... Jem would have run and kept on running. But could not—

No, crippler-boy. Oh no, crippler-boy.

So ... what's going to happen now?

I think Toth's going to get the last crystal, don't you?

And ... reunite the Orokon? Just like that?

No doubt, and begin his eternal reign. Of darkness.

How can you speak of it so ... lightly?

Come, crippler-boy, it won't be eternal. Not really.

What, things might change? In an aeon or two?

That's right, nothing's fixed, everything's in flux—

No! No, I swear it, I won't let this happen, I'll—

Didn't you hear me? You're a crippler, boy.

Time and again did Jem hear these words, but only at the last did they take on their real, their irreducible meaning. His eyes flickered open and he registered, juddering towards him, a jagged, greenish mass. Not until a moment had passed did he make it out as a hedge, its prickly leaves strewn with random flowers. Ah, so he was back in the maze, the maze where he had been before, but...

Jem was not moving. So how could the hedge?

'Such pleasant weather! Lovely, isn't it, Jem?'

'Wh-what?' Jem was in a bath-chair. All he wore was a flannel nightshirt, and wrapped around his knees was a tartan rug. 'My ... my legs! What's happened to my legs?'

'All right, my love?' resumed the cheery voice. 'Not too warm? Not too cold? Don't worry, nearly there now. Just remember, if you get tired, you tell your Aunt Umbecca.'

Jem would have turned round to face his fat aunt, but could not quite manage it; already he was exhausted, as if his life were leaching away.

Wheels crunched round the gravelled path.

'Remember, Jem, should you want a little more *sleepy-treacle—*'

They rounded a corner. But what was this? His aunt let out a delighted cry. Ah yes; they had passed a little grotto, cut out of the hedge; his aunt stepped inside.

Jem heard voices. Or rather, a voice.

386

'What, *me*? Base flatterer, you couldn't be thinking of another lady, could you? Chaplain, I've never known whether to believe you, that's the trouble. Belle of the ball? Silly man, there's no ball today! What's this? A brooch? A glittering little gem, for a glittering occasion? Why, I'm over-whelmed! Pin it on? Well, if you think you could bring yourself … Oh, but your hand is so soft … now, don't tickle! (*Giggles.*) Why, I'll tickle *you*, I'll tickle your … torso! Oh, Eay! Oh, you naughty—'

So disgusted was Jem by all this that he found himself rallying, just a little. His eyes had drifted shut; he forced them open.

That was when he saw Ejard Orange, standing imperiously on the path before him. In his dream, the big cat had been a starved, pathetic thing; here, he was as he had always been. Twitching his tail, Ejard Orange stared at Jem with flashing eyes.

Jem gulped. If he did not speak aloud, nonetheless he was aware of words passing between himself and the mysterious creature.

—Ejjy! I thought you were dead.

—Of course I'm not dead. But are *you*?

—You can see I'm not.

—You can't move your legs. You can't, can you?

—I can't understand it, I'm a crippler again.

—It's easy. Toth's got the crystals, hasn't he?

—That's why I'm a crippler?

—It was the crystals that made you walk, Jem.

—No … don't say that!

—I have to say it. It's the truth.

—But what can I do?

Imploringly, Jem reached out to the cat; instead, he found himself slumping back in his chair as Aunt Umbecca, brooch flashing, returned from the grotto and Ejard Orange vanished through a gap in the hedge.

'Goodness, this maze *is* winding, isn't it, Jem?'

'But you know the way out, Aunt? Don't you?'

His aunt only giggled, just as she had giggled with Eay Feval, or the entity that was like him. Onwards they went; *crunch* went the gravel under the wheels. Puffing, just a little, Umbecca spoke of the splendours to come, as if they were off to another garden party.

'Jem? Are you asleep again?'

His eyelids flickered. They were halfway round a corner, a turn in the maze at a sharp right angle. Slowly Jem breathed in the scent of flowers, of prickly leaves, of sticky, rising sap. He looked ahead; but his aunt, he realised, was turning back, exclaiming again as footsteps came behind her.

'Chaplain, for *me*? But they're magnificent! Why, indeed I shall be belle of the ball, if ball there … What's that? Eyes would always be upon *me*? Naughty man! Come, but fix them around my neck … must I not don these gems at once? That's right … Chaplain, but your hand is lingering!

Haven't forgotten your *morality*, have you? A lady's torso, after all, is ... a lady's torso! (*Giggles.*) Oh, but how delightful! Chaplain ... oh, Eay!'

The giggles were more frenetic, but Jem, by now, was no longer listening. Round the right-angled turn, the sun darkened, clouded by a strange empurpled glow. Then came a sound he had heard in his dreams: a hurdy-gurdy, its music twisting, twining.

Jem's eyes widened. Barnabas?

The hedge rustled and the little man stepped through, grunting under the weight of his boxy instrument. Now, if only Jem could, he might have cast aside his blanket, rushing to embrace this magical dwarf who had been his first, perhaps his greatest friend.

No good; still Jem's legs were useless. But the dwarf, as if to cheer him up, did a clumsy little dance, scuffing at the gravel, turning the hurdy-gurdy's handle all the while. Long ago, as a boy in Irion, it had seemed to Jem that the tongueless dwarf would speak to him through this music; it seemed that way now.

—Jemmy, are you thinking I can't be real?

—Barnabas, I'm just so glad you're here!

—Oh, I'm always here ... always with you.

—You're a spirit? Of the harlequin ... of Tor?

—Just the King's old jester, that's all I am.

—My father's jester? There's a song ... but they killed him!

—Killed? Are you sure?

—I'm not sure about anything, Barnabas.

—You don't need to be. Just remember.

—There's so much. Remember what?

—That you were a crippler. And then you walked.

At this Jem might have cried out at last, as if by his cry he could regain the power to walk. But now came his aunt, turning back brightly as if she had paused just to catch her breath. The purplish light vanished and Barnabas dived back through the hedge.

'Dear me, what was that sound I heard?'

'Sound, Aunt? I don't think I heard a sound.'

'No? But poor Jem, you're still sick. It's those legs of yours, isn't it? One bowed, one buckled! What a burden ... I know, it's too much for a boy to bear.'

'Yes, Aunt.' Jem's voice was dreamy, but not because he was swooning in a treacle-haze. It was Barnabas who had set his mind swimming. *That you were a crippler. And then you walked.*

But how could he ever walk again?

The maze curved in a long, bow-like arc.

'Nearly there, my love, we're nearly ... what's this? One moment, I think I see something *glinting*, just down that fork of the path. A jackdaw's nest, perhaps? Did I ever tell you that my poor sister Ruanna lost her best tiara to a jackdaw? Saw the naughty creature myself, I did, whisking into the window, then out again ... oh, ever so fast! How my eyes popped! How I shrieked! But a moment, a moment.'

Another voice came as Umbecca scurried off:

—Jackdaw, indeed! She stole it herself, I know she did.

—Who ... who are you? But wait, I know you!

—Can't see me, Jem? Just turn your head.

—I ... but I can barely move at all.

—Then I'll have to dance with you. Come, take my hand.

—Harlequin! But my blanket, it's falling away!

—Only in your mind. But it's all in your mind.

—What do you mean? But this is wonderful!

—Everything's in the mind, Jem. Or starts from there.

—Everything? So we're *not* really dancing?

—Perhaps not. But you might, mightn't you?

Jem gave himself up to his wild cavorting, even though he knew it could not be real. He pirouetted, he pranced, the harlequin holding his hand all the while. Music swelled around them; it was the music of Barnabas, who had burst out through the hedge again. Ejard Orange was there too, raised up on his hind legs, capering in time.

In the background, Umbecca quivered with excitement.

'What, Chaplain, a tiara too? But it's too much! Why, this is fit for a Queen! What's that? That I *should* be Queen? I, and not that nasty little baggage, Jeli? Chaplain, really! Queen Umbecca? Queen, nay, Empress? Empress of Ejland? Empress of the World? But your hands ... naughty man, they're under my skirts! (*Gasps.*) Chaplain, really ... oh Eay! But wait ... what's this up ahead? What's this I see? Not ... *Torvester!*'

At once, Umbecca's pleasure was gone. Painfully, she slumped to her knees in the gravel; her heart pounded hard and she clutched her face.

Torvester? Should she pray now?

No; slowly, she uncovered her face. Heat streamed down between the high hedges. 'Why, Jem, I had quite a turn! I thought I saw ... would you believe, Uncle Torvester? Silly, I know ... oh, but your blanket, it's quite disarranged. Those legs, really! They *are* giving you trouble, aren't they, poor boy?'

Jem's eyes glazed and he nodded.

'You know, I *do* begin to think Goodman Waxwell was right?' Leaning close to her nephew's ear, Umbecca spoke softly. 'You'd be happier without them, wouldn't you? It's not as if you *need* them, and they cause you such discomfort. We'll see about getting you a *little operation*, hm? Quite the simplest of procedures, I'm told, and lots of nice sweetmeats afterwards for brave boys who don't cry out. Yes, Jem, it will be *so* much more hygienic ... *so* much nicer.'

And, glinting in her brooch, necklace and tiara, Umbecca fluffed her nephew's head, hummed a little tune and pushed his chair briskly out of the maze.

Chapter 64

A PLEASANT PARK

'Here we are, my love!'

Leaving the maze, they found themselves in a wide green park, a place of neat lawns, flowerbeds and shady trees. It was the glade from the day before, transformed remarkably; later, Jem would recognise a certain yew-tree and hear, in the distance, the babbling of a brook. Now, far distant, he saw only a golden-domed rotunda of stone and stained-glass, rising in the middle of the park; innumerable figures in robes of gold milled on the lawns.

'Just neaten you up a little, hm?' Umbecca touched a hand to her nephew's cheek; then, with a winning smile, she stepped out before him to arrange his blanket.

For the first time that day, Jem noticed what she wore. Again she was all in white, but in place of her simple robes was the ornate, upholstered garb of a fine lady of fashion. In the distance, he realised, the Bearers – if that was who they were – were similarly dressed, only all in gold; hooped skirts glimmered, bonnets flashed, gentlemen bowed urbanely in elaborate frock coats. There were hats, wigs, parasols, canes; acolytes, dressed as golden footmen, carried golden trays.

Jem saw figures in black; others in white.

And then there was a party in red. He stared.

'I wouldn't bother with *them* if I were you,' Umbecca whispered. 'It's terrible, the people who can worm their way into society these days. After your *little operation*, Jem, I dare say we'll often be out and about together, just you and me, cutting a dash in the great world. Why, I should think you'll become quite a well-loved figure, bowling about in your bath-chair (*strapped in*, of course, never you mind). A famous man of wit, I'll be bound ... might even break a lady's heart or two. Just ignore the *parvenu* types, that's my advice.'

Jem faltered, 'But that's ... they're ... isn't that—'

There could be no doubt. Clustered under the yew-tree's shade, looking about uncertainly, the red party consisted of four of Jem's staunchest friends.

Hul ... Bando ... Landa ... Nirry.

'How that slut has the effrontery to show herself I'll never know,' Umbecca burbled on. 'Doesn't she realise I've put her to death? *Dead*, she is, that's right! Hanged, by the neck! I suppose she thinks I'll have her back in my service. *As if*, Nirrian Jubb! A broken-necked maid who's lost her virtue to boot? (Says she's been married, would you believe?) Perhaps you could try out some of your famous wit on her, lovey? A devastating epigram, that's just what we—'

Umbecca would have gone on, but just then a footman appeared, bowing respectfully, extending flutes of glittering Varl-wine. The fat woman quaffed hers eagerly; in the same time, Jem managed only to take his own glass shakily in hand, spilling a little on his blanket. Flushing, he clutched the glass with both hands, not yet daring to bring it to his lips. He gazed upon the crowd. How far away they seemed!

More footmen appeared, this time bearing trays.

'Vol-au-vents? *Lobster?*' Umbecca grabbed one tray, then another. Forgetting herself – and her nephew, too – she slumped to the grass, gorging. In moments, pastry and white flaky meat stuck, scale-like, round her little mouth and tumbled like dandruff down the front of her gown. She moaned, ecstatic. Creamy dressing oozed between her fingers.

Jem heard a voice. 'Shall we have a look around, my child? This might be the time. Well, *you* can look – myself, I'm not quite equipped.'

'Old Wolveron?' Jem squinted into the light. Yes, he was there: the cowl pulled back; the blind, scarred face. 'But you … you're in your dun-coloured robes again. And the staff in your hand … just gnarled, knotty wood. Why aren't you in costume, like the others?'

'My child, it is a question I could ask of you. Take away that tartan rug and what have you left? A nightshirt, that is all. A flannel nightshirt, in blue and red stripes.'

'But you're blind. How can you know?'

'Don't we know many things that we cannot *see*? But let me push your chair. Ah, this staff of mine, do I really need it now? I think not, don't you? Let me just … throw it away, that's what I'll do. There … Careful of that Varl-wine, by the way. You're not going to spill it, are you?'

Jem hoped he would not. A path stretched before them and the old man ignored it, cutting across the lawn towards the rotunda. On the lawn, one would have thought the chair would give him trouble; on the contrary, it gave him none at all.

'I've never known what to make of you,' said Jem.

'There's not a lot to make. And soon, there will be nothing,' the old man added mysteriously. He paused, turning back. 'Dear me, that staff of mine seems to have grown, just *sprung up*, into a large coniferous tree. Quite spoilt the symmetry of the park. Never mind, all things must pass.'

The chair resumed its progress; Jem, by now, felt a gnawing unease. In the grass he saw a rabbit, twitching its nose; there was a squirrel, scurrying; once, he was certain he glimpsed a fox. Why should these add to his unease? A swallow lighted on an arm of his chair, then hopped away again.

'But Aunt Umbecca?' Jem found himself saying. 'Won't she notice you've taken me?'

The old man laughed, almost giggled. 'I doubt it, don't you? There are few things more beguiling than a lobster vol-au-vent. But I dare say you were enjoying a pleasant conversation?'

'She was talking about having my legs amputated.'

'Personally, I've found it quite unnecessary, so long as a boy keeps himself clean. The word *temple* comes to mind, wouldn't you say?'

Jem realised that his companion referred to the rotunda. Up close, the edifice was larger than it had at first appeared. Fluted columns soared above the crowd, rising majestically to the mighty dome; high in the walls, between the columns, were the long, elaborate stained-glass windows. But where, Jem wondered, were the doors?

'Better than the one you had in Irion, hm? I seem to remember a certain boy who blew it up once. Just remember, Jem, what you used to be!'

Ah, but that voice! Now Jem's unease found its focus and he struggled ineptly to turn in his chair. 'You're not Old Wolveron. You're *not*, are you?'

A masked face leant over the back of the chair. 'No, actually. Silas is off with his daughter. Last moments together, and all that, before ... well, I thought I'd better step in and do this bit. You don't *mind*, do you, Jem?'

Jem looked earnestly into the silver mask. 'And you're not Tor, are you? You weren't really Uncle Tor, were you ... ever? You just *look* like him. You're someone else, but—'

'Well, so are you, Prince Jemany. Perhaps.'

The harlequin's fingers, long and bony, hovered almost tauntingly before Jem's face. There was something in the fingers, something flashing. Then it fell.

'Take this, Jem, take it—'

'Your coin! But I thought I—'

Again Jem tried to swivel round, but the harlequin seized the handles of the chair decisively, saying there was someone Jem *really must* meet. He gave the chair a mighty push and Jem found himself whizzing through the crowd. Ladies squealed and a footman dropped a tray.

❊   ❊   ❊   ❊   ❊

The chair came to rest before a figure in red.

Gulping, Jem looked into the figure's face. So, there was a fifth member of the red party; not a friend, this one, but a figure Jem had seen before, if only when these handsome, angular features had been concealed, like the harlequin's, behind a mask. Of course, the face was familiar; for an instant, Jem saw it as his own. He gulped again, looking down at the glass in his hands. Alas, he had spilt the golden Varl-wine; it lay in a pool in his lap, seeping into the tartan.

'You're my father,' Jem said. 'Aren't you my father?'

The Red King did not even look at the crippler-boy in the chair. A drunkard, white-garbed, wove his way towards them, staggering as if drawn by a force beyond his control. It was Ejard Blue. Hate in their eyes, the brothers faced each other over the arms of Jem's chair.

Now Hul was there, Bando too. Protectively they moved towards the Red King as if to shield him from attack. None came. With drunken tears the Blue King reached out, touching his brother with his mutilated hand. Perhaps he thought this might bring accord between them. It did not; the lips of the Red King only curled and all at once his twin's costume, as if at the running of rampant ink, changed colour from white to blue.

Still the brothers faced each other, lost in silence.

A fox, that happened to be weaving its way through the crowd, looked at them curiously; it swished its brushy tail. A large, shambling bear stood blinking at Jem, but Jem did not look into the huge, furry face. Like the fox, he could only gaze up at Ejard Red, then Ejard Blue.

'Can you see me?' said Jem. His voice was small and piping. 'You can't see me, can you? Hul? Bando? Can *you* see me?'

Despair flooded Jem's heart and he thought that somehow, already, he had lost the harlequin's coin. It was only to be expected. He gripped the wheels of his chair. With a struggle, he set himself in motion, rolling towards the temple wall. This time no one screamed, or skittered out of his way.

But then, his chair was much slower this time.

Chapter 65

THAT YEW-TREE'S SHADE

'Tishy?' Jem said nervously.

A woman in black, like a funeral-goer, perched on the plinth of a tall column. A broad-brimmed hat shielded her face, but the book she held was clue enough to who she might be. She reached out a gloved hand. Padding round the side of the column came Ejard Orange.

She stroked his fur; he purred contentedly.

'They're wrong, you know,' she said. 'They think this day is the last day, don't they? End of Atonement? But this, is it not, is 999*e*? And that, I happen to have noticed, is a leap year – six, not five intercalary days. And what do you think *that* might mean, Master Orange, hm?'

The big cat twitched an ear. 'I think it will have *untold* consequences,' he replied. 'Endings never are as neat as people hope, are they?'

'Can you see me, Tishy?' Jem piped up. 'Ejjy, can you?'

The cat's eyes turned to slits. 'I don't think *she* can,' he purred. 'You're fading out of existence, Jem. No one needs you any more – well, only your aunt, perhaps. Right now you look like a ghost to me.'

'Ejjy, no! Could I help losing the crystals?'

'You'd better hope you couldn't, crippler-boy.'

Jem pouted. 'Why aren't you dead, anyway?'

'Me?' preened the cat. 'Why aren't *you*?'

If this was a riddle, Jem could think of no answer. Miserably, he zigzagged into the crowd again, narrowly avoiding the bear. By now, Jem's sodden blanket was askew and his blue and red nightshirt was sticky with sweat. He bundled up the blanket, flinging it aside.

'Ooh, who threw that?'

Nirry, resplendent in red, looked round, affronted. By her side was Landa; the red-garbed women, like their male companions, had worked their way into the crowd.

Stepping away from the blanket, they resumed a discussion which had apparently been going on for some time.

'Come, Nirry, it's really not so bad—'

'She's *with child*, Miss Landa! And Master Jem—'

'The goddess will take care of her,' Landa said piously.

Nirry sniffed, close to tears. 'I don't know about no goddess, Miss Landa, but I will. Do you think I'll see Miss Cata out on the streets? There's always a bed for her at the Cat & Crown – why, I'd go back to the mistress I would, work my fingers to the bone I would, to take care of Miss Cata ... Miss Cata, and her poor, fatherless child!'

At this, Nirry broke down entirely.

A male voice came: 'Tears, my pretty one?'

It was Polty, wholly white; he even wore a white wig, concealing his flaming hair. Jem's eyes blazed. Uselessly he struggled to rise again.

Polty went to Nirry. 'Come, no tears! A kiss, to celebrate my happiness!'

Grinning, brushing Landa aside, he crushed her friend in his arms. Landa retaliated. She ripped away his wig; like a revelation of evil, his hair blazed free. Polty pushed her to the ground. Loudly he whispered in Nirry's ear, and Jem, despairing, heard every vile word:

'Silly little minx, sobbing for Miss Cata! Can't you see that her troubles are over? Tonight I'll have Penge again – what joy shall then be hers ... What, her *own* little accident's got her upset? Silly darling, but I know, I know ... Of course she's been polluted by the crippler's lust! Don't you think we can fix her up? Don't you think we can start all over again? Why, it's the simplest matter – a moment or two with a crochet hook, and innocence is restored! I'll hazard a guess I could do it myself ... add a little *spice* to an intimate moment, hm?'

There would, no doubt, have been more; but just then it seemed that Polty spied Jem staring up at him, white-faced, from his chair. Polty's brow furrowed. He flung Nirry away.

Savagely, Polty leaned over the arms of the bath-chair. Red curls flopping over his eyes, he shoved his face into Jem's. 'What, Vexing, still not dead? Never mind, not long now! But look at you! What's this stain on your nightshirt?'

Polty looked down; so did Jem. To throw away the blanket had done no good; the stain had soaked through. But it wasn't piss, it wasn't!

Polty's breath gusted in his face. 'And you thought you could win ... a piss-a-pants like you? But you're not even *wearing* pants, are you? Not that you'd have much to put in them if you did! Tonight I'll have Penge back ... then just see what I'll do! Just see, Vexing!'

'I'll ... you'll never—'

There was nothing Jem could say. Polty sent the bath-chair spinning backwards. Jem braced himself, thinking he would spill to the ground; instead, his chair came to rest some distance away, further round the side of the many-columned rotunda. He looked at it despondently. A badger waddled by, accompanied by a hopping bird. Jem thought it might have been a snow-tern.

He sighed. On either side of a column were two figures he knew. Both were in black; both sat cross-legged, ignored by the party.

Or ignoring it.

Littler stared into a sphere of glass. 'I can see her.'

Jem said, 'Littler ... but the orb, I thought you lost—'

Rajal cut across him. 'Who? Who can you see?'

'Myla. She's in here, Raj, I swear it.'

'Littler, it's not real.'

'What's real? She's *in* here.'

'So what's she doing?'

'She's beautiful again. She's young again.'

'Littler, must you torment me?' Sadly, Rajal toyed with the amulet on his wrist. Then he added: 'And Jem? What happened to Jem?'

'Raj, I'm *here*, can't you—'

Littler looked up, into the crowd. 'Ejjy!'

He ran off, orb in hand; sighing, Rajal stared beyond Jem's phantom form. Between golden guests came two white-garbed figures, one resplendent, one spindly and awkward.

The Queen sipped champagne. Her voice was high and braying. 'Indeed, serf, I *used* to be in love—'

'Y-Your Majestic Highness?' said Bean. 'B-But how could you stop?'

'A little piss-a-pants, that's all he was. I'll leave him to Catty – if I don't have her head lopped off, of course. They say those legs of his will have to go. Can't you see Catty bathing his stumps, in some grace-and-favour cottage in a squalid provincial town? Me neither. Oh, but what a sweet boy he used to be!'

A mole peeped up from a hole in the ground, swivelled his little head, then vanished again.

'I'd bathe his stumps,' said Bean. 'I mean, if he were mine.'

'You're hardly of *my* class, serf. No, I want another.'

'Another c-class, Your Majestic?'

'Lover, serf, lover!' The Queen reached out, plucking a golden drumstick as if from the air. 'Have you tried these? Mallard duck – delicious … What about that Poltiss fellow? A fine figure of a man, is he not? Not a gangly beanpole like you – *solid*, he looks.'

'I th-think he's taken, Your Majestic. Besides—'

'Taken? Serf, have you forgotten who I *am*? Oh, but what I suffer! Where's that maid of mine when I need her, that's what I want to know!'

And the Queen, turning this way and that, stamped her little foot; Rajal, meanwhile, appeared to be building up the courage to interrupt. He twisted the amulet on his wrist; he gulped, stepped forward, and sank into the mole-hole.

Bean did not notice; the Queen did, and yawned.

'Hm … what about the *red* fellow?' she resumed.

'Which one, Your Majestic?'

'The tall one, serf! Grant me *some* taste.'

'I … I think he's the King … I mean, the King's—'

'Don't talk to me about my husband! Ah, but he *is* a handsome fellow, isn't he?'

'His M-Majesty? Of course—'

'Not him, serf! His brother! Now why isn't *he* King?'

'There ... there was a war to make sure he wasn't, Your Majestic. Thousands died to—'

Jeli rolled her eyes. 'Serf, what do I care about *thousands*? I need diversion, don't I?'

The voices continued, rolling over Jem's awareness; blending, soon enough, with innumerable other voices. Glasses clinked; somewhere there was music. Jem looked about him at the gold that glittered, at the sun pouring down.

Like honey, sticky honey.

And he thought, *Their ears are open, but they cannot hear; their eyes are open, but they cannot see. They think that life will go on; that after today, all will be as before. They are deaf, they are blind; they speak, but they are dumb.*

It was then that Jem heard the hurdy-gurdy, and someone grabbed his chair from behind. He cried out, protesting. At once, the guests were gone and he moved faster, faster; the hurdy-gurdy played faster, faster too.

Rapidly he orbited the doorless temple, flashing by column after soaring column; trees, flowers blurred past his eyes. Somewhere in the park there was a floral clock, its hands spinning around its face. Jem was ecstatic; he thought he might fly – then there was laughter, and the bath-chair overturned.

❄ ❄ ❄ ❄ ❄

Would *she* see him?

Jem, at the foot of a gentle rise, sprawled beneath the spreading yew. At the top of the rise was Cata. He mouthed her name; he called her name aloud. She slumped on the grass, her black dress crumpled round her; Old Wolveron was there too, bent above his daughter in his dun-coloured robes. The sun fell in dapples through the leaves, almost painful in its pattern of black, white, gold. Rabbits, foxes and badgers surrounded them; there was a nervous robin, and a squirrel eating a nut.

Tears ran from Cata's eyes. 'Papa, no—'

The old man clutched her, held her. 'Darling child, there is nothing I can do. For too long, the part of me that is Silas Wolveron has been dying. Why did I hold to this self so tenaciously, if not that I knew you would come to me again? But this, my child, is the end. Grieve not; all things must pass, and you love another, as each man's daughter, in time, must do.'

'Papa, don't say that! You were the only one—'

'Forgetful child! This illusion, I say, will pass; again you will be what you were born to be, I swear it!'

The tears continued, the endearments too, until slowly the old man disengaged himself from his daughter. He reached for his staff, hauling himself to his feet. In a hollow voice he said again that everything was over; that the time had come when he must assume again his eternal identity of Father-Priest Ir-Ion.

'Then Papa, let me ... let me know you that way!'

'Daughter, soon there will be nothing to know.'

Frantically, Cata struggled to stand, but it was as if she were crippled too. Around her, the animals looked on, alarmed; they might have been imploring her to blend her mind with theirs, to draw upon their powers.

It was no good. She sank down, prostrate. Jem clawed at the grass; he scrambled up the rise, legs dragging behind him. If only he were nearer, just a little nearer! Then, he knew, he could embrace Cata again; then, perhaps, she would see him again.

He slumped back. A carp fell from the branches, silver-scaled, glittering. Shaking off water, it righted itself, floundered on its fins and slithered away into a hole in the ground.

Dreamily, Jem rested a cheek on his forearm, gazing at the park beyond the yew-tree's shade. He saw Umbecca, waddling towards them. The fat woman tut-tutted, shaking her head; beyond her, Jem saw the golden-garbed figures, milling, half-unreal, round the gleaming temple. And now it seemed to him that they were rising, vanishing like spirits into the stained-glass windows. The sun surged hotly; an owl flew; on the lawn, curled into a ball, a bear rolled back and forth; an otter heaved itself from the brook, shook itself and rose into the air, paddling frenetically with its little paws.

Somewhere a bell tolled. There was no more time.

Old Wolveron turned towards Jem; despairingly, Jem looked into the ruined face. The old man's voice was soft, tremulous as the fish swimming in the branches. 'Remember, my son, who you are ... remember who you have always been.'

'I ... was Key to the Orokon,' Jem said blankly.

'And still are ... and still will be.'

'But Toth ... but Polty—'

'My son, don't you know what made you the Key? You, and not another? You, and not Poltiss?'

The old man would say no more, but laid his staff in the jaws of the wood-tiger, which had just appeared from behind the tree. Taking Jem's face in his hands, Old Wolveron raised him up; he kissed his eyes, then let him slump back.

And, sinking again into cushiony grass, Jem felt something hard, something metallic on his tongue. He opened his mouth. It was the harlequin's coin.

Cata cried, 'Papa! Papa, don't leave me—'

But already the old man had vanished; then the bell tolled again, and everything vanished.

Chapter 66

THE GOLDEN CRYSTAL

From somewhere came a humming; then it was a mantra.

Light seeped into Jem's eyes and he saw the patterns from the windows – purple, green, red, blue, gold – slanting palely over the stone floor. He looked up, rolling back his neck, to see the Bearers in their tiered ranks, more splendid now than before. In their elaborate garb, one might have thought them row upon row of golden, perching birds, or a gallery of mechanical women and men, poised upon the shelves of some fantastical toyshop. There must have been thousands: circle upon circle, tier upon tier.

Jem still wore only his nightshirt, striped red and blue. He was back in his chair; beside him, breathing heavily, was Aunt Umbecca. Oh, but that must be wrong, mustn't it?

He peered across the rounded vacancy of the floor. Dust floated endlessly in the tinted light, and equidistant round the lowest stalls, pinioned in place like butterflies, were the strangers who had come to this enchanted place.

The red group: Hul, Bando, Nirry, Landa – and Ejland's rightful ruler.

The black group: Cata, Rajal, Littler, Tishy.

But someone was missing from the black group.

Looking to his side, Jem saw that he was ranged with his white-garbed enemies: Polty, red hair exposed; Bean; Umbecca; Jeli, all in white – and Jeli's slobbering husband, glass still in hand, his garb of white turned blue.

The mantra droned on. Jem bit his lip. The harlequin's coin was gone from his mouth. It was not in his lap; it was not in his hands. Could it matter now? He gripped the wheels of his chair. Yes, he would propel himself across the stone-flagged circle; he would be with Cata, be with his friends, while the world ended around them.

Weariness overcame him. He slumped back.

'You're all right, lovey?' Umbecca whispered. With a knowing look she glanced at Jem's lap. 'Haven't had any more little *accidents*, have we? Your poor nerves ... more sleepy-treacle for you, my lad!'

A fat hand fluffed his hair. 'You know, Jem, I'm so looking forward to your *little operation* ... Won't you be *light* without those nasty legs? Why, I'll be able to pick you up like a baby! Think, Jem ... my very own ickle-wickle baby!'

399

'Aunt,' Jem sighed, 'can anyone else see me?'

'I shouldn't think so, dear. Who would look at *you*?'

Trembling, Jem gripped his wheels again. With sudden violence he propelled himself forward, spinning across the floor, whizzing towards Cata. Yes, he would compel her to see him!

Instead, his chair skewed, as if seized by invisible force; his spine jolted. Slammed back against the curving stalls, he slumped forward, trembling, marooned midway between Polty's party and Cata's. Did anyone see him now? Even his aunt?

The mantra was rising; gold glittered sharply amongst the Bearers, and now the light through the windows was darker. Cata gasped; Ejard Blue dropped the glass from his hand as the colours gathered into a figure, into a form.

Old Wolveron, staff in hand, hovered above the centre of the floor. Bright light surrounded him in a sphere; beyond it, the temple had darkened almost to blackness.

Cata staggered forward. 'Papa ... you've come back!'

There was a crack, like a thunderbolt, and Cata sank to her knees. With a cry, Nirry started forward; Landa held her back.

Polty snorted. He stamped, shuffled.

'Stupid girl ... Poltiss, please!' snapped Umbecca. The fat woman was in the grip of emotion, gazing and gazing upon Silas Wolveron – if Wolveron it were.

Jem gritted his teeth. The mantra, turned into a savage music, crashed in the darkness. He clapped his hands to his ears, to no avail; all around, his companions fell to their knees like terrified subjects of an angry god.

The Wolveron-figure raised a hand. A voice came, echoing from every side, booming and distorting:

'BEARERS, SISTERS AND BROTHERS, REJOICE. FOR AEONS, WE HAVE AWAITED THIS MOMENT, WHEN THE BURDEN OF BEING IS TO LEAVE US AT LAST: FOR AEONS, WE HAVE LONGED TO ESCAPE, SEVERING THE TIES THAT BIND US TO THIS WORLD. OUR VIGIL IS AT AN END. TRANSCENDENCE, AT LAST, IS WITHIN OUR POWER: AT LAST, WE WILL RISE LIKE BIRDS INTO THE VAST. NO MORE CAN WE DELAY. THIS IS THE MOMENT WHEN ALL IS TO BE GIVEN. THIS IS THE MOMENT WHEN ALL IS TO BE RECEIVED. LET THE AVATARS STEP FORWARD, THAT WE MAY YIELD UP THE CRYSTAL WE HAVE CARRIED, PERMITTING THE REUNION OF THE OROKON. BLESSED BE THE LORD AGONIS!

'BEARERS, SISTERS AND BROTHERS, GOODBYE!'

Jem shuddered violently. Sweat soaked his nightshirt. Vomit rose to his throat. At any moment, he was certain, he would jerk to the floor, convulsing.

Grunting, Polty staggered to his feet. He straightened the waistcoat of his suit; he sniffed, and pushed back his ragged hair. Slowly, confidence came to him. He leered; he cracked his knuckles; he bounced, just a little, on the balls of his feet. From somewhere, Jem heard a thump, a scurrying.

He looked up: Mauvers, clustered behind the windows.

Of course: it was time, inevitably it was time, for the fifth passing of the Unbeing Bird.

And only now did the true horror begin.

Polty stepped towards the centre of the circle. His four companions, like a phalanx of guards, ranged themselves behind him. One by one they touched their hands to their hearts, and over each heart there appeared a bright glow. Jem might have covered his face, but he forced himself to look, forced himself to drink in the magnitude of his defeat.

On the spindly chest of Aron Throsh, the one they called Bean, was the crystal Rajal had worn. Tears filled Jem's eyes. The purple crystal had been the first that he discovered, in the labyrinth beneath the Temple of Irion. With longing he gazed upon this dark stone, once flung in rage to the skies by Orok, father of the gods. For how long had this crystal lodged in secret, awaiting the crippler-boy who was to be its discoverer, and be rewarded with the power to walk? If only Jem could grasp it again, this gorgeous, glowing Crystal of Koros!

Jem's tears flowed freely down his face; but now, through the tears, was a blur of green. He saw that it came from Aunt Umbecca, and his sorrow gave way to rage. Was Umbecca to possess what had belonged to Cata? Rolling, lolling upon his aunt's huge breasts was the Crystal of Viana, goddess of earth, that Jem had liberated from its hiding place in Zenzau only at the end of his battle with the King and Queen of Swords.

But here, now, were another King and Queen. As if to contrast with his costume of blue, Ejland's shabby ruler wore the red crystal that had been Littler's; his Queen possessed the blue crystal Jem had lost just the day before. Jem dashed his tears from his eyes. Was Ejard Blue, this hated usurper, fit to wear the crystal of the fire god Theron, that once, far away, had fuelled the Sacred Flame? Was Jeli, Cata's faithless friend, to commandeer the crystal Jem had taken, at such cost, from the sea-goddess Javander?

White-knuckled, Jem gripped the arms of his chair.

These, then, were the avatars of the gods.

In arrogant supplication, Polty raised his arms, stepping yet closer to the Wolveron-figure; in return, the robed figure reached out as if to stretch, impossibly, to his golden sisters and brothers. Now Cata might have rallied desperately, burst forward with cries of *Papa!* and *Papa, no!*

There was no time. All around the rotunda, hands were raised in return; from each pair of hands came a rush of power. There was a roar, as of a hundred, a thousand mighty rivers thundering from their banks.

401

Power surged and surged into the sphere of light.

By now, the Wolveron-figure was invisible, but from somewhere impossibly distant came a triumphant cry. The strangers could only look on, helpless, fixed in place. For a time it seemed as if it would never stop, this flowing, this surging, this immensity of power; then, at last, there was a mighty flash and the circle of light became an uprushing column, bursting through the ceiling in golden glory.

Jem sprawled back in his chair, astonished. Since coming to this mystical place in the mountains, he had often wondered where the crystal might be; now he saw that it had been dispersed, hidden not in any single location but instead in every one of the golden Bearers.

Now what had been scattered was united again. The Bearers were gone; their leader was gone; but what was left, where the Wolveron-figure had been, was the fifth and last of the crystals. Glowing with a brilliance that might have shamed the sun, its beauty and splendour surpassed by far the crystals of purple, green, red and blue.

Slowly, just above head height, the golden crystal revolved.

Chapter 67

TRIUMPH OF THE WILL

The windows burst; glass rained down. Mauvers shrieked, and through the devastated dome fell the vast shadow of the Unbeing Bird. Fire burned in Polty's hair and his white suit took on a purplish tinge.

'It's mine,' he cried, 'mine!'

He lunged for the crystal, but a power repelled him, bouncing him back like a ball.

'What's happening? Toth, what's happening?'

Weird lines of light appeared on the floor, radiating from the crystal in a spiral pattern. Angrily, Polty looked this way and that. Again he darted for the crystal; again he was repelled.

Only after a moment did Polty understand.

'Damn,' he muttered, 'I want this crystal with a lust so strong ... how I rage to grasp it ... how I rage to have Penge restored! In that moment, Cata will be mine, and mine for ever! How can I wait, even for an instant? What, but I must follow this path? What game is this? But follow ... how can I not?'

Swiftly he assumed command of himself again. He barked out orders. Compliantly Jeli, Ejard Blue, Umbecca and Bean linked hands behind him, setting out on the spiral path even as the floor expanded beneath them, massively widening the distance they must cover. Gravity, too, became heavier; every step they took would be an effort, the effort mightier as they struggled on. It was as if they were resisting the order of things. And still, tauntingly, the crystal turned and turned; still, far above, loomed the Unbeing Bird, not passing this time, but hovering in wait.

Time stretched. Mauvers screeched. Discords played from nowhere. Slowly, slowly, went Polty and his companions, like prisoners burdened heavily with chains; but the force that bound the false avatars seemed to have liberated something in the others. All this time the black party, and the red party too, had writhed upon the floor like insects skewered on pins. Now Landa struggled to her knees, clasping hands in prayer, calling upon her goddess. Bando tore at the air, as if to free himself from a web. Littler struggled bravely. Mauvers blundered around him and he beat them away, but as he lashed out something fell from his little jacket. He cried out. It was the Orb of Seeing. Glowing, it rose in the air. Crashing and colliding, the Mauvers retreated.

Jem looked on longingly. Could there still be hope?

High above, the shadow of the Unbeing Bird darkened. The temple shuddered. At once there were cracks in the floor, then mighty chasms, zigzagging wildly through the spiral path. Polty called out hoarsely to his avatars. Ejard Blue stood gibbering. Umbecca almost crashed into a yawning chasm. Jem, in his chair, rolled dangerously back and forth.

Littler's orb arced through the air, orbiting the crystal like a compliant planet.

Then it happened.

Rajal's amulet burst into life. Brightness ran up his arm like fire. Mauvers rushed to attack him; he beat them away with the searing arm. He gazed about him wildly; it seemed that all his vision had narrowed to a point. Clutching the amulet, he cried out a name, the one name that consumed him, all and whole:

'*Aron!*'

Bean, on the glowing path, looked back. He staggered; he blinked. Doubt filled his face and he gulped, hard. It was all the encouragement Rajal needed. The gravity that constrained the false avatars had no effect on him. Gripping the amulet, he rushed forward, leaping cracks and chasms that would open, then close, then open somewhere else in the distending, juddering floor.

He skidded into the spiral path.

Polty reared before him.

'Out of my way, Vaga-boy—'

To Rajal, the insult was fuel to the fire. With courage he had never known before, he would have knocked Polty to the ground. His arms were clasped together, his amulet was glowing – but Polty was too strong. The weird gravity made his fist heavy as stone. He struck Rajal a mighty blow, knocking him flying.

Laughing, Polty flung back his head; agonised, Rajal fell to the floor, almost slipping into a sudden chasm. With his glowing arm he pulled himself free, just as Polty charged, grotesque in slow motion.

'Defy *me*? I'll kill you, Vaga—'

Slowly he stamped on the glowing arm; slowly, he kicked Rajal's head. Gasping, Rajal slipped back into the chasm, clinging, clawing, and only his glowing arm prevented him from falling.

But the arm was fading. A few moments more and Rajal would fall.

'No,' Jem murmured, 'please, not—'

'*Rajal!*' The scream was like a clarion bell.

It was Bean. His face contorting, he ripped the purple crystal from his chest. It pulsed in his hand, jerking as if, with the merest impulse, it would soar back to its rightful owner.

Bean shivered, sweated. His fingers loosened.

Polty turned to him, eyes blazing. 'Bean, you traitor! No, you can't defy me—'

'I … I love him, Polty! I can't let you do this—'

'Love? What, for a Vaga? And a *boy*? Bean, you disgust me! I always thought you were such a girl, and now I know just how much! Throw that crystal, and I chop your spine! Your destiny is to obey me, do you understand?'

Bean tore out his words as if each one were an agony. 'No, Polty, that's how it used to be. I know I've been a fool, but I'll be a fool no more. I've got a life of my own, and a mind of my own too. You've crushed me all my life, but I won't let you crush me any more—'

The glow in Rajal's arm was fading, dying.

'The *crystal*—' he moaned. 'The *crystal*, Aron—'

'*Bean!*' Polty's voice burst like thunder. Only the strange, oppressive gravity prevented him from rushing on his side-officer, there and then, and beating him savagely. 'I tell you, Bean, you're mine, mine for ever—'

'No, Polty … no, not any more—'

The fingers slipped, slipped.

'Aron … Aron, *please*—'

Polty sank down, buckling under the gravity. 'Oh Bean, you don't know who I *am*! Didn't you ever guess? Why do you think old Wynda treated me so well after I had to leave Goodman Waxwell's? Why do you think *your* mother loved me so much? Oh, I didn't understand it myself, not for a long time. But Bean, she was *my* mother, too! Do you understand me, Bean? We're *brothers*, Bean—'

Rajal's glow guttered. 'Aron, I'm … dying! Aron … *I love you*—'

Tears burst from Bean's eyes – or rather, from Aron's. But a brief strength surged up inside him, and he flung the crystal with all his might.

The purple stone arced through the air.

Roaring, Polty swung round to seize it. But Rajal was faster. His arm shot upwards, just in the moment when the glow died, when the amulet faded, when he was about to fall.

He grabbed the crystal.

Exulting, Rajal shot into the air, soaring on a blast of magic force to save his slumped lover, spiriting him away from the spiral path just as Polty, glowing-eyed, would have seared the traitor with annihilating rays.

Landa, joyous, rose to her feet. Her gown had turned green.

There was hope, there had to be!

But above, the Unbeing Bird flapped mighty, mocking wings. In the same moment, Ejard Red charged forward, reckless in his urge to attack his lumbering brother. Something flung him back, but it was no human hand. A force repelled him, as if the two Kings were opposing magnets. The Blue King cowered, then laughed insanely as his brother whizzed back through the air.

Ejard Red lay gasping. Bando rushed to him, ardent to protect his master. Contemptuously, the Red King flung him aside. Leaping up, he whipped out his pistol. He spun it on his finger. The floor was lurching. Again he would have charged forward, defying all the powers of evil magic.

'Bob, no—' Bando cried. It was as if they were out on the Wrax Road again, and the King was Bob Scarlet and Bando his man, sworn to protect and defend him from all. The old rebel leapt up, desperate to save his master from death.

A shot rang out. But if the King thought he could shoot his brother here, as all nature's laws bowed and buckled around them, he was mistaken. The bullet skewed. It was Bando who fell, clutching his chest.

Hul blundered towards him. 'No, not Bando—'

Nirry covered her face. 'Those boys, those poor boys—'

There was no hope. Bando's chest was blown away. He died in Hul's arms.

But all was moving too quickly now; there was no time for sorrow. Again, the Unbeing Bird flapped thunderous wings. The heavy gravity was gone; now everything was lighter. Rolling in his chair, Jem felt a twitch, a shudder in his legs. He was close to Cata. She was on the floor, moaning. All at once, her face twisted towards him. She floated upwards. Recognition dawned in her eyes.

It was Nirry who saw what must happen next. She dashed away her tears. Leaping into the spiral path, she flung herself, almost flew, at an astonished Umbecca.

'Give me that crystal, you fat old cow!'

Again Polty bore down, and would have gone for Nirry; but before he knew it Landa was there, kicking at him, clawing at him, beating him away.

'Bitch, bitch—' He whizzed back, clutching his eyes.

Umbecca was enraged. Fat hands circled Nirry's neck.

It was all that Cata needed. Wildly she launched herself upon her evil aunt, pounding her, pummelling her, tearing at the bloated, murderous hands.

But Umbecca was so strong!

A chasm opened around them. The women writhed, tumbled in the air. Then all at once Nirry was skittering free and Umbecca's huge bulk bounced like a ball, then bobbed down into the yawning chasm, just in the moment when gravity returned.

Umbecca clutched, clung, but all her strength was not enough to haul her huge weight free. Piteous cries erupted from her little mouth. 'Catayane ... Nirry! Save me, save me! Think of all I've done for you! My dears, my darlings—'

Jeli rushed back. What impulse seized her, the Queen could not have said; it seemed there was compassion in her after all. Suddenly she knew how much she loved her aunt.

'Save her! Oh, save her—'

But all Cata could save was the green crystal, ripping it from her aunt's enormous bosom just before the fat woman tumbled down and down.

The chasm snapped shut, and Umbecca was gone.

❄ ❄ ❄ ❄ ❄

New powers filled Jem.

But not enough. Staggering up from his chair, he collapsed at once, sprawling on the cracking floor as his chair rolled away, tumbling into a new abyss.

Meanwhile Polty swivelled back in horror. 'Aunt Becca! Not Aunt Becca—' He dashed Landa aside, Nirry too. Grabbing Cata, he shook her, slapped her. Tears burst from his eyes. Spit flew from his mouth. 'Bitch, you bitch, why did you—'

Hair tumbling wild, Cata struggled against him, the green crystal, all the while, tight in her hand. But now the Mauvers whirled backwards, forwards, following the mystic spiral, and again Polty was decisive. Cursing, dragging Cata after him, he lurched through the shattering fields of force, determined at all costs to seize the golden crystal.

Angrily he signalled to his remaining avatars.

Ejard Blue stepped forward nervously. His wife had collapsed, sobbing, desolated at the loss of her aunt. The Blue King took her hand roughly, dragging her to her feet. They must follow!

Ominously, the Unbeing Bird hung overhead. Still Littler's orb circled the golden crystal, and now the orb began to flicker and pulse. It moved faster, cutting a swathe through the Mauvers, just as Ejard Orange appeared, bounding in front of the Blue King. The King tripped, crying out, and the crystal rolled from his neck. At once Littler was there, grasping the gleaming red stone in his hands. He leapt up, triumphant.

Then the orb exploded.

Again, feeling flickered in Jem's legs. Where the orb had been, turning in the air, was a female form, garbed in blue. It was an old, old woman, a repellent crone. But on her head was a gleaming silver band.

The Lichano band! It had to be!

Spinning, the crone plunged back through cycle after cycle of her age, becoming younger, becoming beautiful, becoming younger still…

In moments, she was a small child.

Rajal cried out. 'Aron, it's my sister … Aron, it's Myla!'

Reaching up, Myla dashed the Lichano band from her head. Rays of light burst around her. Power arced from her hands, zapping into the Queen. Jeli collapsed, convulsing, as the blue crystal tore free, whizzing towards Myla.

Grabbing the crystal, Myla scurried back, just a little girl again, huddling with Littler out of the fray.

407

Polty shouted defiance. With all his strength he surged towards the golden crystal, dragging the screaming, struggling Cata.

But nemesis had come.

Jem felt power surge through him. He staggered to his feet, then staggered no more as his strength returned to him, filling him in a joyous, ecstatic rush. Light churned and fractured around him. His blond hair was radiant; his nightshirt billowed.

'The Vexing? Again?' Polty's lips twisted.

Jem rushed towards him, fist flying back, smashing into the hated jaw. All his rage against Polty, accumulated over years, was contained, concentrated, in this blow he dealt him now.

He could only hope it really was so; for in a moment more, the enemy that faced him would no longer be Polty.

Polty was dead, his head cracked open.

'*My brother, my brother*—' Aron tried to rush to him, but Rajal held him back, gripping him tightly as the piteous, animal keenings tore from his chest.

'Oh Jem, Jem—' Cata darted forward.

There was no time. Jem grabbed her hand. Pell-mell they rushed around the spiral circuit, making for the crystal.

No, Toth would not triumph!

But now came renewed thunderings from above, and the walls exploded outwards. Mauvers flew in all directions. Jem and Cata skidded, fell.

'The Unbeing Bird—'

'It's coming down—'

'Coming for *us*—'

'Wait, it's shrivelling—'

Down, down, came the mighty creature, vanishing all the while into clouds of smoke. The smoke billowed, purple, choking, until at last there was only a column of flame, flickering over the prostrate Polty.

Then the flame was Polty's hair; then the flame was Polty; then Polty was rising, transfigured. His clothes had burned away, revealing his naked body, with its big, heavy scrotum bobbing pathetically beneath a mutilated stump. Like the clothes before, the corpse glowed with Mauverlight; the same eerie light burned from the upright, waving hair; it shone from the pits where the eyes had burst; it seared from the mouth with the blackening, crumbling tongue that now flapped hideously open and shut, out of time, mouthing the depraved words of Toth.

Jem and Cata writhed, helpless, fixed in his gaze.

'Fool, Vexing, fool! Did you think you could outwit me? Did you really think you could defeat TOTH-VEXRAH, greatest of all the Children of Orok? All that has passed here has been but a diversion, the better to amuse me before, at long last, I take possession of the Vexing Gem, and the destiny of this world!'

The purple gaze compelled Jem to rise, but not on his legs. They were useless again; limbs dangling, he hung in the air, as if an enormous thumb and finger pinched him round the torso.

Cata reached up, clutching him. 'Jem! Jem, no—'

It was useless. Toth controlled him.

'Go to the crystal, Vexing! Go to it now! Are you not Key to the Orokon? Is that not the ground of your being? Is that not the foundation of your pride? And proud you should be, to be the servant of TOTH-VEXRAH! Ah yes, on you I have depended to retrieve each crystal from the fastness where it hides. Useful you have been, my idiot child. And now you may perform your final act – or, I should say, your *next to* final? Take the crystal, Vexing. Yes, you are there! Reach out, take it now!'

Lurching through the air, Jem could only do as Toth commanded. Around the ruined temple, the others too could only look on, lost in horror, as Jem's hands at last – but mechanically, joylessly – closed around the gorgeous, sun-like jewel that had been the ultimate object of his quest.

Toth's laughter boomed.

Chapter 68

THE GODS ARRIVE

'Wh-where am I?' Jem murmured.

The laughter had died, the light too, and again the scene around him had changed. The temple, what was left of it, was entirely gone. He might have been back in the glade, but the glade stripped of its flowers and trees, transformed into a wild, desolate moor. Cold winds whipped around him, flapping at his nightshirt. The sky was lowering, purple-grey with clouds.

Jem looked down and saw the crystal, pulsing in his hands; he saw his legs, bowed and buckled, hanging in the air. He hovered above a jagged, circular rock, raised above the moor like a stage; looking up at him, miaowing, was Ejard Orange.

'Don't you *ever* die?' said Jem. 'What, not talking this time?'

The big cat only miaowed again. High in the air, human figures appeared, trapped in bubbles of red and blue. The bubbles floated above the rock, buffeted like sails by the strong winds. In the red bubbles were Ejard Red, Hul, Nirry, and Landa; in the blue, Jem saw Ejard Blue, Jeli, Tishy, and Aron.

But where were the others? Where was Cata?

His gaze roved over the moors. By an outcrop of rock he glimpsed a familiar, swishing fox; he saw a rabbit, a badger, a swallow trembling in the cold.

Now Toth came into view, making his way towards them over a heathery hill. Still the corpse-body was naked and glowing, but clutched in its hand was a long staff like a shepherd's, as if Toth had become some depraved parody of Cata's dead father. Obscenely, the big scrotum bobbed and swayed.

Then he was closer, as if time had jumped. Ejard Orange slipped down from the rock, vanishing furtively into the heather just as the evil thing made a second eerie jump. Then there was a third, and the anti-god stood by the rock, looking up at Jem with his purple-glowing gaze.

A bear shambled behind him, scratching at fleas.

'Vexing,' Toth said wryly, 'perhaps you might instruct the avatars – the *real* ones, this time – to come forward?'

Jem's face was blank, golden in the crystal-light.

'Dear me, but I forget: you are entirely helpless.' With a grotesque smile, the anti-god snapped Polty's fingers – once, twice, three times, four – and

Myla, then Littler, Cata, then Rajal snapped back into being, midway in the air. Crying out, they thudded into the green-brown heather.

A number of fish also fell from the sky.

'Come on, Vaga-boy, on your feet,' said Toth. 'Child of Nature, you too ... you as well, you snivelling brats. What's that, Vexing? Oh, don't look so surprised. This *is* the Rock of Being and Unbeing, after all. That's right, underneath the rotunda, all that time. What, you didn't think it would be up in the mountains? Remember, that mountain domain was half-in, half-out of the Vast? Well, this is part of the half that's *in* the Vast. Where else would you keep the Rock of Being and Unbeing? You don't think Father left it lying around in your world, do you, for any old humans who happened along? Come, come. But what's this? Dear me, I think I hear a noise.'

It was a piteous sobbing. It appeared to come from beneath the Rock. With a sigh, the anti-god stepped forward. He bent down, leaning on his staff, and his purple eye-holes grew alarmingly wide.

'Yes, I see! You are positively *wedged*, aren't you? Never mind, my dear, I think a hefty tug might do it. Don't want to be under there, do you, as we bring about the end of the Time of Atonement? What, and miss all the excitement? I don't think so! Let me just set aside my shepherd's crook. Bear, hold this in your paws, hm? Now, my dear, take my hands ... don't *gibber* so, woman, what do you think I'm going to do? And no, my name is *not* Poltiss!'

With that, Toth tugged, then tugged again. He stood up, mopped his brow theatrically, then made a third attempt. This time he succeeded. He stumbled back, collapsing in the heather, as the immense bulk of Umbecca popped free, like a cork from a bottle. Dishevelled, the fat woman sat in the muddy heather, skirts rucked up and legs sticking out, blinking and drooling like a monstrous baby.

'Well, that's *my* good deed for the day,' said the anti-god, struggling back to his feet. 'Now, where were we? Oh, yes: avatars, your time has come. Come here, Vaga-boy. (Yes, resistance *is* useless, isn't it? And tell your thin friend to stop gawping so, up in his bubble. How you could love such an idiot is beyond me.) Now, lay that crystal of yours there on the Rock. See that sort of *hollow* bit there? There happen to be five of those, and I think that one's yours. What, does it make any difference? Damned if I know, but let's just get the crystals *in*, shall we? Just reunite the Orokon, I say, and leave the details to the pedants.'

He looked again at the bubbles, this time to Hul, then Tishy. 'So neither of you thought to bring a notebook? I'd have thought any student of the ancient ways would *kill* to be here today. And here you are, history unfolding before your eyes, and what are you doing? Trusting to memory! Some scholars you are ... Well, I dare say you could milk it for a lecture tour or two – if you'd still be *alive*, that is.'

The taunting voice continued as Toth compelled Cata, then Littler, then Myla to lay their crystals upon the Rock. None, not even the magical Myla, could disobey his commands.

The creature turned to Jem. 'Now yours. Hm, Vexing?'

Still Jem hovered above the Rock. There, entranced by the evil magic, he had watched his friends set their four crystals in place, almost as if they were offerings, laid down for him. Now, as Toth's voice echoed in his skull, Jem knew the true horror of his bondage. Rajal, Cata, Littler and Myla stood before their crystals. One place remained.

The golden crystal burned in Jem's hands.

'Oh give it here,' Toth cried impatiently. Seizing back the shepherd's crook, he swiped at Jem, dealing him a savage blow. Jem flew through the air. The crystal fell, rolling to the edge of the Rock.

Toth grabbed it. 'I know I needed you to *find* the bloody thing, but I'll be damned if I can't stick it in the hole myself. *There!* Damn, why won't it go in? *There!* What? Stupid hole, it's clogged up or something! Curse it, I'll...'

Jem sprawled in the heather. Several fish floundered around him; Ejard Orange ate one. Umbecca, nearby, howled like a baby. Somewhere an owl hooted. Raindrops spattered down.

But something else was happening in the sky. Imprisoned in their bubbles, some, like Ejard Red, had raged; Jeli, inaudible to the others, had screamed, clawing at the translucent walls. Tishy, distraught, had writhed this way and that; Landa had sunk to her knees and prayed.

And still she prayed; she prayed harder, harder, and her red bubble turned green. For a moment, the green glared out, bathing the scene below. Wonderingly, Jem twisted in the waving heather, just as the phantom forms of the gods flickered into being behind their true avatars.

For Rajal came Koros.

For Cata, Viana.

For Littler, Theron.

Javander, for Myla.

For a moment, time was arrested as Jem gazed at these extraordinary presences. In the El-Orokon, Koros was *a being hunched and twisted, garbed in darkness*; the real Koros was dark, but neither twisted nor hunched. Nor was his sister Viana *soft as leaves*, though leaves and vines covered her beautiful green body, and formed a crown for her noble forehead. No, Viana was formidable; while Theron, despite his fiery redness, despite his leathern wings, was perhaps rather less so than one might have feared. As for Javander, Jem had seen her before, with her waving hair circled by a crown of coral, gold and jewels. In the El-Orokon, she was Theron's sister *cool as water*; Jem knew she was very much more.

Toth turned, enraged. With the force from his eyes he would repel the intruders, destroy them. Instead, the four gods raised their hands, channelling strength into their avatars. Rajal, Cata, Littler, Myla gripped the Rock, clung to it. Light surged from the crystals. There was a flash, and the avatars and the gods were one.

They turned upon Toth.

Rain fell more heavily. The power was mounting.

Toth staggered. Still he clutched the golden crystal, tight in his hands.

Thunder crashed. On and on flowed the divine power.

The bubbles – blue, red, green – buffeted wildly.

But where, Jem wondered, was the Lord Agonis?

Just then, Ejard Orange sprang forward. The big cat leapt on to the Rock. He reared up on his hind legs, dancing, dancing; then he was gone, and a human form was there, dancing in its turn, in a particoloured costume and a silver mask.

'The harlequin!' Jem cried. 'But why—?'

The gods faded, dazzled by the dancing form. The avatars staggered back, themselves again, assailed by some new and mighty force.

Toth raised the crystal, as if about to hurl it. 'Impostor,' he screamed, 'I see through your disguise! No, you cannot triumph! No, you have no existence! Agonis-in-the-Vast, you are merely an ideal! How can your Emanation be here?'

Jem was aghast. *The harlequin ... Agonis? Agonis ... the harlequin?*

But what about Lord Empster?

The silver mask flashed, picking up the crystal-rays, then the lightning.

'Agonis, I'll crush you!' Toth cried. 'Agonis, I'll crush you as I crushed you before!'

Light burst from the anti-god's eyes and all at once, shimmering beside the harlequin, was a dazzling vision of female beauty. Staggering, the harlequin broke off his dance, desperate to clutch the Lady Imagenta.

He flung his arms around her; she shimmered free.

Now she was behind him. He turned; she vanished again.

A new voice burst through the thunder and rain. 'Leave her, Emanation! Leave her, she is mine!'

Jem turned. It was Lord Empster.

'You!' Toth burst out. 'I thought you—'

'What, that I vanished with the golden ones? Fallen creature I may be, but still I am a *god*—'

'A half-god, a damaged god—'

'Evil one, then what are *you*?'

'Lord Empster—' Jem began, struggling to stand, but Agonis-of-the-Earth pushed him back in the mud and leapt with mighty, unnatural bounds towards the Rock of Being and Unbeing. Urgently he grappled with his second self, as all the time the vision called the Lady Imagenta played about them, shimmering and slipping like the cascading rain.

Toth reeled. 'No! No, this cannot be—'

413

Imagenta vanished, but still the half-gods struggled. The avatars were forced back, helpless to intervene. Surging with power, Agonis and Agonis rose into the sky, turning and tumbling in the rain above the Rock.

And all the time the golden crystal seared ever brighter in Toth's hands, threatening at any moment to burst free from him, spinning up towards the dazzling contenders.

Suddenly Jem realised what was happening. 'They're – they're fusing! The crystal's power ... it's bringing them together! Toth can't hold it, not for much longer ... they're drawing it towards them, they need it to *unite*—'

Wind howled around the half-gods, but now came the voice of Toth, louder than the wind, crying out his defiance as still he struggled to keep the golden crystal.

'No, Agonis ... no, never! My reign depends on your eternal division! For what did I create the Lady Imagenta, that dream in a glass, if not to damn you to disunity, plunging the earth into chaos? No, even if it must leave my hands, I swear this stone will not fuse you again!'

The anti-god reeled, purple light flaming. Cata struggled towards him, Rajal too. Myla focused her powers; Littler darted round his heels. Toth turned, turned. He would not give way, he would not!

He twisted back, flinging the crystal away. The avatars stumbled, fell. Toth's strength left him; he slithered too, collapsing into the mud, his flames guttering.

The crystal seared, glittered through the rain.

It turned, it tumbled. It smashed into the bubble that contained Ejard Blue.

There was a shattering, like glass; the Blue King screamed, plummeting through the air; at once, Ejard Red was propelled towards him, whizzing on a surge of mystic force.

Jem gasped, 'No—'

Like twin cannonballs the Kings collided, exploding in a nova of red and blue.

In the waves of force, the other bubbles burst – blue, red, green – and the prisoners inside them vanished.

Then the half-gods vanished too.

There was silence above the Rock, a zone of calm where the storm did not rage.

And there, in the silence, the golden crystal returned.

It was Jem's chance. He was numb with shock. Was Nirry dead? Was Hul? Jem could not know; but still, like a curse, his powers came pulsing back. Slithering, hating himself, he scrambled up. He leapt forward, seizing the crystal, plunging it into the Rock of Being and Unbeing.

It was over, all over.

But it was not.

❋ ❋ ❋ ❋ ❋

The five crystals glowed.

Slowly, then rapidly, the Rock began to spin. The avatars rose. Again the four gods flickered into being, as if they would channel their powers again in some last, apocalyptic surge. But now came the anti-god, returning too. He materialised on the Rock, swatting Jem aside.

Jem's legs buckled. 'Toth! But how—?'

'Fool, did you think you had defeated me? Fool, did you think you had triumphed? How could you triumph, when Agonis is destroyed? *Don't you see, I have destroyed Agonis, fairest and greatest of all Orok's children?'*

'I—' Jem's words caught in his throat.

Toth smiled, eyes glowing. 'Ah, Vexing, I always knew I could rely on you! Like the faithful servant you are, you have assembled the Orokon, the guarantee of my power. And now I have no use for you. Five times the Unbeing Bird has passed; five crystals have I clutched in my hands. Now this Time of Atonement is over. Now begins the aeon – nay, the aeons; nay, the eternity – of almighty Toth-Vexrah!'

He flung back his head, laughing insanely. Thunder crashed in the storm-world beyond. Prostrate, Jem clung to the revolving Rock. Here, there were only the crystals, the lights; only the terror of Toth's consuming evil.

The gods had gone.

And Cata? And the others?

Despair filled Jem's heart, bursting like the thunder. But now Toth was growing, changing. There was an uprush of purple light and Polty's corpse burst open, scattering into fragments of bloody meat.

Screeching filled the skies. Again, Toth became the Unbeing Bird; then the creature that had been called Chorassos went whirling backwards, backwards through the tormented air, assuming once more its true, primitive form. Suddenly it was there, immense, filling the skies.

Sassoroch!

Jem was certain that his death had come. He sprawled across the Rock, helpless, as the mighty wingèd serpent swooped for the kill, poison dripping from its fangs, evil glowing from its scales and eyes.

Then came the cry. 'My baby, not my baby—'

It was Umbecca. Keening, the fat woman rushed forward, flinging herself over Jem's prone body. And lolling in paralysis, the breath knocked out of him, Jem watched, horrified, as the serpent swooped up again, up and up through the storm, clamping his aunt between its huge jaws.

For once, Umbecca looked piteously small.

And just once the jaws gnashed, and she was gone.

415

Jem gasped. Tears filled his eyes, bursting forth in sudden, inexplicable grief for this vain, deluded, evil woman who had tormented him from his infancy.

But there was no time for despair. Cheated of its prize, the serpent swooped again. Jem braced himself. There was no escape now. He cried out, screamed and screamed, abandoned himself to pure, blank fear.

Cried out to Cata.

Cried out to the gods.

Screamed, screamed for the harlequin.

And that was when it happened.

Time stopped. Sassoroch froze; the storm froze; and the blasted heath was only a painting, far across a room. An ornate drawing room, a place of gold and velvet, like one that Jem remembered from Lord Empster's house.

And gazing on the painting, there was only Jem.

Only Jem – and the harlequin.

Chapter 69

THE ETERNAL MOMENT

Hey, ho! The circle is round!
Where can its start and its end be—

'Harlequin?'

Still Jem wore his nightshirt, but it was purple, as if the colours had run in the rain. He supposed they had; but now he was dry, warm too, lying on a chaise-longue. On a marble mantelpiece, a clock ticked; a fire crackled brightly, and the harlequin's song was murmurous, like a lullaby. Jem was comfortable, very comfortable.

But still crippled.

The harlequin, perching beside him, removed his mask. Setting it down on a little inlaid table, he turned to look at his young companion with a face, thought Jem, that was nothing at all like Uncle Tor's.

'Aunt Umbecca,' Jem found himself saying, 'is she dead?'

The harlequin smiled. 'I should think so, wouldn't you?'

'And the others? Cata and Raj and—'

'Hush, Jem. Soon, all will be revealed to you. But perhaps there is *one* clue in this chamber now.'

The harlequin's hand – it was bony, Jem reflected, indeed skeletal – gestured towards the fireplace. And there, suddenly, stood a slender feminine figure, a figure Jem had seen before. Face averted, she was dressed in nun-like robes – nun-like, yes, but patterned in stripes.

Would she turn? Jem did not think so.

He looked again at the harlequin. 'I saw *you* die.'

Again the harlequin smiled; then he sighed. 'Jem, you saw nothing of the kind – you saw, rather, the failure of my attempt to heal myself. What has become of my earthly being, it is yet too early to say; all I know is that still I am condemned to be divided.'

'Into how many pieces? Ejard Orange, was he one?'

'I have gone, it is true, by a number of names. *Barnabas* is one you might recall.'

'You were Barnabas, too?'

'And Zady. Remember Zady?'

Jem shook his head, bewildered. 'What about Rainbow? What about … Buby the monkey?'

The harlequin laughed, but with little mirth. 'Let's not go *too* far, Jem. Just remember, I have always been with you, but my being-in-the-world is unstable. Hence my many identities. Hence my disappearances.'

'But you're really Agonis? That one is real?'

'It depends, I suppose, what you mean by real. What Toth said was true. What I am is an ideal, that cannot really exist – *cannot*, that is, while my severed self, the being who has been known principally as Lord Empster, remains abroad in this world. No, Jem, I don't exist. I can't.'

'Can't? Then how *can* you?'

'Ah, but what is real, and what is illusion? Didn't I ask you that once before?'

'I suppose you did.'

Uncertainly Jem gazed again at the painting, far across the room, immeasurably far. A moorland scene, just a moorland scene. Dark. Stormy.

By the fireplace, the rainbow lady shifted a little. Perhaps she *would* turn.

But she did not.

Jem said, 'And what happens now?'

'To Toth? We'll see, soon enough. The Time of Atonement must end in any case. But the new age? I wonder. Remember, I have not been reunited.' The harlequin arched an eyebrow. 'Shall we say, there has been a *different* union?'

Jem was puzzled, but his strange companion made no move to explain. 'Still,' he added, 'I think we might just save the world from the anti-god – this time, at least.'

'*This* time? You don't mean—'

The harlequin raised a staying hand. 'Oh yes,' he went on, 'a new age will dawn, as new ages do. But I doubt it will be an eternity of peace. Perhaps that could never come – not in the earth my father made.'

There was a pause. 'But ... will I be crippled? And Cata? You haven't said about Cata.'

The harlequin, it seemed, would not reply.

'I see,' said Jem. 'And what will happen to you?'

The tall figure stood, pacing the rich, swirling-patterned carpet. He turned back, smiling. 'I dare say I'll carry on as I've always done. What else?'

'And Lady Imagenta? You don't still want to find her?'

The smile faded; the harlequin hung his head and Jem found himself looking, once again, upon the curious vision that was the rainbow lady. His brow furrowed and he wondered, not for the first time, who she was. Could *she* be the Lady Imagenta? Or her Emanation? Or someone else entirely?

He murmured, 'She's just an illusion. Toth said so.'

'And did I not ask what was real, what was illusion?'

'Cata's not an illusion,' Jem said defiantly. 'Cata's real, I know she—'

He bit his lip. The rainbow lady was turning and Jem's heart hammered, as if at last he might see her face. But all he saw was the golden light, streaming from where her face should have been.

There was a knocking at the door.

'That must be Ondon,' said the harlequin.

'Ondon?' said Jem, not remembering the name.

Coolly, the harlequin started towards the door, then turned, as if thinking better of it, and returned to the chaise-longue. The knocking continued as he bent close to Jem's face, whispering, '*Remember, the way has been prepared.*'

'Way? What way?'

But the harlequin only smiled again. Still came the knocking, and the clock ticked in time. He gestured to the painting. 'Time rushes forward, though we think that it does not. Embrace me, child, and leave me for the last time. You know what you must do. You need my help no more.'

'No, harlequin, I … don't leave me, *please*—'

'My coin – take it, just take it. This time, take it.'

And all at once the drawing room was gone, and Jem, coin in hand, was snapped back inside the moorland scene.

But not for long.

Still the storm raged; still Jem, helpless, sprawled upon the Rock. Wildly he gazed, terror rushing back, as the serpent Sassoroch swooped again.

Then, searing with crystal-light – purple, green, red, blue, gold – the Rock rose up, spinning. There was a deafening screech, louder even than the storm, louder than the swooping serpent in its terrifying downward rush. A vortex opened, like a mighty whirlpool of darkness, tearing a hole in the dimensional walls. Jem felt his nightshirt ripping from his back. The purple fabric twisted away. He was naked against the storm, against the dark swirl. Then suddenly Jem, Rock and all, was sucked out of the Vast, hurtling back to the earth.

But not to the mountains.

He screamed and screamed. Still the Rock spun in the air, but now it was ruins that stretched below, bombed out, burned, blackened. There were ragged crowds, fleeing. Explosions. Fires. And still came the thunder, still the wild storm. Lightning zigzagged massively from the clouds, and in the wrenching, booming stormlight Jem knew that he was in Agondon – Agondon, city of his nightmare.

But worse, so much worse.

For now a new wildness crashed through the clouds, bursting into Being, filling the tormented skies above the city. Again Jem could only scream. *Oh Sassoroch, Sassoroch!* All the world was Sassoroch, this serpent of the skies, with its golden coils, its wings, its claws, its fangs, its tail, this avenging anti-god in its true and most terrible form.

And ranged against it? A crippled, naked boy on a spinning stone, no more!

It was the end of everything. In an instant, Jem would be gone, dead, as if he had never existed. He would not matter, nothing would matter.

But no, for then Sassoroch would turn upon Agondon, ardent in a lust for vengeance that could never be appeased. How Jem cursed his weakness! How he cursed fate, time, destiny! With bitter hatred, he cursed the harlequin.

But all at once, Jem knew what he must do.

Clutched in his fingers, tight enough to cut him, was the harlequin's coin. He flung it into the storm, up into the path of the oncoming serpent.

The Rock spun. The coin spun.

And Jem lived through an aeon of time. He rose up, hovering, a tiny, naked thing, the merest insect against Sassoroch's might. But somewhere on the air around him he heard a tentative music. It was a promise of harmony. He would hear it again, and each time, too, he would hear a verse he knew.

This was the first.

> *The Child who is Key to the Orokon*
> *Shall Bear the Mark of Riel*
> *& Have in Him the Spirit of Nova-Riel:*
> *But his Task is Greater as the Evil One is Greater*
> *When the End of the Atonement Comes*

Spin, spin.

Enraged, Sassoroch contorted in the air. Did the creature know, even then, that its triumph was over? Could it not have battered Jem aside, forgotten him like the tiny thing he was? What was Jem to the city below?

But the anti-god, too, was caught in the grip of destiny, time and fate. All was as it had been in the Narrative of Nova-Riel, that old tale that Jem, as a child, had read in a crumbling book. Spiralling up towards the creature's jaws, the crippled boy – but this time it was Jem – made Sassoroch turn, then turn again. And Jem, bedazzled, wondered why it was that he had grown to manhood, only to play the part of a child.

A ringing chord. A verse, once more:

> *For Sassoroch shall come again from Unbeing*
> *& his power shall be a Hundredfold:*
> *But now he shall Bear his True Name & True Visage*
> *That were Hidden from the World*
> *When he was Sassoroch*

Spin, spin.

Jem could have laughed. True visage? How could Toth have a true visage? But even in this the anti-god revealed that he was damned. What was he, really? Nothing! Even now, as his serpent-self turned, and turned again, Toth displayed the impotence that would leave his vengeance undone.

Round and round Jem passed before the slavering jaws; round and round like the turning coin spun the crazed, stupid creature. Riel, in the act that had made him Nova-Riel, had made the monster turn ten times; for Jem, and this monster so much mightier, the turnings must be a hundredfold.

How many now? Ten? Ten already?

But the verse, the verse:

> *& before the return of the Evil one*
> *A time of Suffering shall Descend upon the Earth*
> *& This shall Herald the end of Atonement:*
> *& Only the Power of the Orokon*
> *Shall Defeat the Evil that then shall come*

Spin, spin.

Scales flashed. Eyes flamed fire. Twenty times? Thirty?

Claws struck out. Again, again Jem was almost burned to nothingness, ripped apart, devoured.

It could not be, it could not! The power was with him.

Below, the Rock revolved, as if in time with the coin, and the coin arced higher above the clouds, beyond the vision of Jem, of the serpent, of the onlookers below – for yes, a crowd had clustered, terrified, but intent upon the battle.

Forty times? Fifty?

Soaring, dazzled, Jem looked down.

And saw them. Cata. Rajal. Littler. Myla. They were there, they were all there! And was that Nirry? Was that Hul? Joy filled his heart as he swooped again beyond the serpent's range, avoiding another shattering bolt of power. What was this power, against the gathering harmony? Jem shot behind the monster's head, then out again in front of its blistering eyes.

Round and round. Sixty! Seventy!

The harmony. The verse:

> *& The Child shall find first the Crystal of Darkness*
> *Flung to the Skies by the Father of the Gods:*
> *& He shall Quest through the Lands of El-orok*
> *For the Crystals of Earth Fire Water & Air*
> *That he may Unite them in the Orokon*

421

Spin, spin.

How many times? How many times?

Wild in his excitement, Jem was no longer a naked cripple, hurled through the storm by forces beyond his control. No, he was King, and Cata was his Queen.

Yes, it could still be! Yes, it had to be!

Lightning crashed around him, flames seared from the serpent, but Jem laughed.

Then the serpent, seething in its fury, reared back with new, impossible violence. A claw dashed at Jem, sending him spinning. He crashed against the writhing, coiling body, sticking in a gap between the scales.

Sassoroch whipped round, eyes blazing.

Jem struggled, struggled. He wrenched himself free.

But again the serpent was upon him.

Jem floundered through the storm. He could struggle no more. Bolt after bolt of energy shot past him.

How many times? How many times?

Discords filled the air. The coin was coming down. And down, down bore the slavering monster, tearing apart the skies with its mighty wings.

It was over, it had to be.

But before death, in the instant before, comes a last suspended moment. For Jem, this moment was now. Down he gazed, down through the buffeting snow, past the tattered, tormented clouds, past the spinnings of the crystals in the Rock. What could the crystals mean to him now?

One glimpse of Cata. One glimpse more.

And through the storm he saw her – a glimpse, yes, but it might have been eternal. In the square below, she had risen up, raven hair twisting, dark against the snow. She had flung back her head. And surrounding her in a circle, closing in upon her, were the creatures that had been awaiting her all this time, hovering so near, cleaving so close.

Undoubtedly they were illusory, not real, fantastical in the environs of this ruined city. But there they were – bear, badger, rabbit, tiger – all the old friends, her only friends, from the days when she had been just a child of nature. Back to her came the spirits of the Wildwood. Was the snowtern there? The owl, the robin, the swallow?

All were there – they had to be – and closer they came, closer and closer, vanishing into her very being.

The moment was over. The glimpse was gone. But now Cata shrieked out an inhuman sound, calling on the magic that had always been hers for the taking when the time came.

That time was now.

Longingly, Cata flung up her arms.

Up, up rushed the power through the sky, exploding into Sassoroch in a mighty flash.

The serpent reeled, rallied, then bore down again. But new energies surged through Jem too, feeding on Cata's mystic force. Already he had whizzed away, vanishing into the clouds. The serpent turned, wings whipping, tail lashing madly.

Again Jem swept down, again. Turn, turn.

Exulting, Jem heard the verse again:

> & If he Succeeds a New Age shall Dawn
> & all the Lands of El-orok shall Live in Peace:
> & If he Fails the Horror that has Passed
> Shall be as nothing to the Horror
> That shall come

Spin, spin.

Faster, faster, the coin was coming down.

Ninety times, a hundred, the Toth-creature turned.

He had won! Jem had won! A new vortex opened, ripping apart the skies, and this time it was a vortex of light. Shrieking, Sassoroch vanished into Unbeing.

Jem hurtled, tumbled through the storm.

Then all at once, the storm was gone; instead there was music, just one chord, but this time a harmony so all-encompassing that the very universe might have stopped there and then, all striving over, all passion spent.

And then the world was still.

Radiant, Jem hovered in the clear, cold calmness. He saw the Rock far below him, still revolving; he saw the crystals, shining out their glorious rays.

And Cata? She was lost in the new, strange brightness.

But Jem saw the coin, spinning, spinning down.

The coin struck the Rock.

And that was when an immense, shadowy form rose from the darkness within, filling the sudden calmness of the sky just as Toth, in the guise of Sassoroch, had filled the storm. But this time there was no violence, no sound.

How to describe it, this new, mighty presence? Later, neither Jem nor any of those gathered below could even have attempted to do so. Only for the merest fragment of time could they even gaze upon it, awestruck, before they were compelled to turn their eyes away. All they knew was that they were confronted by a power greater than any they had ever known before, greater than the power of the anti-god, greater than the powers of Koros, Viana, Theron, Javander; greater by far than the Lord Agonis.

It was Orok, the Ur-God.

The form swept round in a mighty arc, wielding an immense sword. From somewhere – as if, impossibly, from within the very silence – came words, words like thunder, but spoken in no human tongue. Perhaps it was a blessing, perhaps it was a curse, raining down on humankind as the sword descended. Then the Ur-God was gone, leaving a desolation that could hardly be explained.

Then the Rock exploded.

At last came cries, screams from below.

Like searing fireworks, the most glorious ever seen, the five crystals of the Orokon soared above the city, scattering again to the corners of the earth. Purple, green, red, blue, gold, the strangest of rainbows filled the skies; at last it dispersed, leaving only a hovering shape, high above, like the sword wielded by the father of the gods. Above it was a pointed arc.

Then the arc-sword vanished, too.

And then Jem was falling.

Chapter 70

THE POWER OF GOODBYE

'Jem – oh, Jem…'

Jem stirred. How could he still be here in this world? Through blurring eyes he was aware of human forms, moving as if in a distant dream. He saw the brightness of the sky, a cold hard azure, and felt the scratchy texture of a blanket … No, it was a coat, certainly a coat; someone must have laid it on top of him. But there was nothing beneath; he had not been moved.

With no particular concern, Jem felt the snowy ground, biting into his naked flesh – the flesh, at least, that could still feel. And how much was that? He tried to move his head but it was a leaden weight; all he knew was that, forming a pool beneath it, spreading round him like a halo in the snow, was something sticky, something not quite cold like the snow.

Something red, undoubtedly red.

'Oh, Jem … Jem—'

He screwed up his eyes. His head, he began to think, was at an angle; a strange one. He saw a ruined chapel, just a jutting spire, no more. And what was that? The hanging, smashed gable of an Elabethan house?

Above the sobbings, the murmurous voices, Jem heard a squeaking. Could it be a rat, one of Agondon's millions of rats? No, the fancy came to him that it was a tavern sign, swaying in the wind; the sign, he was certain, was of a marmalade cat – a cat with a crown…

Jem would have laughed, had he been able. He had fallen to earth somewhere on the Island, somewhere in the square called Redondo Gardens. Should he think it an indignity, to die in such a place? He, Key to the Orokon – he, Prince of Ejland?

No, it was good. No, it was right.

'Jem … Jem, oh—'

'Cata … Cata—' Now Jem saw her, shimmering above him. Close by, he knew, were others of his friends. Good old Raj, he was here, wasn't he? And Littler … and Myla? And Nirry, was she here?

Poor Nirry, had the Cat & Crown been bombed?

Jem would have asked, but did not have the strength. For moments, he was aware only of Cata's hand, stroking his forehead; of her voice, too, choking out endearments between her sobs – endearments, and promises … But promises of what? Perhaps she was speaking of the child they would have, the child that Jem would never see. Could he have spoken,

425

Jem might have said much about this son, or this daughter; but more, much more, about his love for Cata...

He drifted away as if on soft waves. Visions played in his mind, visions of his mother and his Uncle Tor, visions of Barnabas and the harlequin, dancing so strangely on the village green ... Jem saw Rajal, shy and surly on the day they first met; he saw poor, abused Polty; he saw his fat aunt – dear Aunt Umbecca, he could almost have smiled – and the Great Mother and Robander Selsoe and Princess Bela Dona and Pellam Pelligrew and good old Captain Porlo...

What enemies Jem had made! But what friends, too!

A whisper came to his lips. Again, his eyes opened. 'What a life it's been ... what a life, Cata. I can hardly believe it's over.'

'Don't talk like that, Jem.' The voice was not Cata's. Clutched in Nirry's arms, Cata sobbed helplessly; Landa, keening softly, stroked her hair. No, it was Rajal whose voice came now. Taut-faced, he loomed above his beloved companion. 'Nothing's over. Your life, it's just beginning—'

'I'm smashed up, Raj, all smashed up—'

'You'll be well again. Myla's here, her powers—'

Jem would have shaken his head, had he been able. What could Myla do now? His eyes flickered to the side and he became aware of Hul and Tishy hugging each other, looking down at him, their spectacles flashing over anguished eyes. Jem smiled at them as if in blessing. 'And what about your friend, Raj? Is he with you? Did he make it back?'

Rajal gulped. Yes, Aron was here, with them now; shyly, he gripped his lover's hand.

'Be happy, Raj. Just remember, I've loved you too ... in my way. And Myla? Where's Myla? Darling child, what a burden you've had to bear! But it's all over now, you're safe now ... Come, don't be sad for me ... Littler, you're not going to be sad, are you? A brave boy like you? Remember what I told you when Rainbow died – that he'd live on in your heart, safe and sound? Well, I've got a feeling I'll be seeing Rainbow soon, and I'll be right there beside him, Littler, right there ... No, how can you be sad? What an adventure we've had! What friends we've all been! Why, when I was a little boy, I used to dream of all the future might hold. How could I have guessed? Such adventure. Such love. I'd never have believed there could be so much.'

Cata rallied. 'Jem ... Jem, please—'

But by now, Jem was struggling, his eyes closing again; and again his life swam back through his mind, all out of order and mysteriously mingled. He saw the Castle of Irion and the Sanctum of the Flame; he saw the house in Davalon Street, with golden scrolls above the windows and doors. There, a raw boy from the provinces had lived in the guise of Lord Empster's ward. Jem saw himself, absurd in silk and lace, skating on the

River Riel; he saw himself jogging along in a coach. Then there was the *Catayane*, heaving on the waves; then the Temple of Wrax and the flying Isle of Inorchis and Javander's Briny Citadel, deep beneath the waves ... There was so much; there was too much. But always there were the crystals, burning in their brightness.

And always there was Cata.

Jem struggled harder. Death moved closer, but again he opened his eyes; again, the face above him was Cata's. Marvelling, he gazed into the dark, beloved countenace. If only he could have gazed upon her for an age! If only the time before them were not so cruelly short!

'I'm ... I'm shivering, Cata. Burning, too—'

Her tears splashed his face. 'I won't let you die, Jem—'

'My love, it's better this way, can't you see? I was just a pawn in destiny's game; I forgot that for a while, that's all. And now I've done what I was meant to do. I did it well, didn't I? But now it's over ... and I must go. Oh, it wouldn't have been any good, Cata. I'd have just been a crippler ... without the crystals, I'd have just been a crippler.'

Cata gulped back her sobs. 'You fool, Jem, you were never just a crippler with me! Don't you remember, when you came to me in the Wildwood, long before your quest even began? There was magic between us, a magic even then. You gripped my hand, and suddenly your crippled legs didn't matter any more. With me, you rose to your feet. With me, you walked. That wasn't destiny, Jem, that was *me* – you and me. You ran, Jem – with me, you *ran*.'

Cata would have gone on, but Jem was no longer listening. By now, his breath came only in pained gasps, but between the gasps he forced out some last words.

'Loved you, Cata ... want you to know that I always ... loved you. And if I live on ... in a world beyond this, I'll ... love you still, Cata. It can't end, nothing can ... take my love from you ... my love is for ever ... for ever, Cata.'

Jem slumped back, his life leaving him. So this was death, so this was death at last! But yes, he was right: it was better this way. The pain was at an end, and he surrendered gladly.

Distantly, retreatingly, he heard cries:

Master Jem! No, please—

He's gone, he's gone—

No, he can't, he—

Then the cries were gone, and Jem was far away, standing on a hill on a sunlit afternoon, with a broad highway stretching palely before him.

Yes, this was death: this was the way.

But then came something stranger by far. Could this be a trick, some last delusion of departing life? He heard a voice again, coming closer. Perhaps it was a whisper, hot against his ear; perhaps it sounded only in his brain. At first he was joyous, for it was Cata – Cata coming back to him, one last time.

Then the anguish gripped him. Then the pain.

—Jem, I said I won't let you die. And I won't.

—My love, you can't stop me. Not now.

—But I can. All my life, I've had a power within me.

—Of course. Cata, it was *you* who saved the world.

—It was us together, Jem. Your powers. And mine.

—But my powers are gone, Cata. Mine are gone.

—Mine aren't. I'm going to grip your hands, Jem.

—Cata ... Cata, what are you doing?

—Don't sound so fearful. I have to do it. I love you.

—Cata ... *Cata, no! Cata, stop!*

Jem cried these last words aloud. But cries were all around him. Could that be Landa, could that be Myla, pleading with Cata in sudden, terrible certainty? And whose was that voice crying, *Death, it's death*? Whose was that throat opening to the skies, shrieking out in terrible, desolating pain?

Jem was standing naked, the coat falling away. Then there was Cata, falling into his arms.

She clutched him, clung to him.

And then she was slipping, down, down.

He lay beside her, kissed her, as her eyelids closed. Could that be a smile, playing over her lips?

'Oh, my love, what have you done?'

The snow was so cold, terribly cold. Then Nirry was beside him, gasping, convulsing. 'Miss Cata ... there was a light, pouring out of her—'

'She was too weak,' sobbed Myla. 'After Sassoroch, she—'

'Her Essence,' moaned Landa, 'it's ebbing, ebbing—'

Jem could not hear them. All his friends were around him, but they were so far away. There was only Cata; and Cata was lost. He clutched her hard, so hard it seemed he would never let her go. But already she was cold, so cold!

Numb with shock, Jem gazed ahead blankly. It was late afternoon. The light had begun to fail and snow fluttered down again; already, high in the sky, hung a purplish, pock-faced moon.

Then came the vision.

Jem staggered up, startled. For a moment he tried to keep hold of Cata, but could not prevent her from slipping out of his arms. Dimly he was aware of someone – Rajal, perhaps, or Hul – draping the coat around his shuddering shoulders. But he could not draw it about him, only let it fall as he gazed and gazed upon the rainbow robes, the golden face. He heard music, a song. And from somewhere, some cavern deep in his mind, he heard the harlequin's words, telling him that the moment had been prepared.

428

Closer, closer, came the dazzling vision, gliding across the snowy ground. By now, Jem had to screw up his eyes, shielding them with a hand against the light.

Then the light dimmed, fading slowly away. And at last, Jem looked upon the being's face.

He cried out.

Cata. It was Cata.

At once, the vision was retreating again, vanishing across the ruins of Redondo Gardens. Sobbing, crying Cata's name, Jem pursued her. Somewhere behind him were Rajal, Aron, others: but Jem ran too fast.

He stumbled to his knees. It was no good, no good.

The Empress of the Endless Dream had gone, bearing Cata's Essence away with her to the Vast.

※　　※　　※　　※　　※

Jem's hands covered his face. So this was salvation. So this was all it would be.

He breathed deeply. There were no sobs left in his throat; he barely felt the cold that had turned his flesh a mottled bluish-purple. What could he feel but blankness, a blankness that would last for all his life? *Oh Cata, Cata!* Had she known she would die, using up the last of her powers to give him life? Had she really meant to leave him? And to take their child? Jem knew nothing, only that he was alone, and would always be alone, abandoned for ever in this world he had saved.

But not quite alone.

From close by came laughter. Girlish laughter.

Empty-eyed, Jem looked up. It was Jeli. Perched upon a ruined wall, the Queen twisted a lock of blonde ringlets. She bit her lip, gazing upon the naked young man. Coyly, she lowered her eyes; she hummed a little tune, then laughed again.

Jem shook his head. Jeli? Jelica Vance? He had not even wondered what had become of her, nor even cared. He did not care now.

How could Jeli be alive, with Cata dead?

Desolately Jem stumbled to his feet, not even ashamed of his nakedness, only cold. His teeth chattered and he rubbed his shoulders, hugged himself, thinking wryly that he would catch his death. Perhaps he had caught it now; he hoped he had. He supposed that he was now King of Ejland. King! What could it mean to him if Cata were not Queen, to be by his side?

He turned. He must go back to his friends.

But now someone else was standing before him: a tall man, in a costume of purple.

Jem's eyes widened. Horror filled him as he gazed into a face at once familiar and strange.

No. No, it could not be!

But again he thought of the harlequin – or rather, of Agonis-in-the-Vast – telling him of his failure to reunify himself. And he thought again of Toth, flinging the searing crystal from his hands before it could have a chance to do its work. What had it been that Agonis had said? A *different union* – yes, a fusion Jem had never expected ... Red King and Blue, Blue King and Red, for so long they had battered back and forth, bobbed up and down like the little jigging puppets in the booth at the Vaga-fair. But now there was something beyond Red and Blue. Now there was a third way.

'Come, Prince, you'll catch your death.'

It was Jem's thought repeated, this time from the mouth of this familiar stranger. Close by stood a ragged troop of Bluejackets – in the wrong colour now, of course, but fallen in already behind their new master.

Hands came round Jem's shoulders. A draping cape.

Still he could only stare and stare.

'Really, Prince!' said the man in purple. 'Cavorting naked? In Redondo Gardens? Not to mention in weather like this! I dare say there's always been an *eccentric* strand in our dynasty, but this, I think, is going a little far. Just a little, hm? For my son and heir? Oh, but your face! You're really not well ... Come, we must get you back to the palace.'

And Ejard Purple smiled at him fondly.

In the new King's eyes there was a faint, mauve glow.

Chapter 71

A NEW WORLD ORDER

The strangest thing in the world is the way that time passes. After the war, there must have been many who imagined that Ejland would be gripped perpetually in cold, as if the new age could only be an eternity of ice. Amongst the ruins of Agondon, blackened against the snow, such a conclusion might have been irresistible. For ever, it seemed, the river would lie arrested like a looking-glass, and light would fail early in the afternoons. This was the condition of the world. There could be no other.

Jem had no part in these imaginings. For the heir to the throne, the season would be one of fierce, unnatural fires, of feverish swelterings in an overheated chamber. Many would be the whisperings of concern around his bed; many would be the prayers offered up for him, and not just in the palace. For Prince Jemany, there would be vigil after vigil, often by cold, ragged worshippers in tumbledown temples. If few understood the debt they owed him, it was neither here nor there. He was the King's son; that was enough.

For everyone, that is, except for Jem. In his few lucid moments, Jem longed for death. Often he would fancy that it was near, hovering and ready; many were the times that he would beckon it closer, teasing with it, toying with it. If anything could comfort him, it was the thought that soon he would be enfolded in its embrace; that soon he must set out for the undiscovered country with only this dark companion as his guide. As surely as snow would fall, as water would freeze. As surely as daylight would end too soon.

It was not to be. Death, as all know, is persistent, but its triumph can hardly be certain in a young man whose years number not quite twenty; less so when the young man, prior to his illness, has partaken of powerful energies, channelled through the being of his beloved. Perhaps it was those energies that asserted themselves, putting death to rout – even, indeed, combating the ministrations of a certain Master Waxwell. In any event, slowly but certainly, the dark companion took its leave of Jem's chamber – though more than a little disgruntled, one surmises, to find itself cheated of so fair a prize.

Still, death can always avenge itself on others. Elsewhere that season, its harvest was rich. The world of learning, for example, was to suffer a sad loss. Professor Mercol, found lying senseless in the Chamber of Forbidden Texts, was never to recover consciousness, surviving only briefly into the new age. His last act, as his colleagues were soon aware, had been to nominate his candidate for the Aon Fellowship.

His choice was to cause much controversy. Some said, if only in whispers, that the great man's mind had gone; some said his choice must be rejected out of hand. But a university, like any institution, is much given to contemplating its procedures. Neither exhaustive researches in the statute-books, nor the deliberations of several learned committees, could establish any regulation that outlawed the nomination. If there was no precedent to support it, nor was there any against it; although, as some argued, there was a precedent of sorts in the fact that no elector's choice had ever, in the history of the university, been overruled before. In honour of the great scholar's memory, the university authorities had no choice but to obey his dying wish.

Mercol's generation was badly hit that season. Deaths came thickly, almost as if some spirit of the new age, cruelly but efficiently, were clearing a path through the old and infirm. One such was the woman known to us variously as Lady Lolenda or Berthen Waxwell. One morning, bound for the worship which had become the solace of her declining days, she slipped and fell on a patch of ice; lacking a hand, the unfortunate woman had been unable to avail herself of a nearby, convenient railing. This, to be sure, was not enough to kill her; bedridden, she might have lived for many years, but a chill compounded her sufferings and she was to survive neither her former lover, Silas Wolveron, nor her sometime stepson, Poltiss Veeldrop, by more than a moonlife.

Epidemics raged that season, too. While the plague – mercifully for what Eay Feval used to refer to as *the world* – confined its worst ravages to the lower orders, still there were lesser afflictions that respected no such barriers. Influenza, pneumonia and the like flourished far beyond the environs of the poor. For a time that celebrated performer, Harlequin of the Silver Masks – the original, as it were, after which certain other harlequins had been patterned – feared greatly for Clown, his longtime companion; so greatly, indeed, that some said the old rogue had even forsworn his allegiance to the Vaga-god and been received into the Love of the Lord Agonis.

It was a beguiling tale; but neither the rumour, nor the fact that it was true, were enough to save the old entertainer and his friend when the King ordered a new and vicious Vaga-purge. The action was sudden, indeed unexpected, but much applauded in the fashionable world, where some had feared that the reign of Ejard Purple would tend too much to liberalism, even to moral laxity.

News of the purge – things, after all, were getting back to normal – was one of two things that served to cheer the recovery of another eminent personage who had been in a parlous state. This was Lady Cham-Charing, whose second aid to recovery was the intelligence – brought to her personally, and ever so politely, by the new First Minister – that she was to be permitted to return to her family home, commandeered illegally under the old régime. Bursting into tears, Constansia had blessed the new King, thanking the Lord Agonis that justice and mercy had been restored to Ejland. Her prostration was brief, and soon Constansia – sitting up in her sick bed with Pug – was more concerned with the renovation of Cham-Charing House. No expense could be spared, and none would.

Had it not been for Tishy, who was more exasperating than ever, Constansia's happiness might even have been complete. Who, after all, would be Agondon's leading hostess now that Lady Umbecca was off the scene? Mildra Venturon? Hardly. Poor Lady Venturon's sons had been killed in the war; some said her mourning was likely to be endless. As for Baroness Bolbarr, that fine new mansion of hers – tragic it was, tragic – had been levelled to the ground. The Aldermyle residence had also suffered sorely. Cham-Charing House, as Constansia had always known, was built of stronger stuff. Soon, the world would see just how strong.

The *world*, that is, as defined by Eay Feval.

'Won't it, Pug? Won't it, my darling?'

❊   ❊   ❊   ❊   ❊

Happiness of such degree could scarcely have been imagined amongst the lower orders. Making fires in the ruins, avoiding tramping patrols, there were many amongst the poor who found no comfort even in the cessation of conflict, suffering through this season as if it were merely war continuing in another mode. To enumerate the deaths of lesser personages would be the task of an age; besides, a great many have possessed no names in this history, serving only to swell a crowd, or fill the ranks of battle.

Nonetheless there are three one might mention, none of whom would ever have been invited to Cham-Charing House. The first was Nirry's father, Stephel Jubb, who had succumbed rapidly to the ravages of the bottle after Lady Umbecca dismissed him from her service. Reeking of gin, not to mention vomit, he died in a huddled mass in a doorway, one night soon after Jem had saved the world.

His daughter, had she found him, could easily have taken him in: the Cat & Crown, which had sustained little damage, soon flourished again, along with those other trades for which Redondo Gardens is famed. But life in a tavern would hardly have been good for the old man; besides, his condition could only have added to Nirry's distresses. As it was, she would never know what had become of him.

The second obscure death took place far away, in Nirry's native village – and Cata's, and Jem's – where a certain lady who might once have fitted in well in Redondo Gardens was to expire, at last, in the prison cell in which she has languished for much of this tale. Unmourned, Wynda

Throsh – for that was her name – was bundled into a pauper's grave; afterwards, the gravediggers, who had worked up quite a thirst, went off to slake it at an establishment just off the village green. Known as the Lazy Tiger, it was under new management.

Meanwhile another prisoner, in a Vaga-camp in Ara-Zenzau, made up the third of this trio of deaths. An old woman, bent and wizened, for a long time she had lingered at her life's end, barely enduring the privations of a captivity that was, she would say ruefully, by no means her first. Younger people of the tribe, drawn to her aura of power, were sure that only the old woman's magic permitted her to live. For a time, they gathered, she had been in Agondon; in the recent purges, she had been separated from her friends. Often she spoke of her great-children, and sometimes, when she spoke of them, convulsions racked her frame; visions seared her eyes and she could only scream and scream, even when the guards came to beat her into silence. Yet even when she was broken, crushed, still she raged to live; ardently she spoke of the time when, once again, she would embrace her dear Rajal and Myla.

Her wish was not to be granted. Only for so long can nature be denied, even if one happens to be the Great Mother.

✳   ✳   ✳   ✳   ✳

So it was that the cold continued, dashing the hopes of many, fulfilling the dreams of few.

But the season, though a long one – unnaturally long – was not to be eternal. In time it would relent; ice would break, snow would melt; grass would return, and flowers, and leaves to the trees. Days lengthened; birds came back. Gusty rain replaced snow, then the rain cleared away and the sky, at first fleetingly, then lavishly, for day upon day, was a dazzle of azure blue. That year's Theron-season, everyone predicted, would be the most magnificent in living memory. Warmth spread over the land like a gift from the gods; and as it spread, it seemed that indeed a new age, of sorts, had arrived in Ejland.

All over Agondon, there was hammering, plastering, painting and the scrape of cement spreaders. The docks returned to life. Commerce thrived, society too. In Redondo Gardens, Nirry – or rather Wiggler, under Nirry's supervision – set up benches outside the Cat & Crown, greatly increasing trade; Lady Cham-Charing, returning to a house more splendid by far than it had been before, staged an intimate little soirée for – oh, two or three hundred of the best people, which was, so all agreed, a triumph; and in the royal palace, the heir to the throne began first to sit up, then to speak, and then to walk.

It was a patriotic time. The new purple flag had recently been raised, and the forces looked magnificent in new purple uniforms; at the same time, Mr Elgnar's imperial anthem had at last been provided with lyrics

434

by Mr Coppergate, Ejland's greatest living poet. Premiered at the Wrax Opera to massive acclaim, the stirring song would be sung in every barracks and schoolroom in Ejland and all its dominions.

News of Prince Jemany's recovery could only swell this wave of imperial pride. Celebrations broke out all over Agondon, and soon throughout the many realms that fell beneath its sway. At once the Prince, though few had seen him, became an idol of the masses. There were engravings, portraits, busts – none of which, as it happened, looked particularly like him. There were painted tea services and illustrated fans; song-sheets, newspapers, and hastily assembled biographies declaimed, vaguely but fervently, on the role the Prince had played in his father's return to the throne. Fetching young actors impersonated him on the stage, though always in postures of the strictest rectitude; preachers, schoolmasters and parents throughout the empire invoked him as an example of filial duty, heroism and patriotic fervour, exhorting the young to follow in his footsteps.

For the Court, this was an opportunity too good to miss – or so the few cynics were heard to whisper. For it was then that, as if to seize the popular mood, His Imperial Agonist Majesty King Ejard Purplejacket issued a proclamation, declaring that his beloved son – both to celebrate his return to health and symbolise, with appropriate solemnity, his bondage to the empire – was to be granted the title *Prince of Zenzau*.

Better yet, his *Investiture* – so it was called – was to take place on Theron Solstice, in a magnificent ceremony in the newly restored Great Temple of Agonis. Royalty and other distinguished guests from all the known world were invited.

The public's excitement could barely be contained.

Chapter 72

ANTHEM OF THE EMPIRE

Theron Solstice.

Great Temple.

Morven and Crum.

The sentry-post – their particular one, just inside the main doors – was by no means the most enviable. They were almost as far from the altar as could be; there were even pillars to block their view. What of it? This was a place that many would have killed for. Morven and Crum could hear them now, the crowd jostling, cheering, applauding out by the steps, as carriage after carriage disgorged its precious passengers.

Crum said, 'But he's an Ejlander, isn't he? Morvy?'

'Shh! Crum, what are you playing at?'

'Only whispering. Out of the side of my mouth.'

'Fool, have you forgotten where we are?'

'Don't be silly, Morvy, how could I? Anyway, that lot are making enough noise.'

'They're allowed to. We're not.'

Crum sniffed. The commotion outside was all the merest prelude. The crowd awaited the Prince, but he would not appear until the climax of the ceremony, arriving alone in a special coach. Not unreasonably, Crum had wondered how they would time it. The streets were full of people. But then, Crum supposed, they were full of guards too.

He pursued, 'But he *is*, isn't he? Morvy?'

His friend sighed. 'What *are* you talking about?'

'Prince Jem. He's an Ejlander, isn't he?'

'Of course he is, Crum. What else could he be?'

'Well, that's what I don't understand.' Crum gestured to the Imperial Throne of Zenzau, glittering and immense, high on the altar at the end of the central aisle. 'He's Prince of Ejland. So how can he be Prince of Zenzau, too?'

'Crum, really! Haven't I explained this before?'

'You tried. But mostly you talked about Mr Vytoni.'

'And how else, might I ask, is one to understand the science of political economy, without recourse to Vytoni's definitive analysis?'

'His what, Morvy?'

Morven rolled his eyes. 'Crum, Ejland has conquered Zenzau – yes? They've passed the Act of Unity – yes? They've even brought that bloody great monstrosity of a throne all the way from Wrax, which must have been murder on the cart-horses, let me tell you—'

'Farmer Ryle's cart-horse—' Crum began.

'*Hence,*' Morven leapt in, 'this charade. Now shut up. You want us up on a charge?'

Crum, none the wiser, sank into glum silence. Not for the first time, he wished he'd never given Blenkinsop away. Were those boys looking after him properly? Distractedly his eyes roved the many-coloured windows, the fan-vaults, the screens, the monuments. He was more interested in the people. Like a river of silk and jewels and gold, glittering in the brightness of the afternoon, quality-folk swept through the doors, making their way to refurbished pews. Gentlemen doffed their hats. Ladies laughed, flapping fans.

'Stop gawping,' muttered Morven, soon enough.

'I'm … I'm not. It's this collar. It's too tight.'

'You're getting podgy, Crum. It's that tallow-chandler's daughter, isn't it, feeding you all those cakes!'

Crum blushed. 'I'm not *podgy*, am I? It's this uniform. I liked my old one.'

'Really? You could always dye it.'

'*Mor*-vy!'

'Shh!'

A pause.

'But … I'm *not* podgy, am I?'

'Not *diet*, Crum. Dye it. Purple.'

'What? Oh, I see.' Crum grinned, but then he went glum again. 'Zohnny Ryle's sister's husband's sister's baby was this colour, you know. Just like this, and Jumphrey – that was the baby – was born *dead*. Why do we have to be purple anyway? What difference does it make?'

'Oh, Crum, if only we knew!'

'You mean *you* don't know, Morvy?'

Now Morven was glum. 'Crum, shut up. *Please.*'

Crum sniffed again, and wondered if he might scratch his nose. He hoped he wasn't getting hay fever. On the farm in Varl, he got terrible hay fever, just terrible. There wasn't much hay around here, it was true, but fur might bring it on. It was a concern; after all, it would be Morven and Crum whose task it was to take the Prince's ermine train, pacing behind him as he made his way to the altar. Crum supposed it was just as well he didn't have Blenkinsop.

Suddenly he gripped Morven's arm. 'Look!'

Morven shoved him away. 'Idiot! Stop it!'

This time, Crum was undeterred. 'That's Wiggler, Morvy. Didn't you see? Wiggler – and Nirry! Oh, but they didn't see *us* – shall I wave?'

There was a brief struggle. Morven's musket clattered embarrassingly off his shoulder, and a quality-lady – not Nirry – frowned at him.

437

He flushed scarlet.

'You look miserable, Morvy,' said Crum, a little later. 'Buck up. Straighten your musket. And your specs. *You'll* have us up on a charge, you will, and then where will we be?'

Morven supposed it was an olive branch. He was not keen to grip it.

His voice cracked. 'I wish I'd got the Aon. It's so unfair. I just *wish* I'd got it.'

'Never mind, Morvy,' Crum said gently. 'It's better this way. At least I think so.'

'What?' Morven spoke through his teeth.

'You'd have gone back to ... to school, wouldn't you?'

'Yes,' Morven almost shouted.

'Well ... I'd have *missed* you, Morvy.'

Blinking in surprise, Morven looked at his friend. The guests had settled by now, and the stirring tones of the organ rang out.

> *And so we gather here to praise*
> *This godly being on earth:*
> *This princely one whose valour shook*
> *A King mired in a sty*
> > *Of wicked ways,*
> > *Of wicked ways—*

The day's proceedings began with hymns, performed by the Imperial Agonist Temple Choir. Purple-cassocked, the several hundred boys rose as one. Like music of the spheres their massed voices filled the nave, rising to the vaulted ceiling like the spirit of humanity itself, ardent in its longing to transcend this imperfect world.

> *With flags of blue against the sky,*
> *The brother King who took*
> *All goodness, virtue, trust and worth*
> *Proclaimed his reign would raise*
> > *None to defy,*
> > *None to defy—*

'Bit different from our two, eh love?' a certain fellow in a pew off to the side whispered, just a little too loudly, to the lady beside him.

'Wiggler, shh!' returned the lady, whose hat – an elaborate floral creation – was particularly striking.

'But you're right,' she relented. 'I don't think these two would get into that gang. Ooh, but think what a rumpus they'd make,' she added, giggling. 'Eh, Taggle, stop that! Raggle, enough!'

The orphans looked up at her, blinking innocently.

> But like a shepherd with his crook
> The young Prince led the cry:
> The welling evil of those days
> No longer would the earth
>   Of Ejland brook,
>   Of Ejland brook—

A second voice sounded in Nirry's ear. 'So who's *that* one when she's at home then?'

'Baines, don't *point*.' Firmly, Nirry lowered the wizened hand.

Really, who said only boys could be a trial?

'Do you think it's Lady Selinda?' Baines persisted.

'No,' Nirry whispered, 'that's the one with the fat nurse, see? Over there?'

> So with his father in his eye
> The Prince his sword did raise:
> And evil could not dare to look
> But bleeding to the earth
>   Fell down to die,
>   Fell down to die—

'The other one, I think, the one in all that chiffony stuff. Yes, that must be the Shimmering Princess. Representing her old dad, she is. Nob-in-chief of some desert place – Shaker, or Sultana, or whatever they call it.'

'Fond of that companion of hers, isn't she? *Very* fond.'

'Them foreigners have some rum ways, Baines.'

'*Shh!*' – from the row in front.

> But now a new age comes to birth:
> This Purple Empire's ways
> Put trust and virtue back on high
> And open up the book
>   Of peace on earth,
>   Of peace on earth—

After the opening hymns came the speeches.

Inevitable, no doubt, thought Lady Cham-Charing; for all the attendant mumbo-jumbo, it could hardly take long to set one crown, even quite a large, heavy crown, upon the head of one young man.

And some of the guests had come *so* far.

So here was Lector Arden (this fellow who had succeeded to the office of Great Lector after the deaths of Lector Feval, Lector Flonce and Lector Garvice) mounting the lectern, speaking of the sacred duty of the

439

monarch (who was proxy in the world for the Lord Agonis, or was it for the Ur-God Orok?) and, thereby, of the monarch's line; of a vow to be taken, of a covenant to be sealed. In due course would come the First Minister (the unctuous 'Mandy' Heva-Harion), incongruously reading from the El-Orokon; there would be the Archmaximate (robes, mitre, censer) intoning yet more verbiage about the Investiture...

All in all, it *looked* like the most ancient of ceremonies; one would hardly have imagined it had been cobbled together in the Temple College only – what? – a moonlife ago.

Lady Cham-Charing had little interest in ceremonies she had neither devised nor staged herself. She stroked the little terrier that sat on her lap, adjusting the pink ribbon that circled his neck; she studied the stained-glass windows, which her late husband had paid for; she gazed, not for the first time, upon the royal box. In undertones, she resumed a conversation she had been having, on and off, with her old friend Mazy Michan (*née* Tarfoot), who had returned to Agondon after the death of her husband and more or less taken Lady Margrave's place in the Cham-Charing circle.

Lady C. 'No. Really. She *can't* still be Queen.'

Lady M. 'Dowager Queen, do you think?'

'A sort of companion? A consort?'

'Or has she no status – *none*?'

It was an alarming prospect. With furrowing brows the two noble friends inspected the wife of the former King. How brazenly the girl sat in the royal box, twining her golden ringlets round her fingers!

The question of her status had perplexed a great many. Some said the King was to marry her; that he had always secretly loved her; even, that he had married her already. In any case, it was all most unorthodox.

Mazy flapped her fan as if to illustrate the point. 'He *can't* marry her. His brother's wife? Besides, the girl was never up to much.'

'Not with the fat woman around,' said Constansia.

'But then, which of us were? You're *sure* you're all right, Sir Pellion?' Mazy added, turning to the old gentleman on the other side of her. 'Constansia told me you'd never face public life again.'

'One must endure much,' came the reply, 'in a new era.'

'A wise reply, Sir Pellion,' brayed Lady Cham-Charing as the old gentleman coughed into his handkerchief. There was a pause between speeches, and conversation was easier. 'You see now, perhaps, how precipitate you were to shun my little soirée? I too have endured much, have I not, and survived? And is there not much that *still* I must endure?'

With this last remark, the lady's voice took on a steely edge. There was a great deal for which she was thankful, it was true. The renovations were a triumph. There would be a second soirée, and a third. This year's Festival Levee would be the greatest there had ever been. But really, what was to be done about Tishy? If even today – on this day of days – the girl had some mouldering old book on her lap, the case was surely hopeless.

The distraught mother glanced at Freddie Chayn, sitting happily close by with little Miss Quisto. Or rather, with the Princess of Chayn.

Lady Cham-Charing nuzzled Pug.

✻　✻　✻　✻　✻

Twirl, twirl, went the golden curl.

Jeli's mind drifted. Master Waxwell sat in readiness behind a nearby curtain, just in case his services should be required. But already he had dosed her liberally with a certain blackish, sticky substance on which Her Royal Majesty had come, of late, to depend more and more.

With a fixed smile she gazed over the guests, eyes blurring on the strange, dazzling garb of the foreigners. Which one was that – that pig-tailed fellow? The Ambassador, Jeli thought, of Lania Chor. Everyone said he was a fiery fellow. And that one? The Triarch of Hora? Well, one of them … And what – yes, what – of these foreign beauties, fine ladies from lands where, so far as Jeli knew, ladies were constrained even more than here? That Shimmering Princess, honestly! The girl was nowhere near as beautiful as they said.

Jeli giggled. How had some wit put it? *It was all done with mirrors.*

Yes, she must remember that.

Her eyes roved further, over the likes of Constansia Cham-Charing, whom Jeli had always despised, and Mistress Quick, whom she despised even more. Was there no one she could love? With a pang she looked at her old schoolfriends, Huskia Bichley and Erina Aldermyle. Both married now; Erina even had children. Two, already!

Then, of course, there was Jilda Chayn. Jeli's mouth hardened. Jilda! Did the slut think she could wipe out all memory of her ruin? No, she would not forget what she used to be. Jeli would make sure of that.

Very sure.

✻　✻　✻　✻　✻

A nudge. 'Eh, Wiggler! You're scratching it again!'

'No, love,' the whisper came back. 'But I've never much liked a wig on me noggin, you know that. How them quality-gentlemen get on, I can't begin to think.'

'Never mind the quality, just be thankful we're here at all. You know how lucky we are?'

'Not just lucky. Didn't Master Jem have a hand in it?'

'Enough of your Master Jem. *Respect*, Wiggler Olch.'

But Nirry was disingenuous. Wouldn't she always think of the Prince in just that way? Oh, indeed! If only she could see him again, all real and

441

proper, and give him a good long hug! But of course, she never would. What was that word they used? *Proto*-something?

Baines smiled distantly. Tired of exotic guests, she was gazing on the King, far away in the royal pew. Strange, but she really had preferred him in red. Couldn't she just see him twirling his pistol, smiling under his mask, addressing her as his *one-eyed beauty*?

This purple fellow, somehow, was not quite the same.

'What I don't understand,' Wiggler began now, 'is where Miss Landa's gone. How could *she* not be here?'

'Always been an odd one, that girl,' said his wife. 'Odder now. Well, she's gone a bit funny, hasn't she, since—' Nirry stopped herself, but not for the benefit of the snobbish killjoy who shushed her, just then, from the row behind. No, she must not think of Miss Cata. Not now; her paint would run, and then where would she be?

Fortunately, there was another chance to chastise the boys. 'Raggle! Taggle! You've never gone and brought that rat with you, have you? To Temple? Ooh!'

Blenkinsop looked up innocently, his whiskers twitching.

> *And as the young prince crossed the green*
> *The rays of love were brightly seen*
> *Soaring high*
> *In flaming dye—*

And so on.

This was sung by all the congregated, or was supposed to be. Some, not least of all the Ambassador of Lania Chor, were having difficulties. In his case, it was hardly any wonder, since his translator had to apprise him of each line before he could declaim it in his own cater-wauling, barbaric language. One might have thought it would be positively charitable to have the fellow taken outside and shot. But then, thought Constansia, that would probably spark a *diplomatic incident*.

The hymn lumbered to its inglorious end.

Not the best of inspirations. Heads would roll in Temple College, no doubt about it. Constansia took a mental note. Yes, she really must know who was *in* and who was *out*. 'Mustn't we, Pug?' she whispered, with a squeeze for her little terrier.

But she soon had other concerns. As the congregated resumed their pews, she caught a glimpse of her daughter's stockings.

Green? Even today?

What a fool Constansia had been to trust Professor Mercol! Engaged to wean her daughter from such perversities, what had he done but confirm her in them? The Aon Fellowship, indeed! For a girl! No doubt about it, Mercol had been mad – either that, or in love with the girl.

And if the girl had loved him?

Then, thought Constansia, she could love again. What was a mother to do, if not to dream?

She leaned close to her daughter's ear. 'You got on well with Prince Jemany, didn't you, darling? Only ... you do realise that next time there is a gathering *so* distinguished, it is likely to be for ... a royal wedding?'

Tishy flushed. 'Mother! What do you mean?'

'Only ... that a girl would be wise to think of her future.'

'Quite. And mine is the Aon Fellowship.'

Tishy smiled ruefully. What was it Mr Vytoni said? *Few mercies leaven our sufferings at the hands of those who rule us. The best is that our thoughts remain our own: that in our minds, if nowhere else, there is a place where we can be free.* And wasn't she free now? Oh, more than once she had regretted that a fellow scholar, a certain Mr Hulverside, had taken his leave of Agondon. One might have thought he would be glad to remain. Would he not have been an ornament to the Court? Even, perhaps, a fine First Minister? But Mr Hulverside had other plans. And one day, Tishy fancied, she might just help him.

In the meantime, she had much to learn.

'Mother,' she said, just a little spitefully, 'have you given *any* thought to Harlequin and Clown? They're banished, did you know that? Did you even *know*?'

What nonsense was this? Of course Constansia knew. She picked up Pug, kissing his little muzzle.

'They're ... *Vagas*, darling,' she said absently.

❈　❈　❈　❈　❈

The golden curl. *Twirl, twirl.*

Jeli's husband – for of course, he was her husband – leaned close, magnificent in his crown, his ermine, his purple velvet. Expectantly he gestured towards the Zenzan throne, its bejewelled arms gleaming in a shaft of light, rainbow-coloured through the stained glass. Fondly he seized the little twirling fingers. 'He's ready, my dear? You're sure he's ready?'

'Of course, my love.' Jeli had taken her responsibilities seriously. How many times – oh, again and again! – had she checked on the soon-to-be Prince of Zenzau? To look in on him was never a trial; several times that morning, as he readied himself, she had contrived, indeed, to burst into his apartments when he was not *quite* dressed.

Jeli only wished she could have ridden in his carriage. By now, she supposed, he would be gliding through the streets, edging ever closer as the guards, with elegant violence, cleared his path of weeping, beseeching commoners, desperate just for a glimpse of the royal personage.

Yes, he was close now; from outside, Jeli heard an increasing clamour. How he could make this journey alone, she could not imagine. Could he really be engaged, at this moment, in a *time of meditation*? Who had unearthed so foolish a tradition? Could Jeli have meditated on the way to her wedding?

But she did not want to think of that, not now. Much had changed; so, too, had Jem. For a time, as his illness left him, Jeli had feared that he would rave and cry when he learnt of certain measures, *necessary* measures, that the new age entailed. For Vaga-kind, for example: that dusky sister and brother were hardly fit companions for a monarch-to-be. That annoying little boy, the one they called Littler, had been disposed of too; not to mention that vulgar fellow who went by the name of String or Bean or something equally absurd. Let him rot in Oldgate! Jem, after all, was beginning a new life. Were old distractions to worry him, confuse him?

The plan had worked better than anyone dared hope. Why, Jeli had not known him to pine at all! To her delight, he had not even mentioned a particular young lady – a young lady whose name Jeli wished never to hear again. But then, why should Jem think of Catty Veeldrop? It had just been a boyish infatuation, that was all, from the days before he had even *seen* a proper lady … Now, if only he were a little more responsive to other charms … Jeli's eyes misted. The Prince, it was true, must find a bride; but those of high station were hardly to be bound by the morals of their inferiors. Fondly, she imagined the delightful and – yes – *mature* arrangement that might still come to pass.

Not that she was unhappy. Not at all.

Absently, the Queen – *of course* she was the Queen – returned the pressure of the King's hand. Then she quailed a little. Was it happening again? Sometimes his hand – just his hand – would undergo a disturbing, if mercifully temporary change. Jeli could only hope it was an illusion, a side-effect caused by her medicine.

The hand, she was certain, was missing a finger.

Yes, almost time now.

The guards, at the back of the temple, gave a sign. The carriage had come; soon, like a bridegroom – indeed, like a bride – Ejard Purple's long-lost son would make his progress up the aisle.

First, the anthem. What better way to usher in this moment? Filing into place beside the altar, in dress uniforms of the utmost extravagance, came a stately consort of pipes and drums, the finest from the forces of His Imperial Agonist Majesty. Flags unfurled. The choristers reappeared; this time, at their head, complete with spear, helmet-with-horns, and robes patterned like the imperial flag, was the celebrated Zaxon Nightingale, Miss Tilsy Fash.

Applause filled the temple. Boredom was forgotten as the organ heaved, the pipes skirled, the drums thudded and rolled, and soaring above it all came the fulsome soprano of a great diva in her prime:

> *Advance, Ejland ever glorious*
> *Advance upon your foe:*
> *Advance, righteous and victorious*
> *Where but the bold shall go:*
> > *Rule, rule, Ejland!*
> > *Never never never fall:*
> *Ejland, Ejland, over all*
> *Your purple flag you raise:*
> *Each lesser breed with lesser seed*
> *Must bow to you in praise!*

On and on it went, chorus after chorus, tide after tide of patriotic fervour breaking over the temple in an ecstatic rush. Miss Fash, undoubtedly, would soon be Dame Tilsy; by the end, almost all the guests – one exception was Tishy, to her mother's chagrin – had thundered to their feet, joining in, waving little flags. Nirry sang, and Wiggler, and Baines; Raggle and Taggle bounded up and down, raced round the pews and shouted themselves hoarse.

Even Jeli gave a sterling performance, supported by the kindly Master Waxwell, who appeared from behind the curtain just when some had feared the girl might fall.

> *Advance, Ejland, from thy sceptred shore*
> *Defend each tyrant's blast:*
> *Advance, outward ever more and more*
> *Your boundaries will be cast:*
> > *Rule, rule, Ejland!*
> > *Never never never fall:*
> *Ejland, Ejland, over all*
> *By dawn's clear light I read:*
> *In foreign soil with manly toil*
> *You'll plant salvation's seed!*

There was, admittedly, a minor incident when the Ambassador of Lania Chor, after first shouting in outrage at his translator, swept out of a side entrance, eyes flashing fire. It seemed he did not much approve of these latest lyrical fruits of Mr Coppergate's genius.

Not to worry: the scuffle, in the general fray, was barely even noticed. His Imperial Agonist Majesty observed it, it was true, but responded only with a flicker of a smile.

> *Advance, Ejland, mother of the free*
> *And homeland of the brave:*

Advance, spreading unrelentingly
Dominion over wave:
   Rule, rule, Ejland!
   Never never never fall:
   Ejland, Ejland, over all
   Your empire's flag will fly
   No Ejland man or woman can
   As slave or vassal die!

It ended at last. The performers retired; the applause died; but the guests remained standing. For now it really was here, the moment all had awaited. All around the temple pencils were sharpened as the royal artists prepared to sketch the pictures that could – that *would* – make their fortunes. Ladies, even gentlemen, held their breath. How many heads longed to turn, forgetting all decorum, towards the doors?

The silence was intense. Palpable.

Then it happened. The scream.

Heads turned. There were gasps, cries. Jeli blanched. The King was on his feet, blundering down the aisle. What could it mean, these desperate guards, rolling in an ermine train, then staggering up, dragging free the splitting, flopping body of a scarecrow in velvet and lace?

Only after His Imperial Agonist Majesty had struck one of the guards viciously in the face, knocking the fellow's spectacles flying, could the sobbing, slithering fool even try to explain that this – this model, this mannequin, this effigy, this *dummy* – was all, evidently, and so far as one could see, that had been accommodated, that is, enclosed, that is, *contained* within the—

Mercifully, the second guard used simpler words.

'He's gone,' gabbled Crum. 'Prince Jem … he's gone!'